PENGUIN BOOKS

THE WISE WOMAN

Philippa Gregory holds a doctorate from the University of Edinburgh for her research into eighteenth-century literature. She trained as a journalist and worked for the BBC. She lives with her family in West Sussex. Philippa Gregory is best known for her eighteenth-century novels, *Wideacre*, *The Favoured Child* and *Meridon*, which together make up the bestselling saga of the Lacey family and are published by Penguin. Penguin also publish her novel *Mrs Hartley and the Growth Centre*. Her most recent novel is *Fallen Skies*. She has also written several children's books, *Princess Florizella* (Puffin 1989), *Florizella and the Wolves* and *Florizella and the Giant*.

PHILIPPA GREGORY

THE WISE WOMAN

PENGUIN BOOKS

PENGUIN BOOKS

Published by the Penguin Group
Penguin Books Ltd, 27 Wrights Lane, London W8 5TZ, England
Penguin Books USA Inc., 375 Hudson Street, New York, 10014, USA
Penguin Books Australia Ltd, Ringwood, Victoria, Australia
Penguin Books Canada Ltd, 10 Alcorn Avenue, Toronto, Ontario, Canada M4V 3B2
Penguin Books (NZ) Ltd, 182–190 Wairau Road, Auckland 10, New Zealand

Penguin Books Ltd, Registered Offices: Harmondsworth, Middlesex, England

First published by Viking 1992
Published in Penguin Books 1993
1 3 5 7 9 10 8 6 4 2

Typeset by Datix International Limited, Bungay, Suffolk
Printed in Great Britain by Clays Ltd, St Ives plc

One

In my dream I smelled the dark sulphurous stink of a passing witch and I pulled up the coarse blanket over my head and whispered 'Holy Mary, Mother of God, pray for us', to shield me from my nightmare of terror. Then I heard shouting and the terrifying crackle of hungry flames and I came awake in a rush of panic and sat up on my pallet and looked fearfully around the limewashed cell.

The walls were orange and scarlet, with the bobbing light of reflected flames, and I could hear yells of angry rioting men. I knew at once that the worst thing had happened. Lord Hugo had come to wreck us, Lord Hugo had come for the abbey, as we had feared he might come, since King Henry's Visitors had found us wealthy and pretended that we were corrupt. I flung on my gown and snatched my rosary, and my cape, crammed my feet into my boots, tore open the door of my cell and peered into the smoke-filled corridor of the novitiate dormitory.

The abbey was stone-built, but the rafters would burn, the beams, and the wooden floors. Even now the flames might be licking upwards, under my feet. I heard a little whimper of fear and it was my own craven voice. On my left were the slits of open windows and red smoke swirled in through them like the tongues of hungry serpents licking towards my face. I peered out with watering eyes and saw, black against the fire, the figures of men crossing and recrossing the cloister green with their arms full of treasures, our treasures, holy treasures from the church. Before them was a bonfire and while I watched incredulously these Satan's soldiers ripped off the jewelled

I

covers and threw the fluttering pages of our books into the flames. Beyond them was a man on a big roan horse – black as death against the firelight, with his head thrown back, laughing like the devil: Lord Hugo.

I turned with a sob of fear and coughed on the smoke. Behind me were the single cells where the young novitiates, my sisters in Christ, were still sleeping. I took two steps down the corridor to bang on the doors and scream at them to awake and save themselves from this devil inside our gates and his fiery death of burning. I put my hand out to the first door, but the smoke was in my throat and no sound came. I choked on my scream, I swallowed and tried to scream again. But I was trapped in this dream, voiceless and powerless, my feet wading through brimstone, my eyes filled with smoke, my ears clogged with the shouts of heretics wrecking their way to damnation. I tapped on one door with a light hand. I made no sound.

No sound at all.

I gave a little moan of despair and then I picked up my skirts and I fled from my sisters, from my duty and from the life I had chosen. I scuttered down the breakneck spiral staircase like a rat from a burning hayrick.

The door at the foot of the stairs was barred, beside it was the cell where my mother in Christ, the Abbess Hildebrande slept. I paused. For her above them all, I should have risked my life. For all of my young sisters I should have screamed a warning: but to save Mother Hildebrande I should have burned alive and it would have been no more than her due. I should have banged her door off its hinges, I should have screamed out her name, I should never, never have left without her. She was my guardian, she was my mother, she was my saviour. Without her I would have been nothing. I paused for a *moment – a bare half second I gave her – then I smelled smoke spilling under the refectory door and I flew at the bolts on the back door, rattled them open, and I was out in the west garden with the herb-beds around me cool and pale in the darkness.*

I could hear the shouts from the heart of the abbey but out here in the gardens all was clear. I raced down the formal garden paths and flung myself into the slim shadow of the door in the outer wall and paused for one moment. Over the rapid thudding of my pulse I heard the noise of the coloured windows cracking in the heat and then the great crash as they were smashed by a thrown candlestick or silver plate. On the far side of the door I could hear the river flowing, splashing over the stones, showing me my way back to the outside world like the pointing finger of my own especial devil.

It was not too late, I was not yet through the door. For a second, for half a breath, I paused, tested my courage to go back – pictured myself hammering on the doors, breaking the windows, yelling for my mother, Mother Hildebrande, and my sisters, and facing whatever was to come at her side, with her hand in mine, and my sisters all around me.

I waited for no more than a moment.

I fled out of the little garden door, and slammed it shut behind me.

No one saw me go.

Only the eyes of God and His Blessed Mother were on me. I felt their gaze burning into my back, as I kilted up my skirts and ran. Ran from the wrecked chapel and the burning abbey, ran with the speed of a traitor and a coward. And as I ran, I heard behind me a single thin scream – cut off short. A cry for help from someone who had woken too late.

It did not make me pause – not even for a second. I ran as if the very gates of hell were opening at my heels, and as I ran, leaving my mother and my sisters to die, I thought of Cain the brother-killer. And I believed that by the time I came to Bowes village the branches of the trees and the tendrils of the ivy would have slashed at me as I ran – laid their stripes upon me – so that I would be marked forever, as Cain, with the curse of the Lord.

Morach was ready for her bed when she heard the noise at the door of the hovel. A pitiful scratch and a little wail like a whipped dog. She waited for long moments before she even stepped towards the threshold. Morach was a wise woman, a seer; many came to her door for dark gifts and none went away disappointed. Their disappointment came later.

Morach waited for clues as to her visitor. A child? That single cry had been weakly, like an ailing bairn. But no sick child, not even a travelling tinker's brat, would find the courage to tap on Morach's door during the hours of darkness. A girl thickening in the waist, slipped out while her heavy-handed father slept? A visitor from the darker world, disguised as a cat? A wolf? Some misshapen, moist horror?

'Who's there?' Morach asked, her old voice sharp.

There was silence. Not the silence of absence; but the silence of one who has no name.

'What do they call you?' Morach asked, her wit quickened by fear.

'Sister Ann,' came the reply, as low as a sigh from a deathbed.

Morach stepped forward and opened the door and Sister Ann slumped into the room, her shaven head glinting obscenely in the guttering candle's light, her eyes black with horror, her face stained and striped with smuts.

'Saints!' Morach said coolly. 'What have they done to you now?'

5

The girl swayed against the door-frame and put out a hand to steady herself. 'They're gone,' she said. 'Mother Hildebrande, the sisters, the abbey, the church. All gone. Burned out by the young lord.'

Morach nodded slowly, her eyes raking the white, stained face.

'And you?' she asked. 'Not taken for treason or heresy? Not seized by the soldiers, by the young Lord Hugo?'

'No,' she said softly, her breath like a sigh.

'You ran,' Morach said flatly, without sympathy.

'Yes.'

'Anyone see you? Anyone follow you here? Anyone coming behind to burn *me* out, as well as you and your saintly sisters?'

'No.'

Morach laughed as if the news gave her especial, malicious, pleasure. 'Ran too fast for them, did you? Too fleet of foot for the fat soldiers to follow? Faster than your sisters, I'll be bound. Left them to burn, did you? While you hitched up your skirts and took to your heels? That won't get you into the sacred calendar, my little martyr! You've lost your chance now!'

The girl bowed her head at the mockery. 'May I come in?' she asked humbly.

Morach stepped back, eyed her brightly. 'To stay?' she asked conversationally – as if the world were not black as pitch outside her door and a wind with rain at the back of it howling down the valley, gathering speed in the darkness.

Sister Ann nodded, dumb with weariness.

'For long?' Morach jibed.

She nodded again. The dark smears on her bare head and face gave her the look of an old striped plough ox.

'Coming back to live here?' Morach asked, covering old ground again for the pleasure of reviewing the landscape.

Ann raised her head. 'Will you take me back?' she asked. 'My vows are broken – I was not obedient. I ran when the soldiers came – I am a traitor and a coward. My house is broken up and my sisters are dead or worse. I am nothing. I am nothing.'

She paused for a moment. 'My mother is dead,' she said very low. 'Mother Hildebrande, the abbess. She will be in paradise this night, in paradise with all her daughters, with all her true daughters.' Sister Ann shook her head dully. 'This is the only home I have ever known except the nunnery. Will you take me back, Morach?'

Morach paused a moment. The girl was coming back, she had known it the moment she let her cross the threshold. But Morach was a woman whose skills led her to savour each moment.

'I might,' she said, consideringly. 'You're young and strong, and you have the Sight. You were my changeling child, given to me for my apprentice, and I would have made you the next wise woman after me but you chose the nuns. I've not replaced you. You could come back.' She stared at the pale sullen face, the clear shape of the bones. 'You're lovely enough to send a man mad,' she said. 'You could be wed. Or we could sell you to a lover.'

Sister Ann kept her gaze down, her eyes on her muddy boots and the filthy rushes on the earth floor. Then she looked at Morach. Her eyes were not black but a dark, measureless blue. 'I am the bride of Christ,' she said bluntly. 'I can wed no man. I can use no dark arts. There is nowhere for me to go, and I have broke

7

my vows; but I was made a bride of Christ for life, and I am a bride of Christ still. I will be His until the day I die. I will never have any man. I will never use the skills of the devil. I am your apprentice no more.'

She turned her face from the smoking light and took one step towards the door. A sharp scud of rain rattled through the open door and into her face. She did not even blink.

'Come in!' said Morach irritably. 'Away inside! We'll speak of this more. We'll speak of this later. But you can go no further tonight.'

She let Morach take her by the arm, lead her to the little fire in the centre of the room where the banked-down embers glowed under the peat.

'Sleep here,' Morach said. 'Are you hungry? There's porridge in the pot.'

She shook her head and, without another word, sank to her knees before the fire, her hand fumbling in her gown for her beads.

'Sleep then,' Morach said again, and took herself up a rickety ladder to the lóft which spanned half of the room.

From that little eyrie she could watch the girl who did not sleep for a good hour, but kneeled before the cooling fire and prayed very earnestly, moving her lips and telling her beads. Upstairs, in the shelter of a dirty nest of torn blankets, Morach pulled out a bag of carved white bones, and in the light of the smoking tallow candle spilled out three of them and summoned what powers she possessed to see what would become of Sister Ann the nun, now that she was Sister Ann no more.

She laid them in a row and stared at them; her dark eyes narrowed to slits with pleasure.

8

'Married to Lord Hugo!' she said softly. 'Or as good as! Fat eating, soft living.' She leaned forward a little closer. 'Death at the end of it,' she said. 'But there is death at the end of every road – and in any case, she should have died tonight.'

She picked up the bones and slid them back into the little ragged purse, hid them beneath her mattress of straw. Then she pulled a verminous bit of woollen shawl up around her shoulders, kicked off her rough clogs, and slept, smiling in her sleep.

Sister Ann was the first to wake in the morning, alert for the knock of the nun summoning her to lauds. She opened her eyes ready to call *'Deo gratias!'* to the familiar *'Benedicite!'* but there was silence. She blinked when she saw dark rafters and the weave of a thatched roof above her eyes instead of the plain, godly, white plaster of her cell. Then her eyes went darker yet with the sudden flooding-in of awareness of her loss and she turned her face and her bald head into the hank of cloth which served as a pillow and wept.

Softly, under her breath, she said her prayers, over and over with little hope of a hearing. There was no comforting chant of the prayers around her, no sweet strong smell of incense. No clear high voices soaring upwards to praise the Lord and His Mother. She had deserted her sisters, she had abandoned her mother the abbess to the cruelty and rage of the wreckers and to the man who had laughed like the devil. She had left them to burn in their beds and she had run like a light-footed fawn all the way back to her old home, as if she had not been a child of the abbey for the past four years, and Mother Hildebrande's favourite.

'You awake?' Morach said abruptly.

'Yes,' replied the girl with no name.

'Get some fresh water and get the fire going. It's as cold as a saint's crutch this morning.'

She got up readily enough and pulled her cape around her shoulders. She scratched the soft white skin of her neck. All around her neck and behind her ears was a chain of red flea bites. She rubbed at them, scowling, while she kneeled before the hearth. All that was left of the fire on the little circle of flints embedded on the earth floor was grey ash, with a rosy core. She laid a little kindling and bent down her bald head to blow. The curl of wood-shaving glowed red. She blew a little more strongly. It glowed brighter and then a red line of fire ate its way down the curl of wood. It met a twig, lying across it, and the light died as it smouldered sullenly. Then with a little flicker and a puff the twig caught alight, burned with a yellow flame. She sat back on her heels and rubbed her face with a grimy hand. The smell of the woodsmoke was on her fingers and she flinched from it, as if she smelled blood.

'Get the water!' Morach shouted from her bed.

She pushed her cold feet into her damp boots and went outside.

The cottage stood alone, a few miles west of the village of Bowes. In front of it was the dull silver of the River Greta, slowly moving without a ripple. The river rose and sank through great limestone slabs at this stretch, deep and dangerous in winter, patchy in drought. The cottage had been built beside one of the deeper pools which was always filled, even in the driest of summers. When Sister Ann had been a little girl, and everyone had used her given name of Alys, and Morach had been Widow Morach and well-respected, the children from the village used to come out here to splash and swim. Alys played with them, with Tom, and with half a dozen of the others. Then Morach had lost her land to a farmer who claimed that he owned it. Morach – no man's woman, sharp-tempered and independent – had fought him before the parish and before the church court. When she lost (as everyone knew she would, since the farmer was a pious man and wealthy), she swore a curse against him in the hearing of the whole village of Bowes. He had fallen sick that very night and later died. Everyone knew that Morach had killed him with her snake-eyed glare.

If he had not been so thoroughly hated in the village it would have gone badly for Morach after that. But his widow was a pleasant woman, glad to be free of him, and she made no complaint. She called Morach up to the farmhouse and asked her for a poultice to ease her backache, and overpaid her many times to ensure that Morach bore no dangerous grudge. The old farmer's death was explained easily enough by his family's history of weak hearts. Morach took care not to boast.

She never got her land back. And after that day the village children did not come to play in the deep pool outside her door. Those visitors who dared the lonely road and the darkness came huddled in their cloaks, under cover of night. They left with small bunches of herbs, or little scraps of writing on paper to be worn next to the skin, sometimes heads full of dreams and unlikely promises. And the village remembered a tradition that there had always been a cunning woman in the cottage by the river. A cunning woman, a wise woman, an indispensable friend, a dangerous enemy. Morach – with no land to support her, and no man to defend her – nurtured the dangerous superstition, took credit and high payment for cures, and blamed deaths on the other local wizards.

Only Tom still came openly up the road from Bowes, and everyone knew he was courting Morach's little foundling-girl, Alys, and that they would be wed as soon as his parents gave their consent.

For one long summer they courted, sitting by the river which ran so smoothly and so mysteriously down the deep crevices of the river bed. For one long summer they met every morning before Tom went to work in his father's fields and Morach called Alys to walk out over the moor and find some leaf or some weed she wanted, or dig in the stony garden.

They were very tender together, respectful. On greeting and at parting they would kiss, gently, on the mouth. When they walked they would hold hands and sometimes he would put his arm around her waist, and she would lean her golden-brown head on his shoulder. He never caught at her, or pulled her about, or thrust his hands inside her brown shawl or up her grey skirt. He liked best to sit beside her on the river-bank and listen to her telling tales and inventing stories.

Her favourite time was when his parents were working in Lord Hugh's fields and he could take her to the farm and show her the cow and the calf, the pig, the linen chest, the pewter and the big wooden bed with the thick old curtains. Alys would smile then, her dark eyes as warm as a stroked cat.

'Soon we'll be together,' Tom would murmur.

'Here,' Alys said.

'I will love you every day of my life,' Tom would promise.

'And we'll live here,' she said.

When Morach lost her fields and did not get them back, Tom's parents looked higher for him than a girl who would bring nothing but a tumbledown shack and a patch of ground all around it. Alys might know more about flowers and herbs than anyone in the village, but Tom's parents did not need a daughter-in-law who knew twenty different poisons, forty different cures. They wanted a jolly, round-faced girl who would bring a fat dowry of fields and perhaps a grazing cow with a weaned calf. They wanted a girl with broad hips and strong shoulders who could work all day in their fields and have a good supper ready for them at night. One who would give birth without fuss so that there would be another Tom in the farmhouse to inherit when they had gone.

Alys, with her ripple of golden-brown unbraided hair, her basket of leaves and her pale reserved face, was not their choice. They told Tom frankly to put her out of his mind; and he told them that he would marry where he willed, and that if they forced him to it he would take Alys away – even as far as Darneton itself – he would do it and go into service if needs be.

It could not be done. Lord Hugh would not let two young people up and off his land without his say-so. But Lord Hugh was an ill man to invoke in a domestic dispute. He would come and give fair enough judgement, but he would take a fancy to a pewter pint-pot on his way out, or he saw a horse he must have, cost what it may. And however generous he claimed to be, he would pay less than the Castleton butter-market price. Lord Hugh was a sharp man with a hard eye. It was best to solve any problems well away from him.

They ignored Tom. They went in secret to the abbess at the abbey and they offered her Alys. They claimed that the child had the holy gift of healing, that she was a herbalist in her own right, but dreadfully endangered by living with her guardian – old Morach. They offered the abbey a plump dowry to take her and keep her behind the walls, as a gift from themselves.

Mother Hildebrande, who could hear a lie even from a stranger – and forgive it – asked them why they were so anxious to get the little girl out of the way. Then Tom's mother cried and told her that Tom was mad for the girl and that she would not do for them. She was too strange and unlike them. She had turned Tom's head, perhaps with a potion – for whoever heard of a lad wanting to marry for love? He would recover but while the madness was on him they should be parted.

'I'll see her,' Mother Hildebrande had said.

They sent Alys up to the abbey with a false message and she was shown through the kitchen, through the adjoining refectory and out of the little door to where Mother Hildebrande was sitting in the physic garden at the smiling western side of the abbey, looking down the hill to the river, deeper here and better stocked with fish. Alys had approached her through the garden in a daze of evening sunshine and her golden-brown hair had shone: like the halo of a saint, Mother Hildebrande had thought. She listened to Alys' message and smiled at the little girl and then walked with her around the raised flower- and herb-beds. She asked her if she recognized any of the flowers and how she would use them. Alys looked around the walled warm garden as if she had come home after a long journey, and touched everything she saw, her little brown hands darting like harvest mice from one leaf to another. Mother Hildebrande listened to the childish high voice and the unchildish authority. 'This one is meadowsweet,' Alys said certainly. 'Good for sickness in the belly when there is much soiling. This one looks like rue: herb-grace.' She nodded solemnly. 'A very powerful herb against sweat-

14

ing sickness when it is seethed with marygold, feverfew, burnet sorrel and dragons.' She looked up at Mother Hildebrande. 'As a vinegar it can prevent the sickness, did you know? And this one I don't know.' She touched it, bent her little head and sniffed at it. 'It smells like a good herb for strewing,' she said. 'It has a clear, clean smell. But I don't know what powers it has. I have never seen it before.'

Mother Hildebrande nodded, never taking her eyes from the small face, and showed Alys flowers she had never seen, herbs from faraway countries whose names she had never even heard.

'You shall come to my study and see them on a map,' Mother Hildebrande promised. Alys' heart-shaped face looked up at her. 'And perhaps you could stay here. I could teach you to read and write,' the old abbess said. 'I need a little clerk, a clever little clerk.'

Alys smiled the puzzled smile of a child who has rarely heard kind words. 'I'd work for you,' she said hesitantly. 'I can dig, and draw water, and find and pick the herbs you want. If I worked for you, could I stay here?'

Mother Hildebrande put a hand out to Alys' pale curved cheek. 'Would you want to do that?' she asked. 'Would you take holy orders and leave the world you know far behind you? It's a big step, especially for a little girl. And you surely have kin who love you? You surely have friends and family that you love?'

'I've no kin,' Alys said, with the easy betrayal of childhood. 'I live with old Morach, she took me in twelve years ago, when I was a baby. She does not need me, she is no kin of mine. I am alone in the world.'

The old woman raised her eyebrows. 'And no one you love?' she asked. 'No one whose happiness depends on you?'

Alys' deep blue eyes opened wide. 'No one,' she said firmly.

The abbess nodded. 'You want to stay.'

'Yes,' Alys said. As soon as she had seen the large quiet rooms with the dark wood floors she had set her heart on staying. She had a great longing for the cleanness of the bare white cells, for the silence and order of the library, for the cool light of the refectory where the nuns ate in silence and listened to a clear voice reading holy words. She wanted to become a woman like Mother Hildebrande, old and respected. She wanted a chair to sit on and a silver plate for her dinner. She wanted a cup made of glass, not of tin or bone. And she longed, as only the hungry and the dirty passionately long, for clean linen and good food. 'I want to stay,' she said.

Mother Hildebrande rested her hand on the child's warm dirty head. 'And what of your little sweetheart?' she asked. 'You will have to renounce him. You may never, ever see him again, Alys. That's a hard price to pay.'

'I didn't know of places like this,' Alys said simply. 'I didn't know you could be clean like this, I didn't know that you could live like this unless you were Lord Hugh. I didn't know. Tom's farmhouse was the best I had ever seen, so that was what I wanted. I did not know any better.'

'And you want the best,' Mother Hildebrande prompted gently. The child's yearning for quality was endearing in one so young. She could not call it vanity and condemn it. The little girl loved the herb garden as well as the refectory silver.

Alys hesitated and looked up at the old lady. 'Yes, I do. I don't want to go back to Morach's. I don't want to go back to Tom. I want to live here. I want to live here for ever and ever and ever.'

Mother Hildebrande smiled. 'Very well,' she said gently. 'For ever and ever and ever. I will teach you to read and write and to draw and to work in the still-room before you need think of taking your vows. A little maid like you should not come into the order too young. I want you to be sure.'

'I am sure,' Alys said softly. 'I am sure now. I want to live here for always.'

Then Mother Hildebrande had taken Alys into the abbey and put her in charge of one of the young novitiates who had laughed at her broad speech and cut down a little habit for her. They had gone to supper together and to prayers.

It was characteristic of both Alys and Tom that while he waited for her as the sun set and a mocking lovers' moon came out to watch with him, Alys supped on hot milk and bread from fine pottery, and slept peacefully in the first clean pallet she had ever known.

All through the night the abbess waked for the little girl. All through the night she kneeled in the lowliest stall in the chapel and prayed for her. 'Keep her safe, Holy Mother,' she finished as the nuns filed in to their pews in sleepy silence for the first of the eight services of the day. 'Keep her safe, for in little Alys I think we have found a special child.'

Mother Hildebrande set Alys to work in the herb garden and still-room, and prepared her to take her vows. Alys was quick to learn and they taught her to read and write. She memorized the solemn cadences of the Mass without understanding the words, then slowly she came to understand the Latin and then to read and write it. She faultlessly, flawlessly charmed Mother Hildebrande into loving her as if she had been her own daughter. She was the favourite of the house. the pet of all the nuns, their little sister, their prodigy, their blessing. The women who had been denied children of their own took a special pleasure in teaching Alys and playing with her, and young women, who missed their little brothers and sisters at home, could pet Alys and laugh with her, and watch her grow.

Tom – after hanging around the gate for weeks and getting several beatings from the porter – slouched back to his farm and his parents, and waited in painful silence for Alys to come home to him as she had promised faithfully she would.

She never did. The quiet order of the place soothed her after Morach's tantrums and curses. The perfume of the still-room and the smell of the herbs scented her hands, her gown. She learned to love the smooth coolness of clean linen next to her skin, she saw her dirty hair and the wriggling lice shaved off without regret, and smoothed the crisp folds of her wimple around her face. Mother Hildebrande employed her in writing letters in Latin and English for the abbey, and dreamed of setting her to copying and illuminating a bible, a grand new bible for the abbey. Alys learned to kneel in prayer until the ache in her legs faded from her mind and all she could see through her half-closed eyes were the dizzying colours of the abbey's windows and the saints twirling like rainbows. When she was fourteen, and had been fasting all day and praying all night, she saw the statue of the Holy Mother turn Her graceful head and smile at her, directly at Alys. She knew then, as she had only hoped before, that Our Lady had chosen her for a special task, for a special lesson, and she dedicated herself to the life of holiness.

'Let me learn to be like mother,' she whispered. 'Let me learn to be like Mother Hildebrande.'

She saw Tom only once again. She spoke to him through the little grille in the thick gate, the day after she had taken her vows. In her sweet clear voice she told him that she was a Bride of Christ and she would never know a man. She told him to find himself a wife, and be happy with her blessing. And she shut the little hatch of the thick door in his surprised face before he could cry out to her, or even give her the brass ring he had carried in his pocket for her ever since the day they plighted their troth when they were little children of nine.

In the cold morning of her new life Sister Ann shivered, and drew her cape tighter around her. She dipped the bucket in the river and lugged it back up the path to the cottage. Morach, who had been watching her dreaming at the riverside, made no comment, but tumbled down the ladder to the fireside and nodded to Sister Ann to fill the pot and put some water on to heat.

She said nothing while they shared a small piece of bread with last night's porridge moistened with hot water. They shared a mug to drink the sour, strong water. It was brown and peaty from the moorland. Sister Ann was careful to turn it so her lips did not touch where Morach had drunk. Morach watched her from under her thick black eyebrows and said nothing.

'Now then,' she said, when Ann had washed the cup and plate and the tin spoon and set them at the fireside. 'What will you do?'

Sister Ann looked at her. Her dreaming of the past had reminded her of where she belonged. 'I must find another abbey,' she said decisively. 'My life is dedicated to Christ and His Sainted Mother.'

Morach hid a smile and nodded. 'Yes, little Sister,' she said. 'But all this was not sent solely to try your faith, others are suffering also. They are all being visited, they are all being questioned. You were fools enough at Bowes to make an enemy of Lord Hugh and his son but nowhere are the abbeys safe. The King has his eye on their wealth and your God is no longer keeping open house. I dare say there is not an abbey within fifty miles which would dare to open its doors to you.'

'Then I must travel. I must travel outside the fifty miles, north to Durham if need be, south to York. I must find another abbey. I have made my vows, I cannot live in the world.'

Morach picked her teeth with a twig from the basket of kindling and spat accurately into the flames. 'D'you have some story ready?' she asked innocently. 'Got some fable prepared already?'

Sister Ann looked blank. Already the skin on her head was less shiny, the haze of light brown hair showed like an itchy shadow. She rubbed it with a grimy hand and left another dark smear. Her dark blue eyes were sunk in her face with weariness. She looked as old as Morach herself.

'Why should I need a story?' she asked. Then she remembered her cowardice – 'Oh Mary, Mother of God . . .'

'If you were seen skipping off it would go hard for you,' Morach said cheerily. 'I can't think an abbess would welcome you once she knew that you smelled smoke and bolted like any sinner.'

'I could do penance . . .'

Morach chortled disbelievingly. 'It's more like they'd throw you out in your shift for strangers to use as they would,' she said. 'You're ruined, Sister Ann! Your vows are broke, your abbey is a smoking ruin, your sisters are dead or raped or fled. So what will you do?'

Sister Ann buried her face in her hands. Morach sat at her ease until her shoulders stopped shaking and the sobbed prayers were silenced. It took some time. Morach lit a little black pipe, inhaled the heady herbal smoke and sighed with pleasure.

'Best stay here,' she offered. 'That's your best way. We'll get news here of your sisters and how they fared. If the abbess survived she'll seek you here. Wander off, and she'll not know where to find you. Maybe all of the girls ran like you – scattered back to their old homes – perhaps you'll all be forgiven.'

Sister Ann shook her head. The smoke had been hot, the fire close to the cloisters. Most of the nuns would have been burned in their cells while they slept. 'I doubt they escaped,' she said.

Morach nodded, hiding a gleam of amusement. 'You were the first out, eh?' she asked. 'The quickest?' She paused for emphasis. 'Then there is nowhere for you to go. Nowhere at all.'

Sister Ann swayed against the blow. Morach noticed the pallor of her skin. The girl was sick with shock.

'I'll take you back,' Morach said. 'And people will stay mum. It will be as if you were never away. Four years gone and now you're back. Aged sixteen, aren't you?'

She nodded, only half hearing.

'Ready to wed,' Morach said with satisfaction. 'Or bed,' she added, remembering the reading of the bones and the young Lord Hugo.

'Not that,' she said, her voice very low. 'I will stay with you, Morach, and I'll work for you, as I did before. I know more now, and I can read and write. I know more herbs too and flowers – garden flowers, not just wild ones. But I will only do God's work, only healing and midwifery. No charms, no spells. I belong to Christ. I will keep my vows here, as well as I can, until I can find somewhere to go, until I can find an abbess who will take me. I will do God's work of healing here, I will be Christ's bride here ...' She looked around her. 'In this miserable place,' she said brokenly. 'I will do it as well as I can.'

'Well enough,' Morach said, quite unperturbed. 'You'll work for me. And when the young lord has ridden off north to harry the Scots and forgotten his new sport of tormenting nuns, you can step down to Castleton and seek some news.'

She hauled herself to her feet and shook out her filthy gown. 'Now you're back you can dig that patch,' she said. 'It's been overgrown since you left. I've a mind to grow some turnips there for the winter months.'

The girl nodded, and rose to her feet and went to the door. A new hoe stood at the side – payment in kind for hexing a neighbour's straying cattle.

'Sister Ann!' Morach called softly.

She spun around at once.

Morach scowled at her. 'You never answer to that name again,' she said. 'D'you hear me? Never. You're Alys again now, and if anyone asks you, tell them you went to stay with your kin near Penrith. You're Alys. That's your name. I gave it to you once, now I give it to you back. Forget being Sister Ann, that was another life and it ended badly. You're Alys now – remember it.'

Two

In the aftermath of the firing of the abbey there were soldiers and bullyboys chasing the rumours of hidden treasure and golden chalices. They had little joy in Bowes village where the half-dozen families did not take kindly to strangers and where four or five were now out of work with the abbey ruined and no services needed. Morach let it be known that she had a new apprentice, and if anyone remembered the previous girl who had gone four long years ago, no one said. It was not a time for speculation and gossip. There were a dozen vagrants still hanging around the ruins of the abbey – refugees from the nuns' charity with nowhere else to go. The villagers of Bowes locked their doors, refused anyone claiming rights of residence, and chose not to talk about the abbey, or the nuns, or the night of the fire, or the minor thefts and pillaging of the ruined abbey which went on in the later days.

It was said that the firing of the abbey had been a mistake. The soldiers led by the young Lord Hugo were homeward bound from a raid on the mosstroopers, and they stopped at the abbey only to frighten the nuns to do the King's will, and surrender their treasure and their bad popish ways. It had all begun with some wild sport, a bonfire of broken wood and some tar. Once the flames had caught there was nothing that Hugo could do, and besides the nuns had all died in the first minutes. The young lord had been drunk anyway, and could remember little. He confessed and did penance with his own priest – Father Stephen, one of the new faith who saw little sin in stamping out a nest of treasonous papists – and the villagers gleaned over the half-burned building and then started carting the stones away. Within a few weeks of her return to Morach's hovel, Alys could walk where she wished; no one recognized her as the half-starved waif who had gone away four years ago. Even if they had, no one would have taken the risk of reporting her, which would bring Lord Hugh down on the village or – even worse – his son, the mad young lord.

Alys could go freely into the village whenever she wished. But mostly she went up on the moor. Every day, after digging and weeding in the dusty scrape of the vegetable patch, she went down to the river to wash her hands and splash water over her face. In the first few days she stripped and waded into the water with her teeth chattering, to wash herself clean of the smell of sweat and smoke and midden. It was no use. The earth under her fingernails and the grime in the creases of her skin would not come clean in the cold brackish water, and anyway, wading back to the frosty bank with shivery goose-flesh skin, Alys had only dirty clothes to wear. After a few weeks she lost her shudder of repulsion against the odour of her own body, soon she could barely smell even the strong stench of Morach. She still splashed water in her face but she no longer hoped to keep clean.

She rubbed her face dry on the thick wool of her dirty robe and walked upstream along the river-bank till she came to the bridge where the river ran beneath a natural causeway of limestone slabs – wide enough to drive a wagon across, strong enough to carry oxen. She paused there and looked down into the brown peaty water. It flowed so slowly there seemed to be no movement at all, as if the river had died, had given up its life into stagnant, dark ponds.

Alys knew better. When she and Tom had been little children they had explored one of the caves which riddled the river-bank. Squirming like fox cubs they had gone downwards and downwards until the passage had narrowed and they had stuck – but below them, they had heard the loud echoing thunder of flowing water, and they knew they were near the real river, the secret river which flowed all day and all night in eternal darkness, hidden deep beneath the false river bed of dry stones above.

Tom had been scared at the echoing, rushing noise so far below them. 'What if it rose?' he asked her. 'It would come out here!'

'It does come out here,' Alys had replied. The seasons of her young life had been marked by the ebb and flow of the river, a dull drain in summer, a rushing torrent during the autumn storms. The gurgling holes where the sluggish water seeped away in summertime became springs and fountains in winter, whirlpools where the brown water boiled upwards, bubbling from the exploding pressure of the underground streams and underground rivers flooding from their stone cellars.

'Old Hob is down there,' Tom said fearfully, his eyes dark.

Alys had snorted and spat disdainfully towards the darkness before them. 'I ain't afraid of him!' she said. 'I reckon Morach can deal with him all right!'

Tom had crossed his finger with his thumb in the sign against witchcraft and crawled backwards out of the hole and into the sunshine. Alys would have lingered longer. She had not been boasting to Tom, it was true: raised by Morach she feared nothing.

'Until now,' she said quietly to herself. She looked up at the clear sky above her and the sun impartially burning down. 'Oh, Mother of God . . .' she started, then she broke off. 'Our Father . . .' she began again, and again fell silent. Then her mouth opened in a silent scream and she pitched herself forward on the short coarse grass of the moorland. 'God help me!' she said in a grief-stricken whisper. 'I am too afraid to pray!'

It seemed to her that she lay there in despair a long while. When she sat up again and looked around her the sun had moved – it was the middle of the afternoon, time for nones. Alys got to her feet slowly, like an old woman, as if all her bones were aching. She set off with small, slow steps up the hill to where the buds of early heather gleamed like a pale mauve mist on the slopes of the hill. A lapwing called overhead and fluttered down not far from her. Higher again in the blue air a lark circled and climbed, calling and calling, each higher note accompanied by a thrust of the little wings. Bees rolled drunkenly among the early heather flowers, the moor sweated honey. Everything around her was alive and thriving and joyful in the warm roil of the end of summer – everything but Alys, icy Alys, cold to her very bones.

She stumbled a little as she walked, her eyes watching the sheep track beneath her feet. Every now and then she moaned very softly, like an animal in a trap for a long, long night of darkness. 'How shall I ever get back?' she said to herself as she walked. 'How shall I ever get back? How shall I ever learn to bear it here?'

At the edge of the moor, where the land flattened in a curved sweep under the wide, unjudging sky, Alys paused. There was a little heap of stones tossed into a cairn by shepherds marking the path. Alys squatted down on one dry stone and leaned back against the others, closed her eyes and turned her face up to the sun, her face locked in a grimace of grief.

After a few moments she narrowed her eyes and looked southward. The moorland was very flat, bending across the skyline in a thousand shades of green, from the dark lushness of moss around a bog, to the pale yellow colour of weak grass growing on stone. The heather roots and old flowers showed pale grey and green, a bleak landscape of subtle beauty, half pasture, half desert. The new heather growth was dark green, the heather flowers pale as a haze. Alys looked more sharply. A man was striding across the moor, his plaid across his shoulder, his step determined. Alys got to her feet quietly, ready to turn and run. As he saw the movement he yelled out, and his voice was whipped away by the steady wind which blew over the top of the moor, even on the calmest of days. Alys hesitated, ready for flight, then he yelled again, faintly:

'Alys! Wait! It's me!'

Her hand went to her pocket where the beads of her rosary were rounded and warm. 'Oh no,' she said. She sat down again on the stones and waited for him to come up to her, watching him as he marched across the moor.

He had filled out in the four years she had been away. When she had left he had been a boy, lanky and awkward but with a fair coltish beauty. Now he was sturdy, thickset. As he came closer she saw that his face was tanned red from sun and wind, marred with red spiders of broken veins. His eyes, still that piercing blue, were fixed on her.

'Alys,' he said. 'I've only just heard you were back. I came at once to see you.'

'Your farm's the other way,' she said drily.

He flushed a still deeper red. 'I had to take a lamb over to Trowheads,' he said. 'This is my way back.'

Alys' dark eyes scanned his face. 'You never could lie to me, Tom.'

He hung his head and shuffled his thick boots in the dust. 'It's Liza,' he said. 'She watches me.'

'Liza?' Alys asked, surprised. 'Liza who?'

Tom dropped to sit on the heather beside her, his face turned away, looking back over the way he had come. 'Liza's my wife,' he said simply. 'They married me off after you took your vows.'

Alys flinched as if someone had pinched her. 'I didn't know,' she said. 'No one told me.'

Tom shrugged. 'I would have sent word but ...' he trailed off and let the silence hang. 'What was the use?' he asked.

Alys looked away, gripping the beads in her pocket so tight that they hurt her fingers. 'I never thought of you married,' she said. 'I suppose I should have known that you would.'

Tom shrugged. 'You've changed,' he said. 'You're taller, I reckon, and plumper. But your eyes are the same. Did they cut your hair?'

Alys nodded, pulling the shawl over her shaven head a little tighter.

'Your lovely golden hair!' Tom said, as if he were bidding it farewell.

A silence fell. Alys stared at him. 'You were married as soon as I left?' she asked.

Tom nodded.

'Are your mother and father still alive?'

He nodded again.

Alys' face softened, seeking sympathy. 'They did a

28

cruel thing to me that day,' she said. 'I was too young to be sent among strangers.'

Tom shrugged. 'They did what they thought was for the best,' he said. 'No way for them to foretell that the abbey would be burned and you would be homeless and husbandless at the end.'

'And in peril,' Alys said. 'If the soldiers come back they might take me. You won't tell anyone that I was at the abbey, will you?'

The look he shot at her was answer enough. 'I'd *die* rather than see you hurt,' he said with a suppressed anger. 'You know that! You've always known it! There never was anyone else for me and there never will be.'

Alys turned her face away. 'I may not listen to that,' she said.

He sighed, accepting the reproof. 'I'll keep your secret safe,' he said. 'In the village they think only that Morach has a new apprentice. She has said before that she was seeking a girl to do the heavy work. No one has thought of you. You've been forgotten. The word is that all the nuns are dead.'

'Why did you come this way then?' Alys demanded.

He shrugged his shoulders, his coarse skin blushing brick-red. 'I thought I'd know,' he said gruffly. 'If you had died I would have known it.' He thumped his chest. 'In here,' he said. 'Where I carry my pain for you. If you had died it would have gone ... or changed. I would have known if you were dead.'

Alys nodded, accepting Tom's devotion. 'And what of your marriage?' she asked. 'Are you comfortable? Do you have children?'

'A boy and a girl living,' he said indifferently. 'And two dead.' He paused. There were four years of longing in his voice. 'The girl looks a little like you sometimes,' he said.

Alys turned her clear, heart-shaped face towards him. 'I have been waiting to see you,' she said. Tom shivered helplessly. Her voice was as piercing and sweet as plainsong. 'You have to help me get away.'

'I have been racking my brains to think how I can serve you, how I can get you away from that wretched old woman and that hovel!' Tom exclaimed. 'But I cannot think how! Liza watches the farm, she knows to a groat what we have made. My mother and she are hand in glove. I took a risk coming to see you at all.'

'You always did dare anything to be with me,' Alys said encouragingly.

Tom inspected a callus on the palm of his hand. He picked moodily at the hard skin with one stubby fingernail. 'I know,' he said sullenly. 'I ran to you like a puppy when I was a child, and then I waited outside the abbey for you like a whipped dog.'

He shifted his gaze to Alys' attentive face. 'Now you are come out of the abbey everything is changed again,' he said hesitantly. 'The King's Visitors said that you were not true nuns and the lord's chaplain says Hugo did well to drive you out. The abbey is gone, you are a free woman again, Alys.' He did not dare look at her but stared at the ground beneath his feet. 'I never stopped loving you,' he said. 'Will you be my lover now?'

Alys shook her head with an instinctive revulsion. 'No!' she said. 'My vows still stand. Don't think of me like that, Tom. I belong to God.'

She paused, shot him a sideways glance. It was a difficult path she had to find. He had to be tempted to help her, but not tempted to sin. 'I wish you would help me,' she said carefully. 'If you have money, or a horse I could borrow, I could find an abbey which might take me in. I thought you might know of somewhere, or can you find somewhere for me?'

Tom got to his feet. 'I cannot,' he said simply. 'The farm is doing badly, we have only one working horse and no money. God knows I would do anything in the world for you, Alys, but I have neither money nor a horse for you.'

Alys' pale face was serene though she was screaming inside. 'Perhaps you will think of something,' she said. 'I am counting on you, Tom. Without your help, I don't know what will become of me.'

'You were the one who always did the thinking,' he reminded her. 'I just came to see you, running like a dog to the master's whistle, like I always have done. The moment I heard the abbey was fired I thought of you. Then when I heard Morach had a new wench I thought she might be you. I came running to you. I had no plans.'

Alys rose too and stood at his shoulder, very close. She could smell the stale sweat on him, and the stink of old blood from butchering, sour milk from dairying. He smelled like a poor man, like an old man. She stepped back.

Tom put his hand on her arm and Alys froze, forcing herself not to shake him off. He stared into her face. Alys' dark blue eyes, as candid as a child's, met his gaze.

'You don't want me as a man,' he said with a sudden insight. 'You wanted to see me, and you talk sweet, but all you want is for me to save you from living with Morach, just as your old abbess saved you from her before.'

'Why not?' Alys demanded. 'I cannot live there. Morach is deep in sin and dirt. I cannot stay there! I don't want you as a man, my vows and my inclinations are not that way. But I need you desperately as a friend, Tom. Without your help I don't know what I will do. We promised to be true to one another and to always be there when the other was in any need or trouble.' She tightened the rack on his guilt. 'I would have helped you if you had been in need, Tom. If I had a horse you would never walk.'

Tom shook his head slowly, as if to clear it. 'I can't think straight!' he said. 'Alys, tell me simply what you want me to do! You know I will do it. You know I always did what you wished.'

'Find somewhere I can go,' she said rapidly. 'Morach hears nothing and I dare not go further than Castleton. But you can travel and ask people. Find me a nunnery which is safe, and then take me there. Lord Hugo cannot rage around the whole of the north. There must be other abbeys safe from his spite: Hartlepool, Durham or Whitby. Find where I can go, Tom, and take me.'

'You cannot hope to find your abbess again?' Tom asked. 'I heard that all the nuns died.'

Alys shook her head. She could remember the heat in the smoke which had warned her that the flames were very close. She remembered the thin clear scream of pain she had heard as she dived through the garden door. 'I will find a new order, and take a new name, and take my vows again,' she said.

Tom blinked. 'Are you allowed to do that?' he asked. 'Won't they wonder who you are and where you come from?'

Alys slid a measuring sideways glance at him. 'You would surely vouch for me, Tom. You could tell them I was your sister, could you not?'

Tom shook his head again. 'No! I don't know! I suppose I would. Alys, I don't know what I can do and what I can't do! My head's whirling!'

Alys stretched out her soft white hand to him and touched him gently in the centre of his forehead, between his eyes, with all her power in her fingertips. She felt her fingers warm as her power flowed through them. For a dizzying moment she thought she could do anything with Tom, make him believe anything, do anything. Tom closed his eyes at her touch and swayed towards her as a rowan sways in a breath of wind.

'Alys,' he said, and his voice was filled with longing.

She took her hand away and he slowly opened his eyes.

'I must go,' she said. 'Do you promise you will find somewhere for me?'

He nodded. 'Aye,' he said and hitched the plaid at his shoulder.

'And take me there?'

'I'll do all I can,' he said. 'I will ask what abbeys are safe. And when I find somewhere, I'll get you to it, cost me what it will.'

Alys raised her hand in farewell and watched him walk away. When he was too distant to hear she breathed out her will after him. 'Do it, Tom,' she said. 'Do it at once. Find me a place. Get me back to an abbey. I cannot stay here.'

It grew colder. The winds got up for a week of gales in September and when they fell still the moors, the hills, and even the valley were shrouded in a thick mist which did not lift for days. Morach lay in bed later and later every morning.

'I'll get up when the fire's lit and the porridge is hot,' she said, watching Alys from the sleeping platform. 'There's little point in us both getting chilled to death.'

Alys kept her head down and said little. Every evening

33

she would turn her hands to the light of the fire and inspect the palms for roughness. The skin had grown red and sore, and then blistered, and the blisters had broken and then healed. The plump heel of her thumb was toughened already, and at the base of each finger the skin was getting dry and hard. She rubbed the oil from sheep's fleeces into the calluses, frowning in disgust at the rich, dirty smell, but nothing could stop her hands hardening and growing red and rough.

'I am still fit to be a nun,' she whispered to herself. She told her rosary before she went to bed and said the evening prayers of vespers, not knowing the time, far away from the discipline of the chapel bell. One evening she stumbled over the words and realized she was forgetting them already. Forgetting her prayers. 'I'm still fit to be a nun,' she said grimly before she slept. 'Still fit to be a nun if I get there soon.'

She waited for news from Tom but none came. All she could hear in Bowes were confused stories of inspections and changes. The King's Visitors went everywhere, demanding answers in silent cloisters, inspecting the treasures in orders sworn to poverty. No one knew how far the King would go. He had executed a bishop, he had beheaded Thomas More, the most revered man in England, he had burned monks at the stake. He claimed that the whole clergy was his, parish priests, vicars, bishops. And now he was looking to the abbeys, the nunneries, the monasteries. He wanted their power, he wanted their land, he could not survive without their wealth. It was not a time to attempt to enter an order with a false name and a burned gown.

'I am cursed and followed by my curse,' Alys said resentfully, as she hauled water for Morach and pulled turnips from the cold, sticky ground.

Alys felt the cold badly. After four years of sleeping in a stone building where huge fires of split trees were banked in to burn all night she found the mud floor of Morach's cottage unbearably damp and chill. She started coughing at night, and her cough turned to racking sobs of homesickness. Worst of all were the dreams, when she dreamed she was safe in the abbey, leaning back against Mother Hildebrande's knees and reading aloud by the light of clear wax candles. One night she dreamed that Mother Hildebrande had come to the cottage and called to Alys, scrabbling on her knees in the mud of the vegetable patch. 'Of course I am not dead!' Mother Hildebrande had said joyously. Alys felt her mother's arms come around her and hold her close, smelled the clean, sweet scent of her starched linen. 'Of course I am not dead!' she said. 'Come home with me!'

Alys clung to the rags of her pillow and closed her eyes tighter to try to stay asleep, to live inside the dream. But always the cold of the floor would wake her, or Morach's irascible yell, and she would open her eyes and know again the ache of loss, and have to face again that she was far from her home and far from the woman who loved her, with no hope of seeing her mother or any of her sisters ever again.

It rained for weeks, solid torrential rain which wept down out of the skies unceasingly. Every morning Alys woke to find her pallet bed wet from the earth of the hovel and her robe and her cape damp with morning mist. Morach, grumbling, made a space for her on the sleeping platform and woke her once, twice, a night to clamber down the rickety ladder and keep the fire burning. Every day Alys went out downriver towards Bowes where the oak, elm and beech trees grew, looking for firewood. Every day she dragged home a fallen bough of heavy timber and hacked at it with Morach's old axe. Fetching wood for the pile could take most of the hours of daylight, but also there was the pot to be emptied on the sloppy midden, water to be lugged up from the river, and turnips and carrots to be pulled in the vegetable patch. Once a week there was marketing to do in Bowes – a weary five-mile trudge there and back on the slippery riverside track or the exposed high road. Alys missed the well-cooked rich food of the nunnery and became paler and thinner. Her face grew gaunt and strained. When she went into Bowes one day a child shied a stone at the back of her gown and as she turned and cursed him he howled with fright at the blank, mad anger of her eyes.

With the cold weather came sickness. Every day another person came to tap on Morach's door and ask her or Alys for a spell or a draught or a favour to keep away the flux or chills or fevers. There were four childbirths in Bowes and Alys went with Morach and dragged bloody, undersized babies screaming into the world.

'You have the hands for it,' Morach said, looking at Alys' slim long fingers. 'And you practised on half a dozen paupers' babies at that nunnery of yours. You can do all the childbirths. You have the skills and I'm getting too old to go out at midnight.'

Alys looked at her with silent hatred. Childbirth was the most dangerous task for a wise woman. Too much could go wrong, there were two lives at risk, people wanted both the mother and the child to survive and blamed the midwife for sickness and death. Morach feared failure, feared the hatred of the village. It was safer for her to send Alys alone.

The village was nervous, suspicious. A wise woman had been taken up at Boldron, not four miles away, taken and charged with plaguing her neighbour's cattle. The evidence against her was dramatic. Neighbours swore they had seen her running down the river, her feet moving swiftly over the water but dry-shod. Someone had seen her whispering into the ear of a horse, and the horse had gone lame. A woman said that they had jostled each other for a flitch of bacon at Castleton market and that ever since her arm had ached and she feared it would rot and fall off. A man swore that he had ridden the wise woman down in the fog on Boldron Lane and she had cursed him and at once his horse shied and he had fallen. A little boy from the village attested that he had seen her flying and talking with the doves at the manor dovecot. All the country had evidence against her, the trial took days.

'It's all nonsense,' Alys said, coming back from Bowes with the news. 'Chances that could happen to anyone, a little child's bad dream. It's as if they had gone mad. They are listening to everything. Anyone can say anything against her.'

Morach looked grim. 'It's a bad fashion,' she said, surly. Alys dumped a sack of goods on the floor beside the fire and threw three fatty rashers of bacon into the broth bubbling in the three-legged pot. 'A bad fashion,' Morach said again. 'I've seen it come through before, like a plague. Sometimes this time of year, sometimes midsummer. Whenever people are restless and idle and spiteful.'

Alys looked at her fearfully. 'Why do they do it?' she asked.

'Sport,' Morach said. 'It's a dull time of year, autumn. People sit around fires and tell stories to frighten themselves. There's colds and agues that nothing can cure. There's winter and starvation around the corner. They need someone to blame. And they like to mass together, to shout and name names. They're an animal then, an animal with a hundred mouths and a hundred beating hearts and no thought at all. Just appetites.'

'What will they do to her?' Alys asked.

Morach spat accurately into the fire. 'They've started already,' she said. 'They've searched her for marks that she has been suckling the devil and they've burned the marks off with a poker. If the wounds show pus, that proves witchcraft. They'll strap her hands and legs and throw her in the River Greta. If she comes up alive – that's witchcraft. They might make her put her hand in the blacksmith's fire and swear her innocence. They might tie her out on the moor all night to see if the devil rescues her. They'll play with her until their lust is slaked.'

Alys handed Morach a bowl of broth and a trencher of bread. 'And then?'

'They'll set up a stake on the village green and the priest will pray over her, and then someone – the blacksmith probably – will strangle her and then they'll bury her at the crossroads,' Morach said. 'Then they'll look around for another, and another after that. Until something else happens, a feast or a holy day, and they have different sport. It's like a madness which catches a village. It's a bad time for us. I'll not go into Bowes until the Boldron wise woman is dead and forgotten.'

'How shall we get flour?' Alys asked. 'And cheese?'

'You can go,' Morach said unfeelingly. 'Or we can do without for a week or two.'

Alys shot a cold look at Morach. 'We'll do without,' she said, though her stomach rumbled with hunger.

At the end of October it grew suddenly sharply cold with a hard white frost every morning. Alys gave up washing for the winter season. The river water was stormy and brown between stones which were white and slippery with ice in the morning. Every day she heaved a full bucket of water up the hill to the cottage for cooking; she had neither time nor energy to fetch water for washing. Alys' growing hair was crawly with lice, her black nun's robe rancid. She caught fleas between her fingers and cracked their little bodies between her finger and ragged thumbnail without shame. She had become inured to the smell, to the dirt. When she slopped out the cracked chamber-pot on to the midden she no longer had to turn away and struggle not to vomit. Morach's muck and her own, the dirt from the hens and the scraps of waste piled high on the midden and Alys spread it and dug it into the vegetable patch, indifferent to the stench.

The clean white linen and the sweet smell of herbs in the still-room and flowers on the altar of the abbey were like a dream. Sometimes Alys thought that Morach's lie was true and she had never been to the abbey, never known the nuns. But then she would wake in the night and her dirty face would be stiff and salty with tears and she would know that she had been dreaming of her mother again, and of the life that she had lost.

She could forget the pleasure of being clean, but her hungry, growing, young body reminded her daily of the food at the abbey. All autumn Alys and Morach ate thin vegetable broth, sometimes with a rasher of bacon boiled in it and the bacon fat floating in golden globules on the top. Sometimes they had a slice of cheese, always they had black rye bread with the thick, badly milled grains tough in the dough. Sometimes they had the innards of a newly slaughtered pig from a grateful farmer's wife. Sometimes they had rabbit. Morach had a snare and Alys set a net for fish. Morach's pair of hens, which lived underfoot in the house feeding miserably off scraps, laid well for a couple of days and Morach and Alys ate eggs. Most days they had a thin gruel for breakfast and then fasted all day until nightfall when they had broth and bread and perhaps a slice of cheese or meat.

Alys could remember the taste of lightly stewed carp from the abbey ponds. The fast days when they ate salmon and trout or sea fish brought specially for them from the coast. The smell of roast beef with thick fluffy puddings, the warm, nourishing porridge in the early morning after prayers with a blob of abbey honey in the middle and cream as yellow as butter to pour over the top, hot ale at bedtime, the feast-day treats of marchpane, roasted almonds, sugared fruit. She craved for the heavy, warm sweetness of hippocras wine after a feast, venison in port-wine gravy, jugged hare, vegetables roasted in butter, the tang of fresh cherries. Sometimes Morach kicked her awake in the night and said with a sleepy chuckle: 'You're moaning, Alys, you're dreaming of food again. Practise mortifying your flesh, my little angel!' And Alys would find her mouth running wet with saliva at her dreams of dinners in the quiet refectory while a nun read aloud to them, and always at the head of the table was Mother Hildebrande, her arms outstretched, blessing the food and giving thanks for the easy richness of their lives, and sometimes glancing down the table to Alys to make sure that the little girl had plenty. 'Plenty,' Alys said longingly.

At the end of October there was a plague of sickness in Bowes with half a dozen children and some adults vomiting and choking on their vomit. Mothers walked the few miles out to Morach's cottage every day with a gift, a round yellow cheese, or even a penny. Morach burned fennel root over the little fire, set it to dry and then ground it into powder and gave Alys a sheet of good paper, a pen and ink.

'Write a prayer,' she said. 'Any one of the good prayers in Latin.'

Alys' fingers welcomed the touch of a quill. She held it awkwardly in her swollen, callused hands like the key to a kingdom she had lost.

'Write it! Write it!' Morach said impatiently. 'A good prayer against sickness.'

Very carefully Alys dipped her pen and wrote the simple words of the Lord's Prayer, her lips moving in time to the cadence of the Latin. It was the first prayer Mother Hildebrande had ever taught her.

Morach watched inquisitively. 'Is it done?' she asked, and when Alys nodded, silenced by the tightness of her throat, Morach took the paper and tore it into half a dozen little squares, tipped the dusty powder into it and twisted the paper to keep the powder safe.

'What are you doing?' Alys demanded.

'Magic,' Morach replied ironically. 'This is going to keep us fat through the winter.'

She was right. The people in Bowes and the farmers all around bought the black powder wrapped in the special paper for a penny a twist. Morach bought more paper and set Alys to writing again. Alys knew there could be no sin in writing the Lord's Prayer but felt uneasy when Morach tore the smooth vellum into pieces.

'Why do you do it?' Alys asked curiously one day, watching Morach grind the root in a mortar nursed on her lap as she sat by the fire on her stool.

41

Morach smiled at her. 'The powder is strong against stomach sickness,' she said. 'But it is the spell that you write that gives it the power.'

'It's a prayer,' Alys said contemptuously. 'I don't make spells and I would not sell burned fennel and a line of prayer for a penny a twist.'

'It makes people well,' Morach said. 'They take it and they say the spell when the vomiting hits them. Then the attack passes off.'

'How can it?' Alys asked impatiently. 'Why should a torn piece of prayer cure them?'

Morach laughed. 'Listen to the running nun!' she exclaimed to the fire. 'Listen to the girl who worked in the herb garden and the still-room and the nuns' infirmary and yet denies the power of plants! Denies the power of prayer! It cures them, my wench, because there is potency in it. And in order to say the prayer they have to draw breath. It steadies them. I order that the prayer has to be said to the sky so they have to open a window and breathe clean air. All of those that have died from the vomiting are those that were weak and sickly and in a panic of fear in dirty rooms. The spell works because it's powerful. And it helps if they believe it.'

Alys crossed herself in a small gesture between her breasts. Morach would have mocked if she had seen.

'And if they can pay for a spell then they can pay for good food and clean water,' Morach said fairly. 'The chances are that they are stronger before the sickness takes them. The rich are always blessed.'

'What if it fails?' Alys asked.

Morach's face hardened. 'You had better pray to your Lady that it never fails,' she said. 'If it fails then I can say that they have been bewitched by another power, or the spell has failed them because they did not do it right. If it fails I go at once to the heirs and try to buy their friendship. But if they are vengeful and if their cattle die too, then you and I stay away from Bowes, keep our heads down, and keep out of sight until the body is buried and people have forgot.'

'It's wrong,' Alys said positively. 'At the abbey we followed old books, we knew the herbs we grew, we made them into tinctures and we drank them from measured glasses. This is not herbalism but nonsense. Lies dressed up in dog Latin to frighten children!'

'Nonsense is it?' Morach demanded, her quick anger aroused. 'There are people in this village who will swear I can make a woman miscarry by winking at her! There are people in this village who think I can kill a healthy beast by snapping my fingers over its water pail. There are people in this village who think the devil speaks to me in my dreams and I have all his powers at my command!'

'Aren't you afraid?' Alys asked.

Morach laughed, her voice harsh and wild. 'Afraid?' she said. 'Who is not afraid? But I am more afraid of starving this winter, or dying of cold because we have no firewood. Ever since my land was stolen from me I have had no choice. Ever since my land was taken from me I have been afraid. I am a wise woman – of course I am afraid!'

She put the pestle and mortar to one side and then spooned the dust into one scrap of paper and then another, her hands steady.

'Besides,' she said slyly, 'I am less afraid than I was. Much much less afraid than I was.'

'Are you?' Alys asked, recognizing the note of torment in Morach's voice.

'Oh, yes,' Morach said gleefully. 'If they seek for a witch in Bowes now, who do you think they will take first? A little old woman with a few herbs in her purse who has been there for years and never done great harm – or a girl as lovely as sin who will speak with no one, nor court with any man. A girl who is neither maid nor woman, saint nor sinner. A girl who is seen in Bowes very seldom, but always with her cloak around her shoulders and a shawl over her head. A girl who talks to no one, and has no young women friends. A girl who avoids men, who keeps her eyes down when one crosses her path. It is *you* who should be afraid, Alys. It is *you* who they see as a strange woman, as someone out of the ordinary. So it is *you* that they think has the skill to cure the vomiting. It will be *you* they praise or blame. It should be *you* who is afraid!'

'They cannot think these are spells!' Alys exclaimed. 'I told you from the start they were prayers! You asked me to write a prayer and I did! They cannot think that I do magic!'

'Go on!' Morach gestured to her impatiently. 'Write some more! Write some more! I need it to wrap these doses. It is your writing, Alys, that makes the powder work. Ever since you came back, the fennel has cured the vomiting. They say *you* are the cunning woman and I am your servant. They say you have come from the devil. They say that the singed corner of your robe was from the fires of hell – and that you are the bride of the devil.'

'Who says?' Alys demanded stoutly though her voice shook a little. 'I don't believe anyone says anything.'

'Liza – Tom's wife,' Morach said triumphantly. 'She says you've tampered with Tom's sleep. He names you in his sleep – a sure sign of hexing.'

44

Alys laughed bitterly. 'Oh aye,' she said tartly. 'He is calling me to rescue him from her sharp tongue.'

'Curse her then?' Morach's face was bright in the shadowy cottage. 'Try it! Curse her to death and make Tom a widower, rich with her dowry, so that he can return to you and you can use your roughened hands on his land where you will see the benefit. She's a useless, spiteful woman, no one's friend. No one would miss her.'

'Don't,' Alys said quickly. 'Don't speak of such things. You know I would not do it and I don't have the power.'

'You *do* have the power,' Morach insisted. 'You know it and I know it! You ran from your power and you hoped your God would keep you safe if you forgot your skills. But here you are, back with me, and it is as if you were never away. There are no safe nunneries left, Alys! There is nowhere for you to go! You will stay with me forever unless you go to a man. Why not Tom? You liked him well enough when you were young and he has never loved another woman. You could kill Liza. You *should* kill Liza. I can tell you the ways to do it. Hundreds of ways. And then you can live soft in Tom's farmhouse, and wash every day as you long to do, and even say your prayers, and think of how we would eat! A little spell and a great difference. Do it, Alys!'

'I cannot!' Alys said desperately. 'I cannot. And even if I could, I would not do it. I have no power but my learning from the abbey. I will not dabble in your spells. They mean nothing, you know nothing. I shall never use your skills.'

Morach shrugged her shoulders and tied the twists of powder with a thread. 'I think you will,' she said in an undertone. 'And I think you feel your power in your fingertips, and taste it on your tongue. Don't you, my Alys? When you are alone on the moor and the wind is blowing softly, don't you *know* you can call it? Bid it go where you will? Blow health or sickness? Wealth or poverty? When you were on your knees in the abbey, couldn't you *feel* the power around you and in you? I can feel the power in me – aye, and I can feel it in you too. The old abbess saw it clearly enough. She wanted it for her God! Well, now your power is freed again and you can use it where you will.'

Alys shook her head. 'No,' she said determinedly. 'I feel nothing. I know nothing. I have no power.'

'Look at the fire,' Morach said instantly. 'Look at the fire.'

Alys looked towards it, the banks of badly cut peat glowing orange, and the burning log lying on the embers.

'Turn it blue,' Morach whispered.

Alys felt the thought of blue flames in her mind, paused for a moment with the picture of blue flames before her inner eye. The flames bobbed, flickered, and then they burned a steady bright periwinkle blue. The embers glowed like a summer sky, the ashes were a deep dark violet.

Morach laughed delightedly, Alys snapped her gaze away from the fire and the flame spurted and flared orange again.

Alys crossed herself hastily. 'Stop it, Morach,' she said irritably. 'Stupid tricks for frightening children. As if I would be fooled by them after a childhood with you and your cheating arts.'

Morach shook her head. 'I touched nothing,' she said easily. 'It was your gaze, and your mind, and your power. And you can run and run from it as fast as you

46

ran from your holy life. But the two of them will keep pace with you forever, Alys. In the end you will have to choose.'

'I am a nun,' Alys said through her teeth. 'There will be no magic and dark skills for me. I do not want them. I do not want you. And I do not want Tom. Hear me now, Morach, as soon as I can leave here, I will go. I swear to you that if I could leave this very night, I would be gone. I want none of it. None of it. If I could, I swear that I would ride away from this place now and never come back.'

'Hush!' Morach said suddenly. Alys froze into silence and the two women strained their ears to listen.

'Someone outside the door,' Morach hissed. 'What can you hear?'

'A horse,' Alys whispered. 'No, two horses.'

In a quick gesture Morach tipped the pot of water on to the embers of the turf fire. The glow died at once, the room filled with thick smoke. Alys clapped her hand over her mouth so as not to choke.

The banging on the little wooden door was like thunder. The two women shrank together, their eyes fixed on the entrance as if the door would splinter and fall apart. Someone was hammering on it with a sword hilt.

'I'll open it,' Morach said. In the darkness her face was as white as a drowned woman's. 'You get yourself upstairs and hide under my pallet. If it's the witch-taker it'll likely be for me, you might escape. No one will listen to Tom's wife without others to speak against you; and no one has died this week. Go on, wench, it's the only chance I can give you.'

Alys did not hesitate, she fled towards the ladder and upwards like a shadow.

'I'm coming,' Morach said in a harsh grumbling

47

voice. 'Leave an old woman's door on the hinge, can't you?'

She checked that Alys was hidden above, and then swung the wooden latch to open the door.

The two tall men on horseback filled the skyline like giants. Around their shoulders the stars shone and the dark streams of cloud raced past their looming heads.

'We want the young wise woman,' the man said. His face was muffled against the cold, he was armed only with a cudgel and a short stabbing dagger. 'The new young wise woman. Get her.'

'I'm not rightly sure . . .' Morach started, her voice a plaintive whine. 'She is not . . .'

The man reached down and grabbed the shawl at Morach's throat and lifted her up till her face was near his. The horse shifted uneasily and Morach gurgled and choked, her feet kicking.

'Lord Hugh at the castle orders it,' he said. 'He is ill. He wants the young wise woman and the spell against the vomiting. Get her, and no harm will come of it. He will pay you. If you hide her I shall burn this stinking shack around your ears with the door nailed up, and you inside.'

He dropped Morach back on her feet, she stumbled back against the door frame, and turned back towards the cottage, half closing the door.

Alys was looking down from the sleeping platform, her eyes huge in her white face. 'I cannot . . .' she said.

Morach snatched the shawl from her own shoulders, spread it on the hearth and heaped into it handfuls of herbs, a black-backed prayer-book, four of the twists of powder, a shiny lump of quartz tied up with a long scrap of ribbon, and the pestle and mortar.

'You'll have to try or they'll kill us both,' she said

bleakly. 'It's a chance, and a good chance. Others have been cured of the sickness. You'll have to take the gamble.'

'I could run,' Alys said. 'I could hide on the moor for the night.'

'And leave me? I'd be dead by dawn,' Morach said. 'You heard him. He'll burn me alive.'

'They don't want you,' Alys said urgently. 'They would not do that. You could tell them I'm spending the night in Bowes. I could hide by the river, in one of the caves, while they're gone to look for me.'

Morach looked at her hard. 'You've a bitter taste,' she said scowling. 'For all your lovely face you've a bitter taste, Alys. You'd run, wouldn't you? And leave me to face them. You'd rather I died than you took a chance.'

Alys opened her mouth to deny it but Morach thrust the shawl into her hands before she could speak.

'You would gamble with my death, but I will not,' Morach said harshly, pushing her towards the door. 'Out you go, my girl, I'll come to the castle when I can, to get news of you. See what you can do. They grow herbs there, and flowers. You may be able to use your nun's arts as well as mine.'

Alys hefted the bundle. Her whole face was trembling. 'I cannot!' she said. 'I have no skills, I know nothing! I grew a few herbs, I did as I was ordered at the abbey. And your arts are lies and nonsense.'

Morach laughed bitterly. The man outside hammered on the door again. 'Come, wench!' he said. 'Or I will smoke you out!'

'Take my lies and nonsense, and your own ignorance, and use it to save your skin,' Morach said. She had to push Alys towards the door. 'Hex him!' she hissed, as she got the girl over the threshold. 'You have the power, I can feel it in you. You turned the flame blue with your thought. Take your powers and use them now, for your own sake! Hex the old lord into health, Alys, or you and I are dead women.'

Alys gave a little moan of terror and then the man on the horse leaned down and gripped her under both arms and hauled her up before him.

'Come!' he said to his companion and they wheeled their horses around, the hooves tearing up the vegetable patch. Then they were gone into the darkness, and the wind whipped away the noise of the gallop.

Morach waited a while at the cottage doorway, ignoring the cold and the smoke from the doused fire swirling thickly behind her, listening to the silence now that Alys had gone.

'She has power,' she said to the night sky, watching the clouds unravelling past the half-moon. 'She swore that she would go, and in that moment the horses came for her and she was gone. What will she wish for next? What will she wish for next?'

Three

Alys had never been on a galloping horse and she clung
to the pommel of the saddle before her, thrown and
jolted by the horse's great rolling strides. The wind
rushed into her face and the hard grip of the man
behind her was that of a jailer. When she looked down
she could see the heaving shoulders of the great horse,
when she looked forward she saw its tossing mane.
They went over the little stone bridge from the moorland
road to Castleton with sparks flying upwards from the
horses' hooves, and clattered up the cobbled street between the dozen stone-built houses at the same breakneck speed. Not a light showed at any of the shuttered
windows, even the smaller houses, set back from the
main street on earth roads, and the little shanties behind
them on waste ground were dark and silent.

Alys was so shaken that she had no breath to cry out,
even when the horse wheeled around to the left and
thundered up the drawbridge into the great black maw
of the castle gateway. There was a brief challenge from
two soldiers, invisible in the darkness of the doorway,
and a gruff response from the rider and then they were
out into the moonlit castle grounds. Alys had a confused
impression of a jumble of stables and farm buildings on
her right, the round tower of the guardroom on her left,
the smell of pigs, and then they crossed a second drawbridge over a deep stagnant moat, with the noise of the
hooves rumbling like thunder on the wooden bridge,
and plunged into the darkness of another gateway.

The horses halted as two more soldiers stepped

forward with a quick word of challenge and stared at the riders and Alys, before waving them through into a garden. Alys could see vegetable-beds and herb-beds and the bare-branched outline of apple trees; but before them, squat and powerful against the night sky, was a long two-storey building with a pair of great double doors set plumb in the centre. Alys could hear the noise of many people shouting and laughing inside. The door opened and a man stepped out to urinate carelessly against the wall; bright torchlight spilled out into the yard and she could smell hot roasted meats. They rode the length of the building, Alys saw the glow of a bakehouse fire in a little round hive of a building set apart from the rest on their right, and then before them were two brooding towers, built with grey stones as thick as boulders, showing no lights.

'Where are we?' Alys gasped, clinging to the man's hands as he thrust her down from the saddle.

He nodded to the tower which adjoined the long building. 'Lord Hugh's tower,' he said briefly. He looked over her head and shouted. An answering cry came from inside the tower and Alys heard a bolt sliding easily back.

'And what's that tower?' she asked urgently. She pointed behind them to the opposing tower, smaller and more squat, set into the high exterior castle wall, with no windows at all at the base and a flight of stone steps running up the outside to the first storey.

'Pray you never know!' the man said grimly. 'That's the prison tower. The first floor is the guardroom, and down below are the cells. They have the rack there, and thumbscrews, a press and bridle. Pray you never see them, wench! You come out more talkative – but taller! Much taller! Thinner! And sometimes toothless!

Cheaper than the toothdrawer at any price!' He laughed harshly. 'Here!' He called a soldier who stepped out of the shadows. 'Here is the wise woman from Bowes. Take her and her bundle to Lord Hugh at once. Let no one tamper with her. My lord's orders!'

He thrust Alys towards the soldier and he grabbed her and marched her up the flight of stone steps to the arched doorway. The door, as thick as a tree trunk, stood open. Inside, a torch flickered, staining the wall behind it with a stripe of black soot. The castle breathed coldness, sweated damp. Alys drew her shawl over her rough cropped head with a shudder. It was colder even than Morach's draughty cottage. Here the castle walls held the wind out, but no sun ever shone. Alys crossed herself beneath her shawl. She had a premonition that she was walking towards mortal danger. The dark corridor before her – lit at the corners with smoking torches – was like her worst nightmares of the nunnery: a smell of smoke, a crackle of flames, and a long, long corridor with no way out.

'Come,' the man said grimly and took Alys' arm in a hard grip. She trailed behind him, up a staircase which circled round and around inside the body of the tower, until he said, 'Here now,' and knocked, three short knocks and two long, on a massive wooden door. It swung open. Alys blinked. It was bright inside, half a dozen men were lounging on benches at a long table, the remains of their supper spread before them, two big hunting dogs growling over bones in the corner. The air was hot with rancid smoke and the smell of sweat.

'A wench!' said one. 'That's kindly of you!'

Alys shrank back behind the soldier who still held her. He shook his head. 'Nay,' he said. 'It's the wise woman from Bowes, come to see my lord. Is he well?'

A young man at the far end of the room beckoned them through. 'No better,' he said in an undertone. 'He wants to see her at once.'

He pulled back a tapestry on the wall behind him and swung open a narrow arched door. The soldier released Alys and thrust her bundle into her hands. She hesitated.

'Go on,' the young man said.

She paused again. The soldier behind her put his hand in the small of her back and pushed her forward. Alys, caught off balance, stumbled into the room and past the watching men. Before her, through the door, was a flight of shallow stone steps lit by a single guttering torch. There was a small wooden door at the head of the flight of stairs. As she climbed up, it slowly opened.

The room was dark, lit only by firelight and one pale wax candle standing on a chest by a small high bed. At the head of the bed stood a tiny man, no taller than a child. His dark eyes were on Alys, and his hand smoothed the pillow.

On the pillow was a lean face engraved by sickness and suffering, the skin as yellow as birch leaves in autumn. But the eyes, when the heavy lids flew open and stared at Alys, were as bright and black as an old peregrine falcon.

'You the wise woman?' he asked.

'I have a very little skill,' Alys said. 'And very little learning. You should send for someone learned, an apothecary or even a barber. You should have a physician.'

'They would cup me till I died,' the sick man said slowly. 'They have cupped me till I am near dead already. Before I threw them out they said they could

54

do no more. They left me for dead, girl! But I won't die. I can't die yet. My plans are not yet done. You can save me, can't you?'

'I'll try,' Alys said, pressing her lips on a denial. She turned to the fireplace and laid down Morach's shawl. By the light of the fire she untied the knot and spread out the cloth and arranged the things. The little man came over and squatted down beside her. His head came no higher than her shoulder.

'Do you use the black arts, mistress?' he asked in a soft undertone.

'No!' Alys said instantly. 'I have a very little skill with herbs – just what my mistress has taught me. You should have sent for her.'

The dwarf shook his head. 'In all Bowes they speak of the new young wise woman who came from nowhere and lives with the old widow Morach by the river. He'll have no truck with the black arts,' he said, nodding to the still figure in the bed.

Alys nodded. She straightened the black-bound prayer-book, put the herbs and the pestle and mortar to her right.

'What's that?' the dwarf said, pointing to the stone and ribbon.

'It's a crystal,' Alys said.

At once the little man crossed himself and bit the tip of his thumb. 'To see into the future?' he demanded. 'That's black arts!'

'No,' Alys said. 'To find the source of the illness. Like dowsing for water. Divining for water is not black arts, any child can do it.'

'Aye.' The man nodded, conceding the point. 'Aye, that's true.'

'Have done chattering!' came the sudden command from the bed. 'Come and cure me, wise woman.'

Alys got to her feet, holding the frayed ribbon of the crystal between her finger and thumb so that it hung down like a pendulum. As she moved, the shawl covering her head slid back. The dwarf exclaimed at the stubble of her regrowing hair.

'What have you done to your head?' he demanded. Then his face grew suddenly sly. 'Was it shaved, my pretty wench? Are you a runaway nun, fled from a fat abbey where the old women grow rich and talk treason?'

'No,' Alys said quickly. From the courtyard below the window a cock crowed briefly into the darkness and then settled to sleep again. 'I was sick with a fever in Penrith and they shaved my head,' she said. 'I am not a nun, I don't know what you mean about treason. I am just a simple girl.'

The dwarf nodded with a disbelieving smile, then he skipped to his place at the head of the bed and stroked the pillow again.

Alys drew closer. *'In nomine Patris, et Filii, et Spiritus Sancti,'* she muttered under her breath. The stone on the ribbon swung of its own accord in a lazy clockwise arc. 'This is God's work,' Alys said. The stone swung a little wider, a little faster. Alys breathed a little easier. She had never used a pendulum at the abbey, the nuns frowned on it as a supernatural force. The stone was Morach's. By blessing it Alys hoped to stay inside the misty border which separated God's work from that of the devil. But with the old lord glaring at her, and the dwarf's slight malicious smile, she felt in equal danger of burning for heresy as being taken as a witch and strangled.

She put her hand, which shook only slightly, on the old lord's forehead.

'His sickness is here,' she said, as she had seen Morach do.

The dwarf hissed as the crystal broke its pattern of circular swing and moved instead back and forth.

'What does it mean?' he asked.

'The sickness is not in his head,' she replied softly.

'I didn't see your fingers move the crystal?'

'Have done with your chatter,' the old lord flared at the dwarf. 'Let the wench do her work.'

Alys drew back the rich rugs covering the old man. She saw at once how his skin shivered at the touch of the air, yet the room was warm. Tentatively she put the back of her hand against his withered cheek. He was burning up.

She moved her hand cautiously to rest on his flat belly. She whispered: 'His sickness is here?' and at once she felt a change in the movement of the stone. It circled strongly, round and round, and Alys nodded at the lord with renewed confidence.

'You have taken a fever in your belly,' she said. 'Have you eaten or fasted?'

'Eaten,' the old man said. 'They force food on me and then they cup me of the goodness.'

Alys nodded. 'You are to eat what you please,' she said. 'Little things that tempt you. But you *must* drink spring water. As much as you can bear. Half a pint every half hour today and tomorrow. And it must be spring water, not from the well in the courtyard. And not from the well in town. Send someone to fetch you spring water from the moor.'

The old man nodded. 'When you are cold, cover yourself up and order more rugs,' Alys said. 'And when you are hot have them taken off you. You need to be as you please, and then your fever will break.'

She turned away from the bedside to her shawl spread before the fire. She hesitated a moment at the twists of burned fennel and then she shrugged. She did not think they would do any good, but equally they did no harm.

'Take one of these, before you sleep every night,' she said. 'Have you vomited much?'

He nodded.

'When you feel about to vomit then you must order your window opened.' There was a muted gasp of horror from the little man at the head of the bed. 'And read the writing aloud.'

'The night air is dangerous,' the dwarf said firmly. 'And what is the writing? Is it a spell?'

'The air will stop him being sick,' Alys said calmly, as if she were certain of what she was doing. 'And it is not a spell, it is a prayer.'

The man in the bed chuckled weakly. 'You are a philosopher, wench!' he said. 'Not a spell but a prayer! You can be hanged for one thing as well as the other in these days.'

'It's the Lord's Prayer,' Alys said quickly, the joke was too dangerous in this dark room where they watched for witchcraft and yet wanted a miracle to cure an old man.

'And for your fever I shall grind you some powder to take in your drink,' she said. She reached for the little dried berries of deadly nightshade that Morach had put in the bundle. She took just one and ground it in the mortar.

'Here,' she said, taking a pinch of the powder. 'Take this now. And you will need more later. I will leave some for you this night, and I will come again in the morning.'

'You stay,' the old man said softly.

Alys hesitated.

'You stay. David, get a pallet for her. She's to sleep here, eat here. She's to see no one. I won't have gossip.'

The dwarf nodded and slid from the room; the curtain over the door barely swayed at his passing.

'I have to go home, my lord,' Alys said breathlessly. 'My kinswoman will be looking for me. I could come back again, as early as you like, tomorrow.'

'You stay,' he said again. His black eyes scanned her from head to foot. 'I'll tell you, lass, there are those who would buy you to poison me within these walls this night. There are those who would take you up for a cheat if you fail to cure me. There are men out there who would use you and fling you in the moat when they had their fill of you for the sake of your young body. You are safest, if I live, with me. You stay.'

Alys bowed her head and retied Morach's shawl around the goods.

For the next five days Alys lived in a little chamber off the old lord's room. She saw no one but Lord Hugh and the dwarf. Her food was brought to her by the dwarf; one day she caught him tasting it, and then he tasted the food for Lord Hugh. She looked at him with a question in her face and he sneered and said: 'Do you think you are the only herbalist in the country, wench? There are many poisons to be had. And there are many who would profit from my lord's death.'

'He won't die this time,' Alys said. She spoke with real confidence. 'He's on the mend.'

Every day he was eating more, he was sitting up in bed, he was speaking to the dwarf and to Alys in a voice loud and clear like a tolling bell. On the sixth day he said he would take his midday dinner in the hall with his people.

'Then I shall take my leave of you,' Alys said when he was dressed with a black hat on his long white hair, a fur-lined robe over his thick padded doublet, and with embroidered slippers on his feet. 'Farewell, my lord, I am glad to have been of service to you.'

He gleamed at her. 'You have not finished your service,' he said. 'I have not done with you yet, wench. You will go back to your home when I say, and not before.'

Alys bowed her head and said nothing. When she looked up her eyes were wet.

'What is it?' he demanded. 'What's the matter with you?'

'It's my kinswoman,' Alys said softly. 'Morach of Bowes Moor. I had a message that she is ill with a fever in the belly. She is all the family I have in the world . . .'

She snatched a glance at him and saw he was nodding sympathetically.

'If I could go home . . .' she half whispered.

Lord Hugh snapped his thin white fingers. The dwarf came to his side and bent low. There was a low rapid exchange in a language Alys did not know. Then Lord Hugh looked at her with a wide grin.

'When did your kinswoman fall ill?' he asked.

'Yesterday . . .' Alys said.

'You lie,' Lord Hugh said benignly. 'She came here this morning and asked for you at the gatehouse and left a message with David, that she was well, and that she would come next week with more herbs for you.'

Alys flushed scarlet and said nothing.

'Come on,' Lord Hugh said. 'We are going to dinner.'

Halfway to the door he paused again. 'She looks a drab!' he exclaimed to David. Alys' old habit, singed by the fire and trailed in the mud, was tied around her waist with a shawl. She had another grey shawl over her head tied under her chin.

'Get her a gown, one of Meg's old gowns,' Lord Hugh tossed over his shoulder. 'She can have it as a gift. And take that damned shawl off her head!'

The dwarf waved Alys to wait and flung open a chest in the corner of the room. 'Meg was his last whore,' he said. 'She had a pretty gown of red. She died of the pox two years ago. We put her clothes in here.'

'I can't wear her clothes!' Alys exclaimed in revulsion. 'I can't wear a red gown!'

The dwarf pulled a cherry-red gown from the chest, found the shoulders and shook it out before Alys.

Alys gazed at the colour as if she were drinking it in. 'Oh!' she said longingly and stepped forward. The cloth was woven of soft fine wool, warm and silky to the touch. It was trimmed at the neck, the puffed sleeves and the hem with dark red ribbon of silk. Meg had been a proud woman, ready to defy the laws against common-ers wearing colour. There was even a silver cord to tie around the waist.

'I've never seen cloth so fine!' Alys said, awed. 'The colour of it! And the feel of it!'

'It comes with an embroidered stomacher,' the dwarf said, tossing Alys the gown and turning back to the chest. 'And an overskirt to match.' He rummaged in the chest and dragged out the stomacher with long flowing sleeves and fine silver laces up the back, and a rich red skirt embroidered with silver.

'Get it on,' he said impatiently. 'We must be in the hall before my lord comes in.'

Alys checked her movement to take the stomacher and skirt from him. 'I cannot wear a whore's gown,' she said. 'Besides, I might take the pox.'

The dwarf gasped and then choked with malicious laughter. 'Not such a wise woman after all!' he said, tears oozing from his eyes. 'Take the pox from a gown! That's the finest excuse I ever heard.' Abruptly he flung the stomacher and skirt at her and Alys caught them. 'Put it on,' he said, suddenly surly.

Alys hesitated still. In her head she could hear a cry in a voice, her own voice, calling for Mother Hildebrande to come and take her away. To save her from this shame just as she had rescued Alys, all those years ago, from Morach. She shook her head. The loss of the abbey and the loss of her mother were like a nightmare which cast its shadow over every moment of her day. A long shadow of loneliness and danger. There was no mother loving her and protecting her, not any more.

'I cannot wear a whore's gown,' she said in a little whisper.

'Wear it!' the dwarf growled. 'It's that or a shroud, Missy. I don't jest with you. The old lord has his way without question. I'll stab you as I stand here and go to dinner alone if you wish. It's your choice.'

Alys untied her belt and slid her robe to the floor. The dwarf stared at her as if appraising a mare for breeding. His eyes slid over the swell of her breasts under her coarse woven shift, assessed her narrow waist and her smooth young muscled flanks. His lips formed into a soundless whistle.

'The old lord always had an eye for a wench,' he said softly to himself. 'Looks like he saved the pick of the crop for his deathbed!'

Alys flung the gown over her head and pulled it down, thrust her arms through the soft woven sleeves. They were padded on the inside with white silk and slashed so the fine white fabric showed through, caught at each wrist with a little cuff and button made of horn. She turned her back to David and he laced the scarlet laces at the back of the gown and tied them in silence. She turned back and eyed the stomacher and overskirt.

'I don't know how this goes,' she confessed.

David looked at her curiously. 'I thought maids dreamed of nothing else,' he said. 'The overskirt goes on next and ties behind.' He held it out for her and Alys stepped into it, turned under his hands and let him tie the skirt at her waist. It swept from her waist to the floor with a rustle, leaving an open slit at the front for the plain red to show. Alys smoothed her hands down the skirt; the silver embroidery was cold and scratchy under her palms. The skirt was too long – Meg, the old lord's whore, had been a tall woman.

'Now this,' David said. 'Make haste, girl!' He held out the stomacher and sleeves towards her and Alys thrust her arms through the wide-cut hanging sleeves and turned her back again for David to lace her from behind.

'Damned lady's-maiding,' he grumbled, as he pulled the silver laces tight and threaded them through the holes. He tied a firm bow at the base of the stomacher and stuffed the bow out of sight under the boned waist. Alys turned to face him.

'Pull it down at the front,' he ordered. 'And pull the sleeves down.'

Alys pulled the stomacher down at her waist. It was too long for her as well, stopping at the swell of her hips and with the sharply pointed V at the front extending too low. It held her stiffly so that her breasts were flattened into one smooth line from the rich swirl of the skirt to the square neck of the gown which showed at the top of the stomacher. She tugged the oversleeves on both sides. They were long and sweeping, folded back to show the undersleeves like rich slashed pouches beneath them. David nodded.

'And the girdle goes loosely over the top,' he said. Alys fastened the silver girdle and straightened it so the long end fell down in front, enhancing the narrowness of her waist and the pointed line of the bodice, subtly suggesting the desirable triangle at the top of her thighs. She ran her hand over her cropped head where her growing hair was golden and stubbly.

David nodded. 'A sweeter honey even than Meg,' he said to himself. 'Who will stick his tongue in this pot?'

Alys ignored him. 'Is there nothing to hide my head?'

The dwarf rummaged in the chest for a few moments. 'Nothing you could wear without hair to pin it on,' he said. 'You'd best go bareheaded.'

Alys grimaced. 'I suppose no one will look at me,' she said.

'They'll look at nothing else!' he said with malicious satisfaction. 'Half of them think you're a holy healer, and the other half think you're his whore. And the young lord . . .' his voice trailed off.

'What?' asked Alys. 'What of the young lord?'

'He's got a keen eye for a pretty wench,' the dwarf said simply. 'And besides, he's got a score to settle with you. If the old lord had died he could have taken himself to the King's court, put aside that shrew he wed, and made his way in the great world. He'll not thank you for that.'

'The shrew? His wife?' Alys asked.

The dwarf motioned her to follow him through the door and then led her down the twisting stone staircase. As she passed an arrow-slit window Alys breathed in the cold wind which blew from the wintry moorland to the west of them, over the River Tees. It smelled of her home, of her childhood. For a moment she even longed for the little hovel by the river with the moor quiet all around it.

The dwarf grinned. 'She complains of him to the old lord,' he said. 'I've been there, I've heard her. Lord Hugo won't come to her bed, or he won't use her kindly. One time she angered him so that he beat her favourite waiting-woman before her. Too proud to touch his lady, but a temper on him that would scare the devil! The old lord used to keep Hugo on a short leash but they're both weary of the shrew. He used to watch that the young lord didn't abuse her over-much, and kept her supplied with trinkets and perfumes, little sweeteners for her vinegar. But she has called down a storm on them both too often, they both long to be rid of her.'

'They can't do that, can they?' Alys asked, frowning.

David shrugged. 'Who knows what can be done now?' he asked. 'The Church is ruled by the King now, not the vicar of Rome. The King does as he pleases with his women. Why not the young lord? The rightful wife stays barren, but if they dismiss her they lose her entailed lands and her dowry. And in all of Hugo's roistering he's never got a wench with child. So the shrew stays here until they can think of a way to be rid of her and yet keep her wealth.'

'How?' Alys asked.

'If she were taken in adultery,' David said in a whisper. 'Or died.'

There was a cold silence around them as they went through the empty guardroom, and down the flight of steps to the entrance of the great hall.

'And she?' Alys asked.

David hawked and spat disdainfully. 'She'd do anything to take the young lord's fancy,' he said. 'She'd do anything to creep into his bed. She's a passionate woman gone sour, a lustful woman on short commons. There's nothing she would not do for the young lord. I've heard her women talk.

'She's praying every day for an heir to make her place secure. She prays every day for the young lord to turn to her and give her a son. She prays every day for the old lord to cleave to her cause, not to take up the new ways of setting aside wives as lightly as changing hunters. And she's hot for Hugo.' He paused. 'All the women are,' he said.

'And he,' Alys began. 'Does he . . .'

'Sshh,' the dwarf said abruptly. He glanced over his shoulder to see that Alys was ready and at her nod he pushed open one of the thick wooden doors at the side of the great hall.

Four

The great hall was a high arched chamber, dark with
only arrow-slit windows high up in the thick stone
walls. A massive fire was burning against the east wall,
great trunks of trees flung pell-mell and blazing, the
smoke filling the room, smuts and light white ash dancing in the air. Beside Alys, to her left on a raised dais,
was a long table with three empty high-backed carved
chairs behind it, facing the room. Down the length of
the room ran four long tables and benches, soldiers and
guards seated in the best places at the dais end of the
hall; the servants, scullions and women struggled for
places nearest the south door.

The place was in uproar: three or four dogs were
fighting by the east wall, the soldiers were hammering
on the table and yelling for bread and ale, the servants
were shouting to be heard above the noise. In the
brackets on the walls there were burning torches, and as
Alys watched a well-dressed young man stepped up to
the lord's table and lowered a fine candelabra from a
candlebeam and lit sconces of pale golden wax candles.

David the dwarf nudged Alys in the ribs. 'You will sit
in the body of the hall,' he said. 'Come on, I'll find you
a place.' He led the way, with his rolling, half-lame
stride, between the tables. But before he could seat Alys
at an empty place there was a ripple of excitement in
the hall. David turned around and tapped Alys' arm,
directing her attention to the high table. 'Now you
watch!' he said triumphantly. 'You see the welcome he
gets, my Lord Hugh! You see!'

The tapestry behind the table on the dais was drawn back, the little arched door opened, and Lord Hugh stepped through and took his place in the great carved chair at the plumb centre of the table. There was a moment's surprised silence and then suddenly there was a great roar of delight as the soldiers and servants cheered and hammered the table with their knives and drummed their boots against the benches.

Alys smiled at the welcome, and saw how the old lord nodded his bony head in one direction and then in another. 'He looks well!' she thought. After nearly a week of seeing him as an invalid, in the cramped room of the tower, she was surprised to see him now as the lord at his own table. He had flushed a little, with the heat and with pleasure at his howling , yelling welcome. I cured him! Alys thought, with sudden, surprised pleasure. I cured him! They left him for dead but I cured him. Hidden by her drooping sleeves she stretched out her hands, feeling her power flow through her, down to her fingertips.

Alys had cured people before, vagrants and sick paupers in the infirmary, farmers in their heavy beds, peasants on pallets. But the old lord was the first man she had made well and seen rise up and take his power, great power. And I did that! Alys said to herself. I had the skill to cure him. I made him well.

She looked at him, smiling at the thought, and then the curtain behind him moved again and the young Lord Hugo came into the hall.

He was as tall as his father, with his father's sharp bony face. He had his father's black piercing eyes too, and his beaky nose. There were deep lines either side of his mouth, and two lines at the roots of his eyebrows like a permanent scowl. But then someone shouted,

'Holloa! Hugo!' from the benches and his face suddenly lit up as if someone had put a brand to a haystack, in the merriest, most joyful smile. Alys said, 'Mother of God!'

'What is it?' David said, shooting a look at her. 'Have you the Sight? Have you seen something?'

'No,' Alys said, in an instant denial. 'I see nothing. I see nothing. I just saw . . .' she broke off. 'I just saw him smile,' she said helplessly. She tried to look towards David but she could not take her eyes from the young lord. He stood, his hand resting casually on the back of his chair, his face turned towards his father. A jewel on his long fingers winked in the torchlight, an emerald, as green as his bulky doublet, and his velvet cap sat askew on his black curly hair.

'There's the shrew,' David said. 'Coming to sit on my lord's left.'

Alys hardly heard him. She was still staring at the young lord. It was he who had been there at the burning of the abbey. It was he who had laughed as the tiles on the roof cracked like fireworks in the heat and the lead had poured down like a blazing waterfall. It was his fault that the abbey was burned, that Mother Hildebrande was dead, and Alys alone and vulnerable in the world again. He was a criminal, in the deepest and darkest of sin. He was an arsonist – a hateful crime. He was a murderer. Alys looked at his severe face and knew she should hate him as her enemy. But Hugo had charm as potent as any magic. His father said something which amused him and he flung back his head to laugh and Alys felt herself smiling too – as people will laugh with a child or smile for another's upsurging joy. Alys looked down the length of the hall at Hugo and knew that, unseen and unnoticed, her own face was alight with pleasure at seeing him.

'See that woman's pride!' the dwarf said with disdain.

The young lord's wife was tall and looked older than him. She carried her power around her like a cloak. Her face as she scanned the hall was impassive, her welcome to her father-in-law was coolly perfect. She hesitated for a courteous second before sitting so the lords were seated first. Then she looked directly down the hall and saw Alys.

'Bow,' the dwarf said. 'Bow! Get your head down for God's sake! She's looking at you.'

Alys held the woman's cold grey stare. 'I will not,' she said.

Lady Catherine turned to one of the women seated behind her and asked a question. The woman stared at Alys, and then beckoned a servant. Alys was aware of the chain of command, and of the lowliest servant coming towards her, but she did not take her eyes from Lady Catherine's face.

'Two cats on a barn roof,' David said under his breath.

Alys found her palms were tingling from her finger-nails driven into them. She was holding her hands in tight fists, hidden by the sweep of the long sleeves.

'Lady Catherine says you're to go forward!' the servant said, skidding to a halt before her on the dirty rushes. 'Go up to the high table. She wants you!'

Alys glanced at David. 'Go your ways,' he said. 'I'm for my dinner. You go for the cat fight. Come straight to my lord's room after dinner. No dawdling.'

Alys nodded, still not taking her eyes from Lady Catherine's square, sallow face. Then she walked slowly up the length of the hall.

One by one the chattering men and women fell silent to watch her. A great wolfhound growled and then followed Alys up the centre of the hall, up the wide nave between the tables until she was standing with two hundred people staring at her back and Lady Catherine's cold eyes staring at her face.

'We have to thank you for your skill,' Lady Catherine said. Her voice was flat with the ugly vowel sounds of the southerner. 'You seem to have restored my lord to perfect health.'

The words were kind but the look that accompanied them was ice.

'I did no more than my duty,' Alys said. She did not take her eyes from Lady Catherine's face.

'You could tempt me to fall sick tomorrow!' the young lord said easily with a laugh. The officers on the benches nearest the table laughed with him. Someone whistled a long, low whistle. Alys looked only at him. His black eyes were hooded, lazy, his smile was as warm as if they shared a secret. It was an invitation to bed as clear as a mattins bell to church. Alys felt the blood rising to her face in a slow deep blush.

'Don't wish it, my lord!' Lady Catherine said evenly. Then she turned again to Alys. 'Where do you come from?' she asked sharply.

'Bowes Moor,' Alys replied.

Lady Catherine frowned. 'Your speech is not from here,' she said suspiciously.

Alys bit the inside of her lips. 'I lived for some years in Penrith,' she said. 'I have kin there. They speak softer and they taught me to read aloud.'

'You can read?' the old lord asked.

Alys nodded. 'Yes, my lord,' she said.

'Can you write?' he asked, astonished. 'English and Latin?'

'Yes, my lord,' Alys replied.

The young lord slapped his father on the shoulder. 'There's your clerk for you!' he said. 'A wench for a clerk! You can count on her not to rise up in the church and leave you!'

There was a laugh from the head of the long table nearest the dais and a man in the dark robe of a priest raised his hand to Hugo like a swordsman acknowledging a hit.

'Better than none,' the old lord said. He nodded at Alys. 'You may not go home yet,' he said gruffly. 'I need some writing done. Get a seat for yourself.'

Alys nodded and turned to a place at the back of the hall.

'No,' the young lord said. He turned to his father. 'If she's to be your clerk she'd best sit up here,' he said. 'You permit, Catherine?'

Lady Catherine opened her lips on a thin smile. 'Of course, my lord,' she said quietly. 'Whatever you wish.'

'She can sit with your women,' the young lord said. 'Holloa! Margery, shift up and make a place for the young wise woman. She'll dine with you.'

Alys kept her eyes down and went to the side of the dais and climbed the three shallow steps. There was a small table by the dais door where four women were sitting on stools. Alys drew up a fifth stool and sat with them. They eyed each other with mutual mistrust while the servers brought Alys a pewter plate, a knife and a thick pewter goblet stamped with the Castleton crest.

'Are you old Morach's apprentice?' one of them said eventually. Alys recognized a woman who had been left a widow with a fine farm near Sleightholme, but driven out of the house by a powerful daughter-in-law.

'Yes,' she said. 'I lived at Penrith, and then I came to work for Morach.'

The woman stared at her. 'You're her foundling!' she said. 'The little wench. You were living with her when I left to come here.'

'Yes, Mistress Allingham,' Alys said, her mind working rapidly. 'I did not recognize you at first. I left for Penrith just after your son was wed. Then I came back again.'

'I heard you had gone to the abbey,' the woman said sharply.

There was a muffled scream from one of the other women. 'Not a nun's servant!' she exclaimed. 'I won't sit at the table with a nun's servant! This is a godly household, my lord cannot wish us to sit with a heretic!'

'I only stayed there for three days, on my way to Penrith, waiting for the carter,' Alys said steadily, her fingers clasped lightly in the lap of the cherry-red gown. 'I did not live there.'

Mistress Allingham nodded. 'It would have been bad for you if you had done,' she observed. 'It was the young Lord Hugo himself who led the men to strip the abbey. They say he robbed the altar of popish treasures himself, laughing at the sacrilege. They were drunk – he and his friends – and he let his men fire the buildings. But they went too far, it was botched work, all the nuns were burned in their beds.'

Alys felt her hands tremble and clasped them together in her lap. She could still smell woodsmoke. She could still hear that one brief cry. I wish I had died then, she said to herself. I wish I had died in the same fire as my mother and then I would never have had to sit here and hear of her death told as tittle-tattle.

'I'll warrant he did more than that!' one of the other women, the one named Margery, said in a low whisper. 'An abbey full of nuns! He would do more than burn them in their beds!'

73

Alys stared at her in utter horror, but the women were watching Lady Catherine's straight back.

'Sssh,' said one of them. 'She has ears like an owl, that one.'

'I warrant he did, though,' Margery said. 'I can't imagine the young lord hanging back when there was lechery being done. He is as hot as a butcher's dog, that one.'

Another woman giggled. 'He'd have had a round dozen out of their beds before the fire got them!' she exclaimed. 'He would have taught them what they had been missing!'

'Ssshhh!' said the woman more urgently, while the others collapsed into giggles. Alys kept her face turned away and fought the bile which rose unstoppably into her mouth.

'Hush,' said Mistress Allingham in pretended concern. 'This must be distressing for the girl. You stayed with them for three days, and they were your friends, were they not?'

A cock pecking under the tables in the hall squawked as a running servant kicked it aside. 'No,' Alys said, swallowing down vomit. 'Old Morach owed them some labour in their garden in exchange for the use of their herbs. I was sent to work off her debt. I stayed until the work was done and then I came away. I did not know any of them well. I lodged with their servants.'

In the darkness of the hall she could suddenly see the abbess' face, its soft wrinkled skin and the gentle smile. For a moment she could almost feel the touch of her hand as she leaned on Alys' shoulder to walk around the garden. The cool, dry sweetness of the herb garden was very far away now.

'I never even saw half of them,' Alys said, proffering

74

additional detail. 'They were in the middle of some fast or feast and J was kept in the gatehouse. It was a dull three days, I was glad when the carter came and gave me a lift to Penrith.'

A serving-lad stepped up to the dais and presented a silver platter to the old lord, to the young lord, and only then to Lady Catherine. They took slices of dark meat.

'Venison,' Mistress Allingham said with satisfaction. 'David orders a good table.'

'David?' Alys asked involuntarily. 'Does David command the meals?'

'Oh, yes,' Margery said. 'He's the old lord's seneschal – he commands all that happens inside the castle and manages the tenants, commands the demesne, watches over the manors, tells them what crops to grow and takes the pick for the castle. The young Lord Hugo partly serves as seneschal for outside, he rules the villages and sits in justice with his father.'

'I thought David was a manservant,' Alys said.

Mistress Allingham tittered, and Alys flushed. 'Best not let him hear you say that!' she said brightly. 'He's the most important man in the castle after my lord and the young Lord Hugo.'

'And the most dangerous,' one of the women said low. 'As spiteful as a little snake, that David.'

They had to wait a long time for their food. It was brought on thin pewter platters, only the two lords and Lady Catherine ate off silver. They ate the meat with their fingers and knives, and then a bowl of broth and bread with a thick-handled spoon. The bread was a thick trencher of well-milled rye flour. At the top table they had a wheaten loaf, Alys could see its pale, appetizing colour. All the food was tepid, except for the broth which was cold.

Alys set her spoon down.

'Not to your liking?' one of the other women asked. 'My name is Eliza Herring. Is it not to your liking?'

Alys shook her head. 'It's cold,' she said. 'And too salty for my taste.'

'It's made with salted meat,' Mistress Allingham said. 'And from the bottom of the barrel I'll be bound. But it's always cold. They have to carry it from the kitchen. I haven't had hot meat since I left my own home.'

'I daresay you'd rather stay, cold meat and all,' Eliza Herring said sharply. 'From what I hear, the new young wife your son married wouldn't have fed you venison, hot, cold or raw.'

Mistress Allingham nodded. 'I wish the plague would take her!' she exclaimed, then she stopped and looked at Alys. 'Can you work on a woman you don't know?' she asked. 'Could you soften her heart towards me? Or even carry her off? There's much sickness about – no reason why she should not take an ague.'

Alys shook her head. 'I am a herbalist, nothing more,' she said. 'I cannot cast spells and I would not do so if I could.' She paused to make sure that all the women were listening. 'I cannot make spells. All I have is a little skill in herbalism. It was these skills that cured my lord. I cannot and I would not make someone sick.'

'But you could make someone fall in love?' asked the young woman called Margery. Unconsciously her eyes rested on the young Lord Hugo. 'You have love potions and herbs which stir desire, don't you?'

Alys was suddenly weary. 'There are herbs to stir desire, but nothing can change what a man thinks. I could make a man hot enough to lie with a woman – but I couldn't make him like her after he had taken his pleasure.'

Eliza Herring went off into hoots of laughter. 'You'd be no further on then, Margery!' she said delightedly. 'For he has lain with you a score of times and despised you each time until he feels the itch again.'

'Hush, hush!' said the fourth woman desperately. 'She'll hear! You know how she listens!'

A servant came to each of them and poured them ale. Alys looked towards the lords' table. In the clear light of the wax candles she could see the shine on the silver plates. The napery was white linen, unmarked by any blemish. They were drinking wine from glassware. Alys found she was snuffing at the air, breathing in the smell of clean burning wax, clean linen, good food. It reminded her of the abbey and of the overwhelming hunger she had felt when she first saw the cleanness of it, and the order. She had set her heart on having the best, the very best that the abbey could have offered. And she had been well on the way to gaining the best cell, the softest pallet, the best-woven cloak and smoothest robe. She was the abbess' favourite – as beloved as a daughter – and nothing was too good for her. And then the statue of Our Lady had smiled on her, confirming her desire to be there, in a holy place, in a state of grace.

She bowed her head over her plate to hide her face twisted with disappointment. She had lost everything in one night: her faith, her friends, her chance of wealth and comfort, and a life for herself. Alys could have risen to the highest office in the abbey, she could have been Reverend Mother herself one day. But then in one single night it was all gone. Now she was on the outside looking in, again. She had lost her future – and her mother too. Alys forced herself not to think of Mother Hildebrande and shame herself before them all by weeping for loneliness and loss at the dinner-table.

The lords' table was served with fillets of salmon and salad of parsley, sage, leeks and garlic. Alys watched them as they were served. The greens were fresh, from the kitchen garden she guessed. The salmon was as pink as a wild rose. It would have been netted in the Greta this morning. Alys felt the water rush into her mouth as she looked at the pale succulent flesh, shiny with butter. A serving-lad shoved a trencher of bread before her spread thickly with paste of meat sweetened with honey and almonds, and his fellow poured more ale into Alys' goblet.

Alys shook her head. 'I'm not hungry,' she said. 'I want to rest.'

Eliza Herring shook her head. 'You may not leave the table until Father Stephen has said grace,' she said. 'And until the lords and my lady have left. And then you must pour your mess into the almoner's bowl for the poor.'

'They eat the scraps from the table?' Alys asked.

'They are glad of it,' Eliza said sharply. 'Didn't you give to the poor in Penrith?'

Alys thought of the carefully measured portions of the nuns. 'We gave whole loaves,' she said. 'And some-times a barrel of meat. We fed anyone who called at the kitchen door. We did not give them our leavings.'

Eliza raised her plucked eyebrows in surprise. 'Not very charitable!' she said. 'My Lord Hugh's almoner goes around the poor houses with the bowl once a day, at breakfast-time, with the scraps from the dinner and supper table.'

The priest, seated at the head of the table below the dais, rose to his feet and prayed in a clear, penetrating voice in perfect Latin. Then he repeated the prayer again in English. Alys listened carefully; she had never heard God addressed in English before, it sounded like blasphemy – a dreadful insult to speak to God as if he were a neighbouring farmer, in ordinary words. But she kept her face steady, crossed herself only when the others did so, and rose to her feet as they did.

Lady Catherine, the old lord and the young lord all turned towards the door beside the waiting-women's table.

'What a lovely gown you have,' Lady Catherine said to Alys, as if she had just noticed it. Her voice was friendly but her eyes were cold.

'Lord Hugh gave it me,' Alys said steadily. She met Lady Catherine's gaze without flinching. I could hate you, she thought.

'You are too generous, my lord,' Lady Catherine said, smiling.

Lord Hugh grunted. 'She'll be a pretty wench when her hair is grown,' he said. 'You'll have to take her into your rooms, Catherine. She did well enough sleeping by me when I was sick. If she is to stay, she'd best have a bed with your women.'

Lady Catherine nodded. 'Of course, my lord,' she said pleasantly. 'Whatever you command. But if I had known you needed a clerk I could have written your letters for you. I daresay my Latin is a little better than this . . . this girl's.' She gave a light laugh.

Lord Hugh shot a dark look at her from under his white eyebrows. 'I daresay,' he said. 'But not all my letters are fit for a lady to read. And all of it is my own business.'

Two light spots of colour appeared on Lady Catherine's cheeks. 'Of course, my lord,' she said. 'I only hope the girl can serve you.'

'Come to my room now,' the old lord said to Alys. 'Come, I'll lean on you.'

He gestured Alys to his side and she stepped before Lady Catherine. She felt the woman's resentment like a draught of cold air behind her. She held still a shiver which seemed to walk from the base of her spine up to the cropped, cold nape of her neck. Then Lord Hugh's heavy hand came comfortably on her shoulder and he leaned on her as she led him from the great hall, across the lobby behind it, and up to his room in the round tower.

He did not let her go until the door was shut behind them.

'Now then,' he said. 'You've seen the she-dog, my daughter-in-law, and you've seen my son. D'you see now why I let you meet no one, why my food is tasted?'

'You mistrust her,' Alys said.

'Damned right,' the old lord said with a grunt. He slumped into the heavy carved chair at the fireplace. 'I mistrust them both. I mistrust them all. I'm cold,' he said fretfully. 'Fetch me a rug, Alys.'

Alys took one of the fur-lined rugs from the bed and tucked it around his shoulders.

'You have to sleep with her women,' he said abruptly. 'I can't keep you here, it would make matters worse for you if they thought you were my whore. But you will keep your mouth shut about me and my business.'

Alys fixed her dark blue eyes on him and nodded.

'And you will remember that it was I that sent for you, that it is I who command here, and that until I am dead you will be *my* clerk and servant and none other. My spy too,' he said abruptly. 'You can listen to her ladyship and tell me what she says of me, what she plans. And Hugo.'

'And if I refuse?' Alys asked, her voice so soft that he could not take offence.

'You cannot refuse,' he said. 'You either consent to be my clerk, my spy, my cunning woman and my healer – or else I shall have you strangled and dumped in the moat. It's your choice.' He smiled wickedly. 'A free choice, Alys, I won't constrain you.'

Alys' pale lovely face was as calm as a river on a sunny still day in June. 'I consent,' she said easily. 'I will serve you in all that I *can* do – for I cannot make spells. And I will tell no one your business.'

The old lord looked hard at her. 'Good,' he said.

Five

Alys' knowledge of Latin was tested to its full extent by the letters the old lord sent all around England. He was seeking advice on how an annulment of Hugo's and Catherine's marriage would be greeted by his family, and by her distant kin. He suggested that she and Hugo – as second cousins – were in too close kinship, and that was why their marriage was barren, and should – 'perhaps', 'possibly', 'mayhap' – be annulled. His letters were a masterpiece of vague suggestion. Alys translated, and then translated again to hit upon the right tone of cautious inquiry. He was measuring the opposition he would face from his peers and rivals, and from the law.

He was also preparing his allies and his friends for his own death, smoothing the way for his son. He sent two very secret letters by special messenger to his 'beloved cousins' at Richmond Castle and York, commanding them to act if his death was sudden, if it looked like an accident, or if it had been caused by an illness which could be blamed on poisoning. He commanded them to seek evidence against his son's wife; and he implored them to have her tried and executed if any evidence could be found or fabricated which pointed to her. He cast the darkest suspicions on her plans and on her feelings towards him.

If (as a possibility only he mentioned it to them), if the crime pointed to his son – they should ignore it. The inheritance of Hugo was more important than revenge, and besides, he would be dead by then and they would have no thanks from him. Alys, her eyes never lifting from the pages before her, realized that Catherine executed for murder was disposed of as neatly, and indeed more cheaply than Catherine set aside for barrenness. The old lord would not have died in vain if his death could be blamed on his daughter-in-law, his son set free to marry again, and a new Hugh born into the family.

Alys bent her cropped head over her writing as he dictated, and tried to translate blind and deaf, working without taking in the sense of what he was saying, scenting the dangers which surrounded him – and her with him – as a hare senses the hounds and cowers low. She learned for the first time that the land was ruled by a network of conniving, conspiring landlords answerable only to each other and to the King himself. Each of them had one ambition only: to retain and improve the wealth and power of his family; and that could only be done by expanding the boundaries of their manors – and willing it intact to the next heir and the heir after him.

Alys, her quill pen scratching on the downstrokes on the good-quality vellum, realized that the conception of Hugo's son, the old lord's grandson, was not a personal matter between Hugo and his shrewish wife, not even a family matter between the old lord and his son. It was a financial matter, a political matter. If Hugo inherited and then died childless the Lordship of Castleton would be vacant, the manors would be broken up among buyers, the family history and crest revert to the King and be sold to the highest bidder, and the great northern family would fall, its history at an end, its name forgotten. Someone else would live in the castle and claim castle, crest and even family history for their own. For Lord Hugh that prospect was the deepest terror in the world; another family in his place would deny that he had ever been. Alys heard his fear in every line he dictated.

He wrote also to the court. He had a hoard of treasure from Alys' wrecked abbey to be sent south as a gift for the King. The inventory Alys translated was a masterpiece of sleight of hand, as gold candlesticks were renamed silver or even brass, and heavy gold plates disappeared from the list. 'We did the work, after all, Alys,' he said to her one day. 'It was my Hugo that wrecked the abbey, doing the King's work with patriotic zeal. We deserve our share.'

Alys, listing the silver and the gold which she had polished and handled, remembering the shape of the silver chalice against the white of the altar cloth and the sweet sacred taste of the communion wine, ducked her head and continued writing.

If I do not escape from here, I shall go mad, she thought.

'It went wrong at the nunnery,' Lord Hugh said. His voice held only faint regret. 'The King's Visitors told us that the nuns were corrupt and Father Stephen and Hugo went to see the old abbess and persuade her to pay fines and mend her ways. Everywhere else they had been, the nuns or the monks had handed over their treasures, confessed their faults, and Hugo used them kindly. But the old abbess was a staunch papist. I don't believe she ever recognized the King's right to set aside the Dowager Princess Catherine of Aragon.' Lord Hugh said the title carefully. He had called her Queen Catherine for eighteen years and he was careful not to make a slip even when Alys was his only listener. 'She took the oath to acknowledge Queen Anne but I am not sure how deep it went with her.'

He paused. 'She would not discuss her faith with

84

Father Stephen, not even when he charged her with laxity and abuses. She called him an ambitious young puppy.' Lord Hugh snorted in reluctant amusement. 'She insulted him and faced him down and threw them both out – my Hugo and Father Stephen. They came home like scolded boys. She was a rare woman, that abbess.' He chuckled. 'I'd have liked to meet her. It's a shame it all went wrong and she died.'

'How did it go all wrong at the nunnery?' Alys asked. She was careful to keep her voice light, casual.

'Hugo was drunk,' the old lord said. 'He was on his way home with the soldiers, they had been chasing a band of mosstroopers for seven days up and down the dales. He was drunk and playful and the men had been fighting mad for too long, and drunk with stolen ale. They made a fire to keep them warm and give them light to pick over the treasures. They were taking up a fine, it was all legal – or near enough. Father Stephen would not meet them to reason with the nuns, he was still angry with the old woman. He sent a message to Hugo and told him to burn her out – and be damned to her. The soldiers wanted a frolic and some of them thought they were doing Father Stephen's wish. They made the fire too near the hay barn, and then the place caught afire and the women all died. A bad business.'

'Oh,' Alys said. She drew a quiet breath to steady her belly, which was quivering.

'None of them got out,' Lord Hugh said. 'A bad business. Hugo tells me he could hear them screaming, and then a dreadful smell of burned meat. Like a kitchen with a vexed cook, he said.'

'Are these letters to be sent today, my lord?' she asked. Her hand holding the candle beneath the sealing-wax shook badly, and she bodged the seal.

In the afternoon when the old lord rested she was supposed to sit in the ladies' gallery over the great hall and sew. It was a handsome room, the best in the castle. There was a wide oriel window looking out over the inner manse filled with clear and coloured panes of Normandy glass. The beams of the ceiling were brightly coloured: green, red, vermilion and the bright blue of bice. The walls were hung with bright tapestries, and where the wood showed it was panelled and carved with sheaves of wheat, fat lambs, bundles of fruit and goods, reminders of the wealth of the Lordship of Castleton. The doorway was carved with the heavy linenfold pattern which was repeated all around the room and on the window-seat before the oriel window, where Catherine could sit with a chosen confidante and avoid interruption from the others. There was a fireplace as good as the one in the nunnery and a square stone-carved chimney to take the smoke away so the air of the room was clear and the walls stayed clean. The floor had the dark shine of seasoned polished wood and was strewn with fresh herbs which gathered in heaps, swept around by the women's gowns. It was a long room, three-quarters the length of the great hall below it. Catherine's chamber was on the left at the far end, overlooking the courtyard through an arched window fitted with expensive glass. The women slept opposite her, looking out over the river through arrow-slits which admitted draughts and even snow when the wind was in the wrong direction. Next door to them was another small chamber, vacant except for lumber and a broken loom.

In winter, and for many days in the bad weather of autumn and spring, the women spent every hour from breakfast till darkness inside the four walls. Their only exercise was to go up and down the broad, shallow flight of steps from the great hall to the gallery for their breakfast, dinner and supper. Their only occupation in the winter months was to sit in the gallery and sew, read, write letters, weave, sing or quarrel.

Alys pretended she had extra work from Lord Hugh and stayed away whenever she could. She disliked the women's furtive, bawdy gossip, and she feared Lady Catherine, who never threatened Alys nor raised her voice, but watched all the women, all the time. The room was tense with an unstated, unceasing rivalry. In the long hours between midday dinner and supper served at dusk, while Hugo was out hunting, or sitting in judgement with his father, or riding out to collect his rents, or check the manor lands, the women might chatter among themselves, pleasantly enough. But as soon as Hugo's quick steps rang on the stone stairs the women straightened their hoods, smoothed their gowns, glanced at each other, compared looks.

Alys kept her eyes down. There was always sewing to be done in the ladies' gallery. An endless tapestry in twelve panels, which had been started by Lady Catherine's long-dead mother and willed to her daughter. Alys kept her eyes on her hands and stitched unceasingly when Hugo banged open the door and strode into the room. Since the first moment of seeing him Alys had never again looked directly at him. When he came into a room Alys went out, and when she had to pass him on the stairs she would press back against the cold stones, keeping her eyes down and praying that he did not notice her. When he was near her Alys could feel his presence on her skin, like a breath. When a door shut behind her, even out of her line of vision, she knew it was he who had gone out. She was tempted to look at him, she found her gaze drawn always towards him. She was fascinated to see whether his face was dark and silent, in his look of sullenness, or whether he was alight with his quick, easy joy. But she knew that when he was in the room Lady Catherine's gaze swept them all like a sentry on a watchtower. The least sign of interest by Hugo for any woman would be noted by Catherine and paid for, in full, later. Alys feared Lady Catherine's unremitting jealousy, she feared the politics of the castle and the secret, unstated rivalry of the ladies' gallery.

And she feared for her vows. More than anything else, she feared for her vows.

He paused once, while he was running lightly up the stairs as Alys came down, waited on the step beside her and put a careless finger under her chin, turning her face to the arrow-slit for light.

'You're beautiful,' he said. It was as if he were measuring her looks for fault. 'Your hair is coming through golden.'

Alys had a mop-head of golden-brown curls, still too short to fasten back so she wore her hair as a child, loose around her face.

'What age are you?' he asked.

She sensed the quickening of his interest, so tangible that she almost smelled it.

'Fourteen,' she said.

'Liar,' he replied evenly. 'What age?'

'Sixteen,' she said sullenly. She did not take her watchful eyes off his face.

He nodded. 'Old enough,' he said. 'Come to my room tonight,' he said abruptly. 'At midnight.'

Alys' pale face was impassive, her blue eyes blank.

'Did you hear me?' he asked, slightly surprised.

'Yes, my lord,' Alys said carefully. 'I heard you.'

'And you know where my room is?' he asked, as if

that could be the only obstacle. 'In the round tower on the floor above my father. When you leave his room tonight, take the stairs upwards to me instead of down to the hall. And I shall have some wine for you, little Alys, and some sweetmeats, and some gentle play.'

Alys said nothing, keeping her eyes down. She could feel the heat of her cheeks and the thud of her heart beating.

'Do you know what you make me think of?' Hugo asked confidentially.

'What?' Alys asked, betrayed into curiosity.

'Fresh cream,' he said seriously.

Alys' eyes flew to his face. 'Why?' she asked.

'Every time I see you all I can think of is fresh cream. All I think of is pouring cream all over your body and licking it off,' he said.

Alys gasped and pulled away from him as if his touch had scorched her. He laughed aloud at her shocked face.

'That's settled then,' he said easily. He smiled at her, his heart-turning merry smile, and swung around and took the steps upwards two at a time. She heard him whistling a madrigal as he went, joyous as a winter robin.

Alys leaned back against the cold stones and did not feel their chill. She felt desire, hot and dangerous and exciting, in every inch of her body. She gripped her lower lip between her teeth but she could not stop herself smiling. 'No,' she said sternly. But her cheeks burned.

Alys knew she needed to see Morach and she had her chance that afternoon. Lord Hugh wanted a message taken to Bowes Castle and Alys offered to carry it. 'If I am delayed I shall stay the night with my kinswoman,' she said. 'I should like to see her for a little while, and I need some herbs.'

The old lord looked at her and smiled his slow smile. 'But you'll come back,' he said.

Alys nodded. 'You know I'll come back,' she said. 'There's no life for me on the moor now, that life is closed to me. And the one I had before. It's like a journey down a chamber with doors that shut behind me. Whenever I find some safety I have to move on, and the old life is taken from me.'

He nodded. 'Best find yourself a man and close all the doors for good; those before you, and those behind you,' he said.

Alys shook her head. 'I won't wed,' she said.

'Because of your vows?' he asked.

'Yes . . .' Alys started and then she bit the words back. 'I've taken no vows, my lord,' she said smoothly. 'It's just that I am one of those women who cannot abide bedding. It goes with the skill of herbs. My cousin Morach lives alone.'

Lord Hugh coughed and spat towards the fire which burned in the corner of his room, smoke trailing through the arrow-slit above it. 'I guessed some time ago you were a runaway nun,' he said conversationally. 'Your Latin is very weak in profane language, very strong for sacred texts. Your hair was shaved, and you have that appetite – like all nuns – for the finest things.' He laughed harshly. 'Did you think, little Sister Blue-eyes, that I have not seen how you stroke fine linen, how you love the light from wax candles, how you preen in your red gown and watch the light glint on the silver thread?'

Alys said nothing. Her pulse was racing but she kept her face serene.

'You're safe with me,' Lord Hugh said. 'Father Stephen is mad for the new ways and the new Church – he's a fanatical reformer, a holy man. Hugo loves the new Church because he sees the gains he can make: the reduction of the Prince Bishops, fines from the monastery lands, the power that we can now claim – us peers working with the Crown – and the spiritual lords cast down.'

He paused and gave her a brief smile. 'But I am cautious,' he said slowly. 'These turnabouts can happen more than once in a lifetime. It matters not to me whether there is a picture or two in a church, whether I eat flesh or fish, whether I pray to God in Latin or English. What matters more is the Lordship of Castleton and how we weather these years of change.

'I won't betray you. I won't insist that I hear you take the vow of loyalty to the King, I won't have you stripped and flogged. I won't have you examined for heresy and when you fail given to the soldiers for their sport.'

Alys scarcely registered the reprieve.

'Or at any rate,' the old lord amended, 'not yet. Not while you remember that you are mine. My servant. My vassal. Mine in word and body and deed.'

Alys inclined her head to show that she was listening. She said nothing.

'And if you serve me well I shall keep you safe, maybe even smuggle you away, out of the country, safe to an abbey in France. How would that be?'

Alys laid her hand at the base of her throat. She could feel her pulse hammering against her palm. 'As you wish, my lord,' she said steadily. 'I am your servant.'

'Fancy an abbey in France?' the old lord asked pleasantly.

Alys nodded dumbly, choked with hope.

'I could send you to France, I could give you safe conduct on your journey, give you a letter of introduction to an abbess, explaining your danger and telling her that you are a true daughter of her Church,' the old lord said easily. 'I could give you a dowry to take to the convent with you. Is that what it takes to buy your loyalty?'

'I am your faithful servant,' Alys said breathlessly. 'But I would thank you if you would send me to a new home, abroad.'

The old lord nodded, measuring her. 'And serve me without fail until then, as a fee for your passage,' he said.

Alys nodded. 'Whatever you command.'

'You'll need to stay a virgin I suppose. They won't accept you in the nunnery otherwise. Has Hugo been tugging at your skirts yet?'

'Yes,' Alys said precisely.

'What did you tell him?'

'I said nothing.'

The old lord let out a sharp bark of laughter. 'Aye, that's your way, my cunning little vixen, ain't it? So he no doubt thinks he'll have you, and I think you're sworn to my interest and all along you follow your heretical beliefs, or your mysterious arts, or your own sweet way which is none of these, don't you?'

Alys shook her head. 'No, my lord,' she said softly. 'I want to go to a nunnery. I want to renew my vows. I will do anything you ask of me if you will see me safe into my Order.'

'Do you need any guarding against my son?'

Alys shook her head slowly. 'I wish to see my kinswoman. I could stay with her tonight,' she said. 'She will advise me.'

He nodded and rested his head against the back of his chair as if he were suddenly weary. Alys went silently to the door. As she turned the handle she glanced back: he was watching her from under his hooded eyelids.

'Don't poison him,' he said sharply. 'None of your damned brews to kill his ardour. He needs a son, he needs all the vigour he has. I'll tell him to stick it to his wife when he feels his lust rising. You're safe under my charge. And I mean to honour my promise to see you safe behind walls when your work here is done.'

Alys nodded. 'When would that be, my lord?' she asked in a small voice, careful not to betray her anxiety.

Lord Hugh yawned. 'When this damned marriage business is settled, I should think,' he said carelessly. 'When I am rid of the shrew and I have a new fertile daughter-in-law in Hugo's bed. I will need you to work secretly for me until I can see my way clear, but I won't need you after that. If you serve me well in this one thing, I'll put you back behind convent walls again.'

Alys took a deep breath. 'I thank you,' she said calmly, and left the room. She paused outside his door and leaned against the wall, looking out of the arrow-slit. The air which blew in was sharp with the cold from the moor. For the first time in months Alys felt her heart lift with hope. She was on her way back to her home.

She borrowed a fat pony belonging to Eliza Herring to ride to Bowes, confident of her ability to manage the overfed old animal, riding astride with the red gown pulled down over her legs, one of the lads from the castle running beside her. As the pony picked its way around the filth of the wet street she saw a few doorways open a crack to eye her, and a thrown handful of stones spattered on the wall behind her. She nodded. She had no friends in the village. She had been feared as a cunning woman and now she would be reviled as the lord's new whore, a village girl vaulted to the highest place in their small world.

She left the letter with the steward of the castle knowing that even if he dared to break the seal and open it, he would not be able to read the Latin. She ordered the lad to go back to Lord Hugh's castle. She would be safe going on alone. The road from Castleton to Bowes to Penrith ran along dry ground at the crest of the moor. Alys, glancing up the hill from the valley of Bowes, could see the pale ribbon of it running straight as a Roman ruler bisecting the country from east to west. It was empty of traffic. These were wild lands. Travellers who had to make the journey would delay on either side of the moor, at Castleton in the east, or Penrith in the west, so that they could travel together and protect each other. There were wild animals – boar and wolves, some spoke of bears. There were sudden snowstorms in winter, and no shelter. Worst of all, there were brigands and mosstroopers, marauding Scots, sturdy beggars and vagabonds.

Alys avoided the road and set the pony towards the little sheep track which ran from Bowes alongside the River Greta, through thick woods of beech and elm and oak, where deer moved quietly in the shadows of the trees. The river was full and wide here, moving slowly over a broad rocky bed. Underneath the stone slabs a deeper, secret river ran, a great underground lake stocked with fishes that preferred the dark deeps. Even on horseback, Alys could sense the weight of water beneath the ground, its slow purposeful moving in the secret caves.

The pony broke out of the trees, puffing slightly, and then started the climb westwards and upwards through swathes of poor pastureland where sheep could feed and perhaps a few scrawny cows, and then higher again to the moor. Before the plague had come to Bowes and there had been more working men, someone had walled off one pasture from another. The stones had fallen down now and the sheep could run where they wished. At shearing in spring, or butchering in winter, they would be sorted by the marks on their fleeces. Every village had its own brand – but they all belonged to Lord Hugh.

The river was in spate here, a fast-moving swell of water overlapping the stone of the banks and flooding the meadows in great wet sweeps of waterlogged land. Alys rode beside it, listening to the gurgle and rush of the water, and laughed when the little pony shied sideways from a puddle. Bits of wood and weed were tumbled over and over in the peaty water, and at the river's edge the springs bubbled and gurgled like soup pots, spewing out more brown water to swirl away downstream. The branches of ivy nodding at the tumbled drystone walls carried thick heads of dull black berries, a rowan tree glowed with clusters of scarlet berries against the green and grey of the weak winter grass speckled by small brown toadstools on weak leggy stems. Alys kicked the old pony and surprised it into a loping canter. She sat easily in the saddle and felt the wind in her face as the hood of her cape blew back.

The grey stone slabs of the bridge came into sight, the waters backed up behind it and spreading in a great sheet of flood water as shiny as polished pewter. Morach's cottage, like a little ark, stood on a hillock of higher ground away from the waters of the flood. Alys stood up in the stirrups and shouted: 'Holloa! Morach!' so that Morach was standing in the doorway, shading her eyes against the low, red winter sun when Alys came trotting up on her pony.

'What's this?' she asked, without a word of greeting.

'A loan only,' Alys said casually. 'I'm not home for ever, I am allowed to visit this evening. And I need to talk with you.'

Morach's sharp dark eyes scanned Alys' face. 'The young Lord Hugo,' she stated.

Alys nodded, not even asking how Morach had guessed. 'Aye,' she said. 'And the old lord has forbidden me to give him anything to kill his lust.'

Morach raised her black eyebrows and nodded. 'They need an heir,' she said. 'You can tether that animal outside the gate, I won't have him near my herbs. Come in.'

Alys tied the pony to a twisted hawthorn bush which grew at Morach's gateway, picked her fine red gown clear of the muck, and went in.

She had forgotten the stink of the place. Morach's midden was downwind at the back of the cottage but the sweet sickly odour of muck and the tang of urine hovered around the cottage, seeped through the walls. The midden heap was as old as the cottage, it had always smelled foul. The little fire was flickering sullenly on damp wood and the cottage was filled with a mist of black smoke. A couple of hens scuttered out the way as Alys entered, their droppings green and shiny on the hearthstone. Under Alys' new leather shoes the floor felt slippery with damp. The body of flood water only yards from the threshold made the very air wet and cold. At dusk the mist would roll along the river valley and seep under the door and in the little window. Alys gathered her new cloak closer and sat by the fire, taking Morach's stool without asking.

'I brought you some money,' she said abruptly. 'And a sackful of food.'

Morach nodded. 'Stolen?' she inquired without interest.

Alys shook her head. 'He gave it me,' she said. 'The old lord. Gave me these clothes too.'

Morach nodded. 'They're very fine,' she said. 'Good enough for Lady Catherine herself. Good enough for Lord Hugh's whore.'

'That's what they think me,' Alys said. 'But he is old, Morach, and has been very sick. He does not touch me. He is . . .' She broke off as the thought came to her for the first time. 'He is kind to me, Morach.'

Morach's dark eyebrows snapped together. 'First time in his life then,' she said thoughtfully. 'Kind? Are you sure? Maybe he wants you for something and he's keeping it close.'

Alys paused. 'He could be,' she said. 'I've never known a man to plan so far ahead. He has thought of everything, from his deathbed, to the death of the young lord's son who isn't even conceived. He has a place for me in his schemes – to work for him now, he needs a clerk who will keep secrets, and he'll see me safe to a nunnery when my work is finished.' She broke off, meeting Morach's sceptical black glare. 'It's my only chance,' she said simply. 'He says he will get me to France, to a nunnery there. He is my only chance.'

Morach muttered something under her breath and turned to climb the ladder to her sleeping platform. 'Put the water on,' she said. 'I've some chamomile to mash. I need it to clear my head.'

Alys bent her head and blew at the fire and set the

little pot of water on its three legs in the red embers. When the water started to bubble Alys threw in some chamomile leaves and set it to stand. When Morach came down with her bag of fortune-telling bones, she and Alys shared the one chipped horn cup.

Morach drank deep, and then shook the bones in their little purse.

'Choose,' she said, holding out the purse to Alys.

Alys hesitated.

'Choose,' Morach said again.

'Is it witchcraft?' Alys asked. She was not afraid, her blue eyes were fixed challengingly on Morach. 'Is it black arts, Morach?'

Morach shrugged. 'Who knows?' she said carelessly. 'To one man it's black arts, to another it's wise woman's trade, and to another it's a foolish old woman muttering madness. It's often true – that's all I know.'

Alys shrugged and at Morach's impatient gesture took one of the carved flat bones, then another, then a third, from the little pouch.

Morach stared at her choice. 'The Gateway,' she said first. 'That's your choice, that's where you are now. The three ways that lie before you – the castle life with its joys and dangers and its profits; the nun's life which you will have to fight like a saint to regain; or here – poverty, dirt, hunger. But . . .' She laughed softly. 'Invisibility. The most important thing for a woman, especially if she is poor, especially if she will grow old one day.'

Morach studied the second bone with the rune scrawled on it in a rusty brown ink. 'Unity,' she said, surprised. 'When you make your choice you have the chance for unity – to travel with your heart and mind in the same direction. Set your heart on something and stay true to it. One goal, one thought, one love. Whatever it is you desire: magic, your God, love.'

Alys' face was white, her eyes almost black with anger. 'I don't want him,' she said through her teeth. 'I don't want love, I don't want lust, I don't want desire, I don't want him. I want to get back where I belong, to the cloister where my life has order, some peace and some security and wealth. That's all.'

Morach laughed. 'Not much then,' she said. 'Not much for a drab from Bowes Moor, a runaway wench, a runaway nun. Not much to wish for – peace, security and wealth. Not a great demand!'

Alys shook her head irritably. 'You don't understand!' she exclaimed. 'It is *not* a great demand. It is my life, it is what I am used to. It is my proper place, my deserts. I need it now. Holiness – and a life where I can be at peace. Holiness and comfort.'

Morach shook her head, smiling to herself. 'It's a rare combination,' she said softly. 'Holiness and comfort. Most holy roads tend to the stony, I thought.'

Alys shrugged irritably. 'How would you know?' she demanded. 'What road have you ever followed but your own choice?'

Morach nodded. 'But I follow *one* road,' she reminded Alys. 'And they call me a wise woman rightly. This is what the Unity rune is telling you. Choose one road and follow it with loyalty.'   Alys nodded. 'And the last one?'

Morach turned it around, looked at both sides and studied the two blank faces for a moment. 'Odin. Death,' she said casually and tossed the three back into the bag.

'Death!' Alys exclaimed. 'For who?'

'For me,' Morach said evenly. 'For the old Lord

Hugh, for the young Lord Hugo, for you. Did you think you would live forever?'

'No . . . ' Alys stumbled. 'But . . . d'you mean soon?'

'It's always too soon,' Morach replied with sudden irritation. 'You'll have your few days of passion and your choices to make before you come to it. But it's always too soon.'

Alys waited impatiently for more but Morach drank deep of the tea and would not look at her. Alys took the little purse of copper coins from her pocket and laid it in Morach's lap. Morach knocked it to the floor. 'There's no more,' she said unhelpfully.

'Then talk to me,' Alys said. For a moment her pale face trembled and she looked like a child again. 'Talk to me, Morach. I am like a prisoner in that place. Everyone except the old lord himself is my enemy.'

Morach nodded her head. 'Will you run?' she asked with slight interest. 'Run again?'

'I have the horse now,' Alys said, her voice quickening as the idea came to her. 'I have a horse and if I had money . . .' Morach's bare dirty foot stepped at once to cover the purse she had knocked to the floor. 'There *must* be an order of nuns where they would take me in,' Alys said. 'You *must* have heard of somewhere, Morach!'

Morach shook her head. 'I have heard of nothing except the Visitors and fines and complaints against nunneries and monasteries taken as high as the King,' she said. 'Your old abbey is stripped bare – the benches from the church, the slates from the roof, even some of the stones themselves are pulled down, and carted away for walls, or mounting blocks. First by Lord Hugo's men from the castle and now on his order by the villagers. It's the same in the north from what I hear, and the south. They'll have escaped the King's investigations in Scotland, you could try for it. But you'd be dead before you reached the border.'

Alys nodded. She held out her hand for the cup and Morach refilled it and handed it to her.

'The mood of the times is against you,' she said. 'People were sick of the wealth of the abbeys, priests, monks and nuns. They were sick of their greed. They want new landlords, or no landlords at all. You chose the wrong time to become a nun.'

'I chose the wrong time to be born,' Alys said bitterly. 'I am a woman who does not fit well with her time.'

Morach grinned darkly. 'Me too,' she said. 'And a whole multitude of others. My fault was that I gained more than I could hold. My sin was winning. So they brought the man's law and the man's power against me. The man's court, the law of men; I have hidden myself in the old power, in the old skills, in woman's power.'

She looked at Alys without sympathy. 'Your fault is that you would never bide still,' she said. 'You could have lived here with me with naught to fear except the witch-taker but you wanted Tom and his farmhouse and his fields. Then when you saw something better you fled for it.

'They thought Tom would die of grief for you, he begged me to order you home. I laughed in his face. I knew you would never come. You'd seen something better. You wanted it. I knew you'd never come back of your own free will. You'd have stayed forever, wouldn't you?'

Alys nodded. 'I loved Mother Hildebrande, the abbess,' she said. 'I was high in her favour. And she loved me as if I were her daughter. I know she did. She taught me to read and to write, she taught me Latin.

She took special pains with me and she had great plans for me. I worked in the still-room with the herbs, and I worked in the infirmary and I studied in the library. I never had to do any heavy dirty work. I was the favourite of them all, and I washed every day and slept very soft.' She glanced at Morach. 'I had it all then,' she said. 'The love of my mother, the truest, purest love there is, comfort and holiness.'

'You'll not find that again in England,' Morach said. 'Oh, the King cannot live forever, or he may cobble together some deal with the Pope. His heirs might restore the Church. But English nuns will never have you back.'

'They might not know I ran . . .' Alys started.

Morach shook her head emphatically. 'They'll guess,' she said. 'You were the only one to get out of that building alive that night. The rest burned as they slept.'

Alys closed her eyes for a moment and smelled the smoke and saw the flicker of flames, orange on the white wall of her cell. Again she heard that high single scream as she ducked through the gate and kilted up her habit and ran without care for the others, without a care for the abbess who had loved her like a daughter, and who slept quiet, while the smoke weaved its grey web about her and held her fast till the flames licked her feather mattress and her linen shift and then her tired old body.

'The only one out of thirty of them,' Morach said with subterranean pride. 'The only one – the biggest coward, the fleetest of foot, the quickest turncoat.'

Alys bowed her head. 'Don't, Morach,' she said softly.

Morach smacked her lips on a sip of the chamomile tea. 'So what will you do?' she asked.

Alys looked up defiantly. 'I won't be defeated,' she said. 'I won't be driven down into being another dirty old witch on the edge of the moor. I won't be a maid-in-waiting or a clerk. I want to eat well and sleep well, and wear good cloth and ride dry-shod, and I won't be driven down into life as an ordinary woman. I won't be married off to some clod to work my life away all day and risk my life every year bearing his children. I'll get back to a nunnery, where I belong, one way or another. The old lord won't break his promise to me – he'll send me to France. If I can escape the notice of the young Lord Hugo and the malice of his wife, and if I can keep myself a virgin in that place where they think of nothing but lust – I can get back.'

Morach nodded. 'You need a deal of luck and a deal of power to accomplish that,' she said thoughtfully. 'Only one way I can think of.' She paused.

Alys leaned forward. 'Tell me,' she said.

'A pact,' Morach said simply. 'A pact with the devil himself. Have him guard you against the young lord, make him turn his eyes another way. I know enough of the black arts to guide you. We could call up the dark master, he would come for you, for sure – a sacred little soul like yours. You could trade your way into comfort forever. There's your way to peace and order and safety. You become the devil's own and you are never an ordinary woman again.'

For a moment Alys hesitated as if she were tempted by the sudden rush into hell, but then she dropped her face into her hands and moaned in torment. 'I don't *want* to,' she cried as if she were a little girl again. 'I don't want to, Morach! I want a middle way. I want a little wealth and a little freedom! I want to be back in the nunnery with Mother Hildebrande. I am afraid of the devil! I am afraid of the witch-taker! I am afraid of the young lord and of his icy wife! I want to be somewhere safe! I am too young for these dark choices! I am not old enough to keep myself safe! I want Mother Hildebrande! I want my mother!'

She broke into a storm of crying, her face buried in her arms, leaning slightly towards Morach as if begging wordlessly for an embrace. Morach folded her arms and rested her chin on them, gazing into the fire, waiting for Alys to be still. She was quite untouched by her grief.

'There's no safety for you, or for me,' she said equably when Alys was quieter. 'We're women who do not accord with the way men want. There's no safety for our sort. Not now, not ever.'

Alys' sobs weakened against the rock of Morach's grim indifference. She fell silent, rubbing her face on her fine woollen undersleeve. A piece of wood in the fireplace snapped and burned with a yellow flame.

'Then I go back to the castle and take my chance,' Alys said, resigned.

Morach nodded.

'Our Lady once chose me,' Alys said, her voice very low, speaking of a holy secret. 'She sent me a sign. Even though I have sinned most deeply, I hope and I trust that She will guide me back to Her. She will make my penance and give me my absolution. She cannot have chosen me to watch me fail.'

Morach cocked her eyebrow, interested. 'Depends on what sort of a goddess she is,' she said judicially. 'There are some that would choose you to see nothing but failure. That's the joy in it for them.'

'Oh!' Alys shrugged impatiently. 'You're a heathen and a heretic, Morach! I waste my time speaking with you.'

Morach grinned, unrepentant. 'Don't speak with me then,' she said placidly. 'Your Lady chose you. So She will keep you safe to play Her game, whatever it is. Depend upon Her then, my little holy lamb! What are you doing here, drawing the runes and praying for the future?'

Alys hunched her shoulders, clasped her hands. 'The young lord is my danger,' she said. 'He could take me from Our Lady. And then I would be lost.'

'She won't strike him blind to save you?' Morach asked sarcastically. 'She won't put out Her sacred hand to stop him feeling up your gown?'

Alys scowled at Morach. 'I have to find a way to defend myself. He would have me for his sport,' she said. 'He ordered me to his room tonight. If he rapes me I'll never get back to the nuns. He'd have me and throw me aside, and his wife would turn me out. I'd be lucky to get through the guardroom once they knew the young lord had done with me.'

Morach laughed. 'Best keep your legs crossed and your Latin sharp then,' she said. 'Pray to your Lady, and trust the old lord.' She paused. 'If you would stoop to take them, my saint, there are some herbs I know which would make you less sweet to him.'

Alys looked up. 'I may not kill his lust,' she warned. 'The old lord forbade it and he will be watching me. I cannot give Hugo anything to weary him of venery.'

Morach rose from the floor and went to the bunches of herbs dangling on strings from the beams of the sleeping platform. 'It is you who takes this,' she said. 'Make it into a tisane, every morning, and drink it while it cools. It kills a man's desire for the woman that drinks it.'

Alys nodded. 'And what would you use to kill a woman's desire?' she asked casually.

Morach turned, her dark face under the shock of grey hair alight with mischief. 'A woman's desire?' she said. 'But my little nun, my precious virgin, who is this lustful woman? We were talking of the young lord and his persecution of your sainted virginity!'

'Have done,' Alys said sulkily. 'I was asking for one of the women in the gallery.'

Morach chuckled. 'I would have to meet her,' she said slyly. 'This woman, is she young or old? Has she known a man or is she a virgin? Does she long for his love, his devotion – or is she just hot for his body to crush her and his wetness inside her and his hands all over her?'

Alys flushed rosy. 'I don't know,' she said grimly. 'If she asks me again I will bring her to you.'

Morach nodded, her eyes sparkling with amusement. 'You do, pretty Alys,' she said. 'Do bring her to me.'

Alys tucked the bunch of herbs into her pocket. 'Anything else?' she asked. 'To kill Hugo's ardour? Anything else I should do?'

Morach shook her head. 'I have no other herbs, but you could bring me some candlewax when you next come and I'll make images of them all,' she offered. 'We'll make them all into moppets to dance to your bidding, you and me.'

Alys' eyes widened. 'It cannot be done!' she exclaimed.

Morach smiled darkly and nodded. 'I've never done it before,' she said. 'It's deep magic, very deep. But the old woman who was here before me taught me the words. It never fails except . . .'

'Except what?' Alys asked. She shivered as if she were suddenly cold. 'Except what?' she asked.

'Sometimes they misunderstand.'

Alys drew a little closer. 'What?' she asked. 'Who misunderstand?'

Morach smiled. 'You take the little figures and you bind them with deep magic. Understand that?'

Alys nodded, her face pale.

'You order them to do your bidding. You command them to do as you wish.'

Alys nodded again.

'Sometimes *they* misunderstand,' Morach said, her voice very low. 'I heard of one woman who ordered her lover to come alive again. He was dead of the plague and she could not bear to lose him. She made the candlewax moppet while he was lying cold and poxed in the room next door, the sores all over him. When she made the moppet walk, he walked too, just as she had commanded.'

Alys swallowed against a tight throat. 'He was better?'

Morach chuckled, a low chilling laugh. 'No,' she said. 'He was dead and cold, covered with sores, his eyes blank, his lips blue. But he walked behind her, as she had commanded; everywhere she went he walked behind her.'

'A ghost?' Alys asked.

Morach shrugged. 'Who knows?'

Alys shook her head. 'That's foul,' she exclaimed. 'That's black arts, Morach! As foul as your pact with the devil. I'll not touch magic, I've told you before. You tempt me and you bring me no good!'

'Wait till you are in need,' Morach said scathingly. 'Wait till you are hungry. Wait till you are desperate. And then bring me the candlewax. When you are desperate – and you will be desperate, my little angel – you will be glad enough of my power then.'

Alys said nothing.

'I'm hungry,' Morach said abruptly. 'Fetch the food and let's eat. I've only enough wood for another hour, you can gather some more in the morning.'

Alys looked at her resentfully. 'My hands are softening,' she said. 'And my nails are clean and growing again. You can get your own wood, Morach. I've brought you food and money, that should be enough.'

Morach laughed, a harsh, sharp sound. 'So the little virgin has claws, too, does she?' she crowed. 'Then I'll tell you – I have a good woodpile out the back. Now fetch the food.'

Six

As the days grew darker and colder in November Alys'
work as the old lord's clerk increased. He grew more
frail and tired quickly. When a messenger arrived with
letters in English or Latin he would summon Alys to
read them to him, he was too weary to puzzle them out
himself. When young Lord Hugo came to tell him
about judgements in the ward, or disputes over borders,
or news from the wider world, from the Council of the
North or from London itself, he would have Alys by
him, sometimes taking notes of what the young lord
was saying, sometimes standing behind his chair listening. Then when Hugo was gone, with a swirl of his dark
red cape and a mischievous wink at Alys, the old lord
would ask her to tell him, over again, what Hugo had
said.

'He mumbles so!' he said.

The tension between the old lord and the young one
was clear now to Alys. The young lord was the coming
man: the soldiers were his, and the castle servants. He
wanted to make the family greater in the outside world.
He wanted to go to London and try for a place in the
King's court. The King was a braggart and a fool –
wide open to anyone who could advise him and amuse
him. The young lord wanted a place at the table of the
great. He had embraced the new religion. Father
Stephen, another ambitious young man, was his friend.
He spoke of building a new house, leaving the castle
which had been his family's home since the first Hugo
had come over with the conquering Normans and taken

the lordship as his fee and built the castle to hold the land. Hugo wanted to trade, he wanted to lend money on interest. He wanted to pay wages in cash and throw peasants off their grubbing smallholdings and make the flocks of sheep bigger still on long, uninterrupted sheep-runs. He wanted to mine coal, he wanted to forge iron. He wanted the sun shining full upon him. He wanted risks.

Old Lord Hugh stood against him. The family had held the castle for generation after generation. They had built the single round tower with a wall and a moat around it. Little by little they had won or bought more land. Little by little they had made the castle bigger, adding the second round tower for soldiers, and then the hall with the gallery above, adding the outer wall and the outer moat to enclose the farm, a second well, stables and the great gatehouse for the soldiers. Quietly, almost stealthily, they had wed and plotted, inherited and even invaded to add to the lordship until the boundaries of their lands stretched across the Pennines to the east, and westward nearly to the sea. They kept their power and their wealth by keeping quiet – keeping their distance from the envy and the struggles around the throne.

Lord Hugh had been to London only half a dozen times in his life, he was the master of the loyal excuse. He had gone to Queen Anne's coronation, where a man was safer to be seen in support than absent, wearing sober clothes and standing at the back, the very picture of a provincial, loyal lord. He voted by proxy, he bribed and negotiated by letter. When summoned to court he pleaded ill health, dangerous unrest in his lands or, lately, old age; and at once sent the King a handsome present to please the errant royal favour. He knew from his kin at court who were the coming men and who were likely to fall. He had spies in the royal offices who reported to him the news he needed. He had debtors scattered across the country who owed him money and favours. A thousand men called him cousin and looked to him for favour and protection and paid him with information. He sat like a wily spider in a network of caution and fear. He represented the power of the King in the wild lands of the north, and took his place on the great Council of the North, but never more than once a year. He never showed the family wealth or their power too brightly, for fear of envious southerners' eyes. He followed the traditions of his father and his grandfather. They lived on their lands, riding all day and never leaving their own borders. They sat in their own courts. They handed down justice in their own favour. They announced the King's laws and they enforced those they preferred. They did very well as obscure tyrants.

Their greatest rivals were the Prince Bishops and the monasteries, and now the Bishops were fighting for their wealth and could be fighting for their lives. The old lord saw the good times opening slowly for his son, and for his son's unborn, not-yet-conceived heir, and his son after him. Hugo's grandson would be as rich in land as any lord in England, would command more men than most. He could throw his influence with Scotland, with England. He would own a little kingdom of his own. Who could guess how far the family might rise, if they waited and used their caution and their wisdom as they always had done?

But the young Lord Hugo did not want to wait for the great lands of monasteries to come his way in maybe five, ten years from now. He did not want to wait for the sheep to be shorn, the copyholders' fines to be slowly increased, the annual rents brought in. He wanted wealth and power at once. He had friends who owned wagons, one who had a fleet of barges, one who was mining coal and iron ore, another who spoke of ocean-going ships and prizes to be had from countries beyond Europe, beyond the known world. He spoke of trade, of business, of lending and borrowing money at new profitable rates. He never showed his impatience with his father, and Alys feared him more because of this single, uncharacteristic discretion.

'He wants to go to London,' she warned the old lord.

'I know,' he said. 'I am holding him back and he will not tolerate it forever.'

Alys nodded.

'Have you heard more?' the old lord asked. 'Any plots, any plans? D'you think his impatience grows so strong that he would poison me, or lock me away?'

Alys' nostrils flared as if she could smell the danger in the question. 'I have heard nothing,' she said. 'I was only saying that the young lord is impatient to make his way in the world. I accuse him of nothing.'

'Tssk,' the old lord said impatiently. 'I need you to be ready to accuse him, Alys. You are in my daughter-in-law's chamber, you hear the gossip of the women. Catherine knows full well that if she does not conceive a child within the year I will find a way to be rid of her. Her best way would be to get rid of me before I make a move. Hugo is mad for the court and for London and I block his way south. Listen for me, Alys. Watch for me. You go everywhere, you can hear and see everything. You do not need to accuse Hugo or Catherine, either one or the other. You just have to tell me your suspicions - your slightest suspicions.'

'I have none,' Alys said firmly. 'Lady Catherine

speaks of your death as an event in the future, nothing more. I have never heard her admit that she fears a divorce or an annulment. And Lord Hugo comes to her rooms only rarely, and I never see him outside your chamber.'

He was silent for a moment. 'You don't see Hugo outside my room?' he confirmed.

Alys shook her head.

'He does not waylay you?'

'No,' Alys replied.

It was true. Either Morach's tisane had worked, or the old lord had made his wishes plain. When Alys rode back to the castle from Morach's cottage, Hugo had shot her one unrepentant wink, but never ordered her to his chamber again. After that, she kept out of the young lord's way as much as she could, and kept her eyes on the ground when she had to walk past him. But one cold morning, in the guardroom below the old lord's private chamber, she was coming down the little staircase as Hugo waited to walk up.

'Always in a hurry, Alys,' Hugo said conversationally. He took her sleeve in a firm grip between two fingers. 'How is my father today?'

'He is well, my lord,' Alys said. She kept her eyes on the stone flags between his riding boots. 'He slept well, his cough has eased.'

'It's this damp weather,' Hugo said. 'You can feel the mist coming off the river, can't you, Alys? Doesn't it chill you to the bone?'

Alys shot a swift upward look at him. His dark face was bent down towards her, very close, as if she might whisper a reply.

'I have no complaint, my lord,' she said. 'And the spring will come soon.'

'Oh, not for months and months yet,' Hugo said. 'We have long days of darkness and cold yet to come.' He whispered the words 'darkness and cold' as if they were an invitation to the firelit warmth of his room.

'I do not feel the cold,' she said steadily.

'Do you dislike me?' Hugo asked abruptly. He dropped her sleeve and put both hands either side of her face, turning it up to him. 'You told my father that I had invited you and that you were unwilling. Do you dislike me, Alys?'

Alys stayed still and looked steadily at the silvery whiteness of the falling band of his collar, as if it could cool her.

'No, my lord,' she said politely. 'Of course not.'

'But you never came to my room,' he observed. 'And you told tales to my father. So he told me to keep my hands off you. Did you know that?'

He held Alys' face gently. She stole a quick look at his eyes; he was laughing at her.

'I did not know that.'

'So you do like me then?' he demanded. He could hardly hold back his laughter at the absurdity of the conversation. Alys could feel laughter bubbling up inside herself too.

'It is not my place, my lord, to either like you or dislike you,' Alys said primly. Under his fingers her cheeks were tingling.

Hugo stopped laughing, held her face still with one hand, and with a gentle fingertip traced a line from the outside of her eye, down her cheek-bone to the corner of her lip. Alys froze still, unmoving beneath his caress. He bent a little closer. Alys shut her eyes to blot out the image of Hugo's smiling intent face coming closer. He hesitated, a half, a quarter of an inch from Alys' lips.

'But I like you, Alys,' he said softly. 'And my father will not live forever. And I think you would feel the cold if you were back on Bowes Moor again.'

Alys stayed mute. She could feel the warmth of his breath on her face. His lips were very close to hers. She could not move away from his kiss, she could only wait, passive, her face turned up, her eyes slowly, drowsily closing. Then his hands left her face and he straightened up. Alys' eyes flew open; she stared at him in surprise.

'In your own time, Alys,' he said pleasantly, and he swung out of the room and ran up the curving stairs of the tower to his father's room.

No one had seen them, no one had heard them. But Lady Catherine knew.

When Alys was summoned to the ladies' chamber to sew, Lady Catherine waved her to a stool near her own chair, where she could watch Alys' face as the others talked.

'You're very quiet,' she said to Alys.

Alys glanced up with her polite, deferential smile. 'I was listening, my lady,' she said.

'You never speak of your own kin,' Lady Catherine said. 'Do you have any family other than the mad old woman on the moor?'

'No,' Alys said. 'Except those at Penrith,' she corrected herself.

Lady Catherine nodded. 'And no sweetheart? No betrothed?' she asked idly. The other women were silent, listening to the interrogation.

Alys smiled but made a tiny movement of her shoulders, of her head, to signify her regret. 'No,' she said. 'Not now. Once I had a sweetheart,' she glanced to Mistress Allingham. 'You would know of him, Mistress Allingham. Tom the sheep farmer. But I had no portion and I went away to Penrith and he married another girl.'

'Perhaps we should dower you, and send you off to be wed!' Lady Catherine said lightly. 'It's a dull life for you here, where no man sees you and nothing ever happens. It's well enough for us – we're all married women or widows or betrothed – but a girl like you should be wed and bearing children.'

Alys sensed the trap opening up before her. 'You're very kind, my lady,' she said hesitantly.

'That's settled then!' Lady Catherine said brightly. Her voice was as gentle as a diamond scratching glass. 'I will ask my Lord Hugo to look among the soldiers for a good man for you, and I will give you a dowry myself.'

'I cannot marry,' Alys said suddenly. 'I cannot marry and keep my skills.'

'How is that?' Lady Catherine asked, opening her grey eyes very wide. 'You do not need to be a virgin to be a healer unless you deal in magic, surely?'

'I use no magic,' Alys said swiftly. 'I am just a herbalist. But I could not do my work if I belonged to a man. It is time-consuming and wearisome. My kinswoman lives alone.'

'But she's a widow,' Mistress Allingham interrupted, and was rewarded with a swift, small smile from Lady Catherine.

'So you *can* wed and still keep your arts,' Lady Catherine said triumphantly. 'You are shy, Alys, that is all. But I promise you we will find you a fine young husband who will care for you and use you gently.'

Eliza Herring and Margery tittered behind their hands. Ruth, who feared Lady Catherine more than they did, kept very silent and stitched faster, bending low over her work.

'You do not thank me?' Lady Catherine asked; her voice was clear and underneath it – like an underground river – was a current of absolute menace. 'You do not thank me for offering to dower you? And have you married to a good man?'

'Yes, I do indeed,' Alys said with her clear, honest smile. 'I thank you very much indeed, my lady.'

Lady Catherine turned the talk to the gossip of London. She had a letter from one of her distant family in the south which spoke of the King and his growing coldness towards the young Anne Boleyn, his new Queen, even though she was big with his child again. Alys, who blamed the King and the whore, his pretend Queen, for all her troubles, smiled an empty smile as she listened, and hoped that Lady Catherine had been merely amusing herself by tormenting her with promises of marriage.

'And the new Queen was nothing more than a maid-in-waiting in the old Queen's bedchamber when she took the King's fancy,' Eliza Herring said tactlessly. 'Think of that! Serving a queen one day and being a queen yourself the next!'

'And the one he looks to now, Lady Jane Seymour, has served them both!' Margery said. 'Served the old Queen – the false one I mean – and now Queen Anne.'

'A fine place to have at court, a lady-in-waiting,' Eliza said. 'Think how high you might rise!'

Lady Catherine nodded but her face was impassive. She looked at Alys as if to warn her. Alys ducked her head down and sewed.

'Those are London manners,' Catherine said with soft menace. 'And what is right and proper for the King is not always a course for his subjects.'

'Of course not!' Margery said, flustered. 'Besides, if

Queen Anne has a son, he will cleave to her! No King would put aside a wife who gave him a son! It is only barren wives who get that treatment!'

Catherine's face went white with anger.

'I mean . . .' Margery stumbled.

'The King's marriage was annulled because Catherine of Aragon was his brother's wife,' Catherine said icily. 'That was the only reason for the annulment of the marriage, and you have all sworn an oath of allegiance recognizing the King's rightful heir and the truth of his marriage to Queen Anne.'

The women nodded, keeping their heads down.

'Any talk of divorce at the whim of the King is treason,' Catherine said firmly. 'There can be no divorce. The King's first marriage was invalid and against the law of God. There can be no comparison.'

'With what?' Eliza asked dangerously.

Catherine's grey eyes stared her down. 'There can be no comparison between your positions and the Queen's ladies,' she said with acid clarity. 'You are none of you high enough to wear scarlet, whatever borrowed clothes Alys may use. I hope that none of you would want to overset the natural order, the God-given order. Unless Alys hopes to see herself in purple? Married to a lord?'

The women laughed in a nervous, obedient chorus.

'Who did the gown belong to, Alys?' Catherine asked vindictively.

'I was told it belonged to a woman called Meg,' Alys said, clearing her throat and speaking low.

'And do you know who she was, Alys?' Catherine asked.

Alys lifted her head from her sewing. 'Lord Hugh's whore,' she said softly.

Catherine nodded. 'I think I would rather wear brown

than flaunt borrowed colours,' she said. 'I would rather wear honest brown than the gown of a whore who died of the pox.'

Alys gritted her teeth. 'Lord Hugh ordered me to wear this gown, I have no other.' She shot one look at Catherine. 'I hope I do not displease you, my lady. I do not dare disobey Lord Hugh.'

Catherine nodded her head. 'Very well,' she said. 'Very well. But you had best borrow only the gown, Alys, and not the manners of the last owner.'

Alys met Catherine's hard, suspicious gaze. 'I am a maid,' she said. 'Not a whore. And I shall stay that way.'

After that she kept even more carefully away from anywhere that she might meet the young lord. When he came to his father's room she sat in a corner, in the shadows. She put off the cherry-red gown which the old lord had given her, and asked if she might take a new one from the box. She chose a dark blue one, so dark that it was almost black, and wore it with a black stomacher tied as flat as a board across her belly. It was too large for her and came too high up under her chin, hiding the swell of her tight-pressed breasts. She rummaged in the box and found an old-fashioned gable hood in the style which had gone out with the old queen, the false Queen Catherine. Alys scraped back her growing curly hair into a black cap pinned tight. Then she pulled the gable hood on top of the cap and pinned it down. It was heavier than her wimple and hotter with her hair underneath, but it reminded Alys for a moment of the steady pressure of the wimple and the bindings around her face which she had worn for so long.

'You look like a nun,' the old lord said. And when he

saw her swift guarded look at him he said, 'No, wench, you're safe enough. You look like a woman who is trying to be invisible. Who are you hiding from, Alys? Lady Catherine? Hugo?'

'The other gown was dirty,' Alys said evenly. 'I have sent it to be washed. And it is time I wore a hood.'

Lord Hugh raised his white eyebrows. 'You can have your pick of that chest of clothes,' he said. 'And tell David to show you the other chest. You might as well wear them as anyone else while you are here. When you leave they must stay.'

'Thank you,' Alys said quietly. 'Is it not an offence for me to wear scarlet, my lord? I thought only a wife of a landholder could wear red?'

Lord Hugh chuckled. 'I enforce the law of the land. The laws are what I say. And anyway, women don't matter.'

The castle was preparing for the feast of Christmas and the turkeys and geese gobbled innocently on extra feed. The old lord developed a cough which kept him awake at nights and made him tired and irritable during the day. Alys went out in the dawn frost to pick fresh herbs in the little garden outside the kitchen door and bumped into a man, wrapped thick in a cloak, coming in.

He put out a hand to steady her, gripped her arm. As soon as he touched her she knew it was Hugo.

'I gave you a fright.' His smile gleamed from the shadow of his hood. He swept her with him back into the warmth of the kitchen. Servants were sleeping on the floor before the fire and on the benches. Hugo kicked two or three with his booted foot and they staggered sleepily out of his way. He pulled up two stools and thrust Alys down by the glowing embers.

'You're frozen,' he said. He took her hand. Around her fingernails her fingers were blue with cold.

'I was picking herbs with the ice on them,' Alys said. 'Your father's cough is a little worse.'

Hugo took her cold hands and put them between his warm palms. As the feeling came back into her numb fingers Alys grimaced, pulled her hands away and shook them. Hugo laughed softly and leaned forward to recapture them. 'I've been out all night,' he said. His voice was low; no wakeful servant could hear them. 'Don't you want to know what I have been doing, Alys?'

Alys shook her head slightly and looked away from his intent face to the fire.

'I met some friends who think as I do,' he said. 'One of them is the son of landowners, a wealthy man though not noble. Another is the son of a trader. We're all young, we all want a share of the new world which is coming. We are all held back by our fathers.'

Alys made a little movement as if she would rise. Hugo tugged her back to the stool with a handful of her cape. 'Listen to me,' he said softly. 'See how I trust you.'

Alys turned her face away, Hugo kept his hold on her.

'One of my friends plans to set his father aside, have him declared insane and take his land and his wealth. His mother has agreed to support his claim, his wife too. A wicked way to treat your father, is it not, Alys?'

Alys said nothing. Hugo saw that her face was rosy from the warmth of the fire but around her dark blue eyes the skin was white. He knew she was afraid.

'I would not do that, Alys, unless I was tempted very badly,' he said. 'But my father stands in my light – d'you see it, Alys? If it were not for his order that I stay here I would be in London. If it were not for his schemes to keep Catherine's entailed lands I would be free of her. If it were not for his ambition to be hidden, his passion for peace, I would be at court, chancing my life and my wealth for tremendous prizes. Can you see how impatient I am, Alys?'

Alys' lips were pressed together. Hugo had hold of both her hands. If he had not held her fast she would have clapped them over her ears.

'Your chance will come, when God wills,' she said as he waited for her to reply. 'You will have to be patient, my lord.'

He leaned forward so his face was very close to hers. 'And if I am not patient?' he asked. 'If I am not patient and I found someone to assist me? If my father were ill and no one could heal him? If he died? If then I set my wife aside? If I were rid of my wife? Rid of my wife and looking for a woman that I could trust, to hold the castle for me while I was away. A woman who could read, who could write? A woman who would be mine, sworn to my interest, dependent on me? A woman who would be my ears and eyes. Like you watch and listen for my father?'

Alys could not move. His whisper was hypnotic, he was luring her into some trap which she could not foresee.

'I have to be free,' she said in a low voice of longing.

'Do I tempt you, Alys?' he asked softly. 'The wealth and the power?'

He saw her eyes darken slightly as if with desire.

'And pleasure,' he went on. 'Nights and long days of pleasure with me?'

Alys jerked backwards as if he had thrown cold water in her face. She pulled her hands free.

'I have to go,' she said abruptly.

He rose as she did and slid one hand around her waist, holding her close to him. His mouth came down towards her. Alys felt her head tip back, her lips open.

Then he released her and stepped back.

Alys staggered a little, off balance.

'Go now,' he said. His dark eyes were bright with mischief. 'You can go now, Alys. But you are learning who is your master, are you not? You cannot hide behind my father for much longer. I have had many wenches and I know the signs of it. You desire me already, though you hardly know it yet. You have taken the bait like a salmon in the spring flood. You may swim and swim but I shall land you at last. You will dream of me, Alys, you will long for me. And in the end, you will come to me and beg me to touch you.'

He smiled at her white face.

'And then I will be gentle to you,' he said. 'And I will make you all mine. And you will never be free again.'

Alys turned from him and stumbled towards the kitchen door.

'You're in very deep now,' he said softly to himself, as she pulled the door open and fled across the lobby to the great hall. 'You're in very deep, my Alys.'

For twelve nights Alys lay wakeful, waiting for the dawn light to come with winter slowness. For twelve days she moved in a dream through her work for the old lord, writing what he ordered without taking in any sense of the words. She picked herbs for him and brewed them or pounded them according to their potency. She sat in Lady Catherine's chamber and nodded and smiled when they called on her to speak.

For twelve days she waded through a river of darkness

and confusion. She had never longed more for the quiet certainties of Mother Hildebrande. She had never missed those ordered easy days more acutely. For twelve days Alys wandered around the castle like a ghost and when she heard a door bang, and Hugo's merry whistle, she found she was trembling as if she had an ague.

She was by the castle gate when he rode in from hunting one day, his cap lost – blown away on the moor – his face bright. When he saw her he vaulted from the saddle and tossed the reins to one of the men.

'I have killed you a grand dinner, Alys!' he said joyfully. 'A wild boar. They will stuff it and bring its head in and lay it at your feet! And you shall eat rich meat and dark gravy and nibble on the honeyed crackling! My Alys!'

Alys fumbled for her basket. 'I am fasting,' she said breathlessly. 'It is Saint Andrew's day, my lord. I do not eat meat today.'

He laughed carelessly, as if none of it mattered at all. 'That nonsense!' he exclaimed. 'Alys, Alys, don't cling to the old dead ways that mean nothing to anyone any more! Eat fish when you want to! Eat meat when you are hungry! Don't let me ride out all day, and chasing a wild boar too, and then turn your face away from me and tell me you won't dine with me!'

Alys could feel her hands trembling. She held the basket tighter. 'You must excuse me,' she said. 'I . . . '

There was a shout from behind them as someone drove a cart through the narrow gateway. Hugo pressed forward, his hands either side of Alys' head. She shrank back against the wall and then felt him, deliberately, lean his warm body against her. Her stomacher was like armour, her gable hood like a helmet. But when Hugo pressed against her she felt the heat of his body through her clothes. She smelled the clean, fresh smell of his linen, the sharp tang of his sweat. His knee pressing against her legs, the brush of his thick padded codpiece against her thigh, was as intimate as if they were naked and alone together.

'Don't you long for a taste of it, Alys?' he asked, his voice very soft in her ear. 'Don't you dream what it would taste like? All these forbidden good things? Can't I teach you, can't I teach you, Alys, to break some rules? To break some rules and taste some pleasure, now, while you are young and desirable and hot?'

And Alys, in the shadow of the doorway, with the warmth of him all around her and the whisper of his male temptation in her ear, turned her face up towards him and closed her eyes and knew her desire.

As lightly as a flicker of candleflame he brushed his lips against her open mouth, raised his head and looked down into her tranced face with his smiling dark eyes.

'I sleep alone these nights,' he said softly. 'You know my room, in the round tower, above my father's chamber. Any night you please, Alys, leave my father, climb higher up the tower instead of running to be with those silly women. Climb higher up the tower and I will give you more than a kiss in a gateway, more than a taste. More than you can dream of.'

Alys opened her eyes, hazy with desire.

Hugo smiled at her. His wicked, careless smile. 'Shall you come tonight?' he asked. 'Shall I light a fire and warm the wine and wait for you?'

'Yes,' she said.

He nodded as if they had struck an agreeable bargain at last; then he was gone.

That night Alys ate the wild boar when they brought it to the women's table. Hugo glanced behind him and she saw his secret smile. She knew then that she was lost. That neither the herbs nor the old lord's warning to Hugo would stop him. And that no power of will could stop her.

'What's the matter with you, Alys?' Eliza asked with rough good nature. 'You're as white as a sheet, you haven't eaten your dinner for nigh on two weeks, you're awake every morning before anyone else and all day today you've been deaf.'

'I am sick,' Alys said, her voice sharp. Bitter.

Eliza laughed. 'Better cure yourself then,' she said. 'Not much of a wise woman if you can't cure yourself!'

Alys nodded. 'I shall,' she said, as if she had come to a decision at last. 'I shall cure myself.'

On that night, when Alys felt her skin burn in the moonlight and she knew the moon would be lighting the path to Hugo's room through twenty silver arrow-slits, and that he would be lying naked in his bed, waiting and yet not waiting for her, she rose and went to Lady Catherine's gallery where there was a box of new wax candles. Alys took three, wrapped them in a cloth, tied the bundle tight and sealed the string. The next morning she sent it by one of the castle carters to Morach's cottage, telling him it was a Christmas gift for the old lady. She sent no message – there was no need.

On the eve of the Christmas feast one of the kitchen wenches climbed the stone steps to the round tower to tell Alys that there was an old woman asking for her at the market gate. Alys dipped a curtsey to the old lord and asked him if she might go and meet Morach.

'Aye,' he said. He was short of breath, it was one of his bad days. He was wrapped in a thick cloak by a blazing fire and yet he could feel no warmth. 'Come back quickly,' he said.

Alys threw her black cloak around her and slipped like a shadow down the stairs. The guardroom was empty except for one half-dozing soldier. Alys walked through the great hall past half a dozen men who were sprawled on the benches, sleeping off their dinner-time ale, through the servers' lobby to the kitchen.

The fires were burning, there was the smell of roasting meat and game hung too long. The floor had been swept after the midday meal and piles of bloodstained sawdust stood in the corner, waiting to be taken out. The cooks ate well after the hall had been served, the kitchen staff had emptied the jugs of wine and dozed now in corners. Only the kitchen boy, stripped down to his shorts, monotonously turning the handle of the spit roasting the meat for supper, stared at Alys as she walked through, her skirts lifted clear of the muck.

She walked out of the kitchen door and through the kitchen garden. The neat salad beds ran along one side of the path, the herbs were planted on the other, all edged with box-hedging. At the tower which guarded the inner ward the guards let her through with a ribald comment to her back, but they did not touch her. She was well known to be under the old lord's protection. She walked across the bridge which spanned the great ditch of stagnant murky water and then across the outer ward where the little farmyard slept in the pale afternoon sunshine and a blackbird sang loudly in one of the apple trees. There were hives and pigsties, hens roaming and pecking, a dozen goats and a couple of cows, one with a weaned calf. There were sheds for storing vegetables and hay, there was a barn. There were a number of tumbledown half-ruined farm buildings. Alys knew from her work for Lord Hugh that they would never be repaired. It was too costly to run a complete farm inside the castle walls. And anyway, in these days, there was no threat to the peace of the land. Scotland's army never came this far south and the mosstroopers threatened travellers on lonely roads, not secure farms, not the great Lord Hugh himself.

Alys walked through the farmyard area towards the great gate where the portcullis hung like a threat and the drawbridge spanned the dark waters of the outer moat. The gate was shut but there was a little door cut into the massive timbers. There were only two soldiers on duty, but an officer watched them from the open door of the guardroom. The country might be at peace but the young lord was never careless of the safety of the castle, and the soldiers were expected to give him value for money. One of the guards swung the door open for Alys and she bent her head and stepped out into a sudden blaze of winter sunshine. As the shadow of the castle lifted from her, Alys felt free.

Morach was waiting for her, dirtier and more stooped than ever. She looked even smaller against the might of the castle than at her own fireside.

'I brought them,' she said, without a word of greeting. 'What made you change your mind?'

Alys slipped her hand through Morach's arm and walked her away from the castle. The market stalls were set out along the main street of the town, selling fruits, vegetables, meat, fish, eggs and the great pale cheeses from the Cotherstone dairies. Half a dozen travelling pedlars had set out their stalls with fancy goods, ribbons, even pewterware for sale, and they shouted to passers-by to buy a Christmas fairing for their sweethearts, for their wives. Alys saw David walking among the produce stalls, pointing and claiming the very best of the goods and nodding to a servant behind him to pay cash. He bought very little. He preferred to order goods direct from the farms inside the manors which belonged to the castle. Those farmers could not set their own prices, and anything the lord required could be ordered as part of the lord's dues.

She drew Morach away, past the stalls and the chattering women, down the hill, and they sat on a drystone wall which marked the edge of someone's pasture and looked down the valley to the river which foamed over the rocks at the foot of the castle cliff.

'You're getting prettier,' Morach said, without approval. She patted Alys' face with one dirty hand. 'You don't suit black,' she said. 'But that hood makes you look like a woman, not a child.'

Alys nodded.

'And you're clean,' Morach said. 'You look like a lady. You're plumper around the face, you look well.' She leaned back to complete her inspection. 'Your breasts are getting bigger and your face finer. New gown.'

Alys nodded again.

'Too pretty,' Morach said shrewdly. 'Too pretty to disappear, even in a navy gown and a gable hood the size of a house. Has the tisane worn off? Or is it that your looks fetch him despite it?'

'I don't know,' Alys said. 'I think he speaks to me for mere devilry. He knew I did not want him and he knows his wife watches me like a barn owl watches a mouse. He is playing with me for his sport. He takes his lust elsewhere. But the devil in him makes him play with me.'

Morach shrugged. 'There's nothing you can take to stop that,' she said. 'Lust you can sometimes divert, but not cruelty or play!' She shrugged. 'He'll take his sport where he wishes,' she concluded. 'You will have to suffer it.'

'It's not just him,' Alys said. 'That icy shrew his wife says she'll give me a dowry and have me wed. I thought it was just a warning to stay clear of her damned husband, but one of her women, Eliza, is wife to a soldier and she said that Lady Catherine has told one of the officers that she's looking for a husband for me.'

'It can't be done unless the old lord consents,' Morach said, thinking aloud.

'No,' Alys agreed. 'But if the soldier is told that we are as good as betrothed, and Lady Catherine pays over a dowry, and then sees that we are alone together . . .'

Morach nodded. 'Then you're raped, and maybe pregnant or poxed, and you've lost the game,' she concluded with a grim smile. 'No return to an abbey for you with a belly on you or pox-scabs on your pretty face.'

'There's worse,' Alys said miserably. 'He talks to me of his plans and his ambitions, he tempts me to join his cause. He is seducing me while I watch him.'

'For desire?' Morach asked.

'I don't know!' Alys burst out. 'For desire or devilry, or worse.'

'Worse?'

Alys leaned forward and spoke in Morach's ear. 'What if he wants me in his power to suborn me against the old lord?' she whispered. 'What if he wants me to spy on the old lord, to copy his letters? What if he takes me as a pawn in his game to play against the old lord?'

Morach shrugged. 'Can't you tell him "no"?' she asked. 'Tell the old lord what he's doing and claim his protection?'

Alys met Morach's look with a fierce glare. Morach scanned her pale, strained face, and her eyes which were filled with a new expression, a kind of hunger.

'Why, he has caught you and you are ready to own it at last!' she said with sudden insight. She burst into a cackle of laughter. 'You're hot for him! My little nun! You're dragging yourself into hell with desire for him! Your Lady couldn't protect you from the heat between your legs then! Your God has no cure for that after all!'

Alys nodded grimly. 'I desire him,' she said bitterly. 'I know I do now. I feared that I would when I came to you for the herbs. But I thought if I could keep the thought away then I could keep myself safe. Then I thought I was sick of some illness, I was burning up with heat, I could not sleep, I could not eat. When I see him I feel as if I shall faint. If I do not see him I feel sick to my very soul with longing for him. I am trapped, Morach. Damn him – he has caught me.'

Morach whistled softly as if she would summon a storm. 'Have him then,' she said simply. 'It should cure your heat. That's what they always say. Take him like you would take a bottle of wine, drink yourself sick of him and then never touch him again. I can show you a way to have him and not get with child. Have him and satisfy your hunger. Why not?'

'Because I am a bride of Christ,' Alys said through her teeth. 'I cannot taste him and gamble that once or twice or even a hundred times will be enough. I am a nun. I should not even be in the world and *this* is the reason. I should not be able to look on a man. And now I have looked, and seen him, and I want him more than my life itself. But I am *still* the bride of Christ and Hugo must leave me alone. You forget very easily, Morach. You forget my vows. But I do not!'

Morach shrugged, unrepentant. 'Then what will you do?'

'I dare not trust him, and I fear the jealousy of his

wife,' Alys said. 'I have to find a way to have some power in this net they all weave. I am ensnared every way I turn and they play with me – each one of them – as if I were a village simpleton.'

Morach nodded.

'They use me,' Alys went on in a low, resentful undertone. 'The old lord has me as his only friend and real ally. He tells me he owns me outright, he has me trapped, afraid of a charge of heresy, afraid of being exposed as a nun. The young lord wants to ensnare me as a pawn against his father, or else he desires me, or he wants to play for the cruelty of it. And Lady Catherine will throw me to a rapist to punish me for taking the old lord's trust and the young lord's eye. I *must* have some power in this, Morach. I am like an unweaned babe among wolves.'

Morach nodded. 'You need woman's power, as I did,' she said. 'Your Christ will not keep you safe. Not now. Not against real danger and the lusts of men. You need another power. The old power. The power of the old goddess.'

Alys nodded. 'I've no choice,' she said. The cold air around her seemed very still and silent. 'I've no choice,' she said again. 'I have been driven so far and now I am at bay. I have to use what power I can. Give me the things.'

Morach glanced around; the meadow was deserted, the noise of the market was behind them. No one was watching. She unwrapped the cloth bundle and Alys gasped at what she saw.

They were three perfect models, three convincing likenesses, as good as the statues in the chapel. Lady Catherine's flowing gown and her cold sharp face were carved out of the wax as precise and white as a cameo.

Her gown was opened at the front, her legs spread. Morach had scratched the wax at her vagina to give the illusion of hair and the vagina was a deep, disproportionate hole made with a warm bodkin.

'They fit!' Morach said with a harsh giggle. She showed Alys the model of the young Lord Hugo. She had graven his face in his hard look – the one Alys and all the castle dreaded. But around his eyes there was the tracery of lines from his ready smile. Morach had modelled him a penis as big as a codpiece. 'He must wish to be that size!' she sniggered.

She took the two candlewax dolls and showed Alys how they slotted together. 'That'll turn his lust towards her,' she said with satisfaction. 'You'll be safe when he is like this.'

The last doll was the old lord. 'He's thinner than that now,' Alys said sadly. 'Thinner and older looking.'

'I've not seen him for a long time,' Morach said. 'You can shape him how you wish – use a warm knife for carving, and your fingers. But take care.'

Alys looked at the three little statues with distaste. She uncoupled Lord Hugo and Lady Catherine and wrapped them up again. 'What care?' she asked.

'Once you've made them your own, claimed them as models for the life, then whatever you do to them takes place,' Morach said softly. 'If you want the old lord's heart to soften, you cut into his chest, carve out a little piece of wax, mould it into a heart, warm it till it melts, and drip it back into the hole. Next morning he'll be tender as a woman with a new baby.'

Alys' dark eyes widened. 'Is that true for all of them?' she asked. 'I could make Lady Catherine sick by pinching her belly? Or make the young lord impotent by softening his prick?'

'Yes,' Morach gleamed. 'It's a powerful piece of business, isn't it? But you have to make them your own, and you have to make them represent those you mean to change. And – as I warned you – they can obey you too well. They can . . . misunderstand.'

There was a silence in the winter meadow. Alys met Morach's eyes. 'I have to do it,' she said. 'I have no safety without some power.'

Morach nodded. 'This is the spell,' she said. She put her mouth to Alys' ear and chanted over some nonsense words, part Latin, part Greek, part French, and partly mispronounced and misheard English. She said it over and over again until Alys nodded and said she knew it by heart.

'And you must take something from each of them,' she said. 'Something which is close to them, a bit of hair, a bit of fingernail, a paring of skin, and stick it on the part of the doll where it came from. Little fingernail to little finger, hair to the head, skin to where it was cut. Then you have your doll and your power.'

Alys nodded. 'Have you done it before?' she asked.

'No,' Morach said decidedly. 'There wasn't the urgency. I've had women ask me to soften their husband's heart but it's easier done with herbs in his dinner than a wax candle. I've had someone wish a man dead, but I'd never do it. The risk is too great. I always thought the risk was too great to make one of these.'

'Why've you done it now?' Alys asked directly.

Morach looked into her smooth young face and said, 'You don't know, do you? All your learning and all your planning, and you still are ignorant.'

Alys hunched her shoulder. 'I don't know what you're saying.'

Morach put her dirty hand over Alys' clean one. 'I

did it for you,' she said gruffly. 'I did it to give you a chance, to help you gain what you want, and to save you from rape by a soldier or by the young lord or by both. I don't care for your dream of a nunnery but I do care for you. I raised you as my own daughter. I wouldn't see you on your back under a man who cares nothing for you.'

Alys looked into the sharp old face. 'Thank you,' she said simply. She looked carefully into Morach's dark eyes. 'Thank you,' she said again.

'And if it goes against you,' Morach said challengingly, 'if it's found, or if they know they've been hexed, I want my name out of it. You tell them you carved this yourself, it was your own idea. That is the condition. I've made them but I won't take the danger of them. You tell them they are your own if you are ever caught. I want to die in my bed.'

The moment of tenderness between the two women was dispelled at once.

'I promise,' Alys said. She caught the look of suspicion on Morach's face. 'I promise,' she said again. 'I will make you a solemn oath. If anyone finds these I will tell them they are my own, made by me and used by me.'

'Swear on your honour, on your old abbess, and on your God,' Morach said insistently.

Alys hesitated.

'Swear you will say they are yours,' Morach demanded. 'Swear it or I'll take them back!'

Alys shook her head. 'If anyone finds them I am lost anyway,' she said. 'Owning them would be enough to see me hanged.'

Morach nodded. 'Throw them in the moat on your way home if you've changed your mind,' she said. 'If you need magic there's a price to pay. There's a price for everything. The price for this is your oath. Swear by your God.'

Alys looked at Morach with desperation in her face. 'Don't you see?' she demanded. 'Don't you know? I can have no God! My Lord Christ and Our Lady have turned their faces away from me. I ran from them when I left the convent and I hoped to take them with me. But all my efforts cannot keep them by my side. I kept the hours of prayer while I lived with you, Morach – as far as I could guess the right time. But in the castle they are near to being Protestants, heretics, and I cannot. And so Our Lady has abandoned me. And *that* is why I feel lust for the young lord, and why I now put my hand to your black arts.'

'Lost your God?' Morach asked with interest.

Alys nodded. 'So I cannot swear by Him. I am far from His grace.' She gave a harsh laugh. 'I might as well swear by yours,' she said.

Morach nodded briskly. 'Do it,' she said. 'Put your hand on mine and say, "I swear by the Black Master, by all his servants, and in the power of all his arts, that I will own these dolls as my own. I wanted them, I have them, I acknowledge them."'

Alys shrugged and laughed her bitter laugh again – half crying. She put her slim white hand on Morach's and repeated the oath.

When she had finished, Morach captured her hand, and held it. 'Now you are his,' she said slowly. 'You've summoned him now. You must learn the skills, Alys, you must know your master.'

Alys gave a little shiver in the bright wintry sunlight. 'I am his until I can get back to my abbey,' she said. 'I will loan him my soul. I am damned until I can get back to an abbey anyway.'

Morach gave a harsh laugh and struggled to her feet. 'Good Christmas,' she said. 'I'm away to collect my Christmas goods from my neighbours. They should be generous this year, the plague has stayed away from Bowes, and the vomiting sickness has passed on.'

'Good Christmas,' Alys replied and reached in her pocket. 'Here,' she said, offering a silver threepenny piece. 'My lord gave me a handful of coins for fairings. Have this, Morach, and buy yourself a bottle of mead.'

Morach pushed the coin away. 'I'll take nothing from you today but your oath,' she said. 'Nothing but your solemn oath that if they find the dolls you claim them as your own work.'

'I promise!' Alys said impatiently. 'I've promised already. I've promised by the devil himself!'

Morach nodded. 'That's binding then,' she said. Then she pulled her shawl over her head again and turned back towards the town.

Seven

They celebrated the Christmas feast with a series of great dinners at the castle which started on the first day of Christmas and went on till the early winter darkness fell on the twelfth day. They had singers and dancers and a troupe of dark-skinned tumblers who could walk on their hands as well as their feet and whirled around the hall going from hands to feet so fast that they looked like some strange man-beast – an abomination. They had a man with a horse which could dance on its hind legs and tell fortunes by pawing out 'yes' or 'no' on the ground.

On the second day they brought in a bear and forced wine on her and made her dance around the great hall while the young men leaped and cavorted around her – always making sure to keep clear of those huge flailing paws. When they were sick of the dance they took off her mask and baited her with dogs until three hounds were killed. Then Hugo called a halt. Alys saw he was distressed by the loss of one dog, a pale brown deer-hound. The bear was still snarling and angry and her keeper fed her with a dish of cheat-bread soaked with honey and some powerful mead. She went all sleepy and foolish in minutes and he was able to put her mask back on and take her from the hall.

There were some who would have liked to kill her for the sport of it when she was dozy and weak. Hugo, who had been excited by the danger of her and the speed of her sudden charges, would have allowed it but the old lord shook his head. Alys was standing behind his chair.

'Do you pity her? The great bear?' she asked.

He gave his sharp laugh. 'Hardly,' he said. 'But the keeper sells her play very dearly. If we had wanted to kill her it would have cost us pieces of gold!' He glanced back at Alys with his knowing smile. 'Always check a man's purse before you scan his heart, little Alys. That is where most decisions are made!'

The next day the young men went out hunting and Hugo brought back a deer still alive, with its thin legs bound, so that they could release it in the hall. It leaped in terror on to the great trestle-tables, sliding on the polished surface, frantically glaring around the hall for escape, and people ran screaming with laughter out of its way. Alys watched its shiny black eyes bulging with fear as they drove it from one corner to another. She saw the slather of white sweat darken the russet coat until they hustled it forwards and up to the dais so that the old lord could plunge his hunting dagger into its heart. The women all around her screamed with pleasure as the brilliant red blood pumped out. Alys watched the deer fall, its dainty black hooves scrabbling for a foot-hold even as it died.

On the morning of the twelfth day they held a little joust. David had ordered the castle carpenters to build a temporary tilt-yard in the fields of the castle farm, and a pretty tent of striped material for the old lord to sit at his ease and watch the riders. Catherine sat beside him, wearing a new festive gown of yellow, bright in the hard winter sunlight. Alys sat in her dark blue gown on a stool at his left hand to keep the score of hits for each rider.

Hugo was monstrous and exciting in his armour. His left shoulder was hugely enlarged by a great sheet of metal forged into shape and studded with brass nails which terminated in a gross gauntlet. His right shoulder and arm were scaled like a woodlouse with overlapping plates of jointed metal so he could move freely and hold the lance. His chest and belly were covered by a smooth polished breastplate, shaped to deflect any blow, and his legs were encased in jointed metal. He walked stiffly and awkwardly to his horse, the big roan warhorse, which was also plated from head to tail, only its bright, excited, white-ringed eyes showing through the head-piece.

'Is it dangerous?' Alys asked Lord Hugh.

He nodded, smiling. 'It can be,' he said.

Hugo's challenger was waiting at the other end of the lists. Catherine leaned forward, her eyes gleaming with excitement, and dropped her yellow handkerchief. At once the horses sprang forward and the two charged one another. As they came closer the lances came down, and Alys shut her eyes, dreading the sound of lance against body. All she could hear was the thunder of hooves, and then the horses were still. Lord Hugh nudged her.

'No score,' he said. 'Pair of boys.'

In the second run Hugo struck his opponent on the body, on the third he took a blow to his shoulder, and on the fourth his lance hit his challenger smack in his metalled belly and threw him from the horse.

There was a great yell of approval from the watching crowd and the townspeople, who were crowded in at the gate end of the ground, threw their caps in the air and shouted 'Hugo!'

Hugo pulled his horse up and trotted back down the lists. They were bending over the challenger and taking his helmet off.

'Are you all right, Stewart?' Hugo called. 'Just winded?'

The man raised his hand. 'A little tap,' he said. 'But I'll let someone else unseat you!'

Hugo laughed and trotted back to his place. Alys sensed his complacent smile hidden beneath the helmet.

They jousted until the early afternoon and then only went in for a late dinner as the light began to fail. Hugo stripped off his armour at the ground floor of the tower and ran up the spiral stairs in his shirt and hose shouting for a bath. He was washed and dressed in his red doublet in time for dinner and sat at his father's right hand and drank deep. As the lords ate, the mummers sang and danced, and when Lord Hugo called for the bowl and washed his hands and was served with hippocras wine the Lords of Misrule marched in from the kitchen with the lowliest server at their head.

Lord Hugh laughed and vacated his seat at the high table and took a chair at the fireside with Catherine standing behind him. They seated him comfortably and then brought a dirty apron for Hugo and ordered him to serve them all with wine. The women in the body of the hall shrieked with laughter and sent the young lord racing around the hall with one order after another. The serving-lad sat in the lord's chair and handed down commands and judgements. A number of men were outrageously accused of girls' play, and ordered to be tied one on another's back in a long laughing line, to see how they liked a surfeit of it. Several of the serving-wenches were accused of venery and taking the man's part in the act of lust. They had to publicly strip to their shifts and wear breeches for the rest of the feast. A couple of soldiers were accused of theft while raiding in Scotland with Hugo, a couple of the cooking staff were named for dirtiness. A wife was accused of infidelity, a girl who worked in the confectioner's department of the kitchen was accused of scolding and had to wear a scarf tied across her mouth.

The serving-lad giggled and pointed to one servant after another who shrieked against the accusation and could plead guilty or not guilty and was judged by the roar of the crowd.

Then he turned his attention to the gentry. Two of the young noble servers were accused of idleness and ordered to stand on their stools and sing a carol as punishment. One of Lord Hugh's cousins was accused of gluttony – sneaking into the kitchen after dinner begging for marchpane. Hugo's favourite, a young lad who was always in the guardroom talking warfare with the officers, was named a seeker of favours, a courtier, and had his head blackened with soot from the fireplace.

People laughed even more and the serving-lad grew bolder. Someone cast Lord Hugh's purple cape around his shoulders and he stood on the seat of the carved chair, jigging from one foot to the other, and pointed his finger at Hugo who was clowning around at the back of the hall with a tray and a jug of wine.

'Lust,' he said solemnly. The hall rocked with laughter. 'Venery,' he said again. 'I shall name the women you have been with.'

There were screams of laughter, and around Alys at the women's table a nervous ripple of discomfort. The serving-lad was lord of the feast, he could say anything without any threat of punishment. He might name any one of them as Hugo's lover. And Catherine would not be likely to forget, nor pass off the accusation as the fun of the feast.

'How shall you remember them all?' someone yelled from the back of the hall. 'It has been more than three hundred days since last year! That is at least a thousand women!'

Hugo grinned, postured, throwing back the apron to show his embroidered codpiece, thrusting his hips forward while the girls screamed with laughter. 'It's true,' he said. 'More like two thousand.'

'I shall name the women he has *not* had,' the serving-lad said quickly. 'To save time.'

There were screams of laughter at that. Hugo bowed. Even the old lord at the fireplace chuckled. The hall fell silent, waiting to hear what the lad would say to cap the jest.

'There *is* only one woman he has not had,' the lad said, milking the joke. He swung around and pointed to Catherine where she stood beside the old lord at the fireside. 'His wife! His wife! Lady Catherine!'

The hall was in uproar, people were screaming with laughter. Catherine's women, still in their seats at the table on the dais, clapped their hands over their mouths to smother their laughter. Hugo bowed penitently, even the old lord was laughing. Soldiers clung to each other and the serving-lad took off Lord Hugh's purple jewelled cap and flung it in the air and caught it to celebrate his wit. Only Catherine stood, white with anger, unsmiling.

'Now the old lord!' someone yelled. 'What has he done?'

The serving-lad pointed solemnly at Lord Hugh. 'You are very, very guilty, and you become guiltier every year,' he said.

Lord Hugh chuckled and waited for more.

'And every year, though you do less, you are the more guilty,' the serving-lad said.

'A riddle!' someone yelled. 'A riddle! What is his crime?'

'What is my crime?' Hugh asked. 'That I do less and less every year and am more and more guilty?'

'You grow old!' the serving-lad yelled triumphantly.

There was a great roar of scandalized laughter led by Lord Hugh. He shook his fist at the lad. 'I had best not see you tomorrow,' he shouted. 'Then you shall see how old my broadsword is!'

The serving-lad danced on the chair and knocked his skinny knees together, miming terror. 'And now!' he yelled. 'I order dancing!'

He slid from the cape and left the cap on the great chair and led out the dirtiest, lowliest slut from the kitchen to take his hand at the head of the set. Other people, still chuckling, fell in behind them. Alys leaned towards Eliza.

'D'you see her face?' she said softly.

Eliza nodded. 'He's worse than last year,' she said. 'And he was impertinent enough then. But it's a tradition and it does no harm. The old lord loves the old ways and Hugo doesn't care. They always make a butt of Catherine; she's not well liked and they love Hugo.'

One of the mummers came to the ladies' table and laid rough hands on Ruth. She gave a soft shriek of refusal but he dragged her to the floor.

'Here's sport!' Eliza said joyfully, and chased after Ruth to find a partner for herself. Alys went down the hall like a shadow in her navy gown to stand behind Lord Hugh and walk with him back to his chair on the dais.

'Not dancing, Alys?' he asked her over the loud minor chords of the music and the thump of the drum.

'No,' she said shortly.

He nodded. 'Stand behind my chair and no one will call you out,' he said. 'It's rough sport but I love to

144

watch it. And Hugo – ' he broke off. Further down the hall Hugo was on his knees to a serving-wench, half hidden behind a mask of a duck's head. Catherine, unwilling, her face set and pale, was dancing in a set partnered by one of the young knights. 'Hugo is a rogue,' the old lord said. 'I should have matched him to a girl with fire in her belly.'

They danced all afternoon and well into the night. A lad stood and sang a madrigal very sweetly, a gypsy girl came into the hall and danced a wild strange dance with clackers made of wood in her hand, then to a roar of applause the servers came from the kitchen and processed around the hall with the roast meats and set them down on the high table and in messes – four persons to a platter – at all the other tables. It was their final dish of the feast and grander even than all that had gone before. There was swan from the river, roasted and refeathered so that it was as white and complete as a live bird, head rearing up from the serving dish. At the other end of the top table there was a peacock with its tail feathers nodding. The lower tables had cuts of roast goose, turkey, capons, wild duck. Everyone had the best bread at this feast – manchet, a good white bread with a thick golden crust and a dense white crumb. The lords ate with unceasing appetite; Catherine beside them wiped her plate with her bread and took another slice of wild swan, though her face was still set and angry.

The jugs of wine came in, and one dish followed after another. Alys, rocking with weariness, ate little but drank the sharp red wine, cool from the barrels in the cellar. It was midnight when the sweetmeats finally came in, two for the top table. A perfect marchpane copy of the castle with Lord Hugh's flag fluttering over the round tower was put before the old lord. The women got up from the side table to see it and crowded around.

'Too pretty to cut,' Eliza said admiringly.

Before Hugo they placed a little model of a country house set square on a terrace with little sugar deer in a park all around it.

'My plans for the new house!' Hugo exclaimed. 'Damn those servants, they know everything before I know it myself. Here, Sir, see what they have done!'

Lord Hugh smiled. 'Now you can see the two side by side,' he said. 'I know where I would rather live!'

Hugo bowed his head, too full of wine and dinner to quarrel with his father. 'I know your preferences, Sir,' he said respectfully. 'But it's a pretty fancy of mine.'

Hugh nodded. 'Can you bear to eat it?' he asked.

Hugo laughed and took his knife up in reply. 'Who will have a slice of my house?' he asked. 'My pretty little house which I have drawn in an idle moment and then found these kitchen hounds stealing my papers and copying my dreams into sugar?'

'I will!' Eliza said invitingly.

Hugo threw her a smile.

'You would have a slice of anything of mine, Eliza,' he said. 'You would beg for a lick, would you not?'

Eliza gave a little scream of protesting laughter. Hugo smiled at her and then switched the heat of his look to Alys. 'Alys?' he asked. 'Will you taste my pretty toy?'

She shook her head and slid back to the women's table at the rear of the dais. When the others came back with their trenchers Eliza set a piece of the marchpane house before her.

'From him,' she said, nodding at the back of Hugo's chair. 'He served it for you under the nose of his wife.

He has given you the front door. By – you're playing a dangerous game, Alys.'

When the eating was done, and there was nothing on the tables but the voider course of dried fruit and hippocras wine, David stood behind the lord's chair and called one man after another up to the dais for Lord Hugh to give him a gift or a purse of coins. Hugo sat at his father's right hand, occasionally leaning forward with a word. Lady Catherine sat on Lord Hugh's left, smiling her meaningless, small smile. She had given and received her gifts with her women on New Year's Day and she had nothing for any of the castle servants nor for the soldiers. The line of servants and soldiers went on and on. There were a round four hundred of them. Alys, at the women's table at the rear of the dais, unable to see, dozed after the revelry of the Christmas days and the sleepless fortnight which preceded them.

'It's dull this,' Eliza whispered mutinously to her. 'Everywhere else does gifts on New Year's Day. It's only Lord Hugh who is too mean to gather everyone for a feast twice in the bad season!'

Alys nodded, uncaring.

'Let's have another jug of wine!' Eliza suggested. She flapped her hand at a passing serving-wench. Margery frowned. 'You'll get drunk,' she said.

'I don't care!' Eliza said. 'It's the last day of the feast. She won't want us tonight. She'll dress in her best nightgown and lie wakeful all night in her chamber in case the wine has roused Hugo's lust.'

'Hush,' Ruth said with her usual caution.

Eliza giggled and poured from the new jug. 'Maybe his Christmas gift to her is a decent tupping at last,' she whispered.

Margery and Mistress Allingham collapsed into

scandalized laughter. Ruth shot an apprehensive backwards look at their mistress. Alys sipped from her glass.

She liked the smell of wine. They had set glassware on the women's table today in honour of the feast and Alys liked the feel of the cool glass against her lips. At Morach's she had drunk from earthenware or horn, and in the castle she drank from pewter. She had not had the touch of glass against her lips since the nunnery. This wine tasted of itself, without a tang of ill-cleaned metal, the glassware was light and thin, appetizing. Alys sipped again. The drunkenness and the barbarity of the feast days had floated past her. No one had snatched her in a dark corner and tried for a kiss, she had danced with no one. The old lord watched for her, and when a soldier approached her for a dance, the old lord scowled at him and David waved him away. Lady Catherine smiled her thin smile at that and leaned back towards the women's table.

'In the spring we will dance at your wedding, Alys,' she said, her voice acid-sweet. She glanced towards the young man who had gone back to his place. 'That was Peter – a bastard son of one of Lord Hugo's officers. He is the one I have chosen for you. Don't you think I have chosen well?'

Alys looked down the hall towards him. He was well enough, slim, brown-haired, brown-eyed, young. She had seen him stab a knife into a dying dog at the bearbaiting. She had seen him screaming with excitement at the cock-fighting. She thought of what her life would be like as his wife, bound forever to a man with that perilous streak of excitement at the sight of pain.

'Very well, my lady,' she said. She smiled deceitfully into Lady Catherine's face. 'He seems a fine man. Has his father told him?'

'Yes,' Lady Catherine said. 'We must persuade the old lord to find a proper clerk to replace you, and then you can be married. Maybe at Easter.'

'Very well,' Alys said softly and lowered her eyes to her plate so that Lady Catherine could not see the gleam of absolute refusal.

Alys sipped her wine again. All through the days of feasting and the nights of drunken games she had felt the young lord watching her. Lady Catherine watched her too. Alys rested the cold glass against her cheek. She had to break the net, the net that the three of them, the old lord, the young lord and the shrew, had all cast around her. She had to take her power, she had to make the little dolls come alive and dance to her bidding.

Above the table – as it was Christmas – the waiting-women had pure wax candles in the candelabra. On the table was a silver candle-holder with pale, honey-coloured candles. Alys watched the bobbing yellow flame and the pure transparency of the wax. There was the slightest hint of sweetness in the vapour. These were pure beeswax candles. A memory flickered to the surface of Alys' mind and she winced as she realized that the candles would have been made by the nuns at the abbey with beeswax from the abbey hives.

Eliza poured more wine in her glass and she drank again.

In her purse tied on the girdle at her waist were the three candlewax dolls. They knocked against her gently when she moved. Alys had been tempted to fling them from her window down the steep side of the castle to smash against the rocks and tumble into the river below. It was death to be found carrying them and she was too afraid to hide them anywhere in the castle. She had not yet found the courage, or the desperation, to use them. She held to them like a talisman, like a final weapon which would be ready to her hand if their time ever came.

The tart cool taste of the clary wine flooded into her mouth and washed through her. I must be getting drunk, Alys thought to herself. All the voices seemed to come from a long way away, the faces around the table seemed to flicker in a haze.

'I wish . . . ' Alys said thickly.

Eliza and Margery nudged each other and giggled.

'I wish I was Lady Catherine,' Alys slurred.

Ruth, the quiet one, glanced behind her to see that the two lords, watched by Lady Catherine, were still paying out gifts.

'Why?' she asked.

'Because . . . ' Alys said slowly. 'Because . . . ' she stopped again. 'I should like to have a horse of my own,' she said simply. 'And a gown which was a new gown – not belonging to someone else. And a man . . . '

Eliza and Margery exploded with laughter. Even Ruth and Mistress Allingham tittered behind their hands.

'A man who left me alone,' Alys said slowly. 'A man who was bound to me and wed to me, but a man who would leave me alone.'

'Not much of a wife you'll make!' Eliza said laughing. 'Poor Peter will get short commons I reckon.'

Alys had not heard her. 'I want more than ordinary women,' she said sorrowfully. 'I want so much more.'

All the women were laughing openly now. Alys, with her heavy gable hood sliding back off her mop-head of curls and her serious pale face, was exquisitely funny. Her deep blue eyes were staring unfocused at the candles. The young Lord Hugo, who now carried an awareness of Alys like a sixth sense, glanced back and took in the scene with one quick look.

'Your young clerk seems the worse for her wine,' he said softly to his father.

The old lord glanced back. David demanded his attention for another of the soldiers coming up for his gift.

'Get them to take her to her room,' he said briefly to the young lord. 'Before she pukes on her gown and shames herself.'

Hugo nodded and pushed his chair back from the table. Lady Catherine had not heard the soft-voiced exchange and glanced up in surprise. 'My father has an errand for me, I'll only be a moment,' he said softly to her, and then he turned towards the women.

'Come, Alys,' he said firmly.

Alys looked up. Against the candlelight of the hall his face was shadowed. She could see the gleam of his smile. There was a ripple among the women like a flurry in a hen-coop when a fox gets in the door.

'I'll escort you to my lady's rooms,' he said firmly. 'You,' he nodded at Eliza. 'Come too.'

Alys got slowly to her feet. Magically the floor beneath her rolled and melted away. Lord Hugo caught her as she swayed forward and lifted her up. He nodded at Eliza who drew back the tapestry and opened the little door at the back of the dais. They stepped out into the lobby behind the hall, and up the shallow stone steps to Lady Catherine's rooms above. Eliza flung the door wide and Hugo strode into the gallery carrying Alys.

'I'll give you a shilling to keep watch here and hold your tongue,' he said briefly to Eliza.

Her brown eyes were as large as saucers. 'Yes, my lord,' she said.

'And if you gossip I shall have you whipped,' he said pleasantly. Eliza felt her knees melt at his smile.

'I swear it, my lord,' she said fervently. 'I'd do anything for you.'

He nodded to her to open the door to the women's chamber and she scuttled ahead of him and swung it open. He walked the length of the gallery carrying Alys easily. She opened her eyes and saw the moonlight from the window briefly illuminate his face and then they were in shadow again. He pushed open the door to the women's room and laid Alys down on a pallet.

Without any haste, he pulled the pins from her hood and tossed it to one side. Alys fell back on the pillow, her face pale, her eyes closed. 'I feel sick,' she said.

He rolled her to her side, skilfully unlacing her stomacher and the gown below it, so that when he rolled her on her back and lifted her legs and then her body to pull the gown over her head she was stripped down to her shift. Alys dropped back on the pallet, her arms above her head, her golden hair a tangle about her face. Lord Hugo sat back on his heels and scanned her, from her small dirty feet to her outflung hand. Alys snored lightly.

Lord Hugo pulled down his breeches with a little sigh and moved to cover her.

Alys' dark eyes flew open as she felt the weight of him come down upon her and he readied himself to put a hand over her mouth to still her protesting scream; but her eyes, out of focus and hazy, were warm with welcome and she smiled.

'Hello, my love,' she said, as easily as if they had been wed for twenty years. 'Not now, I am too sleepy. Love me in the morning.'

'Alys?'

She chuckled, the warm, confident sound of a woman who knows she is deeply beloved. 'Not now, I said,' she repeated. 'I am tired out with your wants, and your son's wants. Let me sleep.' Her eyelids flickered shut and Hugo watched the lashes sweep her cheek.

'Do you know me?' he asked in confusion.

Alys smiled. 'None better,' she said. She rolled on her side away from him and put her hand back towards him. In a gesture so familiar as to be unconscious, she felt for his hand and then pulled his arm around her and tucked his hand between the warm comfort of her thighs. Hugo, following the demanding tug of her small hands, snuggled up so that his body was cupped around hers. He could feel a deep ache of desire that he would normally have satisfied quickly and roughly on a woman whether she consented or not. But something about Alys' drunken dream made him pause.

'How old are you, Alys?' he asked. 'What year is it?'

'I'm near eighteen,' she said sleepily. 'It's 1538. What year did you think it was?'

Hugo said nothing, his mind whirling. Alys was dreaming of the future two years ahead. 'How is my father?' he asked.

'Dead, nigh on twelve months ago,' Alys replied sleepily. 'Go to sleep, Hugo.'

Her casual use of his christian name brought him up short. 'What of Lady Catherine?' he asked.

'Oh hush!' Alys said. 'No one is to blame. She's at peace at last. And we have all her lands for little Hugo. Go to sleep now.'

'I have a son?' Hugo demanded.

Alys sighed and turned away. Hugo, raising himself up on his elbow, looked down on her face and saw that she was deeply asleep. Gently he pulled his hand away from between her legs and saw a little flicker of regret cross her face. Then she turned deeper into the pillow and slept again.

He sat up on the pallet and put his head in his hands, trying to think soberly enough to understand. Either Alys was drunk beyond belief, dreaming some girl's fantasy of him; or the wine had released in her some of her magic and she had spoken true. In two years' time he would be the Lord of Castleton, Catherine would be gone and Alys would be his woman and the mother of his child.

He leaned forward and stirred up the fire so the light flickered in the little room. Alys' clear, lovely profile gleamed in the half-light.

'What a son we would have!' he said softly. 'What a son!'

He thought of the confident way she had tucked his hand between her legs, and her lazy command of loving in the morning, and he felt himself ache with desire again. For a moment he thought of taking her while she slept, without her consent; but then he paused.

For the first time in his life Hugo paused before taking his pleasure. She had given him a glimpse of a future which was luminous with satisfactions. She had given him a glimpse of a woman who was his equal, who desired him as he desired her. A woman who would plot and scheme alongside him, who had given him a son, and would give him more. He wanted Alys' dream. He wanted that intimacy, he wanted to be on tender terms with her. More than anything else: he wanted her to give him a son.

He chuckled softly in the quietness of the room. He wanted her to call him Hugo, he wanted her to command his loving. He wanted to see her tired with the demands of his son, tired by his lust. Incredulously he looked towards her again. He would do nothing to spoil that promise between them, he thought. He would not force her, he would not frighten her. He wanted her as she was in that glimpse of the future: confident, sensual, amused. A woman of power, confident of her own power to command him, to rule her own life.

He threw a rug over her and she did not stir. He leaned over and gently put a kiss on the smooth curve of her neck, just below her ear. The smell of her skin stirred him again. He chuckled. 'My Lady Alys,' he said softly. Then he got to his feet and walked out of the room.

Eliza was hovering at the doorway, her round face bright with excitement.

'All quiet, my lord,' she said. 'Aren't you having her? Don't you want her now?'

Lord Hugo shot a quick look down the steps to the great chamber beneath them.

'Lift your skirts,' he said tersely.

Eliza's mouth made a little round 'oh' of surprise. 'My lord ... ' she said in a delighted half-protest. He took her gown in one hard hand and wrenched it up to her waist. He backed her against the stone wall and rammed himself into her. Eliza screamed with the sharp pain of it and he at once clapped a hand over her mouth and hissed, 'Fool! D'you want half the castle here?'

Above his hand Eliza's eyes bulged at him imploringly. He thrust into her three, four times, and then he froze, his eyes tight shut, his mouth grim in a spasm of release which felt like anger.

Eliza gasped with discomfort as he released her, and staggered to one side, holding her bruised throat and mopping her gown against her crutch.

Hugo reached into his pocket and threw her a couple

of silver coins. 'You'll keep quiet about that too,' he said. He turned his back on her and sauntered across the gallery and down the steps to the great hall.

She went to the doorway and watched him go down the stairs and pause in the lobby, straightening his clothes, and then she saw his shoulders go back and his smile appear as he opened the door to the dais and went back to sit with his father and his wife.

'God curse you, Hugo,' she said under her breath. She flinched with discomfort and turned towards the women's room. 'A new gown half ruined, half strangled, and tupped for a shilling,' she said miserably to herself. She hunkered down on her pallet and looked across at Alys who lay, still sleeping, as Hugo had left her.

'And all because that damned jade hexed you into losing your manhood with her,' she muttered grimly. 'I saw you, you poxy bastard. I saw you lie beside her and stick your finger in and dare do no more while she muttered spells against you and all your family. And then you stick your cock in me! Damn you,' she grumbled, stripping off her gown and pulling a rug over herself. 'Pox-ridden bastard.'

Alys turned over in her sleep, her hand stretched out, seeking him. 'My love,' she said very softly.

Alys was sick the next day, heavy-eyed, white-faced, poisoned with the wine. She would eat nothing and would drink only water. Indeed, the whole castle, from Hugo down to the poorest scullion, had drunk better than they had drunk all year and were paying the price.

It was not until after dinner that any of the women felt better. Then Lady Catherine commanded them to sit in the gallery and sew while she spun. Alys was ordered to read aloud from a story book.

Alys, nauseous and with her head throbbing, read until the badly printed words danced before her eyes. They were love stories, tales of ladies in castles and knights who worshipped them. Alys let her mind wander as she read the romance – life was not like these stories, she knew.

'Lord Hugo carried you up the stairs last night?' Lady Catherine's arid voice cut into the reading. Alys blinked. 'Carried you all the way to your room, did he?'

'I am sorry, my lady,' Alys said. 'I cannot remember. I was faint and I did not know what I did.'

'Did he carry her?' Lady Catherine turned to Eliza.

'Yes,' Eliza said baldly. She ached inside this morning and she blamed Alys that Hugo's lust had soured into violence.

'Into your room?' Lady Catherine asked.

'Yes,' Eliza said again.

'You were with them?' Lady Catherine confirmed.

Eliza hesitated. She would have given much to have her revenge on Hugo by telling that he had ordered her to stay outside. But the risks were too great. The young lord's anger was swift and unpredictable, and she had stains on her gown and two silver sixpences which would support an accusation against her.

'Yes,' she said. 'He tossed her down on her pallet and told me to watch her and make sure she did not vomit and lie in it like a dog.'

Alys' pale skin flushed crimson.

'How disagreeable for him,' Lady Catherine said in mild triumph. 'I think you had better drink ale in future, Alys.'

'I think so too, my lady,' Alys said quietly. 'I am very sorry.'

Lady Catherine nodded with a glacial smile and stood

while Mistress Allingham moved the spinning wheel for her into a patch of winter sunshine which fell on the wooden floor, brightly coloured from the stained glass of the oriel window.

'Did he do that?' Alys whispered urgently to Eliza. 'Did he throw me down?'

'He lay beside you,' Eliza said spitefully. 'I've saved your skin with my lady by not telling. He gave me two silver sixpences to keep watch. I stood guard at the door while he tossed you down on your pallet and stripped you and lay beside you and stuck his finger in you.'

Alys went white and looked as if she might fall. 'It's not possible,' she said.

'It happened,' Eliza said harshly. 'I saw him do it.'

'But I feel nothing,' Alys said.

'What are you girls whispering about?' Lady Catherine interrupted.

'About the colour of the silk, Lady Catherine,' Eliza said at once. 'I think it is too bright. Alys wants to keep it as it is.'

Eliza lifted up the tapestry which Alys had painstakingly stitched in the previous week and Lady Catherine considered it with her head on one side. 'Rip it out,' she said. 'You are right, Eliza, it needs to be a paler colour, anyone could see that. Alys will have to stop reading and rip it back and do it all again.'

Alys picked up a pair of silver scissors and started snipping at the cloth, the work of seven days to be done all over again. Eliza bent over it.

'It didn't hurt because you wanted it,' she whispered. 'You let him take your gown off and you took his hand and guided it in, just like any slut! And after all you've said about not wanting to go with a man.'

Alys felt her world shift and heave. 'It's not possible,' she said.

Eliza shrugged. 'Don't you remember anything?'

Alys closed her eyes. Vaguely, like a dream, she could remember a sleepy sensuality, a confidence and an affection which she had never felt in her waking life. She remembered a gesture, rolling over on her side and pulling his arm over her, tucking his hand between her thighs. She flushed a sweating scarlet.

'Oh my God,' she said.

'What d'you remember?' Eliza demanded eagerly. 'What did you say to stop him?'

Alys shook her head wordlessly. 'I desired him,' she said. Her voice was hollow with her unhappiness.

'What?'

'I was drunk and I desired him,' Alys said again. 'If he had wanted to take me he could have had me. *You* would not have stopped him, and I would not have wanted him to stop. He could have had me like any little whore in the castle, I would have had no words to stop him. I felt wanton. He could have had me.' She rubbed the back of her hand hard against her eyes. 'I am lost unless I can stop this sickness,' she said. 'I will lose everything unless I can guard myself. I am lost unless I take my power. I must guard myself with all the power I can hold.' Abruptly she threw down her sewing and went to the door.

'Alys!' Lady Catherine commanded. 'What do you think you are doing? How dare you march out of the room without my leave?'

Alys rounded on her, her eyes, her whole face, blazing with anger and despair. 'Oh, go your ways, Lady Catherine!' she said bitterly. 'I have no fear of you now. The one thing you could have taken from me has gone. I was not born to be a woman like you, a woman like these . . . ' She made a sharp, dismissive gesture at the four women whose stunned faces were turned to her, gaping. 'These pitiful slaveys. But now I have seen myself truly. I am no better than any of you. There is *nothing* about me which is special. I am a sinner and I am a fool. But at least now I see my way clearly. Now I am a woman without fear.'

Lady Catherine recoiled from her anger, but then blustered, 'Don't speak to me like that, girl . . . '

'I'm taking my power,' Alys swore. 'You will not call me girl again! You will not rule me! And your husband will not have me as his plaything. You have driven me to it between you and I am taking my power!'

'Stop!' Catherine shrieked. Alys threw her a look like a burning brand and slammed out of the room. They could hear her feet pattering down the stone steps and then the bang of the door of the great hall.

'Is she leaving?' Mistress Allingham asked.

Only Lady Catherine stayed seated, the rest of them crowded to the wide oriel window and craned their necks to see the steps from the great hall below them into the garden, and the path to the gatehouse over the inner moat.

'She's going,' Eliza confirmed. 'She's in the garden heading for the gate. Shall I run after her and order her to be brought back, my lady?'

Lady Catherine's face was pale, her mouth pressed tight as she marshalled her fears and her suspicions.

'Let her go,' she said. 'Let her go.'

The old lord did not miss Alys until that evening just before supper, when he wanted a letter written. David came to the women's quarters to ask for her and Lady

Catherine kept her plain face blank as she told him that Alys was missing.

'I will come in her place,' she said. She threw a dark cloak around her shoulders, pulled the hood over her head, and followed him to the old lord's room in the round tower. On the dark corner of the stairs they passed young Lord Hugo, openly waiting for them. He put out his hand to stop her.

'Alys,' he said. She had never heard that tone from him before, he poured a world full of yearning into the girl's name.

His wife put back the hood of her cloak. Her bony face gleamed hatred at him, her eyes were filled with triumph. 'I thought so,' she said, venom in her tone. 'I thought so.'

Hugo recoiled. 'Madam, I . . .'

David the seneschal exchanged one look with Hugo and went on up the stairs to the old lord's chamber, out of earshot.

'Don't bother pretending,' she said passionately. 'I wondered what hold she had over you and the old man. I suppose she has been bedding you both.' Her mouth worked angrily. 'Bedding you both! Him in his dotage and you who run after anything in a skirt! As soon as I saw her in that whore's dress I knew what was happening. But I waited and I watched. And I saw you eyeing her and I *knew* what you were thinking. God knows I've seen it often enough! God knows I've seen you looking at one woman after another with that smile of yours and that hot look. Then I saw you look at her, and I saw you carry her out of the feast. Carried her to her bed, did you? And paid that fool Eliza to look the other way! Paid that fool Eliza to play blind, and to lie to me, and to laugh at me behind her hand. And paid her to play the slut!'

She rounded on him and hit him hard with her open

palm across the face. Hugo jerked back at the ringing slap and then stood still.

'And what about me?' Her voice rose from a passionate whisper into a muffled scream of rage. 'What about me? You never look at *me* like that. You never come to my room wearing that smile! Every whore in the castle can have a hot look from you! Every slut in the town, every drab in every village can have you between her dirty legs – but me, your own wife, you ignore!' She seized him by the shoulders. 'You ignore me!' she said. Tears were pouring down her face. She shook him hard. 'You ignore me!' she cried again.

Hugo was rigid in her grasp, his whole body rejecting her with its stillness.

'Oh God!' she said in sudden longing. 'Hugo, do to me what you do with her! Take me here!' She drew back into the shadow of the corner of the stair and feverishly pulled up her gown, grasped at the cord of his breeches, tugged at his codpiece, thrust herself against the embroidered padding, moaned as the stiff embroidery touched her. 'Do it now!' she said desperately.

Hugo stepped back and pushed her away from him. In the shadows she could see his face, as unmoved as if it had been carved from stone.

'Have done,' he said, his voice low and level. 'I did not touch the wench, whatever you fear and whatever women's tattle you have heard. I did not lay a finger on her. I carried her to her pallet and I stripped off her gown, covered her with a rug and left her there.'

Lady Catherine staggered as if he had slapped her. She dropped the hem of her skirt and pulled it down over her hips. She was still panting but the coldness of Hugo's voice had entered into her awareness like ice. Her face was white and strained.

'You took off her gown and you did not have her?' she asked, as if she could not believe her ears. Hugo nodded, and turned to leave.

'Hugo!' Lady Catherine ran down the steps after him and clawed on his arm. 'Hugo, tell me you did not desire her. Tell me you did not desire her and that is why you did not have her!'

He paused on the bottom step, smiling his cruel half-smile. 'What now, my lady?' he said acidly. 'First you berate me for tupping her, and now you cannot believe that I did not.'

Lady Catherine gave a little moan and tugged on the fine slashings of his doublet. 'Please!' she begged. 'Tell me truly what passed between you. I cannot bear not knowing. I cannot bear the thought of you . . . '

'You cannot bear what?' he asked acidly. 'You cannot bear me lying with her, and you cannot bear me *not* lying with her. You must tell me, Madam, what I should do to please you.'

She stared at him as if she could not comprehend his speech. 'Oh God, Hugo,' she said hungrily. 'I don't want you to lie with her. But most of all I don't want you to spare her. I'd rather you raped her than spared her. I don't understand what you are doing if you are gentle with her. I don't understand what it means! What are you thinking of if you treat her tenderly? I wish you'd raped her and hurt her! I wish you had torn her inside to slake your lust rather than be tender!'

He looked back up at her and for a moment she flinched from the disdain on his face. 'You'd rather I raped her than spared her,' he said wonderingly. 'You want a little maid of sixteen, in your care, torn inside by your husband's rape? Good God, Madam, you are an ugly woman.'

She gasped and fell back against the stone wall.

'I did not touch her because she was so warm and so loving,' he said, his voice very low. 'She had a dream and she foretold a future for me, a future for me and for her. My father will die and I will be master here. She will give me a son.'

'No,' Lady Catherine moaned and sank to the floor as her knees buckled beneath her.

'Make your mind up to it, lady,' Hugo said remorselessly. 'You struck me for the last time just now. Your days here are done. I shall have the wench from Bowes Moor in my bed.'

'My dowry ...' Lady Catherine said. 'And my lands ...'

'Damn your money,' Hugo swore. 'Damn your lands! And damn you. I want the wench from Bowes Moor and I will risk anything – the castle itself – to have her.'

He flung himself away from her and strode across the guardroom.

Lady Catherine sat on the stairs in the cold for many minutes, then she raised herself up awkwardly, as if she were an old woman. The cold light of the rising moon shone through the arrow-slit on to her beaky, vengeful face. Then she said one word, the most dangerous word of any in her fearful, dangerous world.

'Witch.'

Eight

Lord Hugh was sitting at the fireside in his little stone-walled room when Lady Catherine stormed in, without knocking. He lifted his gaze from the fire as he saw her and raised one eyebrow.

'I sent for the maid,' he said. 'I asked for Alys.'

'She can be your clerk no more,' Catherine said. She spoke softly but her voice trembled with an undertone of passion. 'I have to speak to you, my lord, I have to demand that you find her and bring her to trial.'

'What's she done?' Lord Hugh said wearily. 'Run off? Is something missing from your chamber?'

'Worse than that!' she hissed. 'A thousand times worse than that.'

She waited to see if the old lord seemed impressed. He held his peace.

'My lord, I accuse her of the worst crime of all,' she said. She was panting in her eagerness to ruin Alys. 'I accuse her of a crime worse than murder itself.'

'What's she done?' he asked again.

'She is a witch,' she said.

There was a stunned silence in the hot little room.

'I don't believe it,' he said blankly. But Catherine was on to his momentary hesitation like a striking adder.

'You suspect her yourself!' she said triumphantly. 'You've been closer to her than anyone! And you suspect her yourself!'

'I do not,' the old lord said; but his tone was uncertain.

'Well, I accuse her!' Catherine's voice rang out. 'I

165

accuse her of witchcraft. She has bewitched the Lord Hugo. He has just abused me to my face and said that he will not rest until he has her. That is witchcraft at work, my lord, and your son is the prey.'

A little colour came back into the old lord's face. 'Faith, Catherine!' he said easily. 'I had thought we were speaking of the black arts! You've seen Hugo hot for a wench before now. It'll pass.'

He put a hand out to her and smiled at her with an effort. 'Come,' he said kindly. 'It galls you, I know, but she's just one of Hugo's flirts. There's naught there to cry witchcraft over except the magic a young girl weaves when she's hot. It's no more than that.'

Catherine's face was white with malice. 'No, my lord,' she said venomously. 'You misunderstand me. Lord Hugo tells me that he could have had her and he did not. He has forsworn taking her without her consent. He tells me she cast a spell so that he could see a future with her as his woman. He says that he will throw away my dowry lands, aye, and the whole castle, to have her and the son he believes she will conceive. *That* is witchcraft, my lord, not courtship.'

The old lord shifted uneasily. 'I'll see Hugo,' he said. He reached out to the table beside him and rang a small silver bell. A servant came running and was ordered to find the young lord. Lord Hugh looked at Catherine.

'You may leave,' he said.

'No,' she said.

She met his astounded look without fear. 'I *will* stay,' she said. Her yellow teeth were bared in open malice. 'I say he is bewitched, I say you are half bewitched too. It needs a woman with a clear head here. It needs the witch-taker. I dare not trust your judgement, my lord, for your own safety I dare not trust it.'

The old lord's eyes flared at her. 'You can stay, but you must be silent.'

'Call Eliza Herring also,' Lady Catherine suggested. 'She went with my lord and the witch when he carried her from the hall. She will know what passed between them.'

The old lord nodded.

'And your chaplain,' she urged. 'Father Stephen. He is a holy man, and a true servant of yours. I ask for nothing more than my safety and your safety and the safety of Lord Hugo. If she is a witch as I think then she should be taken, my lord. Taken and tested and strangled.'

'This is nonsense . . .' the old lord started. 'Wind and women's malice . . . When Hugo comes he will explain all.' He gathered his strength. 'And you will say nothing,' he ordered. 'You will hold your tongue. I permit you to stay but if you speak I will have you thrown from my chamber. I can do that, Madam, remember it.'

'I'll be silent,' she promised readily. 'But ask him one thing before you release him and before you believe the lies he will tell for her.'

'What?' he grunted.

'Ask him how you are to die,' Catherine said, her voice strong with spite. 'The witch foretold your death as well as her triumph over me. She said you will die next year.'

Lord Hugh gasped.

'Who should know better?' Catherine asked silkily. 'She gives you your medicine, she handles your herbs. She is by your side when you are ill. If she did not hex you outright she could poison you. And now she has promised him your death.'

Lord Hugh shook his head. 'She is my vassal,' he said, half to himself. 'She is my little maid.'

'But what if she were suborned?' Catherine said quickly. 'What an enemy she would make against you! Think where you have put her, my lord! You have raised her as high as David, your confidant! She knows all your secrets, she nurses you. If she were turned against you by ambition, or lust . . .' The door opened and Hugo came in. Catherine whirled around at the sight of him and fled behind the old lord's chair. With her hand resting on the high back of the chair and her eyes fixed on her husband's face it looked as if the two of them were united against him.

The young lord took in the scene in one rapid glance and beamed in mockery at the sight of his wife's white face.

'Why, Catherine, we meet again,' he said pleasantly. Then he took two swift strides forward and knelt before his father. 'My liege,' he said. 'I'm told you sent for me. I hope I have not kept you waiting?'

The old lord put out his hand and rested it for a moment on his son's dark curly head. Catherine's sharp eyes saw he trembled slightly.

'The Lady Catherine has brought me some troubling news,' he said softly. 'And she has named Alys, my clerk, as a witch. She says you are bewitched, Hugo.'

Hugo got to his feet and shot Catherine a merry glance. 'I think there is no witchcraft here but the magic of a maid,' he said. 'You should not have troubled my father with a quarrel between us, Catherine. It would go ill for you if I ran to him every time I have a complaint against you.'

She took a breath at the warning tone in his voice, but the old lord silenced her with a gesture.

'It's no jesting matter,' he said flatly. 'Catherine says that Alys promised to conceive your son and that I will die. Is this true?'

168

Hugo hesitated. 'She did not know what she was saying . . .'

'Was she in a trance?' The old lord leaned forward, his face grave.

'No.' Hugo hesitated. 'The maid was drunk, or half asleep. It was the wine talking.'

'Witches can use wine to give them the Sight,' the old lord warned. 'Did she know you?'

Hugo hesitated, remembered Alys' confident chuckle and the warmth of her voice as she said 'none better'.

'I don't know,' he said. His mind was racing to see a safe way out for Alys. 'I don't know, Sir. I spoke with her very little.'

'When was this?' the old lord asked. Catherine, restrained by her promise to be silent, leaned forward as if she would suck the words from her husband's mouth.

'Yesterday, after the Twelfth Night supper,' Hugo said unwillingly. 'When I took her to her room – at your command, my lord, you remember. She was drunk.'

Catherine nodded. The old lord shot a look at her over his shoulder. 'Stand a little further off, Catherine,' he said. 'And remember your promise to hold your tongue.'

Hugo's eyes narrowed. 'My Lady Catherine has perhaps mistaken some words I said to her in the heat of a quarrel,' he said to his father. 'It would ill become me to tell you what she said, or did in the darkness of the stairway. Let it suffice that she struck me, and abused me, and angered me and I was perhaps too harsh with her. She begged me to take her like a whore on the stairs and I was offended to see my lady – and your daughter-in-law – hold herself so cheap.' There was a little gasp of horror from Catherine at Hugo's calculated

169

betrayal. 'There is more, Sir, and it is worse,' Hugo said pointedly. 'But I will not weary you with it. I am prepared to ask her forgiveness, and let this quarrel end here.'

The old lord cocked an eyebrow at Catherine. 'Is this all there is?' he asked. 'If Hugo begs your pardon, and makes amends to you as a husband,' he stressed the word 'amends' and the heat of Catherine's constant desire rose up in her sallow cheeks, 'then is the quarrel ended, and Alys can work for me. She need not serve as a lady in your rooms if you have taken against her, Catherine. And Hugo need not see her.'

'No,' Lady Catherine said with an effort. 'Not until Father Stephen has heard this, my lord. And not until we have heard from Eliza.'

At the old lord's frown she leaned forward. 'Lord Hugo says it is naught but a quarrel – but that is the witchcraft speaking,' she said urgently. 'Of course he would try to protect her! We have to inquire further, not just to protect him, but to protect you, my lord. It was *your* death she foretold.'

The old man crossed himself. 'Send for Eliza,' he said to his son. 'And send for the priest.'

Hugo shrugged as if the trouble were hardly worth it and then he opened the door of his father's room and shouted 'Holloa!' down the stone steps to the guard-room. One of the lads came running. 'Fetch Eliza Herring and Father Stephen,' he said.

The three of them waited in awkward silence until the tire-woman and the priest came in. Lord Hugh scowled impartially at them both.

'I have called you, priest, to listen to a discourse,' he said. 'It seems we have need of your wisdom.'

Father Stephen nodded solemnly, his dark, intense

glance taking in Catherine's high colour, and Hugo's concealed rage. Eliza shrank back as near to the door as she could, in a white-faced trance of guilt.

'It's all right, Eliza,' the old lord said kindly. 'No one is accusing you of anything.'

She was trembling so much she could hardly speak. Her black eyes shot from the young lord to her stony mistress.

'All we need is for you to tell the truth,' the old lord said gently. 'Whatever you tell us – *whatever* it is, Eliza – you are under my protection. You can tell the truth.'

'Put her on oath,' Lady Catherine said, trying to speak without opening her mouth.

The old lord nodded and Hugo shot a look at his wife, measuring her courage that she dared speak when she had been ordered to silence.

'On oath then,' the old lord said. He nodded to the priest who stepped forward to the table by the little window and brought a bible forward.

'Do you promise on the Holy Book, on the sacred life of Jesus Christ and His holy Mother and God the Father to tell the truth?' he asked Eliza. 'Remember that the power of the devil is very strong in these disturbed times. You have to be on the side of God or surrender yourself to hell. Will you tell the truth?'

'Amen,' Eliza muttered. 'I promise. Oh God!'

'Tell us what took place when Lord Hugo carried Alys from the hall last night,' the old lord said. 'And tell us everything. And remember you will roast in hell if you lie.'

Eliza crossed herself and shot a quick scared glance at Hugo. He was watching her impassively. She shuddered in her fright.

'The young lord told me to go with the two of them,'

she started. Then she stopped like a sweating filly on a twitch.

'Go on,' the old lord said crossly. 'You're on oath to speak!'

'He told me to wait outside the door of our chamber, to keep watch,' she said. Her eyes were fixed on the old lord.

He nodded impatiently. 'And he took her in and had her? Go *on*, wench, you will surprise no one here!'

Eliza moistened her lips. 'No,' she said. 'I crept after them, to watch. I was curious. Alys spoke so much of her virginity – of her dislike of men. I was curious to see her with my lord.'

She broke off, shooting a quick look at Lady Catherine's marble face.

'Go on,' the old lord said grimly.

'He tossed her down on her pallet and stripped her down to her shift,' Eliza said. 'He pulled his breeches down and he went on top of her.'

Lady Catherine hissed like a snake. The old lord put a hand out to silence her.

Eliza looked quickly from Catherine's suppressed anger to the young lord's threatening black smile.

'I dare not speak!' she burst out.

The old lord leaned forward and snatched her arm, dragged her to her knees before him. '*I* am the master here,' he said. 'Even now in my dotage. I command here still. And I order you to speak and I promise you my protection – whatever you say. Now tell me, wench – what happened when he lay on her?'

'She hexed him!' Eliza said with a little moan. 'I heard her chuckle and she said a spell or something – I couldn't catch it – and then she turned her back to him and fell asleep.'

'He didn't have her?' the old lord asked incredulously. 'Didn't have her when he had stripped her and lain on her?'

Eliza shook her head. 'It was her doing,' she said. 'She reached back to him, and took his hand and wrapped his arm around her, and she put his hand on her . . .' she broke off.

'On her cunt?' the old lord asked frankly.

Eliza nodded, gulped.

'Then what?' he asked.

'He asked her if she knew him, and what year it was, and how old she was,' Eliza said in a little rush, her eyes fixed on the old lord. 'I couldn't hear it all,' she said. 'She spoke very low.'

'Did you hear anything at all?' the old lord asked. 'The truth now, wench!'

She nodded. 'I think she said she was eighteen,' she said. 'I think she said it was 1538.'

Catherine let out her held breath in a long, satisfied sigh.

The old lord looked towards his son.

'Did she foretell my death?' he asked.

Hugo nodded. 'Yes, father,' he said honestly.

'And this other stuff – her conceiving your son. She said all this?'

Hugo shrugged. 'Aye,' he said.

The old lord shrugged. 'Did she say how I'd die?' he asked.

Hugo shook his head. 'I didn't ask. She was talking like one half asleep. I was too surprised to question her and . . .' He broke off.

'And?' the old lord asked.

'I felt very tender towards her,' Hugo said awkwardly. 'I've never felt like that with a woman before, not even a favourite whore. I felt as if I wanted her to sleep. I felt as if I wanted to guard her rest.'

The old lord barked a short laugh. 'That's not witchcraft – that is love,' he said briefly. 'I thought you'd never fall for it, Hugo. You're on a merry road now!'

For a moment the two men grinned at each other, warm with fellow-feeling.

'And for a little drab from the moor,' Hugo said wonderingly.

His father chuckled. 'You can never tell,' he said softly. 'And you'll fall hard, Hugo. I wager you do! She'll lead you a dance, that girl!'

'Never mind that!' Lady Catherine hissed. 'There *is* witchcraft here! What of her naming the year as 1538? What of her calling herself eighteen? How old is she now? Sixteen! And it's 1536! And what of your death? And what of me? She is in league with the devil, she is foretelling our ends – and in only two years unless she is stopped now!'

The old lord nodded. 'What d'you think?' he asked the priest.

The man's face was brooding. 'I know not what to think,' he said. 'It looks very bad. I should want to think and pray for guidance. God will send us a sign to protect us from these terrors within our walls.'

Lady Catherine leaned forward, her eyes glittering in the candlelight. 'Your own lord is threatened with death in a year's time and you know not what to think?' she asked.

The priest stared back at her, unafraid. 'There is malice in the witness against her,' he said levelly. 'Maybe this wench dislikes her, you certainly have reason to hate her, my lady. If she is accursed then it will show in her speech and behaviour. I think we should see her and judge her on her behaviour when she is accused.'

'And let her enchant you all!' Catherine cried out.

'Be still, Madam,' the old lord rumbled. He nodded to Hugo. 'Call for Alys,' he said. 'We'd better have her here.'

The priest looked briefly at Catherine and seated himself at the table in the window. 'She will not enchant me,' he said briefly. 'I have ordered many witches to their deaths. I have watched many women take ordeals where strong men have turned aside sickened. I am merciless in the work of God, Lady Catherine. If she is on the side of the devil then she should surely fear me.'

Hugo strolled to the door, shouted for a servant again and ordered him to seek Alys. 'I believe in none of this,' he said conversationally. 'No magic, no witches, no spells. I believe in the world I can see and touch. All the rest is fairy-tales to frighten little girls.'

Father Stephen exchanged a glance with him. 'I know you like to think so, Hugo,' he said with affection. 'But you go dangerously close to heresy yourself if you deny the fallen angel and the battle against sin.'

Hugo shrugged.

A silence fell for a few moments. Eliza edged nearer to the door.

'May I speak?' Catherine asked.

The old lord nodded.

'I may have been hasty,' Catherine said, her voice level. The old lord bent a piercing look on her face. 'I was angry with my husband and angry with the wench. I may have been hasty in my accusations.'

They waited. Hugo eyed her with open suspicion.

'As you say, my lord, Hugo is not necessarily be-witched. He could be in the grip of desire and tender-ness.' Her voice did not shake with her jealousy, she held herself in iron control. 'I may feel affronted as his wife, but as the lady of the castle, as your ward, it does not concern me,' she said.

The old lord nodded. 'And so?' he asked drily.

'Only one thing in all of this is left to worry me,' she said.

The old lord waited.

'Your safety, Sire,' she said. 'If the girl wishes your death then she is well placed to harm you. And if she is a witch then we are all in danger. We have to know if she has black arts before we can judge whether or no to send her away. If she has powers then we cannot treat her like a naughty servant. She would do us all grave ill. We have to *know*. For our own safety.'

The priest nodded. The old lord glanced at him. 'What do you suggest, Lady Catherine?' he asked.

Catherine took a breath. She did not look at her husband. 'An ordeal,' she said. 'A test for her. To see if she is a witch or no.'

Hugo flinched involuntarily. 'I like not these ordeals,' he said. A glance from his father silenced him.

'Priest?' the old lord asked.

'I think so, my lord.' Father Stephen nodded. 'We have to know if her healing gifts are godly or not. And Lady Catherine is right to think that she can neither be sent away nor kept here while we are all in ignorance. Perhaps a gentle ordeal? Eating sanctified bread?'

A look of disappointment crossed Catherine's face, swiftly hidden.

'Did you hope to swim her, Catherine?' the young lord asked maliciously. 'Or set her in a burning hay-stack?'

'None of that! None of that!' the old lord said impatiently. 'She may well be a good girl and an honest servant with naught against her but your desires, Hugo,

176

and her own special gifts. We'll do what the priest says. She'll take sanctified bread on oath and if it chokes her then we'll know what to do.'

Eliza's eyes were as round as saucers. 'Shall I go?' she asked.

'Stay!' the old lord said irritably. 'Where is the wench?'

Nine

After Alys had flung herself out of the ladies' gallery she ran as far as the outside gate before she hesitated. The air was icy and dry, as if it might snow at any moment. The town was closed and silent. Morach's cottage was half a day's walk away. Mother Hildebrande was gone forever. She could feel the absence of the abbey and the loss of her mother in the arid air, in the low soughing of the winter wind around the castle walls. There was nowhere for her to go.

She turned back at the castle gate and walked slowly across the outer manse. A few thin hens pecked at the cold earth. A fat sow, bulging with piglets, grunted in the sty. Alys shivered as the sun dipped down behind the high round tower. She walked across the second drawbridge, into the inner wall of the castle. Mother Hildebrande was dead, the abbey was in ruins. There was nowhere for her to go but back to the gallery to the spite and triumph of the women.

Her head was still hammering from the wine and from the sudden flood of her anger. She walked slowly, past the herb-beds to the well at the centre of the little garden. She wound up the bucket and drank the icy brackish water, tasted the foulness of it slick in the back of her throat. Then she walked on, past the great hall to the bakehouse, a little building round like a beehive set down between the brooding blackness of the prison tower and the castle physic garden. Alys pushed open the little door and peered curiously inside.

It was warm and quiet. The two great rounded ovens

held their heat like a brickyard. The floor, the tables, the shelves, even the brass tins on their hooks, were covered with a thin white film of flour. The bakers had deserted it after their morning's work – baking the bread for breakfast, dinner and supper in one long sweating shift. They had gone into town to find an alehouse, or into the great hall of the castle to gamble or doze. Alys went quietly inside and shut the door behind her. The room smelled sweetly of new-baked bread. Alys sank to her knees in the white dust at the hearth and found that tears were running down her face. For a moment she was back in the abbey kitchens watching the lay sisters bake and brew. For a moment she remembered the sweet white bread, milled from their own flour, baked in their own ovens, the hot warming taste of fresh-baked rolls for breakfast after prime in the early morning.

Alys shook her head, took up the bulky hem of her navy gown and rubbed her eyes. Then she sat back on her heels and stared into the warm heart of the bakehouse fire for long minutes.

'Fire,' she said thoughtfully, looking to the hearth. She rose up and lifted down two small tins from the wall. One she scooped full of water from the barrel by the table. She placed it before the fire.

'Water,' she said softly.

She took a handful of cold ash, fallen soot and brick dust from the back of the chimney. 'Earth,' she said, putting it before her. Then she pulled the empty tin forwards to complete the square. 'Air,' she said.

She drew a triangle in the spilled flour and ash which covered the stone floor, binding the three points of fire, earth and air.

'Come,' she said in a whisper. 'Come, my Lord. I need your power.'

The bakehouse was silent. Across the courtyard in the castle kitchen a quarrel had broken out, there was the noise of a slamming door. Alys heard nothing.

She drew another triangle, inverted, binding the points for the earth, air and water.

'Come,' she said again. 'Come, my Lord, I need your powers.'

Delicately she stood, lifting her gown as carefully as a woman stepping on stones across a torrent. She stepped across the line, she broke the boundary, she stepped into the pentangle. She turned her head upwards, her head-dress slipped back and she closed her eyes. She smiled as if some power had flowed into her, from the fire, water, earth, air – from the flagstones beneath her feet, from the air which crackled and glowed around her head, from the radiating warmth of the bakehouse which was suddenly hot, exciting.

'Yes,' she said.

There was nothing more.

Alys stood for a long still moment, feeling the power rise through the soles of her feet, inhaling it with every breath, feeling it tingle in her fingertips. Then she straightened her head, pulled up her hood, smiled inwardly, secretly, and stepped out of the shape drawn on the floor.

She tipped the water back in the tub. She set the tins back on their hooks and swept, with one swift, careless movement, the shape of the pentangle from the dust of the floor. She untied the purse on her girdle. Morach's candlewax moppets were cool in her hand. Alys turned them over, smiling at the accurate detail of Hugo's face, her expression hardening when she saw the doll of Catherine with its obscene slit. She went to the pile of firewood stacked at the side of the oven and pulled out a log at the bottom of the pile. She pushed in the candlewax moppets as far as they would go, and then gently put the log back in place. She stepped back and looked critically at the pile. It looked undisturbed. She picked up a handful of dust from the floor and blew it over the log so that it was as pale and dusty as the others. 'Hide yourselves,' she said softly. 'Hide yourselves, my pretty little ones, until I come for you.'

Then she sat before the fire and let it warm her.

It was only then, as if she were only then ready to be found, that the servant came panting across the court-yard and glanced, without much hope, into the deserted bakehouse.

'The lord wants you,' he said, flustered and out of breath. 'At once. I had trouble finding you.'

Alys shrugged indifferently. 'Tell him you couldn't find me,' she said. 'I walked out of Lady Catherine's room without leave. I lost my temper. I don't want to serve her, or him, or anyone. She'll have run to him to complain of me. I won't go.'

The servant shrugged unsympathetically. 'You have to,' he said. 'They're all there. The young lord and the shrew, the old lord and the priest. Even Eliza Herring. Now they want you. You'd best go, and quickly too.'

Alys' blue eyes sharpened. 'What are they all doing?' she asked. 'What is Father Stephen doing there? And Lord Hugo? What do they want with me?'

'It's a row,' he said. 'Lady Catherine is calling up a storm and the old lord is taking her side, I think. But you have to go.'

Alys nodded. 'I'm coming,' she said. 'Run and tell them I am on my way.'

She rubbed her face with the corner of her sleeve and pushed her fingers through her tangle of curls, pushing the longer ringlets behind her ears and pulling the hood forwards into place, so that not a scrap of her hair showed around her face. Then she pulled down the long stomacher of the blue gown, shook out the plain blue underskirt, and then crossed the yard to the door of the great hall. She walked through the hall, where a lad was heaving logs on the fire to keep the room warm and ready for supper, and through the lobby at the back of the dais, to the tower. Up the stairs, through the guard-room with a nod like a queen to the lounging soldiers and a servant, and up to Lord Hugh's door. It stood open. They were waiting for her. Alys, composed, her head high and her face defiant, stepped into the bright room and heard the door swing shut behind her.

She faced the old lord in his chair by the fire. She was dimly aware of Lady Catherine standing behind him, her hand possessively on the carved back of his chair, glittering with triumph. The priest stood away from the fire by the table in the window; before him was a black bible and a silver salver covered with white linen. Next to him stood Eliza, her eyes wide with terror. Alys glanced at her and then saw Eliza's hands. Both of them were clenched into fists with the thumb between the second and third fingers, to make the sign of the cross, the old protection against a witch. Alys' blue eyes became a little darker. She was starting to know what she should fear.

Furthest away from them all was the young Lord Hugo. He was sprawled in a chair with his riding boots thrust out before him, his hands dug deep into the pockets of his breeches, his face dark and sullen under his cap. He met Alys' swift glance with an angry glare which was full of warning.

Alys was silently alert to her danger. She looked back

to the old lord again and scanned his face. He was sallow and his hands resting on the carved arm of his chair were trembling.

'There's a grave accusation laid against you, Alys,' he said. 'The gravest accusation a Christian can face.'

Alys met his gaze squarely.

'What is it, my lord?' she asked.

'Witchcraft,' he said.

Lady Catherine gave a little irrepressible sigh, like a woman at the height of pleasure. Alys did not look at her, but her colour ebbed, her face paled.

'It is said that you have foretold my death,' the old lord said. 'That you have said that you will be the lady of the castle and bear Lord Hugo a son and heir. It is said that you have foretold that all this will happen in just two years from now.'

Alys shook her head. 'It is not true, my lord,' she said confidently.

Hugo leaned forward. 'Was it a dream, Alys?' he prompted. 'D'you remember nothing?'

Alys glanced in his direction, and then turned back to the old lord. 'I did not say it,' she said.

The old lord glanced towards Father Stephen. 'It is possible that the girl was in a trance and is now speaking the truth as she can recall it,' the priest said fairly. 'If she were a true seer she might do that. I have heard of some very saintly prophets who have foretold the future without knowing what words they were saying. There are records in the gospel, the speaking in tongues and other miracles. But also it can be a trap from the devil.'

'D'you have the Sight, Alys?' the old lord asked.

'Hardly,' she said tartly. When they stared at her in surprise she said sharply: 'If I had the Sight, my lord, I would not stand here accused of witchcraft by Lady

Catherine who has hated me since the day she first saw me. If I had the Sight I would have been well away from the castle before this day. Indeed, if I had the Sight I would not have been helpless at Morach's cottage when your men came for me and took me against my will.'

The old lord chuckled unwillingly. 'Then what of these words of yours, these predictions, Alys?' he asked.

Alys, sweating under the dark blue gown, laughed. 'A dream, my lord,' she said. 'A foolish dream. I should have known better than to dream it, and better than to speak it. But I was drunk and very full of desire.'

Hugo, leaning forward, saw the sheen of sweat on her pale forehead. 'You were pretending?' he asked.

She turned and looked straight into his face, her blue eyes as honest as a child. 'Of course, my lord,' she said. 'D'you think I don't know that you take women and use them and cast them aside? I wanted you to desire me, and I wanted you to cleave to me, and I wanted you to think me more than any ordinary wench. So I pretended to have the Sight and I promised you all that your heart desires. I meant only to trick you into being constant to me.'

Hugo's eyes narrowed. 'You have wanted me all along?' he asked.

Alys faced him squarely. 'Oh yes,' she said. 'I thought you knew.'

He heard the lie as loud and as clear as plainsong. But he nodded. 'That explains it then,' he said. 'Wenches' tricks and silly games.' He got to his feet and stretched. His head brushed the carved and painted beams. 'Have you done, Sire?' he asked his father. 'The wench was laying snares to trap me – ' he grinned ruefully ' – I was caught well enough.'

He turned to Lady Catherine. 'I owe you an apology, Madam, I have been cunt-struck – and not for the first time. When we are alone together I will make you handsome amends.' He gave a low seductive laugh. 'I shall treat you as you command me,' he said.

Catherine's hand went to the base of her throat as if to hold her pulse steady. 'It's not over yet,' she said.

The old lord was settling back in his chair, hooking a footstool into place with one foot. 'Why not?' he asked. 'The wench has pleaded guilty to lying and explained her prophecy is a false one. We can see well enough why she should lie. The castle's a big enough place, Catherine, I'll keep her out of your way. You can sleep easy in your bed with Hugo restored to you. The wench is a liar and a strumpet.' He shot a little smile at Alys. 'Nothing worse.'

'She should take the ordeal,' Lady Catherine said. 'That was what we all agreed. She should take the ordeal.'

Alys took a half-breath of fear before she could stop herself. Lady Catherine beamed at her. The colour was draining from the girl's face, she looked ready to faint.

'We are agreed that you should take an ordeal for witchcraft,' Lady Catherine said silkily. 'If you are indeed guilty of nothing worse than a bungled seduction then you will have nothing at all to fear.'

Hugo put out a commanding hand to Catherine and she moved reluctantly from the shelter of the old lord's chair to stand beside her husband. He slid his hand around her waist and looked down into her plain, strained face.

'Come, my lady, have done,' he said. His voice was low. Catherine swayed towards him like an ash tree in a breeze. 'Let us go to your chamber and leave Alys to her clerk duties. I am cured well enough of my lust for her, and if the son by Alys in her prediction was a lie and a bait, then perhaps I shall get a son on you.'

He turned towards the door with his arm still around her waist and she, half drugged with her ready desire, went with him.

It was done. It was nearly done.

Alys froze, afraid to move, conspiring not to break Hugo's spell, willing herself to be invisible. The priest was silent, looking from Catherine to Hugo, and back to Alys' wary stillness, letting them settle it as they chose. Lord Hugh was weary of it all, satisfied with the outcome. It was done.

'No!' Lady Catherine cried with sudden energy. She broke out of Hugo's encircling arm back to the old lord. 'If she is innocent then she need not fear the ordeal. We have to test her before we can leave your health in her care, my lord. That is what we agreed to do. That is what we should do. And I will not leave this room until it is done!'

'Catherine!' Hugo said commandingly. 'You are my wife, I *order* you to leave this matter alone. It is settled to all our satisfaction.'

'Not to mine!' She rounded on him, panting. 'Not to my satisfaction! Not to my satisfaction! You would lead me out of the room like a bleating lamb, my lord. And I know why! It is to spare her the ordeal! Confess it! You do not want me! You have never wanted me! It is to spare your harlot the task of showing she is not a witch! And why?' Her voice grew louder, more shrill. 'Because you are bewitched into shielding her. Shielding her from the rightful anger of your father and you are ready to risk his life, and my life, so that you can have her!'

She dropped on her knees before the old lord. 'Test

her!' she demanded, like a woman begging for a life-time's gift. 'Test the witch! *Make* her take the ordeal.'

The old lord looked at Hugo. 'Tell me the truth,' he said gruffly. 'Are you shielding her from this? If there's any chance she is a witch you should speak, Hugo. We none of us can dare to play with the devil's arts. Not even for love of a maid.'

Hugo gave a ragged, strained laugh. 'There's no chance,' he said carelessly. 'No chance at all. But we shall do whatever you wish, my lord, whatever you wish. I would have thought that we have wasted too long on this matter already. I would have thought you were weary of it. I do not fear the little slut, I see no reason to prolong this more.' He laughed more easily. 'Let's have done and away to our suppers.'

The old lord narrowed his eyes. 'No,' he said gently. 'She can take the ordeal. There's no harm done if she is innocent, and I am not sure of you, Hugo. I am not sure of you in this matter.' He turned toward Alys; her face was greenish white. 'Alys, you are to take an oath,' he said. 'Do as Father Stephen commands.'

Alys shuddered, a tiny movement which betrayed her deep fear. 'Very well,' she said, her voice level.

The priest stepped forward, held out the bible. 'Put your left hand on the Sacred Book,' he said. 'Raise your right hand and say "I, Alys of Bowes Moor, do solemnly swear and attest that I am not a witch."'

'I, Alys of Bowes Moor, do solemnly swear and attest that I am not a witch,' Alys said evenly.

A log fell in the grate sending a shower of sparks upwards. The room was so silent that they all flinched a little at the noise.

'I have never used the black arts,' the priest intoned.

'I have never used the black arts,' Alys repeated.

'I have had no truck with the devil.'

'I have had no truck with the devil.'

'I never looked on his face, nor the faces of his servants.'

'I have never looked on his face, nor the faces of his servants,' Alys repeated. The rhythm of the vows was pressing down on her. She could feel her gown wet under her arms, she could feel a cold sweat down her spine. She fought to keep her face serene. She was sick with fear.

'I have not lain with the devil, nor with any of his servants, nor with any of his animals.'

'I have not lain with the devil, nor with any of his servants, nor with any of his animals,' Alys said. Her throat was tight with fear, her mouth dry. She licked her lips but her tongue itself was dry.

'I have not given suck to the devil, nor to any of his servants, nor to any of his animals.'

'I have not given suck to the devil, nor to any of his servants, nor to any of his animals,' Alys repeated.

'I have made no waxen image, nor cast a spell. I have summoned no ghosts, nor witches, nor warlocks, nor any of the black company.'

'I have made no waxen image, nor cast a spell. I have summoned no ghosts, nor witches, nor warlocks, nor any of the black company.' Alys' voice shook slightly but she had it under control again.

In the utter silence of the little room she could hear her heart beating so loud that she thought they would all hear it and know her fear. The candlewax moppets were so bright in her mind's eye that she thought anyone looking into her face would be able to see them. The fingertip which had drawn the pentangle tingled and stung. There was a tiny scrap of flour beneath her nail.

'And to prove my purity from these devilish skills,' the priest started.

'And to prove my purity from these devilish skills,' Alys repeated. She tried to cough to clear her throat but it was too tight.

'I take this sanctified bread, the body of our Lord Jesus Christ,' the priest said.

Alys stared at him in blank horror. 'Repeat it,' he said, his eyes suddenly sharp with suspicion.

'I take this sanctified bread, the body of our Lord Jesus Christ,' Alys said. She could hold herself no tighter, her voice was a thin thread of fear. Lady Catherine's nostrils flared as if she could scent Alys' terror.

The priest lifted the silver salver and took the linen cloth from it. In the centre of the gleaming plate was a large white wafer with a cross marked on it.

'I take the body of our Lord Jesus Christ, and eat,' the priest said.

'I take the body of our Lord Jesus Christ, and eat,' Alys said breathlessly. She eyed the thick wafer and knew she would not be able to swallow it. Her throat was too tight, her mouth was dry. She would gag on it, and then they would have her.

'And if I am perjured, if I am indeed a witch, then may it choke me; and may those that here witness do what they will with me, for I am damned,' the priest dictated urgently.

The very words stuck in Alys' throat. She opened her mouth but no sound came, she tried to clear her throat but the only noise she made was a harsh croaking sound.

'She's choking!' Lady Catherine said eagerly. 'She's choking on the oath!'

'Say it, Alys,' said the old lord, leaning forward.

'And if I am perjured, if I am indeed a witch' – Alys' voice was harsh, her throat rasping – 'then may it choke me; and may those that here witness do what they will with me, for I am damned.'

'This is the body of our Lord Jesus Christ,' the priest said, and took the bread from the plate and held it towards Alys' face. 'Eat.'

She swayed as she stood, as her knees softened and her terrified blue-black eyes went out of focus. The nausea from last night's wine rose up in her throat tasting like bile. She swallowed it down so that she should not retch and found her throat would not respond. The bile was coming up, upwards. She put her hand to her face and found she was wet with icy sweat. She knew she would vomit if she so much as opened her mouth.

'Eat, wench,' the old lord said with gruff urgency. 'I don't like this delay.'

Alys gulped again. The sickness was unstoppable, her belly was in a spasm of fear, her throat tight with her terror, it was rising up and up, it would spew out the moment she opened her lips.

'She cannot!' Lady Catherine breathed in triumph. 'She dare not!'

Goaded, Alys opened her mouth. The priest crammed the wafer in, the thick handful of papery mush half suffocated her, half choked her. She could feel her lungs heaving for air, she knew she must cough, she knew when she coughed she would spew it all out, bile, vomit and wafer; and then she would be lost.

Alys squared her shoulders and closed her eyes. She was not going to die. Not now. Not at these hands. She chewed determinedly. She thrust a gob of the dry mush towards the back of her throat and forced it down. She chewed some more. She swallowed. She chewed some more. She swallowed. Then she gave one last convulsive gulp and the task was done.

'Open your mouth,' the priest said.

She opened her mouth to him.

'She swallowed it,' he said. 'She has passed the ordeal. She is no witch!'

Alys swayed and would have fallen, but the young lord was at once behind her. He took her by her waist and guided her back to his chair. He poured her a glass of ale from the jug and glanced at the priest.

'I take it she may drink now?' he asked acidly.

When the young man nodded he gave her the glass. For a moment his warm fingers touched her frozen ones, like a secret message of reassurance.

'I am glad,' Lady Catherine said. 'This is the best outcome we could have hoped for. Alys has proved her innocence.'

The old lord nodded. 'She can stay,' he said.

'And live with my women, as she has done,' Lady Catherine said swiftly. 'And she will make me a promise.' She smiled at Alys. 'She will promise me that she will have no more truck with my husband, and that she will tell no more tales of a child for herself from him.'

The old lord nodded. 'That's fair,' he said to Alys. 'Promise it, wench.'

'I swear it,' Alys said, her voice very low. She was still sweating, the lump of communion bread thick and cloying deep in her throat.

'And when I have a child, as I know I will have this year, then we will know that Alys is completely innocent,' Lady Catherine said sweetly. 'Alys can turn her skills towards making me fertile that I may bear an heir.'

The old lord nodded wearily. 'Aye,' he said. 'Alys can have a look at you and see if she has herbs which will help.'

'I am counting on it,' Lady Catherine said. Behind her pleasant tone was a world of threat. Alys, sitting without permission in Lady Catherine's presence, shifted uneasily as she recognized renewed danger.

'My lord will lie with me, not with you, Alys,' Catherine said triumphantly. 'And *I* will bear his son, not you, Alys. And when our son is born then you will be free to leave, Alys.'

'Aye,' the old lord said again. 'Now go, all of you. I'll take a rest before supper.'

Eliza fled for the door and was away downstairs without another word of bidding. Alys rose wearily to her feet. Hugo glanced at her and then went to Lady Catherine, who beckoned imperiously for his arm.

'Let us go to my chamber,' she said. Her look up at his dark face was hungry. She was breathless with lust. He had promised to lie with her, and Alys' defeat had excited her. 'Let us two go to my chamber, my lord.'

Alys, left alone in the room with the old lord, moved slowly towards the door as if she were very, very weary.

'Get her with child, for God's sake,' the old lord said. He was leaning back in his chair, his eyes were closed. 'I'll have no peace until she has a son, or I am rid of her; and I cannot be rid of her inside a year.' He sighed. 'You will be in danger every day of that year until she has a child or until Hugo's eyes are turned away from you. He must be blind to you, and deaf to you, and insensate to you. Get her with child if you can, Alys – or avoid Hugo's desire. Your luck will run out one day. You were perilously close today.'

Alys nodded, saying nothing, then she slipped from

the room and hobbled slowly down the stairs to the guardroom below. Eliza was waiting for her.

'I thought you were going to choke and they would kill you,' she said, wide-eyed.

'So did I,' Alys said grimly.

'Come back with me and tell the others! They won't believe it!'

'No,' Alys said.

'Oh, come on!' Eliza urged. 'They won't believe me if you don't tell them too.'

'No,' Alys said again.

'I thought I would die of fright!' Eliza said excitedly. 'And when you were slow repeating the oath, I thought they would have you! I've never seen anything like it!' She caught at Alys' arm. 'Come on!' she urged. 'Come and tell the others!'

'Let me go!' Alys said, suddenly shaking Eliza off. 'Let me go, damn you! Let me go!'

She pushed Eliza roughly aside and fled down the stairs, through the hall where the servants were putting out great jugs of ale and beer, and out across the yard to the bakehouse. Only there, when she had slipped through the door and slammed it behind her and sunk down to the hearthstone, did she let herself weep. And then, to her horror, she felt her vomit rising, rising up in her throat again.

She kneeled and faced the embers of the bakehouse fire and felt her throat clench against the rising tide of bile. Then she vomited, spewing it out into the ashes. Six times she heaved and puked until her belly was empty and her mouth sour.

And it was then that Alys knew fear. For in the embers of the fire, whole and untouched, unblemished in its white circle, was the sanctified wafer. Not a mark on it, as whole as when she had sworn an oath and chewed it and swallowed it. It had choked her as she had known it would.

Ten

The night drew in, darker and colder, and Alys, still hidden in her refuge at the bakehouse, heard the shouts and clatter of supper and then the querulous voices of tired servants clearing up. From the courtyard she could hear the shouts of servants who were leaving the castle and going into town, she could hear the march of the soldiers coming from their duty at the castle gates, a few steps in rhythm and then a disorderly straggle towards the guardroom, a few shouted jests and then the numbing silence of night. Still Alys waited, shrouded in silence and darkness, waited for the moon to rise above the dark squat bulk of the great hall, waited for the last flickering candles to go out at the little windows. Waited for the peak of the night, sitting on the cooling hearthstone of the bakehouse fire.

As it grew more and more chill she took a ragged old coat from the back of the door, wrapped it around her thin shoulders and put a few little pieces of kindling into the embers. When they flickered into flame she tossed on a dry log. Then she sat very still, watching the flames and saying nothing. Alys sat still and silent in a little island of solitude, as if she were waiting for something to come to her – some clarity or some hope. She knew that she was a sinner; far, far from the God of her mother, from the God of her innocent childhood in the nunnery. Despite the hours on her knees, despite the smile on the face of the statue, she would not be forgiven for running from her sisters when the fires of hell had opened around them. She would not be forgiven for the sin of lust. She could not take the devil on loan. She was so far from the peace of Christ that she vomited if she ate his bread.

Alys threw on another log. The firelight flickered and threw ominous moving shadows around her. Out in the yard someone screamed in mock fright and cried out 'Jesu save me!' but Alys did not cross herself. She knew that she alone, of all the castle, could never be saved. She squatted at the stone hearthside like a stone herself, and watched the flames burn up her hopes, her chance of returning to the abbey, her chance of forgiveness. All night she watched and waited by the dying fire as a mother will watch by the bed of a dying child. All night Alys watched her future cool and crumble, and finally faced her despair.

'I'm lost,' she said softly, just once.

All her plans – of escape from the castle, of return to an abbey, of the revival of the Church of Rome and a haven for her – they were all gone. Alys knew that she would never be an abbess nor even a novitiate again. She could not trust herself in a holy place. God had put his mark on her – as she had feared – during that panic-stricken run. She could not whisper in the confessional, she could not eat the sacred bread. Holy wine would curdle if she came close – and turn to blood. Holy water would ice over. The holy bread would rise up in her throat and choke her and if she vomited it out on the chancel steps they would all see, everyone would see, the wafer untouched by her soiled, sinful mouth. No abbess could miss the signs of a woman mired in sin, a woman given over to the devil. She could not coax nor lie her way back to sanctity. She could not confess and be absolved. She was in too deep. She was in too deep. She was black as the deeps of the river at midnight.

Alys breathed out a long, slow sigh of despair. The old life was gone indeed, as surely as Mother Hildebrande – and all her wisdom and love and kindness – was blown away on the moorland winds in a puff of white ash and charred gown. The old life was gone and Alys would never have it back.

She sat and mourned for it, for two long hours, with her eyes on the flames and the white consecrated wafer gleaming palely among the red hot embers. Alys watched it – unburned, not even charred – and knew she was far from Christ, and from His mother, and from her own mother, the abbess. She was as far away from them already as if she were in hell.

At that thought she paused and nodded. 'I'm damned,' she said wonderingly. 'Damned.' She had a moment of pity for herself. In quieter times, in an easier world, she would have made a good nun, a holy woman, a wise woman. As wise and beloved as her Mother Hildebrande. 'I'm damned,' Alys said again, tasting eternal judgement on her tongue. 'Damned without hope of forgiveness.'

She sat still for a few moments longer, then she reached for the fire tongs and hooked the unburned wafer out of the flames. It was cool to the touch. Alys looked at it and her face was stony in the presence of a miracle. Then she took it between her hands and tore and ground it until it broke into one, twenty, a thousand pieces, and she fed each little piece to the flames until they caught and burned and were gone. Alys smiled.

'Damned,' she said again, and this time it sounded like a direction for her to follow.

She knew now she would stay in the castle until she could see which way the wind blew for the old lord and for young Hugo. There could be no abbey, no convent in the future. Alys would be in the world forever and she would take her power in the world with her woman's strengths and the power of a woman damned to hell. She had to turn the eyes of Hugo from her. She had to make him lie with his wife. Catherine had to conceive. Any other outcome from today's black business would end badly for Alys, she knew. Her only chance of using the castle as a stepping stone to higher things, her only chance of escape, was to see the man she desired turn away from her and return to his wife. To watch her triumph, and to see a son in her arms.

Alys nodded, her face brightening in the firelight. If she could accomplish that – then she would be safe for months, even years. She was high in the old lord's favour, she would earn Catherine's gratitude. Between the two of them she might build a reputation which could take her to the highest houses in the land. Even if she only stayed with Lord Hugh and won his complete trust she would eat well and sleep warm and be free to travel when and where she wished. But Lady Catherine must conceive. If she did not conceive, and soon, she would look around her for a scapegoat. There would be another ordeal. And then another after that. And in an ordeal by water, or an ordeal with fire, or an ordeal with holy wine, in any one of them Alys would fail. And then she would face a nightmarish death.

'I have no way out,' she said softly to herself.

In the early hours of the morning, when the bake-house was as dark as pitch, and reason and the learned code of morality at its lowest ebb, Alys leaned forward and pulled out the log which hid the candlewax figures.

With the cloak as a shield around her shoulders she ranged the three figures on the lap of her blue gown and started to chant the spell Morach had taught her. The words meant nothing to her but as she whispered them into the silence of the darkened bakehouse they seemed to shroud her in power, a new power, one she could claim as her own. The rhythm of the words was like a song. Alys said them over and over, three times, in a low monotone. As she said them she stroked the wax dolls with her fingers until the wax grew as warm as skin, and took the glow from the fire. Three more times Alys whispered the spell to them, and caressed them, and made them her own, then she thrust her hand into the purse at her girdle and brought out a twist of paper. Wrapped in it were three hairs. The long brown one Alys stuck on the head of the doll to represent Lady Catherine, the short black hair was from Hugo, and Alys had one long silver hair from the old lord's comb.

The dolls gleamed in the firelight, each one with a strand of hair, each one moving slightly as Alys stroked them and whispered to them, naming each one of them and claiming them for her own. The embers sighed and settled in the fireplace like the whisper of a ghost. In the dim firelight and the shadows of Alys leaned forward to see more clearly. The little wax torsos moved very, very slightly under her gentle fingertips.

The dolls were breathing.

They were alive.

Alys let out a little sigh of awe and fear. She leaned over them and looked at them more closely. Then she put the one to represent the old lord carefully down on the hearthstone. 'I want nothing from you,' she said softly to it. 'I want you to be well and strong. And I want you to care for me and protect me for as long as I wish to stay here. And then I want you to let me go.'

The little doll's face was impassive in the firelight. Alys watched it for some moments. Then she took up the doll which was the young lord. For a moment she looked at it, at the clear features and the strong arrogant face. Then gently, very gently, she drew her fingernail across its right eyeball.

'Don't see me,' she whispered. 'Don't watch for me. Don't look at me with love. Don't notice me when I come into a room, don't turn to catch sight of me. Be blind to me. Be blind to me!'

She stroked her finger gently over the other eye. 'Don't look at me, don't notice me, don't watch for me! Be blind to me! Be blind to me!' she said again.

She blinked to clear her own gaze and was surprised to find tears on her cheeks. She rubbed them aside with the back of her hand. The little figure of Hugo was sightless, a smooth smear where each eye had been. Alys nodded. She felt shrouded in her own power. The tender, longing part of her was stilled, hidden. Her eyes gleamed in the darkness, her face shone with a sense of her own magic. She looked witchy. She licked her lips like a cat.

She held the little figure of Hugo closer, then she started to work on his fingertips. With delicate little movements she started to scrape the tips of his fingers away.

'Don't long to touch me,' she said. 'Don't touch me. Don't long for the feel of my skin. Don't stroke your hand against my face. Don't caress my hair. Don't reach for me, don't hold me. I am stealing away your desire to feel me. I am stealing your power to feel me. Don't touch me, don't reach out for me, don't caress me.'

The fingertips of both hands were flattened; the fingernails, so delicately carved by Morach, had melted away.

'Don't touch my body, or my face, or my hair,' Alys

said. 'Don't put your hand between my thighs, or on my breasts, or hold the nape of my neck. Don't desire the feel of me. Don't touch me.'

She laughed, a low delighted laugh, at the tingling sense of her own power which flowed so powerfully from her belly to her fingertips, down to the soles of her feet. Then she heard the echo of her laugh in the deserted bakehouse and looked around her fearfully. She hitched her cloak a little closer, turned the doll of Hugo to one side and started stroking at his ear.

'Don't listen for me,' she said, her voice a low whisper. 'Don't hear my voice. Don't have pet names for me. Don't recognize my voice among all others. Don't listen for my singing. Don't waken when you cannot hear my breathing in the bed beside you. Don't harken for me when I am away. Don't listen for my step when I am close.'

Delicately she stroked at one ear until it was smoothed quite away, and then she turned the doll around and stroked and rubbed the second ear until it too was gone.

Then she put the doll on its back on her lap again and pressed her index finger to its lips. 'Don't speak to me,' she said. 'Don't whisper to me, don't sing for me, don't joke with me, don't pray for me.' With jerky little motions she scratched at Hugo's mouth. 'Don't call me,' she said. 'Don't call me. Don't dream of me and speak my name, don't wake and say my name. Don't let my name come to your lips.'

His mouth was a smooth smear, but still Alys rubbed and rubbed at it.

'Don't kiss me,' she said. 'Don't put your mouth on mine. Don't put your tongue to my lips. Don't lick me, or kiss me, or bite me. Don't take my body into your mouth. Don't suckle at my nipples until my breasts ache for you. Don't bite my neck or my shoulders or my belly. Don't take me in your mouth and tease me with your tongue and suck me till I cry out in pleasure and beg you to do more.'

Hugo's mouth was a shapeless hollow. Alys had rubbed his lips until there was nothing there. The wax had melted and the mouth was eroded. An ugly little monster was all that was left of what had been a miniature copy of Hugo. An ugly little monster, blinded like some cave-dwelling fish, fingerless like an aborted baby, earless, toothless, gumless, lipless, with just a gaping hollow where his mouth had been.

Alys laughed again and her laughter was harsh with a wild panic.

'And now you, my Lady Catherine,' she said softly.

Very gently, with infinite care, she took up the doll which was Catherine and set it on her lap beside the doll of Hugo. She turned them to face one another and jiggled the grotesque penis against the female doll. She rubbed it against the doll's mouth, rubbed it against her neck, her belly. Then she rocked them together in an obscene dance. She pressed the dolls together, and then took them apart again. She slipped the gross wax penis into the female doll, and took it out again. Then she laid the female doll on her back and pressed the male doll down on top of her so the penis slipped into the monstrous maw, and they stayed together.

Alys took a scrap of ribbon from the purse at her girdle and fastened the two dolls together. In the fire-light, the little female doll seemed to gleam with contentment, the flickering light made her cheeks pink and warm. On top of her, tied fast, was the eyeless, earless, fingerless, mouthless monster which was Hugo. Alys let them rest together on the floor at her feet and stared at the fire.

After long, long minutes she shook herself from her reverie and bent down and took the two of them up.

'So,' she said. 'Hugo is hot for Catherine. He cannot let her alone. He is like a man obsessed. He is a man half mad with desire. He itches constantly for the feel of his cock inside her.

'And she . . .' Alys said slowly. 'She is contented. She is his beast. She is his brood mare, his whore, his dog for the whipping. He can do what he likes with her, she feels he can do no wrong. She forgets everything else – everything else,' Alys said with emphasis. 'She forgets fears and rivals and enmities because she is exhausted and drained and then filled with joy again as her husband runs back to her like a thirsty dog runs to his trough of water.'

The bitterness of Alys' vomit was still on her tongue. She hawked and spat into the flames.

'He looks at no other woman,' she said. She jiggled the two dolls together. 'He desires no one else. He thrusts into her as if he would fuck his way to paradise.'

'And she loves it,' she said with distaste.

She held the little dolls together for a moment longer and then untied the ribbon which bound them. They fell apart at once, as if the male doll were glad to be rid of the binding. Alys frowned a little, wondering what it meant. Then she set the doll Hugo down beside his sire on the hearthstone and started to stroke the female doll's belly.

'His seed is in you,' she said softly. 'And you conceive a boy. You get fatter, the baby grows.' Alys' clever fingers moulded the wax into a new shape. Catherine became monstrously large. 'You grow and grow,' Alys said. It sounded more like a curse than a spell for fertility. 'Nothing will stop you. No fear, no shock, no accident. You grow larger and larger and your appetites are gross. And then . . .' Alys paused. 'You take to your bed in labour. And from your pain and travail you bring forth a son who is the image of his father.'

Alys paused. Her lovely face was twisted with anger and with jealousy.

'And then you reward me,' she said sternly to the grossly swelling doll. 'You pay me a purse of gold and your blessing. You give me enough money for me to go far away, wherever I will. And you and I part and I never have to see you or your husband again.'

Alys gathered the three dolls on her lap.

'The spell is done,' she told them. 'And you brought it all on yourselves. These are the destinies you desired, or the destinies you forced me into making for you. The spell is done and it starts to work this very day.'

She slid the three into her purse again and slipped down from her stool to the hearthstone before the fire. She pulled the cloak around her and closed her eyes. Within seconds she was asleep.

As dawn broke, and the cocks crowed and the animals called and then the people awoke, Alys slept on. She slept without dreams to remember. But all night and all the early morning, the tears welled up from under her closed eyelids in a constant unstoppable flood. And her hands remained clenched in fists, the thumb between the second and third fingers, in the old, old ineffectual sign against witchcraft.

When the bakers' lad came in just after dawn to stoke the fire he found her there, her tangle of golden hair dirty in the ashes, and when he shook her awake and she sat up, the ashes still clung to her, so that she looked like Morach, an old woman with a wild shock of grey and white hair. Her face was dirty and in the shadowy dawn the smears looked like hard lines from years of longing and no satisfaction. The bakers' lad had never seen Alys before and he recoiled from her.

'I beg your pardon, dame!' he said swiftly, and when she struggled to her feet he took to his heels and was off into the courtyard where the grey light of dawn made the castle appear icy and white.

Alys followed him out of the open door as far as the well in the centre of the yard. She crooked a finger at him. 'Pull me water,' she said, her voice a hoarse croak.

The boy came nervously towards her but stayed out of reach. 'Promise you won't hex me?' he said.

Alys laughed, a bitter sound, and hawked and spat. 'I promise,' she said. Then she looked at him and her blue eyes gleamed with malice. 'Not this time, at any rate.'

The boy trembled but came closer and wound down the bucket. Three times he had to drop it before it smashed through the ice in the well. Then he wound it up, filled to the brim. Alys cupped her hands and scooped up the icy water and drank greedily.

'Now go to your work,' she said. 'But tell no one you saw me.'

'I won't, lady! I won't,' the boy promised eagerly.

Alys looked at him until he nearly shrivelled with fear. 'I shall know if you do,' she said with emphasis. Then she turned away from him and went wearily to the women's quarters to wash and change her gown and comb her hair. The purse with the three candlewax dolls knocked at her thigh with every step she took.

Eliza fell on her the moment she was through the door, with the others not far behind.

'Where have you been? You've been out all night!'

Eliza exclaimed. Then, when Alys started to reply, 'Never mind that!' she said impatiently. 'Never mind! You'll never guess what's been happening here. All night! All night!'

The other women, bright-eyed and half hysterical, collapsed into laughter. Alys felt herself smiling, catching their amusement despite her weariness.

'What?' she asked.

'Lord Hugo!' Eliza said. 'You'll never guess. He's been here, with my lady, all night long. And we saw, we saw . . .'

'Tell it right!' Margery reproved. 'Tell it from the beginning.'

'I'll not hear it,' Ruth said. 'Lady Catherine is sure to come in and catch you tattling, Eliza.'

'Well go sit with her then!' Eliza said impenitently. 'And if she comes – cough so we can hear you. But I've *got* to tell Alys. I shall die if I don't.'

'Silly girl,' Mistress Allingham said indulgently. 'Not that we didn't have a night of it! Indecent!'

Ruth went out of the room and Eliza dragged Alys to a footstool and sat at her feet.

'After supper,' she began breathlessly, 'Lord Hugo came up here and said he would like to hear us singing and playing. Ruth played the mandolin and I sang, and then Margery sang. He said my voice was very sweet and he smiled at me – you know how he does!'

'Yes,' Alys said wearily. 'I know his smile.'

Eliza winked. 'Well, *you* would of course. My, you're a sly one! I never knew you were hot for him. I thought you were wedded to the single state! And there you were all along . . .'

'About last night . . .' Margery interrupted.

'Yes!' Eliza said. 'Well, after we had sung he called

for some mead and he made us all have a glass with him, and then he took the bottle, as bold as you please, and said to Lady Catherine. "I think we will have need of this to quench our thirsts this night."' Eliza's eyes grew wide with double meanings. 'Then he said, "Though I will give you enough to drink, my lady, I promise you! Your mouth will run over with it!"'

Alys swallowed convulsively. 'Vile,' she said softly.

'There's worse than that!' Eliza said with delight. 'They went into the room together and we were just left there, imagine how we felt! We didn't know whether to go or stay. Ruth was for going but I said – we haven't been dismissed, he might want something – so we stayed.

'Then we heard it. First of all we heard them talking, quietly, so we couldn't hear the words. Then we heard Lady Catherine say, "I beg you, my lord, I beg you to give me a son. Do it to me!"' Eliza gave a squawk of laughter and clapped a hand across her mouth.

'Ruth left then, you know how she is. But we stayed. And then we heard Lady Catherine moaning. She sounded like she was in pain so we thought we should go in, but then we thought not. Over and over again she was saying: "Hugo, Hugo, please, oh please."'

'What was he doing?' Alys asked. She thought she knew.

Eliza licked her lips. 'We peeped,' she said. 'We opened the door really and she had the curtain drawn across it so they didn't know. I peeped around the curtain, I thought I could say we were worried for her if they caught me. Catch me! They wouldn't have noticed if we'd danced in singing.'

'What was he doing?' Alys asked. She was very white.

'He had made her kneel before him,' Eliza said, her

voice a delighted whisper. 'He had his cock out and he was hard as a spear – I saw it! And he was rubbing it all over her face, her eyes, her ears, her hair, everywhere. And rubbing himself on her neck and the front of her nightgown.'

Alys was very still, she was thinking of the little dolls and the obscene dance she had made them do before she had tied them together with the ribbon.

'He ripped her gown,' Eliza said. 'And she just knelt there and let him do what he wanted. And he rubbed himself against her breasts. She was shameless. She was there with her gown ripped to her navel and her arms tight around his bum just moaning and moaning for more.'

Alys put a hand to her forehead, she was cold and wet. 'And then?' she asked. 'I suppose he had her?'

Eliza shook her head. 'Worse,' she said.

'What?' Alys said.

'He told her to get on the bed and spread herself wide,' Eliza whispered. Alys shut her eyes briefly.

'She looked disgusting!' Eliza said in delighted shock. 'She stuck her legs right out and she opened herself with her hands.'

Alys shook her head. 'Oh, enough, Eliza! I don't want to know.'

Eliza was unstoppable. 'And he climbed on the bed and he rammed inside her as if he hated her,' she said in an awed whisper. 'Then he pulled out again and walked away.'

'What happened?' Alys asked.

'She screamed,' Eliza said. 'She screamed when he thumped in and then she screamed again when he pulled out. She was writhing on the bed like a barrel of eels. She was wild! She kept begging him and begging him to do it to her.'

'Did he?' Alys asked tersely.

Eliza shook her head. 'Not properly, not like she wanted. Over and over again he went to the bed and mounted her once, and then pulled away. And again and again she screamed for more. Then he made her get off the bed.'

Alys waited in silence.

'He made her strip naked and tear her shift into pieces,' Eliza said. 'Then he told her to knot the pieces into a rope.'

'Good God!' Alys said impatiently. 'Why did you not stop him? Why did you not at least call to her?'

Eliza looked at her. 'Don't you know?' she asked. 'Are you so cold that you don't know that? She was loving it. She wanted him to treat her like that. She wanted to be his brood mare, his whipped dog. She was not his wife; she was his whore.'

Alys sat very still and let the echo of her spell wash over her and around her. She wondered how deep an evil she had done.

'He made her crawl up and down the floor,' Eliza said. 'He made her crawl on her hands and knees. He tied the shift over her eyes so she could not see and he made her crawl around. Sometimes he entered her from behind, sometimes he went to her head and forced her mouth on to him. And whatever he did,' – Eliza's voice was soft with delighted shock – 'she cried for more.'

'All night?' Alys asked coldly. She was thinking of the two dolls tied together and then their abrupt falling apart.

Eliza shook her head. 'He took the blindfold off her and he put it around his own back,' she said. 'He did it around her so they were bound together. Then he lifted her up and lowered her on to him.'

Alys could feel vomit again rising in her throat from her empty belly.

'She screamed,' Eliza said. ' A long really loud scream, as if he had really hurt her that time. And the two of them dropped to the floor and he humped her on the rushes until her back bled.'

Alys hawked and spat into the embers of the fire. 'Give me some ale, Margery,' she said softly. 'This story of Eliza's makes me sick to my very heart.'

'It's done,' Eliza said with quiet triumph. 'The story's done. I said you should have been here.'

Alys sipped the ale. It was warm and stale from standing all night in the pitcher. 'Did he spend the night in her bed?' she asked, but she already knew the answer.

Eliza shook her head. 'He untied the rope when he had done with her and sprang away from her as if he hated her,' she said. 'Lady Catherine was still lying on the floor and he slapped her – one cheek and then the other – and then he pulled up his breeches and left her, like that. With her back all bruised and bloody and his hand print on both her cheeks.'

Alys nodded. 'And is she grieved?' she asked, detached.

Eliza shook her head. 'She was singing this morning when I took her cup of ale in to her. She had her hands on her belly and she told me she is sure she has conceived a child. She is sure she is going to bear him a son. She has begged her way into paradise and she is content.'

Alys nodded and sipped at the ale again.

'Good,' she said. 'Hugo is back with his wife, his wife is carrying his child. Neither of them will trouble me, I am spared her foul jealousy and his dangerous lusts. I can do what I ought to do – clerk for my lord and keep him and his household well.'

She got up from the stool and shook the dust from her gown. 'It has a bitter taste,' she said quietly to herself. 'I never knew it had a bitter taste.'

'What has?' asked Eliza. 'The ale? It should be sweet enough.'

'Not the ale,' Alys replied. 'The taste of victory.'

Eleven

It was bitterly cold all February. The river froze into great long slabs of grey and white ice. When the ladies walked along the path beside the river they could see the water dashing along beneath the thick skin. Alys shuddered and drew as far back as the snowy banks would allow. In the second week a thick mist blew across the moors from the south-west and the women stayed indoors for one long winter day after another. It was dark when they woke, then pale and cloudy and brooding all day, then dark again at three in the afternoon. Sounds were muffled in the fog and from the window in the gallery you could not see the river below – from the old lord's room high in the round tower you could neither see nor hear the castle courtyard.

Alys spent all the time she could with the old lord in his little room in the tower. It was warm there and the lord and his steward David were quiet easy company. She wrote as she was bid, restrained condolences to the Princess Mary for the death of her mother, the Dowager Princess Catherine of Aragon, she read to the old lord from bawdy, unlikely Romances and listened to his anecdotes and memories of battles and jousting and of the time when he was young and strong and Hugo had not even been born.

The mood in the women's gallery above the great hall was ominous. Lady Catherine plunged from hysterical gaiety, when she commanded the women to play and sing and dance, into a deep sullen anxiety when she would sit at her loom without weaving and sigh. The women bickered among themselves with the fretful irritation of caged animals. And once or twice a week, like a water-wheel turning against its will, Lord Hugo would come to the women's chamber, bearing a jug of mead.

The evening would start merrily enough, with the women dancing and Lady Catherine in a flutter of excitement. Hugo would drink deep, his jokes would grow more bawdy. He would grab Eliza if she was within reach and fondle her openly, before his wife and the other ladies. Then he would up-end the jug and fling it towards the fireplace, take Lady Catherine by her wrist and drag her off to the bedchamber. As the women tidied the room, sweeping up the broken pottery and setting the glasses to one side on the cupboard, they would hear Catherine's loud shrieks of pain and then her gasping unrestrained sobs of pleasure. At two in the morning, without fail, Hugo would loose his wife from the rope of linen which he always tied around them, and stagger, blear-eyed and foul-tempered, for his own bed.

'Tisn't natural,' Eliza said one night to Alys. The candle was out, they were lying in the dark. In the other corners of the room they could hear the quiet breathing of Mistress Allingham and a rumbling snore from Ruth. Eliza had long ceased to laugh at the antics of Lord Hugo and his lady. All the women were appalled at the turn the two had taken.

'Did you hear her this evening?' Eliza asked. 'I reckon she's bewitched. It isn't natural for a woman to beg for a man like she does. And she lets him do anything he wishes to her.'

'Hush,' Alys said. 'It's her way. And she'll sleep well tonight and be sweet-tempered in the morning. And soon we'll know if she's in foal.'

'Whelping,' Eliza said with a sleepy giggle. 'But it isn't natural, Alys. I've seen bruises on her that he's made with his belt. And when I showed them to her she gave me a smile ...' She paused. 'A horrid sort of smile,' she said inadequately. 'As if she was proud.'

Alys said nothing more and soon Eliza was breathing deeply, sprawled out across Alys' side of the bed. For an hour Alys lay sleepless in the darkness, watching the cold finger of moonlight move across the ceiling, listening to Eliza's snuffling snores. Then she slipped quietly from the bed and went out to the gallery, and threw a couple of logs on the fire, and a handful of pine twigs.

The twigs spurted little flames and a sharp resinous scent filled the room. Alys sniffed at it and sat down on the warm fleece before the fire to watch the flames.

The castle was wrapped in utter winter darkness and utter night-time silence. Alys felt she was the only being awake or even alive in the whole world. The embers of the fire formed into little castles and caverns. Alys stared deep into their red glow, trying to make out shapes, pictures. The sweet tangy scent of the burning pine reminded her of Mother Hildebrande and her quiet study where the little fire had been made of pine cones. Alys used to sit at her feet and lean against her knees while reading, and sometimes Mother Hildebrande would rest her hand gently on Alys' head and lean forward to explain a word, or chuckle tolerantly at a mispronunciation.

'What a clever girl,' she would say in her soft voice. 'What a clever girl you are, my daughter Ann!'

Alys took the sleeve of her nightshift and rubbed at her eyes. 'I won't think of her,' she said into the silence of the room. 'I must go on not thinking of her, stopping myself thinking of her. I will be without her now. Without her, forever.'

She thought instead of Morach and the cold dark little cottage at the foot of the moor. Morach's hovel would be up to the eaves in snow by now. Alys grimaced remembering the long, dark, winter days, and the ceaseless unrewarding labour of digging out a track from door to midden to carry the slops.

'Whatever I am doing now,' she whispered, 'whatever it costs me – it is better than that life. Mother Hildebrande would know that. She would understand that. She would know that even though I'm very deep in sin ... she would know ...' Alys broke off. She knew that the abbess would never have accepted an argument which said that hardship justified a sinner in one sin after another, down to the very doors of hell itself.

'I won't think of her,' Alys said again.

She sat in silence for a little while, then the fire shifted and roused her from her daydream. She tossed a little log on to the soft embers at the back and watched it glow and then blacken and flame.

Very quietly behind her, the door of Lady Catherine's bedroom opened and Hugo came out. He was wearing only breeches, his chest and back bare, carrying his boots, his shirt and his doublet. He checked in surprise when he saw Alys, so still at the fireside. Then he came on.

'Alys,' he said.

'Hugo,' she replied. She did not move her head to look at him, she had not started at the sound of a voice in an empty room.

'Did you know I was there?' he asked.

'I always know when you are near,' Alys said. Her voice was dreamy. Hugo felt himself shiver as he came near her, as if all around her was some circle of deep power.

'I have not seen you for days,' he said. 'I have not seen you, to speak with, since the night of your ordeal.'

Alys thought of the purse on her girdle with the little figures still safe inside, stuffed under her pallet in her room. She thought of the blinded model of Hugo knocking and rubbing against the fat belly and cavernous slit of the doll of Catherine.

'No,' she said.

'You lied, didn't you?' Hugo asked gently. 'When you told them that you were hot for me, and that you had made up a false prophecy to snare me?'

Alys shrugged as if it hardly mattered. 'That was a lie, but I don't know the truth,' she said slowly. 'I truly cannot remember that night. I remember you carrying me from the hall but that is all. After that it was just sleep.'

Hugo nodded. 'So you did not desire me?' he asked. 'You were lying when you said it. You did not desire me then and you do not desire me now?'

Alys turned her head and looked at him. One side of her face was rosy with firelight, the other side in flickering shadow. Hugo felt the breath catch in his throat.

'Oh yes,' she said softly. 'I desire you. I have wanted you, I think, since the moment I first saw you. I came into the great hall and your face was graven deep with hard lines – and then I saw you smile. I fell in love with you then, in that instant, for the joy in your smile. I hate her being with you, I hate the thought of you touching her. I cannot sleep when I know you are with her. And I dream of you, constantly. Oh yes, I desire you.'

'Alys,' Hugo breathed. He put out his hand to touch her cheek, cupped his palm around her face as if she were a rare and lovely flower. 'My Alys,' he said.

Alys hissed an indrawn breath. 'Can you feel me?' she asked. She took his hand from her cheek and examined it carefully.

'Are you telling my fortune?' Hugo asked, amused.

Alys turned the hand over and looked at the clean short fingernails. She turned the hand back and looked at the perfect idiosyncratic whorls on the fingertips.

'Can you feel me?' she asked again. 'Can you feel my touch?'

'Of course,' Hugo said, puzzled.

'With every fingertip? With every one?' she asked.

He laughed a little. 'Of course,' he said. The words spilled out from him as if he had held them back for too long. 'My little love, my Alys, of course I can feel your touch. I have waited and waited for you to reach out your hand to mine. Of course I can feel you!'

'When I whisper, like this,' Alys said, hardly breathing the words, 'can you hear me?'

'Yes,' Hugo said, surprised. 'Of course I can. My hearing is good, Alys, you know that.'

Alys put her hand out to his face and stroked with infinite tenderness his eyelids and the delicate lined skin around his dark eyes.

'Can you see me?' she asked. 'Can you see as well as you ever did?'

'Yes,' Hugo said. 'What is this, Alys? Are you afraid I am ill?'

Alys clasped her hands in her lap and looked back towards the fire.

'No,' she said. 'It is nothing. I thought for a time that I wanted you blind and deaf to me. I know now, this night, that is not true. It never was true. Maybe my desire for you is stronger than anything else. Maybe my desire for you is stronger than my wish for safety.

Perhaps even stronger than . . .' She broke off. 'Anything else,' she said weakly.

Hugo frowned. 'What "else"?' he asked. 'What d'you mean "anything else"? Is it some herbalism or some old women's trickery?'

Alys nodded. 'I wanted you to look away from me,' she said. 'I feared Lady Catherine's jealousy. After that time – when she made me take the ordeal – I knew she would catch me at something, force me to some test. And sooner or later I would fail.'

Hugo nodded. 'And so you cast some silly girl's spell to keep me away from you, did you?' he asked, half amused. 'You must despair of your powers, Alys. For here I am, seeing you, touching you, hearing you and desiring you.'

Alys glowed in the darkness like a pearl suddenly opened to the light.

Hugo chuckled. 'Of course,' he said easily. 'What other end could there be between you and me? I love you. I looked down the hall and saw you in that red gown which was too big for you, and your poor shorn head and your clear little face and your night-blue eyes and I wanted to take you and bed you at once. And I have waited and waited for the lust to pass – and instead of passing it has become love.

'I would have had you that night – Twelfth Night. I would have taken you when you were drunk and you could neither refuse nor consent. But when I touched you I saw you smile, and you said my name as though we had been lovers for years. And as soon as you did – I wanted that. I didn't want to take you like a whore. I didn't want to force you. I want to make a life with you like that. I don't believe you have the Sight. I don't believe in that stuff. I don't fear you are a witch or a magician or any of that silly mountebank stuff. But I do believe in a life for the two of us. No – three of us. Me, you and my child: a son for me.'

Alys was silent for a moment. She looked again at his fingertips and then she put out her hand to his face and gently touched the soft skin around his eyes.

'And your wife?' she asked softly.

'None of her business,' Hugo said promptly. 'What you and I are to each other is none of her business. Besides, she's well served these days. Soon she must conceive.'

Alys turned her face towards him and looked steadily at him. 'And why is that?' she asked.

Hugo shrugged. 'Because I go to her,' he said impatiently.

'And why is that?' Alys asked again.

'I don't . . .' Hugo stopped the sentence short. 'D'you think it's your doing, Alys?' he asked, near to laughing.

Alys glanced behind her at the darkened room and at Lady Catherine's chamber where the woman lay asleep, smiling even in her sleep at his abuse of her; bruised, drained, satisfied.

'I don't know!' she said sharply. 'I can't tell! How would I know? I'm not trained in the black arts, I know nothing more than I saw old Morach do, up on the moor, to frighten stupid women out of their money. I don't know why you lie with her. Nor do I know why you hurt her and abuse her. It disgusts me, Hugo. I don't know why it should be like that between you two. I would not have made it like that between any man and woman – not even if I hated her. I hexed you to lie with her – I admit that! But I did not plan that you should beat her and spit on her and force her into abominable acts. I did not plan that she should love you for it!'

'I don't know why it is like that,' Hugo conceded. He moved to sit closer to Alys and laid his arm around her shoulder. She leaned towards him. 'It disgusts me too,' he said, his voice very low. 'I've never treated any woman like that – not the poorest whore. But something in me drives me to slap her and ride her and whisper curses to her . . . ' he broke off. 'And the more I do, the worse I am, the more she adores it.'

He shook his head. 'It sickens me to my soul in the morning,' he said. 'And I can only touch her when I am drunk. Alys, you should see her. She lies before me and begs me to hurt her in any way I please. It makes me feel . . . fouled.'

Alys nodded. 'I made a spell that you would give her a son,' she said softly. 'I am sorry that I touched you. I'm sorry that I made such a spell. I felt driven to it, I did not know what else to do to make myself safe here. I wanted my power. But now I wish I had not done it, Hugo.'

'D'you think it is your magic which is driving her?' Hugo looked from the fire to Alys' clear profile. He kissed her temple where a tendril of golden hair curled. 'I don't think it is your spell, my lovely Alys. I think Catherine's tastes have always been for pain. She was hot for our marriage even though she knew I did not care for her. She has always begged me to lie with her, even when we were quite little children. She has always allowed me to abuse her. It has never been as bad as this before. But I have never felt so angry with her before. I never felt constrained before now.'

'Constrained?' Alys asked.

Hugo nodded. 'You know why,' he said. 'Your safety lies in her conceiving. You cannot stay here with her waiting to trap you. She has to be satisfied. You were driven to your little spell, I am driven to lie with her. I know she has to be satisfied for her to leave you alone.'

'The spell made no difference?' Alys asked. She turned and looked at him and he saw her face lightening as if he was taking some guilt away from her.

'No difference at all,' he said honestly. 'It is all nonsense, and you should not fear your power like this. I am acting as I wish. I am doing what I decide. I am doing my duty by Catherine as I should have done long before. I do it without desire, so I do it drunk and cruelly. And she – by some twist in her own appetites – likes me to be drunk and harsh with her. So she is well served. There is no magic in it.'

Alys gave a little sigh. 'I have been afraid,' she admitted. 'I was afraid it was all my doing, and the ugliness and the bitterness of my spell had made you ugly and bitter with her.'

Hugo gathered her into his arms and settled her on his lap, his arms around her, her cheek against his.

'Fear nothing,' he said. 'I want a future for us. But I don't believe in magic and all the old spells and fears. It is a new world we are building, Alys. A world free of superstition and fear. A world we can explore, full of new lands and adventures, full of wealth and opportunity. Don't cling to old dark ways, Alys. Come out with me into the light and put that all behind you.'

Alys turned her face to him and laid her cheek against the warm stubble of his chin.

'You are so strange,' she said with half a smile. She pulled back and touched his face, her fingers tracing the lines around his eyes, the deep cleft between his eyebrows. 'You are so strange to me and yet I feel I have known you all my life.'

'My friend, Lord Stanwick, told me I was cunt-struck!' Hugo said with a low laugh. 'I was drinking with him the other day and I told him I loved a girl so much that I was in danger of a breach with my wife, with my father, and with my duty. He laughed till he wept and said he must meet you. He could hardly believe in the existence of a girl who could turn me from hunting and whoring and scheming for the future.'

Alys smiled. 'And you?' she asked. 'Are you – what d'you call it? Cunt-struck? Or is it something real which will last?'

He tightened his grip around her. 'It will last till I die,' he said simply. 'You have my heart, Alys, I am yours till death.'

Alys stirred at once. 'Don't say that!' she said. 'Don't speak of death! I want us to live forever, I want us to be young forever. I want this night to last forever!'

He laughed. 'God! You're fey, Alys. We will love while we are young, and while we are old, and then we will grow older and die and go to heaven and be two angels together. What is there to fear in that? Did you think I might go to hell for my few little sins? I have confessed! I am cleared! And you can never have sinned in your life. Not with a face as clear and as sweet as yours. Not my little maid Alys.'

Alys hesitated. She wanted to tell him of the abbey, of the smoke, of her panic in the firelit darkness. She wanted to tell him that she had run from her sisters and left them to burn. She wanted to tell him that she had once loved someone and been beloved. That she was not truly an orphan for she had been held and taught and loved by a mother. And that she had betrayed her and then denied her. Left to die in her sleep, shrouded with smoke, eaten alive by flames.

'What is it?' he asked.

222

'Nothing,' she said.

She did not dare.

'Will you surrender your magic?' he asked. 'The little spells and charms?'

Alys hesitated. 'Why d'you ask it of me? You keep the things that give you power – your weapons, your wealth. My magic is all the power I have. it keeps me safe here.'

Hugo shook his head. 'It does nothing except frighten you and make you feel that all the world's sins are at your door,' he said roundly. 'Keep your herbs and your crystal and your real skills, the ones you have used to make my father well. Keep your medicines and throw away your spells, Alys. There is real danger for you when you play with them. Not because they are true – for they are nothing but nonsense to frighten peasants! – but because they give your enemies a handle on you. Throw away the magic and keep the medicine.'

'All right,' Alys said reluctantly. 'I agree. Unless I have need of them, unless I have need of that power, I will stop.' She thought of the figures in her purse, stuffed deep in the mattress in her room. 'I never know whether it works or not,' she said honestly. 'I was sure I had hexed you and Catherine, and now you tell me it is your own tastes.'

He nodded. 'We were always like that,' he said. 'No spell on earth could make me use a woman so if it were not to her taste as well as mine.'

'I will throw it away,' Alys said. 'I should never have started but for that ordeal. I was afraid and I wanted some power – at any price.'

Hugo tightened his arm around her shoulders. 'Don't be frightened,' he said, his voice low. 'I love you, I will protect you. You have my power around you now.'

He took her hand and turned it palm upward. As if he were sealing a bond he planted a kiss in the centre and folded her fingers over. She took his hand to do the same for him. She kissed each fingertip one by one, as if to bless them, as if to keep them whole. Then they sat by the fire until the darkness of the arrow-slits started showing pale.

'I must go,' Hugo said.

Alys held her face up for his farewell kiss. He took it in both hands and kissed her lips, and then very gently, both eyelids. 'Sleep,' he said and his voice held a tenderness she had never heard from him before. 'Sleep and dream again of the time I will be with you night and day and no one will come between us.'

'Soon,' Alys whispered.

'I swear it,' Hugo said.

'I want to be your wife, Hugo,' Alys said softly. 'I want to belong here, as you do, without question. And I want to have your son, as I said in my dream.'

He chuckled. 'Marriage is something else, my darling,' he said softly. 'You and I were made to be lovers, we should be together. But marriage is business: land, property, dowry. Not for lovers like us. I want you to freely love me, to freely be mine. Not marriage, my darling, but long nights and days of love; and a son for me. Now sleep and dream of it.'

He kissed her again and went from the room. Alys stayed for a moment, listening to his soft steps down the stair and then went into the women's room and quietly closed the door.

She looked swiftly around. None of them had stirred, they were still all four deeply asleep. Noiselessly she crossed to her pallet on the floor and fumbled among the straw, pushing her arm deep into the bed. At last she found it and drew out the little purse with the three candlewax figures. She threw her cloak around her shoulders and went, barefoot, to the door.

The stone stairs beneath her feet were icy cold. She passed like a ghost out of the doorway and towards the gate which guarded the drawbridge. The soldiers were sleeping, there was no danger to watch for. Alys tiptoed across the bridge, her feet numb, and went to the moat-side.

She thrust her hand deep into her purse and pulled out the first doll she found. It was the Lady Catherine doll, grotesquely ugly with its monstrous sexuality and bursting belly. Alys shuddered as she held it in her hand and then she tossed it into the moat.

She had expected it to sink, to sink down into the green water and disappear. No one ever drained the moat, no one fished with nets. All sorts of rubbish and offal were thrown into it every day. Alys had thought the little dolls would sink to the bottom and no one would ever find them. Or if they did, the wax would be blurred and broken, and no one would ever think they were anything but candles, wastefully dropped by some negligent servant.

The little wax doll sank beneath the freezing water, and then, as Alys watched, it bobbed up again. Lady Catherine's mocking, ugly smile stared at Alys. The little candlewax eyes looked at her.

'No!' Alys cried aloud. 'Get down.'

An icy breeze rippled across the moat. The wax doll bobbed in the waves. The face of Lady Catherine seemed to smile as if she was enjoying Alys' fear.

'Sink, damn you!' Alys dropped to her knees on the frozen bank, leaning out towards the bobbing doll. 'Sink down! Go down!'

The fitful little wind blew the doll closer inshore.

'Go down!' Alys breathed. 'Drown!'

At once she caught herself. 'Oh God! I didn't mean that!' she said. In a frenzy of sudden anxiety she reached out towards the little doll. 'I meant the doll to sink, that's all!' she said, as if she were explaining herself to the darkness all around her. 'I didn't mean drown. I just want to be rid of it.'

The breeze was taking the doll away. At the same moment Alys heard someone hammering on the outer gate: servants coming to work, demanding admission.

Alys bunched up her nightshift in one hand and stepped into the glassy cold water. She gasped at the icy touch and reached out towards the little doll. It bobbed out further, just beyond her reach.

'I've got to get it,' she said.

She gritted her teeth and stepped out a little deeper. The water was swirling around her knees. Her feet were aching to the very bones with the cold. Something slimy and icy flickered across her calf. 'I've got to get it,' she said again.

The doll bobbed out further. Her little waxen white head turned away from Alys as if she were obstinate, as if she were playful.

'Come here,' Alys said. She clamped her teeth together to stop them from chattering, the cold seemed to be eating away at her feet, her legs, and now up to her thighs as she stepped further out.

The little doll bobbed in the winter dawn breeze and the face turned back to Alys. The doll was smiling at her.

Alys took one step further out and the little doll's smile widened as if it were about to burst into tinkling, malicious laughter. Her little arms came out above the water, she reached towards Alys. Alys stretched, her fingers just fractions of an inch away from the little wax hands. Alys took one more step forward and then stumbled on the greasy rubbish of the underwater bank of the moat. She heard the doll's tiny peal after peal of laughter as the steep side of the moat suddenly plunged downwards and fell away beneath her feet. Enticed into the depths of the moat Alys dropped like a stone into the slimy icy water, her scream cut short as water rushed into her mouth. Her hand closed over the little doll, her other hand was clenched on the purse. She thrashed helplessly in the water.

Alys had never learned to swim, she sank and then bobbed up gasping for air in a frenzy of panic. When her face broke free of the water she snatched at a breath but then choked helplessly and felt herself going down again.

The cold was her enemy. The icy green waters of the moat were eating her, her legs had gone numb and her thrashing thighs were powerless. Deep in her belly the cold moved in. Alys sank beneath the water and came up, coughing and retching. She opened her mouth to scream and a wave of icy green water swept into her face.

'No!' Alys cried out. She snatched for a breath but it was water she gobbled and it rushed into her lungs and weighed her down, thrust her under the surface. Alys choked and retched and breathed in a lungful of water. Then suddenly there were a pair of hard hands on her arm, and then under her armpit.

'Got you, wench,' a voice said from far away.

Painfully, Alys was dragged from the water and beached, whooping and vomiting on the bridge.

'There, lass, there,' the man said.

He flung his cape around her and rubbed her roughly, drying her and warming her at the same time.

'Holloa!' he shouted towards the guardroom. 'Let us in!'

He scooped Alys into his arms and carried her into the guardroom where a frowsy-faced lad threw open the door. 'Lass tried to drown herself,' he said tersely. 'Get some hot mead for her, quickly. And a sheet to wrap her in. And another cloak.'

The lad went running. Alys, hidden in the man's cloak, retching and vomiting, fumbled with her shift and thrust the dangerous little doll into her purse with the others.

The man held her. Water poured from Alys' mouth, she wept moat water, she pissed wetness into the wet shift, and her urine was as icy as the rest.

The man thumped her hard on the back and Alys struggled for breath, caught a gulp of air and then vomited a basin of water.

'Head down,' he said.

Water gushed from Alys' nose, her hair stuck like waterweed to her icy face. Remorselessly he held her, head down, until she had stopped choking, then he lifted her upright and thrust her into the chair and chafed her hands.

The lad burst in with a steaming jug and a billowing sheet.

'Good,' the man said. 'Wait outside.'

He ripped Alys' nightshift from hem to collar and rubbed her body hard with the warm sheet. Her skin was rough with gooseflesh and her feet and fingers were blue. From thigh to ankle she was bleeding sluggishly from a hundred little cuts and scratches from the rubbish in the moat. Then the man wrapped her tight in his thick cloak, sat her in the chair, and held a mug of hot mead to her mouth.

Alys twisted away. The liquid was scalding. But he held her again and forced her to drink. It went down her sore throat like liquid fire.

'Here, don't I know you?' the man asked.

Alys blinked up at him. Her teeth were chattering so badly and she was shivering so hard she could hardly make him out.

'Father Stephen,' she said, when she recognized the priest. 'It's me, Alys. Lady Catherine's woman. Lord Hugh's clerk.'

'More mead,' the priest commanded. He handed her the mug and Alys wrapped her hands around it. She was shuddering with deep chilled shivers.

'Drink it,' he said. 'I insist. It'll drive out the cold. You're looking better already.'

Alys nodded. 'I'm grateful you were there,' she said.

He frowned. 'Why did you do it?' he asked gently. 'It's a painful death, a nasty way to go. And hell at the end of it, for sure.'

Alys nearly denied it, then she caught herself.

'I was afraid,' she improvised quickly. 'After the ordeal . . . Lady Catherine is suspicious of me . . . I am afraid of another ordeal, or another. She can make what claims she wishes against me. I could not sleep in the night and then I woke full of dread. I did not know what to do.'

Her teeth chattered as if denying the lie. Alys clenched them on the mug and sipped.

He looked distraught. 'Child, I had no idea,' he said. 'I am to blame for this! I had no idea that the lady's personal vengeance against you went so deep. I would never have allowed an ordeal to satisfy mortal malice!

It's a sin to use the ordeal to pay some grudge. I should have known! And to drive you to despair!' He broke off and took two swift strides down the room.

Alys pushed her hand through her hair and squeezed out some of the icy water. She watched him, trying to measure his mood and the extent of her danger.

'You must confess,' he said. 'Confess and pray for the sin of attempting to take your life. It is a mortal sin, God forbids it by name. You must wrestle with your despair and your fear. And I will also ask you to forgive me. I have been too rigorous. I have sought for wrong-doing too eagerly. It is a sin.' He thought for a moment. 'It is the sin of vanity,' he said. 'I have been proud of my record of witch-taking, of hunting heresy. Many have come before me and few have escaped justice. But I must guard against pride.'

'I am innocent,' Alys said eagerly. 'And I was afraid that Catherine would force me to another ordeal. That you would support her and question me. And that some mistake – some innocent mistake – would mean my death.'

He nodded, stricken. 'I have been at fault,' he said. 'I am glad to be a scourge to the wicked, but not to an innocent like you. You must forgive me. I will never set an ordeal for you again. You can have my word. I will protect you against malice. You have proved your innocence, once with the ordeal of bread, and once in the moat. For if you were a witch you would have floated and you were assuredly drowning when I hauled you out.'

Alys nodded, and wrapped the cloak a little tighter around her. Father Stephen caught the movement and handed her another cup of mead. 'Drink,' he said. 'And then you must go to your chamber and make sure you are warm and dry. Fear no more, you are safe from any ordeal ever again. I will never try you and no one will ever test you while I am near to protect you. You were drowning like a Christian, you are no witch.'

Alys nodded again, a small gleam of satisfaction hidden behind the mug.

'Will Lady Catherine be awake? Will she trouble you with questions when you go to your chamber?'

Alys glanced at the slit window of the guardroom. It was grey with the winter dawn. 'She may,' she said. 'She is suspicious of all her women. I have more freedom than the others because I serve the old lord. But she watches us close, and she fears all of us.'

Father Stephen nodded. 'She has much to fear, poor lady,' he said. 'Hugo does not always use her kindly and the old lord is weary of her complaints. He has asked me to speak to my bishop about having her set aside and the marriage annulled.'

Alys felt her interest quicken. 'Can your bishop decide?' she asked.

Father Stephen glanced quickly behind them to see that they were not overheard. 'Of course not!' he said. 'The King is the supreme head of the Church. All matrimonial decisions go before the Church Court and finally to him. But the young lord and Catherine are in close cousinhood, and their grandparents were cousins also. I daresay it could be argued that the marriage was invalid.'

Alys drew a little breath. 'If you were to recommend it, would the bishop do as you advised?' she asked.

Father Stephen smiled. 'I have a degree of influence with His Grace,' he said smugly. 'But I have not yet decided what advice I should give. I have to pray and think on it, Alys. I am Hugo's friend, but in this I have to be God's man before any other claim.'

Alys nodded sympathetically. 'It is a heavy responsibility for you, Father Stephen,' she said. Her face was turned up to him, her dark eyes guileless. 'It would be so wonderful if you could get the young lord released,' she said. 'The castle would be a happier place! And Lady Catherine would be spared the pain she suffers now.'

Father Stephen nodded. 'Marriage is a sacrament,' he said. 'It lasts until God ends it – unless it was invalid from the first. There can be no argument about suiting a man's or a woman's whim.'

Alys nodded. 'But no one knows what my lady endures,' she said. 'Dreadful acts against her. And she so deep in sin that she glories in them like a beast.'

Father Stephen looked appalled. 'That should stop,' he said. 'Whatever the means, I should stop that. That is mortal sin.

'Here!' he said, breaking off. 'You are shivering. Get to your chamber and some dry clothes.'

Alys turned to go.

'Alys,' he said hesitantly. She turned. 'Swear that you will never think to kill yourself again,' he said. 'It is an awful sin, the most dreadful sin. And it would lead you to a terrible judgement and an eternity in hell. An eternity, Alys! Think of it.'

Alys bowed her head, the sodden purse with the magic dolls safe in her blue hands. 'I do think of it, Father,' she said dully. Then she turned and went.

Twelve

In the warm chamber the women were still asleep. Alys cast off the cloak and crept naked into bed. She stuffed the sodden purse with the candle dolls beneath her pillow, and pushed her damp hair away from her face. Then she slept and dreamed of the castle as her own, her own ladies calling her Lady Alys, and Hugo's warm body sleeping beside her. She turned in her sleep and said his name very softly, and smiled. Even when Eliza roughly shook her awake Alys stayed within the joyful confidence of her dream. She smiled at Eliza. He loves me, Alys thought. He loves me and he has promised to find a way for us to be together.

'My lady wants you,' Eliza said dourly. 'She's shouting for you, complaining you're late. Best make haste.'

Alys shook off her lazy contentment, jumped out of bed, threw on her dark blue gown and stuffed her hair in a dark blue cap, and fled across the gallery to Lady Catherine's bedroom.

'My lady?' she asked as she opened the door.

Catherine was sitting up in bed, her fine linen shift torn beyond mending at the front, her bedding rumpled.

'Alys,' she said and bared her yellow teeth in a smile. 'Alys, I have need of your skills.'

'Of course, Lady Catherine,' Alys said evenly. 'What may I do for you?'

'I think I am with child,' Catherine said. She gleamed at Alys. 'Hardly surprising I suppose!'

Alys nodded, saying nothing.

'My lord has been insatiable these last weeks,' Catherine said. She licked her lips like a gourmet savouring a dish. 'It seems he cannot leave me alone. And now he has put me with child.'

'I am very happy,' Alys said thinly.

'Are you?' Catherine taunted. 'Are you really? I find that surprising, Alys. I thought you hoped for a little of Lord Hugo's attentions yourself! But he has had eyes for no one but me. Isn't that true?'

'I know he has been much with you, my lady,' Alys said. She could feel anger rising up in her and the blood drumming softly in her head. 'All your ladies have been aware that my lord has visited you often. We are all glad for your happiness.'

Lady Catherine's laugh rippled out into the chamber. 'I'll warrant,' she said nastily. 'And you, Alys? Have you given up all hope of him looking your way?'

'Yes,' Alys lied easily. 'I am here to serve the Lord Hugh as his clerk and his herbalist when he needs me. When he has finished with my services I will return to my home. I am a servant to his son, and to you, my lady. Nothing more.'

Catherine nodded. 'Yes,' she said, underlining the point. 'You are Hugo's servant. He might use you or throw you aside. It does not matter.'

Alys curtsied in silence.

'He can have you if he wishes,' Catherine said simply. 'It does not matter now. I have been jealous of you and I was afraid you would take him from me. But now I am with child no one can take him from me. He can lie with you if he pleases, he can take his pleasure on you or desert you. But I have won him, Alys. Do you understand? He is mine now. I am the mother of his child. And neither the old lord nor Hugo will think of you as anything but a diversion.'

Alys kept her gaze down on the floor. When Catherine fell silent she looked briefly up.

'Do you understand?' Catherine asked.

Alys nodded. She could not speak, she was willing the news to be untrue. She was willing Catherine to be barren, to stay barren. She did not need Catherine to tell her that if Hugo had a legitimate heir then Catherine had won and Hugo's soft-voiced promises of last night would be set to one side.

'I have need of you,' Lady Catherine said in a different tone. 'My own mother is dead as you know, and I have no women friends to advise me. My old wet-nurse died last year and there is no one in the castle who can tell me how to care for myself and the health of the child. Lord Hugh swears you are skilled with herbs, the best healer he has ever known. I expect you to care for my health and advise me. And I will expect you to deliver my child. I want a son, Alys. You will be responsible.'

Alys moved a little closer to the high bed. 'My lady, you need a physician and a midwife,' she said. 'I have had some experience in childbirth but for your health and the health of an heir you should have a physician.'

Catherine shrugged. 'Nearer the time I shall have one attend me,' she said arrogantly. 'But in the meantime I shall have your advice and your constant attendance. You have attended births, I suppose? You are skilled?'

Alys shook her head stubbornly. 'I am only sixteen,' she said. 'My Lord Hugh has been kind enough to trust to my herbs but he had thrown out his medical advisers and would see them no more. It pleased him to use me instead of them. But you have no quarrel with the wise women and midwives around the castle, my lady. You should speak with them.' She did not say that she would rather die than care for Catherine but the dislike between the two women was as tangible as Catherine's sprawling, half-naked body.

'What about that old woman at Bowes?' Catherine asked, prolonging the discussion for the pleasure of watching Alys' pale tense face and hearing Alys searching for excuses. 'Would she care for me well?'

Alys fell into the trap. 'My cousin Morach?' she asked. 'Oh yes, indeed. She is skilled. She has attended many births. She could come and see you at once and care for you. She is an excellent midwife.'

Catherine nodded. 'I'll have you both then,' she said in careless triumph. 'I'll send the soldiers to take Morach up. She can live with us here. She can guard my health and you can both serve me. I shall have you wait on me night and day, Alys. And now I want you to look at me and tell me. Am I with child? Is it a boy?'

Alys dipped a curtsey, hiding her anger and her fear, and went to fetch her little bundle from the women's room.

'What did she want you for?' Eliza demanded as soon as she stepped in the door. 'Is she foul today? Hugo stayed with her all night, did he not?'

'I don't know,' Alys said. 'He's not with her now. She's full of joy. She thinks she's with child. I am to confirm it.'

The other women exclaimed, Eliza's eyes grew round. 'At last,' she said. 'Hugo's done his duty at last.'

'Yes,' Alys said drily. 'Praise be. And what an act of love it was!'

'Is it true?' Eliza asked. 'She's had false alarms before. And if ever spite could stop a baby settling then she would be the one to do it.'

236

'I doubt it's true,' Alys said. 'She has every reason to lie. But I'll tell her "yes" or "no". And I'll tell the old lord too. If she is lying, I will tell him at once.'

'Hush!' Ruth said instantly. 'Go along, Alys, she'll be waiting for you. Shall I come too?'

'Yes,' Alys said. 'She's been scratching at me until I am heartsore. Come with me, Ruth, and she'll mind her tongue.'

'What are you going to do?' Ruth asked curiously as Alys took the prayer-book and the crystal from her bundle.

'I shall see if I can dowse for a baby,' Alys said easily. 'Don't look so amazed, Ruth, it's a common enough skill.'

She led the way back into Lady Catherine's room. Catherine was looking at herself in a beaten silver hand-mirror.

'What is this mark on my neck?' she asked Alys.

Alys looked a little closer. 'It is a bruise, my lady,' she said evenly. She could see the marks of teeth. He had bitten her and sucked her. Hugo had done this.

Catherine sighed luxuriously. 'How could it have come there?' she asked innocently. 'What sort of bruise, Alys?'

'A bite,' Alys said briefly.

'Ohh,' Catherine sighed. 'I had forgotten. That was Hugo. He snatches at me and he bites me and sucks me as if he would eat me up. We will have a lion, not a son, Alys! For he mounts me like a lion!'

Alys nodded coolly, but her cheeks were scarlet. Catherine did not miss the signs of jealousy. She rarely missed anything.

'Are you a virgin still, Alys?' she asked. 'I could forward the match we spoke of. The young soldier is still willing. I should hate to think of you becoming old and dried-up and unloved. To have a man mad for you is a wonderful thing, Alys. When Hugo comes to my bed I feel as if I am a queen. And when he takes me in his arms and covers my whole body with his kisses! I can't tell you, Alys, how it feels! It is a pleasure so deep that it feels wicked – like a mortal sin.'

Alys felt her anger rising like vomit in her throat. 'You are blessed in your love, my lady,' she said. 'Now can you tell me when you last had your times?'

Catherine frowned at the interruption. 'Five, no, six weeks ago,' she said.

'Are you at all sick?' Alys asked.

Catherine shook her head.

'Are your breasts tender or enlarged?' Alys asked. She felt her cheeks stinging with heat as she forced herself to speak coolly about Hugo's love-making with his wife – the fat sow, Alys said inwardly.

Catherine laughed. 'Of course they are tender!' she said rejoicingly. She opened her shift so Alys could see her. Her large, brown-tipped breasts were marked on both sides with thin red strips, like little lines of blood blisters.

Ruth gasped. 'Are you hurt, my lady?' she asked.

Catherine closed her eyes, revelling in the memory. 'Oh, he hurt me,' she said, her voice very low. 'He bound me, and tied me, and mounted me from behind.'

She opened her eyes; they were dark with remembered desire. 'Don't you wish he would do that to you, Alys?' she asked. 'Wouldn't you love him to cover you? To mount you like a wild stallion on a willing mare?'

Alys cleared her throat. Her mouth was suddenly very dry. 'No, my lady,' she said simply. 'The ordeal you forced on me has cleared my head as well as my character. I no longer look for the young lord. In any case,' she said icily, 'my tastes do not run that way. I should never revel in pain.

'Now, I shall lay my hand on your belly and see if I can dowse for a baby, my lady,' she said. 'It is the same as water-divining, many people do it. There is nothing to fear.'

Catherine nodded, irritated at the coolness of Alys' voice. 'I fear nothing,' she said. 'No one can hurt me but him.'

Alys took out the prayer-book and muttered a few words of nonsense in Latin. She did not dare to bless the work as she used to do. The memory of the fragile communion wafer which had to be torn into pieces like skin before it could burn was still very bright. She dared not invoke the name of the Lord or His Mother. But she waved the prayer-book around and whispered low so that no one could say later that she had done the work unblessed.

She touched Lady Catherine's round belly with her icy small hands and noticed with malicious satisfaction how the slack flesh quivered to her touch.

'This woman is with child,' she said aloud. The crystal revolved in a lazy right-hand arc. Alys bit her lip and tasted her own blood, as warm and salty as a tear. Catherine was pregnant.

'What does it say? What does it say?' Catherine asked.

'You may be with child,' Alys said slowly. She longed with all her heart to deny the child. But nothing would stop it growing in Catherine's fat belly. It could not be wished away.

'Ask if it's a son!' Catherine demanded.

'The child is male?' Alys asked.

The crystal swung again.

Catherine gave a little delighted crow. 'Is that yes? Is that yes?' she demanded.

Alys nodded.

'Send for the young lord!' she said to Ruth. 'You stay here,' she said to Alys. 'He may want you.'

Alys gathered up her crystal and prayer-book and went over to the window. Outside a brisk wind was blowing, bringing snow down from the moor. The little herb and flower garden of the inner manse below was drifting with whiteness, snow swirling between Alys in the second storey and the frozen ground below. Out on the moors Morach's cottage would be white, with great drifts banked up against the door. If it snowed hard and long the soldiers from the castle would not be able to get through. Alys had a great longing to be out there, in the cold and loneliness of the moor. Anything rather than be here, in this little hot room with this spiteful, corrupt woman, and with the man she loved obeying his wife's bidding.

Hugo walked in without knocking. Catherine did not cover herself. Her shift was open, her breasts splayed wide, her belly showing. The fine linen sheet of her bed only half covered the bush of hair. She looked at Hugo as if she expected him to start love-making again, before Alys, before Ruth.

'You sent for me, lady?' he said tersely. He did not look at Alys.

'I have some news for you,' she said. She patted her bed. 'Come and sit a little closer.'

Hugo made no move. 'Your pardon, Madam, but I cannot wait,' he said. 'I am riding out hunting today and they are waiting for me. If I delay, the horses will be chilled. There's a bitter wind.'

'Stay home then,' Catherine said invitingly. She shrugged down a little deeper in the bed. The nipples on her breasts had hardened at the sight of him. Alys found herself staring. 'I can find sport to amuse you here,' Catherine suggested.

Hugo nodded. 'Tonight, Madam,' he said. 'I have promised my father venison for his dinner next week. I must hunt it today.'

'I'll be quick then and tell you our news. I have good news for you. I am with child and Alys here thinks it is a boy.'

There was a stunned silence. Hugo still did not look at Alys.

'That is the best news I could hear,' he said levelly, his voice under tight control. 'I congratulate you, Madam. I hope we have a healthy son. And now I must go.'

'Where are you riding?' Catherine asked.

'Bowes Moor,' he said from the doorway.

'Oh, stop then!' she said, as if she had just thought of it. 'Stop, my lord. Go to Alys' kinswoman's cottage and bid her come to the castle. Send one of your men back with her. I need her skill, Alys needs her advice. Isn't that true, Alys?'

'Morach has greater skill than I,' Alys said. She did not look up from the floor. She knew Hugo was not looking at her. 'But you will have no need of her until the birth, my lady, in October. You should summon her then.'

'My lord would want me to take no chances with my health,' Catherine said positively.

Hugo shook his head. 'Whatever you wish, Madam. I can fetch her today. But perhaps she will not be ready to come.'

Catherine opened her pale eyes very wide in surprise. 'Then take her, my lord,' she said simply. 'If we agree that we need her, what else should we do?'

Hugo bowed. 'Very well, my lady,' he said and turned for the door again.

'You have not said good day to Alys,' Catherine said silkily. 'She will be indispensable to me now. You must treat her with courtesy, Hugo! Whatever jade's tricks she may have played in the past, she is my favourite lady-in-waiting now!'

With an effort he turned. He met Alys' inscrutable blue gaze.

'Of course,' he said coldly. 'Forgive me.' The lines at the roots of his brows and the corners of his mouth were deep. 'Good day, Alys.'

'Good day, Lord Hugo,' Alys replied. She felt a deep coldness as if the waters of the moat had seeped from her belly through all her limbs. There would be no chance of displacing Catherine now. There would be no annulment of the marriage, there would be no love-making in the big, well-lit chamber. Hugo would never sleep the night in comfort at her side. Catherine had won. And it was Alys' own magic that had helped her to it.

Hugo met Alys' eyes in one hard angry look, and then he turned and was out of the door before Lady Catherine could detain him any longer.

'Fetch my rose and cream gown, Alys,' Lady Catherine said contentedly. 'He loves me in that colour. And call a servant to bring hot water and hot sheets. I will have a bath. He loves me sweet-scented.'

Alys curtsied like a servant and did as she was bid.

Alys was surprised to find she was eager to see Morach.

She waited around the outer gateway for the soldiers who would bring Morach back from Bowes Moor. It was a bitterly cold afternoon, with a sulky half-light of dense greyness. The snow-bearing grey clouds lay belly-down over the grey forbidding walls of the castle. The mist in the moat was white-grey, the slivers of snow whirling constantly in the wind were the only source of light in the world. Alys wrapped her cloak closely around her and held her cold hands up inside her sleeves.

She heard them before she saw them. The rattle of hooves on the cobbles and then the hollow sound of them crossing the drawbridge. She stepped out of the archway as the man pulled his horse to a standstill and tossed the bundled Morach down as if he were glad to be rid of her.

'There, old lady!' he said. 'Have done spitting at me! Here's Alys come to greet you and to show you your quarters. Blame her for fetching you away from your smoky fireside. Don't blame me!'

'Hello, Morach,' Alys said.

Morach shook herself down and pulled her shawls around her bent shoulders.

'Alys,' she said. She looked at the girl critically, noting the strain on her white face.

'Hard times,' she said. It was not a question.

'I am sorry if they brought you against your will.' Alys said. 'It was Lady Catherine's idea and order. Not mine.'

Morach nodded. 'With child, is she?' she asked.

Alys nodded.

'It was the dolls did it?' Morach confirmed.

Alys drew Morach into the shelter of the wall and put her mouth close to her ear.

243

'I don't know,' she said. 'How can you tell? Hugo said he went to her for choice, but he never went to her like that before I did the spell. And there was something so . . . ' She broke off. 'Something very unnatural about the way they are together.'

'Unnatural?' Morach asked with a sharp laugh. 'Since when could you limit Nature, child? What d'you mean? That he mounts her like a dog? That he beats her? That he blows his hunting horn when he comes?'

Alys gave an involuntary giggle. 'Not that!' she said. 'But the rest. And he couples with her when they are tied together with a strip of linen. I tied the dolls together with a ribbon. D'you think this is my doing?'

Morach shrugged, stoical. 'Could be,' she said. 'Could be just his nature. Take me in, child, I am cold.'

Alys nodded at the guard and held Morach's arm and little bundle as she took her across the outer manse, over the inner drawbridge which spanned the ghostly, mist-filled moat, and across the dripping garden of the inner manse, then into the main body of the castle. She led Morach through the great hall without stopping, though Morach dawdled and looked all around her.

'Tell me of the household,' she said as Alys tugged her onward. 'This is Lord Hugh's hall?'

Alys nodded.

'I've been here before when I was a witness in a case of theft against Farmer Ruley,' Morach said. 'The old lord sat behind the table on his great carved chair.'

'He holds the quarterly court here,' Alys said tersely. 'And he has dinner and supper here.' She drew Morach up the steps to the dais and opened the tapestry at the rear of the little stage. 'This is where we come in,' she said. 'This lobby outside is where we wait for the lords and my lady if we are too early. Sometimes they gather here and talk.' She nodded to one doorway. 'This way leads to Lord Hugh's round tower where his room is, his soldiers, and where the young lord sleeps.' She drew Morach up the flight of stairs to their left. 'These are the stairs up to the gallery, the ladies' gallery which is set above the hall. These are the women's quarters – we stay here. You're not welcome in the round tower except by the lords' command.'

Morach nodded, following Alys up the flight of stairs, examining the tapestries which hung on either side.

'I am to have a new room to share with you,' Alys said. 'But we are still housed in the women's quarters. Lady Catherine sleeps off the gallery, the other women share a room opposite, and we are to have a new little room next door. They used to store lumber in it; I told them we needed space to distil herbs and make our goods. I'd rather we could have been in the round tower with the old lord. But Catherine watches me close.'

'Because of the young lord?' Morach asked, her breath coming short as they climbed the stairs.

Alys nodded. 'She was jealous,' she said in a sudden rush. 'And she put me through an ordeal. She was trying to get rid of me, Morach. Hugo had told her that he loved me. And last night we were alone together and he promised ... he promised ... ' Alys broke off, her face hard with grief. 'None of it matters now,' she said unsteadily. 'It does not matter what he said to me, nor what plans we made. I dreamed of being his lady here. But it meant nothing. She is with child now. Her position is untouchable.'

Morach nodded. Alys led her into the ladies' gallery and opened the door in the right-hand corner of the room. 'Lady Catherine's chamber is opposite,' she said gesturing. 'It overlooks the inner courtyard, it's warmer.

The other women sleep next door to us, looking out over the river. Our room matches theirs. We look out over the river too.'

Morach stepped inside and looked around. 'A bed,' she said with satisfaction. 'I've never slept in a bed.'

'Half a bed,' Alys said warningly. 'We're to share.'

'And a good fire and a chest for our things,' Morach said, making a rapid inventory of the room. 'A little mirror and a cupboard. Alys, this is greater comfort than the cottage for the winter.'

'And greater danger,' Alys said warningly. 'The ordeal was no jest.'

Morach cocked a bright, unsympathetic eye at her. 'You lied your way clear,' she stated.

Alys nodded. 'I paid a price,' she said, her voice very low. In her mind she could still see the undamaged consecrated wafer which she had chewed, swallowed and then vomited up into the hearth without marking it. 'I am outside the grace of God,' she said. 'That was when I commanded the dolls.'

'The only thing to do,' Morach said briskly. 'If one seigneur will not protect you – you have to seek another. How else could you survive? If you are outside the grace of your God then you have to use magic. You might as well go out into a storm in your shift. You need some power around you.'

Alys nodded. 'Hugo promised to protect me,' she said. 'Only last night he swore that he loved me – he has said he would give up Catherine, even the castle itself to be with me. It is as you foretold, Morach, and as I dreamed. He said he would set Catherine aside for me. And I said I would give up magic, he and I are safer without it.'

Morach flapped a dirty, dismissive hand. 'All these

promises,' she said with mocking respect. 'But now he knows that his wife is with child.'

Alys nodded. 'Yes,' she said dully.

'Spoken to him since?' Morach asked brightly.

'No,' Alys said. 'Anyway, we weren't alone.'

'Gave you a sign, did he? Tipped you the wink? Caught you on the stairs and said "never fear, sweetheart!"'

'He's out hunting,' Alys said defensively.

'Sent you a message to say that even though the rich Lady Catherine is carrying his son and heir, you are still his love and the promises stand? That he will send her away and put you in her place?'

Alys shook her head dumbly.

Morach gave a cracked laugh. 'Better pray for a stillbirth then,' she said agreeably. 'Or an idiot, or a weakling, or a sickly girl from a ruptured womb that can never bear child again? What'll it be, Alys? Something a little stronger than prayer? A little spell to make Catherine miscarry? Herbs in her dinner? Poison on her sheets to make her skin swell and blister, to pox the babe as it comes out?'

'Hush,' Alys said, glancing towards the thick door. 'Don't even speak of it here, Morach. And don't think of it either. I've come too close to my power already. I've stood inside the pentangle. I've felt my power from the soles of my feet to my fingertips.'

Morach breathed a deep sigh of pleasure. 'You came to it,' she said. 'At last.'

'I don't want it,' Alys said in a passionate whisper. 'I felt the power of it and the delight of it and I loved it. I know what you mean now, Morach, it was like the strongest wine. But that will not be my way. I will trust Hugo. I will trust to what he promised. And I will keep my promise to him to rid myself of magic. I want rid of that power, I want to be an ordinary woman that can be bedded by an ordinary man and feel delight, as great as Catherine feels, when he has her. I want that life and those pleasures. Not yours.'

Morach chuckled to herself as if it did not much matter.

'I *will* keep faith with Hugo,' Alys said. 'However hard it is over the next few months. Even if he wavers. *I* will keep faith. We have made promises. I have given him my love, I shall stay true to him.'

Morach shrugged dismissively. 'Maybe,' she said, unimpressed. 'But what of the dolls? Are they safe?'

'I want rid of them,' Alys said in a whisper. 'I threw one in the moat last night, but it floated. I had to go in and get it out. It nearly drowned me, Morach. It was the doll of Lady Catherine and I felt that it dragged me in. I felt it wanted me drowned. I heard it laugh as I went down. I heard it laugh, Morach! I want rid of the dolls. You must take them back.'

Morach pulled a stool up to the fire and looked into the flames for a moment. When she looked up her old face was sallow. 'They're yours,' she said. 'Your candles, your commands, your dolls. I'll not have them around me. I'll not claim them. I'm not surprised they tried to drown you. There's a shadow around them that I can't clearly see. But it looks like water.'

'Much water?' Alys asked. She looked in the fire, like Morach. All she could see were the dark squares of turf and the red embers.

'A lungful is enough,' Morach said dourly. 'Too much if it is your lungs. Anyway, the dolls are yours.'

'Can I bury them?' Alys asked.

Morach shrugged. 'You might do. The shadow I see is Water not Earth.'

'Can I throw them on the fire and let them melt and burn?'

Morach put her head on one side and looked at the fire. 'It's a perilous gamble,' she said.

'What am I to do with them then?' Alys demanded in irritation.

Morach laughed unkindly. 'You should have thought of that first,' she said.

Alys waited.

'Oh well,' Morach said. 'When the weather lifts we'll go up to the moor and drop them down one of the caves. If their shadow is water they will have their fill then. We'll maybe be able to do some spell to take their power away. Where d'you keep them?'

'On me,' Alys answered. 'In my purse on my girdle. I had no room of my own, I was afraid they would be found.'

Morach shook her head. 'That's not safe,' she said positively. 'You don't want them close to you, listening to your voice, hearing your worst thoughts. Is there nowhere you can hide them?'

Alys shook her head, thinking. 'I am nowhere alone!' she said impatiently. 'I am with someone all day and every day. Even when I am in the herb garden there is always someone near by, a servant or a gardener or one of the scullions.'

Morach nodded. 'Hide them somewhere foul,' she advised. 'In the castle midden or under a close stool. Somewhere that not even a child would pry.'

'Out of the garderobe!' Alys exclaimed. She pointed to the corner of the room where a round hole had been cut into the wall and covered with a wooden lid. 'You take your ease there,' she said. 'And the shit falls down into the moat. No one would search there. I can hang them on a piece of cord from underneath the seat.'

Morach eyed the corner seat. 'That'll do,' she said. 'In time they'll get marked and foul. No one will see them. And whatever power your spell has laid on them I cannot see them hexing your Lord Hugo to hang outside the castle wall while you shit on his head.'

Alys gave a sudden giggle and her whole face lightened. For a moment she looked like the girl who had been the favourite of the whole abbey. 'I'm glad you're here,' she said. 'Now I'll call for hot water for you. You'll have to have a bath.'

Thirteen

Morach was unruly about bathing, ashamed of being naked before Alys, certain that water would make her ill.

'You smell,' Alys said frankly. 'You smell disgusting, Morach. Lady Catherine will never have you near her smelling like this. You're as bad as a dungheap in August.'

'Then she can send me back to my cottage,' Morach grumbled while the servants came up the stairs with the big bath and the cans of hot water. 'I didn't ask for some lout of a man to come riding all over my garden and snatch me off to come to help a woman in childbirth for a baby that's only just conceived.'

'Oh, hush,' Alys said impatiently. 'Wash yourself, Morach. All over. And your hair too.'

She left Morach with the steaming bath and when she returned, with a gown from the chest, Morach was wrapped in the counterpane from the bed, as near to the fire as she could get.

'Folks die of wetting,' she said dourly.

'They die of dirt as well,' Alys retorted. 'Put this on.'

She had chosen a simple green gown for Morach, a working woman's gown with no stomacher and no overskirt; and when she was dressed and the girdle tied, and a foot of material stitched up into a thick hem, she looked well.

'How old are you, Morach?' Alys asked curiously. She seemed to have stayed the same age for all of Alys' life. Forever bent-backed, forever greying, forever lined, forever dirty.

'Old enough,' Morach said unhelpfully. 'I'm not wearing that damned cap.'

'I'll just comb your hair then,' Alys said.

Morach fended her off. 'Stop it, Alys,' she said. 'I may be far from my hearthside, but I don't change. I don't want you touching me, I don't want to touch you. I am a hedgehog, not a coney. Keep your hands off me and you won't get prickled.'

Alys recoiled. 'You've never wanted me touching you,' she said. 'Even when I was a little girl. Even when I was a baby I doubt you touched me more than you had to. I can't remember sitting on your knee. I can't remember you holding my hand. You're a cold woman, Morach, and a hard one. And you brought me up longing and longing for a little tenderness.'

'Well, you found it, didn't you?' Morach demanded, unrepentant. 'You found the mother you wanted, didn't you?'

'Yes,' Alys said, recognizing the truth of it. 'Yes, I *did* find her. And I thank God I found her before I had tumbled into Tom's arms for gratitude.'

Morach gleamed. 'And how did you repay love?' she asked. 'When you found your mother, when you found the woman to hold you and kiss you goodnight and tell you stories of the saints, and teach you to read and to write? What sort of a daughter were you, Alys?'

Alys turned a white face to Morach. 'Don't,' she said.

'Don't?' Morach asked, deliberately dense. 'Don't what? Don't say that all this love counted for so much that at the first sniff of smoke you were away like a scalded cat? Don't remind you that you left her to burn with all your sisters while you skipped home at an easy pace? Don't remind you that you're a Judas?

'I may be cold, but at least I'm honourable. I decided

to feed you and house you and I kept my promise. And I did more than that – it suits you to forget it now. But I did dandle you and tell you stories. I kept you safe as I promised I would. I taught you all my skills, all my power. From your earliest days I let you watch everything, learn everything. There's always been a wise woman on the moor, and you were to be the wise woman after me.

'But you were too clever to be wise. You had to find your own destiny, and so you promised to love your mother and her God forever; but at the first hint of danger you ran like a deer. You ran from her, back to me; and then you ran from her God, back to magic again. You're a woman of no loyalty, Alys. It's whatever will serve a purpose for you.'

Alys had turned away and was looking out of the window where the sun was coming through the snow-clouds, hard and bright. Morach noted her hands on the stone window-sill, clenched until the knuckles showed white. 'I am not very old,' she said, her voice shaking. 'I am not yet seventeen. I would not run again. I have learned some things since the fire. I would not run now. I have learned.'

'Learned what?' Morach demanded.

'I have learned that it would have been better for me to have died with her than to live with her death on my conscience,' Alys said. She turned back to the room and Morach saw that her face was drenched in tears. 'I thought that as long as I survived, that was all that mattered,' she said. 'Now I know that the price I paid for my escape is high, too high. It would have been better for me to have died beside her.'

Morach nodded. 'Because you are now alone,' she said.

'Very, very alone,' Alys repeated.

'And still in danger,' Morach confirmed.

'Mortal danger, every day,' Alys said.

'And deeply enmeshed in sin,' Morach finished with satisfaction.

Alys nodded. 'I am beyond forgiveness,' she said. 'I can never confess. I can never do penance. I am beyond the pale of heaven.'

Morach chuckled. 'My daughter after all,' she said, as if Alys' despair was the stuff of rich comedy. 'My daughter in every detail.'

Alys thought for a moment and then nodded. The bowing of her head was an acceptance of defeat.

Morach nodded. 'You may be a wise woman yet,' she said slowly. 'You have to watch everything go. You have to see everything slip away from you, before you can be wise enough to do without.'

Alys shrugged sullenly. 'I have Hugo,' she said stubbornly. 'I have his promise. I am not a poor old witch on the moor just yet.'

Morach gleamed at her. 'Oh yes,' she said. 'I was forgetting that you have Hugo. What joy!'

Alys released the grip of her hands. 'It *is* a joy,' she said defiantly.

Morach grinned. 'Did I not say so?' she demanded. She laughed. 'So then! When do I see her? Catherine. When do I see her?'

'You call her Lady Catherine,' Alys warned. 'We can go and see her now, I suppose. She's sewing in the gallery. But watch what you say, Morach. Not one word of magic or she will have us both. She no longer fears me as a rival, but she would not resist the temptation to get rid of me, if you gave her the evidence to put me through another ordeal.'

Morach nodded, the old slyness back in her eyes above the green shawl. 'I don't forget,' she said. 'I'm not bought with a whore's gown. I'll keep my silence until I'm ready to speak.'

Alys nodded and opened the door. The women were sitting at the far end of the gallery with the yellow wintry sun shining through the arrow-slits on their work. They all turned and stared as Alys led Morach into the room.

'Anyway,' Morach said behind her hand, 'it wasn't me that used the magic dolls was it, Alys?'

Alys shot Morach one furious glance and walked forward. 'Lady Catherine,' she said. 'May I present to you my kinswoman, Morach.'

Lady Catherine looked up from her sewing. 'Ah, the cunning woman,' she said. 'Morach of Bowes Moor. I thank you for coming.'

Morach nodded. 'No thanks are due to me,' she said.

Lady Catherine smiled at the compliment.

'Because I didn't choose to come,' Morach said baldly. 'They rode up to my cottage and snatched me out of my garden. They said it was done on your orders. So am I free to go if I wish?'

Catherine was taken aback. 'I don't . . . ' she started. 'Well . . . But, Morach, most women would be glad to come to the castle and live with my ladies and eat well, and sleep in a bed.'

Morach gleamed under the thatch of grey hair. 'I'm not "most women", my lady,' she said with satisfaction. 'I am not like most women at all. So I thank you to tell me: am I free to come and go as I please?'

Alys drew breath to interrupt, but then hesitated. Morach could take what chances she wished, she had clearly decided to haggle with Lady Catherine. Alys chose to avoid the conflict. She left Morach standing alone in the centre of the room and went to sit beside Eliza and looked at her embroidery.

'Of course you are free,' Lady Catherine said. 'But I require your help. I have no mother or family near to advise me. Everyone tells me you are the best cunning woman in all the country for childbirth and cursing. Is that true?'

'Not the cursing,' Morach said briskly. 'That's just slander and poison-talk. I do no curses or spells. But I am a healer and I can deliver a baby quicker than most.'

'Will you deliver mine?' Lady Catherine asked. 'When he is born in October? Will you promise to deliver me a healthy son in October?'

Morach grinned. 'If you conceived a healthy son in January, I can deliver him in October,' she said. 'Otherwise . . . probably not.'

Lady Catherine leaned forward. 'I'm certain I have conceived a son,' she said. 'Can you tell? Can you assure me? Alys said it was a boy, can you see for sure? Can you tell if he is healthy?'

Morach nodded but stayed where she was. 'I can tell if it is a boy or girl,' she said. 'And later on I can tell if it is lying right.'

Lady Catherine beckoned her closer.

'If I want to,' Morach said unhelpfully. 'I can tell the sex of a child – if I want to.'

There was a ripple of subdued shock among the women. Ruth glanced over at Alys to see how fearful she was of her kinswoman's temerity. Alys' face was serene. She knew Morach always drove a hard bargain with a customer and Lady Catherine's private score with Alys could not be worsened.

'Alys, tell your kinswoman to watch her tongue or I

will have her thrown to the castle dogs,' Lady Catherine said, her voice sharp with warning.

Alys raised her head from Eliza's embroidery and smiled at Lady Catherine without fear. 'I cannot command her, my lady,' she said. 'She will say and do as she pleases. If you dislike her you should send her home, there are many wise women in the country. Morach is nothing special.'

Morach cocked an eyebrow at the barb but said nothing.

Lady Catherine hunched her shoulders in irritation. 'What do you want then?' she asked Morach. 'What d'you want, to tell the sex of the child, to minister to me in the months of waiting, and deliver me a boy?'

'A shilling a month,' Morach said, ticking off her requirements on her fingers. 'All the ale and food I want. And the right to go in and out of the castle without any hindrance or question, day and night.'

Lady Catherine chuckled reluctantly. 'You're an old huckster,' she said. 'I hope you deliver babies as well as you bargain.'

Morach gave her a slow dark smile. 'And a donkey, so I can get to my cottage and back again when I need,' she added.

Lady Catherine nodded.

'Do we have an agreement?' Morach asked.

'Yes,' Lady Catherine said.

Morach stepped forward, spat in her hand and held it out to shake. Ruth, who was sitting at Catherine's feet, shrank back as if from an infection, but to Alys' surprise Lady Catherine leaned forward and took Morach's hand in a firm grip.

'Funny old lady, your kinswoman,' Eliza said under her breath.

'She's an old hag,' Alys said, stirred with a sudden unreasonable irritation. 'I wish she had never come.'

'My lord was asking for you, Alys,' Lady Catherine said, scarcely troubling herself to glance over. 'Lord Hugh is in his chamber. He has some clerk's work for you.'

Alys rose to her feet and curtsied. She glanced over towards Morach. The old woman was the only idle one in the room. All of them, even Lady Catherine, had needlework or a distaff in their hands. She winked at Alys and hitched a footstool a little nearer the blazing fire.

'Your kinswoman will do well with us,' Lady Catherine said. 'I have some plain sewing which you can do, Morach.'

Morach smiled at her. 'I don't sew, my lady,' she said pleasantly.

There was another ripple of subdued shock among the women but Lady Catherine looked amused. 'Will you sit idle, with empty hands then? While all of us work?' she asked.

Morach nodded. 'I am here to watch over you and the child,' she said grandly. 'I need to be able to see – with my healer's vision. If you want some fool –' she smiled impartially at the busy women ' – some fool to net you a cap, there are many of them. There is only one of me.'

Catherine laughed. Alys did not even smile. She curtsied to Catherine and went from the room. Only when she was in the round tower climbing the little turret staircase to Lord Hugh's bedchamber did she realize that her jaw had been set with irritation and it ached.

Lord Hugh was seated at a table, a thin, densely written piece of paper unfurled before him.

'Alys!' he said as she came in. 'I need you to read this. It's written small. I cannot see it.'

'From London?' Alys asked.

The old lord nodded. 'The bird brought it to me,' he said. 'My homing pigeons. Clever little birds, through all this bad weather. It must be urgent for my man to send them out into snow. What does it say?'

The letter was from one of Lord Hugh's informants at court. It was unsigned, with a code of numbers to represent the King, the Queen, Cromwell and the other lords. Lord Hugh had his own methods for making sure that his sovereign sprang no surprises on his loyal vassals.

Alys read it through and then glanced up at Lord Hugh. 'Grave news,' she said.

Hugh nodded. 'Tell me.'

'He says the Queen was taken to her bed. She was with child, a boy child, and he is lost.'

'Oho,' Lord Hugh said softly. 'That's bad for her.'

Alys scanned the paper. 'Sir Edward Seymour is to become a member of the privy chamber.' She glanced at Lord Hugh. He was nodding, looking at the fire.

'The Queen blames the miscarriage on a shock from His Majesty's fall,' Alys read. 'But there is one who says that he heard the King say that God will not give him male children with the Queen.'

'That's it then,' Lord Hugh said with finality.

Alys looked up at him questioningly. 'That's it for the Queen,' he said, speaking low. 'It will be another divorce I suppose. Or naming her as a concubine and returning to Rome. He's a widower now that Catherine is dead.'

'He could return to the Pope?' Alys asked incredulously.

'Maybe,' Lord Hugh said softly. 'Queen Anne is on the order of her going, that is for certain. Miscarriage, blame . . . ' he broke off.

'He could restore the priests to their power?' Alys asked.

Lord Hugh glanced at Alys and laughed shortly. 'Aye,' he said. 'There might be a safe nunnery for you yet, Alys. What d'you think of that?'

Alys shook her head in bewilderment. 'I don't know,' she said. 'I don't know what to think. It's so sudden!'

Lord Hugh gave his short laugh. 'Aye,' he said. 'You have to skip very fast to keep pace with the King's conscience. This marriage is now against the will of heaven too, it seems. And Seymour's star is rising.'

He nodded towards a leather pouch of letters. 'These came by messenger,' he said. 'Scan them and see if there is anything I should know.'

Alys broke the seal on the first. It was written plainly in English and dated in January.

'From your cousin, Charles,' she said. 'He says there are to be new laws against beggary,' Alys read.

Lord Hugh nodded. 'Skip that bit,' he said. 'You can tell me later.'

'It is the coldest winter ever known,' Alys read. 'The Thames is frozen and the barges cannot be used. The watermen are suffering much hardship, starving for lack of work. Some of them have their boats stuck fast in the ice and the boats are being crushed. There is talk of a winter fair.'

Lord Hugh waved a hand. 'Read me that later,' he said. 'Anything which affects the north? Any new taxes?'

Alys shook her head. 'He speaks of the King's accident, a fall while jousting.'

'I knew of it already. Anything else?'

'He suggests that you write pressing your claim for the monastery lands which abut your manors,' Alys said. She could feel her lips framing each word precisely as she thought of the wide fertile fields either side of the river. Mother Hildebrande used to like to walk in the meadows before haymaking, smelling the heady scent of the flowers growing wild and thick among the grass. On a summer evening their perfume stole across the river to the gardens, to the chambers, even to the chapel, like a sweet, natural incense. Now these lands were spoil – up for offer.

'He says, "You and Hugo are well praised for the goods you have sent south and for your loyal zeal. Now is the time to prompt the King to reward your labour. He is also open to money bids for the land, beneficial leases, or land exchanges. They are saying that a lease of three lives will pay for itself over and over."'

The old lord nodded. 'Twenty-one-year leases,' he said softly. He shook his head. 'It would see me out, but what of Hugo? Anything else?'

Alys turned the page. 'Prices of corn, coal and beef,' she said. 'Prices of furs and wine.'

'Anything else about the north?' Lord Hugh asked.

'No,' Alys replied. 'But the laws about vagrants will affect your lands.'

They were silent for a moment, the old lord looking deep into the fire as if he would see his way clear through the changes which were coming.

'This other letter,' he said abruptly. 'Translate it for me. It's from the bishop's clerk and he writes in Latin. Read me it in English.'

Alys took the paper and drew up her stool to the table. It was a letter from the bishop's clerk outlining the acceptable causes and reasons for an annulment of the marriage between Lady Catherine and Lord Hugo. Alys felt the sudden heat come into her face. She looked up at the old lord. He was looking at her quizzically.

'I can send the old shrew away,' he said. 'Barren old shrew. Send her away and free Hugo.' A wide smile as bright as his son's cracked his grave face. 'I've done it!' he said. 'I've freed Hugo. Now he'll have a plump new wife with a fat new dowry and I shall live long enough to see my heir!'

Alys' face was sour. 'You don't know then?'

'Know what?' he asked, his face darkening. 'Out with it, girl, you're my source for women's tattle. You should come to me with whatever news you have the moment you get it.'

'She's with child,' Alys said. 'I suppose that changes everything.'

For a moment he hardly heard her, then his face lit up with joy. 'With child!' His fist banged down on the forgotten, redundant letter. 'With child at last!' He threw back his head and laughed. Alys watched him, her mouth pressed tight.

'With child at last!' he said again. Then he checked himself. 'Is she sure? Have you looked at her? This is no ruse, is it, Alys? Does she think to save her skin for another few months with pretences?'

Alys shook her head. 'She's pregnant. I checked her. And she sent for my kinswoman, Morach, who is to stay with us until the birth. They've just struck their deal.'

'Boy or girl?' the old man asked eagerly. 'Tell me, Alys. What d'you think? Boy or girl?'

'I think it's a boy,' Alys said unwillingly.

'Has she told Hugo?' the old lord demanded. 'Curse the lad! Where is he?'

'She told him,' Alys said. 'He's out hunting venison for you, my lord. I don't know if he's back yet.'

'He went out without telling me?' the old lord asked, his face suddenly darkening. 'He gets the shrew in pup and then he goes out without telling me?'

Alys said nothing, her hands clasped in her lap and her eyes down.

'Hah!' Lord Hugh said. 'Not best pleased, was he?'

Alys said nothing.

'She told him this morning and he went straight out?' Lord Hugh checked.

Alys nodded.

'In a rage I suppose,' the old lord said ruminatively. 'He was counting on an annulment. He'll know that's not possible now.'

The fire crackled. The old lord sat silent in thought.

'Family comes first,' he said finally. 'Duty comes first. He can take his pleasures elsewhere – as he always has done. But now that his wife is with child, she is his wife forever. The child is well – d'you think?'

'These are early days,' Alys said. Her lips were cold and the words came out carefully. 'Queen Anne herself can tell you that many a baby is lost before birth. But as far as I can tell, the child is well.'

'And a boy?' the old man pressed her.

Alys nodded.

'That is well!' he said. 'Very well. Queen Anne or no! This is the nearest to an heir that we have ever come. Tell Catherine to wear something pretty tonight, I will drink her health before them all. She can come to my room as soon as she is dressed. I will take a glass with her.'

Alys nodded. 'And me, my lord?' she asked. 'These other letters?'

Lord Hugh waved her away. 'You can go,' he said. 'I have no need of you now.'

Alys rose from the chair, curtsied and went to the door.

'Wait!' he said abruptly.

Alys paused.

'Thrust those papers from the bishop in the fire,' he said. 'We don't want to risk Catherine seeing them. She would be distressed. We cannot risk her distress. Burn them, Alys, there will be no annulment now!'

Alys stepped forward and gathered the thick manuscripts into her hands. She pushed them into the back of the fire and watched them flame and blacken and crumble. She found that she was staring at the fire, her face blank and hard.

'You can go,' the old lord said softly.

Alys dropped him a curtsey and went out, closing the door softly behind her. David the dwarf was coming up the stairs, his sharp little face curious.

'You look drab, Alys,' he remarked. 'Are you sick? Or heartbroken? What's the old woman doing in the ladies' chamber? Are you not glad to have your kinswoman take your place?'

Alys turned her head aside and went down the stairs without answering.

'Is it true?' David called after her. 'Is it true what the women are whispering? Lady Catherine is in child and Hugo is in love with her, and she is high in the lord's favour again?'

Alys paused on the turret stair and looked back up at him, her pale face luminous in the gloom. 'Yes,' she said simply. 'All of my wishes have been fulfilled. What a blessing.'

'Amen,' said David, his face creasing into ironic laughter. 'And you so joyful!'

'Yes,' Alys said sourly, and went on downstairs.

Hugo was late from hunting and came to the high table when they were eating their meats. He apologized gracefully to his father and kissed Catherine's hand. They had great sport, he told them. They had killed nine bucks. They were hanging in the meat larder now and the antlers would be brought in for Lord Hugh. The hides, tanned, perfumed and soft, would make a cradle, a new cradle for the new Lord Hugo.

He did not once look at Alys, and she kept her gaze on her plate and ate little. Around her the babble of excited women's talk swayed and eddied like a billowy sea. Morach was silent too – eating her way through dish after dish with determined concentration.

When supper was over both Hugo and the old lord came to the ladies' chamber and the women played and sang for them and Catherine sewed as she talked. Her colour was high, she was wearing a new gown of cream with a rose-pink overskirt and a rose stomacher, slashed, with the cream gown pulled through. In the candlelight with her hair newly washed and dressed and her face animated with happiness she looked younger, prettier. The old bony greedy look had gone. Alys watched her glow under Hugo's attention, heard her quick laughter at the old lord's jests, and hated her.

'I need to pick some herbs in the moonlight,' she said quietly. 'I must ask you to excuse me, my lords, my lady.'

Catherine's bright face turned towards her. 'Of course,' she said dismissively. 'You may go.'

The old lord nodded his permission. Hugo was dealing cards and did not look up. Alys went down the stairs and across the hall, out through the great hall doors and into the yard of the inner manse and then turned to her right to walk between the vegetable- and herb-beds.

She needed nothing, but it was good to be out of the hot chamber and under the icy high sky. She stood for minutes in the moonlight, holding her cape tight around her, her hood up over her head. Then she walked slowly the length of the garden and back again. She was not planning. She was not thinking. She was beyond thought and plans or even spells. She was hugging to her heart the great ache of loneliness and disappointment and loss. Hugo would remain married to Catherine, they would have a son. He would be the Lord one day and Catherine the Lady of the castle. And Alys would be always the barely tolerated healer, clerk and hanger-on. Disliked by Catherine, forgotten by Hugo, retained on a small pension from the old lord because in that large household one mouth more or less made little difference.

She could marry – marry a soldier or a farmer and leave the castle for her own little cottage. Then she would work from sunrise until hours after dark, bear one child after another, every year until she fell sick and then died.

Alys shook her head as she walked. The little hovel on Bowes Moor had not been enough for her, the abbey had been a refuge she thought would stand forever, the castle had been a step on her way, and her sudden unexpected desire for Hugo and his love for her had been a gift and a joy she had not anticipated. And now it was gone.

Behind her the hall door opened and Hugo came out.

'I can't stay long,' he said in greeting. He took her cold hands in his warm ones and held them gently. 'Don't grieve,' he said. 'Things will come out.'

Alys' white, strained face looked up at him. 'Hardly,'

she said acidly. 'Don't comfort me with nonsense, Hugo, I am not a child.'

He recoiled slightly. 'Alys, have a heart,' he said. 'We both thought that you would be safer here if Catherine were with child. Now she is content and her position assured and you and I can be together.'

'In secret,' Alys said bitterly. 'In doorways. here in the kitchen garden in darkness, wary of watchers.'

Hugo shrugged. 'Who cares?' he demanded. 'I love you, Alys, and I want you. I have done my duty by Catherine, she will ask no more. I will get you a house in the town if you wish, and spend my nights there with you. We can be lovers at least! I want you, Alys, I care for nothing but that!'

Alys pulled her hands away and tucked them under her cloak. 'I wanted to be your wife,' she said stubbornly. 'Your father had a letter from the Prince Bishop today telling how an annulment could be done. We were very near to being rid of her. I wanted her gone. I wanted to lie with you in the Lady's chamber, not in some little house in town.'

Hugo took her by the shoulders and shook her gently. 'Careful, my Alys,' he said warningly. 'You are sounding to me like a woman who wants to leap to the top of the ladder. I would have taken you for love, I desire you in my bed. I would lie with you in a ditch, on the herbs here and now. Is it me you want or my name?'

For a moment Alys held herself stiff, then she moved into his arms. 'You,' she said. He held her tight and the coldness and the pain in her belly melted in a great rush of desire. 'You,' she said again.

'We'll find some way,' Hugo said gently. 'Don't be so afraid, Alys. We will find ways to be together, and we will love each other. Don't fret.'

Alys, held warm and close inside his cloak, rested her head against his shoulder and said: 'If she were to die . . . '

Hugo was instantly still.

'If she were to die . . . ' Alys said again.

He held her away from him and scanned her face, her blue innocent eyes. 'It would be a tragedy,' he said firmly. 'Don't think that I would welcome that route away from her, Alys. Don't make the mistake of thinking I would permit it. It is not a strange thought to me, I admit. I have wished her dead many and many a time. But I would never do it, Alys. And the man or woman who hurt Catherine would be my enemy for life. I have hated her – but she is my wife. She is Lady Catherine of Castleton. I owe her my protection. I command you, I *demand* that you keep her as well and as happy as it is in your power to do. She is a woman like you, Alys. Full of desire and longing like you, like any. She may be greedy, and she and I may lie together in all manner of perverse ways. But she is not a bad woman. She does not deserve death. I will not consider it. And she is trusting in your care.'

Alys nodded.

'Do you swear to protect her?' Hugo asked.

Alys met his intent gaze. 'I swear it,' she said easily. She felt the arid taste of the empty oath in her mouth.

'I must go,' Hugo said. 'They will be watching for me. Meet me tomorrow, Alys, come to the stables in the morning, my hunter is sick, you can look at him for me and we can be together.' He kissed her gently, quickly, on the mouth and then he turned and was gone. She heard the hall door slam as he went inside, leaving her alone in the garden.

'If she died . . . ' Alys said softly to the moonlit garden in the icy light. 'If she died he would marry me.'

Fourteen

Next day Alys could not get away to the stables until just before noon. Lady Catherine had an ache in her back and ordered Alys to rub it with oils and essences. Alys worked on the broad fleshy back with mounting impatience. Lady Catherine, prone and sighing with contentment, would not let her go. Alys' hands were hard, unloving on the other woman's flesh, drained of their healing magic by Alys' spite. She had to restrain an urge to pinch. After she had finished rubbing in the oil, Catherine's smooth white back was striped with red.

'That was good, Alys,' she said, in a rare moment of contentment.

Alys curtsied, collected her oils into her basket and shot from the room like a tom-cat. She half threw her basket at Morach and fled for the stairs, down the winding stony treads, across the hall, out of the kitchen door and around to the stables.

It was no good. Hugo had left. The simple lad who worked with the horses smiled his empty smile at her.

'Where is the young lord?' she asked abruptly. 'Was he here?'

'Gone,' the boy said. 'Long, long gone.'

Alys shivered and snapped her fingers under cover of her sleeves to recall her from a shadow of superstition.

'Long, long gone,' said the lad again.

Alys turned and went back to the castle. The stall for Hugo's favourite horse was empty, he had waited for her only a moment. She ached with resentment at his leaving so readily; and disappointment that he could so

269

easily go. Alys knew that if she had been waiting for him she would have been there all day.

She saw him at dinner at midday and he gave her a rueful grin and a wink but they did not speak. In the dying light of the afternoon he took his horse and his great deerhounds down the valley, riding fast by the flooding river, and she did not see him again until suppertime. Alys sat at the little table with the other women and watched the back of Hugo's neck where the dark hair curled. She imagined the feel of that silky hair beneath her fingers and how it would be to grip the nape of his neck in one hand. She felt as if she could grip him and shake him with desire – and with anger too. They left the supper table early and Hugo joined them in the ladies' gallery.

'My back aches again,' Catherine said faintly and Alys watched as she leaned on Hugo's arm and walked slowly into her bedroom. As the door closed Alys' keen eyes saw Hugo's arm go around his wife's waist. Alys waited for him to bid her goodnight and come out again to Alys as she sat with the other women at the fireside. The door stayed shut. Alys felt Morach's mocking black eyes smiling at her. There was no sound from Catherine's bedroom.

'Aye, he's very tender all of a sudden,' Eliza said, her mouth muffled by a thread of embroidery silk. 'There'll be no more slaps and curses now she's in foal.'

Alys looked towards the door again. It stayed shut. 'He's bound to try to keep her sweet,' she said unwillingly. 'He has to have an heir, Catherine has to have her way – at least in these early months.'

Morach hawked and spat into the fire. 'He likes it,' she said contemptuously. 'He'll like the taste of her when she's big with his child. He'll like the thought of a baby in her belly. He'll like her breasts getting fatter and the richness of her body. Men are just babies themselves. He'll suckle from her breasts and roll on her round belly like a new-born infant himself. He's not a man right now, he's a little boy with a new toy.'

Eliza giggled. Alys said nothing. The women sewed in silence, each of them craning their heads to hear what passed in the next room.

The door opened. 'My lady is tired,' Hugo said. He looked towards Morach. 'You or Alys, prepare her a tisane to help her sleep. She needs her rest.'

Morach nodded towards Alys. Hugo smiled at her, one of his open-hearted sweet smiles. 'Thank you, Alys,' he said pleasantly. 'You can bring it in when it is ready.' Then he turned on his heel and went back to his wife.

When the tisane was ready Alys gave it to Ruth to take in. She waited by the fire to see if Hugo came out again. He did not. That night, for the first time in their long, loveless marriage, he stayed in his wife's bed all night long. For the first time in her life Catherine slept with her head on her husband's shoulder and her brown hair tangled across his chest.

Alys sat by the fire with the others and sewed. When she went to bed, with Morach's warm bulk beside her, she did not sleep. She watched the arrow-slit of silver light walk from one end of the chamber to the other as the moon nonchalantly traversed the sky. Alys lay on her back, her eyes open, seeing nothing, thinking nothing. She endured jealousy, as she might endure an attack of deadly ague, stoically; sickened to the heart, saying nothing.

The weather itself was against her, confining her to the castle. March was wild and full of rainstorms and flurries of thick wet snow which clogged doorways and blew into the west-facing windows, leaving puddles on the stone floors. The sky seemed lower than usual and it was dark every afternoon. The castle seemed to shrink in on itself, besieged by winter.

Alys was never alone. Morach shared her bed at night, Lady Catherine ordered her to the ladies' gallery very often, and the old lord took to sitting with them in the afternoons, so Alys could not escape to his chamber in the round tower. Hugo rode out every day, going further and further afield, as restless as a mewed falcon. They heard stories of his adventures: of an alehouse which had been a nest of poachers burned down and the men and women turned out on to the snow-driven moor, of a pitched battle on the highway with some beggars, of a small riot in a bawdy house with mummery and masquers and lechery in the street.

'He is a rogue!' the old lord said proudly when he heard of Hugo's ready violence.

Alys did not seek Hugo and neither did he summon her. A deep secret gulf of silence had opened up between them. She did not waylay him on the stairs, or even attempt to catch his eye when he was sitting with Catherine and her ladies. Alys waited, like the living water beneath the frozen ice of the river, for better times.

He was gentle with Catherine and she, eating well, sleeping well, attended by her ladies and popular with her father-in-law, gleamed with satisfaction. Hugo lay with her once or twice, and though the women listened they heard no screams of pain and pain-shot pleasure. On those two nights Alys sat up all night by the arrow-slit, watching over the white landscape on the other side of the river, chilled to the bone by the icy wind which blew off the high moor. All night she stared out over the desert of snow, white-faced and wide-eyed as a barn owl, seeing nothing. In the morning Morach exclaimed at the ice of her hands and the deep violet shadows in folds of skin beneath her eyes.

Towards the end of the month of March, Hugo came back from his ride, found his father in the ladies' gallery and asked him for permission to go away to visit his friends in Newcastle. Alys froze and kept her eyes on her sewing. Catherine was all smiling interest.

'Of course you must go!' she said confidently. 'We will be well enough here! Your father will guard us and Morach and Alys will keep me well!'

Hugo smiled at them all. Alys felt his eyes on her and did not look up.

'Then I shall go with a clear conscience and come back with a light heart,' he said pleasantly. 'And you and all your ladies must make me a list of things to bring you from the city.'

'I should like some silk,' Catherine said consideringly. 'And David will certainly need tea and spices.'

'I shall ride like a pedlar,' Hugo said smiling. 'Alys, can I bring anything for you?'

Alys looked up, her face indifferent. 'No thank you, my lord,' she said coolly. 'I want for nothing.'

He nodded. The other women asked for little fairings, coloured silk ribbons for a gown, a purse of spices. Hugo wrote down their requests seriously and tucked the list inside his doublet.

'I'll leave at daybreak,' he said. 'So I'll bid you farewell now.' He took Catherine's hand and kissed it. 'Stay well, my dear,' he said. No one could have been deaf to the tenderness in his voice. 'Stay well for the sake of my son, and for yourself.'

Alys got quietly to her feet and left the room. Pausing outside the door she heard his farewells to the others and then she went down to the lobby between the stairs and the entrance to the round tower where he must pass.

He came light-footed down the stairs, whistling.

'Alys!' he said, as she stepped forward into the light. 'I'm glad you waited for me.'

There was a brief silence between them as Hugo assessed Alys' stony face.

'I am sorry,' he said frankly. 'I know these days have been hard on you. As hard for you as for me. I've seen you growing pale and thin, Alys, and it has cut deep into me. I need to be away, I need to be away from here, Alys. I am sick of these wintry days and these long evenings with women. I know you are in pain, watching Catherine as you do. I know how it must hurt you.'

Alys turned her head away from him, but her cold hand gripped his.

'I *have* to endure this,' Hugo said urgently. 'Catherine is my wife, she is carrying my son, I have no choice, Alys. And I cannot long for you and look for you, and snatch little moments with you. I want to be either with you or without you; this half-life of occasional desire is worse than nothing.'

Alys nodded unwillingly.

'I need to put some leagues between this place and myself,' Hugo said urgently. 'Enmeshed between one duty and another I feel myself being pulled a thousand different ways at once. Some days I feel I want to run away!'

'You are fortunate in having the freedom to run,' Alys said drily.

He smiled at her. 'Don't scratch at me,' he said softly.

'I am going away to think, Alys. When I come back I shall tell my father that you and I must have some time together. We can make arrangements. We can find somewhere for you to live in comfort near by, where I can be with you. I am going away to think of how it can be managed. Wait for me.'

Alys turned her pale, unsmiling face towards him. 'I have to wait for you,' she said grudgingly. 'There is nowhere else for me to go. I love you.'

He beamed at that, but there was no joy in either Alys' face or her voice. 'It seems I am just a woman like any other,' she said sulkily. 'Neither your vows to me nor my magic have kept me safe from this pain.'

'Sweetheart . . . ' he started and drew her closer to him. Then the door above them on the stairs opened and he dropped her hand and went by without another word. Alys looked after him with a desire so sharp that it felt like hatred.

In the long month he was away he wrote every week to his father and it was Alys' task to read his scrawled letters. He spoke of his friend's trading company – Van Esselin and Son – and his plans of expansion. He spoke of Lord Newcastle's son, and nights of roistering along the waterfront. He wrote well and the old lord and Alys would sometimes laugh together in the middle of a letter, when Hugo wrote of a struggle which ended in the River Tyne, or a mountebank on a street corner with a dancing bear. His letters made him vivid in Alys' mind and she wanted to hear his voice tell his stories, and see that sudden smile warm and lighten his dark face. She forgot the weeks of longing and looking for him and the nightly walk of moonlight across her bedroom wall. She forgot the sour taste of curdled desire, and the passion which felt like hatred, not love. Instead she laughed with his father and thought – without consciously thinking – if he and I were married, it would be like this.

The old lord would wipe his eyes and tell Alys to read the section again, and then he would laugh again. 'He's a rogue!' he exclaimed. 'But there's no one in the world who could resist him! Don't you think so, Alys?'

And Alys, alone in the tower room with the father of the man she loved, would lean back against his chair and nod. 'Irresistible,' she said.

The old lord tweaked one of her curls which tumbled from the back of her hood. 'You hot for him still?' he asked.

Alys nodded, turned her head and smiled at him. 'I love him,' she said. 'And he loves me.'

The old lord sighed, his face kindly. 'He has to have his heir,' he said gently.

'I know,' Alys said. 'But we can love each other.'

'Maybe,' the old lord said, with a lifetime of whoring and loving and fighting behind him. 'Maybe for a while.'

Catherine had her letters too. He wrote asking after her health every week and telling her those things of Newcastle that he judged fit for her ears.

I know the real Hugo, Alys would whisper to herself while Catherine read his letters aloud to the circle of ladies. I know what he was really doing that night, when he tells Catherine that they went for a night sail and then early to their beds. He writes the truth to his father, and he knows I will read his letters, his true letters. Catherine does not know him, not as I know him.

Alys was happier in the long cold days while Hugo was away. She slept at nights, a deep sleep so sweet that she could hardly bear to wake in the morning. She dreamed that Hugo was home, that she was wearing Catherine's rose and cream gown, that she was leaning on Hugo's arm as they walked in the garden, that it was summer, high summer, and the sky was smiling down on them both. She dreamed that she was sleeping in Catherine's big bed with Hugo's arm possessively around her. She dreamed that she was sailing on Hugo's tall-masted trader, sailing to the very edge of the world and Hugo was at the wheel, laughing with her, with his eyes screwed up against the glare of the sunlight on the long rolling waves. She dreamed that she was taking Catherine's seat at the high table in the great hall. Hugo drew back her chair for her because she was big with child. All the faces turned towards her were smiling. They were cheering her because she was carrying the heir. As she woke she heard them shout 'Lady Alys!'

Catherine was happy and busy while Hugo was away. Pregnancy suited his wife. Her temper was sweet as fruit and she laughed and sang in the mornings. Her colour had risen in her cheeks and she looked rosy when she read Hugo's letters and came to the end and said, 'There is a little piece here I will not tell you. It is for my eyes only.' Then she would slip the letter in the purse at her girdle and pat it, as if to keep it safe.

Alys would turn her head from that. Catherine would leave the letter spread out on her pillow, ostentatiously reading it when Alys was combing her hair, inviting Alys to pry. Alys resorted to icy indifference, she would not stoop to spy on Catherine's letter and besides, she knew Hugo could promise anything. Words of love were light currency to him.

It means nothing, Alys said to herself softly. He is planning our life together, his life with me. He said he needed time to make his plans. And while he is planning he is keeping her sweet with a few little words. I will not begrudge her a few little words. They are like nonsense spells. They mean nothing. They mean nothing.

'By God, you look sour,' Morach said cheerfully as they went to bed one evening. 'Pining for the young lord?'

Alys shrugged a thin shoulder, jumped into the bed and pulled the covers up to her ears.

'Painful, ain't it?' Morach said. 'This nonsense of love? You'd have done better to keep him at arm's length forever than to love him and lose him without even having him. You'd have done better to forget your promise to him to surrender magic, just as he has forgotten his promise to you.'

'He hasn't forgotten,' Alys said fiercely. 'You know nothing about it, Morach. I haven't lost him. He asked me to wait for him and I am waiting. When he comes home it will all be different. I am waiting. I am happy to wait for him.'

'You look it,' Morach said ironically. 'You're losing your looks, your face is white and strained. You get thinner every day. Your breasts are less and less, your belly is as flat as a dice-board. If you wait much longer you'll be worn out with waiting.'

Alys lay down and turned her face to the wall. 'Bank up the fire before you come to bed,' she said coldly. 'I'm going to sleep.'

Morach and Lady Catherine had made a surprising alliance. Every day and every evening they chattered and gossiped in the overheated gallery. Alys sat as far as she could from the fire and watched the two of them. 'Like a pair of old hags together,' she said under her breath.

Morach was not afraid of Catherine like the rest of the ladies; and Catherine, a bully by nature, was amused to have met her match. One day Morach insisted on going to her cottage though the snow was thick and wet and the sky low and threatening. Lady Catherine forbade it. 'You can go tomorrow,' she said.

Morach nodded, and went to her chamber and came out with a cape around her shoulders and a shawl over her head.

'I said you could go tomorrow,' Catherine said impatiently.

'Aye,' Morach said, unmoved. 'I *could* go tomorrow, and I *could* go the day after, or next week. But it's my desire to go today.'

Catherine snapped her fingers. 'You'd best learn, Morach, that in this castle you do things by my desire. Not yours.'

Morach gleamed her slow secret smile. 'Not I, my lady,' she said. 'I am different from the rest of them.'

'I can still have you whipped,' Catherine threatened.

Morach met her angry look without fear. 'I wouldn't advise it, my lady,' she said. Then she turned her back and went from the gallery as if she had permission to leave and Catherine had wished her 'God speed'.

There was a stunned silence and then Catherine burst into loud laughter. 'God's truth, the old woman will be hanged,' she said. The women chimed in with the laughing, exchanging scared glances. Alys alone sat silent. When Morach came back in the evening, after having completed her own mysterious business, Catherine behaved towards her as if they had never disagreed.

One day, at the end of March, Hugo sent a letter to Catherine saying he would be home within a few days. She flushed pink with pleasure.

'Hugo is coming home,' she announced. 'And within the week! I have missed him.' She smoothed her gown over her rounded breasts. 'I wonder if he will see a difference in me. What d'you think, Alys?'

Alys was watching the logs in the fire. 'I expect so, my lady,' she said politely.

'D'you think he will desire me as he did before?' Catherine asked. 'D'you remember those wild nights when our son was conceived? D'you think he will still be mad for me?'

Alys turned a blank, insolent face towards Catherine. 'Maybe,' she said. 'But you had best have a care, lady. It would be a sad end to your ambitions if your rough games shook the baby out of your belly.'

Catherine shot a look at Morach. 'That can't happen, can it?' she asked in sudden fear. 'That can't happen?'

Morach pursed her lips. 'Depends what you do,' she said. 'Depends how he likes it.'

Catherine laughed a ripple of excited laughter. She leaned towards Morach and whispered in her ear. Morach chuckled. 'That shouldn't harm the baby,' she said out loud. 'Not if it pleases you!'

Catherine put her hand on her heart and smiled broadly. Then the two of them put their heads together and whispered like village girls outside an alehouse.

Alys felt unreasonably irritated with Morach. 'Will you excuse me, my lady?' she said rising to her feet. 'I have to read to Lord Hugh before dinner.'

Catherine barely looked up to nod dismissal. Morach was whispering something behind her hand.

'And then he did what?' Catherine asked incredulously. 'I did not know that men could do that. What did his wife say – in heaven's name?'

Alys shut the door behind her and leaned back against

it and closed her eyes. She could hear the ripple of laughter even through the massive wood. She turned wearily and went down the stairs, through the lobby and up the winding narrow staircase of the round tower to Lord Hugh's chamber.

Hugo was there. He was sitting on a stool at his father's feet as Alys walked into the room and he sprang up to greet her. Alys staggered and her face went white and then blushed red.

'I did not think to see you for days yet,' she said. 'Hugo, oh Hugo!'

He took her hand and squeezed it tight to warn her to be silent. The old lord looked from Alys' thin flushed face to his son's bright smile.

'I came home early,' Hugo said levelly. 'I have a great scheme to lay before my father and I wanted to see you all again. How is my wife? Is her pregnancy going safely?'

'She is well,' Alys said. She could hardly speak for breathlessness and she did not want to speak of Catherine. She wanted to hold him, to touch his face, the soft skin around his eyes, to kiss his merry smile. She wanted to feel his arms around her as he had held her that one night, that first night, and his kisses on her hair.

'What is this scheme of yours, Hugo?' the old lord asked. He beckoned to Alys to stand behind his chair and she crossed the room to his side and watched Hugo's animated face as he talked.

'It's Van Esselin,' he said. 'He has plans to fit a ship for the longest voyage they have ever undertaken – around Africa, even as far as the Japans. He has the ship's log from a Dutch pilot that shows a clear passage. I have seen it, it is true. And he plans to take goods and baubles to trade all along the way and to come back with a cargo of spices and silks and all the rich trade. It's a great opportunity for us, Father. I am certain of its success.'

'Trade?'

'It's not huckstering in the butter-market,' Hugo said quickly. 'It's honourable trade. It's a great adventure, as exciting as a war, as distant as a crusade. The world is changing, Father, and we have to change with it.'

'And what if this great ship sinks?' the old lord asked cynically.

Hugo shrugged. 'Then we have lost the wager,' he said. 'Van Esselin asks us only for a thousand pounds to back him. We can gamble a thousand pounds for the rewards this promises to bring.'

'A thousand pounds?' Lord Hugh repeated incredulously. 'One thousand!'

'But think of the return, Father!' Hugo said urgently. 'We would get it back twenty, maybe fifty times over. If they bring back spices and silks they can sail into London and make a fortune in a sale on the quayside itself. Or they can bring it back to Newcastle, or even take it up to Scotland. People are desperate for spices – think of the prices we pay in the kitchen! This is the way for us to make our fortune, not struggling to get our rents from snow-bound farmers!'

Lord Hugh shook his head. 'No,' he said slowly. 'Not while I am lord here.'

Hugo's face grew dark with one of his sudden rages. 'Will you explain to me why?' he asked, his voice shaking.

'Because we are lords, not traders,' Lord Hugh said with disdain. 'Because we know nothing of the sea and the trade your friend does. Because our family's wealth and success has been founded on land, getting and keeping land. *That's* the way to a lasting fortune, the rest is mere usury in one shape or another.'

'This is a new world and things are different now,' Hugo said passionately. 'Van Esselin says we do not even know what lands the ship may find! What riches it might bring back! There are tales of countries where they use gold and precious stones as playthings! Where they desire our goods above anything else!'

The old lord shook his head. 'You're a young man with a young man's ambitions, Hugo,' he said. 'But I am an old man with an old man's love for order. And while I am alive we will do things in the old way. When I am dead you may do as you please. But I imagine that when you have a son of your own you will be as unwilling to gamble with his inheritance as I am unwilling to gamble with yours.'

Hugo made an impatient noise and flung himself towards the door. 'I have as much power here as a woman!' he shouted. 'I am thirty-two years old, Father, and you treat me like a child. I cannot bear it! Van Esselin is a year younger than me and he runs his father's company. Charles de Vere's father has given him his own house and retainers. I cannot be your lapdog, Sire, I warn you.'

Lord Hugh nodded. Alys glanced at him, expecting him to fire up, but he was sitting very still in thought. 'I understand that,' he said levelly. 'Tell me, Hugo. When does this Van Esselin want the money?'

'This time next year,' Hugo said. He came back towards his father in his eagerness. 'But he needs to have the firm promise of it by the autumn.'

'I'll do this for you then,' the old lord said. 'If Catherine has a son safely delivered in the October, then I'll find the thousand pounds for you. And it shall be your money and your son's money. A gift to celebrate his birth. You may do as you wish with it. Buy land in good heart and with set rents, or throw it to the winds and the seas with this venture. Let us see how your judgement is, when you have a son in your arms to be provided for, another generation to come after you.'

'If Catherine has a son, I have a thousand pounds?' Hugo asked.

The old lord nodded. 'You have my word,' he said.

Hugo stepped quickly towards his father, dropped to one knee and kissed his hand. 'I shall make my fortune then,' he said delightedly. 'For Catherine is certain she is carrying a boy. Isn't she, Alys? You think so, don't you?'

Alys nodded stiffly. Her neck was tight with strain.

'I'll go to her now and see how she fares,' Hugo said delightedly. He bowed to his father, nodded blithely at Alys and strode from the room. Alys did not move as the door shut behind him.

The old lord chuckled. 'I shall have some peace in this castle yet,' he observed. 'I shall set myself up as a marriage broker. Wait till you see how he cossets her now that she means an heir, a future and a thousand pounds for him!'

Alys moved her stiff lips in a smile, and took up the book she was reading to him.

Fifteen

Alys spent the evening on the other side of the ladies'
gallery fireplace from Hugo and watched with an impassive face as Catherine tapped him on the shoulder in
reproof at a jest, rested her hand on his shoulder and
twisted one of his dark curls around her finger.

Alys was ordered to bring Hugo some more Osney
wine from the sideboard. She went down on one knee
to serve him. He smiled down at her.

'Are you well, Alys?' he asked under his breath, so
that only she could hear. 'When I wrote to my father of
all my doings I thought of you, reading the letters. I
wrote to you as well as to him, you know.'

Alys' hand pouring the wine shook a little and the
bottle rattled on the lip of the cup.

'When I lay with a whore I thought of you, Alys,' he
said, his voice very low. 'I wondered if you were playing
with me. If you have played with me all along, and with
my father, and with my wife. What dark games do you
have, Alys? Have you truly given up play and magic
after all, as you promised?'

He glanced swiftly round. No one was watching them.
'I went away half mad for you,' he whispered. 'Everywhere I went in Newcastle the edge was off my pleasure.
I kept wondering what you would think of a thing, how
you would like it. And then I was angry with you, Alys.
I believe you bewitched me after all. I believe you have
played with me to spoil my peace.'

'I have no magic, my lord,' Alys said stiffly. 'I have a
little skill with herbs, sickness and childbirth.' She shot

a quick look at him from under her eyelashes, then she stood with the bottle of wine still in her hands. 'And my peace is spoiled too,' she said.

Hugo laughed up at her, his white teeth sharp in his smile. 'I'm ready to be witched,' he said. 'I'm ready to be tempted! But see how I am placed now, Alys! There can be nothing in my life till October – I get everything then. We could make merry till then, you and I. But in secret.'

'What are you saying?' Catherine interrupted. 'What are you saying to my lord, Alys? Don't you think she has grown thin, Hugo? Thin and white. I am afraid we are not feeding her well enough. She was so pretty when she first came to the castle and now she is as boney as a spinster at her distaff!'

The women laughed in an obedient chorus. Alys met Hugo's quick scrutiny with a look of blank resentment.

'Are you unwell?' he asked neutrally so that they could all hear.

'No,' Alys said in a tone as level as his. 'I am weary with being indoors so much. That is all.'

'Leave us now,' Catherine interrupted. 'One of you check that my bed is warm.' She shot a look at Hugo. 'Though I will be hot enough in a moment, I reckon,' she said in a loud whisper.

Hugo laughed and took the hand she reached out for him. 'Away to bed, my lady,' he said caressingly. 'You must rest for the health of my son. You don't know what a fortune I have riding on him!'

Eliza went into Catherine's bedroom and checked there were fresh herbs on the floor and under the pillows. Then she bobbed a half-curtsey to the two of them before the fire and she, and all the ladies, went to their rooms.

'Not so hot for you these days,' Morach commented as she and Alys stripped off their gowns and scurried into the cold bed in their shifts.

'No,' Alys said shortly.

'Why's that d'you think?' Morach pried.

'I don't know,' Alys said.

'I wonder why,' Morach said, undeterred.

'The old lord has him fast,' Alys said, in sudden impatience. 'He did it today, I heard every word. He will make Hugo's fortune if Catherine bears a healthy son. He has promised him a thousand pounds for his own free use.'

Morach gave a low whistle. 'So Hugo's bought off!' she said. 'No future for you then, Alys. I reckon that work you did with the moppets worked better than you thought!'

'I've wished that away a thousand times,' Alys said.

'Why?' Morach asked. 'Because you love him and desire him now? Because you want him so much that you will risk everything to lie with him? While you look at him so coldly and walk past him without looking back, are you praying he will put her aside and come to you; as hot for you, as you are for him?'

Alys pushed back the covers and jumped down to the cold floor.

'Yes,' she said through her teeth. She rattled the wood basket and threw a log on the fire. 'I am sick to my very soul for him. I cannot eat, I cannot sleep, and now tonight he lies with her again, and after this child there will be another, and another, and all there will be for me will be the leavings from her dinner.'

Morach chuckled delightedly. 'Pass me my shawl,' she said. 'And put on another log to bank up the fire. It's as good as the mummers, life in this castle. You're lost now she's with child, you know. Even without the money he wouldn't stop going with her. He has the taste of her now.'

Alys threw the shawl to Morach. 'What d'you mean?' she asked. She took a comb from the chest of clothes and a steel mirror and started to comb her hair. It was shoulder length now, a tangle of brass and gold. Alys picked impatiently at the knots.

'The taste of her?' Morach asked. 'Oh, men are trapped by it. When their women are carrying a child. Men see their women's breasts grow fuller, their rounded bellies. They like the evidence of their own rutting, even as they do it. It's two parts male swagger, and one part something else. Something old, deeper. And Hugo has it badly.'

Alys pulled at her hair mercilessly and coiled it into a rough plait. 'Badly?' she asked.

Morach cocked an eyebrow at her. 'Sure you want to hear?' she asked.

Alys nodded.

'He had her this afternoon,' Morach said. 'After he had been with his father. You were still in the old lord's chambers. He came striding down here and shooed all the women out of the room and he took her like he was possessed. If this is your magic moppets then they've done their job well. He can't leave her alone. First this afternoon and then tonight again.'

Alys' face was shocked. 'How were they together? Was he as rough with her as ever? He was never tender with her?'

Morach shook her head. 'He didn't bind her this time,' she said. 'But he did everything else he had a mind to do. He slapped her a little and he pulled her hair. Then he made her take him in her mouth. He's careful for the child so he would not lie on her. He thrust himself into her mouth and bellowed like a bull with pleasure.'

'Stop it,' Alys said abruptly. 'You're disgusting, Morach. How d'you know all this? You're lying.'

'I watched,' Morach said, smiling, tucking the fine shawl around her shoulders and moving the pillow behind her tousled head. 'I needed to know. Of course I watched.'

Alys nodded. Nothing Morach could do would surprise her.

'And what about her?' Alys said abruptly. 'Why does she permit it? Now that she has his child. Why is she still so demanding?'

Morach chuckled 'She's not demanding – you silly little virgin!' she exclaimed. 'What should she demand? She's getting everything a woman could want – and more than a decent woman would admit to wanting. She lies there, like a pink soft mountain, and lets him crawl all over her.'

Alys scowled. 'He said he would go to her no more once she was pregnant,' she said. 'He said he had to have a son, and then he would come to me. Then he said he would go to Newcastle to think what to do – that he longed to live with me and yet he had to keep her sweet. All this time I have been waiting and waiting. All this time, Morach! Waiting and waiting for him.'

Morach looked at her without sympathy. 'Go to him then,' she said. 'You cannot fight her whelping heat with your convent coldness. Go to him and tell him you want him, and that he's to leave her. Hex him, promise him darkness and passion. Pain beyond pain and pleasure beyond pleasure. There are things you could give him, there are things you could do, that he has never even dreamed of with his little drabs. Tell him you're a witch and that if he comes to you you can give him pleasures that mortal men only dream of. He's like any man – they all long for witchery and wickedness at night. If you want him, Alys, take him! You don't have much time, you know.'

'Time?' Alys asked instantly. 'You've foreseen something, Morach?'

'Away.' Morach flapped her hands, fending Alys off. 'You've not much time while you're young and beautiful. The plague could come any day and mark your face. The wind could blow and scar you. You could fall sick and lose the clear colour of your skin and your eyes and hair. You're getting thinner every day with this passion burning up inside you – a month from now and you'll be a plain spinster. If you want something you should get it at once. Waiting is a trial for no one but yourself.'

Alys nodded. 'I am on a rack of desire for him,' she said softly.

'Shall I tell him?' Morach asked. 'I'm the last person to leave them at night. I could take him to one side and tell him that if he leaves Catherine's room he can come here. And I'll keep guard till the two of you are done.'

Alys turned towards the bed and looked at the old woman. Her face was suspicious. 'Why?' she asked. 'Why would you risk offending Lady Catherine – you who stand so high in her favour, paid twice what the rest get, free to come and go, eating like a pig and free to speak your mind to her? Why risk it?'

Morach chuckled. 'It's a game, child,' she said indulgently. 'It's like casting the runes, or reading the cards, or making herbs. It's a game. What will happen next? All magic is the question – what will happen if . . . ? I want to know what will happen to you when Hugo has you. I want to see that happen. It takes my fancy, that's all.'

'Can't you see it?' Alys asked. 'Why can't you see the future as you used to see it, Morach?'

The old woman shrugged. 'I can see you don't have long; that should be enough for you. When I look, it all goes dark, I can see nothing except darkness and water. So you'd best act as any woman would – never mind the Sight. What will it be? Shall I tell him you want to see him?'

Alys paused. 'Yes,' she said, with sudden decision. 'Now. Call him out now. Get him away from Catherine now. I can't bear him to lie with her tonight.'

The old woman nodded and slipped from the bed, spread the shawl around her shoulders and crept through the door. Alys took up the mirror again, ruffled her hand through her thick hair, watched the colour rise in her pale cheeks. Across the gallery she could hear Morach's peremptory knock on the door and her call: 'Lord Hugo! The old lord is asking for you. He said you were to come at once!'

She heard Hugo's muttered oath and his quick step to the door. She heard him call to Catherine, telling her to sleep, and then the bedroom door slam behind him. He stepped out into the gallery.

Alys tossed aside the mirror and went out of her room to meet him.

'Lord Hugh does not need you, I sent Morach to call you out,' she said. She held her head very high and her hair fell in a ripple of gold away from her face. Hugo stared at her, at the thin cotton of her nightgown and at the rapid pulse beating at the hollow of her neck under the half-open gown.

'Alys,' he said softly.

He could see the muscles in her neck move as she swallowed.

'I cannot bear you to lie with her,' Alys said. 'You told me to wait until you came back from Newcastle and I have waited. I want you as my lover. I have dreamed and dreamed of you coming home to me.'

Hugo's dark gleam of a smile came, and faded. 'You heard my father,' he said. 'You know how much I need an heir. You know that my future and my family's future depends on an heir to this castle and these lands. And he has promised me that money, Alys. I cannot distress Catherine when she is carrying the child I need more than anything else in the world!'

'What about me!' Alys broke out. 'I see what Catherine needs – aye, and gets! And I see what you need! But what about me?'

Hugo looked at her, his smile crinkling around his eyes. 'You want me,' he said. It was not a question.

Alys nodded.

'Is Morach gone from your room?' he asked.

Alys did not look up; she nodded again.

'Come then,' he said and slid his arm around her waist, and she let him lead her to her bedroom, swing her off her feet and lay her on the bed.

He pulled up her gown to see her naked and gave a little grunt of pleasure at the sight – like an animal, Alys thought. She closed her eyes and thought of the nights and days she had longed for him, had longed for this moment.

'This is Hugo,' she said to herself. 'Hugo, that I have dreamed of and longed for, and desired more than I have ever desired anyone in my life.'

It did not help. She felt cold and arid. She was nervous of the pain and the weight of him.

Hugo hitched his nightshirt up around his waist. 'If you were a witch indeed then you would enchant me,' he said. 'They were talking of witchery in Newcastle. They say if a man so much as touches their skin then no other woman can ever excite him again.'

Alys shook her head. 'I'm no witch,' she said. 'You told me to put all that aside, I did as you bid me. I cannot enchant you.' She was getting cold, half naked before him.

Hugo dropped on top of her and Alys was crushed beneath his weight. He had eaten spicy meat at supper and his breath was sour. She threw her arms around his broad shoulders and said, 'Hugo,' thinking how she had longed for this moment – that it *must* be what she wanted, since she had wanted it for so long.

'If you were a witch,' Hugo said, rubbing himself gently against her, 'what pleasures would you give me, Alys? Do you think witches can make men fly? Do you think they can make them lust all night and all day? Would you conjure for me virgin after virgin? All of them wet with desire, all longing for me. All lying with me and with each other? A great rolling bed of women with mouths and hands and bodies for my pleasure alone?'

As his words excited him he arched his back and leaned up on his hands and pushed into her. Alys screamed – a sharp scream of pain – and wriggled at once away from him. 'No!'

Hugo laughed, put his hands on her thin shoulders and said breathlessly: 'Take it, Alys! It's what you've been hot for! It's what you've been pining for! What did you expect? A touch as gentle as your own busy little fingers? This is what a man does, Alys! Learn to like it!'

At every word he spoke he thrust deeper into her.

Alys scrabbled frantically against him, trying to pull herself up and away from his greedy lust. 'Oh!' Hugo said suddenly, and he fell heavily on her.

They lay very still for a few moments. The pain inside her eased a little and she felt his cock grow limp and slide away. She smelled her blood and felt it trickle on her cold thighs. She felt the skin around her eyes tighten and grow cold with drying tears. She moved a little and Hugo rolled off her, like a pig in a wallow, and lay on his back, gazing blankly at the ceiling.

Alys crept a little closer and put her warm head on his shoulder. She could hear his heart thudding and slowing. His arm came around her and held her.

'I hurt,' Alys said in a little voice, like an injured child.

Hugo chuckled. 'Not a witch then,' he said. 'You've done no shagging with the devil, that's for sure.'

'I told you I was no witch,' Alys said impatiently. 'I was a virgin. You have taken my virginity. And you hurt me, Hugo.'

He nodded, as if it did not matter much. 'It always hurts maids the first time,' he said indifferently. 'What did you expect?'

Alys said nothing, but the world of her expectations was laid out before her in bitter colours.

Hugo gave a yawn and sat up. 'Give me a cloth,' he said. 'I cannot go back to Catherine like this.'

Alys slipped from the bed and walked awkwardly over to the linen chest. She could feel a trickle of blood flow warm down her thigh. She passed him a length of linen. 'Go back to Catherine?' she said stupidly.

'Of course,' he said. He mopped at his crutch with quick, hard gestures, wiping her blood away. Wiping the smell of her away. He looked up at her shocked face and shrugged.

'Come on, Alys,' he said impatiently. 'You heard my father, you know what this child means to me. Every night of my life until the baby is born I shall sleep in Catherine's bed. I shall make her as content and serene as I can. I owe it to my son, I owe it to my line and, by God, I owe it to myself! I have waited to sire a son for eighteen years! One woman after another has been barren with me. Now my wife, my own legal wife, is with my child and they all say it will be a son. Of course I shall watch over her, and anything she wants will be hers!'

'I dreamed of a son that we would have,' Alys started. 'You and me.'

Hugo leaned forward and patted her white cheek. 'When you are pregnant with my son *you* will be my favourite,' he said carelessly. 'While Catherine carries my son I am hers to command. Right now there is only one thing in the world which could keep me from Catherine.'

'And what is that?' Alys asked. Her throat was aching from holding in her anger and her pain.

Hugo grinned. 'The rutting I have dreamed of with you!' he said, laughing. 'Ever since I saw you, and especially since they all thought you were a witch, I thought you would take me – like witches are said to take men. I thought you would ride me like I mount a horse. I thought you would know ways which would drive me mad with lust for you.'

Alys shook her head slowly. 'And instead, I was just another virgin,' she said softly. 'An ordinary girl.'

Hugo stood up, tossed aside the bloodied cloth and drew Alys into his arms. 'Ordinary girls give pleasure too,' he said consolingly. 'Another time, sweetheart, when I am not wearied with travelling and sated with Catherine. Another time it will be better for us both.'

Alys nodded, hearing dismissal in his voice.

'But don't send Morach for me again,' he said warningly. 'Catherine is bound to find out and distress could harm the baby. I will come to you when I can leave her without her knowing. I will come to you when she sleeps.'

'In corners,' Alys said. 'In doorways. Hidden in secrecy.'

Hugo gleamed. 'I love it like that,' he said 'Desperate and quick. Wouldn't you like me to take you like that, when we're too hot to wait for a proper time?'

Alys turned her head away so that he could not see the anger and resentment in her eyes. 'Like any ordinary girl,' she said.

He put an arm around her waist and kissed her carelessly on the top of her head.

'I must go,' he said. 'Sweet dreams.'

The door shut softly behind him. Alys walked wearily to the bed, flung herself down on her back and watched the flicker of the firelight on the ceiling. She did not turn her head as the door opened. She knew it was not Hugo.

'Fool,' Morach said companionably. 'I thought you were hot for him. I could have told you it would hurt, lying with a man you hate.'

Alys turned her head slowly on the pillow. 'I don't hate him,' she said slowly. 'I love him. I love him more than life itself.'

Morach gave a little crow of laughter and hitched herself up into the high bed.

'Aye, you say you do,' she said agreeably. 'And you think you do. But your body says different, child. Your body said "no" all the way through, didn't it? Even when you kept trying to tell yourself you were in heaven.'

Alys raised herself up on one elbow. 'Help me, Morach,' she said. 'It hurt and I hated him touching me like that. And yet I used to tremble when he so much as looked at me.'

Morach chuckled and heaved the blankets over to her own side. 'He's a disappointment to you,' she said. 'And you hate Catherine. You're torn different ways at once. And you don't consult your own pleasure. Get hold of your power, Alys! Find what you want and take it. You lay there tonight and asked him to rape you. What he wants is a woman to drive him mad – not another victim.'

Alys pulled the blankets back and turned on her side with her back to Morach. 'And you watched,' she said irritably.

'Of course,' Morach said calmly. 'And I can tell you, he had more pleasure with Catherine's wanton joy than he did with you.'

Alys said nothing.

'If it had been me,' Morach said thoughtfully to Alys' stiff back, 'I'd have taken my time and given him wine, and taken a glass myself. I'd have drugged him maybe. I'd have used earthroot which makes a man dream of desire until he is mad with it and makes him hard with no chance of ease for hours. I'd have told him bawdy stories, I'd have let him watch me touch myself. I'd have told him I was a witch and that if he touched me he would go mad for my touch forever. And when he was half pickled with lust *then* I'd have let him have me. I wouldn't have whimpered beneath him like a ravished scullion.'

Alys shut her eyes and hunched up her shoulder.

'But I wouldn't have done any of that until I'd decided whether I wanted him or not,' Morach said to

297

the quiet room. 'I wouldn't have a man when we had a score to settle. I wouldn't tup a man who was lying his head off to me. I wouldn't let him roll on me and then wash himself clean as if I was dirt. I'd make him choose between me and his wife. And I'd use my magic to make him choose me.'

Alys turned around and looked at Morach. 'There is no magic in the world that can stand against an heir,' she said bitterly. 'All I can hope for is for the bitch to die in childbirth and the heir to die with her.'

Morach met her look. 'And me here to see she does not,' she said equably. 'It's a fine net you've meshed yourself in, little Alys.'

Alys turned her back on Morach again and thumped down into the bed.

'You must wish you were back at the abbey,' Morach said, rubbing salt in the old wound. 'You'd have been safe from all this uncomfortable reality there. Safe with your mother in Christ.' She paused. 'Pity,' she said cheerfully.

Alys had thought herself unhappy before, but after that night her days were harder still. The weather was against her through a long wintry April. Alys thought that the long season of darkness and cold would never end.

She had known harder winters in her childhood with Morach when food and even firewood had been scarce, and for frozen day after frozen day Morach had sent her out of the door of the snowed-in shanty to scoop a bucket of snow and set it to thaw on the little precious flame. At night they had huddled together for warmth and listened for the cry of the wolf pack which came nearer at twilight and dawn. Morach would throw another turf of peat on the fire and a handful of herbs and laugh as if the bitter cold and the pain in her belly and the long lonely cry of the wolves amused her.

'Learn this,' she would say to Alys – wide-eyed and thin as an orphan lamb. 'Learn this. Never cross a powerful man, my Alys. Find your place and keep it.' And the little child with the great blue eyes too big for her white face would nod and clench her little chicken-foot hands in the old sign against the evil eye.

'That farmer was a bad man,' she said solemnly.

'He was that,' Morach replied with relish. 'And dead now for his injustice to me. Find your place and keep it, Alys! And then avoid the hard men with power!'

Alys had been cold then with a deep iron coldness which had stayed with her for all her life like some incurable growth of ice in her belly. All the petting at the abbey, all the banked fires of blazing logs, all the sheepskin rugs and the wool tapestries could not cure her of it. When the wind howled around the walls of the abbey she would shiver and look up at Mother Hildebrande and ask:

'Was that wolves? Was that wolves, Mother Hildebrande?'

And the old abbess would laugh and draw the child's head against her knees and stroke her fingers through her fair curly hair and say, 'Hush, my little lapwing. What if there are? You are safe here, behind the thick walls, are you not?'

And the child would reply, with deep satisfaction: 'This is my place now.'

And now I have no place, and I am cold again, Alys said to herself.

She was seated on the kitchen step, her hands dug deep into her sleeves, her face turned up to the thin yellow light of the winter sun. All the other women were indoors, chattering and laughing in the warm gallery. Morach was singing some bawdy ditty to amuse them and Catherine was laughing aloud with one hand held over her swelling belly.

Alys had left them with an irritable shiver to run down to the garden to gather herbs. The old lord had a cough at nights which made him weary and Alys wanted the heads of lavender for him to help him rest. They were stunted and frozen, they should have been picked when the juice was in them, fresh and violet and sweet in midsummer.

'They were neglected and left, and now they are cold and dry,' Alys said, turning the arid handful in her lap. 'Oh God, Hugo.'

Between Catherine's demands for company and the needs of the old lord who sank one day but rallied the next, Alys should have been busy, with no time to brood. But all those long weeks, as it snowed deeper, and then thawed, and then snowed again, Alys moped at the fireside, at the arrow-slit window, or shivered on her own in the frozen garden.

'What ails you, Alys, are you sick?' the old lord asked.

David the dwarf peeped at her and gleamed his malicious smile. 'A sick physician? A foolish wise woman? A dried-out herbalist?' he asked. 'What are you, Alys? A gourd rattling with dried seeds?'

Only Morach in the dark room which they shared at night put her dirty finger precisely on the root of Alys' pain. 'You're dying for him, aren't you?' she said bluntly. 'Dying inside for him.'

Hugo barely noticed her in his busy days. He wrote a stream of letters to London, to Bristol and to Newcastle, and cursed like a soldier at the delay in their delivery and replies. He supervised the pulling-down of the big keystones of the abbey and the men dragged them over the snow on sledges to make a heap where he planned his new house. 'Not a castle,' he told Catherine. 'A regular house. A Tudor house. A house for a lasting peace.'

He drew plans for his new handsome house. It was to have windows, not arrow-slits. It was to have chimneys and fireplaces in every room. He would have had the men dig foundations, but no one could drive so much as a knife into the frozen ground. Instead, he measured up and drew it, and showed it to David, and argued about kitchens and the bakehouse and the number of rooms and the best aspect. When he strode into the castle, as the wintry darkness came down in the afternoon, all the women in the castle fluttered – like hens in a shed with a fox beneath the floor. Hugo let his dark laughing eyes rove over all of them, and then took his pick in a shadowed doorway for a few minutes of rough pleasure.

He rarely had the same woman twice, Alys saw. He never wilfully hurt them or played the mad cruel games he had done with his wife. He treated them with abrupt lust and then quick dismissal.

And they loved him for it. 'He is a rogue!' 'He is the old lord reborn!' 'He is a man!' she heard them say. He put his hand out to Alys once with a quizzical smile and a dark eyebrow raised. Alys had looked through him, her face as inviting as frozen stone, and he had laughed shortly and turned away. She heard him whistle as he ran down the stairs, accepting her rejection as lightly as he had accepted her invitation. She no longer ran deep in Hugo's blood – he had too many diversions. He never came again to her room while Catherine slept –

Alys never expected it. She had taken a gamble on her desire and lost him, and lost her desire too.

All she had left to her was a nagging knowledge that she needed him, at a level which ran deeper than lust. Alys felt she had tried his lust and found it wanting. In his easy dismissal of her she felt her power – over him, over herself, over all of them – drain away like the pale sunsets which bled light from the narrow line of the western horizon in the early afternoons of the dark winter days.

One day the crystal on the thread hung downwards heavy and still, like a plumb-line, when she laid her hand on the old lord's chest.

'Have you lost your power, Alys?' he asked sharply, his dark eyes wide open, alert as a ruffled old eagle owl.

Alys met his gaze unmoved. 'I think so, my lord,' she said, cold to her very bones. 'I cannot get the thing I desire, and I cannot learn not to desire it. I've no time nor appetite for anything. Now it seems I've no ability either.'

'Why's that?' he asked briefly; he was short of breath.

'Hugo,' Alys said. 'He wanted me to be an ordinary woman, a girl to love. Now I am so ordinary he passes me by. I threw my power away for love of him and now I have neither the power nor the love.'

The old lord had barked a sharp laugh at that which ended in him coughing and wheezing. 'Get Morach for me then,' he said. 'Morach shall tend me instead of you. Catherine says that she trusts her with everything. That she is a great healer, an uncanny herbalist.'

Alys nodded, her face pinched. 'As you wish,' she said. The words were like flakes of snow.

The old lord used her as his clerk still, but there were only a few letters he cared to write during his sickness,

302

during Lent. But when she was sitting at the wide oriel window of the ladies' gallery on the Wednesday after Easter Day Alys saw a half-dozen homing pigeons winging in from the south, circling the castle in a broad determined swoop and then angling, like a flight of sluggish arrows, towards their coops on the roof of the round tower. It meant urgent news from London. Alys bobbed a curtsey to Catherine and left the ladies' gallery. She arrived at Lord Hugh's door as the messenger came down the stairs from the roof of the tower with the tiny scrap of paper in his hand. Alys followed him into the room.

'Shall I read it?' Alys asked.

Lord Hugh nodded.

Alys unfurled the little scrap. It was written in Latin. 'I don't understand it,' Alys said.

'Read it,' Hugh said.

'It says: *On Easter Tuesday the Spanish envoy refused an invitation to dine with the Queen. The King took mass with him and the Queen's brother was ordered to attend him.*'

'That all?'

'Yes,' Alys said. 'But what does it mean?'

'It means the Boleyn girl has fallen,' Lord Hugh said without regret. 'Praise God I am friends with the Seymours.'

He said it like an epitaph on a gravestone, and closed his eyes. Alys watched his hard, unforgiving face as he slept and wondered if Queen Anne yet knew that she was lost.

After that day there was little work for her in the castle except reading to the old lord and sitting with Catherine. She could not be trusted to sew an intricate pattern – she lacked attention, Catherine complained.

She had lost her intuition for herbs and Catherine shivered at the touch of her cold fingers. Day after day Alys had less and less to do but watch and wait for Hugo – and then see him pass by her without noticing her in the shadows.

She grew thinner and she took to drinking more and more wine at dinner as the food stuck in her throat. It was the only thing which helped her sleep, and when she slept she dreamed long wonderful dreams of Hugo at her side, and his son in her arms, and a yellow gown slashed with red silk and a snow-white fur trim.

As snow turned to sleet and then rain, the ground grew softer. At the end of April the young lord rode out every dawn and did not come back till dusk. They had started digging the foundations for the new house and on the day they had completed the outline he came home early, at midday, dirty with mud, bursting into Catherine's gallery, where she was sewing a tapestry with Morach idly holding the silks on one side of her and Alys and Eliza and Ruth stitching at the border.

'You must come and see it!' Hugo said. 'You *must*, Catherine. And you shall see the rooms I have planned for you and for our son. She can come, can't she, Morach? She can ride the grey palfrey?'

His glance flickered past Alys to the older woman. Alys kept her eyes on her work but she could feel him near her as a trout can feel a fisherman's shadow.

'If it's a very quiet horse,' Morach replied. 'Riding will not harm either of them, but a fall could be fatal.'

'And all your ladies,' Hugo said expansively. 'All of them! You must be pining to go out – mewed up here like fat goshawks! Wouldn't you like to smell the moorland air again, Alys? Feel the wind in your face?'

Catherine smiled at Alys. 'She won't leave your

304

father,' she said. 'She is always with him or running errands for him. She can stay. And also Margery and Mistress Allingham. I will come, and Eliza and Ruth and Morach.'

'As you wish,' Hugo said readily. 'As you wish. We'll go tomorrow. I'll walk out with you today, after dinner.' He caught sight of Alys, face down-turned to her work. 'You don't begrudge us our pleasure, Alys?' He had a wish, as wilful as a teasing child, to see her face and her eyes and to hold her attention.

She did not look up at him. 'Of course not, my lord,' she said, her voice thin but steady. 'I hope you and my lady have a pleasant day.'

'You must be thirsty, my lord,' Catherine interrupted. 'Alys, call for some wine for my lord before you leave us. You are bid to go to Lord Hugh, are you not?'

Alys rose to her feet and went to pull the bell.

'Is my father ill?' Hugo asked.

'Oh no,' Catherine reassured him. 'Alys does not tend his health now. She has lost her skill. Isn't that strange? Morach tends him now. But he likes Alys to read to him. Doesn't he, Alys?'

Alys shot a quick look at Hugo from under her eyelashes. 'Yes,' she said. 'May I go now?'

Hugo smiled, his eyes resting on her, his look thoughtful, and nodded her away. Alys, her eyes on the floor, her face pale, went out of the heavy door and closed it quietly behind her.

'Not long now,' Morach said, watching Hugo's eyes following Alys to the door. 'Not long now,' she said with malicious satisfaction.

'What?' Catherine demanded impatiently.

Morach's grin was irrepressible. 'I said, not long now. I was thinking of a game I know.'

Sixteen

The old lord kept Alys with him after dinner, he had a letter by messenger from his cousin in London. The man had come slowly, overland up the Great North Road, travelling with others delayed by snowdrifts. The news he brought was a week old. But gossip and rumours have a long life. Lady Jane Seymour had been given her own apartments at Greenwich Palace – as grand as those of the Queen. Rochford, the Queen's brother, was not to be elected to the Garter. That honour was given elsewhere. The King had danced with Lady Jane Seymour all evening. The King and the Queen were to watch a May Day joust together but the court was seething with stories of a quarrel between the Queen and King when she had stripped the baby Princess Elizabeth naked and thrust her at him, demanding if he could find a flaw, a single flaw, on the chubby little body. Another perfect child would follow the first, she swore. But the King had turned away.

Alys read the letter to him and then burned it when he nodded to the fire. There was also a letter from the College of Heralds. Lord Hugh wanted to add a quartering to his shield to greet his new grandson. There was a precedent for the honour in Catherine's family and the old lord and the college were haggling about the justice of the claim and the price that would have to be paid for the added lustre to Hugh's name. He shook his head at their demands. 'I must watch my ambition,' he said. 'See what ambition is doing to the Boleyns, Alys. The safest place to be is halfway down the hall. Not too near the top table.'

There was a lease sent from the Bowes manor for his inspection. A tenant was resisting a change of his holding from entry and occasional fines to an annual rent. He wanted to pay his fines in goods but the castle was hungry for cash. Alys read the medieval Latin of the lease slowly, stumbling over the archaic words. Lord Hugh watched the flames in the fireplace, nodding first with concentration and then with weariness, and then his eyes slowly closed. Alys read on a few sentences more and then softly laid down the parchment and looked at him. He was fast asleep.

She rose quietly from her chair and went softly to the arrow-slit in the westward wall and looked out. Below her on the far side of the river-bank she could see Lady Catherine walking awkwardly, wrapped in furs, one hand on Hugo's arm. He was leaning towards her so that he could hear what she said above the rushing of the water. Even at that distance Alys could see Catherine's adoring gaze up at Hugo and her smile.

The old lord was dozing behind Alys, the fire crackled in the grate. Alys watched how Hugo leaned towards Catherine and how he helped her across the muddy parts of the path. At a distance Morach followed, with a basket on her arm and Eliza Herring walking at her side. The other ladies must have stayed indoors. Behind them were two armed servants on horseback. Hugo was taking no chances with the safety of his wife and unborn son.

Alys felt her hands hurting and looked down. She had clenched them into fists and her nails had marked four deep red sickles into each palm. 'Oh God, this jealousy is my crucifixion,' she whispered, but she stayed watching, unable to leave the window.

Catherine slipped a little on the mud and Hugo

caught her with one arm around her waist. Alys could almost hear her laugh as Hugo held her, then she turned her face up to him and his dark head came down and he kissed her.

Alys felt her cheeks burn. Somewhere, from the back of her mind, came the memory of the doll which she had thrown in the moat. The three dolls were hidden in the purse on a piece of string dangling out of the garderobe, waiting for the time that they could be buried. Alys had kept her mind away from them with the same disciplined blindness that she stopped herself thinking of the nunnery, of her mother, or of fire.

But when she saw Catherine slip, so near to those deep icy waters, she thought again of the little doll of Catherine which she had thrown far out into the green waters of the moat and which had bobbed and turned its face to her, and then smiled at her and nearly drowned her from its own power and malice.

'Oh, but I'm safe now,' Alys said aloud. 'I'm safe here indoors, while you are out there.'

She glanced back into the room. The old lord was snoring, his cap askew, his head on one side. The warm glow of the firelight flickered red on the stone walls. The deerhound dozed before the fire, paws twitching now and then in his dream.

'Nothing could hurt me here,' Alys said. She looked back out of the window. 'But you . . . ' she whispered to Catherine. '*You* are very near the water. And the spell on the dolls was very potent. So potent that your husband went to you and loved you with such passion that he has forgotten all about me. It was my power in the dolls that drew him to you. It was my power in the dolls that put that baby in your belly. And the doll for you was drowning, Catherine. Your doll was drowning.'

Alys was silent for a moment, her bewitching whisper falling into the quietness of the room.

'I had a Seeing of Hugo and me together,' she murmured. 'Perhaps that meant you died, Catherine. Perhaps you're going to die. Perhaps you're going to drown. Perhaps you're going to drown now.'

Walking a short distance behind the couple Morach paused and put her head on one side as if listening to some distant noise.

'Perhaps it will happen now,' Alys whispered. She was pressing up against the window-sill, leaning her whole body against the cold stone, forcing her will through the very walls of the castle.

'Perhaps now, Catherine,' she said. She started humming, very deep in her throat, a powerful sleepy noise like a swarm of toxic bees. 'Perhaps now,' she whispered yearningly. 'The water is very deep and very cold, Catherine. The rocks are very sharp. If you slip and fall now, you will be swept downriver and by the time they get you out, your lungs and your belly will be filled with icy water. You nearly drowned me. I know how it feels. And soon, you will know it too.'

Morach was standing as alert as a hound listening for the horn. Then she whirled towards the castle and stared towards it, raking the arrow-slits with her stare as if she were looking for Alys, almost as if Alys had called loudly and clearly towards her. She looked straight towards the narrow slit of window in the great tower where Alys stood. For a moment the two women stared towards each other and Alys knew that – despite the distance, the narrowness of the arrow-slit and the darkness of the room – Morach was looking into her eyes and reading her mind. Then Morach yelled a wordless warning and started running towards Catherine.

Hugo turned at the shout and his hand went to his sword. Catherine swung around and lost her footing on the mud of the path, stepped backwards, and with the awkward misbalance of pregnancy stumbled on the very edge of the path. Her arms flailed like a helpless child. Alys, watching with burning eyes, was humming louder and louder, deep in her throat; and it was as if the power of the sound was pressing down on the little figure, wrapped tight in bulky furs. Catherine clawing helplessly at the air, her mouth wide in a scream, fell slowly backwards. Then she was gone – head over heels, clear over the rocks at the edge of the river, into the deep pool and down into the fast flooding waters.

Hugo tore at his sword and flung it aside, yelled at the soldiers for help, and jumped down on to the rocks and boulders at the river's edge, throwing himself towards the water. But Morach was quicker. In an instant she dived out over the rocks, deep into the pool, and went down below the water like a questing otter. She came back up and duck-dived again.

'Get out of the way, Morach,' Alys breathed through the window, shaking with dismay. 'You're *my* kin, not hers. You're working for my interests, not hers. Leave her, Morach. Leave her be!'

Morach shook her head, as if to rid herself of a voice in her ears, and dived. There was a flash of white as her feet kicked in the air and then a flurry of colour of drowned cloth as she surfaced with Catherine in her arms. Hugo waded in, waist deep in the water, and grabbed Catherine. Alys could see that she was limp, perhaps stunned. She knew the woman was not dead. It would have been a rare piece of luck if she had broken her neck or staved in her head on a rock.

Hugo gathered Catherine into his arms and then

reached out a hand for Morach. One soldier jumped down and passed the two women up to his fellow on the bank. Alys watched it all, dry-eyed, white-faced. She watched Hugo scoop Catherine back into his arms for a stumbling run towards their horses. She saw Catherine grab the pommel of the saddle with one limp hand as she was handed up on to the horse, and Morach was tossed up behind one of the soldiers. The little cavalcade moved out of sight around the curve of the tower and Alys guessed they would hurry back into the castle by one of the sally-ports. At any moment now there would be an alarm and people running, and everyone worried about Catherine and praising Morach.

Alys pushed herself stiffly away from the window and pulled out a footstool to sit at Lord Hugh's feet and watch the flames of the fire. She shivered a little as she remembered the icy greenness of the moat. Then she leaned forwards and put her chin on her hands and stared with blank, unseeing eyes into the very heart of the redness – and waited for the noise and the shouting to start.

She did not wait long. Lord Hugh jumped out of his sleep at the yell from the great hall which echoed up to his room.

'What is that? What is that?' he demanded. 'Alys! Are we under attack? What is that noise?'

'I'll go and see, my lord,' Alys said smoothly.

She went to the door but as she opened it David came in. 'Nothing to alarm you, my lord,' he said swiftly. 'The Lady Catherine had a fall in the river and Lord Hugo has brought her safe home. She is being put to bed by her women. Her wise woman says she thinks the child is not hurt.'

'God be praised!' the old lord said, crossing himself.

'Tell her I'll come at once. Alys! D'you hear that! Catherine near-drowned and the heir with her! God's breath! That was a narrow escape!'

'I'd best go to her,' Alys said.

'Yes, yes. Go and see how she is and come straight back to me. I'll come and see her myself when she permits. And tell Hugo to come to me as soon as his wife is settled.'

Alys slipped from the room and ran down the stairs to the ladies' gallery. The place was in uproar. Servants were running around with wood-baskets, ewers of hot water, jugs of mulled wine and hot mead. Catherine's women were shrieking orders and then cancelling them, snatching up Catherine's hands to chafe and kiss. Hugo, supporting Catherine, was yelling for them to put a warming-pan in Catherine's bed and clear the room so she could be undressed. Morach, ignoring the hubbub, dripped a wet path to Alys' chamber. She checked when she saw Alys in the doorway and their eyes met.

'You swim like a witch,' Alys said, not caring who heard her.

'And you curse like one,' Morach replied, venom in her voice.

'Why meddle?' Alys asked, dropping her voice so her words were lost in the shouting. 'You heard my power, you know what I was doing. Why meddle in my work?'

Morach shrugged. 'That's a death I'd wish on no one,' she said. She shuddered as if she was chilled to her soul. 'I'd hate to die by water,' she said. 'I couldn't stand by and see a woman die by water. Not a young woman, not a young woman with child, not one that I'd served. You're a harder woman than me, Alys, if you could have stood by and watched her drown.'

'I was holding her under with all the power I have,' Alys said through her teeth.

'And I pulled her out,' Morach said, blazing. 'There are some deaths no woman should suffer. I'd rather any death than drowning. I'd rather any death in the world than going under the water and choking my way to hell.'

Alys glanced around her. Eliza Herring was within earshot, though screeching instructions to a servant. 'Thank God you were there,' Alys said loudly.

Morach gleamed under her dripping mat of grey hair. 'Thank you for your good wishes.' She pushed past Alys and went into their little room, slamming the door.

Alys turned and clapped her hands together. 'You men!' she said, her voice clear above the noise. 'Out! All of you! We cannot get Lady Catherine abed with you all here. Eliza! Turn down her bed. You girl!' – to a passing maid – 'Get those warming-pans into her bed. And you' – to another – 'see the fires are banked high in her chamber and this one.'

The room emptied at once. 'Out of the way!' Alys said crossly to the maidservants and to Catherine's ladies who still cluttered the room. She took Catherine's other arm and she and Hugo led the shivering woman into her chamber and lowered her into a chair by the fire.

'Fetch towels and sheets,' Alys ordered Hugo, without looking at him. She pulled off Catherine's sodden fur cloak and dropped it on the floor. Then she unpinned her head-dress, undid her gown, and stripped her with hard hands until the woman was naked.

Hugo passed her the towels and both of them rubbed her hard all over until her white skin glowed pink and the roughness of the gooseflesh had subsided. Then Alys wrapped her tight in the warm sheets and Hugo lifted her into bed. Alys piled rugs on top of her and pulled the warming-pans out to refill them with fresh embers, while Hugo gave her hot mead to drink. Her teeth chattered pitifully on the cup. Alys, at the fireside, shovelling embers, hunched her shoulders.

'I'm cold,' Catherine said.

Hugo shot a despairing look at Alys. The room was as hot as a bread-oven. Alys' face was flushed, her forehead damp with sweat. The mud on Hugo's boots was dried to dust by the heat, his wet clothes were steaming.

'Drink some more mead,' Alys said, without turning round. She slammed the scorching lid of the warming-pan and then wrapped it in a towel and thrust it into the bed under Catherine's feet.

'I'm so cold, Alys,' Catherine said. Her voice was high and thin, like a child. 'I'm so cold, Alys. Can you not give me something to make me warm?'

Alys turned to the chest and pulled out one of Catherine's great fur cloaks with the hood. 'Sit up a little,' she said. 'We'll put this around you like a shawl, and you can have the hood over your wet hair. You'll soon warm up.'

Together they raised her in the bed. Alys looked away when her robe fell open and the rounded part of her belly was exposed. She looks like a mead-pot, Alys thought irritably, all gross curves. Beside the plump naked woman, Alys felt herself to be a shadow, a spectre of darkness. She tucked the thick furs around Catherine and then pulled the bedclothes up again.

'Warmer?' she asked.

Catherine nodded and tried to smile, but her face was still white. Hugo held her cold hands in his own. He turned them over, her fingernails were blue.

'Should she be blooded?' he asked Alys. 'Should we sent for a surgeon and bleed her?'

Alys shook her head. 'She needs all her blood,' she said. 'She's choleric in humour. She'll warm up.'

'And the baby?' he asked. He turned a little away from the bed so Alys could hear him, but Catherine could not. 'The baby is the most important thing. Will the baby be all right?'

Alys nodded. She had a very sour taste in her mouth. She did not want to put her face too close to Hugo, she thought her breath would smell foul. 'I doubt this will harm the baby,' she said. 'You will be laughing about this in a few days. Both of you.'

Hugo nodded but his face was dark with worry. 'Pray God that's so,' he said.

Alys turned away. 'I have to go to your father,' she said. 'He sent me to find news of Lady Catherine. Shall I send one of the other women in to sit with her?'

Hugo shook his head. 'I'll go to him,' he said. 'And I'll come back at once. You stay here and watch over her. I trust you to care for her, Alys. You know how much this child means to me. He will be my future – and my freedom. He will make my fortune this autumn if we can get him through to a safe birth and to his grandfather's arms.'

Alys nodded. 'I know,' she said.

Hugo turned back to the bed where Catherine lay, her arms wrapped around herself, shivering in the baking heat of the bedroom. 'I am going to tell my father that you are safe and well,' he said. 'I will leave Alys here to care for you, and I will come back in a few moments.'

Catherine nodded and lay back, her jaw clenched to keep her teeth from chattering. Against the dark furs her skin was white as thick vellum. The door shut quietly behind Hugo as he went out.

The two women were alone. The room was silent. In the gallery outside the bedroom door, Catherine's other women waited around the fire twittering like nervous birds. Catherine did not have the strength to call them, she could not reach out her hand to the bell. She was as much in Alys' power as if Alys had her bound and gagged and a knife whetted ready for her throat.

Alys turned from the door and came slowly to the foot of the bed. Catherine's pale brown eyes looked up at her.

'I felt as if I was pushed,' she said. Her lip trembled, like a little child that has suffered some unimaginable unkindness. 'I felt as if someone pushed me. But there was no one there.'

Alys looked back at her, her face impassive.

'I heard a humming noise, a loud humming noise – like bees, or like a person humming – and then I felt someone push me, push me hard, push me into the water,' she said.

Alys' lovely face was clear, her blue eyes confident. 'These are fancies,' she said, her voice lilting, sweet as a song. 'You have had a grievous fright. Pregnant women have these fears, my lady. There was no one near you, my lady. How could anyone hum and throw you in the river?' She laughed gently.

Catherine put a hand out of the nest of furs towards Alys. 'Will you hold my hand, Alys?' she asked pitifully. 'I am afraid. I feel so afraid.'

Alys came a little closer. She could hear the humming in her own head now, like a drowsy hive. She knew that if she touched the smallest fingertip of Catherine's white cold hand she would succumb to temptation and snatch up the pillow and crush it down over her frightened face. The humming was too loud to resist.

'I have been cruel to you, Alys,' Catherine said, her voice a thin thread. 'I have treated you unkindly and tormented you. I was jealous.'

Alys kept her face blank, and held on to the noise of the humming. Louder and louder the noise swelled, while Catherine beckoned her closer.

'I am sorry,' Catherine said softly. 'Please forgive me, Alys. Hugo looked on you with such desire I could not bear it. Please forgive me.'

The humming was drowning out thought. Catherine was reaching out for her. Alys' hands trembled with the desire to lock around her fat neck and squeeze and squeeze until there was no breath left in that plump, white, indulged body.

'Please, Alys,' Catherine said pitifully. 'You do not know what it is to feel jealousy such as I felt for you. It led me into the sin of unkindness to you. I know I taunted you and tormented you. I am afraid I made an enemy of you. Forgive me, Alys. Please say you forgive me.'

Alys stepped a little closer. Catherine's face was pitiful. Alys found herself smiling, warm with joy at what she was about to do. Catherine reached out for her murderer with imploring hands. Alys took another step closer, stretched out her own hands . . .

'For the sake of Our Lady,' Catherine said. 'Take my hand, Alys, and say you forgive me.'

At the name of the Holy Mother Alys checked, closed her eyes for a second and shook her head. She took a deep breath. The humming sound burned angrily in her head for a moment and then rumbled softly away, deep and soft, as if a dark swarm had gone back to a cave, to hide for a while, until their time should come again.

Catherine reached out for her. Alys stepped forward and reluctantly took her outstretched hand.

'I was jealous,' Catherine went on eagerly. 'You were so beautiful when you first came to the castle, Alys. And Hugo was so cold to me. You are so clever and so learned, and the old lord liked you – and he never really liked me. And I was afraid that you were taking them from me, both of them. My husband and my guardian. I was afraid you would take my place from me. Then I would have had nothing, Alys.' She was breathing very fast but there was no trace of colour in her cheeks. She was as white as a candlewax doll.

Alys, holding Catherine's cold hand, holding on to her own power, felt the dark swarm flowing back through her, through her veins, through her head, out through her deadly fingertips.

Her hands became icy, colder than Catherine's, colder than the winter river itself. Alys gave a little tremble of excitement and put her other hand over Catherine's clinging grip.

'I think I'm dying,' Catherine said breathlessly. 'The room is dark, so very dark, Alys. Hold my hand a little tighter, I can hardly see you.'

Alys tightened her grip as she was bid. A fierce hungry smile spread across her face. She could feel the coldness and the darkness pouring from her, pouring out through her hands into Catherine. 'Are you cold?' she asked.

Catherine shuddered. 'I am freezing, Alys! Freezing!' she exclaimed. 'And all the candles are out! And the fire out! Why is it so cold? Why is it so dark? I feel as if there is no one here who loves me or cares for me at all. Hold my hand tighter, Alys! Talk to me! I am afraid! I am afraid!'

Alys laughed, a cold ripple of sound in the brightly lit steaming room. 'I am here, Lady Catherine,' she said.

'Can you not see me? The fire is banked high, it is terribly hot. Can you feel nothing? And all the candles are lit – the lovely bright beeswax candles. The room is as bright as day, as bright as sunlight. Is it all dark for you? Is it all dark for you at last?'

'Alys!' Catherine said imploringly. 'Hold me, Alys, please! Hold me close! I feel as if the waters are taking me under. I am drowning, Alys! I am drowning in my bed.'

'Yes!' Alys said exultantly, her own breath coming fast. 'You caught me like this last time, in the moat. You called me to you and then you pulled me down! But this time it is me drowning you! I need not put my hands to your throat. I need not do more than hold your hands as you wish, and you will go down, Catherine. You will go down alone, you will drown in your bed!'

'Alys!' Catherine cried. Her voice was as thin as a thread, and at the end of the word she choked, as if a wave of green icy water had slapped her in the mouth.

Alys laughed again, madly, recklessly. 'You're drowning, Catherine!' she said, amazed at her own power. 'Morach could pull you out of the river but nothing and no one can save you from drowning! You're going down, Catherine! You're going down! You are drowning in your bed!'

The door clicked behind them and Alys whirled around. It was Hugo. Behind him was the old lord and David. He looked from one woman to the other and his face was puzzled.

'What's wrong?' he asked.

Alys took a deep breath. The bright hot room seemed to swirl around her like the colours in a swinging crystal. 'She is fearful,' she said. Her voice seemed to come from a long way away. 'And she is holding on to me so tight! I tried to call for the women but they did not hear. And I am faint.' She swayed as she spoke and Hugo stepped quickly forward. Alys lurched towards him; but it was David the seneschal who stepped forward and caught her as she fell.

Hugo did not even turn around to look at her. He had Catherine gathered in his arms and she was sobbing on his shoulder.

Seventeen

Catherine was ill for many days, through the springtime weather of May when the sun rose clear and early, and the birds sang till dusk, till the end of that storm-filled, sunshine-filled month; but she did not complain. She lay quietly in her bed which was carried across to the little window so she could sit up on her pillows and see the courtyard and the garden and the life of the castle going on. She wearied easily and she liked to have Alys by her side to read to her. 'I cannot see the print,' she said. 'My head aches so. And Alys reads so sweetly.'

Lord Hugh passed her books and poems to read, and even some of his letters from London which told of Queen Anne's trial and her execution. '"By the hand of a French swordsman, especially trained and brought over from that country,"' Alys read to Catherine.

Catherine shook her head. 'I never liked her,' she said softly. 'I was named for Queen Catherine, you know, Alys. I always thought Anne Boleyn would fall. She was an adulteress, first with the King, and then with his courtiers. I won't mourn for her. Her rise was ungodly swift.'

'No swifter than Jane Seymour's,' Alys said logically. 'She was lady-in-waiting to them both. And she will be queen in her turn. If a man is king, or even master of his destiny, he will choose the woman he wants. And she can rise as he wishes.'

Catherine turned her head on the pillow and smiled at Alys. 'A marriage for love is best,' she said contentedly. 'A marriage for love between equals is best.'

Hugo came to her every morning and sat with her until dinner. He dined with her in her chamber at noon, and the table in the big hall seemed strangely empty without them. Alys often waited on them in Catherine's chamber as they ate. Hugo took her service without noticing her. He only watched Catherine, pressing her to eat the finest things, to drink little glasses of good red Mount Rose wine from Gascony to strengthen her blood. It was Catherine who thanked Alys.

In the afternoon while Hugo went out hunting, Alys would sing to Catherine and play the lute. She would read to her and copy passages from books which Catherine wanted to learn. 'I am so glad you are here, Alys,' Catherine said sweetly one day. 'I am so glad you are here to care for me. I feel so weak, Alys, I can tell you – but don't tell Hugo. I feel so weak I feel as if I will never be strong again. I am glad to have you care for me. I don't think I would have survived my drowning without your care.'

Morach, sitting idly at Catherine's bedroom fire, shot a quick amused glance at Alys' face. Alys looked blandly back.

'Who would have thought that you two girls would have become so close?' Morach wondered aloud. 'Such friends as you now are!'

Alys drew her lips back in a smile. 'It makes me very happy to be your friend, my lady,' she said stiltedly. 'Perhaps you should have your rest now.'

Every afternoon Catherine slept in her high bed until supper-time, when she dressed to go down to the hall with her ladies. The women and the men, gathered for their supper, gave a little mutter of approval to see her strength growing every day.

'It was a near thing,' Morach said with satisfaction,

as she reached for another slice of manchet bread on the ladies' table. 'A near-run thing indeed. I thought for a little while that we might lose her.'

'It's a miracle,' Ruth said devoutly. 'A miracle that she should be snatched from drowning and then not die of the cold nor lose the baby. I have thanked God for it.'

'It's a miracle she should turn out so sweet,' Eliza whispered blasphemously. 'She was as sour and as full of acid as a lemon until her dunking. Now she's all honey. And kindly to you.' She nodded at Alys.

'Will the baby have a fear of water?' Mistress Allingham asked curiously. 'I remember a child in Richmond whose mother fell in the river and she could never touch water without shivering.'

'I remember her,' Morach nodded. 'Aye, sometimes it takes them that way, sometimes they swim like little fishes in the flood. D'you remember Jade the Idiot? His mother was drowned and I myself reached inside her dead body and pulled him out like a little lamb from a dead ewe. We wrapped him on the very bank of the river while the great flood was up high! And he could swim like he was more fish than man!'

Margery nodded eagerly and spoke of another fine swimmer. Alys leaned back a little and let the talk wash around her. The beeswax candles were very clear and bright tonight and the wine was sweet. Looking to her left she could see Hugo's back, the padded broad set of his shoulders, the swirl of his cape. On the nape of his neck his dark hair curled tight, his cap was set askew in the new fashion. She stared as hard as she could, willing him to be aware of her, to turn, to see her.

She could not do it. He had lost his sense of her.

'You're pale, Alys,' Eliza said. 'Are you sick again?'

Alys shook her head. 'No, I'm well,' she said. 'A little weary, that's all.'

Margery blew on her trencher of bread, piled high with her portion of savoury meat mortrews, and bit into it with relish. 'You've been sick since the Christmas feast, I reckon,' she said. 'You were so bright and bonny when you first came to the castle and now your skin is pale as whey.'

'She'll bloom in the summer,' Morach said. 'Alys never liked being cooped indoors, and the reading and the writing she does would weary anyone.'

''Tisn't natural, for a woman to have such learning,' Mistress Allingham said roundly. 'No wonder she looks so thin and plain. She's working all the time with her mind and not growing plump and bonny like a girl should.'

'Plain?' Alys repeated, shocked.

Eliza nodded, mischievously. 'Why did you think you were so high in my lady's favour? Because Hugo never looks your way no more! You're all thin and bony, Alys, and white as frost. He bundles up with Catherine and folds himself around her fat belly and thanks God for a bit of warm flesh in these cold nights.'

'She'll bloom in summer,' Morach said again. 'Leave the girl alone. The long cold dark days of this spring would weary anyone.'

The talk moved on at Morach's bidding but later that evening after supper, Alys slipped into Lady Catherine's room while the rest of them were drinking mead around the fire in the gallery. She carried a candle with her and set it down before the glass to see her face. It was a large handsome mirror made of silvered glass and the reflection it gave was always kindly, forgiving. Alys set down the candle and looked at herself.

She was thinner. The gown of Meg the whore was wider than ever, the girdle spanned her waist and hung down low and the stomacher, laced as tight as it could go, flattened her slight breasts but was loose over her belly. She slipped her shawl back. Her shoulders were as scrawny as an old woman's, her collar bones like the bones of a little sparrow. She stepped a little closer to see her face. There were dark shadows beneath her eyes and lines of strain around her mouth. She had lost her childish roundness and her cheeks were thin and pale. Her blue eyes looked enormous, waif-like. She radiated coldness and loneliness and need.

Alys made a sour face at the mirror. 'I'll not get him back looking like this,' she said under her breath. She stepped a little closer. The shadows under her eyes were as dark as bruises. 'I'll not get him back at all,' she said softly. 'He could have loved me when I was straight off the moor, taught by my Mother Abbess, and skilful like Morach. He could have loved me then and been true to me then, and none of this misery would ever have happened. Now I've set my hand to magic and he's been witched, and she's been witched, and something is eating me away from the inside, like some great greedy worm, so all my strength drains from me and all I have left is my longing for him.'

The face in the mirror was haggard. Alys put her hand up and felt the tears on her cheek. 'And my magic,' she said softly. 'Longing and magic enough to hurt and wound. That's all I have left me. No magic to summon a man to love me.'

She sighed and the candleflame bobbed at her breath and spat a trail of smoke. Alys watched it wind towards the bright-painted timbered ceiling.

'I dipped very deep to be rid of him,' she said softly

to herself. 'I used all the power I had to turn his eyes from me and his mind from me. I'll have to go that deep again to get him back.'

The candleflame quivered, as if in assent.

Alys leaned forward. 'Shall I do it?' she asked the little yellow flame.

It dipped again. Alys smiled, and her face lit up with her youth and her joy again.

'Flame-talking!' she said softly. 'A flame as a counsellor!'

The room was very still; in the gallery she could hear someone take up a lute and strike a few chords, trying the sound. The chords hung on the air as if Alys was holding back time itself while she made her decision.

'It's more deep magic,' she said thoughtfully. 'Deeper than I know. Deeper than Morach knows.'

The candleflame flickered attentively.

'I'll do it!' Alys said suddenly. 'Will it win me Hugo?'

The flame leaped and a tiny spark shot out from a fault in the wick. Alys gave a start of surprise and then clapped her hands over her mouth to hold in a ripple of laughter.

'I win Hugo!' she said delightedly. 'I get what I want!'

She snatched up the candlestick and turned to go from the room. As she walked the flame billowed out like a streamer, lighting the walls and Hugo and Catherine's big curtained bed so its shadow leaped up and jumped like a huge stalking animal. Alys opened the door to the gallery and stepped into the brightly lit room and the music. In its stick, unnoticed, the candleflame winked and went out.

The women were gathered around the fireside. Catherine, round and warm, was leaning back in her chair, her eyes closed, listening to Eliza plucking at the lute. Alys passed like a pale cold ghost through the room, carrying a darkened candlestick, and slipped into her bedroom.

She closed the door behind her but still Eliza's careless off-key warble came through. She leaned her back against the door as if she would blockade the room from them all. Then she shrugged, as a gambler does when he has nothing more to lose, crossed to the garde-robe and rolled her sleeves up. Wrinkling her nose at the smell, she reached down the gap in the wall to feel for the string and the bag of the candle dolls. The bag was stuck to the castle wall, caked with muck. Alys' fingers scrabbled, trying to get a grip. She got hold of one corner and tore the purse away from the wall and up into the room.

'Faugh!' she said under her breath. She carried it over to the stone hearth and pulled at the neck of the purse. The stiff string was stubborn but snapped at last and the candle dolls spilled out on to the hearth.

Alys had forgotten how ugly they were. The little doll of Catherine with her legs spread wide and her grotesque fat belly, the old lord with his beaky, hungry face, and Hugo – beloved Hugo – with his eyelids wiped blind, his ears rubbed away, his mouth a smear and his fingers clumsy stumps. Alys shivered and tossed the purse on the fire; it sizzled and a rank smell of midden filled the room. Alys pulled a stool closer, put the three dolls on her lap and gazed at them.

Very quietly the door behind her opened and Morach came in, soft-footed.

'Oh,' she said gently. 'I felt your magic even while I was gossiping about London news out there. But I did not think you would have turned to the dolls again.'

Alys looked at her, blank-faced. She did not even try to hide the horrors she had made of Morach's little statues.

'Taking your power again, are you?' Morach questioned.

Alys nodded, saying nothing.

'You heard what they said of your looks at dinner,' Morach said, half to herself. She hunkered down on the hearth-rug beside Alys. 'You heard what they said about you, that Hugo loves Catherine, that Catherine fears you no more because you have lost your looks.'

Alys remained silent, the little dolls side-by-side on her lap. Morach took the poker and stirred the fire so the log fell backwards and she could see a deep red cave of embers. 'Bitter that was for you,' she said, looking deep into the fire. 'Sour and bitter to know that your looks are going and you have had so little joy from them.'

Alys said nothing. The dolls in her lap gleamed wetly in the glow from the fire as if they were warming back to life after their long cold vigil hung outside the castle wall.

'And you've taken Hugo's desertion badly,' Morach said softly. She did not look at Alys, she looked into the heart of the fire as if she could see more there. 'You saw him dive into the river and pull Catherine out. You saw him wrap her warm and bring her back as fast as his horse would go. You saw him hold her and kiss her, and now you see him, unbidden, at her side every day and in her bed every night. And how she grows and beams and thrives on his love! While you – poor sour little Alys – you are like a snowdrop in some shady corner of the wood. You grow and flower in coldness and silence, and then you die.'

The smell from the burning purse eddied around the two of them like smoke from the depths of hell.

'So you want your power,' Morach said. 'You want

to make the dolls yours again, you want to make them dance to your bidding.'

'Fashion him again,' Alys said suddenly, holding out the mutilated doll of Hugo to Morach. 'Make him whole again. I commanded him not to see me, not to hear me, not to touch me. I commanded him to lie with Catherine and get her with child. Lift my command off him. Make him whole again and passionate for me. Make him back to what he was at Christmas when he carried me from the feast, to lie with me whether I would or no. Make him how he was when he faced her down and swore false oaths to keep me safe. Make him what he was when he sat by the fire – in that very room where she sits now – and told me that she disgusted him, that he lay with her only to keep me safe, and that his body and soul craved to be with me. Make him that again, Morach! Make him new again!'

Morach sat very still, then she slowly, almost sadly, shook her head. 'It cannot be done,' she said gently. 'There is no magic that can do it. You would have to turn back time itself, turn back the seasons to Christmas. All that has happened here since then *has* happened, Alys. It cannot be undone.'

'Some of it can be undone,' Alys insisted, her face small and pinched, her voice venomous. 'The child can be undone, Morach. The child can be undone in its mother's belly. The child can be stillborn. Catherine can die. Then even if he does not love me – at least he does not love her. And when she is gone, and the child is gone, he will turn back to me.'

Morach shook her head. 'I won't do it,' she said softly. 'Not even for you, Alys, my child, my poor child.' She shook her head again. 'I've aborted babes and I've given women miscarriages,' she said. 'I've blighted cattle, oh yes, and men's lives. But they were always people who were strangers to me, or those I had reason to hate. Or the babies were unwanted and the women desperate to be rid of them. I couldn't blight the child of a woman I live with, whose bread I eat. I couldn't do it, Alys.'

There was silence. The last remnant of the burning purse flickered and fell into ashes.

'Then tell me how to do it,' Alys hissed. '*I* can do it to her. I would have drowned her that day if you had not meddled, Morach. I will make an end of her now. And I warn you not to meddle.'

Morach shook her head. 'Don't, Alys,' she said warningly. 'I cannot see the end to it, and there is so little time . . .'

Alys looked sharply at her. 'What have you seen?' she demanded. 'What time? What little time?'

Morach shrugged. 'I can't see,' she said. 'I see a hare, and a cave, and coldness and drowning. And little time.'

'A hare?' Alys asked. 'A March hare? A magic hare? A hare that is a witch in flight? What does it mean, Morach? And a cave? And a drowning? Was that what should have happened to Catherine? Drowning in a cave, swept underwater and buried underground by the river?'

Morach shook her head again. 'A hare, a cave, a coldness, a drowning, and very little time,' she repeated. 'Don't question me, Alys, for I won't act unless I can see my way. I know danger when I am thrust towards it. I know fear of fire and fear of water. Don't force me forwards when I can sense danger ahead, Alys.'

There was a silence filled with fear in the room. The women sat, as still as sighted deer, waiting for their sense of terror to pass by. It was moments before either of them spoke. Then it was Alys, and her voice was not like her voice at all.

'You have to do something,' she said slowly. She was looking down at the dolls on her lap. And her face was alight with a mixture of fear and exultation.

'Why?'

'Because the dolls have come alive,' Alys said. As she spoke she leaned closer and could see their little chests rise and fall in a slow languid rhythm of breathing. 'They are alive,' she said. 'We will have to do something with them, Morach, or they will start acting on their own.'

Alys had never before seen Morach afraid. The woman seemed to hunch into herself as if she were cold, as if she were hungry. The long, hard years on the moor, living off the vegetable patch and the few begrudging gifts seemed to have laid their mark on her after all, and the gloss and the comfort of the weeks in the castle fell away as if they had never been.

They had the dolls hidden beneath their pillow. At night Alys could feel them squirm beneath her head. During the day she felt their eyes follow her, through the pillow, through the rug, as she went around the room. They lived beside the two women, three monstrous little ghosts summoned into life and now impossible to kill.

The two women were afraid. Both Morach and Alys were afraid that someone would see the cover on the bed stir and lift. They feared a scrupulous maidservant coming unbidden to shake the covers. They feared the prying eyes of Eliza Herring or a surprise visit from Father Stephen. The little dolls were so vivid in their minds they could hardly believe that no one else saw them, that no one else felt their presence, that no one else heard the occasional little cry muffled by the pillow, from behind the closed door.

'What are we to do with them?' Alys asked Morach, at dawn on the third day.

Neither woman had slept; the little dolls had stirred beneath the pillow all night. In the end they had wrapped themselves against the cold dawn air, thrown more wood on the fire, and sat at the hearth, huddled together, as the flames flared up.

'Can we burn them?' Alys asked.

Morach shook her head. 'I dare not,' she said. 'Not now they're so lively. I don't know what they would do.' Her face was drawn and grey with fear and fatigue. 'What if they leaped out of the fire and came running, all melting and hot after us?' she asked. 'If the dolls themselves did not burn us, then Lord Hugh would have us for witchcraft. I wish to all the gods that I'd never given them to you.'

Alys shrugged. 'You taught me the spell to give them power,' she argued. 'You must have known we would be stuck with them, lively, forever.'

Morach shook her head. 'I never heard of it like this before,' she said. 'I never heard of it so powerful. It's your doing, Alys. It's your power. Your power and the great hatred you poured into them.'

Alys clenched her hands on her blanket. 'If I have all this power why can I get nothing I want?' she demanded. 'I can make mistakes so powerful that my life is at risk. I can betray my mother and all my sisters. But the little skill to win a man from a woman I can't do. I get little joy from my power, Morach.'

Morach shook her head. 'You're all contradictions,'

she said. 'That's why your power comes and goes. One after another you have loved and betrayed. And now you want Hugo. What would you do if you had him?'

Alys closed her eyes for a moment. Behind them, under the pillow in the shadowy bed draped with thick curtains, the little dolls lay still as if they too were listening.

'I would love him,' she said, her voice languid with desire. 'I would make him my love, my lover. I would make him so drunk with me, so drugged with me that he would never look at another woman. I would make him my servant and my slave. I would make him mad for me.'

Morach nodded and hitched the blanket a little closer. 'You'd destroy him too then,' she said.

Alys flinched and opened her mouth to argue.

'No,' Morach said. 'It's true. If you take a young lord and make him your slave then you destroy him as much as an old lady left to burn to death. You're a darker power than any I've ever known or heard on, Alys. I wonder where you came from that dark night when I found you, abandoned at my door.'

Alys shook her head. 'All I want is the things that other women have,' she said. 'The man I love, a place to live, comfort. Catherine is laden with goods. I want nothing more than she has. What right has she that I have not?'

Morach shrugged. 'Maybe you'll get it,' she said. 'In your little time.'

'How little?' Alys asked urgently. 'How long do I have, Morach?'

The old woman shrugged, her face a little greyer. 'I can't see,' she said. 'It's all gone dark for me. The bones, the fire, the crystal, even the dreams. All I can see is a hare and a cave and coldness.' She shivered. 'As cold as death,' she said. 'I am learning fear in my old age.'

Alys shook her head impatiently. 'I am afraid too,' she said. 'Every day we are in greater danger with the moppets here. Let's decide and be done with them. We dare not keep delaying.'

Morach nodded. 'There's that holy ground, a little preaching cross, on the moor outside Bowes,' she said slowly. 'The other side of the river from my cottage.'

Alys nodded. 'Tinker's Cross,' she said.

'Aye,' Morach said. 'Sanctified ground. That's the place for them. And the cross is near a lonely road. No one ever goes there. We could leave here in daylight, be there at midday, bury them in the holy ground, sprinkle them with some holy water, and be back here by supper.'

'We could say we were fetching plantings,' Alys said. 'From the moorland, heather and flowers. I could take the pony.'

Morach nodded. 'Once they're buried in holy ground they're safe,' she said. 'Let your sainted Mother of God take care of them instead of us.'

Alys lowered her voice to a whisper. 'They won't bury us will they?' she asked. 'remember what I told you about the doll of Catherine? She pulled me into the moat, Morach. She meant to drown me when I tried to sink her. The little dolls won't find a way to bury us in revenge?'

'Not in holy ground,' Morach said. 'Surely, they'd have no power on holy ground? And I made them and you spelled them. Working together, we must be their masters. If we take them soon and put them in holy ground, before they gather their power . . .'

Something in Alys' stillness alerted her. Her voice tailed off and she looked at Alys, and then followed Alys' fixed gaze. On the cover of the bed, out of hiding, the three candlewax dolls stood in a row, leaning forward as if to listen. As the two women watched, silent in horror, the three took one hobbling little step closer.

Eighteen

They had the ponies saddled and harnessed as soon as the grooms were awake. They left a message for Lady Catherine and trusted to Morach's reputation for stubborn independence as their excuse for leaving without notice and without permission. They were both pale and silent as they trotted the ponies out of the castle gate. On one side of Alys' saddle she had slung a spade, and tied to the pannier was a sack which bulged and heaved.

The ponies fretted all the way through the little town, shied at shadows and threw their heads about. Morach clung on with little skill.

'They know what they're carrying,' she said quietly.

As they left the cobbled main street of Castleton and started westwards down the country lanes, the bag went still and quiet and the ponies went more steadily.

'It's as if they wanted to betray us,' Morach said, bringing her pony alongside Alys and speaking very low. 'There is powerful hatred in them.'

Alys was white-faced, strained, her blue eyes black with fear. 'Hush,' she said. 'Did you get some holy water?'

'Stole it,' Morach said with quiet satisfaction. 'That Father Stephen is careless with his box of tricks; he left it behind in his room, he thinks himself safe in the castle. I could have had some bread from the Mass too, but I thought better not.'

'No,' Alys said. She remembered the last time she had tasted communion bread, and the undigested wafer coming up whole in her throat. 'Better left alone.'

The two women rode on in silence. It was a day of swirling fog which suddenly cleared in bright patches like little islands of sunshine along the road, until the fog came down like a grey wet night again.

'If this fog thickens we can do our business without fear of being seen,' Morach said, pulling her shawl up over her mouth. 'All finished and done and back to the castle in time for supper.'

Alys nodded. 'It will thicken,' she said with certainty. 'I am going to get through this day without danger. I am going to escape the malice of these dolls. I am coming out of this with a whole skin.'

Morach shot her a look, half rueful, half amused. 'You have the power,' she conceded. 'Call up the fog then, and safety at any price.'

Alys nodded, half in jest. 'A thick fog,' she repeated. 'And my safety at any price, and ...' She paused. 'Hugo in my arms before the day ends!'

Morach chuckled and shook her head. 'Impatient whore,' she said smiling. 'You want everything, and always at once!'

The fog lifted for a moment and the ponies trotted out more quickly along the road. Their unshod hooves made little sound on the soft mud. On either side of the track great bushes of gorse flowered, bright yellow, empty of perfume in the cold air.

A flock of lapwings lifted from a meadow by the track and wheeled across the sky, calling into the wind. All around them the fog lay grey and thick but above the two women was an eye of brilliant blue sky and a bright sun.

'Feel the warmth of that sun!' Morach said in delight. 'I love the sun after a cold winter. I've been chilled to my bones these last few days. Chilled and shaking. It's good to be out in the sunshine again.'

Alys nodded, pushing the hood of her cape back. Her hair, free of a hood or cap, tangled into golden-brown curls. The colour was back in her cheeks. 'The castle is like a prison,' she said resentfully. 'Whether Catherine is sweet or sour it is wearying to wait on her.'

Morach nodded. 'As soon as the babe is born, I'm away,' she said. 'Back to my cottage.'

Alys nodded. 'You'll just be in time for winter then,' she observed. 'The child's due in October.'

Morach grinned. In a bush ahead of them a blackbird thrust out his chest and warbled a long rippling call. Morach whistled back, exactly the same notes, and the blackbird, half angry, half puzzled, repeated his song even louder.

'I know,' she said carelessly. 'But I'd rather die of cold on the moor than spend another winter in that castle.'

'Would you?' Alys asked. 'Would you really?'

Morach looked around at her and the smile died from her face. 'No,' she said. 'I cannot abide the cold at the moment. I'd do anything rather than be cold and in the dark.'

Alys shrugged her shoulders. 'You've a whole summer ahead of you,' she said carelessly. 'Don't fret.'

Morach shrugged off the shadow which had touched her, lifted her face to the sunlight and half closed her eyes. 'And you?' she asked. 'Will you wait for Hugo? When this task of ours is done? Will you fatten up and learn to smile, wait for him to weary of his tired wife and puking babe? I thought you had grown impatient with waiting, I thought you were turning to magic again?'

Alys looked straight ahead at the swirl of mist before them which hid their road. 'You saw me with Hugo in

338

the runes, and I dreamed of him and me together, and a son we would have. I want him, Morach, and both you and I have seen it. It must be there, waiting to happen. Tell me how I can get him.'

Morach pursed her lips and shook her head. 'You have your power,' she said. 'And you're young, and when you're not lovesick you are as beautiful as any girl in the country. Why wait and pine for Hugo? There are other men.'

Alys looked out along the straight lane ahead of them, stretching along the shoulder of the hill. 'I want him,' she said steadfastly. 'The moment I saw him I knew desire. I was straight out of the nunnery, Morach, and he was the first man I had ever seen in my life who was a match for me. I wanted him then as a bird seeks a mate. Nothing could stop me. Nothing could stop him.'

Morach gave a cracked laugh, hawked and spat. '*You* stopped him!' she exclaimed. 'Stopped him in his tracks. Turned him cruel and twisted, a monster to his own wife. Set them dancing a wicked little dance. And now he loves her.'

Alys' eyes narrowed, her whole face looked pinched and mean. 'I know,' she said through her teeth. 'I should have taken the risk of him loving me and not meddled with magic. I should have trusted him to care for me. But I was anxious for my own safety . . .' she broke off. 'I wouldn't take the risk,' she said.

Morach grinned. 'Still the same story then,' she said cheerfully. 'You run to save your own skin and then find you have lost the one thing you needed.'

Alys' pony checked and side-stepped at her sudden grasp on the reins. 'Yes,' she said sharply, as if Morach's wit had struck as hard as a stone. 'Yes. My God, yes.'

There was silence for a moment. 'Best give him up,' Morach said. 'That's the other lesson your life is teaching you. When something is gone – it's gone. Even if you lost it by your own folly or cowardice. You've lost your Mother Abbess and you've lost Hugo. Give them both up. Let them go. The past belongs to the past. Find another love, Alys, and hold on to it this time. Take a risk for it.'

Alys shook her head. 'I have to have Hugo,' she said. 'There are too many promises between us. I had a Seeing. I can give him a son and I still think that Catherine will not. I have to be the lady at that castle, Morach. It is what I want and it is where I belong. I have dreamed of it over and over. Even if the love is gone, even if I have twisted and changed him – even twisted and changed myself. I want the castle. I want to be first with Hugo and the old lord. I want the dream that I dreamed, even if I am no longer fit for it.'

Morach shrugged, watching Alys enmesh herself.

'How can I get it?' Alys pressed her. 'Good God, Morach, lovelorn wenches are your speciality. How can I get him, him and the castle? There are spells, surely?'

Morach laughed shortly. 'There are none to make a man love you,' she said. 'You know that as well as I. There are no tricks to make love come and stay. All magic can do, all herbs can do, is to summon lust.'

'Lust is no good,' Alys said impatiently. 'He's lusty enough. And with everyone else. I want him to want only me. Only me.'

Morach smiled. 'Then you have to give him some pleasure that no other can give,' she said. 'You have to take him out of his mind with desire. You have to let him ride the goddess.'

'What?' Alys demanded.

Ahead of them the mist was like a grey, wet wall. 'So much for sunshine,' Morach said, and hunched her shawl around her shoulders so they trotted into the darkness and it enveloped them.

The ponies' feet were even quieter on the soft wet mud. Around them the leaves of the hedgerows dripped wetly. The dark green of the hawthorn was flecked with white buds. Then the hedgerows gave way to open moorland and they could hear the distant sighing sound of the river.

'What d'you mean, ride the goddess?' Alys asked, her voice muffled and low.

'Poison,' Morach said matter-of-factly. 'There's a toadstool, the little grey one – earthroot, it's called.'

'I know that,' Alys interrupted. 'You give it dried and pounded in food to cure feverish dreams and lustful visions.'

Morach nodded. 'Take it fresh, or baked so it is sweet, and it will cause a fever, aye, and dreams like madness,' she said. 'If you want a man so badly that you do not care what it costs, you trick him to eat the earthroot, and then you whisper wild dreams and visions. You dance for him naked, you lay him on his back, you lick him all over like a bitch with a puppy. You do whatever enters your head to give him pleasure, any way.'

Alys was breathing fast. 'And what does he do?' she asked.

Morach laughed shortly. 'He sees visions, he dreams dreams,' she said. 'He may think you are the goddess herself, he may think he is flying high in the skies and having his lust on the stars. Any dream you whisper to him he will take for his own – delight or nightmare, the choice is yours.'

'And after?' Alys asked. 'When he has taken his pleasure and awakens?'

Morach chuckled her slow malicious chuckle. 'Then you use your power as a woman,' she said. 'No witchcraft is needed then. You swear that all he dreamed was true – that you are a witch and you have led him into the wild places that only we know. If he is fool enough – and you are barefaced enough – he will never go with another woman. Other women are the earth to him after that, plain and ordinary. You are fire and water and air.'

Alys' face was alight. 'I'll have him,' she said. 'I'll trap him with that. It's what he wanted from me from the first.' She paused for a moment. 'But the cost,' she said, suddenly cautious. 'What's the price for all this, Morach?'

Morach laughed wildly. 'You should have been a usurer, not a witch, Alys. A usurer. You never touch a thing but you have to know the price. You never take a risk. You never gamble all! Always careful, always counting. Always self-preserving.'

'The cost,' Alys insisted.

'Death,' the woman replied easily. 'Death for the man.'

At Alys' sharp look she nodded. 'Not at once, but after a while,' she said. 'A few doses may make little difference but if you drug him again every week, say, for six months, then his body cannot live without it. He needs it like other men need food and water. He needs it *more* than he needs food and water. He is your slave then, your dog. You do not have to bed with him unless you please, he needs the world of dreams with or without you. He is a dog begging for its bowl of food. And he lives as long as a dog will live – five, six years.'

'Have you used it?' Alys asked curiously.

Morach's smile was hard. 'I have used everything,' she said coldly.

Alys nodded, and they rode on in silence for a little while, the noise of the river growing louder as they came nearer.

'Is the river in flood?' Alys asked, her voice muffled by the cloth she had wound around her face.

'Not yet,' Morach said. 'But it's rising. If it rains in the hills then it will spout out of the caves and flood the valley. It's been a wet winter this year.'

'Will the bridge be clear?' Alys asked, peering ahead.

'We have a few hours yet,' Morach said. 'But if there is a storm on the hills we won't have long to do our business and get home dry-shod.'

'Not much business to do,' Alys said. The bundle of dolls stirred as if to contradict her.

'Here then,' Morach said and went to turn off the mud lane. The ponies hesitated at the muddy track down the hillside. Morach peered at the churned mud beneath their hooves. 'This track was used recently,' she said. Her eyes went to Alys' face. 'Several horsemen,' she said. 'And dogs.'

'Hugo,' Alys said. 'He must have come hunting this way yesterday. It doesn't matter, Morach. We are well ahead of him this day. He usually sits with her until after dinner.'

Morach scowled. 'I wish he'd stay home all day,' she said. She kicked her pony irritably and the animal jolted forward, slipping and sliding down the track. Alys followed.

'We'll be finished and headed for home before he sets out,' she said. 'And there's nowhere else for us to go. Tinker's Cross is the only sacred ground nearby. We can hardly dig up the chapel graveyard.'

Morach's pony flinched at another kick. 'I don't like it,' she said irritably. 'If he sees us with a muddy spade, even after we've finished, he'll ask why.'

'We'll hide the spade,' Alys said reassuringly. 'It'd be as hard to get it back as it was to steal anyway. We'll hide the spade and the sacking and the pannier bag and ride home with a bunch of heather and herbs. No one will challenge us, they all know we need grasses from the moor to keep Catherine well. No one doubts us, Morach.'

'Hide it where?' Morach asked stubbornly.

Alys shrugged. 'I don't know! Why are you so sour? Aren't there caves enough along the river-bank where you could hide half an army? We'll shove it down one of the caves and wedge it tight so the river cannot wash it out again. The waters are rising, it'll be high summer and drought before anyone can go down the caves again. The waters will hide it for us.'

Morach shivered and spat over her left shoulder. 'You can hide it,' she said. 'I'll not go near a cave, nor deep water. Look around you for a likely place as we cross the river.'

Alys nodded. 'I'll go first,' she said. 'The ponies may be afraid of the bridge.'

It was the natural stone bridge upstream of Morach's old cottage, formed out of great slabs of limestone, with the river bubbling, like brown soup, below. When the river was in spate great gouts of water would fountain up from the cracks in the river bed as the underground torrents burst out, and every cave and pothole along the bank would be a boiling spring of melt-water and storm-water, forced up from the underground lake to wash into the surface river. On either side of the river-bank, as much as six feet away from the water, was the high-water line of sticks and straw and rubbish from the last flood. The ponies put their heads down and sniffed suspiciously at the stone slabs beneath their hooves, then delicately stepped across, as light as goats, ears forward, listening to the rush of the water beneath them.

'There's a good place,' Alys said. The mouth of the cave was a little way along the river-bank. She slipped from the saddle and threw the bridle at Morach. Both ponies dropped their heads to the short moorland grass and cropped. Alys scrambled up the little slope and peered inside the cave.

'It goes back miles,' she said, her voice echoing. 'I can't see the end of it. It could go for miles into the hill-side.'

She came out again and took the reins from Morach.

Morach's face was strained. 'Did you hear the water rising?' she asked. 'I'm afraid of it coming up early. We don't want to be cut off this side of the river if the water is rising.'

'I heard it, but it was far away down at the bottom of the cave,' Alys said. 'We'll have enough time. Come on.'

The two ponies straggled up the hill on the far side, stepping out on the dry ground, floundering in the bogs. Ahead of them, on the track, they could see the mark of horses' hooves.

There was a cairn on the top of the hill and the wide, dry moorland stretching all around them. Morach pushed her shawl off her face and looked around her.

'That's better,' she said. 'Tinker's Cross is this way.'

She led the way, kicking her pony into a trot. Alys' pony trotted behind, the pannier bumping at every step. The mist had cleared now they were on the top of the moor, though it clung to the valley sides. Ahead of them, Alys could see the thin finger of the old Celtic cross pointing upwards. Around it was a little circle of stones, the edge of the sanctified ground. When Alys came up to the cross Morach had already dismounted and was tying her pony to a holly bush.

'Give me the dolls,' she said to Alys. 'And dig them their grave.'

Alys untied the pannier bag from the saddle and handed it, unopened, to Morach. Morach hunkered down on the wet turf and held the bag in her arms. Quietly she crooned a little tune at the dolls, while Alys untied the shovel from the other side of the saddle.

'If you remember any of your prayers you should say them,' she remarked, without raising her eyes. 'The holier the act of burying them the better.'

Alys shrugged. 'I remember them,' she said. 'But coming from me they might as well be said backwards. I am far from the grace of God, Morach. You'd be closer to heaven than me.'

Morach shrugged almost regretfully. 'Not I,' she said. 'I've not set foot in a church in twenty years, and I never understood what they were saying even then. I made my choice. I don't regret it. But I'll never work with deep shadows again as you have done here. It's too powerful for me.'

Alys thrust the spade hard into the holy ground and twisted it out tearing at the tough roots of the grasses. 'I went as deep as I was driven,' Alys said. 'You counselled me to it. You said if I lost one god I should seek another.'

'Hush,' Morach said, looking around. The bag on her lap stirred and she held them tighter. 'Keep your voice down,' she said. 'There is older magic here than the

346

cross. That holly tree was planted to mark this place before the cross was raised. The old magic runs very strong here. Don't wake it now.'

'It was your bidding,' Alys insisted in a whisper, thrusting the spade in deeper. 'It was my choice to use it, but it was your spell.'

Morach looked up at her, her dark eyes gleaming. 'We had an agreement,' she said.

Alys was silent, digging hard. She was through to the stone soil now, the grave for the dolls was a spade's width across.

'You ordered them, you took responsibility for them,' Morach insisted. 'They are your dolls. I made you swear that you would not blame me for them, whatever they did.'

Alys said nothing, turning out shovelfuls of damp soil into a little heap.

'By rights I need not be here,' Morach said resentfully. 'Your dolls, your magic, and your bitter power that has made them so lively.'

Alys rested on the handle of the shovel and pushed back a lock of hair with one grimy hand.'Have done,' she said. 'Is this deep enough?'

Morach leaned forward. 'A little more,' she said. 'We want them to sleep well, the bonny little things.'

Alys thrust the spade deep again and then jerked her head up.

'What's that?' she demanded. 'Did you hear?'

'What?' Morach asked quickly. 'What?'

The mist was closing down again, swirling around them. Alys shrank back. 'I thought I heard something,' she said.

'Heard what?' Morach said. 'What d'you hear, Alys?'

'Horses,' Alys said, so softly that Morach could

scarcely hear the words. 'What'll we do, Morach? What'll we do if someone comes?'

'I hear them!' Morach said urgently. 'I heard a horn!'

There was a sudden blast of a hunting horn, very near them, and then out of the mist two great deer-hounds leaped, dashed past Morach, nearly knocking her over, and bayed, savagely, terrifyingly, at Alys.

Alys flung herself back till the cold stone of the cross at her back stopped her. She pressed back against it and the dogs, their hackles high and prickly on their great backs, opened their mouths and roared at her like lions.

'Hugo!' Alys screamed over the noise. 'Hugo! Save me! Call your dogs off me! Save me!'

The horn blasted loud again and then a great roan stallion leaped out of the mist towards them and reared to a standstill. Hugo jumped down with his riding whip in his hands and beat his dogs back.

Alys flung herself towards him and he caught her up in his arms.

'Alys?' he said in amazement.

The other huntsmen rose out of the fog, one of them slipped a leash on each of the dogs. 'Alys, what are you doing here?' Hugo looked around and saw Morach, rising to her feet, her face a sickly grey and a bag which kicked and squirmed in her hand.

'What d'you have there?' he rapped out.

Morach held the bag fast and shook her head. She seemed to have lost her tongue in her terror. She shook her head harder and harder like an idiot child incapable of speech.

'What d'you have there?' Hugo demanded again, his voice hard with his own fear. 'Answer me! Answer me! Tell me what you have in that sack!'

Morach said nothing but the bag went suddenly still.

Then Alys screamed, a sharp, piercing scream of pure terror, and pointed. The bag was splitting open, from bottom to top, like the rancid skin of a rotten peach. Splitting and bursting open. And out of it, marching like a row of crippled soldiers, came the three dolls. The scrawny, beaky, old lord, the grossly pregnant woman doll, and the sightless, fingerless, mouthless, earless Hugo.

'She did it!' Alys screamed, the words pouring out of her mouth like a river in flood. 'She did it! She made them! She hexed them! Morach did it! Morach!'

Morach stared Alys in the face for one full, incredulous second, then she whirled around and plunged into the fog, skirts snatched up, running as fast as she could like a hunted animal, into the deepest fog in the valley.

'Holloa!' Hugo yelled. 'A witch! A witch!' He jumped up into the saddle, seized Alys' arm, and hauled her up behind him. The horse was dancing to be off and Alys grabbed at Hugo's shoulders. The huntsman unleashed the dogs and they bayed and circled the hunters, as if they could not catch the scent. One of them pawed up at Alys, reaching for her, its wide mouth open, its breath hot. Hugo kicked it down with an oath. 'Holloa! Holloa!' he yelled again. 'A witch! Find the witch! Seek the witch! Seek her!'

The big dog bayed again and flung himself at Alys but then the huntsman blew his horn in a great discordant shriek and the dogs broke away into the mist. Hugo's huge stallion wheeled and dashed after them. Alys pressed her face to Hugo's back and clung around his waist, weeping in her terror.

Morach was ahead of them, scrambling downhill, slipping in the mud, crawling over the stones, and then up again, running for her life. The dogs sighted her and bayed a deeper note. She whirled around when she heard it and they saw a glimpse of her white face, then she fell to her hands and knees and dropped out of sight for one moment.

'A hare!' a young huntsman called. 'A hare! She'll change herself into a hare!'

As he spoke a hare broke from the ground beneath their feet, black-tipped ears laid smooth, head flung back, and tore away down the hill towards the river.

The dogs shot off on the new scent, yelping like mad puppies as the hare gained on them.

'She'll make a circle!' Hugo yelled. 'Cut her off! Turn her back!'

Alys, gripping while the horse leaped and bounded beneath her, was screaming into the wind, 'No! No! No!' but Hugo could not hear her. The huntsman was blowing his horn, the hounds were yelping and the brown hare, her long legs pounding, was sailing across the ground in great bounds, her eyes white-ringed with terror.

'She's heading for the river, Sir!' a huntsman yelled. They were closing on the prey but not fast enough. 'She'll get down one of those holes and we'll never get her out.'

'Faster!' Hugo shouted. 'Cut her off! Don't let her get to the river-bank! Drive her into the river!'

The hounds surged forward but the hare jinked and turned and snatched herself away. The horses stumbled and slithered down the steep hillside, the riders urging them on. The hare was headed for the stone bridge; they could see her clearly, racing across the grey stone slabs, and the hounds, a few lengths behind her and going faster on the stones. Then she leaped down from the bridge and flew off to the left, leaving the dogs snapping at the empty air, and dived into the deep cave Alys had found earlier. Baying with anger the hounds flung themselves at the opening.

'Whip them off! Whip them off!' Hugo yelled. 'They'll get stuck. She'll lure them down there and trap them.'

He flung himself from his horse and strode towards them, his whip hissing. The hounds fell back, snarling and dripping from their red mouths, and went to the huntsman. Hugo, shaking with excitement, went slowly to the mouth of the cave and cautiously peered in.

'Mortal deep,' he said. 'I'd go down there for a beast but not for a witch-turned-hare.'

The men nodded. 'She could turn back,' one warned.

'Or change into a snake in the darkness,' another nodded.

'What'll we do?' the young one asked. Instinctively they looked towards Alys. She was clinging to the pommel as the horse shifted restively, and when she looked up her face was tear-stained, wild.

'Wait,' she said, her voice shaky and shrill. There was a rumble of thunder and a crack of lightning over the high dark hills to the west, the source of the river.

Hugo came back to the horse's side and looked up at Alys.

'Wait?' he asked. 'What d'you mean? Wait?'

Alys laughed hysterically. 'The storm is come,' she cried. She looked westward. A few fat drops of rain fell sluggishly from the sky, then more, then more.

'So?' Hugo asked.

'The water is rising,' Alys said. Her voice shook and then she was laughing, laughing too much to speak, while the tears poured down her face. 'The water is rising. While you wait out here, dry-shod, she waits in there. Listening.'

Hugo gaped at her. 'Listening?' he repeated.

'She will hear the roar of the underground lake rising up, she will hear the gurgle of all the little streams flowing towards her, and then she will feel the rush and suck of the torrent around her ankles, and then, rising quickly, around her knees.

'She may try to come out, she may struggle to climb up, but her head will touch the stone roof of the cave and the water will come up, and up, and up, until it bursts over her face and there is nowhere for her to hide and nothing but flood water for her to breathe.'

Hugo was pale. 'We swim her underground?' he said.

Alys' face was gaunt with horror. Her voice was the high cackle of madness. 'Look,' she said, pointing to the high-water line of the debris of branches and straw. It lay like a ribbon along the river-bank, a clear yard above the entrance of the cave. 'Nothing will swim out of there,' Alys said, laughing and laughing. 'Nothing! You guard the entrance and the storm will do your work for you. The rain will be your torturer. The deep flooding river will be your executioner. Morach is dead! Dead as she feared to die!'

Nineteen

There was silence for a long minute, then there was a dull roll of thunder and a livid purple-yellow flash of lightning which outlined the horizon of the western hills. The sky above them was greenish yellow, as bright as decay, and rolling in quickly from the west were clouds as dark as midnight.

Hugo looked up at Alys. Her face was ugly with strain. Her heart was pounding. All she could think of was how to survive. How to escape the charge of witchcraft which must come next. Her laughter had been blown away by the ominous breeze which was blowing the storm towards them, but her cheeks were still wet.

'Don't cry,' Hugo said. He pulled off his leather gauntlet and put up his hand to brush her cheek.

'I was afraid,' Alys said. When his hand touched her face she turned towards it so that his palm brushed her lips.

'Afraid of what?' Hugo asked softly. 'I'd not hurt you.'

Alys shook her head. 'No,' she said. 'I know that.'

'Then what did you fear?' Hugo asked.

'Her.' Alys nodded to the dark mouth of the cave. 'She had made some dolls, she said they would do her bidding. She said that if she made the dolls sick then the people would be sick.'

Hugo nodded. 'I saw them,' he said. 'They were vile.'

'You saw them as she shook them out of the bag,' Alys said quickly, 'as she let the bag open and shook them out. She told me that she would be mistress of the castle, that she would command your father, and you, and me, and Lady Catherine. With the dolls.'

Hugo looked at Alys and she saw an old superstitious fear cross his face. 'This is nonsense,' he said uncertainly. 'But you should have told me.'

Alys shrugged. 'How could I? I never see you alone now. Your father is too old and frail to be frightened with such dark fears. And I would not trouble Lady Catherine, not now.'

Hugo nodded. 'But what were you doing with her?' he asked. 'When I rode up?'

'She had agreed to stop,' Alys said. 'She promised to bury them in holy ground, to put away the magic. But she would not come out alone. She forced me to come too. She did not dare stand on the holy ground. She made me dig the hole. Only I could step on holy ground, because she was a black witch – leagued with the devil – and I am not.'

Hugo nodded. 'You must have been very afraid,' he said. He put his warm hand out and closed it over hers as she gripped the pommel of the saddle.

Alys looked down at him, her face alight with joy at his touch. 'I am afraid of nothing now,' she said. 'And I have my power, my white power, good power, which is dedicated to you and to the service of your family. I was using my power for you, to keep you all safe. I was struggling with her evil – and none of you knew.'

Hugo put a foot in the stirrup and swung into the saddle behind Alys. 'Come,' he said over his shoulder to the men. 'We'll go home. I have to speak to my lord and to Father Stephen about this matter. Alan, you block the hole with rocks, boulders as big as you can carry, and wait here with Peter until the water rises and covers it. You can keep the dogs with you.'

The men nodded.

Hugo hesitated. 'As you love me ...' he said. 'No word of this to anyone. If you want to follow me to Newcastle, on my travels, or to London – not one word. We tell everyone that the woman fell into the river and was drowned. All right?'

The young men, grave-faced, nodded.

'If you gossip,' Hugo said warningly, 'if you chatter, like silly girls, then I will not know which of you has whispered this story.' He looked from one to another. 'I will turn all of you away, and you will never find service with a noble house again,' he said. 'You will go back to your fathers, my cousins, and I will tell them that you are not worthy to be in my family.'

The men nodded. 'You have my word,' they said, one after another, like an oath. 'You have my word.'

Hugo nodded and clicked to his horse. The young huntsman fell into line behind Hugo. They rode up the moorland path to Tinker's Cross again. Hugo tightened his arms around Alys.

'I have missed you,' he said in sudden surprise. 'I have been planning this voyage so carefully, and been so busy with the farms and the castle and the new house, and watching so much over Catherine that I had forgotten the pleasure of your touch, Alys.'

Alys nodded. She leaned back against him, feeling his warmth, the way he moved easily with the strides of the big horse.

'I saw you pale and quiet and I thought nothing of it,' Hugo said remorsefully. 'I thought you were sulking with me, because of that night. And I felt angry with you, for refusing me a second time.' He dropped his head forward and pressed her to his cheek. 'I am sorry,' he said simply. 'I have not cared for you as I should.'

'I have been very unhappy,' Alys said, her voice low.

Hugo held her close. 'That's my fault,' he said. 'I wanted to be free of your love, of the promises I had made you. It all seemed – ' He broke off. 'Oh, I don't know! Too complicated. There was Catherine near-drowned and sick. There's my father failing but looking as if he will live forever. There's my new house, which I want more than anything in the world, and my father won't give me the funds! And then there you were, looking at me with your big eyes like some vagrant deer. I am selfish, Alys, that's the truth. I didn't want more troubles.'

Alys turned her head a little and smiled at him. 'I am not your trouble,' she said confidently. 'I'm the only one who can help you. I'm the only one who cares for you. I have grown sick this winter nursing your father, caring for your wife, and fighting this great evil of Morach which Catherine insisted on bringing into your family. If it had not been for me and my white power I don't know what Morach would have done.'

Hugo shook his head. 'I'd like to believe it can't be so,' he said. 'But I saw her. And then I saw the hare. This is a bad business, Alys.'

'Well ended,' Alys said firmly. 'We'll think no more of it. I fought against her and you have killed her, and the thing is done.' Her hands on the pommel of the saddle were white with tension, her fingers ached.

'Yes, it's done and we'll keep it quiet,' Hugo said. 'I don't want to distress Catherine, not at this time. And my father would be disturbed. We'll collect those little dolls and give them to Father Stephen. He'll know what to do with them. And we'll say no more on this.'

Alys nodded again.

'You are lucky it was me that found you,' Hugo said.

'If it had been anyone else they would have tried to catch two witches, not just the one.'

Alys shook her head. 'I have taken an ordeal,' she said coldly. 'I am no black witch. I counselled Lady Catherine against having Morach in the castle, and I warned her that though I am just a herbalist and a healer, Morach always had a reputation for dark work. I warned her and I warned you. No one would listen.'

Hugo nodded. 'That's true,' he conceded. He was silent for a moment while his horse walked up the path to the high moor. 'It must have been an odd childhood for you, Alys, all alone on the moorland with a woman like Morach as your mother.'

'She was not my mother,' Alys said. 'I am glad of it.' She paused. 'My mother, my real mother, was a lady,' she said. 'She died in a fire.'

Hugo pulled his horse to a standstill and looked down at the ground.

The spade lay where Alys had dropped it, beside the little hole. The pannier bag was on the ground, split from top to bottom. But there were no little wax dolls anywhere.

The wind stirred the heather all around them and the rain began to fall in great thick drops of water. Alys pulled her hood up over her head and felt the wind tug her cape. There were no little dolls anywhere on the sodden ground.

Hugo jumped down from the horse and kicked around in the clumps of heather. 'I can't see them,' he said. 'Hey! William! Come and help me search for them.'

'Search for what, my lord?' William asked, dismounting and leading his horse forward.

'For the dolls, the dolls that the old woman had in her sack,' Hugo said impatiently. 'You saw them.'

The young man shook his head. 'I didn't see anything, my lord,' he said. 'I just saw the old woman running off and then the hounds followed a hare and ran it to ground.'

Hugo squinted against the driving rain. 'You saw nothing?' he asked.

'No, my lord,' William said, his round face wet, his hair plastered to his scalp.

Hugo hesitated, not knowing what to say, then he laughed shortly and slapped him on the back. 'Mount up, we'll go home,' he said and swung back into the saddle himself. 'Lead those ponies back to the castle.'

'Will you not hunt for the dolls?' Alys asked, her voice low.

Hugo shrugged his shoulders and turned his horse homeward. 'If they were made from lye or tallow they'll melt quick enough,' he said. 'They were maybe broken under the horses' hooves. Maybe they were fancy and cheating like half the rest of witchcraft. They're on sanctified ground – for what *that* is worth – let's forget it.'

Alys hesitated for a moment, glancing back at the holly tree. There was something white at the root; she leaned forward to see. Hugo tightened his grip around her waist.

'Don't fret,' he said. 'Let's away, it's going to pour with rain.'

He turned the horse but Alys did not take her eyes from the roots of the holly tree. She saw a tiny little white root, like a worm, like a little candlewax arm. She saw a tiny, misshapen, white hand. It waved at her.

'Let's go!' she said with sudden impatience.

Hugo wheeled the horse and it reared forward into a great loping canter, all the way across the top of the moor until it slowed for the ford south of the castle.

'What shall we tell Lady Catherine and your father?' Alys asked, her words whipped away by the wind.

'That Morach fell in the river and drowned,' Hugo said. 'And when the baby comes, you will be able to deliver him, won't you, Alys? You will care for him and for Catherine?'

'Yes,' Alys said. 'I was at every childbirth Morach attended since I was two years old. And I have delivered several babies on my own. I didn't want to care for Catherine while she hated me, but I can do well enough now. I will care for him as if he were my own child.'

Hugo nodded and held her more closely. 'I thank you,' he said formally.

'I won't fail you,' Alys said. 'I shall use all my powers to keep Catherine well. Your baby will be born and I will keep him well. For you, Hugo, and for me. For your fortune and your freedom depend on him. And I love you so well that I want you to be rich and free.'

Hugo nodded, and Alys sensed he was smiling. She leaned back into the rich warm jerkin and felt his body heat warm her through, and his arm tighten around her waist.

'I have news for you that I have been saving,' she said. She hesitated on the lie for no more than a moment. 'I am with child, Hugo,' she said. 'I am going to bear your child. We lay together only once but I am fertile for you and you are lusty and strong with me.'

Hugo was silent for a moment. 'Are you sure?' he asked incredulously. 'It's very soon.'

'It's nearly two months,' Alys said defensively. 'He will be born at Christmas.'

'Christmas!' Hugo exclaimed. 'And you're sure it is a son?'

'Yes,' Alys said determinedly. 'The dream I had at

359

the Christmas feast last year was a true Seeing. You and I will have a son and we will be lovers, we will be as man and wife.'

'Catherine is my wife,' he reminded her. 'And she is carrying my son.'

'But I am carrying another son,' Alys said proudly. 'And your son on me will be strong and handsome. I know it already.'

Hugo chuckled. 'Of course,' he said soothingly. 'My clever Alys! My lovely girl! He will be strong and handsome and brilliant. And I will make him wealthy and powerful. He and his half-brother can be companions for each other. We will bring them up together.'

Hugo loosened the reins and the big horse moved forward faster in its rolling canter. 'My father will be glad,' Hugo said, raising his voice against the wind in their faces and the rain. 'His own whores had sons by the quiverful – but his own wife had only the one.'

'And who loved him the best, and who did he love the best?' Alys challenged.

Hugo's broad shoulders shrugged. 'That matters not at all,' he said dismissively. 'Love is not for us. Land, heirs, fortune – these are the things that matter for lords, Alys. The poor can have their loves and their passions. We are interested in weightier things.'

Alys leaned back and rested her head against his shoulder. 'One day you will love as passionately as a peasant,' she said softly. 'One day you will be mad for love. You will be humbled to dirt for it.'

Hugo laughed. 'I doubt it,' he said. 'I doubt that.'

They rode in silence for a little while, Alys weighing the lie of pregnancy, which should guarantee her safety whatever anyone in the castle said against her or against Morach. Hugo would never lose the chance of another son, even if a proclaimed witch were carrying it. While he thought she was carrying his child he would die to protect her. But once the lie was discovered . . .

Alys shook her head, she could plot no further than one move at a time, plot and trust to her dreams of herself in the garden in Catherine's rose and cream gown. A scud of rain hit her in the face, and a low rumble of thunder sounded around the western hills and rolled nearer.

Alys had a sudden vision of Morach listening to the sound of the storm in the dark cave, her head against the stone ceiling, the water roaring and washing around her knees, and the hounds waiting for her outside. She blinked. For a moment she could feel the hard unyielding stone on the back of her own neck as she pressed upwards, away from the water. The water around her legs was icy cold, storming with currents, a rising torrent which tumbled around her knees, and poured unstoppably to pull at her skirt around her thighs. Some driftwood banged against her roughly and she stumbled and fell into the water and sprang up again, drenched and trembling, clumsy with the weight of the water in her gown.

It was as if the water had tasted her now and wanted more. A great wave buffeted the cave, hitting her sideways, and she knocked her face against the rock wall and felt the weight of the earth all around her. It was now nearly too late to crawl out and face the men but the terror of drowning was suddenly greater than her fear of the hounds, and she scrabbled at the wall, trying to find her way back out. Her hands, bruised and bleeding, battered against the wall of the cave and then suddenly stretched out into a void of water where the river beat its way outwards. She stretched out her hands like a blind woman, pummelling the swift current, longing for the cold touch of air. Then her knuckles scraped the roof of the passage out of the cave.

She had left it too late. The narrow hole out of the cave was already filled to the ceiling with the tumbling roil of flood water. All that was left for her was the little pocket of air trapped in the roof of the cave, and as she turned her face upwards to breathe into it another surge of water bellowed into the cave and the level of water leaped from waist-height to her shoulders. Her gown was filled with water, the current swirling around her whole body. Pushed and pulled by the torrent she lost her footing and fell, with a roaring noise in her head as the water rushed into her ears, her nose and her mouth. Hunger for life threw her upwards again, to the last little hollow of air in the roof of the cave. But as she reached for it her head cracked against the ceiling of the cave and her open choking mouth tasted only water. Alys moaned.

'What's the matter?' Hugo's voice pulled her back to the present, to her dangerous gamble, to his arm comfortingly around her. 'Did you say something?'

'Nothing!' Alys said brightly.

A great squall like a dark curtain spread down along the valley, blotting out the hills all around them.

'The river's up,' said Hugo with satisfaction. 'The witch is drowned.' He shook the water out of his eyes and pressed the roan horse into a canter. 'All speed for home,' he said.

Gossip about Morach's sudden departure from the castle could not be prevented. Too many people had known that she had ridden out with Alys, and seen Alys return alone with Hugo. William had seen nothing, but the other huntsmen had seen that notorious sight – a witch change herself into a hare – and would not remain silent for ever. But the word could be kept from Catherine. Hugo summoned the women into the gallery while Catherine slept before supper and told them that if he heard one word – one word – spoken out of turn about Morach in Catherine's presence, he would beat that woman and turn her out of the castle in her shift.

The women opened their eyes wide and muttered among themselves.

'She is drowned,' Hugo said baldly. 'With my own eyes I saw her fall into the river and drown. And the man or woman who denies that is calling me a liar.' His hand lightly touched his belt where his broadsword would hang. 'I would kill a man for that, and beat a woman. I cannot stop you chattering among yourselves' – he swept them with his dark accusing look – 'no power on earth could prevent that. But one word of suspicion or doubt before Lady Catherine and you will wish you had been born mute.'

Only Eliza found the courage to speak up. 'What about Alys?' she asked.

'Alys stays with us,' Hugo said. 'She is a good friend to our family. She will care for Lady Catherine now, and for my son when he is born. It will be as it was before Morach came to the castle. You can forget Morach. She is gone.'

He waited in case there should be a reply and then he smiled his joyless commanding smile and walked from the gallery to seek his father.

Alys was there before him, sitting in the twilit chamber on a stool at the feet of the old lord, giving him the news before Hugo should come.

'Morach's gone,' she said without preamble.

The old lord looked sharply at her.

Alys nodded. 'She and I were up on the high moor together. She was making some mischief with candlewax dolls and I went with her, to stop her. Hugo was out with his hounds and they saw her, and chased her down a cave and left her there to drown.'

The old lord said nothing, waiting.

'She was a witch,' Alys said harshly. 'It's good that she's dead.'

'And you are not,' the old lord said slowly.

Alys turned her pale face up to him. 'No, my lord,' she said gently. 'Not at my ordeal, when Catherine hated me and tested me so harshly; and not now. I have made my peace with Catherine and I am her friend. I am in love with your son, and I love and honour you. Tell me that I can stay in your household, under your protection. I am free of Morach and I am free of the past.'

The old lord sighed and rested his hand on her hand. 'What of your power?' he asked. 'You lost it when Morach came and when Hugo would not love you.'

Alys gleamed up at him. 'I have it back,' she said. 'Morach had stolen it from me and stolen my health as well. She knew I would stand between her and you. She knew I would protect you and yours from her witchcraft. She made me ill and weak and she was starting to work her ill will against you all. Now that she is dead I have my power back and I can keep you safe. Tell me that I may live here under your protection, as your vassal.'

The old lord smiled down into Alys' bright face. 'Yes,' he said softly. 'Of course. I wanted you by me from the first day I saw you. Don't make trouble between Catherine and Hugo, I want a legitimate heir, and after this one I want another. You and Hugo can be what you will to each other – but don't distress my daughter-in-law while she is carrying my grandson.'

Alys nodded obediently, took his caressing hand and kissed it. 'I have news for you,' she said. 'Good news.'

The old lord waited, his eyebrows raised.

'I am with child,' Alys said. 'Hugo's child. He lay with me the night he came home from Newcastle. I am not like Catherine, hard to please, hard to conceive. I am with child to Hugo. I have missed two times. The baby will be born near the Christmas feast.'

The old lord gleamed. 'That's good!' he said. 'That's good news indeed. And d'you think it will be a son, Alys? Can you tell if it will be a boy?'

Alys nodded. 'A boy,' she said. 'A strong, handsome boy. A grandson for you, my lord. I shall be proud to be his mother.'

The old lord nodded. 'Well enough, well enough,' he said rapidly. 'And it means that Hugo will likely stay here until your child is born. Between you and Catherine, I shall keep him fast at home.'

'Yes,' Alys said eagerly. 'Catherine could not keep him home but he will stay for me. I will keep Hugo home for us both, my lord. I want him to leave for London or on his voyage as little as you do.'

The old lord barked his sharp laugh. 'Enchant him then,' he said. 'And keep him by you.' He paused for a moment and looked at her with pity. 'Don't overleap yourself, Alys,' he said gently. 'You will never be his wife. You will always be Catherine's lady. Whatever goes on at court – and I say nothing about that – whatever goes on at court, we are simple people here. Catherine is your mistress, you serve her well. Hugo is your lover and also your lord. I don't deny I am fond of you, Alys, but if you forget what is owed to your masters I would throw you from the castle tomorrow.

'Serve Catherine honourably and well and let Hugo take his pleasure with you when he wishes. That was how I kept my women. A wife for the heirs, and a woman for pleasure. That's order and sense. That's how it should be done.'

Alys kept her head down and her resentment hidden.

'Yes, my lord,' she said submissively.

David took her by the sleeve as she passed him by on the ill-lit stairs.

'I hear your kinswoman is dead,' he said softly.

'Yes,' Alys replied steadily. Her voice did not quaver, her face was serene.

'A hard death for a woman – drowning in cold river water,' David said.

Alys faced him down. 'Yes,' she said.

'And what of you now?' David pursued.

Alys smiled into his face. 'I shall care for Lady Catherine,' she said. 'I shall serve and honour Lord Hugh, and his son. What else?'

David drew her a little closer, pulled at her sleeve so that she leaned down and his mouth was near to her ear. 'I remember you when you were a fey wild thing off the moor,' he said. 'I saw you naked, changing your rags for the whore's shift. I heard that you took the ordeal for witchcraft. I saw you sicken and pine for the young lord. *Now* I ask you. What next?'

Alys twitched her sleeve from his grip, straightened up. 'Nothing,' she said blandly. 'I will serve Lady Catherine and help her during the birth. I will obey my Lord Hugh and honour his son. There is nothing more.'

The dwarf nodded. His smile gleamed at her in the

darkness. 'I wondered,' he said. 'I truly wondered about you. I thought you had the power to turn this castle on its ears. When you brought in the old woman, the witch, with all her power, I thought you were about to act. I have been watching you and wondering when you would make your move. I have had you in my mind for the new lady of the castle. So close as you are to the old lord! So powerful in your witchery to tame Hugo's wildness! And if you had a child – as you foresaw in your dream – such a wife you would be for him!'

Alys took a sharp breath but she held her gaze steady on his dark, angry, little face.

'What went wrong?' the dwarf asked curiously. 'What went wrong between you and the old witch? You were on your way, weren't you? The old witch was within Catherine's confidence, you and she would have attended the birth alone. What would it have been? Stillbirth? Strangled with the cord? Breech? Coming backwards and drowning in the blood?'

He laughed, a sharp cruel laugh.

'But you were in too much of a hurry, weren't you?' he said. 'Wanted Catherine dead and out of the way and Hugo all your own? I saw you pining and fading and losing your looks. It was eating you inside like a bellyful of worms, wasn't it, little Alys? So you hexed Catherine into the river, didn't you? Hexed her into deep water, wearing her thick furs so that she would drown.'

Alys was as white as skimmed milk. 'Nonsense,' she said bravely.

'And the old one pulled her out,' the dwarf said. 'D'you know? I rather liked the old one, your mother.'

'She wasn't my mother,' Alys said. Her whole face felt stiff, unnatural. 'I just lived with her. My real mother died in a fire.'

'Fire?' the dwarf said acutely. 'I never heard that before?'

'Yes,' Alys said. Her voice held a depth of despair. 'My mother, my real mother, died in a fire. And nothing has ever been right for me since she was gone.'

The dwarf cocked his head on one side, viewing her like some strange specimen. 'So now you've lost one to fire and one to water,' he said unsympathetically. 'But shall I call you Lady Alys yet? Will Catherine go the way of your two mothers? Fire? Water? Or by earth? Or by air? And what of you? Will it be the castle or a hidden place in town – a bawdy house in everything but name?'

Alys took one angry step down the stair and then turned on the step and looked back up. Her face was bright with spite. 'You *will* say Lady Alys to me,' she said passionately. The dwarf recoiled from her sudden rage. 'You will say Lady Alys to me – and I shall say "Farewell!" to you. For I shall be Hugo's wedded wife. And you will be a beggar at my gate.'

She turned and pattered down the stairs, her fine gown floating after her, not looking back. David stayed on the step listening to her footsteps going down and around the curving stone stair.

'I doubt that,' he said to the cold stone walls. 'I doubt that very much indeed.'

Catherine was heartbroken at the loss of Morach. She wept and clung to Alys when she was told, and Alys put her arms around her and they held each other like a pair of orphan sisters.

'You must stay with me now,' she said. She could scarcely speak for sobbing. 'You have her skills, you were there to help me just as she was there to help me when I was nearly drowned, when I nearly lost my life. You're her daughter, I loved you both. Oh! But Alys! I shall miss her.'

'I shall miss her too,' Alys said. Her blue eyes were flooded with unspilling, convincing tears. 'She taught me all that she knew, she gave me all her skills. It's as if she handed the care of you over to me before she left us.'

Catherine looked up trustingly. 'Do you think she knew?' she asked. 'Do you think she knew with her wisdom all along that she would leave us?'

Alys nodded. 'She told me she saw a darkness,' she said. 'I think she knew. When she took you from the river I think she knew then there would be a price to pay. And now the river has taken her.'

Catherine wailed even louder. 'Then she died to save me!' she exclaimed. 'She gave her life for me!'

Alys smoothed Catherine's hair with one soft, hypocritical hand. 'She would have wanted it that way,' she said. 'She, and I, are glad to make that sacrifice. I have lost my mother for you and I do not,' her voice gave a little pathetic quaver, 'I *will* not regret it.'

Catherine was sobbing without restraint. 'My friend, Alys!' she said. 'My only friend.'

Alys rocked her gently, looking down at the puffy, tear-blotched face. 'Poor Catherine,' she said. 'What a state you are in!'

She raised her voice and called for the women. Ruth came at once.

'Send for Hugo,' Alys said. 'Catherine needs him.'

He came at once and recoiled as Catherine, blubbering, reached out her arms to him with a wail of grief. He dropped to his knees before her chair and held her.

'Hush, hush,' he said gently into her hair. He looked

up at Alys, not seeing her. 'Have you nothing you can give her?' he asked. 'Nothing that can calm her? It cannot be good for the child for her to distress herself so.'

'She needs to calm herself,' Alys said distantly.

Catherine sobbed and held Hugo closer. 'I know,' she said, sniffing. 'But she made me laugh. She made it seem as if everything was a jest. She told me things about her life that made me laugh till I cried. I can't believe she won't walk in now and laugh in our faces.'

Alys shot one quick look at the door. The tapestry quivered. For a moment it seemed all too likely that Morach would walk in, trailing water and icy river weed, and laugh in their faces with her blue drowned mouth opened wide.

'No,' Hugo said quickly. 'She won't do that, Catherine. She is drowned. Try not to distress yourself so.' He turned to Alys. '*Surely* you have something to calm her?' he said.

'I can give her a distillation of the flower of Star of Bethlehem,' Alys said coldly. She went to her room. In the linen chest were the little bottles and powders and herbs which she and Morach had amassed. On the bed was Morach's white cotton nightshift. In the draught from the open door it billowed for a moment and raised itself a little up on the bed, as if it would get up and walk towards her. Alys stared at it hard for several moments. The arms shifted slightly as if they would point at her accusingly. Alys leaned back against the door and stared it down until she could force it to lie flat and limp again.

'Here,' she said, coming back into the gallery.

Hugo took the glass from her without looking up and gave Catherine sip after sip, watching her face and talking to her in a low, gentle voice. When she stopped sobbing, sat up, and wiped her face with her handkerchief, he looked around at Eliza and said, 'Here! Make her ladyship's bed ready! She should sleep now.'

Eliza ducked a curtsey and went through to Catherine's room.

'Have you anything to help her sleep?' he asked Alys over his shoulder.

She went back to the room she had shared with Morach. A log had shifted on the little fire and the shadows leaped and danced around the bed. For a moment it looked as if there were someone sitting on the chest at the head of the bed with their face turned towards the door. Alys leaned back against the door and pressed her hand hard against her heart. Then she fetched the drops of crushed poppy seeds for Lady Catherine, so that her ladyship might sleep well in the comfort of her great bed.

Hugo took the draught without thanks and led Catherine – one arm around her thick waist – out of the gallery and into her bedroom.

Alys watched them go, saw Catherine's head droop to Hugo's shoulder, heard her plaintive voice and his gentle reassurances. Alys tightened her lips, curbing her irritation.

'Won't you be afraid to sleep tonight on your own?' Eliza asked Alys as the door shut behind the couple.

'No,' Alys said.

Eliza gave a little scream. 'In a dead woman's bed!' she exclaimed. 'With the pillow still dented with her head! After she had drowned that very day! I'd be afraid she would come to say her farewells! That's what they do! She'll come to say her farewells before she rests in peace, poor old woman.'

Alys shrugged her shoulders. 'She was a poor old

woman and now she's dead,' she said. 'Why should she not rest in peace?'

Ruth looked sharply up at her. 'Because she is in the water,' she said. 'How will she rise up on the Day of Judgement if her body is all blanched and drenched?'

Alys felt her face quiver with horror. 'This is nonsense,' she said. 'I'll not hear it. I'm going to bed.'

'To sleep?' Mistress Allingham asked, surprised.

'Certainly to sleep,' Alys replied. 'Why should I not sleep? I am going to get into my nightshift, tie the strings of my cap and sleep all the long night.'

She stalked from the room and shut the door behind her. She undressed – as she had said she would – and tied the strings of her nightcap. But then she pulled up her stool to the fireside and threw another log on the fire, lit another candle so that all the shadows in the room were banished and it was as bright as day, and waited and waked all night – so that Morach should not come to her, all cold and wet. So that Morach should not come to her and lay one icy hand on her shoulder and say once more: 'Not long now, Alys.'

The next day Alys summoned a maid from the kitchen and they cleared the room of every trace of Morach. The kitchen maid was willing – expecting gifts of clothes or linen. To her horror at the waste of it all, Alys piled it all up and carried it down to the kitchen fire.

'You're never burning a wool gown!' The cook bustled forward, eyeing the little pile of clothes. 'And a piece of good linen!'

'They are lousy,' Alys said blankly. 'D'you want a gown with a dead woman's fleas? D'you want her lice?'

'Could be washed,' the cook said, standing between the fire and Alys.

Alys' blue eyes were veiled. 'She went among the sick,' she said. 'D'you think you can wash out the plague? D'you want to try it?'

'Oh, burn it! Burn it!' the cook said with sudden impatience. 'But you must cleanse my hearth. I cook the lord's own dinners here, remember.'

'I have some herbs,' Alys said. 'Step back.'

The cook retreated rapidly to the fire on the other side of the kitchen where the kitchen lad was turning the spit, leaving Alys watched, but alone. Alys thrust the little bundle into the red heart of the fire.

It smouldered sulkily for a moment. Alys watched until the hem of Morach's old gown caught, flickered and then burst into flame. Alys pulled a little bottle from her pocket. 'Myrrh,' she said and dripped one drop on each corner of the hearthstone, and then three drops into the heart of the fire. 'Rest in peace, Morach,' she said in a whisper too low for anyone to hear. 'You know and I know what a score we have to settle between us. You know and I know when we will meet again, and where. But leave me with my path until that day. You had your life and you made your choices. Leave me free to make mine, Morach!'

She stepped back one pace and watched the flames. They flickered blue and green as the oil burned. On the other side of the kitchen the cook drew in a sharp breath and clenched her fist in the sign against witchcraft. Alys paid her no heed.

'You cared for me like a mother,' she said to the fire. The flames licked hungrily around the cloth and the bundle fell apart and blazed up, shrivelling into dark embers. 'I own that now. Now it is too late to thank you or to show you any kindliness in return,' Alys said. 'You cared for me like a mother and I betrayed you like an enemy. I summon your love for me now, your mother-love. You told me I did not have long. Give me that little space freely. Leave me to my life. Morach. Don't haunt me.'

For a moment she paused, her head on one side as if she were listening for a reply. The dark smoky smell of the myrrh filled the kitchen. The kitchen lad kept his face away from her and turned the spit at extra speed, its squeak rising to a squeal.

Alys waited.

Nothing happened.

Morach had gone.

Alys turned from the fire with a clear smile, nodded at the cook. 'All done, clothes burned and the hearth cleaned,' she said pleasantly. 'What are you making for the lord's dinner?'

The cook showed her the dozen roasted chickens waiting to be pounded into paste, the almonds, rice and honey ready for mixing, the sandalwood to make the mixture pink. 'Blanche mange for the main course,' she said. 'And Allowes – I have some good slices of mutton. And Bucknade. Some roasted venison. I have some fish, some halibut from the coast. Would you want me to make something special for Lady Catherine?' she asked ingratiatingly.

Alys considered. 'Some rich sweet puddings,' she said. 'Her ladyship loves sweet things and she needs all her strength. Some custards, perhaps some leche lombarde with plenty of syrup.'

'She's growing very fat and bonny,' the cook said admiringly.

'Yes,' Alys said sweetly. 'She is fatter every day. There will scarce be room for my Lord Hugo in her bed if she grows much bigger. Send a glass of negus and some custards and some cakes up to her chamber, she is hungry now she is in her fifth month.'

The cook nodded. 'Yes, Alys,' she said.

Alys paused on her way to the door, one eyebrow raised.

The cook hesitated, Alys did not move. There was a powerful silence as the cook met Alys' blue eyes and then glanced away. 'Yes, Mistress Alys,' she said, unwillingly giving Alys a title. Alys looked slowly around the kitchen as if defying anyone to challenge her. No one spoke. She nodded to the kitchen boy and he scrambled from the spit to open the door for her into the hall. She passed through without a word of thanks.

She paused as the door closed behind her and listened in case the cook should cry out against her, complain of her ambition, or swear that she was a witch. She heard a hard slap and the spit-lad yell at undeserved punishment. 'Get on with it,' the cook said angrily. 'We don't have all day.'

Alys smiled and went across the hall and up the stairs to the ladies' gallery.

Catherine was resting in her room before dinner, the women gathered around the fireside in the gallery were stealing an hour of idleness. Ruth was reading a pamphlet on the meaning of the Mass, Eliza was daydreaming, gazing at the fire. Mistress Allingham was dozing, her head-dress askew. Alys nodded impartially at them all and walked past them to her own chamber.

The maid had swept up the rushes from the floor as she had been ordered, and left the broom. Alys took it up and meticulously swept every corner of the room, sweeping the dust and the scraps of straw into the centre of the room. Carefully she collected it all and flung it on the fire. Then she took a scrap of cloth and wiped all around the room, everywhere that Morach's hand might have rested or her head brushed. Every place where her skirt might have touched or her feet walked. Round and around the room Alys went like a little spider spinning a web. Round and around until there was no place in the room which she had not wiped. Then she folded the cloth over and over, as if to capture the smell of Morach inside the linen – and flung it into the heart of the fire.

The maid, complaining, had brought new rugs and a spread for the bed and Alys smoothed them down over the one solitary pillow. She shook out the curtains of the bed and tied them back in great swags. Then she stepped back and looked around the room with a little smile.

As a room for two healers, two midwives for the birth of the only son and heir, it had been generous. It was as big as the room next door where the four women slept, two to a pallet-bed. As a room for one woman, sleeping alone, it was noble. It was nearly as big as Lady Catherine's, the bed was as large, the hangings nearly as fine. It was colder than Catherine's room – facing west out over the river – but airier. Alys had chosen not to scatter new herbs and bedstraw on the floor, but the room smelled clean. It was clear and empty of the clutter of women, no pots of face paint, no creams, no half-eaten sweetmeats like in Catherine's room. Alys' gowns, capes, hoods and linen were in one chest, all her herbs, her pestle and mortar, her crystal and her goods were in the other.

There was one chair, with a back but no arms, and one stool. Alys drew the chair up to the fire, rested her feet on the stool, and looked into the flames.

The door opened. Eliza Herring peeped into the room. 'There you are!' she said awkwardly.

Alys raised her head and looked at Eliza, but said nothing.

Eliza looked around. 'You've swept it,' she said, surprised.

Alys nodded.

'Aren't you coming out to sit with us?' Eliza asked. 'You must be bored in here on your own.'

'I'm not bored,' Alys said coolly.

Eliza fidgeted slightly, came a little further into the room and then stepped back again. 'I'll come and sleep in here with you, if you like,' she offered. 'You won't want to be on your own. We could have some laughs, at night. Margery won't mind me moving out.'

'No,' Alys said gently.

'She really won't,' Eliza said. 'I already asked her, because I guessed you would want company.'

Alys shook her head. Eliza hesitated. 'It's bad to grieve too much,' she said kindly. 'Morach was a foul old woman but she loved you – anyone could see that. You shouldn't grieve for her too long, Alys. You shouldn't sit here all alone, grieving for her.'

'I'm not grieving,' Alys said. 'I feel nothing. Nothing for her, nothing for you women, nothing for Catherine. Don't waste your worry on me, Eliza. I feel nothing.'

Eliza blinked. 'You're shocked,' she said, trying to excuse Alys' coldness. 'You need company.'

'I don't want company and I cannot have you sleeping in here,' Alys said. 'Hugo will want to be on his own in here with me very often. I have prepared the room for the two of us.'

Eliza's eyes widened, her mouth made a soundless 'O'. 'What about my lady?' she demanded when she could find her voice. 'She may not be well, Alys, but she has enough life in her to throw you back into the street.

Hugo would never cross her while she is carrying his child.'

Alys' lips smiled without warmth. 'She will become accustomed,' she said. 'Everything is going to be different now.'

Eliza blinked. 'Just because Morach drowned?' she asked.

Alys shook her head. 'It is nothing to do with Morach. I am expecting Hugo's child. It will be a son. Do you tell me that he will let Catherine rule me, when she is carrying one son and I another?'

Eliza gasped. 'But hers is legitimate!' she protested.

Alys shrugged. 'What of that? You can never have too many sons and Hugo has no other. I think they will treat them both as heirs until they know that the succession is safe, don't you?'

Eliza held the door against her and peered around it. 'Is this dukering?' she asked. 'Divining and dukering?'

Alys laughed confidently. 'This is mortal woman's knowledge,' she said. 'Hugo has been lying with me ever since he came back from Newcastle. Now I am with his child I want a room to myself and perhaps a little maid to wait on me. Why should Catherine object? It will make no difference to her.'

'She made it bad enough for you before,' Eliza warned.

Alys nodded. 'Yes,' she said. 'But now she is ill and weary all the time, and I am the only one who can quiet her fears. She would cling to me whatever I did. And I will care for her kindly enough.'

Eliza nodded with begrudging admiration. 'You've come a long way, Alys,' she said.

'They call me Mistress Alys now,' Alys said. 'Would you ring for a tub and a pitcher of hot water? I shall take a bath.'

'Ring yourself!' Eliza exclaimed, instantly indignant.

Alys whirled up from the chair and took Eliza by the shoulders, shook her and held her, putting her angry face very near. 'I will warn you once, Eliza,' she said through her teeth. 'Everything is different here now. I am Alys no more. I am carrying Lord Hugh's grandchild by his son who is barren with every other woman but me and his wife. I am second only to his wife. I can count you as my friend, or I can count you as my enemy. But you will not live here long if we are enemies.'

The fight went out of Eliza in a rush. 'You're very lucky,' she said with half-hearted resentment. 'You came as nothing and now you're to be called Mistress Alys.'

Alys shook her head. 'I came as a learned woman, a healer and my lord's clerk,' she said proudly. 'I am the daughter of a noble lady. I am fit for this. I am as fit to be the Lady here, as Jane Seymour is for the Crown. Now ring for hot water, I shall take a bath.'

Eliza nodded, slowly. 'Yes, Mistress Alys,' she said.

Two menservants carried the big barrel up the winding stairs and into Alys' room and set it down close to the fire. A kitchen maid came with a sheet of linen and spread it over the sides and bottom of the bath. Two men behind her brought great buckets of scalding water. They poured it in and went back for two more. Alys sent them for a fifth to leave by the side of the barrel with a ladle to add more hot water as she wished. She shut the door behind them and opened the chest where she kept the herbs. She had dried honeysuckle and rose petals in a purse of linen and she took a handful and scattered them on the water. She had a tiny bottle of oil of chamomile and she rinsed her hair with it. She sat in the hot water with her head resting against the back of the barrel and rubbed her hands all over her body, crushing the flower petals against her skin. Her hands went over and around her breasts until the nipples stood hard and tingled to her touch. She shook out her wet hair and let it tumble over the side of the barrel and drip carelessly on the floor.

As the water cooled she roused herself from the bath, wrapped herself in a warm sheet and sat in solitary silence before her fire. She sniffed at the skin of her forearm, like a sensuous little animal. She smelled of meadow flowers from the petals, and her fair hair smelled of honey. Her body was lithe and slim and lovely. Her face was grim.

'Tonight,' Alys said softly to herself. 'Tonight, Hugo.'

Twenty

Alys, washed, scented, oiled, and dressed in a simple blue one-piece gown with a blue ribbon at her waist, had to wait with what patience she could simulate all through a long and tedious day. Lady Catherine was still too grieved to come down to dinner. She whimpered for company; and Hugo, looking in at the ladies' gallery on his way to the hall, was prepared to dine with her in her room. That left the old lord eating on his own, solitary, at the centre of the long high table, glowering under his dark eyebrows. When the meats were taken away Alys left the women's table and went to him and leaned over him to ask a question. The women heard his sharp laugh and a low-voiced reply to Alys. Then he nodded her, casually, to a stool further down the table, and talked with her until the meal was ended. David's gaze, as he watched them served with the voider course of wafers, fruit and hippocras wine, was bright.

'Is Alys to sit with Lady Catherine's women no more?' he asked the old lord. 'Is she your guest now, my lord?'

The old lord gleamed under his eyebrows. 'I was bored,' he said uncompromisingly. 'And there was no one to talk to. If my daughter-in-law has forgotten her duty to dine at my table and my son takes to her chamber with her like a maid-in-waiting – what am I to do? Sit dumbstruck?'

David nodded. 'I asked only so that I would know where to order her cup placed for her,' he said apologetically. 'If you wish the woman to dine with you I shall set her pewter here.'

The lord banged the table with his fist. 'When Catherine is absent Alys can have her plate, can't she?' he demanded irritably. 'When in all my life have I not had a woman to watch when I wished? And Alys is the best-looking woman in the castle. She shall sit with me when Catherine is not here, and she can drink from glass and eat off silver. Is that clear?'

David bowed in silence. When he straightened up he saw Alys watching him, her blue eyes bright with amusement. 'Thank you very much, David,' she said coolly. 'You are kind to consider my comfort. I would never have had that invitation but for you.'

The old lord laughed briefly and snapped his fingers for more wine. Alys took the flagon from the wine-server and poured it for him, leaning forward so that he saw the promising swell of her breasts at the neck of her gown.

'Pretty whore,' the old lord said with a smile, and threw back his head to drain the glass.

Alys, unashamed, smiled back.

When dinner was over she went with the Lord Hugh to his chamber and wrote letters to his dictation until the light had gone. He had to re-form his alliances now that Jane Seymour's family were in favour, and there were rumours that the hastily wedded bride was with child. She was said to be trying to reconcile the King and his daughter Mary. 'A popish Princess at court again,' Lord Hugh said thoughtfully. 'And everything sliding around like a whore's blanket.'

Alys rang for candles and a glass of mulled wine for the old man.

'I'm weary,' he said frankly. 'It's a long time coming, this baby of Catherine's. When is yours due?'

'End of November,' Alys said. 'As we start preparing for the Christmas feast.'

The lord nodded, his eyelids drooping. 'That will be merry,' he said. 'For us at any rate. And what d'you think of Catherine? Will she have another soon after this?'

Alys shrugged. 'She's from sickly stock,' she said disparagingly. 'But there's no reason why she should not have more. She may take time to conceive though, she's not very fertile, is she? This one took her nine years!'

The old lord moved restively. 'I should have matched him elsewhere,' he said irritably. 'But it was so easy, with the wardship in my hands and all. But if I had known she would have been so slow to take, I would never have put her with Hugo.'

Alys went behind his chair and stroked his forehead. He lay back against the hard chair back, quietened by her touch.

'Don't fret,' she said. 'By this time next year you will have two grandsons – hers and mine. By this time next year I shall be pregnant by Hugo again.'

'Setting up a stud?' he asked, chuckling with his eyes closed.

'I want to stay here,' Alys said frankly. 'And I want Hugo. And I want your protection. What better way?'

The old lord shook his head. 'There is no better way,' he said. 'While you are carrying my grandson I am yours to command. You know what this child means to me.'

Alys nodded. 'I know,' she said.

The old lord sighed and sat quietly for a little while. With slow easy strokes Alys dragged her fingers across his forehead, feeling the soft ridges of the lined old skin under her fingertips.

'I shall give you land, Alys,' Lord Hugh said,

luxuriating in her sure touch. 'When your son is born. I shall endow you with some land. A woman like you should have a little wealth, a little power.'

Alys smiled, her touch on his forehead never hesitated. 'I should like the farm next door to old Morach's cottage,' she said, without hesitation. 'It's a pretty place and Morach had a claim to some of the fields. It would please me to take the whole farm off them. It will repay them for their robbery of Morach.' She gave a soft little laugh. 'Some symmetry,' she said.

'Maybe,' Lord Hugh replied. 'I'll have David or Hugo look into it.'

Alys nodded, the gentle pressure of her fingertips slowing to keep time with his deeper breathing. In a few moments he was asleep, and she pulled up a stool to the foot of his chair and sat down, leaning back against him, watching the fire.

In his sleep his hand stretched out and touched her head. Alys untied the hood and put it to one side and let his hand rest on her rumpled curls. They sat together for a long while. Alys watched the fire and felt the comfortable warmth of his hand on her head like a benediction. She closed her eyes. The warm, safe, clean smell of the room and the touch of a hand on her head was like the abbey and Mother Hildebrande's touch. Alys closed her eyes too and waited.

He was not long. Hugo came striding in, his cape pushed back off his shoulders and his cap askew from his ride, and checked on the threshold at the picture they made: his father's familiar profile softened in sleep and Alys' young beauty under his protection.

'Hush,' Alys said, getting to her feet and drawing Hugo from the room. 'He is tired. I have been writing letters for him all afternoon.'

'I've been riding,' Hugo said. 'Catherine was weary after dinner.'

'Then only we two are awake,' Alys said, with a little secretive smile. 'Only we two, awake, and ...' She paused, glancing at Hugo with a look which promised everything. 'Only we two, awake and ... restless,' she said.

Hugo shot her a quick, measuring look from under his dark eyebrows. 'Where are Catherine's women?' he asked. 'I left Ruth and Margery sitting in Catherine's bedchamber. Where are the others?'

'Gone into Castleton,' Alys said. 'You could walk into my room and there would be no one to see you pass.'

Hugo nodded. 'Go ahead of me,' he said. 'See that Catherine is still asleep and her door is shut.'

Alys nodded and led the way down the winding staircase and through the antechamber before the great hall, and then up to the ladies' gallery above. The fire burned low in the grate. The door to Catherine's chamber was closed. Alys and Hugo slipped across the gallery and into Alys' room, as silent as ghosts.

Hugo shut the door behind them and dropped the bolt home. 'Here is a change, Alys,' he said. 'After that first time I thought you found I was not to your taste.'

Alys shook her head to loosen her hair and it tumbled around her face in a shower of brass and gold. She tossed it from her eyes and smiled confidently at Hugo, measuring his rising desire.

'You took me as a virgin, an ordinary girl,' she said. 'It will never be like that again. I withdrew from you to learn my skills. I had to find my teachers, I had to know some deep arts before I could lie with you.'

'What arts?' Hugo asked; his voice shook slightly.

'You know of them,' Alys said simply. 'You have dreamed of them, you have hardly believed they could be possible between a man and a woman.'

Hugo touched his lips with his tongue. 'I have heard,' he began, 'of arts that a woman, a skilled woman, can use which can make a man crazy for her. And I have heard that if you lie with a witch she can take you to the very borders of heaven – and beyond. And I've heard that you feel unearthly pleasure, pleasure beyond that any ordinary woman can give you.' He gave a nervous excited laugh. 'All lies and trickery, I suppose?'

Alys shook her head slowly, her hair swung forward. Hugo leaned towards her. 'You smell of honey,' he said.

'All those things I can do,' Alys promised. She paused, weighing her words. 'If you dare.'

'I dare,' Hugh said quickly. 'I desire them.'

Alys smiled and crossed the room. Hugo followed her with his eyes. She opened the chest of herbs and took out a flagon of spiced wine and two cups. As he watched she poured a cup for both of them, turned aside for one second – half a second only – and palmed a fat pinch of crushed earthroot into his cup.

'I drink to your desire,' she said. 'May it bring you all that you dream.'

Hugo raised the cup and downed it in three impatient gulps. 'And your desire, Alys?' he asked. 'When you last lay with me you had no desire.'

Alys shrugged. 'I was an ordinary maid,' she said. 'You asked me to put aside my power for love of you – and so I did. But then you found – did you not? – that there are many ordinary maids in the castle. But only one witch.'

Hugo laughed, a little shaky. 'A witch,' he repeated.

'With witches' skills.' He moistened his lips with his tongue. 'I scarcely believe in witchcraft, Alys. You will have to deal with a modern man, an unbeliever.'

Alys smiled, confident in Morach's herbal skills. 'Oh, Hugo,' she said, a laugh in the back of her voice. 'You believe and disbelieve at will. But when you are out on a cold moor with the mist around you and the river rising, you see dark magic and know fear. And when you are here with me, in this room, you will be enchanted and know your deepest desires.'

'You've changed,' he said.

Alys nodded. 'I have found my mistress, the dark mistress of all wise women, and I have learned from her. I had to become one with her as if I were her lover. And now I know her skills.'

'What are they?' Hugo asked. 'Your mistress' skills?'

Alys put her hands to the back of her gown and slowly, almost casually, began to untie the ribbon laces. Hugo watched in silence as she shrugged it off her shoulder. She was naked underneath. She pushed it down over her hips and stepped out of it. She wore no shift, no undergown. Hugo hissed an indrawn breath at the sight of her body and at the realization that she had planned this seduction. She had dressed herself after her bath so that she would be naked before him this day. He reached out to snatch at her but Alys gestured to the chair.

'Be seated, Hugo,' she said, magnificently formal in her nakedness.

Hugo stepped obediently towards the chair, stumbling as he reached it. Alys watched him intently.

'Is it hard for you to walk, Hugo?' she asked.

He opened his mouth to frame a reply, moving slowly.

'Hard for you to walk, or talk, or reach for me,' Alys said. 'All you can do is watch.'

Hugo, slack-muscled, entrapped by the drug, lolled in the chair, his eyes, darkly dilated, never leaving Alys' white body with the bush of golden hair.

'I will tell you what my mistress taught me,' Alys said, her voice a low, hypnotic song. 'She taught me to dance so that a man cannot move for desire.' Alys' hair fell in a fair curtain over her shoulders, over her breasts, she stretched to one side and then another. Hugo could not take his eyes from her moving body.

'I can't move,' Hugo said thickly.

'She taught me to summon my sisters to touch me,' Alys said. Her hands cupped her own face, closed over her throat, smoothed down together over her breasts. The nipples, rosy and hard, flickered through the curtain of hair. Alys threw her head back so her throat was bared, cupped both her breasts in her hands and walked towards Hugo. 'I will always have pleasure,' Alys whispered. 'I will always have pleasure for the asking. My sisters will come to me at any time, any time I ask. And they will stroke me and lick me and kiss me. Can you see them yet, Hugo? They are coming to us both. They come to pleasure me and to please you.'

His mouth fell longingly open. Alys stood astride him and rubbed first one breast and then another against his lips. Hugo quested for her touch, turning his head like a baby. His hands clenched on his thighs but he could not reach out and hold her.

'My mistress has come now,' Alys said in an awed whisper. 'She is in the room with me now. Oh God! D'you see her, Hugo? She is naked like I am, and her hair is black. Her touch burns my skin like fire and her kisses make me long for more and more. With her are my sisters, ten, twenty girls, all naked. All come to dance for you, Hugo!'

Hugo could not take his eyes from Alys but he felt in every corner of the room the gathering of women. He sensed their eyes upon him and the growing heat of their bodies. Alys, watching him all the time, stroked her hands down across her belly to the perfect indentation of her navel.

'Can you feel me, Hugo?' she asked. 'Can you feel me, and all my sisters and my cunning mistress? Can you see us, all naked, can you see the stars in our hair and our smiles?'

Hugo shuddered, a great involuntary shiver which shook his whole body. 'Alys.'

Alys' hand smoothed down her belly to the golden bush of hair. 'Look, Hugo,' she said. 'In all your nasty little games with Catherine, has she ever stood proudly before you and let you see her?'

Wordlessly, Hugo shook his head.

'Then look at me,' Alys said. 'I am not ashamed, I am not afraid. No man hurts me, no man torments me. My sisters and I give each other delight that no man could ever match. But we will let you be with us, Hugo. We will let you roll with us, play with us, excite us.' With both hands she parted the hair and rubbed her forefinger delicately against her pink opening flesh.

'Let me,' Hugo said urgently. 'Let me, Alys.'

She raised her head again and smiled at him, mockingly. 'Ah! You must wait,' she said. 'You must wait until you can see us all. All my sisters want you to taste them, all of them want to touch you. We are all hungry for your touch, Hugo. My sisters and me. D'you see us? Do you see us now?'

'I can see you,' Hugo said. 'And I can feel them, I can feel their hands on me.'

Alys came closer at once. 'On your hair and on your face, Hugo,' she whispered. 'Can you feel their lips on your face and on your neck? Can you smell their perfume, Hugo? The scent of their hair and their sweat and their wetness? They're ready for you. They are longing for you. D'you think you can please us? Do you think you can please us all?'

Hugo rolled his head back and groaned. Alys teased his open mouth with one nipple, then another, and she slid her wet fingers into his mouth. 'This is the taste of her,' she said. 'This is the taste of my sister the Sky Goddess. D'you like her?'

Hugo was sucking frantically, his forehead was damp with sweat, his dark curls sticking to his face, desperate with unsatisfied lust. 'Yes,' he said. 'I can see her now! I can see her white body and her hair.'

Alys leaned forward and rubbed her breasts against his face, gasping a little as his stubble scratched across her nipples. 'This is my sister the Sun Witch,' she said. 'D'you feel the warmth of her skin? She is shameless, Hugo! She cares for nothing but heat and pleasure!'

Hugo groaned aloud and butted his head against Alys' moving breasts. 'Give me your heat, Sun Witch,' he demanded. 'I want your shamelessness.'

Alys lowered herself a little to his lap, her slim thighs astride him. 'She is coming to sit on you,' she whispered. 'The Star Goddess, she wants to feel your body between her legs.'

The drug of the earthroot held Hugo passive. He could only arch his back as Alys lowered herself and pulled away, lowered again, and then succumbing to her own lust, gripped him with her thighs and rubbed herself against his breeches, against his padded codpiece.

'I want ... I want ...' Hugo stammered. Saliva drooled from his mouth, his eyes were turned up in his head, only the whites showing.

'You want us all,' Alys said. 'Every one of us in every way you can dream of.'

'Yes,' Hugo said. 'Alys, please!'

Alys untied the codpiece, pulled away the flap of his breeches; he was naked underneath. He thrust upwards and she dropped her body down to meet him. As they joined she felt a great surge of pleasure bounding up through her, and she clung to the thick padded shoulders of his jacket while the waves of it washed over and over her.

'She is here!' she said triumphantly. 'The mistress of all of them has you in her thrall. Open your eyes and look at her. You are planting your seed in her, open your eyes and see the mistress you will never match, never replace, never reject.'

Hugo, drugged to the point of blindness, forced his eyes open and saw her.

'Mistress ... my lady ... Alys!' he exclaimed in surprise.

'I am my own mistress,' Alys said, joyful in her power. 'I am my own mistress at last.' She fell forward and clung around his neck and heard his harsh gasp as his body tightened and throbbed inside her, and then quietened.

As they grew cool she lifted herself away and pulled her cape around her shoulders, and tossed a handful of pine cones on the fire. She put the flagon of wine and the glasses back in the chest, all the time watching Hugo's deep, trance-like sleep and his flickering eyelids, as he dreamed of more and more extravagant orgies. He groaned once or twice and thrust his hips upwards, into the empty air.

Alys put another log on the fire and scattered pine needles on it so that the room smelled resinous and sweet. Then she drew up the stool and sat, hugging her knees and waiting for Hugo to wake from dreams of colours so bright, smells so pungent and touches so intimate, that they were more vivid than reality. Alys watched the man she loved rear upwards in his chair and thrust his hips into nothingness in a drugged ecstasy, calling her name once, and then again; and she felt as far away from him as if she were walking alongside the cold river-bank on the snow-blown moorland and he were dead and still in his grave.

He came to his senses slowly. He blinked and stared disbelievingly around him, shook his head in bewilderment, and then focused on Alys, calmly seated at the fireside, her hair tumbled over her naked shoulders, the cape thrown back, her bare skin warmed into a thousand tones of peach by the firelight.

'Alys,' he said. 'What hour is it? And how long did I sleep? I had such a dream!'

Alys smiled steadily, her eyes mysterious. 'It is nearly time for supper,' she said. 'You have not slept, it was no dream. I was here, you were here, all of them were here with us for all of that time.'

Hugo leaned forward, grabbed her hands. 'They were?' he demanded. 'It was no dream? They were here, your sisters? And we were together, all of us?'

Alys laughed a deep ripple of pleasure. 'Oh yes,' she said silkily. 'We were all here and you enjoyed every one of us. It was such pleasure, Hugo, wasn't it?'

'Yes,' Hugo assented, dazed. 'Oh yes. My God, Alys. I've heard of such things but I never dreamed they could happen. But I saw them! I touched them.'

'You touched them!' Alys agreed, smiling. 'You

392

touched us all. I promised you a time beyond all the times you had ever had. What did you expect, Hugo? Some whorish tricks? Or your nasty cruelties with Catherine? I can give you your dreams – the cream of your desires – nothing less.'

Hugo leaned back in the chair and closed his eyes again. 'I feel drunk,' he said. 'I feel as if I drank for a week and then dreamed for a year.'

Alys shrugged. 'Time means nothing when you are with us all,' she said. 'And my kisses and my sisters' kisses are powerful wine for a man.'

Hugo opened his eyes and looked at her, his gaze suddenly piercing. 'Is this a trick?' he asked acutely. 'Is it a trick you have played on me? With herbs or poisons or some stuff? Tell me the truth, Alys. I never want more pleasure than you gave me – but I am awake now and want to know the truth. I am not some country clown at a fairground to be fooled. It makes no difference to my love for you – so tell me. Was it the wine you gave me? Or some trickery?'

Alys laughed. 'You tell *me*, Hugo,' she said. 'You have been drunk many times – have you ever been potent like that in drink? Have you ever seen my sisters before when you were drunk or sober? Have you ever woken clear-headed, feeling strong after drinking?'

She gambled on the power of the earthroot. 'You *know* what you saw. You know what you did! Was it one woman or twenty? Did you have the pleasure of one woman, or did you have the pleasure of twenty? Was it me, or was it me as the mistress of your dreams, and all of my wicked, desirable sisters?'

Hugo nodded, leaned back and closed his eyes again. 'Deep, deepest magic,' he said. 'There were many, many of you. And you, Alys, as mistress of them all.'

Alys smiled and rose up from the stool and stood before him. 'Yes,' she said calmly. 'I am mistress of them all. I am in my power. And the pleasure you have with us I can give you whenever I wish. Whenever you ask and whenever I consent.'

Hugo's eyes darkened with the remainder of the drug and with desire. 'They will come again?' he asked.

Alys smiled. 'Whenever I summon them,' she said. 'My sisters and I – we like to play with you, Hugo.'

Hugo smiled. 'Alys,' he said. 'My love.'

Twenty-one

All through the next week, and the week after, Catherine was sluggish and tired. In the morning her women found her pillow damp with her sweat and tears. She slept badly at night, dreaming of her long-dead mother, and her father who had been reported for speaking treason against the King and died in the cold cells of York prison while waiting for his trial. During the day she mourned Morach – the only friend she had made in all the years she had spent as Lord Hugh's ward and young Hugo's wife. It was as if the loss of Morach had added to all the losses she had felt in her life and her grief for all of them overflowed and oozed from her eyes, from between her legs, from the very pores of her skin, in a steady unstoppable, cold dampness.

Catherine, who had been a tyrant to her women and a bully to the servants, ceased giving orders or making demands. Alys had nothing more to do than sit with Catherine in the morning before dinner, and then again in the afternoon while Hugo went riding alone. Catherine drank deep of clary – a French red wine – which Alys assured her would build her blood, and ate at dinner and supper like a pig in farrow, with shameless gluttony. Dazed and sleepy from the wine, belching with rich food, and weary as her pregnancy entered its fifth month, Catherine dozed on her bed every afternoon after dinner, and fell asleep immediately after supper every night. If Hugo desired, he and Alys could be together all afternoon and all evening while his wife dozed and – after she fell into a drunken sleep – all night.

He did desire. The earthroot worked its potent magic nearly every day and Alys found he needed smaller and smaller doses to fall into his waking dreams of desire. When he came out of them, blear-eyed and slack-muscled, he always told Alys that she was his love, his only love. After a month of drugged hallucinatory love-making he seemed as addicted to Alys herself as to the earthroot. She had no need to weave dreams and fantasies – the smell of her, the taste of her, the pleasure he took in her body was enough to throw him into his feverish lust. Alys had him enthralled in the deep tangled forests of his own desires and Hugo never struggled to be free.

'Got him on your line, have you?' the old lord asked her one morning as she watched Hugo crossing the courtyard below the round tower window.

'My lord?' she asked, without looking round. Watching Hugo warmed her heart with a sweet glow of possession: Hugo was hers now, no one else even tempted him. His quick lusts and careless satisfactions in dark doorways were finished, all the women in the castle knew it. Hugo was infatuated, mad for Mistress Alys. The only woman who did not know it was Lady Catherine.

'On your line,' the old lord repeated. 'Hooked, netted and landed. Does he thrash much in the net, pretty Alys? Or is he one of the steady ones – a couple of thrusts and he is spent?'

Alys giggled involuntarily. 'Hush,' she said. 'That is no way to talk of the young lord.'

'And does he talk much more of London?' the old lord demanded. 'Going to the court and leaving me? Or that damned voyage of his?'

Alys' smile was proud. 'Not at all,' she said. 'The

voyage is still in his mind, his heart is still set on the thousand pounds. But other men will sail the ship, he will not leave the castle now. I can hold him.'

'Hold him until that ship is left port and you will have my gratitude,' the old lord growled. 'Can you keep him till next spring?'

'He will not leave me when I am carrying his child,' Alys said. 'And I know Hugo, when he sees the son I shall give him he will not be able to tear himself away. I will keep him safe for you, my lord.'

Lord Hugh nodded. 'See you do,' he said. 'But don't keep him from his work on the land. He should be out there, talking with the men. There are markets where they are skimming the fees they owe us. There are farms months behind in their rent. There are tenants dying, wedding, birthing, changing their leases and not paying us the proper fines. In every village there is an agent who reports to us and pays us the fees. Every one of them is taking his share of what is rightfully ours. There's his new house being built and the workmen taking their time, I'll be bound. He should be out there, enforcing our rights, not playing hunt-the-flea in your shift, Alys.'

Alys shook her head. 'It is Catherine he sits with during the day,' she said. 'I would ride out with him, what could be better for us all than my eyes and ears on the land as well as his? But Catherine keeps him home during the hours he used to be abroad. If you complain of him neglecting his work on the land then it is Catherine you should blame.'

The old lord scowled. 'Still sickly is she?' he demanded impatiently. 'What ails her?'

Alys shrugged. 'She is weary,' she said. 'She feels weak. She is eating to keep up her strength but the more she eats the heavier she gets and the lazier she feels. Her strength and her power seem to be fading away. Perhaps she will be better when the weather is warmer. She needs the sunshine. And she misses Morach still.'

The old lord hunched his shoulders irritably, like a ruffled bird of prey. 'Misses that old witch! She should be ashamed of herself.'

Alys smiled faintly. 'Odd is it not?' she said. 'You would think that she was grieving for a mother. And I, who was raised by Morach, I know her for what she was, and I have little sorrow.' She paused. 'As if I were the lady and not her,' she said.

The old lord cocked a shrewd eyebrow at her. 'No,' he said shortly.

Alys looked at him.

'Don't think of it,' the old lord advised her. 'Be glad with what you have won, *Mistress* Alys. You have climbed as high as you will go in this castle. I like to have you by me, Hugo is mad for you, even Catherine likes you and needs you now, and you are carrying my grandson in your belly. But if you try to overturn the natural order, try to leap up to nobility, I will have you thrown back to the midden. We are not the King's court here. You cannot make your fortune on your back.'

Alys' blue eyes sharpened with anger but she said nothing.

'Hear me?' the old lord insisted.

'I hear you,' she said levelly.

'And you'll keep your ambitions for your son,' the old lord reminded her.

Alys smiled at him. 'As you wish, my lord,' she said pleasantly. 'What a child he will be!'

'Yes,' the old lord said, still irritable. 'Ring the bell for Father Stephen, I want him to read to me. I have missed him in his travels away from us.'

'I'll read,' Alys offered, moving towards the table and the books.

'I'll have Father Stephen,' the old lord said. 'I want a man's voice. Women are very well in their place, Alys. But you can grow weary of them.'

'Oh yes,' Alys agreed. 'I grow very tired of the chatter in the gallery at times – such gossip and nonsense! Such a clatter the foolish women make who have nothing better to do but eat and grow fat and lazy. I will fetch Father Stephen at once for you, and I will send Hugo to you when he comes home. He can tell you about the new house, he is riding out today to see the builders.'

The lord grinned wryly, noting how Alys turned his complaint.

'Clever little whore,' he said gently.

Alys smiled back, swept him a seductive curtsey, and flicked out of the room.

In the ladies' gallery Catherine had not risen from her bed though it was near noon and time for dinner. Ruth was in her room showing her one gown after another, Catherine pettishly waving them all aside.

'They don't fit,' she said. 'This baby is getting bigger and bigger. You should have altered them, you should have let out the seams, Ruth. I told you to do so and you have been lazy and negligent.'

Ruth shook her head. 'I did alter them, my lady,' she said in her quiet, frightened voice. 'I altered them as you asked me. But that was last week, my lady. You seem to have grown again around your waist.'

Catherine sighed and leaned back. 'I am swelling like

399

a bubble,' she said plaintively. 'This baby exhausts me.' She shot a look towards Alys in the doorway. 'Can't you help me, Alys?' she asked pitifully. 'I am so tired.'

'Are you eating well, have you your appetite?' Alys asked, coming forward and laying a hand on Catherine's forehead. Her skin was oily and damp. Catherine turned her face towards Alys' touch.

'You're so cool,' she said. 'Your hands are so cool and sweet-smelling. I wish I was cool.'

'Have you drunk your negus?' Alys asked. 'And eaten your biscuits?'

'Yes,' Catherine sighed. 'But I don't feel hungry, Alys. I don't want my dinner.'

'You must eat,' Eliza Herring interrupted. 'You must keep up your strength, my lady.'

Alys nodded. 'She is right, my lady. You have the baby to think of. And your own health to maintain. You must eat.'

'My legs ache,' Catherine complained.

Alys turned back the covers of the bed. Catherine's ankles were swollen and flushed pink, her calves, her knees, even her thighs, were spongy with extra fat and the skin was white and puffy.

'You need to walk,' Alys said. 'You should be up and walking every day, my lady. Walking in the fresh air, or even riding. You could ride a gentle horse.'

Catherine turned her head away from the window where the sky was showing blue with some strips of white cloud blowing away to the east. 'I'm too tired,' she said. 'And I told you, Alys, my legs ache. What sort of healer are you? When I tell you my legs ache, you tell me to walk! If I told you I was blind would you tell me to look harder?'

Alys smiled sympathetically. 'Poor Catherine,' she said sweetly.

Ruth started at the use of Catherine's given name but Catherine's face lit up. 'Morach used to call me that,' she said wistfully. 'And I can remember my mother calling me that: "poor Catherine".'

Alys nodded. 'I know. Poor, poor Catherine,' she said tenderly.

'I feel so tired! I feel so unhappy!' Catherine burst out. 'Ever since Morach has been gone I have felt as if nothing is worth any effort. I cannot be troubled to get out of bed, I cannot be troubled to dress. I wish Morach were here. I wish she were still here.'

Alys held Catherine's hand and patted it gently. 'I know,' she said. 'I know. I miss her too.'

'And Hugo doesn't even care!' Catherine exclaimed. 'I told him how much I miss her and he just says that she was a poor old woman and if I have a fancy for a peasant there are a thousand like her on our lands. He doesn't understand!'

Alys shook her head. 'Men don't understand,' she said. 'Morach was a very wise woman, a woman who had seen much and understood the world. But she taught me all of her skills, Catherine. And I will be here all the time. I cannot take her place in your heart, but all that she could do for you and your baby I will do, when the time comes.'

Catherine snuffled wetly and hunted for her handkerchief. 'And I don't have to get up for dinner, do I?' she asked. 'I feel so weary. I'd rather eat up here.'

Alys shook her head, still smiling. 'No, of course not,' she said tenderly. 'Get up tomorrow and take a little walk when you feel stronger, but the hall is noisy and crowded and people stare so. You don't have to go down to dinner if you don't want to. Your health is more important than anything else.'

'And they tell me that you sit with the old lord?' Catherine asked. 'When I am not there?'

Alys nodded. 'He asked me, and I thought it best,' she said. 'He is a man of whim and powerful fancies. I did not want him insisting on company, your company and the young lord's. I knew you two wanted to dine alone up here. I thought if I talked to the old lord and kept him cheerful he would not insist that you come downstairs.'

Catherine nodded. 'Thank you, Alys,' she said. 'I like to eat my dinner with Hugo up here. I am weary of going down to the hall. Keep the old lord amused so that Hugo and I can be alone together.'

Alys' smile was sisterly. 'Of course, Catherine,' she said. 'Of course.'

In the afternoon, when Catherine was drowsy from a large dinner and too much wine, Alys met Hugo in the ladies' gallery and asked if she might go with him to see the new house.

'Can we not go to your room?' he asked in an undertone.

Alys shook her head. 'Catherine's women will be here all afternoon,' she said. 'You will have to wait till tonight, my lord!'

Hugo made a face. 'Very well,' he said. 'You can ride the little grey mule, or one of the ponies.'

Alys threw a cape around her shoulders. 'What about Catherine's mare?' she asked. 'She's quiet enough, isn't she?'

Hugo hesitated for a moment. 'Yes,' he said. 'Catherine has not ridden for months, but she has been exercised by one of the lads every day.'

'I'll ride her then,' Alys said.

Hugo hesitated again. 'Catherine might take it amiss,' he said.

Alys stepped a little closer so that he could smell the perfume on her hair, and raised her face to him. 'There are many things of Catherine's which give me pleasure,' she said silkily. 'Many things.'

Hugo glanced quickly around them. Ruth was sitting at the fireside sewing. As she caught his glance she dipped her head over her work again and stitched furiously.

'Don't tease me, Alys,' he said under his breath. 'Or I shall insult my wife by throwing you down and taking you on the threshold of her bedroom.'

Alys' eyes narrowed and she smiled. 'As you please, my lord,' she said in a low-voiced whisper. 'You know that I desire you. I can feel myself grow wet just at the thought of you.'

Hugo gave an exclamation and turned and picked up his cloak.

'I am taking Mistress Alys out to see the new house,' he said shortly to Ruth. 'I need her to write some orders for the builder for me.'

Ruth rose to her feet and bobbed a curtsey but kept her head down as if she were afraid to see the desire on their faces.

'Tell my wife when she wakes that I will be home in time to take supper with her,' Hugo said. 'I will send Alys home ahead of me when she has finished her work.'

Ruth nodded. 'Yes, my lord,' she said.

Hugo turned and strode from the room. 'I'll order the horses,' he said over his shoulder.

'Tell them to put a saddle on Catherine's mare,' Alys said. 'I don't like the pony.'

*

Alys sat uneasily in the saddle as the mare walked quietly across the drawbridge and down the little hill into the town. She had ridden the ponies in the stable often, but the pace of the bigger horse was longer and more rolling, and the ground looked very far away. Gritting her teeth, Alys regretted the vanity which had made her insist on riding Catherine's horse.

On either side of the road people turned to look at the horses going by and women dipped into grudging curtsies and men pulled their caps off their heads. Hugo smiled from one side to another as if the tokens of respect were willing tributes. Alys, swelling with pride, looked straight ahead as if she were too grand to either see or hear them.

At the corner of the street a barrow was halted selling fresh fish. Alys saw a girl of about her own age, seventeen. She was barefoot with a brown shawl around her shoulders and a dirty grey gown underneath. At her skirt clung a whey-faced toddler and she carried another child on her hip. Her face was marked with sores, and there was a dark bruise around her eye. Her hair, uncombed and unwashed, hung in thick rats' tails over her shoulders. She bobbed a curtsey as the two of them and the two servants rode by. Hugo did not even look at her.

That could have been me, Alys thought, her face impassive, her eyes looking straight ahead. That could have been me – married to Tom, accepting his fists and his lust. That could have been me – Morach's apprentice, always dirty, always poor. That could have been me – sickly, pregnant, exhausted. Anything I have done is better than that.

Hugo, ahead of her, rode confidently and easily. His blue cloak flickered behind him, matching the deep blue of his puffed breeches and the slashed lining of his blue jacket. His riding boots were deep, luminous black, the best leather well polished. His blue suede gloves with the gold embroidery would have kept any family in this town in food for months. Alys watched his back, torn between desire and resentment. He turned in his saddle. 'Horse going well?' he asked.

Alys flashed him her most brilliant smile. 'Oh yes,' she said, confidently. 'You must buy me one of my very own, Hugo. A roan to match yours.'

Hugo nodded absently. 'You haven't seen the new house before, have you?' he asked.

Alys hesitated and let him change the subject. 'No,' she said. 'I saw the plans when you were drawing them. And I saw the letters from the men in London who are planning houses in the new style.'

Hugo nodded. 'It's a fine house,' he said. 'We have dug deep down into the ground and we will have cellars below ground level. That will keep things cold even in the hottest of summers.'

Alys nodded. The cobbles of the town ended abruptly and the road was hard-packed earth, an old Roman road running north. The horses walked more smoothly on the easier ground and Alys was getting used to the mare's long-legged pace.

'It faces south for the sunshine,' Hugo said. 'It's built in the shape of an "H" with the entrance door set fair in the middle. There's a parlour for Catherine and her ladies on the left as you go in. No great hall at all, no great dining-room for everyone. No more eating with the soldiers and servants.'

Alys smiled. 'It will be a great change,' she said.

Hugo nodded. 'It's the new way,' he said. 'Outside London they never build castles for noblemen, just houses, beautiful houses with wide, lovely windows. Who wants a pack of servants – a private army? I'll always train the peasants for soldiers, I'll always have men I can call on. But we don't need a great castle ready for a siege at any moment! These are peaceful times. Neither the Scots nor the reivers come raiding this far south any more.'

'And you save money!' Alys said teasingly.

Hugo grinned, unrepentant. 'And there is nothing wrong with that!' he said. 'It's my father's way, the old way, to think a man's power can only be measured by the number of people who have to trail after him when he rides out. I would rather be a lord over fertile lands. I would rather have ships out on the sea. I would rather have the men who take my wage working for me – working every day, not lounging around in the guard-room in case I need them in a year's time.'

Alys nodded. 'You'll have house servants though,' she said. 'And some kind of retinue.'

'Oh aye,' Hugo said. 'I shan't ask Catherine to cook her own dinner!'

Alys smiled. 'No, I can't see Catherine working for her keep,' she said.

'I'll have house servants, and grooms for the stables, and Catherine will keep her ladies and David will stay with us, of course. But the soldiers can go, and the smith, and the master of horse, and the bakery and the alehouse. We can brew our own ale and bake our own bread, but we do not have to feed the whole castle any more.'

Alys nodded. 'Your new house will be just for you,' she said. 'Just for you and the people you choose to have by you.'

Hugo nodded. 'I'll get rid of the hangers-on who do nothing for their keep but idle and eat,' he said.

Alys laughed, a little ripple of laughter. 'You will be rid of the ladies' gallery then!' she exclaimed. 'For more idleness and eating goes on there than anywhere else in the castle!'

Hugo grinned. 'I will see if Catherine can make do with fewer ladies,' he said. 'But I would not wish to deprive her of companions.'

Alys shrugged. 'She takes little pleasure in anything these days,' she said. 'All she does is lie abed and sigh and eat. She has not sewn in the gallery for days. She only gets up to have dinner with you. You do not know, Hugo, how idle she has become.'

Hugo frowned. 'It cannot be good for the child,' he said.

Alys shook her head. 'I have begged and begged her to make an effort and get out of bed and walk a little, even if it is only in the gallery. The weather is growing more fair, she could sit in the garden and take the air. But she will not. She feels tired all the time and she weeps for Morach and for her parents. You will have to be patient with her, Hugo. She is old to conceive a first child and she was barren for many years. Her body is not young and lithe and strong. And her humour is melancholy.'

There was a little silence for a few moments.

'Shall we canter?' Hugo asked abruptly. 'You can manage Catherine's horse, can you?'

Alys laughed. 'I feel as if she were my own horse,' she said. 'Of course we can canter. Have I not told you that I fear nothing when we are together?'

Hugo smiled back at her. 'Well, I fear enough to want to keep you safe when you are carrying my son,' he said.

Alys shook her head. 'He is safe inside me,' she said.

'And I never felt better or happier in my life. With your love I have everything I ever wanted. I can canter! I feel as if I could fly!'

Hugo laughed and touched his hunter slightly with his heels. At once the big horse surged forwards. Alys' mare followed quickly, her stride rapid. Alys bounced in the saddle, clinging to the pommel, praying that Hugo would not look back and see her white-faced and afraid.

He did not. They rode for some minutes along the track, the servants cantering along behind them. Then Hugo pulled up the roan and the mare stopped abruptly, throwing Alys forward on to the neck. She held on by a firm grip on the saddle, and heaved herself back into place.

'Here,' he said. 'Here will be the gates. I shall build a great wall all around this area and leave the land inside as it is: trees and shrubs and grass. I shall have deer roaming inside the wall, maybe even some boar for me to hunt. I shall have a cottage here at the gates and a gatekeeper. No guardroom, no soldiers. And then from here I shall make a track to the front door.' He pointed ahead of them. Alys could see about twenty men digging and carrying.

'Is it to be of brick or stone?' Alys asked.

'The main pillars of the house are stone, but it will be faced with brick,' Hugo said proudly. 'It's a pretty brick, a warm colour. It looks well against the stone. They are making the bricks and firing them here.'

'And the stone?' Alys asked idly, looking around.

'From the nunnery,' Hugo said. 'I had them bring the stones up here. Some of them are handsomely carved. I shall use the slates from their roof as well, and some of their beams that were not burned. Shall you laugh, Alys, to be my whore under a nun's roof?'

Alys felt her skin grow cold. She turned away. 'And not far from the river!' she said. Her voice was strained but Hugo was unaware.

'I may divert it and dam it and make some little lakes,' he said. 'For fish and for pleasure. I love the sound of water. It's the only thing I will miss when we leave the castle, the sound of water.'

Alys nodded. 'And you must plant pretty gardens,' she said. 'I shall supervise a herb garden, a proper knot garden, an orchard and an aviary!'

Hugo laughed. 'Yes, you shall,' he said.

'And a still-room,' Alys said. In her mind she could smell the clean, light smell of the still-room at the nunnery. 'We shall have a physic garden, a herb garden, and a still-room where I shall make medicines for you and me and our family.'

'You can have some of the gear from the nuns,' Hugo said. 'A lot of it was brought away safe. Pestles and mortars and measuring bowls and the like. Some good glass bottles, too, with golden labels.'

Alys felt her mouth grow dry. Then she nodded, shook her head back and laughed, a high reckless laugh. 'Yes,' she said. 'Why not! Everything that the nuns had and that you took from them we can use. Why should it go to waste? Why should anything be spoiled? Let us take and take anything we need until we have the house just as we want it!'

Hugo jumped down from his horse and held out his arms to her. Alys slid off her horse down to him and leaned against him as he held her close. 'I love you, Alys,' he said. 'I love your hunger for life. You would rob an old nun of her very shift, wouldn't you – if you had need of it?'

Alys looked up into his dark smiling face. 'I would,'

she said. She felt at once a fierce, destructive joy. 'I have no patience with nuns, always confessing and forbearing, and avoiding sin. I want to live now. I want to have my joys now and my pleasures. If I am a damned sinner then at least I shall go to my punishment with the taste of everything I wanted still warm on my tongue.'

Hugo laughed with her. 'You must make some magic here,' he urged. 'When the workmen leave one evening we will come and you can summon your wild sisters and we can lie on the half-built walls and on the ground together and we can claim the very stones and the slates back from the nuns and dedicate the house to ourselves and to our pleasure!'

'Oh yes!' Alys said hollowly. 'Yes.'

Twenty-two

'I want a green gown,' Alys said idly. She and Hugo were sprawled on the high bed in her room. There were new hangings on the wall to match the new curtains on the bed. A fire burned in the grate with sweet-smelling pine cones and a pinch of incense. Outside the summer sky was striped with gold as the sun slowly set. 'I want a green silk gown for summer.'

Hugo lifted a hank of Alys' golden-brown hair. 'You're an expensive wench,' he said idly. 'I have given you yards and yards of cloth for one gown after another. Anyway, you have no right to wear silk.'

Alys chuckled, a low, lazy laugh. 'You can give it to me as a portent,' she said. 'Your father has promised me land and money when our son is born. Then I will be a freeholder.'

'Has he?' Hugo looked surprised. 'You have him under your thumb, my little witch, don't you? I've never known him give land away before. Not even Meg, his favourite whore, had land from him! He has you very close to his heart, doesn't he?'

Alys looked smugly at him. 'He loves me as if I were his daughter,' she said with quiet pleasure. 'And he wants me to go out with him when you cut the last of the hay. And *I* want a new green gown. A trader showed it to me yesterday. It's pure silk, it will cost a fortune. He brought it to show Catherine but she would not fit a wagon-cover. He showed it to me instead and I long for it, Hugo!'

Hugo chuckled. 'Persistent wench! You have as many gowns as Catherine – I swear it.'

Alys sighed and dropped a kiss on his bare shoulder as he lay naked and at peace on her bed, his long limbs gilded with the sunlight from the arrow-slit. 'No,' she said. 'Catherine has more gowns than me. She has all the gowns from her mother's chests. And you have bought her more gowns than you have ever bought for me.'

Hugo shook his head. 'Damned if I can think when,' he said. 'No more than one a year for all the years we have been married. But you, Alys! You want a gown a week!'

Alys smiled. 'Why should I not have as many gowns as Catherine?' she asked. 'You would rather see me in a new gown than her, wouldn't you? And you would rather strip me, than her, wouldn't you?'

Hugo shrugged. 'How many does she have?' he asked in mock weariness.

'Twelve,' Alys said.

Hugo rolled over on to his belly. Alys saw that his eyes were bright and he was laughing. 'And how many do you have, my little witch?' he asked.

'Eleven!' Alys said triumphantly. 'And now I want a green gown!'

'*Then* will you be satisfied?' Hugo demanded.

Alys sat up, threw back her hair and swarmed up along his body so she was lying along his back. She pressed her hips forward slightly, pushing against Hugo's warm, naked buttocks.

'Do you want me satisfied? Satisfied and plump? Plump and tired? Boring?' she asked. She thrust a little harder with each word. Hugo groaned and closed his eyes.

'Witch,' he said under his breath. 'You would make a dead man feel desire.'

Alys laughed and put her arms around his waist. Her hand slid between his belly and the rumpled sheets of her bed. She found his penis and held him, hard. Hugo groaned and tried to turn over.

'No,' Alys said, whispering into his ear. 'I have you in my power, Hugo. I will have you like this!'

Hugo struggled for only a moment and then as Alys' hand insistently pressed him he plunged his face and his body deeper into the bed and felt her push and push him from behind, her hand working, until with a slow groan he lay still. Alys laid her cheek against his sweating shoulder blade, and rested, lying like a long, naked snake along his back.

Hugo shook his head like a man waking from a powerful dream and rolled over. 'Alys, my love,' he said.

She smiled at him. 'The green gown,' she stipulated. 'And ribbons and gloves to match.'

He took her in his arms. 'A thousand gowns,' he said, kissing her neck, the hollow of her collar bone and the rumpled mass of her hair. 'A thousand gowns of green, of silver, of royal purple or gold. Whatever you wish.'

Alys lay back and shut her eyes. Hugo kissed her breasts and then nuzzled her belly.

'You're very thin still,' he said thoughtfully.

Alys' eyes opened, she smiled at him. 'I wondered when you would notice,' she said.

He sat up. 'Notice what?' he asked. 'What should I notice?'

Alys stretched like a cat. 'Why, that Catherine's baby makes her fatter and lazier every day and that my baby has left me as slim as a virgin.'

Hugo shrugged. 'I thought only that different women took their pregnancy in different ways. But what of it, Alys?'

413

'I lied to you,' Alys said coolly. 'I lied to you and to Lord Hugh. I said I was pregnant when I was not.'

Hugo choked. 'You did what!' he exclaimed.

'I lied,' Alys said again simply.

Hugo put his hand out and turned Alys' face towards him. The lines at the roots of his eyebrows were growing deep, his mouth was grim. 'You said that you were carrying my son and you lied to me and to my father?'

Alys nodded fearlessly.

Hugo pushed her away from him and got up from the bed. He flung his jacket around his shoulders and stared out of the arrow-slit at the river and the green hills behind.

'Why?' he demanded, without turning around.

Alys shrugged. 'Morach had just died,' she said. 'I was afraid you might blame me, too, and have me sent away. Catherine hated me when she first met me, if she knew we were lovers she would have turned against me again. Your father cares for nothing as much as a son to come after you. I needed something to keep me here safe.'

Hugo turned back to see her. 'You are a schemer,' he said with dislike. 'You have tried to entrap me.'

Alys sat up, threw her shift over her head and slipped from the bed, tying the strings of the white linen gown at her shoulders as she walked towards him. 'You entrapped yourself,' she said. 'Your desire for me has trapped you in a way that no lie could ever do.'

Hugo reached out his hand and touched the base of her neck. Her pulse beat steadily, unhurried by any alarm, under his finger.

'You are not carrying my child,' he said, showing his disappointment.

Alys smiled at him. 'I *was* not carrying him when I

414

first said,' she said. Her blue eyes twinkled. 'But I am a liar no more! I am with child now, as I foretold. I missed my term this month and soon I shall be as fat as you could desire.'

Hugo's face warmed, the deep frown lifted.

'Our son will be born in April,' Alys said with unshaken confidence. 'I am glad it is this way, Hugo. The first time we were lovers it was not good. You had lain with Catherine and you went back to her bed. Our son could only be conceived when you lay with me heart and soul. And I only want a son conceived in my passion.'

Hugo drew her to him. 'And you think it is a son?' he asked.

Alys nodded. 'I know it is a son,' she said. 'He will be born when the strongest lambs are born, when the weather is good. He will be born in your grand new house if you make haste and build me a beautiful chamber with wood panelling and big bright windows. Build me a room which overlooks the river where I can have sunshine all day, and I will give you a son that will be the best of both of us. Your courage and my skills. Think of a lord who could play with magic, Hugo! He could rise and rise until he was the greatest lord in all the land.'

He tightened his grip on her. 'What a boy he would be!' he said.

Alys smiled up at him. 'How high he could go!' she said. 'And the daughter who will come next – think who her husband could be, Hugo! How high our family could rise with our noble, magical children!'

They were silent for a moment. Alys could see the ambition in Hugo's face. He and his father had craved sons, but this reign had taught men the value of pretty women as pawns in the power game.

Hugo checked himself and returned to the present. 'Never lie to me again,' he said. 'I shall feel a fool telling my father and everyone around the castle will know. I don't like to be teased by you, Alys. Don't lie to me again.'

Alys chuckled idly. 'I promise,' she said easily. 'I needed to lie then, but I will never need to lie again. I am safe now. I am safe enough in your love, am I not? There is nothing I could do to lose your love, is that not so, Hugo?'

He closed his arms around her and buried his face in her hair. 'That is so,' he said. 'There is nothing you could do which would lose my love.'

'And I am your father's best companion and most trusted friend,' Alys said contentedly. 'And now I am carrying his grandson. There is nothing which can threaten me now.'

Hugo rocked her gently, feeling her lightness, his tenderness and desire rising again.

'Nothing can threaten you,' he said gently. 'I am here.'

Alys put her arms around him and held him close. The breeze through the window smelled of hay and meadow flowers. She closed her eyes and smiled. 'I am safe now,' she said.

'But don't lie to me,' Hugo said with residual resentment. 'I hate women who lie.'

Next day was the last day of haymaking and Alys and Hugo rode out to watch them making hay in the high meadows between the moorland and the river. Half of the castle went with them, the cooks and serving-maids and lads, the soldiers, their women, the young pages and girls who worked at sewing or baking or brewing or spinning. Even the old lord came out for the day, riding a stocky old war-horse, with David, very smart in a dark velvet suit, riding beside him. A hundred people took a holiday from the castle, walking in a laughing, singing crowd across the stone bridge at the foot of the castle to the fields on the far side, and before them all rode Hugo and Alys on her new roan pony, wearing her new green gown.

She wore her hair brushed loose, tumbling over her shoulders and down her back, trimmed with ribbons of green and gilt, in defiance of the fashion of the new modest Queen. The silver gilt glinted like real silver in the sunlight and the green ribbons flickered around her head. She wore light leather gloves for riding trimmed with green ribbons, and new tan leather boots. The roan mare which Hugo had bought cheap at the Appleby sales was quiet and Alys rode confidently, with her head up, smiling around her as if she owned the fertile fields and the singing people. When Hugo leaned over and spoke softly to her she laughed aloud as if to tell everyone that the young lord shared his secrets with her alone.

Catherine had stayed behind with Ruth and Margery, a handful of servants, a couple of cooks and the soldiers on guard. 'She doesn't want to come,' Alys had told Hugo. 'She is too tired she says, she is always too tired for anything. It will be better without her.'

Hugo did not hide his concern. 'She has three months before the child is born,' he said. 'If she takes to her bed now, what will she be like by October?'

Alys had giggled. 'She will be a haystack,' she said unkindly. 'Have done, Hugo! She is tired, she wants to rest; you cannot force her to come. Sit with her in the evening when we come home and tell her all about it. It is no kindness to her to drag her out of her chamber and into the hot sunshine when she is so gross and weary.'

It was the last hayfield to be cut of the demesne and Hugo was to cut the last swathe. They had left a narrow strip of pale green grass standing, ready for Hugo to come and scythe it down. The party from the castle scattered around the edges of the field, the serving-girls and lads started spreading cloths and unpacking big jugs of ale and unwrapping loaves of bread and meat. Half a dozen musicians stood in one corner of the field, tuning their instruments for the dance, making a clamour like howling cats. The labouring men and their women had been waiting in the hot sunshine since before noon. They had cut down branches and bent them into an arbour and placed a seat inside for the old lord. He was helped down from his horse and went to sit in the shade while David scuttled around the field, missing nothing, ordering everything for the feast.

They had a scythe ready sharpened for Hugo, and the bailiff who had ordered and overseen the haymaking was dressed in his best, his wife beside him, ready to hand the scythe to the young lord. Hugo jumped down from the saddle and threw his reins to a page-boy. Then he turned and helped Alys down. Hand in hand they went towards the farmer and his wife; Alys kicked at the long piles of cut grass, sniffing at the sweet, heady smell of the meadow flowers and the new-mown hay. Her new green gown rustled pleasantly over the stubble. Alys raised her head to the sunshine and strode out as if she owned the field.

'Samuel Norton!' Hugo said pleasantly as they drew close. The bailiff pulled off his hat and bowed low. His wife dropped down in a weighty curtsey. When she came up her face was white, she did not look at Alys.

'A good crop of hay!' Hugo said pleasantly. 'A grand hay crop this year. You will keep my horses in good heart for many winter nights, Norton!'

The man mumbled something. Alys stepped forward to hear what he was saying. As she did so the woman flinched backwards in an involuntary, unstoppable movement.

Alys checked herself. 'What's the matter?' she asked the woman directly.

The farmer flushed and blustered. 'My wife's not well,' he said. 'She would insist on coming. She wanted to see you, my lord, and the Lady Cath . . .' he broke off. 'She's not well,' he said feebly.

The woman curtsied again and started to step backwards, her Sunday-best gown brushing the cut hay, picking up seed heads.

'What's this?' Hugo asked carelessly. 'You ill, Goodwife Norton?'

The woman was white-faced, she opened her mouth to reply but she could not speak. She looked from her husband to Hugo. She never once glanced at Alys.

'Forgive her,' Farmer Norton said hurriedly. 'She's ill you know, women's time, women's fancies. All madness in the blood. You know how women are, my lord. And she wanted to see the Lady Catherine. We did not expect . . .'

Hugo's bright cheerfulness was dimming rapidly. 'Did not expect what?' he demanded ominously.

'Nothing, nothing, my lord,' Farmer Norton said anxiously. 'We mean no offence. My wife has a present for the Lady Catherine – some lucky charm or women's nonsense. She hoped to see her, to give it to her. Nothing more.'

'I will give it to her,' Alys said, her voice very clear.

She stepped forward, the folds of the green silk shimmering around her. She held out her hand. 'Give me your gift to Lady Catherine and I will give it to her. I am her closest friend.'

Goodwife Norton clenched the little purse she wore at her waist. 'No!' she said with sudden energy. 'I'll bring it up to the castle myself. It's a relic, a girdle, blessed by St Margaret to aid a woman in childbirth, and a prayer to St Felicitas to ensure the child is male. It has stood me in good stead, half a dozen times. Lady Catherine shall have it. You shall have it, my Lord Hugo, for your son! I will bring it up to the castle and I will put it in her hands.'

'Give it to me!' Alys said, her anger rising. 'I shall give it to her with your compliments.'

She reached out towards the woman and Goodwife Norton flinched backwards as if from a dangerous animal.

From the waiting men and women all around the field there was a hiss, like a cat as it senses danger.

'Not into your hands!' The woman suddenly found her voice, sharp and shrill. 'Into any hands in the world but yours! It's a holy relic saved from the nunnery. The holy women kept it safe for the good of wives, married women! For women carrying their husbands' children in matrimony. For childbirth in the marriage bed. It's not for the likes of you!'

'How dare you sneer at me!' Alys said breathlessly. She reached again for the little bag in Goodwife Norton's hand.

Now she could see it more clearly. It was a little velvet purse, rubbed smooth in the middle by the kisses of women praying for an easy childbirth. She remembered it from the nunnery. It had been kept in a golden casket near the altar and when a woman big with child came into the chapel she could whisper to one of the nuns that she wanted to kiss it. No one, however poor, however needy, was refused. Alys found she was staring at the gold stitching on the purse. She remembered the Mother Abbess herself had stitched it. *My* mother,' Alys thought. The sudden sharp pain made her angry.

'You're nothing better than a thief yourself!' Alys said. 'That belongs in the nunnery, not hawked around a hayfield. Give it to me!'

'Witch!' Goodwife Norton spat. She leaped back so Alys could not reach her and then she said the word again – 'Witch!' She spoke under her breath but it was as loud and clear as if she had screamed it. The whole haymaking gang froze into silence.

Alys felt the world grow still around her as if she were a painted piece of glass on a fragile leaded window. Nothing would move, nothing would make a sound. Goodwife Norton should not have said that word and she should not have heard it. The haymakers, the village people, the townspeople, and the people from the castle should not have that word in their minds. It should not have been said. Alys did not know what to say or do to take the sudden danger out of the innocent morning.

Hugo stepped forward. 'Norton?' he prompted softly.

The bailiff said briskly, 'I beg your pardon, Lord,' and seized his wife by the elbow and marched her rapidly across the field. At the first woman he stopped and thrust his wife towards her with a rattle of low-voiced orders. The two of them bent their heads and scuttled from the field like rats fearing the scythe. Farmer Norton strode back, his red face furious.

'Damned scolds,' he said, as one man to another.

Hugo was unsmiling. 'You should have a care,

Farmer Norton,' he said. 'A wife with a tongue as loose as that will find herself charged with slander. These are serious accusations to fling around. A noble lady should not have to listen to such.'

The man said nothing. He looked stubborn.

'I do not think you have been presented to Mistress Alys,' Hugo said smoothly. 'She is a dear friend of my wife, she is my father's clerk. She is my chosen companion today. I will lead the dancing with her.'

Norton flushed a deep brick-red of shame. Alys glared at him, her eyes blazing blue with her challenge. He dropped his head in a deep bow.

Alys waited. Then she held out her hand.

He took it reluctantly and kissed the air just above her skin. She felt his hard, callused hand tremble underneath her touch.

He straightened up. 'We've met before,' he said bravely.'I knew your mother, the Widow Morach. I knew you when you were a child, playing in the dirt of the lane.'

Alys gave him a cold, level stare. 'Then you know she was *not* my mother,' Alys said. 'My real mother was a lady. She died in a fire. Morach was a wet nurse to me, a foster-mother. Now she is dead and I am back where I belong. In the castle.'

She turned to Hugo. 'I shall sit with Lord Hugh,' she said pleasantly, 'in the shade, while you cut your swathe of hay. Bring me a handful of hay and flowers!'

She spoke clearly enough for all to hear her ordering the young lord as a mistress orders her lover; and then she turned on her heel and walked across the soft stubble of the hayfield to where the old lord sat in the shade. It was a long, long walk with the eyes of the haymakers and the castle people on her every step. The new gown swept the hay around her. Green, the colour of spring, of growth . . . and of witchcraft. Alys, wishing that she had worn a gown of another colour, kept her head up and smiled around at everyone. Wherever her gaze fell people turned away their heads, shuffled their feet. She walked across the field like a new, dangerous dog walking through a flock of sheep. People shifted like wary old yows to keep their distance.

But they whispered. Alys could hear the soft susurration of dislike, as quiet as the wind shifting in the uncut hay. 'Where is Lady Catherine?' someone called from the back, louder than any other. 'Where is Hugo's wife? We want the lady to come from the castle for hay-making, not the castle slut!'

Alys kept her head high, her eyes steadily flicking around the watching field, the smile unwavering on her mouth. Never could she catch someone speaking. Always their faces were blank and fearful. There was no one she could name as her slanderer. However quickly her gaze went from one stubborn face to another the whisper preceded her. Underneath her arms she could feel the gown growing damp. She nearly stumbled as she reached the bower like a criminal running to sanctuary. Then she checked. There was no chair for her. David and the old lord were sitting down.

'I will trouble you for your chair, David,' she said bluntly. 'It was hot in the sunshine and I wish to sit.'

For a moment, for half a moment only, it seemed as if he would refuse her.

'Let the wench sit,' the old lord said irritably. 'She's carrying my grandson in her belly.'

David rose reluctantly and went to stand behind the old lord's chair.

'What was all that about?' the old lord asked.

Alys sat still, her hands quietly in her lap, her face composed. 'Country gossip,' she said. 'They envy me, those who knew Morach and the nasty little cottage. They cannot understand how I should move from there to here. They make up fancies of witchcraft and then they frighten nobody but themselves. That fat old shrew, Goodwife Norton, has taken it into her thick head that I have bewitched the young lord and supplanted Catherine. She sought to insult me.'

The old lord nodded. Out in the field Hugo had stripped off his thick, costly jacket. A pretty girl with brilliant golden hair had stepped forward and was holding it for him. As they watched she held it to her cheek. They heard Hugo's flattered laugh. Farmer Norton handed him a scythe. Hugo rolled up his white linen sleeves, spat on both palms, and took it in a firm grip. There was a ragged cheer from the crowd. Hugo was popular this year, with high wages for the labourers at his new house and his wife pregnant.

'Strange how the word "witch" follows you,' the old lord said. He was watching Hugo scything down the grass. The young girl carrying his jacket and Farmer Norton and the other haymakers walked slowly behind him, laughing. The mood had lightened. The musicians had started playing a ragged tune with a thumping beat, a lad was singing.

Alys said nothing.

'It's a bad word to have hung around your neck,' the old lord said neutrally. 'It looks bad. For you – but not only for you. For me and Hugo also.'

'It's gossip and nonsense,' Alys said shortly.

'Perhaps they heard of the ordeal?' David suggested helpfully. 'Or of Alys' dream of her and Hugo? Or maybe they suspect her learning – unusual in a girl from

424

a country hovel? Or the sudden drowning of old Morach? I heard a rumour that *she* was a witch and drowned while running away.'

The sun on the field was very hot, but Alys in the underwater green of the arbour shivered as if she were cold.

'I am carrying Hugo's son,' she said steadily. 'I am the second woman he has ever got with child in all his life. If anything were to happen to Catherine or her child then my baby would be your *only* grandchild, my lord. I do not think it befits us to gossip like common people about witchery and sorcery and nonsense. Hugo and I are lovers, and I am the mother of his child. If an old fool like Goodwife Norton wishes to make a scene and spoil a day why should we have our peace disturbed?'

The old lord nodded. 'No wonder it is to be a long pregnancy, Alys, since this baby protects you from all ills. Thirteen months by my reckoning?'

Alys smiled. 'He has told you then,' she said easily. 'I have begged his pardon for my mistake. It was a natural mistake. I wanted Hugo's child so much that I mistook the signs. But I am sure now. You will see me growing soon. But never growing, I hope, as big as the Lady Catherine!'

The old lord chuckled. 'Vixen,' he said without heat. 'Don't scratch at her. There can never be too many sons. There is room for you both.'

Hugo had reached the end of the line. He stooped and picked up a bunch of the grass and the spindly sweet-smelling flowers. The blonde girl ran forward with his jacket and held it out for him to slip it on. As he put it on he turned around and put his arm around her shoulders, kissed her heartily on both cheeks, and tucked the flowers into the neck of her gown. The girl leaned back against his arm and smiled at him. She was young and bright, dressed in her best gown of bright blue, cut very low and square across her creamy, plump breasts.

'Looks as is you have lost your flowers, Mistress Alys,' David observed.

Alys stood up and smiled at him. 'Then I shall make Hugo pick me some more,' she said recklessly.

She turned her back on both of them and walked out into the bright sunlight, smiling. All around her people were spreading white cloths on the newly cut grass, the scything gang were raking the hay into long rows to dry in the wind and the sun. Jars of ale were opened and earthenware mugs thrust forward for filling. Alys walked towards Hugo across the field with her flat belly thrust forward to make it look bigger, smiling, gambling on her power. And as she came close, the girl with the flowers stuffed in the bodice of her gown twisted out of Hugo's careless grip and fell back to avoid Alys' glance, and then slipped away.

'Alys,' Hugo said grimly.

'You have thrown away my flowers,' Alys said. The smile was still on her face.

Hugo bent to the heap of hay at his feet and picked up a swatch of grass mixed with flowers. 'Here,' he said ungraciously. 'Take these, I am going to open the dancing.'

'With me?' Alys asked.

Hugo's face was grim. 'Since you have started a storm which I shall have to calm, I shall dance first with you and then with every wench in this field, until they are all content.'

Alys' smile never wavered. She took Hugo's out-stretched arm and together they walked towards the musicians. Other couples fell into place behind them. But they moved quietly, as if they were bound to dance and too obedient to refuse.

Alys stepped back and faced Hugo, waited for the music to begin, and froze. Behind Hugo's shoulder was a face she knew.

It was Tom, and a hard-faced woman hanging on his arm beside him.

Alys' face never flickered. Her eyes went past him without a glimmer of recognition, her clear bright smile impartial, unchanging – Tom brushed his wife Liza off his arm and came towards the dancers. Alys' face was a lighthearted mask, her head on one side, listening to the music, her foot tapping to the beat. Tom, unbidden, walked unstoppably forward.

'Alys!' he said.

Hugo spun round. Tom was standing immediately behind him, but he did not even look at the lord, did not uncover his head. He ignored him as if he were a post in the hayfield. All he could see was Alys in her new green gown, her green and gilt ribbons plaited into her golden-brown hair, heartbreakingly lovely.

'Alys,' he said again.

Alys looked at him as if noticing him for the first time. She put her head on one side as if she were viewing some strange specimen.

'Yes?' she said interrogatively.

Tom gulped. 'I will take you away,' he said, in a sudden awkward rush of speech. 'I will take you, Alys. I will take you away. I've heard what they said of you . . . it's not safe for you here. I will take you now.'

Alys threw back her head and laughed. A clear brittle sound like breaking glass. She tossed her head and smiled at Hugo.

'Who is this?' she asked. 'Is he simple? Does he mistake me for someone?'

Tom blenched as if she had struck him. 'Alys!' he said in a hoarse whisper. Hugo tapped him on the shoulder, his face grim. 'You interrupt the dancing,' he said. 'Go your ways.'

Tom seemed not to feel the touch, he did not hear his lord. He did not take Hugo's warning. His eyes were fixed on Alys' bright, unconcerned face.

'I want to save you, Alys!' he said desperately. 'They have called you a witch – you are in danger. I'll take you – I'll take you away, cost me what it will!'

Liza behind him said, 'Tom!' in a hard, sharp command.

'Who is this?' Hugo asked her. 'Some friend of yours?'

Alys turned her bright clear gaze on him. 'I don't know,' she said, detached. 'I don't know him.'

'I will take you,' Tom said again. 'I won't fail you. I will leave my farm and my wife, even my little children. I will save you, Alys. You need not stay in the castle with those people and their vices. I will take you away. I have some money saved. We will find a little farm somewhere and I will keep you safe. You will be as my wife, Alys! I will be true to you and guard you with my life!' He broke off. 'You will be a virtuous woman again, Alys,' he said softly. 'You were a good girl, I loved you then. You are a good girl still. You will be my little sweetheart once more.'

She stared at Tom in open amazement and her gaze never wavered. She looked straight through him, as if he were a man of straw, a man of water, as if he were not even there. The smile lilting on her lips never even flickered.

'You're babbling, goodman,' she said coolly. 'I know you not.'

'Alys!' Tom exclaimed, and then he stopped short. He could not believe that his playmate, his childhood love, should look through him as if he were clear glass. As if he were nothing to her. As if he had never been anything to her. He stared at her for one long moment, and her face never altered, never changed from bright-eyed indifference.

Then he spun on his heel and tore away from her, tore away from her empty, smiling face, through the crowd, vaulting the gate at the corner of the field and plunging out of sight.

Alys laughed again, a merry, carefree laugh, and waved at the musicians who had lost the beat and were falling into silence.

'Why do we wait? Let's dance!' she cried gaily. 'Let's dance!'

Twenty-three

Catherine was sleeping when they came home. Alys and Hugo went quietly past her closed door to Alys' bedroom and told Eliza to call them as soon as Catherine awoke. Hugo strode over to the arrow-slit and looked out. Alys took the ribbons from her hair and pulled down her gown to show her warm creamy shoulders.

'My lord?' she said softly.

Hugo glanced around. 'Not now,' he said coldly. 'Who was that lad in the field?'

Alys ignored his rejection. 'No one I know,' she said.

'The maid I danced with, the little blonde one, said he was an old lover of yours. His wife speaks against you. Says you have stolen his peace, says you hexed him into loving you and he can neither sleep, nor eat, nor love her.'

Alys laughed. 'Not I,' she said. 'But from what you say I guess it must have been Tom of Reedale. We were playmates when we were children, I've not seen him in ten years. He married a shrew. She'd blame anyone for the dryness of her marriage. It can't be laid at my door.'

'It looked bad,' Hugo said.

Alys shrugged, tossing her hair back off her shoulders. Hugo turned away from her, looking out of the arrow-slit window again. Alys hesitated. She stepped forward and put her arms around his waist, pressed against his back. 'Tonight,' she said softly, 'tonight, Hugo, I will summon my sisters to be with us. My sisters and I will play together tonight. I will summon them and they will spread their smooth bodies over me and lie down on me and give me endless, endless pleasure.' She felt his arousal in the tension of his shoulders, but he did not turn round.

'And what for you?' Alys asked coquettishly. 'No, nothing for you! Not a touch, not a kiss, Hugo! You will lie as if you are enchained, and you will watch while they bury themselves – fingers, lips, tongues – in me. And you will watch my body writhe under their caresses, and you will hear me cry out with pleasure.'

Hugo sighed with desire, leaning his head forward so it was touching the cool stone of the lintel.

'I will let them bind me,' Alys said thoughtfully. 'You will see me on a rack of their pleasure. You will see me strain and pull against their silken knots as they penetrate me and pleasure me and make me cry for release.'

Hugo turned around in her arms and pressed her close to him, nuzzling her naked shoulders, inhaling the scents of her skin and hair; but his face was still sombre.

'That was an ugly scene in the field,' he said. 'You must be more careful.'

Alys pulled away from him, irritated. 'There's nothing I can do to prevent gossip,' she said. 'People will become accustomed to the change. When they see the son we have, when they grow used to me being always at your side, when they know that I am always here – the lady of the castle in everything but name.'

Hugo shook his head, unconvinced. 'I want Catherine to take her supper in the hall tonight,' he said. 'There's been too much gossip. There's been too much ugly talk about witchcraft and Catherine being set aside.'

Alys shrugged and smiled up at him. 'I don't care what they say,' she said confidently. 'I know that I am carrying your child and that I am well and strong.

People can say what they like, they can think what they like. It does not matter what they say. You will protect me, your father will protect me. Old women gossiping in chimney corners cannot hurt me.'

Hugo shook his head. 'It hurts us all,' he said bluntly. 'You're a fool if you think yourself safe, Alys. Every word said against me, every whisper against my name, is a threat to the peace of the country. These are times when people will make a mob over anything. These are times when people are anxious about witchcraft, fearful.

'There are vagrants everywhere thrown on to the roads by the closing of the monasteries, stirring up anger about the loss of sanctuary. There are changes that no one could have foretold. The little monasteries and nunneries are going and there is anger among the people – they cling to the old religion, they cling to the old superstitions.

'I don't like to be gossiped about. I like to ride out and see smiles. I like a little honour done my name. I like a pretty wench to curtsey to me and not to fly away the moment you come near for fear your shadow falls on her. You did badly at the field today, Alys. You were named as a witch before many people and you did not deny it.'

'And what about you?' Alys demanded, her anger mounting. 'What about you who are desperate for my witchcraft, who beg me to work magic on you? You have bidden me to call my sisters to your new house – to christen it backwards! You, who want me to spread my magic all around your new house, to destroy the holiness of the stolen stones. You want all the pleasures and none of the pains, Hugo! You want bedroom witchcraft and daylight sainthood. You can't be a person out of the ordinary, out of the crowd, and then expect them

432

to call down blessings on your name when you ride by on your big horse.'

Hugo shook his head. 'You don't understand,' he said again. 'For all your learning, you are a foolish slut in this. Why d'you think it is death to speak against the King? Not because he is not safe on his throne! Not because he lacks soldiers! But because danger lies in gossip and rumour. Treason starts with whispers. And they are whispering about *you*.'

Alys walked away from him, to the chest for her clothes, and took out her comb. 'They always talk of the special ones,' she said in a low angry voice. 'I have been special all my life. I have been the favourite for all my life. People have always envied me and wondered what powers I have. I will ride it out. I am the favourite in the castle, I am like a daughter to your father. I am your lady.'

Hugo said nothing, but he shook his head.

Alys pulled up a stool to the fireside and half turned her head from him. She ran her fingers through the thick tresses of her hair to free them from the curls of the plaits, and then started to comb it over and over, until the comb was running smoothly. Hugo, still angry, found himself watching the hypnotic strokes of the comb sliding through the silky golden mass of thick hair. Alys sat on her stool before the empty fireplace and closed her eyes and hummed a song softly in the back of her throat. Hugo leaned back against the wall, arms folded, and watched her, his face impassive. Alys, acutely aware of him even though her eyes were shut, thought that in a few moments she would give him some wine with a pinch of earthroot. It had been some days since Hugo had been drugged into madness and desire. She felt a need, like a tingle in her fingertips, to

433

pull the strings and set Hugo's lust dancing once more. And this time she would make him crawl towards her begging for a taste of her. Alys smiled with her eyes still shut. Hugo would not call her a slut and a fool without paying for it with agonizing desire.

The knock on the door startled them both from the beginning of Alys' sensual spellbinding. It was Eliza Herring.

'Mistress Alys! Lady Catherine is awake and asking for you.'

Alys pulled up the shoulders of her gown and shook the creases from the skirt. She threw her hair away from her face. 'I'll go and sit with Catherine,' she said irritably. 'I'll tell her that she must go to the hall for supper. She exposes us all to abuse if she will not do her duty.'

She could read nothing from Hugo's face. 'I don't think it is your place to instruct the Lady Catherine on her duty,' he said softly. 'You may tell her that I request it. Your wishes are of little weight in this matter.'

Alys hesitated, unbalanced by Hugo's irritability. 'Tonight . . .' she said.

Hugo shook his head. 'I will have you tonight, or whenever I choose,' he said sharply. 'But it makes no difference to your service to Lady Catherine. You should not keep her waiting.'

Alys shot one level glance at him. Hugo stared back, without fear, without affection. Alys, her face dark with anger, put down the comb and went to Catherine.

She was propped up on her fine embroidered pillows. Her face was flushed from her sleep and her eyes were red.

'I've been lonely,' she said without preamble.

'I'm sorry to hear that,' Alys said, suppressing her

irritation. The room was stifling. It faced east over the courtyard and grew dark in the afternoons, though the summer sky was pale and golden through the window. Catherine had ordered the fire to be banked high and hot in the grate; candles burned on the table. There was a crowded, sour smell to the room. The strewing herbs on the floor were limp and scentless. On the cupboard there was a clutter of sweetmeat plates and Catherine's pots of creams, salves and perfumes, a goblet on its side, the dregs sticky on the shelf, and an empty pitcher of ale.

'I had a bad dream,' Catherine said. 'I dreamed that Hugo had left me, gone to London. Gone to the King's court.' She gave a little sob. 'Like Father,' she said.

Alys sat on the bed, taking Catherine's plump, damp hand. 'Don't grieve,' she said. 'He has not gone. He is not going anywhere. Think of the baby. It is bad for the baby if you cry. Hugo is settled and happy here. He is not planning to leave. And anyway, even if he did, Henry is a gentle king. Hugo could do no wrong at court.'

Catherine lay back against the pillows. Her face was flushed, a little trickle of sweat ran down between her fat breasts inside her night-gown.

'My back hurts,' she said pitifully. 'It aches again.'

Alys concealed her impatience. 'Have you been in bed all day, Catherine?' she asked.

Catherine nodded.

'If you do not walk around you will get heavy and tired, and of course you will ache,' Alys said. 'Let me help you up.'

Catherine shook her head again. 'I can't walk around,' she said fretfully, 'I am lame. My ankles hurt and my knees. My legs hurt all over. You don't understand, Alys. I am too old and too tired to carry and bear this baby. I am not strong.' She gave a little snuffly sob. 'I am not strong,' she said again.

Alys leaned forward and stroked Catherine's forehead, brushing back the brown hair which clung in limp tendrils to her face.

'What about a bath?' Alys suggested. 'I could tell them to bring a hot bath up for you, with some herbs in it to make you feel less tired. I could wash your hair and you could put on a pretty gown for supper tonight. Wouldn't that help?'

Catherine turned her face towards Alys' caressing hand. 'Yes,' she said, like a child trying to please. 'All right. Tell them to bring me a bath.'

Alys sent the serving-maid down with orders to bring the biggest bath-tub draped with the finest linen cloth to Lady Catherine's room. Sheets must be aired to dry her and wrap her. Alys went to her room to fetch dried flowers and some verbena oil to pour into the bath water and to set before the fire to scent the room.

Hugo was dozing on Alys' bed as she came in, his feet up with his dusty boots on the cover. He opened one lazy eye when he saw her but did not trouble to move. 'What are you doing?' he asked. 'Is Catherine well?'

'She's fretful,' Alys said. 'I thought a bath would soothe her. She's complaining that we left her all day alone. She has not dressed. She has not even washed today. I will give her a bath and wash her hair and get her dressed for supper.'

'Good,' he said. He stretched out and closed his eyes again. The dirt from his boots was smeared all over Alys' new counterpane.

She hesitated for a moment, resentful. Everyone in

the castle has their own way with their lives but me, she thought. Hugo can rest and dream of the stupid fairheaded peasant. Catherine can waddle into a bath. I have to run between the two. She nodded without speaking and took the herbs and the oils to Catherine's bedroom. Eliza followed her, holding the door.

The great bath-tub lined with linen had been set before the fire and was filled to the brim with steaming water. Eliza put the herbs and oils beside it, and at Alys' nod helped Catherine from the bed.

Catherine's legs were worse. Around her knees and around her ankles the skin was white and swollen. Her large belly stood out from the rest of her body with the navel protruding. Her breasts were tight and hot, blue-veined and distended. The nipples had swollen and were brown and bruised. Her hands were swollen too, with a deep red mark where her wedding ring was cutting into her finger. Alys took her hand.

'Does this hurt?' she asked.

Catherine nodded. 'It's grown too tight,' she said. 'It throbs.'

Alys held her hand and put one arm around Catherine's wide waist to guide her into the water. Catherine sank, like a beached whale returning to the deep, and sighed with pleasure.

'Fetch your lute,' Alys said to Eliza, 'and sing to us.'

Catherine laid her head back against the edge of the tub. Alys folded a thick square of linen and placed it under Catherine's solid white neck. 'There,' she said. 'That's more comfortable for you.'

Catherine shut her eyes but her mouth quivered. 'I'm so tired,' she said plaintively. 'So tired.'

Alys took a handful of soft waterlogged herbs and scrubbed Catherine's shoulders in a gentle circular motion. Catherine languidly raised one arm and then another for Alys to wash and rub. When she reached Catherine's fingers she massaged them with oil and pulled gently at the wedding ring. It was stuck tight. They would have to call a blacksmith to cut it off. Hugo's wedding ring would have to be cut off Catherine's hand. Alys hid a smile.

Catherine leaned forward in the bath, grunting as she bent over her fat belly while Alys washed her back. Then Alys went around the tub and lifted and washed one leg after another. The skin was yielding, spongy to the touch. Both ankles were swollen as thick as if they were sprained, and both knees. Alys pressed them hard. Catherine did not complain of any discomfort. Alys' fingers left dark red marks.

Eliza tuned her lute and started to play very softly. Catherine lay back in the tub, one white foot in Alys' hands, and shut her eyes. Alys, feeling her healing power welling and pouring through her fingers, rubbed at the sole of Catherine's swollen foot. She sensed Catherine's lack of balance, an unevenness about her body, something sickly, something poisonous inside her. She took up the other foot and rubbed it gently with oil.

When she had finished with Catherine's feet she went to the head of the tub and very gently poured water over Catherine's thick brown hair, concentrating on the skin of the scalp and the temples, washing it with soap and then rubbing it with oil, and then rinsing it all until the hair was clean.

The discontented look of a lonely child had drained away from Catherine as if Alys' touch was a panacea. Her face was rosy. When Eliza's song had finished, she hummed the chorus and then waved her hand:

'Sing it again!' she said. Eliza shot an irreverent wink at Alys and took up the lute for a second time and sang the song through once more.

Catherine sighed with pleasure.

'The water is growing cold,' Alys said. 'You must come out, Catherine, or you will chill.'

Eliza laid down the lute and opened the door for a serving-girl. Alys held up the warmed sheet and draped it around Catherine from the front, Eliza threw a warmed sheet over her shoulders and back.

'Clear this,' Alys said abruptly to the serving-girl and Eliza.

She guided Catherine to the bed and patted at her face and hands and shoulders until they were dry, then she combed her fine brown hair and spread it out around her on the warmed sheet so that it would dry without tangles.

Catherine lay like a painted statue, pink from the heat, smiling. Alys dropped the bed-curtains from their bags and drew them around the bed. The serving-men came and took the bath away. When they had gone, slopping water and swearing, the room was very quiet. Alys tied back the curtains at the head so Catherine could see the fire crackling and the flames burning brightly, sweet-smelling with Alys' incense.

The door behind Alys opened and Hugo came into the room.

He stepped up to the bed and put an arm around Alys' waist to keep her at her place.

'Are you well, my Lady Catherine?' he asked gently.

Catherine's eyes fluttered open. She smiled her delight at seeing him.

'Hugo,' she said. 'You have been away from me for so long!'

He nodded. 'I have neglected you,' he said. 'I left you to care for yourself and the child and Alys here tells me that you are not taking the exercise you need.'

Catherine looked at Alys and smiled. 'She takes very good care of me,' she said.

'And she has a wonderful touch, has she not, Catherine?' Hugo asked.

Alys looked quickly at him. He was smiling, there was some heat at the back of his smile. Alys could smell his lust like woodsmoke on an east wind. She tensed and tried to move aside. Hugo's grip tightened on her waist and his smile never faltered.

'Oh yes,' Catherine agreed. 'She has been rubbing my back and my feet and my head. Alys has healing in her fingers, her touch is like silver.'

Alys could feel Hugo's heat through his doublet. She felt danger massing around her, clotting in corners of the room, thickening and rolling closer like woodsmoke from green wood.

'I will leave you,' she said. 'I will leave you two alone and order your supper to be served here tonight.'

'No,' Hugo said, not taking his eyes from Catherine's rosy, relaxed face. 'I have a fancy to see you massage my wife with your oils, Alys.'

Catherine's eyes widened, but she said nothing.

'It is not fit . . .' Alys started.

'Do it,' Hugo said softly. 'You have done everything else I have ever desired. Now I desire this.'

He lifted the sheet which covered Catherine and dropped it to one side. Catherine, revelling in his attention after weeks of neglect, lay still and let him look at her, let his eyes wander over her bloated pale body, distended with her pregnancy.

'I please you?' she asked humbly.

Hugo placed his hand on the mound of her belly. 'You do,' he said. 'And this pleases me most of all.'

He glanced at Alys who was motionless, watching the two of them together.

'Do it, Alys,' he said. It was an order.

Alys went slowly to the table and poured lavender and almond oils into the palm of her hand and rubbed them to make them warm. She was thinking feverishly how to escape from the two of them, how to get herself out of Catherine's chamber and into the safety of the ladies' gallery where the others were sitting around the fire and chattering about the haymaking. She glanced at Hugo as she walked around to the other side of the bed. His dark eyes were very bright. He looked capable of anything. Alys smelled danger as sharp as a curl of smoke from a spark in a haystack.

She started gently and softly to stroke oil into Catherine's white puffy shoulders and arms. Catherine lifted her head to expose her thick neck, closed her eyes and lay still.

With a little laugh Hugo walked to the door. Alys heard the click of the lock as he turned the key and then the rustle of his doublet as he threw it off. When he came back to the bed on the other side, he had rolled up his shirtsleeves and poured a handful of oil into his own hands.

'I will copy you, Alys, and learn your skills,' he said. His voice was like silk; Alys heard the tone of his rising lust and did not look across at him.

Catherine's nipples were hardening as they stroked her shoulders and her neck.

'A little lower?' Hugo suggested, a ripple of laughter in his voice.

Alys stroked, with gentle small touches, down to the

swell of Catherine's breast. Hugo copied her movements exactly. Catherine arched her back slightly on the bed, her stomach raised, her breasts moving towards their hands.

Hugo chuckled. His palm moved confidently down and Alys watched her lover cup his hand over his wife's plump breast.

'I should leave you now,' she whispered. She could not drag her eyes away from his confident, caressing hand. Catherine sighed with pleasure, her eyes still closed.

'You do it, Alys,' he told her, smiling his mischievous smile at Alys' tense, anxious face.

'Do it,' he said again.

Gently she stroked the slope of Catherine's breast.

'I command it,' Hugo said softly.

Alys slid the palm of her hand over Catherine's plump nipple and felt the nipple harden beneath her touch with a delicious responsiveness. Catherine moaned.

'Rub me,' she said.

'You do it,' Hugo demanded. He reached across Catherine and took Alys' other hand and placed it on Catherine's other breast. At Alys' touch Catherine smiled. Her face, warm with pleasure, shadowed in candlelight, was lovely. Alys stroked gently all around Catherine's hot breasts, rubbed the nipples with the flat of her palm, felt a sudden rising desire to press harder, to stroke and pummel Catherine's warm, bulging, newly washed skin, to pinch her, tease her, see her squirm and arouse her desire.

'I have to tell you, my lady, that I have lain with Alys,' Hugo said quietly.

Alys gasped and froze, but Catherine, her head arched

back, her breasts pushed upwards to Alys' hands, was not distracted from her greedy sensuality.

'I could not resist her,' Hugo said gently. 'She is a most delicate whore.'

Catherine laughed, a breathless laugh, deep in her throat. 'You must take your pleasure where you will, Hugo,' she said. 'You are a man. You are the lord. You must have all that you desire.'

'I am going,' Alys said abruptly. She turned for the door but Hugo was quicker. He blocked her way in a moment and she stood, outraged, her eyes blazing.

Hugo's smile was as feckless and wicked as she had ever seen.

'Turn around, Alys,' he said.

For a moment she hesitated and he took her gently by her shoulders and turned her back to Catherine's sprawled wanton bulk on the bed. Catherine opened her eyes and smiled at Alys; she looked ready to eat her. Alys shuddered – partly from distaste, partly from a rising, unwanted desire. She was trapped by Hugo's lust, in Hugo's fantasy, as she had so often entrapped him.

Gently he pushed her back to the bed.

'Touch her, Alys,' he said softly. 'Touch my wife again. You can stroke her – or even pinch her. You can slap her if you wish. I imagine you would like to slap her. She will not mind. She likes it.'

He pushed her gently and Alys leaned forward and slid her hand, still slick with oil, from Catherine's thick throat down to her fat breasts. Catherine groaned softly and reached her arms out for Alys.

Hugo's skilful hands went to the back of Alys' gown and untied the lacings, loosening them swiftly. Alys straightened up to protest, but Catherine, without

443

opening her eyes, still smiling, caught one of her hands and pulled it back on the warm, squashy breast.

'Rub me,' she said. 'Alys, rub me.'

Hugo chuckled, his wicked spoilt-boy chuckle, held Alys more firmly around her waist and pulled the lace from the holes with a swift hiss. The green stomacher and wide sleeves tumbled off. Hugo pushed down the white linen chemise so Alys' breasts and arms were bare. She made a soft, inarticulate protest.

'*My* gown,' he reminded her. 'The new green gown. Mine to strip from you, as we agreed.'

He untied the strings of the overskirt and dropped the expensive brocade to the floor. He untied the green silk underskirt and it fell in a ring at Alys' feet. Alys, held by Hugo's careless hand around the waist, both hands captured by Catherine, stood leaning over the bed wearing nothing but her fine linen shift.

'On the bed,' Hugo ordered. He pushed her gently, and when she resisted he pushed her harder. 'I mean it, Alys,' he said. There was an unmistakable threat in his low voice. 'You have no choice, Mistress,' he said.

Reluctantly Alys climbed on the bed beside Catherine. Catherine turned her face to her and smiled. 'Pretty Alys,' she said. Her voice was slurred with desire. 'Take her shift off, Hugo,' she said. 'Strip her.'

Hugo pulled Alys' shift up from her hips and over her head in one smooth motion as Catherine reached out for her and pulled her down beside her.

'I may not enter you, my lady,' Hugo said thickly to Catherine. 'It would be dangerous for the baby and bad for your milk. But I can give you some pleasure, I think.'

Catherine laughed, a delighted, indulged laugh. 'You bring me your whore?' she asked. 'Hugo, you are wicked! You bring me your whore to please me with her silver fingers?'

Hugo chuckled. 'I am a little wicked,' he conceded. They sounded as if they were flirting in some elaborate courtly ritual. Alys between them, naked and shivery, shrank back as Catherine's scented damp body pressed forward.

'But she would tempt a saint, wouldn't she, Catherine?' Hugo asked agreeably. 'You can't blame me for falling into temptation with Alys.'

He took a handful of Alys' hair and pulled her head back. He put his mouth over hers and Alys felt his tongue slide shamelessly into her mouth as he kissed her deeply and fully while Catherine watched. Incredulously, through her own rising desire, she heard Catherine's low aroused chuckle.

Hugo released her. 'See how I share my secrets with you, Catherine!' he said. 'You are my lady! This is my whore.'

Catherine took Alys' limp hand and put it to her breast again. 'Touch me again,' she said. 'Like you were doing before.'

'I won't be commanded as if I were a toy,' Alys said. She tried to speak with her power in her voice, but she sounded soft, petulant. She felt her power draining from her, mauled by the two of them. She pulled back, away from Catherine's grasping hands, but Hugo was up on the bed behind her and pressing her forwards. His arms came round her waist and caressed her breasts. Alys felt the warmth of his familiar hands stroking her, cupping her breasts, gently pulling at her hardening nipples. Catherine's hands were on her belly, spanning and pinching Alys' narrow waist.

'Don't,' Alys said weakly. She heard consent in her

own voice. She felt her rising desire to be taken by them both, to have them both use her as they wished. As if they were two rich, indulged children, and she a new toy for them to finger and destroy. As if she were without value, a nothingness, which they might tease, abuse, reject. If the two of them played with her to destruction, tore her to pieces between their greedy mouths and working fingers, it would be just. It would be her deserts.

'Don't,' Alys said softly. Hugo heard her assent and laughed. 'Little whore,' he said tenderly and nudged her forward, his penis pressing hard against her back. 'Alys, I think you long to see how low you can fall.'

Alys leaned forward over Catherine's big belly and nuzzled at the fat breasts and licked, with the tip of her tongue, at Catherine's nipples. The oil was sweet and pungent, it furred Alys' tongue. She felt trapped in a nightmare of heady sickly tastes and new forbidden sensations.

Catherine shuddered with pleasure at the touch of Alys' tongue, and took Alys in her arms. She snatched at Alys' hand and pushed it down between her legs. Alys, flinching with contradictory repulsion and lust, felt Catherine's bush of thick hair and then a deep slippery canal drenched in liquid, feeling her own thighs grow sticky and wet.

Catherine was breathing fast. Her hands pressed Alys' hand against her body more and more urgently. She arched her back and rubbed herself against Alys' hands, groaning as she did. Alys gave a little gasp of distaste and of desire. She was surrounded by Catherine and Hugo. Catherine squirming beneath her, Hugo bearing down on her from behind. The two of them were playing with her like two malicious cats with a mouse.

And at the same time Alys felt a leap of desire that she should be between them, that Catherine's hands should be pawing her, one at her breast, and one, horribly, delightfully, between her legs. That Hugo should be pressing himself at her back – as hard as a spear – probing between her legs, hard and slippery with her wetness, and then she felt Hugo rear up behind her and plunge himself inside her, at the same moment as Catherine snatched Alys' hand, ground her hot wet flesh against it and thrust it deep inside her.

Catherine and Hugo groaned together, repeatedly thrusting at the same time, as practised lovers reaching release together. Alys, hot with desire, suddenly frantic, twisted and turned between them, but Hugo slackened and stilled, grew small and released her.

Catherine rolled away, her breathing deep and easy, her face rosy and relaxed. Hugo dropped face down into the pillow with a deep sigh. Alys lay between the two of them, silently raging and unsatisfied. The small bones of her hand were aching where Catherine had crushed it against her flesh. Inside her body she was hot and sore, between her legs she was drenched and unsatisfied.

She looked from one to the other; they were both smiling, sated. Neither of them looked at her, neither of them cared whether or not she had any pleasure. The question of Alys' irritable, unsated desire was of no importance. Alys' sensation of drowning in corruption was of no interest. Catherine pulled the covers a little closer, her face slack with sleep and satisfaction. She slept.

The fire crackled gently, the scent of lemon verbena was very sweet in the room. The three of them – the two naked pregnant women, and the half-dressed young lord – lay still. The lord and his lady slept.

*

447

Catherine came down for supper in the great hall, rosy in her pink and cream gown, her face smiling, fat as a pudding, her hair spread out over her shoulders, her appetite sharp. Hugo had her on his arm as they walked into the dining-hall and there was a shout of appreciation and welcome from all the diners. Alys took her old place at the women's table and cast a hard look around at all of them to warn them not to mock her for her return.

'Welcome back,' Eliza said irrepressibly.

Alys met her bright eyes with a cold stare. 'I am happy to dine with you, Eliza, and with you all,' she said levelly. 'But do not forget that I am carrying Hugo's son in my belly – something each one of you would give a year's pay for. Don't forget that when Catherine takes to her bed again I shall be sitting next to the old lord and that I am his favourite. Don't forget that I am Mistress Alys to you and every one of you. My fortunes may rise and fall, but even at their ebb they are higher than you could dream.'

All the women looked at their plates and supped their broth in silence. Alys let the silence go on and on. She watched Hugo. Half a lifetime ago it seemed that she had sat here with Morach beside her, and watched Hugo's back with a desire so strong that she had thought she would die of it. Now she looked at his shoulders and his neck and the set of his head with silent hatred.

'Are you not eating, Mistress Alys?' Ruth asked quietly.

Alys glanced down at her bowl. The broth had grown cold, thick lumps of grease floated in it. Alys took a sip of wine tainted with the metallic taste of the pewter cup. David the steward had seen that her place on the women's table was laid with pewter, like theirs. Glass was only for the top table, and she had lost her place there.

'I am not hungry,' she said briefly. 'I will ask Hugo to send me something to my room later.' She rose from the table and went to the high table, to the old lord.

'I wish to leave the table,' she said softly in his ear. 'I have some pains and I feel sick. I wish to go to my room.'

The look he turned on her was kindly enough, but he smiled as if he could see straight into her heart. 'Don't be envious, vixen,' he said softly. 'You come second to Catherine. We always told you that. Go and sit at your place and drink and eat from pewter. She will keep to her room again some time and you can queen it up here then. But when she chooses to eat with us in the hall where she belongs, you take your place at the women's table – where you belong.'

Alys glanced across at Hugo. He was listening to some jest a man was shouting to him from a table further down the hall. He caught the end of the riddle and threw back his dark head in a shout of laughter.

'No,' the old lord said, following her glance. 'There is no appeal against my decision. I am master here still, Alys. Go and sit where you are bid.'

Alys smiled her sweetest smile. 'Of course, my lord,' she said. 'I did not wish to spoil the good cheer and merry company at the ladies' table with my illness. But if you wish it, of course I will sit with them.'

Lord Hugh glanced back at the table and barked a sharp laugh at the four sour faces. They were straining to hear what Alys and the old lord were whispering about.

'Oh, go your ways,' he said indulgently. 'I will spare you the merry cheer of that crew. Go to your room now, but another time you must sit with the silly bitches.'

Alys dipped him a curtsey and slipped out through the tapestry-hung door behind them. She caught Eliza's eye as she left and remembered her first dinner in the castle when they had told her that no one could leave before the lord.

'Things are better for me now than they were then,' Alys said to herself grimly. She mounted the stairs to the ladies' gallery, pushed open the door and pulled up a chair before the fire. 'It is better for me now than in Morach's ugly cottage.' She threw another log on the fire and sat watching the sparks fly. 'I have forced them to see me for what I am,' she said defiantly to herself. 'I came here as a nobody and now they call me Mistress Alys and I have twelve gowns of my own. I have as many new gowns as Catherine.'

The quietness of the room gathered around her. 'I have forced them to see me for what I am,' Alys said again. She was silent for a moment, watching the flames.

'They see me as his whore,' she said softly. 'Today I became Hugo's whore. And everybody knows.'

Twenty-four

Alys was alone in her bedroom when the others came up to the gallery. She heard them talking and laughing, she heard the clink of jug on pewter. She sat by her little fireside, her door firmly shut, and listened to them playing a card game as Eliza sang. Then the chatter died down as one by one the women excused themselves and went to their room. Alys listened for Hugo's voice and heard him call 'Goodnight' to one of them. She sat by her fireside and waited.

He did not come to her.

In the early hours of the morning, when the darkness was still thick and the moon was setting in the west, Alys wrapped a shawl around her and crept across her floor to the door. She opened it and peeped out. The fire in the long gallery had died down, the ashes cold. Catherine's door was shut. There was no sound.

Alys paused for a moment by the hearth and remembered the time when she had sat there absorbed in her longing for Hugo and he had come from Catherine's room and put his arm around her and told her that he loved her. Alys shrugged. It was a long, long time ago. Before Morach's death, before her deep magic had come to claim her, before she had played the wanton with him – and had him take her at her word.

She crept to Catherine's door and turned the handle gently. Opening it a crack, she could hear deep rhythmic breathing. She slid through the door like a ghost and peered into the room.

The room was dark. All the candles were out and the

fire had died away in the darkened grate. The little window faced the castle courtyard and garden and no moonlight shone. Alys blinked her eyes, trying to see through the shadows.

In the great high bed was Catherine, sprawled on her back with her high belly making a mountain of the covers. One arm was thrown carelessly above her head; Alys could see the thick clump of dark hair in her armpit. The other arm was cradling the man lying beside her. Alys stepped a little closer to see. It was Hugo. He was deep asleep, lying on his side with his head buried into Catherine's neck, his arm thrown proprietorially over her body. They lay like a married couple. They lay like lovers. Alys watched them without moving while they breathed steadily and peacefully. She watched them as if she would suck the breath out of their bodies and destroy them with the weight of her jealousy and disappointment. Hugo stirred in his sleep and said something.

It was not Alys' name.

Catherine smiled, even in the darkness Alys could see the calm joy of Catherine's sleepy smile, and gathered him closer. Then they lay still again.

Alys closed the door silently, and crept back, across the empty, cold gallery to her own room, shut the door behind her, drew her chair up to the fire, wrapped her shawl around her and waited for day to come.

In the half-light of dawn, before the sun was up but while the sky was pale yellow with the promise of sunshine to come, Alys went over and opened the chest of her magic things. Tucked away in the corner was Morach's old bag of bones – the runes.

Alys glanced behind her. Her bedroom door was shut, no one in the castle was stirring. She glanced out of the arrow-slit window. In the pale light she could see strips of mist hovering and rising from the silver surface of the river. As she watched they rose and billowed. One of them looked like a woman, an old woman with grey hair and a shawl wrapped around her.

'No,' Alys whispered, as she recognized her. 'I am not calling you. I will use your runes for I need to know my future. But I am not calling you. Stay in the water. Stay out of sight. You and I will both know when your time comes.'

She watched the mist until it billowed and ebbed and lay flat and quiet again, and then she turned from the arrow-slit and sat on the rug before the fire.

She shook the bag like a gambler shakes dice and then flung them all out before her. Without looking at the marks she picked three, carefully considering each choice, her hand hovering over one and then moving to another.

'My future,' she said. 'Hugo uses me as his whore and now I am nothing here. There must be more for me. Show me my future.'

She spread the three of her choice before her, one beside another, and gathered the others into their purse again.

'Now,' she said.

The first one she had drawn was face down. The back was blank and she turned it over. The front was blank as well.

'Odin,' she said surprised. 'Nothingness. Death.'

The second was blank. She turned it over, and then turned it over again. 'It is not possible; there aren't two blank runes,' Alys whispered to herself. 'There *is* only one blank rune. All the rest are marked.' She flipped over the third. It was smooth and plain on both sides,

453

one side as empty as the other. Alys sat very still with the three faceless runes in her hand.

Then she raised her head and looked towards the arrow-slit. The mist quivered as it lay on the river, quivered and formed the shape of a resting woman. 'You knew,' Alys said in a low whisper towards the mist. 'You told me, but I did not hear. Death, you said. Death in the runes. And I asked you "how long?" and you would not tell me. Now your runes are blank for me too.'

She tipped out the purse. The other bones spilled out on to the floor. Each one was smooth and as innocent of any mark as an old polished skull.

Alys shuddered, as if the cold river water was pressing around her, as if the green deep wetness of it was coming up to her chin, lapping over her mouth. She gathered the runes together with one hasty gesture, slung them into the bag, and tossed the bag into the corner of the chest. Then, with her shawl wrapped tight around her, she crept into bed. She could not sleep for shivering.

Hugo went out riding at first light, Catherine slept late. The women in the gallery eyed Alys sideways when she came out of her room, her face serene, her red cloak around her shoulders.

'I'm going up to the moors,' she said to Eliza. 'I need some more herbs for Catherine. Is she sleeping still?'

'Yes,' Eliza said. 'When will you be back?'

Alys looked at her coldly. 'I shall be home in time for supper,' she said. 'I will take my dinner with me and picnic out on the moors.'

'I'll come with you to the stables,' Eliza said.

She and Alys went down the stairs, across the hall

and out of the great door to the gardens. Eliza trotted to keep pace with Alys as they walked through the gateway, over the bridge and across the grass to the stables.

'It's a pretty mare,' Eliza said enviously as the stable-boy brought Alys' new pony out.

'Yes,' Alys said with grim satisfaction. 'Yes, she is. She was expensive.' She snapped her fingers to the stable-lad. 'Fetch me some food from the kitchen. I'll dine on my own on the moors.' The lad dipped a bow and ran off.

'Hugo slept with Catherine all night,' Eliza said in a confidential undertone, watching the lad run to the kitchen door.

'I know,' Alys said coldly.

'Has he turned away from you now?' Eliza asked.

Alys shook her head. 'I am carrying his son,' she said coldly. 'My place is safe.'

Eliza looked at her with something very close to pity. Alys caught the look and felt herself flush.

'What is it?' she demanded. 'What are you staring at?'

'You'd have been safer married to that soldier Lady Catherine picked out for you,' Eliza said shrewdly. 'If you wanted to know where you were with a man, he would have been the one for you. Hugo is as changeable as weather. Now he's back with Catherine again, next it'll be another woman. You can't ever call yourself safe if you trust in Hugo.'

The stable-lad was running back with a small leather bag in his hand. He tied it to the saddle and brought the mare forward. 'He bought this for me, didn't he?' Alys said to Eliza, pointing to the pony. 'And I have a chest full of gowns. And I am carrying his son in my belly. I am safe enough here, aren't I?'

455

Eliza shrugged, holding Alys' herb sack while the lad helped her up. 'He's fickle,' she said again. 'A woman who lives as a whore should keep a big bag of savings. It's a chance-made business. You've ridden very high, Alys, but I think you're coming down now.'

'Mistress Alys to you!' Alys flared. She shook out the skirts of her red gown, smoothed the rich embroidered overskirt, and gathered her reins in her hand. She looked down at Eliza as if she were a beggar at the gates and Alys a fine lady. 'I am Mistress Alys to you,' she said again.

Eliza shrugged her shoulders. 'Not any more, I reckon,' she said. 'I reckon you're falling, Alys. I reckon you are on your way down.'

Alys wheeled the mare around, her face set, and kicked her towards the castle gateyard. As she trotted past the soldiers they shouldered their pikes in a salute but Alys looked neither left nor right. Down the little hill of Castleton she spurred the pony and then around the base of the cliffs at the foot of the castle to cross the bridge over the river and up to the moors. She did not pull up the pony until they were on the far side of the river-bank and it was blowing hard and out of breath. Then she drew rein and looked back at the castle, grey and lovely in the summer sunlight. Alys stared at it, as if she would swallow it up, gobble the whole place to sate her hunger, lords, ladies, servants and all.

Then she turned the pony around and headed up for the moorland.

She had not planned to ride to Morach's cottage, she had headed west from the castle, heading for the moors without any sense of purpose. The herb bag had been an excuse but as the hedges fell away from the side of

456

the road and the land became more wild Alys saw a little clump of windflowers on the side of the road and pulled up the horse. She slid from the saddle and picked them, wrapped them in dock leaves, and then, leading the horse by the reins, she walked down through the field towards the river, watching the thick meadow grass under her feet for any other herbs or flowers she could use.

The river was at its summertime ebb, sluggishly winding along the stone slabs, standing still in deep brown peaty pools, disappearing down the cracks of the river bed and then welling up in a narrow drying stream a few yards on. A redshank flew up from a pool calling and calling a clear sweet sound. Further downriver the water would have drained from Morach's grave, her body would be rotting, busy with flies. Alys shrugged and turned her thoughts away from it.

Alys walked along the river-bank, leading her horse, watching the banks for herbs and for the innocent faces of the small meadow flowers. The smell of wild thyme was sweet and heady, the harebells stirred as the steady ceaseless moorland breeze breathed through them. The little darkfaced Pennine violets bobbed as the red skirts of Alys' long gown brushed them. Away on the higher ground, white, mauve and blue clouds of lady's-smock swayed together on their long stems. Alys walked as if she could walk away from loneliness, walk away from need, walk away from the love of her life which had turned sour as soon as she had twisted it to serve her purpose.

With her little mare dawdling behind her, Alys walked, wishing she were far away from the castle, far away from Hugo, far away from her own ceaseless ambition. Alys walked, her eyes watchful for healing herbs, her mind at a loss as to her next step. God had failed her, love had failed her, magic had entrapped her. Alys, sure-footed on the familiar paths, was lost. All she could still feel was her hunger to survive – as keen and as vivid as ever; and behind that her old grief for her mother – Mother Hildebrande – that stayed with her, sharp and alive even when the runes read blank and Alys was as unsighted as any ordinary woman. On the clear sun-filled day, with larks climbing as high as heaven and lapwings calling and curlews crying, Alys walked alone in her own world of darkness, coldness and need.

She stopped abruptly. She had walked nearly as far as the deep pool before Morach's old cottage. She shaded her eyes against the bright morning sunlight and looked up the hill towards it. It was in the same state that it had always been. The stone-slated roof looked ready to slide off into a heap, the one tiny horn window was dark and abandoned. No smoke eddied from the window or the door. Alys walked towards it and tied her horse to the hawthorn bush laden with creamy-white sickly flowers at the garden wall. She hitched up her skirt and climbed through the little sheep gap. Morach's vegetables were sprouting, burdened with weeds, in their bed. Alys stared at them for a moment, remembering that she had planted them, all those months ago in the autumn. It seemed odd that Morach should be dead, long dead, and yet her turnips were growing in their bed. The front door was unfastened; the little hook had never held it firm, it was banging in the light breeze. Alys guessed that the bravest of children from Bowes village might have pushed open the door to look inside and then scattered, breathless with terror. None of them would have dared go nearer.

'I dare,' Alys said aloud. But she stayed, waiting on the outside.

The door squeaked and banged. Inside the cottage something softly rustled. Alys thought that there would be rats in the cottage, grown fat on Morach's seed store, nesting in the rags of her bed. Alys waited on the doorstep, almost as if she expected to hear Morach's irritable voice calling her to stop dawdling and come in.

The rustling noise in the cottage had stopped. Still Alys paused, delayed pushing open the door, stepping over the threshold. Then, as she hesitated, she clearly heard the noise of someone moving. Someone moving, inside the cottage. Not a rat, not the rustle of a small animal. Alys heard footsteps, someone walking heavily and slowly across the floor.

Involuntarily Alys stepped back, her hand reaching behind her for the reins of her horse. The footsteps inside the cottage paused. Alys opened her mouth to call out, but no sound came. The horse dipped its head, its ears pressed back as if it smelled Alys' fear and the uncanny eerie smell of death from the cottage.

There was another noise, a dragging noise, like someone pulling a stool up to the fireside. Bright in Alys' mind was the image of Morach, dripping with river water, blue with cold, her skin puffy and soggy from months underwater, climbing out of her cave as the river level sank, walking wetly upstream to her cottage and pulling her stool up to her cold fireside to hold her white waterlogged hands towards the empty grate. A damp smell of death seemed to swirl outwards from the cottage. Alys imagined Morach's half-rotten body decaying as she walked, falling off her bones as she waited for Alys to come to her. As she waited in the darkness of the cottage for Alys to open the door.

Alys gave a little moan of terror. Morach was indoors waiting for her and the moment of reckoning between the two of them was to be now. If Alys turned and fled she knew she would hear the swift squelch of rotting feet running behind her and then feel the icy cold touch of fingers on her shoulder.

With a cry of terror Alys stepped forward, wrenched open the door, and flung it wide. At once her worst nightmares became real.

She had not imagined the noise.

She had not imagined the footsteps.

In the shadowy cottage she could see the figure of a woman seated before the fireplace, a stooped figure of a woman shrouded in her cloak. As the door banged open she slowly straightened up and turned around.

Alys screamed, a breathless, choked-off scream. In the darkness of the cottage she could see no face. All she could see was the hooded woman rising to her feet and coming nearer and nearer; coming towards her and stepping over the threshold so the sun shone full on her face. Alys half closed her eyes, waiting for the glimpse of ghastly blue puffy flesh, waiting for the stink of a drowned corpse.

It was not Morach. The woman was taller than Morach had been. The face she turned to Alys was white, aged and lined with pain. Half-hidden by the hood of her cloak was a thick mane of white hair. Her eyes were grey. Her hands, stretched out to Alys, were thin and freckled with age spots. They shook as if she were sick with the palsy.

'Please . . .' was all she said. 'Please . . .'

'Who are you?' Alys said wildly, her voice high with terror. 'I thought you were Morach! Who are you? What are you doing here?'

The woman trembled all over. 'I am sorry,' she said humbly. Her voice was cracked with age or grief but her speech was slow and sweet. 'Forgive me. I thought this place was empty. I was seeking . . .'

Alys stepped closer, her anger flowing into her like hot wine reviving her. 'You've no right to be here!' she shouted. 'This place is not empty. It is no shelter for beggars and paupers. You will have to leave.'

The woman raised her face imploringly. 'Please, my lady,' she started and then a clear light of joy suddenly flooded over her face, and she cried out, 'Sister Ann! My darling! My little Sister Ann! Oh, my darling! You are safe!'

'Mother!' Alys said in a sudden blinding moment of recognition and then fell forward as the arms of Mother Hildebrande came around her again and held her as if she had never been away.

The two women clung to each other. 'Mother, my mother,' was all Alys said. The abbess felt Alys' body shake with sobs. 'My mother.'

Gently Hildebrande released her. 'I have to sit,' she said apologetically. 'I am very weak.' She sank down to a stool. Alys dropped to her knees beside the abbess.

'How did you come here?' she asked.

The woman smiled. 'I think Our Lady must have brought me to you,' she said. 'I have been ill all this long while, in hiding with some faithful people in a farm a little way from Startforth. They told me of this little hovel. There was an old woman living here once, but she has gone missing. They thought that if I lived here and sold medicines to those that asked it of me, that it was my best chance for safety. In a little while, we thought, no one would distinguish one old woman from another.'

'She was a witch,' Alys said with revulsion. 'She was a dirty old witch. Anyone could tell you apart.'

Mother Hildebrande smiled. 'She was an old woman with more learning than was safe for her,' she said. 'And so am I. She was a woman wise beyond her station, and so am I. She must have been a woman who by chance or choice was an outlaw, and so am I. I shall live here, in hiding, at peace with my soul, until the times change and I can again worship God in the Church of His choosing.'

She smiled at Alys as if it were a life that anyone would prefer, that a wise woman would envy. 'And what of you?' she asked gently. 'I have mourned you and prayed for your immortal soul every night of my life since I last saw you. And now I have you back again! Surely God is good. What of you, Sister Ann? How did you escape the fire?'

'I woke when the fire started,' Alys lied rapidly. 'And I was running to the chapel to ring the bell when they caught me. They took me into the woods to rape me, but I managed to get away. I went far away, all the way to Newcastle searching for another nunnery, so that I could keep my vows; but it was unsafe everywhere. When I came back to look for you or any of the sisters, Lord Hugh at the castle heard of me and employed me as his clerk.'

Mother Hildebrande's face was stern. 'Has he ordered you to take the oath to deny your Church and your faith?' she asked. Her hands were still palsied and her face was that of a frail old woman. But her voice was strong and certain.

'Oh no!' Alys exclaimed. 'No! Lord Hugh believes in the old ways. He has sheltered me from that.'

'And have you kept your vows?' the old woman

asked. She glanced at Alys' rich gown, the red gown of Meg the whore who died of the pox.

'Oh yes,' Alys said quickly. She turned her pale heart-shaped face upwards to Mother Hildebrande. 'I keep the hours of prayer in silence, in my own mind. I may not pray aloud of course, nor can I choose what I wear. But I fast when I should and I own nothing of my own. I have been touched by no man. I am ready to show you my obedience. All my major vows are unbroken.'

Mother Hildebrande cupped her hand around Alys' cheek. 'Well done,' she said softly. 'We have had a hard and weary trial, you and I, daughter. I have thought often that it was easier for the others, those who died that night and are in paradise today, than for me trying to hold to my vows and struggling with a world which grows more wicked every day. And it must have been so hard for you,' Mother Hildebrande said gently. 'Thank God we are together now. And we need never be apart again.'

Alys hid her face in Mother Hildebrande's lap. The old woman rested her hand on Alys' bright head.

'Such lovely hair,' she said gently. 'I had forgotten, Sister Ann, that you were so fair.'

Alys smiled up at her.

'I have not seen your hair since your girlhood,' Mother Hildebrande remembered. 'When you first came to me, out of the world of sin, with your bright curly hair and your pale, beautiful face.' She paused. 'You must beware of the sin of vanity,' she said gently. 'Now you are thrust out into the world in your womanhood. Now that you wear a red gown, Sister Ann, and with your hair worn loose.'

'They make me dress like this,' Alys said swiftly. 'I

have no other clothes. And I thought it right not to endanger Lord Hugh, who protects me, by insisting on a dark gown.'

Mother Hildebrande shook her head, unconvinced. 'Very well,' she said. 'You have had to make compromises. But now we can make our own lives again. Here, in this little cottage, we will start. We will make a new nunnery here. Just the two of us for now, but perhaps there will be more later on. You and I will keep our vows and lead the life that is appointed to us. We shall be a little light in the darkness of the moorland. We will be a little light for the world.'

'Here?' Alys said, bemused. 'Here?'

Mother Hildebrande laughed her old laugh, full of joy. 'Why not?' she said. 'Did you think that serving Our Lady was all rich vestments and silver and candles, Sister Ann? You know better than that! Our Lady was a simple woman, She probably lived in a home no better than this! Her son was a carpenter. Why should we want more than Her?'

Alys felt she was gaping. She tried to gather her thoughts together. 'But, Mother Hildebrande,' she said, 'we cannot live here. In summer it is well enough but in winter it is dreadfully hard. We have no money, we have no food. And people will talk about us and then the soldiers will come . . .'

Mother Hildebrande was smiling. 'God will provide, Sister Ann,' she said gently. 'I have prayed and prayed for you, and I have prayed and prayed to live once more under the rules of our Order, and now, see, my prayers are answered.'

Alys shook her head. 'They are *not* answered,' she said desperately. 'This is not the answer to your prayers. I know what it is like here! It is dirty and cold. The garden grows nothing fit to eat, in winter the snow banks up to the door. God does not want us to be here!'

Mother Hildebrande laughed, her old, confident laugh. 'You seem to be deep in His counsels that you speak so certainly!' she said gently. 'Do not fret so, Sister Ann. Let us take what He gives us. He has given us each other and this roof over our heads. Surely He is good!'

'No! It's not possible . . .' Alys urged. 'We must go away. We must go to France or Spain. There is no place for us in England any more. We court disaster if we stay here and try to practise our faith.'

The old abbess smiled and shook her head. 'I have sworn to practise my faith here,' she said gently. 'I was commanded to lead an order here, in England. No one ever said that if it became hard I should run away.'

'We would not be running!' Alys urged. 'We would find another nunnery, they would accept us. We would be obeying our vows, living the life we should lead.'

The abbess smiled at Alys and shook her head. 'No,' she said softly. 'God gave me thirty years of wealth and comfort, serving Him in luxury. Now He has called me to hardship. How should I refuse Him?'

'Mother Hildebrande, you *cannot* live here!' Alys raised her voice in exasperation. 'You know nothing about the life here. You do not understand. You will die here in wintertime. This is folly!'

There was a moment's shocked silence at Alys' rudeness. Then Mother Hildebrande spoke with gentle finality.

'I believe that this is the will of the Lord,' she said. 'And I am bound by my vows of obedience to do His will.' She paused for a moment. 'As are you,' she said.

'But it's not possible . . .' Alys muttered mutinously.

'As are you,' Mother Hildebrande said again more slowly, her voice warning.

Alys sighed and said nothing.

There was a silence between the two women. Alys, glancing up from where she knelt at her mother's feet, saw that the abbess' eyes were filled with tears.

'I . . .' she started.

'When can you join me here?' Mother Hildebrande demanded. 'We should start our new life at once. And there are many things we need which you can provide.'

Alys' moment of penitence was brief. 'I don't know when I can come,' she said distractedly. 'My life at the castle is so uncertain . . .' She broke off, thinking of Hugo and Catherine, and her own baby growing in her belly. 'I could come next week perhaps,' she said. 'I could come for a few days next week.'

Mother Hildebrande shook her head. 'That is not enough, Sister Ann,' she said gently. 'You have been away from our holy Order for many months, but before then you lived with us for many years. You cannot have forgotten our discipline so soon. You may go now, but you must come back tomorrow, wearing a plain dark gown and bringing with you whatever Lord Hugh is prepared to give gladly. For the rest, we will grow our own food and weave our own cloth. We will make our own rushlights and write our own books from memory. We will make bread and sell it in the market, we will fish, and sell what we catch. And we will make simple medicines and remedies and sell or give them to people who are in need.'

Alys kept her eyes down so Mother Hildebrande could not see her panic and her immediate utter refusal.

'It looks very dark for our Church,' Mother Hildebrande said. 'But this is how it was for Saint Paul himself, or for Saint Cuthbert when the English Church

466

was nearly destroyed before, by the pagans. Then, as now, the Lord called His people to serve Him in darkness and secrecy and want. Then, as now, their faith triumphed. God has called us for a special mission, Sister Ann, only He knows how great our work will be.'

Alys said nothing. Mother Hildebrande no longer looked like a weary old lady. Her face was radiant with her joy, her voice strong with certainty. She broke off and smiled at Alys, her familiar, loving smile.

'Go now,' the abbess said gently. 'It must be near the time for sext. Pray as you ride back to the castle and I will pray here. You have not forgotten the offices of the day, Sister Ann?'

Alys shook her head. She could not remember one word of them. 'I remember them all,' she said.

The abbess smiled. 'Say them at the appointed hours,' she said. 'The Lord will forgive us that we are not on our knees in His chapel. He will understand. And tomorrow, when you come, you will confess to me your sins and we will start afresh.'

Alys nodded dumbly.

The abbess rose from the stool. Alys saw she walked very stiffly, as if her back and her hip bones and legs all ached.

'I am a little weary,' she said, as she caught Alys' look. 'But once I start working in the garden I shall grow fit and strong again.'

Alys nodded and went out of the door. The abbess stood on the threshold. Alys untied the pony's bridle and then remembered her bag of food.

'Here,' she said. 'I brought this for my dinner, but you can have it.'

The abbess' wise old face lit up with a smile. 'There, my child!' she said delightedly. 'The Lord has provided for us, and He will provide for us over and over again. Don't be faint-hearted, Sister Ann! Trust in Him, and He will bring us to great joy.'

Alys nodded dumbly and climbed up the step of the sheep gate and stepped into the saddle.

'That's a very fine horse,' the abbess observed. 'Too good for a clerk, I would have thought.'

'It's Lady Catherine's horse,' Alys said quickly. 'She is carrying the young lord's child and cannot ride. They like me to ride her mare to keep it in exercise.'

The abbess nodded slowly, looking from the horse to Alys. For one moment Alys was gripped with a chilling certainty that the old woman understood everything, could see everything. The lies, the witchcraft, the walking wax dolls, the murder of Morach, and the bed with three writhing, greedy bodies. Hugo's laugh when he called her his wanton whore echoed in the sunny afternoon air around them.

Mother Hildebrande looked into Alys' face, unsmiling. 'Come tomorrow,' she said gently. 'I think you have been very near to very grave sin, my daughter. Come tomorrow and you can confess to me and with the guidance of God I will absolve you.'

'I have not been near sin,' Alys said breathlessly. She managed a clear honest smile. 'Nowhere near, praise God!' she said lightly.

Mother Hildebrande did not smile in return. She looked from the expensive, elegant pony in the rich, well-made harness to Alys in her red gown with the silver embroidered stomacher and her cherry-red cape; and her old face was drained of its earlier joy. She looked as if she had been cut to the heart.

'Tomorrow at noon,' she said firmly and turned and went back inside the cottage.

Alys watched the door shut on the frail figure and stayed for a moment longer. There was no sound of a tinderbox, no smoke drifted out of the barred window. There would be no dry kindling in the hut, perhaps only one or two rushlights. Morach might have hidden her tinderbox. But even if there had been one – Mother Hildebrande would not have known how to light a fire.

Alys wrenched the mare's head around towards home. 'Come on!' she said sullenly. She kicked it hard and the animal flinched and lunged forward, nearly unseating her. 'Come on!' she said.

Twenty-five

When Alys rode up to the inner castle gate Eliza came dashing down the stairs, pushing past the soldiers and dragging her from the saddle.

'Come at once! Come at once!' she said in an urgent undertone. 'It's Catherine! She's in pain. None of us know what to do! Thank God you're back now! They were about to send the soldiers out to look for you!'

Alys let Eliza grab her and rush her across the draw-bridge, through the great hall and up the stairs to the ladies' gallery.

The place was filled with people. Servants were dodging in and out carrying trays. Sheets were airing before the fire. Someone had let Hugo's deerhound into the room and it growled when it saw Alys. Two serving-men were labouring up the stairs with the bath-tub, another two coming behind with churns of hot water.

'She said she wanted a bath,' Eliza said. 'She wanted you to bath her again, like you did yesterday. Then she said she felt pains in her belly. She was walking around to ease them. We made her get into bed. Hugo has only just come in himself, we were afraid you were off together and would be gone all day. David has just gone to tell Lord Hugh. Catherine's in her bedroom – go to her, Alys! Go to her!'

Alys clapped her hands. 'Out of here!' she shouted. All of her anger and fear and frustration boiled over in one releasing burst of rage. 'Out of here, you useless toss-pots!' she yelled. She took one of the servants by the shoulder and spun him around and thrust him out of the room. He staggered on the stairs and collided with another, hurrying up the stairs with extra sheets. Alys grabbed a page-boy by the ear and pushed him out of the room. One of the serving-wenches was giggling helplessly at the chaos. Alys smacked her hard across the face and watched with vicious pleasure as the red marks of her fingertips showed on the girl's cheek.

'Now get out,' Alys said to them all. 'I will call you if I need any of you.'

She left them scrambling for the gallery door and stalked towards Catherine's bedroom.

Hugo was at the head of the bed, holding Catherine's hands. Her women, Ruth, Mistress Allingham and Margery, were on the other side of the bed. Ruth was swinging a censer of silver which Alys recognized as part of Hugo's haul from the nunnery. The air was thick with the throat-rasping smell of incense. Margery was sponging Catherine's head. She was tossing on the pillow, with her eyes shut. Every now and then she gave a gasp of pain and strained her body upwards as if some giant hand had gripped her in the middle and hauled her to the roof.

'Stop that,' Alys said irritably to Ruth. 'And open a window. The place stinks.'

Hugo looked up, his scowl disappearing. 'Thank God you're back, Alys,' he said. 'No one knew what to do, and the physician in Castleton is away all week. I was on the edge of sending for the wise woman from Richmond.'

'When did the pains start?' Alys asked.

Catherine opened her eyes at Alys' voice. 'This morning,' she said. 'When I woke.'

Alys nodded knowledgeably, though she knew nothing more. 'I'll have to look at her,' she said. 'You'd better wait outside.'

Hugo leaned over Catherine's bed and pressed a kiss on her forehead. As he passed Alys he laid a hand on her shoulder. 'Save my son,' he said in an undertone. 'Nothing in the world is more important than that.'

Alys did not even look at him. 'Of course,' she said curtly.

Hugo's pat on her shoulder was that of a man to a trusted comrade. Alys, remembering his hands cupped on her breasts as he thrust her towards Catherine's smothering embrace, shot him an angry glare, but he was looking at Catherine. He did not even see her.

'Give her something to ease her pain,' he said softly. 'She's being very brave. I'll be outside all the time. I'll come in if she wants me.'

'Certainly,' Alys said frigidly.

Hugo led the way out of the room, the women scuttling after him.

'Shall I stay?' Eliza asked.

'What could you do?' Alys asked cruelly. 'You know nothing. What use could you be? Tell them to bring the chest of my things from my room.'

Catherine moaned again and Alys went swiftly to her side.

'What sort of pain is it?' she asked.

'Like opening,' Catherine gasped. 'Like opening up and splitting. Alys, help me!'

There was a tap at the door. Two serving-men came into the room carrying Alys' chest of herbs and oils, put it gently on the floor and went out. Alys opened the chest and took out a twist of powder in a piece of paper.

'On the right side or on the left?' she asked.

Catherine groaned again. 'All over,' she said. 'I feel strange, Alys. As if this were not me. I feel in the grip of something else.'

'Open your mouth,' Alys said. Deftly she tipped the powder down Catherine's throat and then held a glass of water for her to sip. At once Catherine's colour came back into her cheeks and she breathed a little more easily.

'What can it be, Alys?' she asked. 'It's something wrong with the baby, isn't it?'

'It's coming before its time,' Alys said. 'Could you have been mistaken with the dates, Catherine? You are only nearing your seventh month. It should not come yet.'

Catherine gasped as another pain seized her. 'I could be, I could be,' she said. 'But not two or three months wrong. There's something wrong. I can feel it!'

'What can you feel?' Alys asked urgently. Hidden away at the back of her mind was the thought that perhaps Catherine's pregnancy was going wrong. That the child would not be born, or would not be a son. Or would be born dead. Or if Catherine were to die . . .

'I feel strange,' Catherine said. Her voice sounded unreal, as if she were calling from a long way away. 'Help me, Alys! You love me dearly I know! Help me, Alys! I feel as if the child is slipping out of me, melting and slipping away!'

Alys stripped back the covers. Catherine's plump, puffy legs were stained with veins of blue, flushed pink with heat. Alys pulled up Catherine's shift with reluctance and peered at her. The lower sheet was stained with a pale, creamy juice.

'Is this your waters? Have your waters broken?' Alys asked.

Catherine shook her head, her body twisted as a spasm of pain took her. 'I don't know, I don't think so,' she said. 'I have had nothing but this oozing.'

'No blood?' Alys asked.

'No,' Catherine said. 'Alys, keep the baby inside me. I can feel it melting.'

Alys pulled Catherine's shift down and rested her hand on Catherine's round belly. 'You are being foolish,' she said firmly. 'Foolish and hysterical. Babies do not melt. I can see you are in pain and I can help you bear your pain; but there is no blood and your waters have not broken. Your baby is still inside you and he is well. Babies do not melt.'

Catherine started up on the bed, half-supporting herself with her arms. She glared at Alys and her face was wild, her hair tossed around her face, her eyes bulging. 'I tell you he is melting!' she screamed. 'Why won't you listen to me, you fool! Why won't you do as I tell you! Do something to make the baby safe! He is melting. I feel him melting! He is melting inside me and slipping away!'

Alys pushed Catherine back down on the pillows and held her hard by the shoulders. 'Hush,' she said roughly. 'Hush. That cannot be, Catherine. You are mistaken. You are gibbering nonsense.'

She rested her hand on Catherine's rounded belly and then snatched it away again in instinctive horror. Catherine gave another groan. 'I told you,' she wept.

Alys put her hand back, she could hardly believe what she had felt. Under the palm of her hand she distinctly felt the round fullness of Catherine's belly reduce and subside. Something under the thick layer of flesh shifted and bubbled. As it did so, Catherine groaned again.

'The baby is going,' Catherine said despairingly. She was groaning deep in her throat, an animal growl, not like a woman at all. 'I cannot hold him. He is going,' she said.

474

Alys pulled Catherine's shift up and looked again at the woman's parted legs. The pool of creamy white juice had spread over the sheets. Alys gagged and swallowed her saliva.

'I don't know what this stuff is. I don't know what to do,' she muttered.

Catherine did not even hear her. She was straining her body upwards, and as she thrust her belly towards the ceiling Alys could see the shape of the rounded bump flowing and changing like river slime.

'Lie still, lie still,' Alys commanded helplessly. 'Lie still, Catherine, and nothing will happen!'

'He's going!' Catherine cried. 'I cannot hold him in. I cannot hold him. Ohhh!'

As she groaned, Alys saw the birth canal open, widen. She caught a glimpse of pale body and thought for a sudden moment of hope that the baby would be born whole, that she might even save it, that Catherine might have her dates all wrong and the baby was ready to be born.

'I see him!' she said. 'Let him come, Catherine, let him come. You are ready to give birth to him. Let him come!'

Catherine bore down, her stomach muscles fighting to push her baby out into the world. Alys slid her small skilled hands into the birth canal and gently gripped the tiny body inside. For a moment she felt the baby, small, well-formed; felt his rounded buttocks and a firm, muscled leg. Her hands slid over his perfect shoulder and felt his little arm, his hand clenched in a fist. He was slightly askew. Alys smiled through her concentration and felt upwards, along the warm, wet body to find the head, to guide him outwards, to bring him head outwards for his little journey. His shoulder was rounded and smooth to her touch. Alys' gentle hands went up to his rounded, hard skull and sensed the delicate shaping of his face.

Catherine groaned again as her muscles contracted. Alys slipped her hands away from the clamp of the muscles and then slid in again to turn and guide the little body. He was turning, he was coming right, head first into the world. She took either side of his skull in a gentle firm grip and pulled him towards her, out of the slippery tight canal of Catherine's body.

'Yes,' she said. 'I have him safe.'

Alys had forgotten that this was her rival, that this was Hugo's heir which would threaten her own safety, her own son. She was entranced by the desire to aid the birth. She was moving in the unconscious rhythm of all wise women who go deep into a mother to bring a baby out, safe, into the light. Alys pulsed with the baby, moved with Catherine, timed her touches and her tugs to the rhythm of the birth. 'He is coming!' she breathed excitedly. 'He is coming.'

The little body turned again, Alys reached deep inside Catherine, gripped the skull and the little shoulder and steadily, carefully, pulled.

With a sickening jolt her fingers broke through the soft crust of his skull and punctured his body, as soft as lye soap. An arm came away in her hand, a gout of liquid cascaded into her palm. Alys screamed with horror.

As she screamed, Catherine pressed downwards again and there was an explosion of white slime into Alys' face, hot and wet, in lumps against her mouth, her lips, her eyes, sticking to her hands, her hair, her dress.

'No! No! No!' Alys screamed, batting both hands against the horror of Catherine's bed. 'No!'

Again and again Catherine pressed down and lump after lump of the white foam was voided from her body until the sheets were covered with the mess of it and the room stank of tallow.

'It's wax!' Alys said in utter horror. 'Oh my God, it's candlewax!'

She backed against the window, her hands caked with wax, hiding her face, where little blobs of wax were drying hard on her skin. 'Oh my God, oh my God,' she said over and over again. 'It's wax. It's candlewax.'

Catherine gave one last groan and then lay still.

'My God! It's candlewax!' Alys repeated till the words lost their meaning and became nothing more than a howl of horror. 'Candlewax! Candlewax! Candlewax!'

Alys picked at her face, scratching the drying spots off her skin, shuddering at the wax under her fingernails. She scratched at the backs of her hands, at her palms. She was coated in the stuff. 'I'll never be clean,' she said in the high sharp tones of uncontrollable hysteria. 'Candlewax! I'll never get it off!'

Catherine lay on her back, deaf to Alys' insane whimperings. Her body had expelled its muck and she was exhausted and empty. It was long moments before she moved and then she put up her hand and patted her belly, disbelievingly. It had lost its shape. It was still fat, fleshy and loose; but it no longer jutted proud. Her baby was gone. She pushed herself slowly, laboriously, up the bed to rest on the pillows and looked down at the mess on the sheets and at Alys, backed against the wall, hair and face drenched in candlewax, her eyes black with horror, her hands feverishly picking, picking, picking – at her skin, her hair, her dress.

'What is this?' Catherine asked, her voice thin with horror. 'What is this stuff? What has happened to me?'

Alys swallowed and gagged, swallowed again. She looked down disbelievingly at her working hands and stilled them with an effort. She took a deep breath. 'You have no baby,' she finally croaked. 'Your baby has gone.'

Catherine leaned forward and pushed a finger into one of the white gobbets. 'My baby was this?' she asked.

Alys shook her head. 'It never was a baby, not a flesh and blood baby,' she said. 'This is wax from your body. There never was a real baby at all.' Her voice broke into a little shriek at the end, and she clapped a hand over her mouth to still the noise. 'Just a flux,' she said softly. 'Not a baby.'

Catherine's face was gaunt. 'No baby?' she asked. 'No son for Hugo?'

Alys shook her head, not trusting her voice.

The two women stared at each other for a moment, silenced with horror.

'Don't tell him,' Catherine said. Her voice was cracked, near madness. 'Don't tell him that it was like this.'

Alys found she was rubbing her hands together. The wax clotted into strips as she rubbed, and dropped away like dried skin. 'Damn it,' she said. 'Damn the stuff!'

'Don't tell anyone it was like this,' Catherine said again, with more urgency. 'Tell them it was a miscarriage. I don't want anyone to know about this. I don't want anyone to know of this . . . this horror!'

Alys nodded slowly in silence.

'If they know about this . . .' Catherine broke off. Her eyes searched Alys' downcast, horrified face. 'If they knew about this they would get rid of me,' she said, very low. 'They would say I am – unnatural.'

Alys was wringing her hands, rubbing the foul wax away. It had clogged between her fingers. With quick, nervous movements she was picking at her fingernails.

Catherine stared at her. 'How could such a thing be?' she demanded. 'Alys? You have seen many births. How could such a thing happen?'

Alys paused. The memory of the Catherine doll made of wax, with its round belly made of wax, and the little lumps of candlewax she had moulded to shape the roundness of the belly was very vivid in her mind. She had coupled the wax doll of Catherine with the gross wax penis of the Hugo doll. She had commanded the doll, telling it that the baby would be the image of his father, his candlewax father. Morach's warning that 'sometimes they misunderstand' surfaced in her memory.

'I don't know,' she said, her instinct to save herself conquering her terror. 'It must be some vile illness in you. It must be some corruption in your body. You are sterile and all you can conceive and all you can void is this muck.'

Catherine barely flinched, she was so deep in horror. 'My fault,' she said slowly as if she were learning a lesson almost beyond her understanding. 'Something wrong inside me.'

'Yes,' Alys said, careless of Catherine's foundering shame.

They were silent again.

'Hide it,' Catherine said. 'I want no one to know.' She glanced towards the fire. 'Burn it.'

Alys nodded. Catherine dragged herself up from the bed, gasping with the effort, and the two women pulled out the lower sheet, ripped it into half and then ripped it again. Each piece they rolled up and put on the little fire. It smouldered darkly, and when the wax caught fire it flickered and spat, burning with an ominous yellow flame. The smoke smelled like a tannery.

'Your hair,' Catherine said, her voice shaky. 'And your face.'

Carefully she picked the wax out of Alys' hair. Alys rubbed at the skin of her face until it was free of the little white scabs. She shuddered as she picked them off her skin.

'Your gown,' Catherine said.

Alys' red sleeves were white to the elbows with the stuff, the front of her gown was spattered with white dots. Alys stood while Catherine undid her gown and then she stepped out of it. From Catherine's chest she took an old gown which Catherine had not worn since her pregnancy. Catherine laced her into it silently. Alys took a clean sheet from where it was airing by the fire and made up the bed.

'They'll have to come in and see you,' she said.

Catherine nodded. 'They'll ask for the body,' she warned.

Alys nodded. She took a bowl and poured in a little water, tore up a napkin and tied it into little knots, tossed in half a cup of red wine and threw the rest on the bed. It spread in a deep red stain. Then she covered the bowl with a cloth from the table. 'No one will look too close at that,' she said. 'You may get away with it.'

Catherine had gone a sickly yellow colour. 'I feel faint,' she said.

Alys nodded. 'See them, and then you can rest,' she said with scant sympathy. 'How do you think *I* feel? I am ready to vomit.' She went to open the door.

'Alys,' Catherine stopped her. Alys turned.

'Swear you will never tell anyone. Never anyone!' Catherine demanded.

Alys nodded.

'Especially not Hugo,' Catherine said. 'Swear to me that you will never tell Hugo that I had . . .' she broke off. 'That I had a monster inside me,' she finished.

Alys' face was hard. 'He will have to know that you cannot conceive,' she said tightly.

Catherine paused. She looked at Alys at if she was seeing her for the first time, reading the coldness of Alys' grim face.

'Yes,' Catherine said slowly.

'I won't tell him that it was monstrous,' she said. 'He will never know from me that you voided lumps of white clay. Smelly lumps of clay.'

Catherine dropped her eyes. 'I am ashamed,' she said, very low.

Alys looked at her without pity. 'I will keep your secret,' she said. 'I won't tell him about that.' She paused for Catherine's reply. When none came she slipped out of the door.

Hugo was waiting nearest the door but at Alys' entrance everyone in the crowded gallery stopped talking and looked towards her. The old lord and David came towards her at once. Alys clasped her hands together and looked down.

'My lord,' she said. 'Lord Hugo. I have some very sad news. The Lady Catherine has been brought to bed too early and she has lost the child.'

There was a buzz of conversation and comment. Hugo's eyes burned into Alys' face, his father was as black as thunder.

'She is able to see you,' Alys said to Hugo. She met his look with one of infinite tenderness. 'I am so sorry, Hugo,' she said. 'There was nothing anyone could do for Catherine. She was too sterile and sickly from the start.'

He pushed past her and went into Catherine's room. The old lord came up and took Alys by the sleeve.

'What caused the miscarriage?' he demanded. 'She came down to supper yesterday, did she overtax her strength?'

Alys leaned her mouth towards his ear. 'The child would have been malformed,' she said. 'It's as well it is gone.'

The old lord looked as if he had been struck. 'God, no!' he said. 'No! A filthy cripple from my stock! And after all these years of waiting!'

'Can she have another?' David the steward pressed close to Alys. 'In your opinion, Mistress Alys? Will Lady Catherine conceive again?'

Alys met his gaze. 'I think not,' she said. 'You should summon a physician perhaps to judge. But in my mind I am certain. She can conceive no normal child.'

The old lord slumped down into a chair, rested both his hands on his cane and gazed into the distance.

'This is a bitter blow, Alys,' he said softly. 'A bitter blow. Catherine's baby gone, and her chances of another. All in one afternoon. A bitter blow.'

Catherine's door opened again and Hugo came out. His face was set. The line between his eyebrows was deep, his mouth grim. 'She'll rest now,' he said. 'Someone go and sit with her.'

Eliza and Ruth dipped a curtsey and slipped into the room.

'She said she'd see you, Sir,' Hugo said to his father. 'She wanted to ask your blessing.'

'Blessing be damned,' the old lord said, struggling to his feet and thumping his cane on the floor. 'I'll not see her. She's barren, my son! And she's wasted more years in this castle than I care to count. I'll see her when she's fertile. No point sitting by the sick bed of a barren woman. No point in a barren woman! Twenty-three bastards I sired, to my knowledge; and three legitimate children, one son. I've never looked twice at a barren woman by my knowledge, and I never will.'

He snapped his fingers for the page to open the door and stamped towards it. The people in the chamber drew back to let him pass, fearful of his rage.

'You,' he said, pointing to Alys. 'Come to my room! I've got work to do!' Then, as Alys moved towards him, her belly thrust forward against the flowing lines of the gown, he checked himself. 'No, ' he said. 'I had forgotten. Go and rest yourself. Go and sit down and sew or sing or something. But keep yourself well, Alys.

'David! Pick her out a maid to do her fetching and her carrying for her. And see she has a comfortable chair in her room. She must rest. She must rest. She must stay well. She's carrying Hugo's child. And see that she has what she fancies to eat. Get her whatever she wants! Anything that she wants she must have!'

David bowed, his quick, sharp smile raking Alys. 'Yes, my lord,' he said.

The old lord nodded. 'Keep her safe,' he said. 'No more riding out for you, Alys, you must stay home in safety.' He looked at Hugo. 'Don't let her get as fat as the other one,' he said. 'That was the problem there. Keep her like you would a good brood mare, well-fed but not gluttonous. She's to sit beside me at table every night so I can see what she eats.'

Hugo nodded, unsmiling. 'As you wish, Sir,' he said coldly. 'I am taking my horse out for a while. I am sick to my soul of these women's doings.'

The old lord nodded. 'Damn right,' he said irritably. 'All that talk and all that expense and then a barren sow at the end of it.'

The two of them left the room, Hugo clattering loudly down the stairs and shouting for his horse. Slowly, the serving-women and men and the off-duty soldiers and the pages straggled from the room, whispering as they left, whispering slander, scandal, ill-willed rumours. Alys stood in the centre of the room, unmoving. As everyone went out they dipped a low curtsey or a bow to her. Alys did not smile, did not acknowledge the homage beyond a curt nod of her head. Then David and Alys were alone.

'Is there anything you would order for supper tonight, Mistress Alys?' David asked slyly.

'I will have the best,' Alys said simply. 'I will have the best of whatever there is,' she said. 'The very best of whatever there is.'

Twenty-six

Catherine woke in the night screaming and only Alys could soothe her. She was sweating from her nightmare and from a fever. Alys gave her a little of the dried berries of deadly nightshade and watched her till she fell asleep. Three times Catherine's nightmares woke her – and all the ladies. Three times a waiting-woman came and knocked on Alys' door and said that Lady Catherine was crying and carrying on and she must have Alys with her. The third time Alys gave her a fat pinch of sleeping powder in a cup of brandy-wine and left her on her back, snoring.

In the morning Catherine was quiet and drugged. Hugo called in at her chamber. She held out her arms to him with the tears running down her fat face.

'You must excuse me, Madam,' he said coldly. 'You have not been churched.'

Catherine gave a gasp of disbelief and looked at his face. He was without pity.

'Hugo!' she exclaimed. 'I am so grieved . . .'

He stepped back towards the door, keeping himself far from her as if she had the plague.

'You are unclean,' he said precisely. 'I may not touch you. Alys will assist you.'

'But I thought you did not believe in that . . .' Catherine wailed. Hugo bowed minimally and passed out through the door, ignoring her, ignoring Alys. Alys stepped back to let him pass and shut the door behind him with quiet satisfaction.

The old lord would not see Catherine at all, though

she asked for him. He said he was too busy to come to the ladies' gallery. When Catherine was fulfilling her duties as the lady of the castle she could see him whenever she chose. In the meantime, he had no skills in the sick-chamber and could not wait on her.

Catherine, fallen from favour with both lords, wept again, sluggish, warm tears which rolled down her face.

'They hate me because the baby died,' she whispered to Alys. 'They both hate me because the baby died.'

Alys persuaded Catherine to eat some breakfast and sit up in bed and comb her hair. She did as she was told, like a lumpish child. But they could not stop her weeping. All the time, the waxy ooze dripped from between her legs, staining the sheets, and slow, oily tears rolled down her cheeks. She did not sob, she did not moan. She sat quietly and did whatever they asked of her. But she could not stop her tears.

Alys sat with her until dinnertime and then went down to the great hall, leaving Ruth and Mistress Allingham to dine with Catherine in her chamber. She entered by the tapestry-covered door at the rear of the high table. As she let the curtain fall behind her and moved to her seat on the left hand of the old lord's chair she heard a ripple of approval from the men in the hall. Now she was the only woman carrying Hugo's child. She was the only hope for an heir. The women in the castle might fear her and resent her, and outside, in the shadow of the castle, they might talk sourly of witchcraft and the young lord hexed into madness and lust; but a son came before everything. Anything would be forgiven the woman who gave Hugo a son.

The old lord came in, his face grave, Hugo at his side. Alys stood behind her chair until they were seated and then took her place. She did not look at Hugo. She knew he was in a rage too deep to speak. She bent her head and broke her bread. Hugo would come round.

'I shall need you to write some letters this afternoon,' the old lord said. 'And you shall sit in my chamber and read to me.'

Alys inclined her head. 'Gladly, my lord,' she said.

He grunted. 'Not too tired are you?' he asked. 'Sleep well?'

'I had to attend Lady Catherine in the night,' Alys said, her voice neutral. 'She was weeping and asked for me. I was called to her three times.'

Lord Hugh waved his hand at David for the wine-server. 'Drink this,' he said gruffly to Alys. 'Drink deep. It'll give the baby good blood.'

He paused. 'That must stop,' he said abruptly. 'Running around after the barren woman is too tiring for you. It must stop. Catherine can weep on someone else's shoulder.

'Hugo?' Hugo raised his face from studying his hands clenched on the table before him. The old man nodded. 'You see to it. Tell Catherine she may not disturb Alys. Alys can't wait on her any longer. Alys must not get over-tired.'

Hugo nodded. 'As you wish, Sire.'

'Aye, you're sour,' the old lord said gently. 'It's not to be wondered at. Nine years waiting and then nothing. But I tell you what, my boy. Our wager still stands. If Alys gives you a son I'll give you a thousand pounds. One son is as good as another when there's no choice. You shall still have your fortune. How's that?'

'I thank you,' Hugo said. 'You are generous. But I wanted the money to finance the sailing of the ship. Alys' child will not be born until April. My friend will have found other, more eager backers by then.'

487

The old lord nodded, crumbled his bread thoughtfully. 'I have some ideas I'll broach with you later, Hugo,' he said. 'You may find you have the money in time. I have a plan or two still in mind.'

Hugo managed a cold, sulky smile. 'You are a great schemer,' he said.

The old lord nodded. 'Music!' he said sharply to David. 'And send for someone to make us laugh. We are sick with melancholy over nothing. A barren woman is a disaster for no one but herself. Get me the new wine, the Flemish wine, and send to Castleton for tumblers or jugglers or a bear, for God's sake. Even a cockfight if there's nothing else to be had! I won't mourn for Catherine. I have new plans! Find someone to make me laugh!'

David nodded and snapped his fingers to one of the pages. He tossed a silver coin high into the air and the lad leaped for it and snatched at it and raced from the hall, the dogs barking and snapping at his heels at the sudden excitement. Half a dozen men scrambled from the benches and fetched their instruments, started to tune them discordantly and cursed each other in their hurry. Then they started to play and the serving-wenches got up to dance, a circle dance, an old village dance. Alys, remembering the music from her childhood, watched them, her foot tapping.

'Dance with them!' the old lord said. 'Take the ladies and dance with them!'

Alys flashed him a smile and beckoned to Eliza and Margery. They broached the circle and then joined in. One of the girls danced in the middle while the others circled her, then she chose a partner and they led the others around in pairs, then the second girl danced alone in the centre of the circle. The girls arched their necks and tossed their heads, conscious of the watching men. They stamped their feet in time to the music and when they took the long sweeping steps around the circle they put their hands on their hips and swayed seductively. Alys, her fair hair flying, danced with one eye on Hugo. When it was her turn in the centre of the circle she danced and bobbed with her head held up, her colour high, and the proud curve of her belly thrust forward. When he looked at her she smiled confidently at him.

He grinned, the blackness of mood lifted from him, the crease between his eyebrows vanished. With a word to his father he jumped down from the dais and broke into the circle. When the time came for Alys to choose a partner he stepped forward and there was a little ripple of applause. Following Hugo, the other men from around the hall stepped into the circle and danced too. The circle grew too wide for the space between the tables and broke into two circles, then four. The music grew louder and more insistent, the beat of the tambour more and more compelling. Alys, in her green gown, whirled in a spell of triumphant sensuality, Hugo leaping and dancing around her. When the music stopped in a cascade of bells she fell into his arms and he swept her off her feet and up to the dais.

Catherine, in her chamber above the hall, heard the music, the laughter, the shouts of applause for Alys, and the joyful thud of dancing feet. Sitting alone in her great bed with her dinner untasted before her she listened, while the fat tears rolled down her cheeks.

The old lord had a swathe of letters for Alys to write in the afternoon. She sat at the little table in the window, in her green gown with a green French hood covering her hair, a green shawl around her shoulders.

'You are like a hayfield in springtime,' the old lord said. 'I like watching you, Alys.'

She smiled at him, saying nothing.

'Now to work,' he said briskly. He sat erect in his chair, one hand outstretched leaning on his cane. Without looking at Alys he reeled off a list of the men who were to receive his letters. Alys, dipping her quill into the inkpot, wrote as fast and as clearly as she could.

She forced herself to keep writing at the rapid speed of the old lord's speech. She forced herself to keep translating his curt, idiomatic English into classical Latin. She forced herself to keep her head down, to play the part of the loyal clerk, the doltish scribe; while Lord Hugh begged support from all of his friends currently holding high places in the King's court for his son's forthcoming divorce from his wife on the grounds of her being too close kin.

Six letters the old lord dictated, then he broke off.

'Father Stephen will have to write the letter to the Supreme Court,' he said. 'He will know how it has to be framed, the way the rhetoric has to be done, all of that clerkish nonsense.'

'Will he do it?' Alys asked doubtfully.

Lord Hugh shot her a wicked grin. 'He has no choice, my dear. He is in my hands. I have given him, free of any charge, all the benefices in my lands. He is a worldly man, an ambitious man, as well as a fervent churchman. He has hitched his star to my Hugo, they are two of a kind. Hugo's rise will carry him upward as well. He knows the price – he is my man at the church courts.'

'And what will happen to Catherine?' Alys asked, her voice soft.

Lord Hugh shrugged. 'Lord knows,' he said carelessly. 'If it were the old days she could have gone into a nunnery. Now I don't know. She has no family to speak of. I suppose I might find someone to marry her. A widower with sons already who can afford a barren wife might do. She's a personable enough woman, and warm in bed, Hugo says. I'll give some of her dowry back. Or I could give her a little household somewhere in my lands. She could take a couple of her women and some servants.' He nodded. 'As she wishes. She'll be free to do as she pleases. If she does not stand against me she'll find me generous.'

'Does Hugo know of this?' Alys asked.

The old lord shook his head. 'No; and he's not to know it from you either, my pretty wench. I'll tell him when I get my replies. If they're favourable we'll go ahead with this plan. Take these letters to David for me and tell him they're to be delivered at once. The messengers are to wait for the reply and come straight back. Tell him I'll give a silver shilling to every man who is prompt. And tell the messengers to neither eat nor drink within the city of London. There's plague in the town again, I don't want it brought back here.

'And then go and lie down. Rest. If Catherine calls you, tell her it is my wish that you rest in the afternoons.'

Alys nodded, gathered up the papers and left.

She had not forgotten Mother Hildebrande. At noon, as Alys had smoothed her hair, looking in the mirror before going down to dinner, it was Mother Hildebrande's stern face she saw. She saw her mother, standing in the doorway of the little cottage, shading her eyes against the sun, looking downriver, scanning the riverside path, waiting confidently for the daughter she had found again, certain that she would come, trusting the strict training, the habit of discipline, and – more than anything else – trusting the love which was between the two women. She would wait for an hour, her old legs and her tired back aching. The path would stay empty. She would be puzzled at first – Alys the novice nun had never been late for any lesson, never scuttled in after the others to chapel. Then she would be afraid for her daughter – fearing a fall from the horse, or an accident, or danger for Alys. Then she would turn slowly back into the damp cottage to sit by the empty fireplace and put her hands together and pray for the soul of Alys who had not come, though she was bound by every oath in the world to come; who had failed in her duty to her God, who had failed her mother, the only person left in the world who loved her.

Alys could see Mother Hildebrande in her imagination when she heard the ripple of pleasure at midday dinner as she had come through the door to the hall, with her belly thrust forward, to take Catherine's place. When her food was put before her, Alys had a sudden vision of Mother Hildebrande struggling with damp firewood in Morach's cottage, and the dry taste of stale bread left from yesterday. Alys was aware of her when Hugo's dark scowl lightened and he drained his glass and jumped down to dance; even when his hand slid down her spine and rounded over her buttocks and Alys stood still and leaned into his caress, her long eyelashes sweeping down to hide the pretended arousal in her eyes.

When she translated the letters, using the skills Mother Hildebrande had taught her, part of Alys' mind was still with the old woman. The sides of the river-banks were steep now the river was at its midsummer low – she would not be able to get water. When the bread from yesterday was gone there would be nothing to eat unless she climbed the hill and begged from passers-by on the road. Alys thought of the woman she had loved as a mother, with her hand held out to strangers and her quiet dignity insulted by pedlars.

Alys gave the letters and the instructions to David, making special emphasis of the danger of London's plague, and went to her own room, shut the door, kicked off her shoes and lay down on her bed. She gazed upwards at the green and yellow tester like a ceiling above her head, elaborate, luxurious, expensive. She knew, as she had known from the moment when she sat at Mother Hildebrande's feet on Morach's dank earth floor, that she would not go back to live in the little hovel by the river. Alys would never again feel the empty-bellied misery of the poor in winter. Alys would never again break the ice on the river to pull out a bucket of stormy brown water. Alys would never again break her fingernails and bruise her hands scrabbling in frozen earth for icy turnips. Not if she could control her fate.

'I can't go back,' Alys said aloud. 'I won't go back.'

She thought of her mother, the woman she had longed for, whose loss had grieved her every day, and she found that the deep wound of pain had gone, vanished. When she thought of Mother Hildebrande now it was with fear of her intrusion, it was with irritation, it was with anxiety. Mother Hildebrande was no longer a dead saint to be mourned. She was a lively threat.

'She should go away,' Alys said softly. 'She should go away to a proper nunnery. I would go with her if she would only go to a proper nunnery. Even now, even with Catherine being set aside and everyone recognizing

493

Hugo as my lover, and me as the mother of the heir; I would go with her if she went to a proper nunnery.'

Alys paused. She thought of the peace and deep pleasure of her girlhood as Mother Hildebrande's favourite in the abbey by the river. She thought of the quiet lessons in Latin and Greek, of her pleasure in learning so quickly; of being the best. She thought of the stillroom and the smell of the herbs and the tinctures. She thought of the herb garden and the raised beds and the stalky secret leaves of the herbs, of the smell of lavender when she rubbed it in her hands, of the feathery touch of sage, the tang of mint when she plucked a stalk and bit deeply.

Alys shook her head, still staring at the tester and the bed curtains, but seeing the little girl with the fair hair who longed for peace and plenty and who had loved the Mother Abbess who had given her both.

'No,' she said finally. 'No, I wouldn't. I wouldn't go with her, not even if she went to another abbey. That was the life of my girlhood, just as Morach was the life of my childhood. I will not go backwards to those old places. I am finished with them both. I wish they were both dead and gone.'

The door opened without knocking and Hugo came in.

'Resting like a lady, Alys?' he slurred, holding the door for support. He had stayed in the great hall after Alys and his father had left. The musicians had played on and on, the jugs of wine had gone around. The serving-wenches had come out from the kitchen and danced wildly. Hugo and the soldiers had drunk deep, shouting at the women, snatching one out of the circle and pulling her about. While Alys and the old lord had been working, writing and planning for the future,

Hugo had been playing in the hall. There was no work for Hugo. He was an idle child.

Alys raised herself on one hand. 'Your father ordered me to rest,' she said carefully.

Hugo levered himself from the doorway, shut the door, and came sideways into the room, his feet hastening to keep up with him.

'Oh yes,' he said nastily. 'You're his great favourite now, Alys, aren't you?'

Alys said nothing, measuring Hugo's drunkenness, judging his dampened-down anger.

'God knows why!' he exclaimed. 'Your damned country wise woman meddling lost me my child! Lost him his grandson! If we'd had a physician, a proper man who had studied and read these things, from York or from London, Catherine would still be carrying that child now! And I would get my money in the autumn, and have an heir to follow me.'

Alys shook her head. 'The baby was sick,' she said. 'It would never have gone full term whoever you had waiting for the birth.'

Hugo's dark eyes blazed at her. 'Wise woman nonsense,' he said roundly. 'You swore to me he was healthy. You swore to me it was a healthy boy. You are a liar and a cheat. And all the words you say to me are lies and cheats.'

Alys shook her head, but said nothing, watching his anger rise and curdle to malice.

'Get your gown off,' Hugo suddenly said.

Alys hesitated.

'You heard me,' Hugo snapped. 'Get your gown off. *My* gown, remember? The one that brought your tally of gowns up to Catherine's dozen. The one you begged for like a whore.'

Alys stood up and unfastened the gown, slipped it off, hung it carefully over the foot of the bed, opened the cold linen sheets and slid into bed, watching Hugo all the time.

Hugo undid his codpiece, untied his knitted hose, dragged them down. 'Here,' he said. 'Was it our romp that made Catherine lose the baby?'

Alys shook her head. 'No,' she said, hiding her apprehension of Hugo's temper. His sexuality, which had been in the palm of her hand, had escaped her. He had looked at the girl in the hayfield and desired her. He had taken Alys without her consent, and revelled in having her and Catherine at once, as if they were two of a kind: two slavish women. He had humbled Alys as if she were nothing more than his whore – a toy for Catherine. He had freed himself from Alys' dominance and now he could use her as he wished.

He clambered on the bed and kneeled over Alys. His breath was thick with wine and onions from dinner. He kissed her, kneading her breasts roughly with his hands. Alys felt her muscles tensing and the warm dampness between her legs drying and cooling.

'I took you like a whore then,' he said.

Alys closed her eyes and put her arms around his neck in a loveless charade of desire.

'You loved it,' Hugo said. 'All women are whores at heart. You, Catherine, the yellow-haired girl at haymaking. All whores.'

'I am not,' Alys asserted. 'I am carrying your child, I am the only woman who can carry your child. And I can enchant you, Hugo. Have you forgotten how you feel when my sisters come to me?'

Hugo shook his head. 'It's a wife I need, not a scheming witch,' he said angrily. 'It's a legitimate son I need, not a bastard child from a woman with no name, with no family. I don't know how to command my life any more. I look at Catherine and think how mad she is for me, and I look at you and think how mad I was for you. And it's all worthless. It's a mess. All the things I need escape me. All the things I truly want are forbidden me. All I can do is play mad games with you, and get a son on you who will be of no good to anyone, and serve nothing but my private pride.'

'You could command your life,' Alys said cautiously. Hugo was soft with drink, irritable. Alys felt him thrust against her ineffectually. His hand went down and he fumbled against Alys' cold refusing dryness.

'If Catherine were gone,' Alys said quickly, 'and I had a son, your son, and instead of thinking of me as a whore and trying to reduce me to your whore, you saw me as I am – a woman of great power. I need no family behind me, no name. I need bring no fortune with me. My skills and my power are all the dowry any man would desire. We could be married – just as I dreamed. And your house, your new and lovely house, would be our house, and our son's house. And we could live in the new way, as you wished, together.'

'And have more sons,' Hugo said with drunken enthusiasm. He thrust once more at her. Alys felt him, flabby and damp, against the tightly closed muscles of her body. She could smell him, the thick, clotted smell of his linen. Her teeth gritted with distaste.

'Yes, we could have more sons,' she said. 'You would be the sire of a line. Legitimate sons.'

'More sons than my father had! More sons than my grandfather had!' Hugo babbled. 'I am sick of what they are saying about me – that I cannot father a child. We'll marry and move to the new house and have a hundred sons.'

'Marry?' Alys asked softly, ready to spring a trap of a verbal betrothal on Hugo. A promise of marriage was the most binding promise of all, an honourable man could not withdraw. 'Do you ask me to marry you?'

'Hundreds of sons!' Hugo said, with a sudden swing to drunken cheeriness. 'Hundreds of them.'

'Shall we marry?' Alys whispered insidiously. 'Marry and have legitimate sons. Do you want to marry me, Hugo?'

For a moment she thought he would answer her, and she would have his word of honour and a chance to blackmail him with his own meticulous code. But he gave a sigh and pitched forward on his face, buried his way into the pillows and started snoring.

Alys slithered out from underneath him, threw a rug around her bare shoulders and pulled over a chair to the hearth. She watched the flames. 'Odin,' she said, thinking of the blank runes. 'Death of the old way and the birth of the new. The old lives have to die. The old precious loves have to make way. There has to be a death.'

A log shifted and flamed, its yellow light flickering into Alys' face making her look entranced, witchy. 'Death of the old ways,' she said again. 'There has to be a death.'

She sat in silence for a moment.

'A death,' she said softly. 'Not my death, not Hugo's, not the old lord's. But there has to be a death. The old loyalties must be changed. The old loves must die.'

She said nothing more for a long while but watched the flames in silence. Alys knew that the runes were foretelling a death – she hoped to buy them off with a symbolic death of her old love and her old loyalty. But in her most secret heart Alys knew that the runes would want blood.

'Not my blood,' she said softly.

When Hugo woke he was clear-headed and anxious to be off hunting. Alys helped him on with his doublet, patted the thick padded back and shoulders and pulled the rich silk lining through the slashings on the sleeves and chest. Even with the shadows under his eyes from the drink and the dark haze on his chin, Hugo looked very fine. Alys did not correct him when he assumed that he had made love to her. She walked with him to the door of the ladies' gallery and watched him run lightly down the stairs, then she nodded to Eliza sitting at the fire.

'Bring me Catherine's writing desk,' she said and took a stool with them. Mistress Allingham was sewing the long tapestry they had been working ever since Alys came to the castle. Catherine's mother and her women had started it, Catherine and her ladies had worked it. Alys fancied that she and her women would be working it long after Catherine had left the castle in disgrace. It was only a quarter completed. Idly Alys pulled out the folds and looked at the intricate bright colours of the design.

'Where are Ruth and Margery?' she asked.

'Gone out to the garden,' Mistress Allingham replied. 'Lady Catherine is sleeping, but she was asking for you after dinner.'

Alys shrugged. 'I was with Lord Hugh,' she said. 'Catherine cannot have me at her beck and call.'

Mistress Allingham raised her thin eyebrows but said nothing.

Eliza brought Catherine's ivory writing desk. A quill stood ready in the matching pot of ink, there were smooth sheets of paper and a short candle for the sealing wax, with some scraps of ribbon. Alys took it on to her lap with satisfaction, touched everything, smoothed the paper, brushed her fingertip against the feathers of the quill.

She took up the pen and wrote.

I am sending these things to you by messenger because I cannot come today as I intended. Lady Catherine at the castle is ill and I am commanded to care for her. For your safety and my own I will not endanger us nor bring us to their attention by insisting otherwise. I will come as soon as I can. Say nothing to the messenger. Send me no reply. I will come as soon as I can.

When she had finished writing she folded the paper three times and dripped sealing-wax in three puddles along the join, pressing the little seal into each one. The seal was a miniature version of Hugo's family crest, used by the ladies of his family for generations. Alys carefully drew an elegant 'A' underneath each seal and then let it dry.

'What are you writing?' Eliza asked, unable to contain her curiosity any longer.

'There is a new wise woman come to Morach's old cottage,' Alys said. 'I don't know who she is or where she comes from. But I am sending her some things. When my own time comes I shall need a wise woman to deliver my child. If she is skilled and good-natured I shall summon her.'

'The one at Richmond has a fine reputation for childbirth,' Mistress Allingham offered.

Alys nodded. 'Then I will send a gift to her too,' she said. 'It is well to be prepared.'

'It couldn't happen to you, could it?' Eliza nodded

towards Catherine's door where Catherine lay asleep in bed, tears sliding out from under her closed eyelids, her sheets soaked with white, creamy slurry.

Alys shook her head.

'They are saying that it is a weakness in Hugo,' Eliza volunteered. 'That he cannot get a woman with child and that if he does the child does not take.'

Mistress Allingham pursed her lips. 'This miscarriage is like none I have ever seen before,' she said. 'Lady Catherine does not bleed.'

Alys lowered her voice to match theirs. 'There is a corruption in her humours,' she said. 'Remember how the child was conceived. She is always too hot or too cold. I did what I could to bring her into balance but the child was conceived in heat and dryness and lost in damp and coldness. I can make Catherine well, but I cannot change her nature. No one can make her fertile. No one can make her clean.'

'Then he'll put her aside,' Eliza hissed, her face alert.

Alys nodded and put a finger across her lips.

The two women exchanged one bright look.

'And you carrying his child!' Eliza noted.

Alys smiled at her and got to her feet, shaking out the folds of the bright green gown. 'And you said I was falling,' she reminded Eliza. 'You were taunting me with falling low. You called me a whore.'

Eliza flushed red. 'I beg your pardon,' she said. 'I spoke wrongly to you, Alys . . . Mistress Alys. I spoke too freely, and I was mistaken.'

Alys nodded. She went to her chamber and took the old dark blue gown from her chest, the gown the old lord had given her from the leavings of his whore Meg. Alys shook out the folds. It would drape around Mother Hildebrande – she had grown so slight and stooped. But it was made of good thick wool and would keep her warm, even in that damp cottage. Alys folded it up and went downstairs through the deserted great hall, to the kitchen.

The place was quiet. The cooks and servers had slipped out to Castleton, to lie in the fields by the river, to visit friends, to carouse with the off-duty soldiers. The kitchen-lad was there, dozing by the spit he turned all day. There was a big cooked haunch of beef on the spit, left from dinner.

'Wake up,' Alys said peremptorily.

He was on his feet in a second, rubbing his eyes with one grimy hand. When he saw Alys he shrank back.

Alys smiled at him. 'I am sending some food to a wise woman on the moors, and a gown,' she said. 'You may take it for me. You may ride my mare out.'

The lad blinked.

'Put together a basket of everything you can find which is good to eat,' Alys said. 'A big cut off that joint, bread, fruit, some sweetmeats and a pitcher of wine.'

The lad hesitated.

'Go on,' Alys said. 'I will tell the cook I ordered it.'

He nodded and went to one of the beams where a dozen baskets were hanging. He lifted one down and went to a larder set against the cool outside wall of the castle.

Alys looked around her. The floor was strewn with herbs. Dried and old, they had not been changed for months. Some hens and a cockerel pecked around on the floor, their white and moss-coloured droppings marked the stone slabs. The fire on the other side of the room smouldered around a great trunk of pine. It would be stoked up for supper and then banked in

502

overnight. One side of the kitchen wall was a block of stone with half a dozen hollowed sinks for burning charcoal to scald sauces and heat little pans. Everything around it was covered with a light coating of black dust.

There were no locks on the cupboards. Every store-room was open, the flesh room, the fish room, the confectionery room. Even the ale cellar was open. Alys thought of Hugo's plan to move to his new house and cast off the free-living retainers, and saw something of the savings he would make.

'Get a jug of wine with a stopper,' she said. 'The best wine.'

The lad came out of the larder, the basket filled with food: half a round cheese, two loaves of bread, a cut of the meat, a bowl of early cherries, a thick slice of ham, a pot of almond paste with currants.

'There's a pot of bucknade,' he offered.

It was one of Mother Hildebrande's favourite dishes but she would not eat meat on a saint's day or a holy day. Alys could not remember the church calendar which had once been so familiar to her.

'No,' she said. 'Is there any blanche mange?'

Blanche mange was mashed chicken or rabbit, sweet-ened with honey and served with a pinch of sandalwood to make it pink. Mother Hildebrande would eat white meat on a fast day if they could get no fish. The lad nodded and went to the larder, filled a pewter bowl and came back into the main kitchen tying a coarse linen napkin over the mouth of the bowl.

He put the basket on the table and then went to the wine cellar for the wine. It was stored in huge casks, chocks hammered in underneath one end so the wine flowed downwards to the tap. Alys could hear the wine pouring into the jug, then the lad came back into the roasting kitchen, pushing the stopper home and wiping the jug on his smock. Alys took it from him, folded the gown around it to keep it safe in the basket and then led the way to the stables.

The simple lad was there, sprawled on a hay bale in the sunshine, picking his teeth with a straw.

'Put a saddle on my mare,' Alys said to him. 'This boy is doing an errand for me.'

He jumped to his feet and nodded, grinning and laughing at her.

'And see him through the gate,' Alys said. 'He is carrying those goods on my orders.'

She handed the letter to the spit-boy. 'Give this to the old woman,' she said. 'She will not harm you.' She paused for a moment, waited for him to feel her power. 'You may not speak with her,' she said slowly, impressively. 'If she speaks to you say nothing. Just shake your head. She will think you are mute. You may not say one word to her.'

The boy nodded. 'Not one word,' Alys said slowly, softly. 'And do not wander on the way or eat the food. I shall know if you deliver less than you set out with. I shall know if you have disobeyed me and spoken with her.'

He shook his head and gulped nervously.

'Do you know where the wise woman of Bowes Moor lives?' Alys asked. 'The cottage by the river, before you come to the stone bridge?'

The lad nodded.

'Take these goods there,' Alys said. She drew the letter out and tucked it down the side of the basket so it was completely hidden. 'This letter too. Don't show it to anyone and don't lose it. I shall know if you do.'

The lad nodded again.

Alys smiled at him. 'When you return this afternoon I shall give you a sixpence,' she said.

The boy looked at her.

'Yes?' Alys asked.

'Could I have instead a scrap of ribbon of yours?' he asked. 'Or something you don't need. An old kerchief?'

'Why?' Alys asked.

He dropped his gaze to the floor. 'To ward off beatings,' he said. 'In the kitchen they say that you have the power to get anything you want. That you can do anything you like. I thought if I had a relic of yours . . .'

Alys shook her head. 'I am just an ordinary woman,' she said. 'A healer with special skills, holy skills. Nothing of mine is a talisman. I am just a healer with holy powers. I do nothing for my own ends.'

The lads exchanged one secret, disbelieving look. Alys chose to ignore it.

'Be as quick as you can,' she said, walking from the stable yard. 'And send word to me when you are safe back.'

Twenty-seven

Despite Alys' careful instructions, Hildebrande sent a letter back with the kitchen-lad. It was written on coarse paper, the back of a bill from an inn with a stub of lead. It was unsealed. Alys' lips compressed when she saw it. Anyone could have read it on its journey to her and she would not even know. It was typical of Hildebrande to care nothing for their safety, she thought. The woman was mad for martyrdom, rushing towards exposure and danger. She had been so long out of the world she had no idea of the dangers, the peril she was forcing on Alys. Alys gave the lad the sixpence she had promised and tucked the letter into her sleeve. She went out into the herb garden to read it.

The warm evening sun gilded the enclosed garden. Surrounded by the castle walls, the garden was sheltered from wind, a trap for heat. Drowsy bees stumbled from plant to plant. Alys walked down the narrow paths, her green gown brushing against the herbs, releasing their scent. Ahead of her, in the flower garden, Ruth and Margery were sitting in the shade of a bower. They glanced towards Alys but did not approach her. The bakehouse to Alys' left was quiet and cold. The old round prison tower behind it was silent. Alys perched on the walled edge of a bed of mint and let the sun beat down on her uncovered head. The purple flowers sweated their scent into the still air. In the orchard beyond the flower garden there were birds singing piercingly sweet. Beyond the orchard, in the outer manse, a horse whinnied in greeting.

Alys slid the letter from her sleeve, and spread it on her knees to read.

'Dear Daughter in Christ,' Hildebrande had begun, incriminating Alys in the first three words. Alys glanced around. There was no one near. She tore off the top of the letter before even looking at the rest, scrumpled it in her hands, pushing her sharp fingernails through the soft paper, shredding it as she stuffed every scrap into her purse.

I do not discuss with you the reasons for your delay. There can be no reasons for delay when the will of the Lord is plain to us. Tell Lady Catherine to be of good heart and trust in Our Lady who knows her pains well. You may visit her later and care for her. I expect you this evening.

There was a gap in the writing, then, in a more rounded hand as if the mother was speaking to her daughter, not the abbess to a disobedient nun, the letter went on:

Please come at once, Ann. I am fearful not for myself, though I am weary and I cannot light the fire or draw water, I am fearful for you. What are you doing in that castle which makes you so slow to obey?

'I *knew* she would not know how to light the fire,' Alys said irritably. She smoothed the letter out on her lap. In the sunlight of the garden, Hildebrande aching with arthritis, struggling with a tinderbox, too frail and too old to lug a bucket of water up to the cottage from the steep river-bank, seemed a long way away.

Alys scrunched the paper into a ball in her hand and thrust it into her purse to burn later, then she stretched out her legs before her. The green gown fell elegantly around her. Alys turned her face up to the sunlight and closed her eyes.

'You will turn brown, Mistress Alys, brown as a peasant,' a voice said softly.

Alys opened her eyes. David the steward stood before her, at his side was a young woman of about sixteen. She was fair, golden-headed; her hair brighter than Alys', her eyes a lighter, more sparkling blue. Her body was full; Alys noticed the tightness of the bodice over her firm young breasts and the shortness of the skirt of her gown as if she were still growing.

'This is Mary,' David said, gesturing to the girl. 'She is to be your maid, as Lord Hugh ordered.'

Alys nodded, staring at the girl. The girl looked back, taking in every inch of Alys' gown, her long golden-brown hair, her green hood.

'Has she been in service long?' Alys asked coldly.

'All her life,' David said promptly. 'She was serving in a tradesman's house in Castleton. She caught my eye because she is bright and quick. I thought she would suit you. I didn't want one of the drabs from the kitchen to wait on you. They are as slow as oxen and as dull.'

Alys nodded again.

'You're very pretty,' she said to the girl; she made it sound like an insult. 'How old are you?'

'Sixteen, my lady,' the girl answered.

'You call her Mistress Alys,' David corrected sharply. 'Mistress Alys is not the lady of the castle. She is Lady Catherine's woman only.'

Alys gave David a look which would scratch glass. 'Since she is to be my maid I suppose she can call me what she pleases, as long as it pleases me.'

The dwarf shrugged his strong shoulders. 'As you wish, Mistress Alys.'

'Are you betrothed or married?' Alys asked the girl.

'No, my lady,' she said breathlessly. 'I am a virgin.'

Alys shot a hard, suspicious look at David. He smiled blandly at her.

'You can wait in the ladies' gallery until I send for you,' Alys said abruptly. The girl dipped a curtsey and went into the castle.

David remained. He took a pinch of lavender and sniffed it, savouring the smell, demonstrating his ease and comfort.

'She is very beautiful for a peasant girl,' Alys observed.

'Yes, indeed,' David replied.

'Very like the girl in the field who took Hugo's flowers at haymaking.'

'Her sister, actually,' David said. He squinted up at the blue sky. 'Very like her, now I come to think of it,' he said thoughtfully.

Alys nodded. 'Do you think to supplant me with some plump sweeting, David? Do you think Hugo would put me aside for a sudden fancy, when I carry his child and he has been besotted with me for months?'

David opened his eyes in amazement. 'Of course not, Mistress Alys! I merely obeyed Lord Hugo. He said you should have a maid of your own, my task it was to find you one. If she is not to your liking I can send her away. I will tell the young lord that the maid I suggested was too pretty for your liking, and I will find some plain old woman. It is no trouble at all.'

'It is no matter,' Alys said abruptly. 'I am not afraid, David. You can bring a hundred such as her and throw them into Hugo's path. They will not conceive his child.

They will not take my place. They may amuse him but they will not sit at the high table. D'you think the old lord will prefer a village wench to me?' She laughed sharply, enjoying the small man's angry face. 'I will employ the girl. She can do my sewing for me and run errands.'

'Up to Bowes Moor perhaps?' David asked quickly. 'To see the new arrival there? Another wise woman, in your old cottage. Who is she, Alys? Another kinswoman who is no kin at all? Or Morach returned from the dead?'

'Hardly a ghost!' Alys said, swiftly recovering from the change of tack. 'No, it is a travelling wise woman who has a fancy to stay at the cottage. I sent her some goods and a message because I shall need a wise woman in the spring, when my time comes. Either she or the one at Richmond will have to come out to me.'

'I see.' David turned to go. Alys breathed out in relief at having come through his questioning so well.

'And why should the kitchen-boy pretend to be mute?' David asked. 'Why could he not speak to her? Does she know secrets that she might share if someone asked her?'

Alys laughed aloud, a note as blithe as the birdsong from the orchard. 'Oh, the silly lad!' she exclaimed. 'I ordered him not to tire her with his chatter, nor eat the food on the way, nor stop to play with his friends. And next thing he thinks he has to act like one struck dumb! I wish I had been there to see him acting like a mute simpleton!'

David smiled thinly. 'He is a fool that boy.' He nodded his head to Alys and left her. Alys watched him go, her face stiff with her unconcerned smile until he was gone.

The sun was burning on her back. Alys felt flushed, her thick mane of hair made her neck and her head hot. She was sweating. Her green gown was strapped too tight, the stomacher too stiff. She went indoors for the cool and the shade. As she climbed the stairs to the ladies' gallery she felt a deep weight of pain in her head and the skin behind her ears tightened on her skull like pincers.

Mary was in Alys' bedchamber, straightening the counterpane on the bed, gawking out of the window.

'Everything so fine, my lady!' she exclaimed as Alys came in. 'So fine and so pretty!'

'Unlace me,' Alys said, turning around. The girl unfastened the stomacher and then the gown and caught them as Alys slid them off and let them fall. 'I have a headache,' Alys said. 'Close the shutters over the window and go and sit in the ladies' gallery. I want to be alone. Call me an hour before supper.'

'I'll put your gown away,' Mary said. She took the green gown and moved towards the chest of Alys' herbs and oils.

'Not that one,' Alys said sharply. 'I am a herbalist, a healer. I keep all my medicines in there. You must never go to that chest. You must never touch it. Some of the tinctures are very delicate and they would spoil if anyone but me touched them. The other chest is for my clothes.'

The girl bobbed a curtsey and folded Alys' gown carefully into the chest. She shut it with a bang. 'Sorry, my lady,' she said.

Alys lay back on the pillows and closed her eyes.

'I was told to tell you that Lady Catherine wanted to see you,' the girl suddenly said. 'I forgot to tell you at once.'

'Tell her I have a headache and I am resting,' Alys said, without opening her eyes. 'I will come to her at suppertime.'

Mary bobbed another curtsey and went out. The draught from the open windows of the gallery caught the door and banged it shut. Alys winced. Through the door she could hear Mary speaking to Eliza.

'My Lady Alys is lying down,' she said. 'She will see Lady Catherine at suppertime.'

Even in her pain Alys smiled. 'My Lady Alys,' she said to herself. 'My Lady Alys.' Alys knew she had to see Hildebrande. She could not trust anyone in the castle with messages – David's information was too precise, too accurate. He knew everything that went on within the castle and without. She dared not send another message, she could trust no one. And Hildebrande, the fool, was as capable of sending a verbal command as an unsealed letter. She sat by the old lord at supper and picked at the food on her plate.

'You are not eating, Alys,' he said at once. 'Are you unwell?'

Alys summoned a smile. 'A little sickly, my lord,' she said. 'And I have run out of the powders I need.'

'Someone shall get you whatever you need,' he said. 'They can get them immediately. It is bad for the baby if the mother does not eat. You shall have whatever you want.'

Alys shook her head. 'I need some powdered bark from an elm tree,' she said. 'It's a special tree I know. I could not direct anyone to it; it grows in a copse by the river at the foot of the moor. There must be a dozen elm trees there. Only I know which one I use.'

'Do you wish to go out there?' the old lord asked. 'I would send you in a litter. It is not safe for you to ride.'

'I would do well on a mule,' Alys said. 'I would not fall, and I would not do more than a walk. No harm could come to me or the child. And I do indeed need the powders.'

'A couple of the men-at-arms shall go with you,' Lord Hugh decided. 'And your new maid. David said he has brought you a bonny wench who was anxious to serve you. You could go tomorrow morning and be back by dinner.'

'Yes,' Alys said. 'Or we could take our dinner with us. It should be fine again tomorrow, and then I will not have to hurry. I do not want to have to trot or canter.'

'No, no,' the old lord said hastily. 'Take all day if you wish, Alys, as long as you are safe. Stay out of the bright sunlight and take care that you do not overtire yourself.'

'Very well,' Alys said agreeably. 'As you desire, my lord.'

Hugo did not come to the ladies' gallery nor to Alys' room that night. Mary, the new maid, slept in Alys' room on a little truckle bed which rolled out on wooden wheels from underneath the big bed. Alys lay in the darkness listening to Mary's steady breathing with rising irritation. At midnight she shook her awake and told her to go and bed down in the gallery. 'I cannot sleep with you in the room.'

'Very well, my lady,' the girl said. Her fair hair was tousled into ringlets, her cheeks rosy. She blinked owlishly at Alys, still half asleep. Her shift, open at the neck, showed the inviting curves of her breasts.

'Go,' Alys said irritably. 'I shall not sleep until I am alone.'

'I'm very sorry, my lady,' Mary said. She went as quietly from the room as she could, picking her way in the darkness. She closed Alys' door with silent care and then clattered into a stool in the gallery. Then there was silence. Alys rolled over and slept for the rest of the night.

In the morning she ordered Mary to bring her ale and bread and cheese, and ate it sitting up alone in the great bed. She told Mary to pour hot water into a ewer and bring it to her, and to warm a bath sheet before the fire for Alys to dry herself. Mary went to the chest of gowns.

'The brown gown,' Alys said. 'And the black stomacher and the black gable hood.'

When she was dressed she looked at herself in the hand-mirror. The stomacher flattened her belly and her breasts into one smooth board. Hildebrande would not see the curve of her pregnancy. The old-fashioned gable hood rested low on her forehead at the front and covered her hair completely at the back. The brown gown was a rich, warm russet, elegantly cut – but as unlike the cherry-red gown of Meg the whore as any Alys owned.

'Can you ride?' she asked Mary as they came down the stairs.

Mary nodded. 'My father once owned a little farm,' she said. 'He kept many horses. He bred them for the gentry.'

'Does he have it no longer?' Alys asked, leading the way through the inner gate, across the drawbridge, and across the other manse to the stables.

Mary shook her head. 'They were lands belonging to the abbey,' she said. 'When the abbey was wrecked the land was bought from the King by my Lord Hugh. The rents were too high for us, we had to leave.'

'What does your father do now?' Alys asked idly.

Mary shook her head. 'The loss of his farm was like death to him,' she said. 'He does a few jobs – shearing in summer, haymaking. Digging in winter. Most of the time he is idle. They live very poor.'

'You can ride my pony,' Alys said. 'I'll take a mule. We can swap when we are out of sight of the castle. Lord Hugh worries too much about my safety.'

Mary nodded, and the stable-lad led the horses out. She mounted easily, shaking out the skirts of her grey gown with as much grace as if she were noble enough to wear colours. The lad whistled at her and Mary tossed back her blonde ringlets and smiled at him. Alys was lifted to the mule's back and kicked the animal into a walk.

Two men-at-arms joined them as they passed through the gateway into Castleton. One walked before them, one behind.

They went briskly over the bridge and up the hill. The sun was bright on the straight, pale road before them, it would be another hot day. Alys, feeling the weight of the gable hood and the heat of the cloth on her neck, looked enviously at Mary who sat easily and confidently on the mare, looking all around her at the rye turning yellow in the fields, and the pale green of the wheat.

'Harvest soon,' she said pleasantly. 'It's been a good year for grains. And it'll be a good autumn for fruit, my father says.'

'Pull up, ' Alys said abruptly. 'I'll ride my own horse now.'

Mary stopped and the soldiers helped the two women exchange mounts. They rode on in silence as the road climbed higher and higher and the fields gave way to

rough pasture land – good for nothing except sheep –
and then they were out in the thick heather-purple haze
of the open moorland. The hills around them stretched
forever into the distance, the sky above them arched
like a massive bowl of blue. Larks spiralled upwards,
singing and singing. Over a cliff face on the right-hand
side, broad-winged buzzards hung effortlessly on the
warm air. Higher still above them was a circling dot in
the sky, a golden eagle.

The river was gone, hidden underground as if it had
secrets too dark for the sunshine. The hard, white
limestone river bed threw back the light of the sun in a
stony glare. Alys was glad when they rode into the
green shadow of the coppice.

'You can sit here and eat your dinners,' she said to
the three of them. 'I am going deeper into the wood for
the bark of a special tree. Wait here for me. I may be
some time, I will have to find the best tree and cut the
bark. Don't come searching for me, I shall be perfectly
safe and I don't want to be disturbed.'

The two soldiers hesitated. 'Lord Hugh said to keep
you safe,' one of them objected.

Alys smiled at him. 'What could harm me here?' she
asked. 'There is no one on the road and no one in this
wood. I was brought up here, I know these parts better
than anyone. I shall be safe. I shall not be far. I shall
hardly go out of earshot. Rest here until I return.'

She rode down the slope, her mare stepping carefully
over the roots in the path, and drew rein when she was
out of sight. She waited for long moments. No one was
following. Alys turned the horse's head upstream and
kicked her into a trot and then into a canter along the
grassy bank of the river and up to Morach's cottage.

Mother Hildebrande was sitting in the doorway, her

tired old face turned to the sun as if she were soaking in the warmth. She opened her eyes when she heard the noise of the pony and stood up, hauling herself up the frame of the door.

Alys dismounted, tied the pony to the hawthorn bush, and stepped over the sheep stile.

'Mother,' she said. She glanced around swiftly. The open moorland all around the cottage was bare and empty. Alys knelt on the threshold and Mother Hildebrande rested her trembly hand on Alys' head and blessed her.

'You are come at last, daughter,' Mother Hildebrande said.

Alys stood up. There was determination in the old woman's eyes.

'I cannot stay,' Alys said gently. 'Not yet. That is what I came to tell you.'

The old woman eased herself down on the stool at the doorstep. Alys sat at her feet. Mother Hildebrande said nothing. She waited.

'*I* am not unwilling,' Alys said persuasively. 'But Lady Catherine is ill, near to death, and no one there can care for her. She has miscarried her child and is scouring with a dreadful white fluid which they say is a curse upon her and upon Lord Hugh's house for the sacrilege of destroying our nunnery. A holy woman is needed there. She needs me to protect her from fear. No one knows what to do. She is mortally afraid and for no fault of her own. I cannot believe that our merciful Lord would want me to abandon her. And anyway, they would not let me go. Even now I am only released from the castle to fetch some herbs and some elm bark for her.'

Mother Hildebrande said nothing. She sat very still,

watching Alys' clear profile as Alys sat at her feet, leaned back against her knees as she always used to sit – and lied.

'The old lord is tender with my beliefs,' Alys said urgently. 'He does not care which faith he follows. But his son is a Protestant, an unbeliever. It was he who wrecked our abbey, and now he is turning his attention to every religious house for miles around. His father is Sheriff of the County but it is Hugo who rides out and does the King's sacrilege. He believes in nothing, he trusts nothing. He hates the true faith and he captures and imprisons believers. If he knew you were here – the Mother of an Order he had wrecked – he would hunt you down and hurt you until you were driven to deny your faith.'

Mother Hildebrande looked at her steadily. 'I do not fear him,' she said gently. 'I fear nothing.'

'But what good does it do?' Alys demanded passionately. 'What good does it do to risk danger, when with a little care and caution and delay you could get away to safety? Isn't *that* the Lord's work? To get to safety so that you can live according to His laws again?'

Mother Hildebrande shook her head. 'No, Sister Ann,' she said. 'Saving your own skin is not the Lord's work. You are speaking with the persuasive voice of the world. You are speaking of clever practice and winning by deceit. The way we are promised is not that way. The Lord's work is to proclaim Him in words and to demonstrate Him in our lives. I have never been skilled with words, I have never been a clever woman; but I can be a wise woman. I can be a woman who can show by her life a lesson which a more learned woman would write in a book. I cannot argue truths – but I can demonstrate them. I can live my life, and die my death, as if there were some things which matter more than clinging to goods and staving off death.'

'It is not wise to die!' Alys exclaimed.

Mother Hildebrande laughed gently, the dry old skin of her face wrinkling easily with her smile. 'Then all men are fools!' she said softly. 'Of course it is wise to die, Alys. Everyone will die, all that we can choose is whether we die in faith. Whether your dangerous young lord comes for me today, or whether I die surrounded by my friends in a comfortable bed, does not matter to my immortal soul, just to my frightened body. Wherever and whenever I die, I want to die in my faith and my death will show that the most important thing in my life was keeping my faith.'

'But I want to live!' Alys said stubbornly.

The old woman smiled. 'Oh, so do I!' she said, and even Alys could hear the longing in her voice. 'But not at any price, my daughter. Both of us took that decision when we took our vows. Those vows are harder to keep now than it seemed when you were a little girl and the abbey was the finest home you could have hoped for. But the vows are still binding, and those who have the wisdom to hold to them will have the joy of knowing that they are one with God and with His Holy Mother.'

They were both silent.

'Go back to your comrades,' the old woman said gently. 'Tell them that Catherine will have to get well without you. And then come back here. If your monstrous young lord comes after you then we will face him with what courage the Lord gives us. If he does not, then we will make a new life here in peace.'

'I am under guard!' Alys exclaimed. 'I cannot come away. They will not let me.'

Mother Hildebrande looked at her. 'Then stay here,'

she said simply. 'Let us wait for them to seek you here and we can face them together.'

Alys shook her head. 'They would come at once and take us both prisoner,' she said. 'We would have no chance at all!'

'No one can take a wise woman prisoner,' Hildebrande said. 'Her heart and her mind belong to herself. If you obey your vows then all the obstacles on your path will fall away.'

'You don't know what they will do when they catch you!' Alys exclaimed.

Mother Hildebrande smiled and shook her head. 'Alys, I have been in hiding for ten months, ever since the sack of the abbey. I know exactly what they will do to me. They will question me as to my faith, they will beg me to recant. Then they will show me the instruments of torture. Do you have a torture dungeon at the castle?'

'I don't know,' Alys said unwillingly. 'I suppose so . . . I don't know. I've never been there.'

Mother Hildebrande smiled. 'And it is I who am called blind!' she said. 'Then I will tell you, Alys. Lord Hugh does indeed have a torture room at Castleton castle. It is in the prison tower in the eastern corner of the inner manse. You can see the roof of the tower from the market-place in Castleton. It is opposite the round tower where Lord Hugh has his rooms. If you do not know of it, then you must be blind indeed.

'They say that it is a room like a cellar, with no way in and no way out except narrow stairs with a trapdoor into the guardroom, guarded by the soldiers. They have pincers to tear the fingernails and toenails from the hands and feet, they have great shears to crop ears, to slit tongues. They have a little blacksmith's forge to heat the brands to burn flesh, and they have a rack to stretch and stretch your body until all the bones are wrenched from their sockets and you are a cripple in every limb.'

'Stop it,' Alys cried with her hands over her ears. 'Stop it!'

'They have a press made of carved wood to crush the breath out of your body and break your ribs. They have a gag which holds your mouth open with sharp metal plates. They have a collar with spikes facing inwards which they tighten and tighten until the spikes are driven through your skin into your throat.'

'I won't hear this! I won't listen!' Alys exclaimed.

Mother Hildebrande waited for Alys to put her hands down from her ears. 'I know the dangers I am facing,' she said gently. 'It would be a poor act of faith if it were done by accident, would it not? I know what they can do to me if they take me. It is right that I should know the tortures I may face. Our Lord knew all His life what would come to Him. And my pains will be no worse than a crucifixion. No worse than the pains Our Lord suffered willingly for us. If He calls me to do it for Him, how can I say "no"?'

Alys shook her head dumbly.

'Is it fear, Sister Ann? Are you afraid to travel this road with me?' Mother Hildebrande asked, and her voice was filled with pity. 'Tell me if it is so and we will find you another way, a safer way.'

There was a long silence. Then Alys shook her head. 'No, Mother,' she said slowly. 'I have been your daughter from the moment I first saw you. Where you lead I have promised to follow. If it is God's will and your belief that we must risk this, then I cannot refuse.'

Mother Hildebrande put her hand gently on Alys'

head in a silent blessing. 'Then why is it I feel that you hesitate?' she said softly. 'Is it the young lord, Sister Ann? Has he become dear to you?'

Alys shook her head in denial but Mother Hildebrande never shifted her gaze. 'Are you in sin, Ann?' she asked gently. 'Have you looked at a married man and forgotten his vows to his wife, and your vows to Our Lord? God forgive me, but when I saw you first in that red gown I feared you had become his whore.'

'I am not!' Alys said in a whisper.

'He is young and handsome and they say that he loves lust and young women. If he forced you, Ann, or even if he seduced you into consent, you can tell me, and we will find a penance for you. You can expiate your sin. Our Lady is merciful, she will intercede for you.'

'I have done nothing,' Alys said defiantly. She looked up at Hildebrande and for one moment the old abbess saw the hungry child of the herb garden who swore she had no kin and no one to prevent her coming to the abbey.

The old woman paused a moment longer, searching Alys' clear, open face. 'I pray that it is so,' she said at last. 'Go now, Alys, and tell them you are not returning to the castle with them. We have to start our new life here at once. God is not to be delayed with excuses. His call comes before that of a lady in a castle – whoever is her husband.'

Alys rose reluctantly. 'Do you have enough food?' she asked.

The abbess smiled. 'I feasted like a prince on your gift,' she said. 'There is plenty, and when that is gone Our Lady will send plenty once more. We will not hunger here, Sister Ann. We will not be cold and lonely.

The Lord will guide us. I trust Him to set a table for me, and my cup will run over.'

'I'll light the fire,' Alys said.

'You can do it when you come back,' the abbess said.

'I'll do it now. The cottage needs airing. The sooner the fire is lit the better.'

The abbess let her go inside, closed her eyes to the sunlight and murmured a prayer of thanksgiving that Sister Ann was found, the finest child of the abbey, found and restored to God once more. Whatever her sins – and there must have been many sins during ten long hazardous months out in the world – the girl would confess them and expiate them. It was a joy as great as that of a holy conception to have the child, her beloved daughter, returned to her. 'Like the prodigal son,' the abbess whispered softly. Under her closed eyelids she could feel the prickle of tears. Sister Ann had been spared the fire and been spared rape, and had been led home.

'It's alight,' said Alys tersely, coming out into the sunshine again with dirty hands. 'In a few moments you can put some of the wood on. Put only one piece at a time, it's damp.'

The old woman nodded, smiling. 'I shall walk along the river to meet you as you come back from your escort,' she said. 'The river here flows underground, you can sometimes hear it as you walk along the banks, Ann, did you know? It made me think of our faith – sometimes underground and sometimes above, but always flowing.'

Alys nodded. She could not look at the caves uncovered by the drought without thinking of Morach's drowned body trapped and rotting in the crooked darkness of one of the holes. She could not sense the deep, secret, wetness of the water under the rocks. All she could see was the glare from the limestone slabs. All she could feel was their merciless aridity.

'I won't be long,' she said.

Twenty-eight

Alys rode towards Castleton without looking back. Mary, mounted on the pony again, rode behind her. The soldiers, rested after their dinner in the wood, stepped out blithely. The leading soldier whistled softly through his teeth.

The fine weather was breaking up, there was a mist lying in swirls along the river, clumping over the still pools. The air was colder in the west, behind them there were long thick strips of cloud gathering.

'Best make haste,' the soldier in front said over his shoulder. 'It's going to rain and you have no cape.'

Alys nodded and the man broke into a slow, steady run. The mule trotted behind him, the dust beneath its hooves as white as salt. Alys, watching its long, doltish ears, jogged uncomfortably along. Behind her she heard the rapid, light sounds of her pony cantering, held in on a tight rein by Mary. Alys could taste the dust of the road in her mouth, could feel its stony dryness on the skin of her face, in her hair. She felt its crystalline deadness all around her as she rode away from Hildebrande and left her alone on the high moor.

The horses' hooves rang hollowly on the Castleton bridge. The soldier slackened his pace as they walked through the town. The market traders were gathering up their goods, a sharp flurry of wind whipped the cloth on a weaver's stall into a dozen flags. The pony shied but Mary, sitting easily in the saddle, moved with it; the mule waggled his long ears at the sight.

'Just got home in time,' the soldier said. The guards

at the gates barred their way with pikes and then lifted them up in a salute to Alys. Behind them came the dull rumble of thunder.

'Here comes the rain,' the soldier said. 'You were lucky to get home dry, Mistress Alys.'

Alys nodded and let him lift her from the saddle under the shelter of the gateway.

'Someone lend me a cape,' she said abruptly.

A scud of rain raced across the courtyard before them. Mary put a soldier's cape around Alys' shoulders and Alys pulled it up over her stiff gable hood. Ducking her head against the driving rain she ran across the yard, through the second gate, across the inner manse and into the great hall.

She paused inside the hall as a crack of lightning made the hall as bright as midday and then a loud peal of thunder exploded outside. A soldier at the fire jumped and crossed himself. 'Christ save us!' he said. 'That was right overhead.'

'Where is the young lord?' Alys asked him. 'Where is Hugo?'

'With his father, Mistress Alys,' he replied. 'A messenger came from the King and they are reading the letters.'

Alys nodded and went through the hall, through the lobby, to the round tower. As she climbed the tower steps her way was suddenly bright as the lightning exploded again. Alys stumbled and clung to the wall as the thunder rocked the building. 'I *will* do it,' she said through her teeth.

Her gown had been soaked in the brief run across the courtyard and now it clung to her thighs, dragging her down. It was as cold and wet as the gown of a drowned woman. 'I *will* do it,' Alys said again.

She went up a dozen more stairs into the circular guardroom below the old lord's room. There were two soldiers playing at dice. 'Is the young lord with his father?' Alys asked them.

'Yes, Mistress Alys,' said the younger, standing to speak to her and pulling off his cap.

Alys nodded. The thunder rolled dully as if it had sped away to rage around the other tower, the prison tower.

'The storm has gone,' the lad said. 'What a clap that was just now!'

'It's not gone yet,' Alys said. She turned from the room and went up the next flight of stairs, clinging to the stones at the side of the stairs as if her knees were weak.

She had been right about the storm. As she raised her hand to the latch of the old lord's door a knife of white light sliced through the arrow-slit to Alys' feet and then a great angry roar of thunder shook the stone tower. Alys, flinching back, almost fell into the room.

Hugo, his father and David were seated at the fireside.

'What a storm!' the old lord said. 'Are you wet, Alys? Are you cold?'

'No, no,' she said. She heard that her voice was too sharp, too alarmed. She took a breath and steadied herself. 'I had to run across the courtyard but we were home before the rain started,' she said.

Hugo looked up at her. 'You should change from your wet clothes,' he said. 'My father and I are busy with messages from the King's council.'

'I won't disturb you then,' Alys said. 'I shall be ready to come and clerk for you, if you wish, my lord.'

Lord Hugh nodded.

'I just thought I should tell you,' Alys said. 'The new wise woman at Morach's cottage on Bowes Moor. She is very strange. I met her in the woods when I was fetching the elm bark. She talked very wild. She frightened me.'

Hugo looked up. 'Did she do you harm?' he asked.

Alys shook her head. 'No, but I would not have her near me when I am at my time,' she said. 'I had sent her some goods and thought she might be of service to me. But she talked so wild and looked so strange. I don't like her. I don't like her being in Morach's cottage.'

The old lord was watching Alys curiously. 'Not like you to be fearful, Alys,' he said. 'Is it your condition?'

Alys shrugged. 'It must be,' she said. 'But the woman mistook me for someone else. She called me Ann and conjured me to go and live with her. She ordered me to go to the cottage and she said I would be in danger if I did not join her. She made me fearful.'

'Was she hexing you?' the old lord asked.

'No,' Alys said firmly. 'Nothing like that. I suppose it was nothing more than my foolish fancy. I do not swear against her, I make no accusation. But I cannot like her living here so close to us. Nor living there – where I like to collect my plants. And it was old Morach's cottage and now it is mine. I don't want her living in my cottage.'

'Move her on?' the old lord said, cocking an eyebrow at Hugo.

Hugo laughed shortly. 'We'll dump her over the border into Westmorland,' he said. 'They have enough mad old women there for her to merge into the crowd.'

Alys put her hand on her belly. 'I would not do her harm,' she said. 'I would not cause her to be hurt. I want you to move her gently, Hugo. I am only nervous because of my time and I do not want ill-wishing around me.'

'Oh aye,' Hugo said. 'I'll send a half-dozen men out tomorrow. They can put her on a horse and send her over the border. You'll not see her again. She'll not trouble you.'

'Tell them not to hurt her,' Alys said. 'I feel it would be bad luck for me if they hurt her.'

Hugo nodded. 'I'll tell them to be gentle with her. Don't fret, Alys.'

She nodded. 'I'll leave you to your business then, my lords.' There was another flash of lightning as she put her hand on the door, and a deep rumble of thunder overhead.

'This storm will do your work for you and blow the old hag across the border,' Lord Hugh said.

'Going the wrong way,' Hugo said briefly. 'It'd blow her to Yorkshire and I'd wish that on no one.'

The old lord chuckled and Alys closed the door behind her softly.

The storm did not cease circling the castle all night. Alys went down to supper with her way lit by flashes which made the candles into sticks of black with flames of shadows. Catherine stayed upstairs, whimpering with fear at the storm and cringing when the thunder rolled. Her window was barred tight shut, with the hangings drawn, but still the quicksilver brightness of the lightning drew a rapid silver line around the curtains for one sharp second before the thunder crushed the world into blackness.

Alys' colour was high, she sparkled as if she had been brushed with lightning herself. She was wearing a bright yellow gown and her hair combed loose over her shoulders. She laughed and leaned towards the old lord, smiled across him to Hugo, nodded at the soldiers at their table at the back of the hall who gave her a ragged cheer. She drank deep of the dark red wine the old lord urged on her. She ate well.

'The elm bark settled your belly then,' the old lord said approvingly. 'The baby will do well with you, Alys. No jade's tricks of miscarriages, eh?'

Alys gleamed at him. Outside the lightning smashed the darkness and the thunder roared in reply. A woman down in the body of the hall screamed.

'No, my lord,' she said brightly. 'Not if my skill can prevent it. You will have a fine babe on your knee when the spring comes in.'

Hugo nodded. 'I'll drink a toast to that,' he said.

There was a sharp flash of lightning and a loud clap of thunder. One of the serving-wenches screamed in fear and dropped a tray of meat, and the dogs, who had been cowering beneath the trestle-tables, dashed out into the hall, snatched up the bones, and cowered back into their shelters again.

Alys laughed gaily.

'This rain will beat down the wheat,' Hugo said gloomily. 'We may lose some unless it blows over swiftly and the wheat can recover and stand tall again.'

The old lord nodded. 'Summer storms never last long,' he said encouragingly. 'This one will blow out overnight and in the morn you'll see a bright yellow sun to dry out the wheatfields.'

'We must go out when they cut the wheat,' Alys said. 'And celebrate harvest home.'

A page stepped up to the dais to speak to the old lord. He leaned back in his chair to give an order. Hugo spoke across him to Alys.

'Perhaps you had better stay home,' he said. 'You were not pleasantly greeted last time you went out to the fields.'

The lightning flashed like a sword into the hall. Alys met Hugo's narrowed judging gaze with a brilliant smile which did not waver even when the roll of thunder drowned out his words.

'I care for nothing!' she said, her voice very low. 'Not with the storm raging all around us! Come to my room tonight, Hugo, come to my room and I shall take you for a ride in the storm which you will never forget. My sisters go out to play on nights like this and I would be with them. You have forgotten my power, Hugo, but when I stretch my hand out there is nothing which can stop me. I do not fear these village people with their patches of land and their pig in the sty and their hive of bees. I do not fear anything they say nor anything they can do. I fear nothing, Hugo. Come to my room tonight and see how it is to play with a thunderstorm.'

Hugo lost his hard, critical look and was breathing swiftly. 'Alys,' he said longingly.

'After supper,' Alys commanded. She turned her head from him. David was at her side and the server of meat bent his knee and proffered the silver plate.

'Give me plenty,' Alys cried over the rumble of the storm. 'I am hungry. I shall eat all I need. Give me plenty!'

Supper was concluded swiftly, the noise of the storm made talk impossible, and even the least superstitious were edgy and fearful. For a little while the thunder slackened as it rolled off up the valley. But at the head of the valley by the great waterfall it turned and came raging down the river's course again, gathering speed and blowing the waters of the river out of course, flooding over their banks. The women did not choose to sit in the gallery where the windows rattled with the wind and the fire spat and hissed with falling rain. They went early to their beds, Ruth sleeping on a truckle bed in Catherine's room, holding her hand against her night-terrors. Alys laughed openly at the thought of it, flung open her door to Hugo, and then barred it behind them.

He had caught her mood, his eyes were shining. He waited for her to command him.

'Drink,' Alys said, handing him the wine with a small pinch of earthroot. She drained her own glass. 'And strip, Hugo, my sisters will only take you skyclad.'

Hugo dragged his clothes off slowly, the earthroot spreading through his body, making his limbs heavy and uncontrolled. Alys could see his dark eyes go blacker yet as the pupils dilated with the drug.

'Alys, my witch,' he slurred.

'Lie on the bed,' she said in a whisper. 'They are coming, my sisters. They will come at the next roll of thunder. Listen for them, Hugo! When the lightning splits the sky they will tumble down from the clouds, screaming and laughing, their hair streaming behind them. They are coming now! Now! Now!'

Alys stood naked before the arrow-slit window, her arms outstretched. 'I can see them,' she said. 'Across the brightness of the sky they're coming, Hugo! Here, my sisters! Here I am! Take me out in the storm to play with you.'

The wind gusted through the arrow-slit. Alys, burning up with guilt, with desire, with feverish excitement, laughed madly as the rain lashed her body. 'Oh, that is good!' she said. The cold, hard rain stung her nipples, in a thousand prickling blows. 'Oh, so good!' she said.

She turned to Hugo, driving herself beyond caution. 'Let's go outside,' she said recklessly. 'To the top of the round tower.'

'Outside,' Hugo said thickly.

Alys threw her dark blue cape around her nakedness, and put a blanket around Hugo's shoulders. He stumbled as she led him across the gallery, down the stairs and across the lobby to the round tower. The old lord was still in the hall, there was no one in the guardroom. Alys and Hugo slipped through, and up the narrow dark stairs, past the old lord's room, past Hugo's chamber above it, and up the stairs and out to the top of the tower.

In a sheltered corner the pigeon coops were battened down to keep the messenger pigeons safe. Alys wanted to release them – to fling the precious birds out into the random winds so that they would be tumbled and lost and never find their way home. Apart from the coops, the roof-top was empty, slate-floored and inhospitable, a tower pointing upwards into the very vortex of the storm. The air was howling around them, the wind buffeting them so strongly that their words were whipped from their mouths and they were deafened with the hurrying gale. Alys stepped across to the parapet and looked down.

The walls were high and straight as a plumb line. Alys could barely see the foot of the tower where it grew, like some strange crag, from the sheer rock of the cliff above the river. As the lightning flashed, Alys could see the cliffs, shiny and wet in the darkness as they fell away, in a sheer drop down to the river bed. Each crag was as pointed as a pike, and below them the river crashed and foamed over more sharp rocks, breaking in waves of black water and white spume. Alys let her cape fly out behind her and turned her face up to the drenching rain.

'They are here!' she yelled. 'My sisters are taking us to play with the storm! Can you feel them, Hugo?'

The wind had torn Hugo's blanket from his shoulders and whipped it away like a ribbon. The rain lashed his stocky white body. He flung his head back and laughed as the wind tore against him and the rain poured down on his nakedness.

Alys pressed against him, squeezed his thigh between her legs as they stood, drenched in the storm. The lightning dazzled them for a moment and then plunged them into blackness.

'Feel my sisters,' Alys said urgently. 'We are riding in the storm with them. See how the winds pull and throw us around. We are out in the storm, tossed by the air, bruised by the lightning. The storm is our lover. Be the storm, Hugo! Be at one with the storm and take us all.'

The earthroot was twisting and turning Hugo's brain. His body was icy from the rainwater and burning from his own heat and the earthroot fever. He savagely snatched up Alys and pressed her against the turret wall and forced himself into her. Alys, her body crushed against the stone wall, her shoulders and head above the parapet in the full force of the storm, laughed aloud.

'You are the storm, Hugo, you are the storm!' she cried. 'Love me into madness. I have thrown away everything for you. Everything is lost for you!'

Hugo buried himself into her, withdrew, thrust forward again. At every move Alys was pushed nearer and nearer the edge of the turret wall where it dropped down from full height to waist height. Below them the river was in a spate of deep dark water and wind-lashed foam. Alys saw the movement into fatal danger and laughed again. Deep inside her, desire and madness were building together. She clenched her legs around Hugo's waist and leaned back on the wall. Hugo, blind to everything but his fantasy of witches and storms and magical lust, forced himself into her again and again.

One final movement flung Alys from the support of the turret wall out into nothing, over the precipice. Hugo held her hips, her legs were around his waist, but her body was half falling from the top of the tower. And then Alys, mad for satisfaction and mad for release from her fear and her guilt, let go of Hugo's shoulders and stretched her arms out, over her head, reaching out into the abyss. The lightning flashed, lighting Alys' insane, laughing face and Hugo's tranced grimace of pleasure as Alys flung herself, head first into nothingness, with only her legs still gripping Hugo. She screamed at her pleasure and the sound was torn away from her mouth by the wind. She opened her eyes and looked downwards. She was dangling from the top of the tower, below her was a maelstrom of boiling winds, seething rain and the tumbling torrent of the river over boulders. Alys stretched her arms out into nothingness and laughed aloud, longing for the final terror of the tumbling fall and then blackness.

Then her belly clenched with lust and she groaned, instinctively she tightened her legs around his back, forcing him closer and closer, deeper and deeper inside her, wringing every second of pleasure from him. Hugo, not knowing what he did, caring neither for her safety nor her danger but only his own pleasure, snatched her back from the precipice and bore down on her on the stone flags of the turret roof. The rain poured down on the two glistening bodies as they rolled together, knotted with lust. Then the thunder rolled again and Hugo groaned, and fell away from her.

Alys lay, mouth open, drinking in the rain. Her hair was a puddled wet mass behind her neck, Hugo a spent weight on her body. She pushed him away and sat up slowly. Her head was swimming with the wine from supper and with the powerful drugs of lust and terror. She pushed herself to her feet and hobbled over to the edge of the tower. She was sober now, as a drunkard who suddenly sees the danger he was in will turn sober and cold in a second. She held on to one of the turrets and peered down the dizzying drop. She could not see the foot of the tower, it was too dark and too high. But she could hear the rush of the river water as it broke its back on the rocks. When the lightning cracked the sky again Alys could see the rocks far, far below her, where they formed a cliff of breakneck height down to the raging vortex of the river bed. Alys stepped back from the edge of the tower and pulled her cape around her. She shuddered.

'That was too close,' she said. 'Too close. Too near to the edge. Too close.' She shook her head like someone coming out of a deep trance. 'The blank rune, the blank rune,' she whispered. 'Oh God! The blank rune. Odin.'

For a moment she stared down and then she looked out towards the moor. The storm was raging out eastwards; when the lightning struck she could see the rain like a wall of water spreading over the moor up towards the high fells. The river would be filling fast, Morach in her cave would be drowned all over again. The river might spill out in the darkness, flood over its banks and hungrily eat the little hovel and the old arthritic woman, sweep them away before the soldiers came.

'Sleep well,' Alys said ironically to the darkness.

'Both my mothers. Sleep well. May the thunderstorm take both of you, may the rain wash you both out of my life, may the winds blow you far away from me.' She laughed in a high cracked voice at her own black humour and then turned slowly back to Hugo.

He was lying where she had left him, his skin cold and wet. Alys wrapped her cape tightly around her and lifted up the trapdoor in the flagstones. In the pigeon coops under the little rickety roof half a dozen tiny red eyes watched her anxiously, the birds stirring fretfully as she passed. Alys stepped down the narrow stone stairs and dropped the trapdoor back into place. She went past Hugo's room and past the old lord's chamber. Halfway down the stairs to the guardroom she met one of the soldiers.

'Fetch a comrade and go and get Lord Hugo,' she said briskly. 'He is drunk and would go out on the roof to see the storm. See that his servants warm him and dry him and put him to bed. He is dead drunk and cannot walk.'

The soldier grinned. 'Yes, Lady Alys,' he said. He ran down to the guardroom ahead of her and Alys heard the quick ripple of male laughter. She walked down the stairs, through the guardroom, where the soldiers stood back to let her pass, sneaking a look at her bare white feet, and across to the stairs up to the ladies' gallery.

Mary was waiting by Alys' bed when she came into the room. Without comment she took the soaking cape from her and wrapped Alys in a warm sheet. Alys, too tired and dazed to be bothered with her nightshift and nightcap, slipped between her sheets wrapped and warm like a swaddled baby.

'Goodnight, your ladyship,' Mary said carefully, and blew out the candle.

That night Alys had a dream. It came from the thunder-storm and the pouring rain outside the castle. It came from the boiling flood of the river around the rocks of the castle's foundation. It came from the blank rune. It came from Morach – dark and deep and hidden in her drowned cave. It came from Hildebrande – praying in the darkness with the tears pouring down her old face for the lamb which had lost its way, for the daughter who had turned traitor.

Alys dreamed she was on the road to Castleton from Morach's cottage. She dreamed she was riding her mare. It was a fine day, sunny and bright and the mare was stepping smartly along the white road. Alys dreamed she saw the bluish leaves of wild sage in the bank at the side of the road and pulled up the mare to pick the fresh florets.

The mare stopped, Alys slipped from the saddle and bent down over the plant. Then she recoiled. The bank was alive with worms. It was seething with white mag-gots, tiny and thin, writing together in a huge mass of corruption. As she fell back against the horse's shoulder she saw that the bank on the other side of the road was filled with worms as well. She was trapped between two feasts of writhing, silent maggots.

Alys went to leap up on the horse but, in the way of dreams, there was no saddle and no stirrup. She could not get up. She fumbled at the horse's back, then she went around to the other side, hoping there might be a saddle on the other side. There was nothing, and she could feel the banks coming closer. The whole mon-strous hedgerow of maggots, crawling over every flower, thick in every hole, was coming closer, closer.

Alys screamed as loud as she could and her scream tore through the fabric of the dream, ripped her sleep open. She opened her eyes and she was sitting upright in her bed, sweating with terror.

'My God, my God!' she said into the darkness.

The castle was in silence, the storm gone. Outside there was the soft patter of summer rain and the sky was pale with the rising, cloudwashed sun.

'My God,' Alys said again.

She turned her pillow over, it was damp with sweat. She pulled the covers a little closer. She felt as chilled and as trembly as if she had just come in from the storm.

'What a dream!' Alys said to herself in the silence of her room. 'What a nightmare. And all nonsense. All nonsense.'

She shook her head and lay down on the pillow again, clutching the covers around her for warmth.

'Nonsense,' she said to herself softly. 'All nonsense.'

Within minutes she was asleep. Within minutes she was dreaming again. Once more she was riding down the road on her pretty mare. Once more she saw the herb, pulled up the horse, and leaned towards the flower-studded bank. There was something white moving under the leaves.

Alys recoiled, thinking it must be some worm, perhaps a snake. Then she saw more clearly.

A little white hand.

Alys screamed aloud, but made no sound except a soft groan.

As she watched, the little hand parted the curtain of a dock leaf and the little wax doll walked out. It was the doll of Hugo – the worst of the three. Eyeless, earless, fingerless, mouthless. It waddled on little legs through the thick leaves and flowers of the bank and down to the road. Behind it, like tiny toy soldiers, came the other two. The doll of Lord Hugh, stooped and more tired, but marching determinedly behind Hugo, and behind him came Catherine. With helpless fascination Alys leaned down from her horse to see better. The doll of Catherine had changed. The great fat belly had gone, torn away. There was a ragged edge to the doll's body and a cavernous hole where the belly had been. At every step the doll took it left a little trail, like the slime of a snail, where molten candlewax dripped from the wound.

'Where are you going?' Alys moaned.

The Catherine and the Lord Hugh dolls checked at her voice. But the little doll of Hugo could neither hear her, nor see her, feel her, nor speak to her. It trudged on like a little unstoppable toy.

'To Castleton,' the two little dolls said in their piping, innocent voices. 'To find our mother who made us.'

'I buried you!' Alys shouted at them. 'I left you on holy ground. I left you there. Lie quiet! Lie quiet, I command you!'

'We want our mother!' they said in their high, bright voices. 'We want our mother, our mother, little Sister Ann!'

'No!' Alys' scream broke through her sleep. She heard her door bang open as Mary came into the room, asking if she were ill.

'No!' Alys said again, the dream fading as she felt Mary's hand on her arm.

But she heard their reply, from three miles out on the Castleton road. 'We want you, mother,' they cried joyfully. 'WE WANT YOU!'

Twenty-nine

The morning was clear and sun-filled, just as the old lord had predicted. The storm had drenched the mist and blown away the clouds. Alys, waking from a second sleep, went over to the arrow-slit and stared out towards the moor where the white ribbon of the road snaked westward.

For long moments she stood staring towards the moor as if she thought that she might see something coming along the road. Then she shrugged and turned away.

'I fear nothing,' she said under her breath. 'Nothing. I have not come this far to be fearful of dreams. I am not a fool like Catherine. I shall fear nothing.'

Mary tapped at the door and came in, laden with a platter of bread and meat, and a pitcher of ale. Alys went back to bed and ate heartily, sitting up in bed, and reviewing one gown after another as Mary took them from the chest and spread them out before her.

'The new blue gown,' she said at last. 'And I'll wear my hair loose.'

Mary laid out the dress, poured hot water from a ewer to a basin, and helped Alys lace tight into the gown. It had been remade from some blue silk in Meg's box, sewn by the castle sempstresses in the style favoured by the new Queen Jane. Alys smiled. The dress might have come into fashion precisely to show off her growing belly. The stomacher was cut short, it pressed across the breasts and laced at the back like a bodice. In the front the fullness of the gown was gathered across the belly.

Even virgins wearing such a fashion would look pregnant; Alys, with the curve of her belly emphasized by the folds of silk, looked like a queen of fertility. She opened the door, bid 'good day' to the ladies and strolled across the gallery to visit Catherine.

Catherine was still in bed. Her breakfast tray was pushed aside, she was drinking from a mug of ale. She put it down when Alys came in the door and held out her arms to her. Alys bent over the bed and allowed Catherine to hold her and nuzzle her damp face into Alys' neck.

'Alys,' Catherine said miserably. 'You must help me.'

Alys pulled up a chair to the bed without invitation or permission and sat down. 'In what way, Catherine?' she asked pleasantly. 'You know I would do anything in my power for you.'

Catherine snivelled weakly and hunted in the pillows for her handkerchief. She rubbed her eyes and her moist nose. 'I cannot stop weeping,' she said thickly. 'All day and even all night. Alys, I weep even in my dreams.'

Alys examined her clasped hands against the blue of her robe. They were as smooth and as white as a lady's. No one would look at them now and think Alys had ever plied anything heavier than a needle. 'Why do you weep?' Alys asked, without much interest.

Catherine pressed the backs of her hands against her pink cheeks to cool them. 'Hugo will not see me,' she said flatly. 'He will not see me and he refuses to touch me because I have not been churched. But Father Stephen is not here so I cannot be churched. Hugo knows that. He is using it as an excuse to snub me. I know it. I know it.' She broke off, her voice had risen high and angry. She took a deep breath.

'I do not even know if Father Stephen believes in

churching,' she said resentfully. 'If he calls it superstition and refuses to do it, and Hugo still will not touch me until it is done, then what can I do? It is a trick. Hugo is punishing me for losing his child. But it is not my fault! I am not to blame!' Her voice had grown high and shrill again. She took a quivering breath, trying to calm herself. Alys barely looked at her.

'The old lord will not see me,' she said. 'He says he will see me when I am well again and fit to be seated at table; but I know he is angry with me.' She hesitated, her voice very low. 'I suspect him,' she said softly. 'I suspect him of trying to have me put aside.'

Alys glanced up at her but said nothing.

'You *must* know,' Catherine said with sudden energy. 'You write his letters for him, he tells you his business. Is he writing to have me set aside and the marriage annulled?'

'Yes,' Alys said precisely. 'If his friends at court will support his application.'

The flushed colour went from Catherine's face, leaving her waxy white. 'On what grounds?' she whispered.

'Too close kinship,' Alys replied.

'There was a dispensation . . .' Catherine began.

'Bought from the Pope,' Alys answered. 'The King decides these matters now. Not the Pope.'

Catherine was silent, staring at Alys. 'What does Hugo say?' she asked. 'Does he love me still? Does he want to keep me? Will he stand against his father?'

'Hugo doesn't know,' Alys answered. 'But I doubt he would go against his father's will in this matter.'

'No,' Catherine said, shaking her head. 'He would not. He married me because his father ordered it, and he lay with me because they needed an heir. Now I cannot give an heir I am of no use to anybody. So they will throw me away.'

Alys looked at her fingernails. They were pale pink and regular, with clear white tips and little half-moons of whiteness at the base. Alys inspected them approvingly.

'I am lost,' Catherine said hollowly.

Alys waited, indifferent to Catherine's pain.

'What will they do with me?' Catherine asked.

'You could marry again,' Alys suggested.

A little of the colour came back into Catherine's cheeks. 'After Hugo?' she demanded.

Alys nodded, conceding the point. 'Or you could have a little house of your own, with your own servants on your dowry land. Perhaps a little manor, a farmhouse.'

Catherine's plump face trembled with her grief. 'I have been the lady of the castle,' she said. 'The wife of Lord Hugo. Do they expect me to live in a cottage and keep ducks?'

Alys smiled. 'Could you fight them?'

'I'd lose,' Catherine replied promptly. 'Catherine of Aragon could not sway them, a princess in her own right. The Boleyn woman's own uncle found her guilty and sent her to be killed. It's not likely that they would listen to me! The King's council do not like to hear about male impotence, male infertility. It is easier for them to blame a wife.'

Alys glanced behind her to see that the door was safely shut. 'That's treason,' she said flatly.

Catherine looked defiantly at her. 'I don't care,' she said. 'They have used me like a toy and now they will throw me on the midden. Hanging as a traitor could not hurt me worse than this betrayal.'

There was silence for a few moments. Alys saw that Catherine's constant tears had dried on her cheeks.

Underneath the rosy plumpness of Catherine's face the old hard lines were beginning to show again.

'Who will they marry him to?' Catherine asked. 'Have they written to anyone?'

Alys kept her voice level, her joy and confidence concealed. 'Lord Hugh has made no approaches,' she said. She waited for Catherine to guess that Alys would be the new lady, waited for her explosion of rage, of jealousy which would carry her out of the castle in a fit of pique and then beach her outside, never to return, in a little manor farm, visited only now and then by David with unwanted goods from the castle. Impoverished. Alone.

'I suppose they will wait until the annulment has gone through,' Catherine said. Alys smiled inwardly at Catherine's stupidity. 'Then they will look about them for a girl, a young girl, fertile and strong and wealthy. That's who they will wait for. Some noble little thing who will fall passionately in love with Hugo as I did. And then wear away her life with longing and jealousy – as I have done. And then wait and wait for a child from him. For it is *he* who has no seed. It is *he* who is corrupt.'

Alys kept her face down so Catherine could not see her smile. There was no young noble bride in the offing. There was no list of candidates. Alys was as close to Lord Hugh as anyone in the castle. If there had been marriage plans for Hugo then Alys would have known – even before Hugo himself. The annulment was planned. A second marriage would be left to Hugo's desires, to Lord Hugh's preference. Alys knew that when Catherine left the castle the new lady would be Alys.

Catherine threw back the covers of the bed and went

to the window. She drew back the curtains and flung open the shutters. The morning sunlight poured into the room, the dust from the strewing herbs dancing in the sunbeams.

'Look at him,' she said with deep resentment. 'Blithe as ever.'

Alys went to her side. In the courtyard below, Hugo was detaining Alys' new serving-girl, Mary, with one casual hand on her arm.

'Who is she?' Catherine said in a half-whisper.

'A new girl, my maidservant. David found her in Castleton to wait on me,' Alys said. She could feel herself getting breathless; deep in her belly she felt her pulse speeding with jealousy.

Hugo's laugh echoed around the courtyard, they could see Mary toss back her hair and smile at him.

From the round tower behind them, the prison tower, a soldier came out of the little doorway and strolled down the external stone stairs, calling some jest to Hugo. The watching women could see Mary shrug her shoulders and laugh.

'So now *you* know,' Catherine said triumphantly. 'Now you know how I felt when they brought you in, straight off the moor, and I saw Hugo turn and watch you every time you crossed a room. They called you one of my ladies but I knew you were here for *their* delight – Hugo's and the old lord's. It killed me inside to see him burning for you. And now you can watch your maid, a silly ignorant girl, and see Hugo burning for her. And every time she walks across the room you will see him turn his head away from you and watch her.'

Alys leaned against the window-sill and looked down, the stone wall cold and hard against her. Hugo had his arm around Mary's waist, he was whispering in her ear. Mary had leaned back along his arm, her neck seductively stretched, the tops of her breasts showing over her bodice. As Hugo's wife and Hugo's mistress silently watched, Hugo dropped his dark head and kissed her neck and her breasts. They heard Mary's ripple of laughter and then she pushed him away. She ran a few steps from him, as if she were unwilling, and then she glanced at him over her shoulder, inviting the chase. When he did not follow, she set her basket on her jutting hip and swayed across the courtyard. Hugo stood and lazily watched her walk away until she was out of sight.

'How long do you think she will hold out against him?' Catherine asked. 'A month? A week? Until tonight?' She gave a cracked, bitter laugh and leaned back against the bedpost. 'It was always better, I found, if they gave in swiftly. He gets bored then. The worst agony for me was when he was hot for you. You delayed so long. It was such pain for me, waiting and waiting for him to have his fill of you and come back to me.'

Alys shook her head. She could not match the torment and storm-lit madness of last night with Hugo's prosaic flirtation in the sunny courtyard.

'Only last night we were lovers,' she said unguardedly. 'How could he want a slut like her today? We were together in madness last night. How could he wake and want her?'

'He used to go from my bed to yours without even pausing,' Catherine replied. 'Hugo's infidelities happen at speed. You, of all people, should know that.'

Alys nodded. 'But last night . . .' she said. She broke off. Catherine was right. Of all women she should have known of the fickleness of men's desire. From her earliest childhood she had heard Morach warning girls wanting love potions that you can arouse lust but not liking. You can hex someone to obsession but not to affection.

'Do you love him?' Catherine asked curiously.

'No,' Alys replied absently. 'I did, at first. I was sick with love for him, I gambled everything – my soul itself – to make him love me. But since then . . .' She sighed. 'I sometimes desire him,' she said. 'And I need him now to keep my place here. I like to be the lady here, I like to be first with him and with his father. But I cannot say I love him tenderly. I have only loved one person tenderly.'

She thought of the old woman in the cottage on the moors coming out into the innocent sunshine at the sound of the horses, and then the soldiers taking her roughly and bundling her on a horse behind some lad who would crack jokes and call her 'Grandma' and then sling her down like a sack in Appleby market. 'And I think I may have failed in my love for her,' Alys said evasively.

'Morach?' Catherine guessed.

Alys thought of the old corpse rolling round and round in the roiling waters of the cave. 'Not Morach,' she said. 'But it is true that I failed her too.'

Catherine slid an arm around Alys' waist. 'When I go will you come with me? To the manor farmhouse? We could live together, Alys, you could practise your healing. We would be comfortable.'

She hesitated, glancing sideways at Alys. 'I would care for you. I would protect you. I would be like a husband to you. I desire you, Alys. I wanted you the night that Hugo brought you to me, and I had desired you before. It was my idea that he should have us both. He tempted me into telling my desires once, and I told him that I longed for you.

'Even when you were my rival I hated you and wanted you, all at once. I used to think of Hugo lying with you and I longed for you both, I envied you both. You – because you had Hugo at your beck. And he – because he could lie on you and master you. I longed to see you together, your body and his. But now, since I lost the baby, I hate Hugo. I hate the thought of him and his foul seed. But I still want you. I dream of you.'

Alys stepped out of Catherine's cuddling arm, her mind whirling with possibilities. 'I don't know,' she said, playing for time. 'I never thought.'

Catherine's face was eager. Alys felt her power flowing through her as she saw Catherine's need for her, Catherine's desire. Alys laughed softly, seductively. 'I never knew you desired me, Catherine,' she said. 'I never knew.'

Catherine reached out for Alys once more, pulled at her waist. 'I would keep you safe,' she said urgently. 'Here in the castle, if Hugo tires of you, you are lost. When the old lord dies they will blame you for his death, perhaps charge you with witchcraft. Have you thought of that? But with my money on my land I can keep you safe.'

'I am safe here,' Alys objected. 'Hugo may flirt with a serving-wench but he desires no one but me. I will have a place here long after Mary is out on the streets of Castleton plying her trade as a whore. Hugo will never tire of me.'

Catherine nodded. 'Not now,' she said. 'But later. When the new wife comes in, she may demand that you are sent away. If she is young, noble and beautiful,

Hugo will do everything he can to please her. She will snub you and insult you. She will bring her own women and you will have nothing to do in the gallery. They will tease you and abuse you. And when Hugo comes to sit with them they will laugh and say you are awkward and foolish and out of fashion. Your gowns will be wrong, Alys, and they will laugh at your speech and even at your healing. They will mortify you and humble you and then laugh at your pain. I can save you from that, from humiliation when the new wife comes in. And I would like to live in a manor-house with you. Far from Hugo, far from his father. Just you and me with a little farm, Alys!'

Alys felt her skills slick and warm at her fingertips. She felt her power around her like a puppet-master's cloak when he spreads it wide as a backcloth and sets his little dolls dancing. She slid her arm around Catherine's broad waist and felt the big woman yearn towards her. 'If I agree to come to you when Hugo's new wife arrives, will you go peaceably now?' she asked. 'The old lord has said he will be generous with money if you accept the end of the marriage graciously. You could get all the money we need by obliging him.'

Catherine stiffened. 'Make it easy for them!' she exclaimed.

'Make it easy for us,' Alys corrected her. 'Take their money, and then, when you are safe in your own little manor – take me too!'

Catherine drew Alys to her, drenched her neck in kisses, moved her lips up across Alys' face towards her mouth. 'Then I can have you, like Hugo used to have you,' she said. 'I used to dream of what he did with you, I used to burn up with jealousy and desire dreaming of him with you. Now I cannot have him and he hates me, and he has made me foul to myself. But at least I can steal his whore from him. At least I can take you.'

Alys forced herself to stand still, her hands on Catherine's puffy hips, while Catherine's grip tightened around her waist and her other hand stroked the top of Alys' breasts.

'Do you want me for desire of me, or revenge on Hugo?' Alys asked curiously.

'Both,' Catherine said honestly. 'I will humble him as he has humbled me. I lost my child but he will lose his whore. I shall steal you away from him as if you were his best possession. I shall take you as I would poach his mare. I shall make you mine and every time I lie on you I shall have all my pleasure and his as well.' She turned towards the rumpled bed, her hand insistently pulling Alys. The sheets were stained with wax and smelled sour.

Alys froze, hiding her disgust. 'Not now,' she said quickly. 'Tonight, Catherine. If I can get away from Hugo I shall come to you tonight.'

Catherine paused and beamed. '*We* deceive *him*!' she said, laughing with delight. 'Just when he thinks he has beaten me to the ground and has you as his whore. We steal away together and laugh at his pride. And we will find pleasure that Hugo in his cruelty has never dreamed of.'

'Yes,' Alys said. 'I will come tonight if I can sneak away from him. And I will come to your manor as soon as you are settled.' She kept her eyes down to hide the flare of triumph. 'I promise.'

'Do you swear on Our Lady?' Catherine asked urgently.

Alys took the oath as lightly as a butterfly sipping nectar. 'I swear.'

Catherine reached out both arms. 'I agree,' she said.

'I agree, Alys. Now let me hold you again.' Her grip tightened. 'Let me hold you,' she said.

Alys stood still in Catherine's embrace for a long tedious moment; her face, hidden from Catherine, was radiant. Then she gently stepped back.

'You should rest,' she said. 'Go back to bed and eat a good dinner. I have to go and write letters for Lord Hugh. The King's messenger came yesterday, they will need replies today.'

Catherine reluctantly released her. 'Come to me when you are free this afternoon,' she commanded. 'And we will talk about the manor-house. I will tell David to fetch me the books of accounts and we can choose our home together.'

Alys nodded. 'If I can come I will,' she temporized. 'You go to bed now.'

'I love you, Alys,' Catherine said. She looked like a little girl, climbing into the high bed. 'I know you don't love me. But when you are hurt by Hugo and banished from here, I think you will turn to me. Do you think you could love me?'

Alys shaped her lips into a smile. 'I love you already,' she said. 'And I look forward to the day when we are in our manor-house together.'

Catherine held out her arms. 'Hold me again,' she said.

Alys stepped forward, put her arms around Catherine and let the woman rest her head on Alys' unwelcoming shoulder. Alys drew back and pulled up the covers, tucking Catherine into bed.

'I will tell the girl to change your bedding,' Alys said.

Catherine beamed at her. 'How you care for me, Alys!' she said gratefully. 'How gentle and loving we will be together when we are far from here.'

*

Alys glanced out of the arrow-slits in the tower on her way to Lord Hugh's chamber. The high hills of the moor glowed like purple mist in the bright sunshine. The air was clear and clean as it blew gently through each arrow-slit, so Alys, hastening up the spiral stairs, went from sharp moorland air to stale castle smells as the sunlight fell briefly on her face and then left her in darkness. The white road was empty of travellers. She paused and looked carefully. There was nothing stirring the dust. Nothing.

She breathed slowly at the final window before she went in to the old lord.

He was wearing a light summer robe and sitting in his chair before a small fire. The room was crowded. Hugo was there and as Alys opened the door he laughed at some jest and she saw his dark head thrown back and his face merry. When he saw her he gave her a swift wink and came forward to draw her into the room. As his fingertips touched hers they both felt a tingle of last night's desire. 'Give you good day, my Alys!' Hugo said warmly.

Behind Hugo was the priest Father Stephen, still in his travelling cloak, thinner and more intense than before. David stood beside him, holding rolls of manuscript letters.

'Ah, Alys,' Lord Hugh said genially. 'Come in, come in. Here is our own good Stephen with news of his preferment. He has been made archdeacon! You must congratulate him.'

'Indeed I do,' Alys said prettily. She put her hand to Stephen. 'I can think of no better man for the task,' she said.

Stephen bowed slightly over her hand. His eyes flickered from her face to her belly. He had heard gossip that Alys was carrying Hugo's child. Now he saw that it was true.

'I have much work to do,' the old lord said. 'Stephen, you will take your old rooms? And talk with me this afternoon after dinner?'

'Certainly, my lord,' Stephen said.

'Come riding with me now,' Hugo said. 'We can take the hounds and go up over the moor, get some meat.'

Stephen grinned. 'Still hunting Hugo?' he said. 'Always some prey or another.'

It was a private joke. Both men grinned like schoolboys. 'No preaching now,' Hugo said. 'Not on your first day back with us!'

Stephen laughed and nodded. They swirled from the room in a flurry of coloured capes and David went quietly after them, shutting the door.

Alys settled herself at the table in the window, smoothed her blue gown over her knees, turned her head and smiled.

'You're looking very contented,' the old lord said approvingly.

'I have been talking with Catherine,' Alys said. 'I think I have done you a service which will please you.'

He cocked an eyebrow at her and waited.

'If you will settle a decent-sized manor farm on her, and give her a pension, then I can persuade her to let the annulment go through without protest,' Alys said calmly. 'She is ready to leave at once.'

'Christ save us!' the old lord exclaimed. He hauled himself up on his cane and walked around his chair. 'Why?' he asked. 'Why should she surrender Hugo after clinging to him for all these years?'

'She feels unclean,' Alys said. 'She felt the miscarriage very deeply, she has wept without ceasing until today.

She feels your anger and Hugo's. She wants to please you and she wants to get away. She knows she is barren and she will have to go.'

The old lord nodded. 'But I always thought her so lustful,' he said. 'I thought we would have to lever Hugo out of her arms.'

Alys looked down and smiled complacently. 'She is a woman of unnatural desires,' Alys said simply. 'She now desires me.'

The old lord gave a crack of laughter. 'God help us!' he said. 'Hugo will be mortified! She's had his cock between her legs and she prefers the peck of a hen! Wait till I tell him! He will die of shame! Catherine will let the marriage go if she can have his whore!'

He sobered in a few minutes. 'And what of you?' he asked. 'Playing both sides against the middle, as usual, I suppose?'

Alys looked up at him. 'My lord?' she asked innocently.

'What light oaths have you pledged?' the old lord demanded. 'Come now, girl, I need to know the terms, all the terms that Catherine is setting.'

'I have promised to live with her should I ever leave here,' Alys said.

The old lord nodded. 'And she was satisfied with that? Sounds very thin to me.'

'She thinks Hugo will take another wife from far away,' Alys said. 'She does not know that I carry Hugo's child in my belly. She is a fool. Her own worries and her own fears blind her. Not even her ladies have dared to tell her that I carry Hugo's child. She is so selfish, so drowned in her own needs, that she does not even see me. She understands nothing. She thinks I am a passing fancy, she does not see clearly enough to see me as Hugo's lady.'

The old lord had turned away, Alys could not see his face. But the stillness of his back warned her.

'You thought that you would be the new wife?' he asked.

Alys found that her breath was coming fast. The sense of fear and anger in her belly which she had felt while watching Hugo flirting in the courtyard was flooding back. She felt her face grow cold and then flushed.

'Yes,' she said bravely. 'I may not be noble and I bring no dowry. But I am the only woman ever to conceive and to carry his child. When my son is born he will be the only heir you have. You know as well as I that Catherine is not infertile – you have had physician after physician to look at her. You know it is Hugo's seed which is weak. If you bring another wife you will only have another barren marriage. It is *only* I who can conceive with Hugo. *Only* I who can carry his child full term. When I give birth to a son in the springtime you do not *dare* not to have us wed by then, and the child legitimate!'

The old lord, his back still turned, threw back his head and roared with cruel, mirthless laughter. Alys smiled nervously, hoping to share his humour.

'I dare?' he asked, turning around to face her. 'You tell me: I do not dare? Oh, my pretty slut, I dare greater things than that!' He stepped across the chamber and thrust his bony hands in front of her face, counting off points on his fingers. 'One: Hugo is not to marry a base woman from God knows where, of God knows what family or parents. Two: I don't take gambles on appearances.' He patted her lightly in the belly with the back of his hand. 'You could have a cripple in there, like Catherine had. You could have a girl.' He spoke as if cripple and girl were equally abhorrent. 'You could have a dead baby or an idiot boy.'

Instinctively Alys put her hands over her belly as if to block out the words. He pushed her hands away. 'Or wind. You could fail to go full term,' he said cruelly. 'You could miscarry like Catherine. You have six months to get through yet, my little whore, it's not likely I'll buy without seeing what I'm getting, is it?'

Mutely Alys stared up at him, her hands in her lap, palms uppermost. 'And thirdly,' he said loudly. '*If* it is a son, and hale and hearty, Hugo does not marry you, you little fool. We make the son legitimate! I adopt him as my heir. We want the child, we don't want you! We never wanted you except for clerking and Hugo's pleasure!'

Alys was white-faced, her hands were shaking.

'What made you think you could snare me, you little slut? Have you forgotten who I am? You seem to have forgotten your own base blood as soon as you had colours on your back. But me? Have you forgotten who I am? I am the lord of all the land around me for hundreds of miles! My family was planted here by William the Norman King himself, and I have fought and schemed for every acre under my foot. You might forget yourself – God knows you're not memorable! But me? Have you forgotten my family? Have you forgotten my power? Have you forgotten my pride? Have you forgotten who I am?'

Alys rose unsteadily to her feet. 'I am unwell,' she said. She could feel her face trembling. It was hard to form the words. 'I will leave you, my lord,' she said.

'Sit down, sit down,' Lord Hugh said impatiently, his anger blown away in a moment. He thrust her into the chair and stamped over to the table and poured her a glass of wine. Alys took it and sipped. He watched the colour creep back into her cheeks.

'I warned you,' he said gently. 'I warned you not to try to overleap the boundaries, God's own boundaries, between the noble and the rest.'

The wine was steadying Alys. 'Hugo loves me,' she insisted softly.

The old lord shook his head. 'Alys, don't talk like a fool!' he begged. 'You please Hugo. You are a pretty woman, desirable and hot. Any man would want you. If I were not frail and old, I'd have you myself. But don't think these things are decided on whim, on pleasure in a face, or a night's lust. Not even the King himself consults his appetites in this. It's a political decision, always political. Hunting for heirs, hunting for new alliances. Making power, consolidating power. Women are just pawns in this game. Hugo knows as well as I that the next marriage has to be done well, to our advantage. We need a connection with a rising family of the south-east – someone close to the King. Hugo is right – the King is more and more the source of power, of wealth. We need a family high in favour at court.'

Alys put down the glass. 'And do you have one in mind?' she asked bitterly.

'I have three!' the old lord said triumphantly. 'The de Bercy family, they have a wench of twelve they would let us have, the Beause family – they have a girl too young, only nine – but if she is big and forward for her age she might do. And the Mumsett family – they have a girl on their hands whose marriage contract has collapsed. She's twenty. The right age for Hugo. I need to know why her engagement failed, but she might do.'

The wine was spreading through Alys' body like despair. 'I did not know,' she said dully. 'You never spoke of these to me. You never wrote to them. You never received letters from them. I did not know. How have you made these arrangements? I never wrote for you.'

Lord Hugh chuckled. 'Did you think you saw all my letters?' he asked. 'Did you not think that David writes for me, in Latin, aye, in English and Italian, or French too? Did you not think that Hugo writes for me sometimes? Did you not think that when it is deep, deep secret then I write for myself and send it out by a bird, releasing the bird with my own hands so that no one knows but me and a clever, secretive bird?'

Alys shook her head. 'I thought you trusted me alone,' she said. 'I thought I was close to your heart.'

The old lord looked at her with compassion. 'And they call you a wise woman!' he said with gentle mockery. 'You are a fool, Alys.'

She bowed her head.

'What will become of me?' she asked.

'I'll keep you as my clerk,' the old lord offered. 'There will always be a place for you in my hall. You will nurse your child for the first two years. I will not take him away from you before then. When he has tried his first steps I shall take him for my own and you can please yourself.'

'I can stay here?' Alys asked.

'As his nurse, if you watch your tongue. As long as Hugo's new wife does not object. She will have the rearing of your son. He will be brought up as her child.'

'She gets Hugo and the castle and my son,' Alys said numbly. 'This girl you do not even know. She gets Hugo *and* the castle *and* my son and I get nothing.'

Lord Hugh nodded. 'I could send you to France to a nunnery when the baby is taken from you,' he offered. 'I'll give you a dowry and the name of a dead man. You could go back to the nunnery as a widow. I will do that for you.'

'I have lost my faith,' Alys said with weary dignity. 'Step by step in this castle I have fallen into sin and lost what little faith I ever had. The life I have led here would have robbed the faith of a saint.'

The old lord laughed shortly. 'Forgive me,' he said. 'I am just a layman, I cannot dispute these things. But surely the life you lived here would have *proved* a saint. This should have been a good test for a little fledgling saint.'

Alys bowed her head under his mockery.

'Well then, you have your final haven,' he said, a ripple of laughter in the back of his voice.

Alys looked at him dumbly.

'Catherine and the manor-house!' he said, his laughter spilling out. 'And the rest of your nights with Catherine's fat body bouncing up and down on you and poking in her fingers where you want a cock!'

He exploded into laughter, unstoppable, genuine guffaws, ignoring Alys sitting frozen at the table. Then he broke off and mopped his eyes. 'What a haven, my little one!' he said. 'But you could do worse. You were born for a meaner estate than that, after all. It's a triumph for you, in its way. I'll settle some land on you as I promised, and Catherine shall have a fine enough manor. It is better than nothing, Alys; and you were born to nothing.'

Alys sat in silence, her eyes on the table, her cold hands clasped across her belly.

'Now to work,' Lord Hugh said briskly. 'We're holding a sheriff's court this afternoon in the great hall. I want to see the cases which are coming up before me. And these letters have come from the King's council. An armful of new instructions – pursuit of heretics, witchcraft, papists. Treatment of paupers, upkeep of roads, bridges. Numbers of big horses each tenant must keep, numbers of sheep on lands. Training of young men as archers, banning of the crossbow. Control of enclosures, Lord knows what else.' He dumped an armful of papers before Alys on the table. 'Sort them into two piles,' he said. 'The ones that require an answer at once, that we have to deal with today. And those that can wait. I'll read the cases which will come before me this afternoon.'

Alys bent her head over the papers, smoothed out their creases, stacked them on one pile or another. She was not plotting, nor scheming how to turn the plans for the marriage to her advantage. She felt as if she had lost her ability to turn anything to advantage. She was up against the power and authority of men. There was no chance of anything but defeat.

Thirty

Alys worked until dinner. Lord Hugh trusted her to draft his replies to routine letters and then read them back to him for his scrawled signature and the stamp of his seal. However, some things he kept to himself. There were letters from London which came in a packet of linen with the seams stitched and sealed. He cut it open, sitting in his chair by the fireside, and burned each of the secret pages after he had read it.

At noon David came to the chamber. 'Dinner is ready, my lord,' he said.

Lord Hugh started up from his thoughts and stretched his arm out to Alys. 'Come away, Alys,' he said kindly. 'Come down to dinner with me. This is weary work for you, are you sure you are not too tired?'

Alys rose from the table and followed him from the room. She saw David's acute glance at the whiteness of her face and the slope of her shoulders.

'Does it fare merrily with you, Alys?' he asked. 'Merrily, merrily?'

She looked at him without bothering to conceal her dislike. 'I thank you for your wishes,' she said. 'I hope they come back to you threefold.'

The dwarf scowled. He clenched his hand into the fist with thumb between second and third fingers, the old protection against witchcraft, crossed himself with the fist, and kissed his thumb.

Alys laughed in his glowering face. 'Mind Father Stephen does not see you,' she said. 'He would accuse you of popish practices!'

The dwarf muttered something behind her as Alys, with her head high, followed the old lord down the stairs and into the great hall.

Hugo and Stephen were placed either side of Lord Hugh, Stephen on his right in honour of his return to the castle and to mark the old lord's favour. And the power of the new Church, Alys thought sourly. Alys was seated on the other side of Stephen.

She said nothing while the servers brought the silver ewers and bowls and Lord Hugh and then all of them washed their hands and dried them on the napkins. David watched over the pouring of the wine and then the pottage was served.

'Are you well, Mistress Alys?' Stephen asked her courteously.

'I thank you, yes,' Alys replied. 'A little weary. My lord has made me work hard this morning. He had to reply to the King's letters and we have the sheriff's court here this afternoon.'

'Hugo and I have added to the burdens of the court,' Stephen said. 'We took up a witch today.'

The tables nearest to the high table fell silent, the diners strained forward to listen. Most people crossed themselves. Alys felt her throat tighten.

'My lord!' she exclaimed. She glanced down the table at Hugo. 'God keep you both safe and well!'

'That is my prayer,' Stephen said. 'And it is my duty to preserve myself and my bishop's diocese from these evil creatures.' He glanced around him and raised his voice so that they could all hear him. 'There is no defence against witchcraft except fasting, penitence and prayer,' he said. 'No subscribing to another witch to protect you. That way you fall deeper and deeper into the hands of the one who is their master, who stalks this

563

earth seeking for souls. The True Church of England will protect you by seeking out all witches and destroying them, root and branch, even down to the smallest, least twig.'

There was silence. Stephen was impressive.

'Yes,' Alys said. 'We must all be glad of your vigilance.'

He turned his head to her. 'I have not forgotten the injustice of your ordeal,' he said softly so that no one else could hear. 'I carry it with me in my heart, to remind me to avoid popish practices like the ordeal and to keep my own conscience in these matters. I never use the ordeal in my work. I question – question with sight of the rack, and then with torture only where necessary – but I never test a witch with an ordeal any more. I made a mistake that day in giving way to Lord Hugh and Lady Catherine. I have never made that mistake again.'

'But you torture?' Alys asked. Her voice trembled slightly. She sipped her wine.

'Only as it is ordered, for those suspected of felonies,' Stephen replied gently. 'The law is strict in this matter. First comes questioning, then showing the rack to the prisoner and questioning again, and then, and only then, is questioning under torture allowed. When I know I am doing God's work in this godless world, and obeying the law in this lawless world, I can do my duty without anger or malice; or fear that I am doing wrong through my own blindness.'

Alys stretched her hand to her wine again. She saw it was shaking. She hid both her hands in her lap, out of sight under the damask tablecloth.

'And who is this witch you took up today?' she asked.

'The old woman you accused,' Stephen said. 'The old woman who lives by the river on the moor. We were riding out that way hunting and we met with the soldiers who were taking her over the border to Westmorland – as you desired.'

'There must be some mistake,' Alys said breathlessly. 'I never accused her of being a witch. She frightened me. She came on me alone in the wood. She called me by another name. But she was a harmless old woman. No witch.' Alys could hardly speak over the noise of her pulse in her head. She had no breath for anything more than short sentences.

Stephen shook his head. 'When we stopped to see that they handled her gently – soldiers like a game, you know – she asked who we were and when we told her Hugo's name, she cursed him.'

'She would not!' Alys exclaimed.

Stephen nodded. 'She named him as the destroyer of the nunnery and of the holy places. She said that he would die without an heir because he had done blasphemy and sacrilege and that the vengeance of her god was upon him. She called on him to repent before more women voided the devil's slime, which is all that he can father. And she begged him to release a woman named Ann. That was the last thing she said – let her go!'

'This is awful,' Alys said. 'But just the ravings of a mad woman.'

Stephen shook his head. 'I have been appointed by my bishop to search out these witches,' he said. 'There is one in every village, there are dozens in every town. We must root them out. People are frail, they run to these wizards in times of trouble instead of fasting and praying. The devil is everywhere and these are troubled times. We have to fight against the devil, we have to fight against witches.'

Alys gave a trembling little laugh. 'You are frightening me!' she protested.

Stephen broke off. 'Forgive me,' he said. 'I did not mean to. I am hot in the pursuit of evil, I forgot your condition and the delicacy of your sex.'

There was a little pause.

'And this mad old woman,' Alys said lightly. 'Won't you let her go? I should be sorry if my complaint against her brought her to this charge.'

Stephen shook his head. 'You misunderstand the seriousness of her crime,' he said. 'When she speaks of her god it is clear she is speaking of the devil, for we know that the Holy God does not curse men. He sends misfortune to try them, for love of them. When she speaks of Hugo as a destroyer of the popish false church, it is the devil crying out against our glorious crusade. We are snatching souls from the devil every day. He enjoyed an easy time with the Romish priests feeding people with lies and fears and superstitions and magic of all kinds. Now we are pushing the light of God across the country and casting the devil – and his followers like this old woman – into the fiery furnace.'

The brightness of the sunlight through the high east windows dazzled Alys, the room was spinning around her as Stephen spoke. 'Oh don't!' she said, in sudden agony. 'Stephen, remember how it was for me when you gave me the ordeal. Remember my terror! Spare this poor old woman and send her away, send her to Scotland! Send her to France! Spare the foolish old thing. She did not know what she was saying, she is mad. I saw it when I met her. She is mad.'

'Then how did she know of Catherine's illness, if not through sorcery?' Stephen asked. 'It has been kept most quiet. Only you and Catherine's ladies and Hugo knew

566

of it. Not even my Lord Hugh knew of her scouring white slime.'

'These things are talked of,' Alys said rapidly. 'Gossip is everywhere. She is probably one of those horrible old women who sit in the chimney seat and chatter all day. I sent her a gown and some food, she probably gossiped with the messenger. Don't burn her for being a foolish, ugly, old woman, Stephen!'

'We won't burn her,' Stephen said.

Alys looked up into his pale, determined face. 'You won't?' she asked. 'I thought you said you would cast her into the fire.'

'I meant that when she dies she must face the flames of hell, the fire of the afterlife,' Stephen said.

'Oh,' Alys said. 'I misunderstood you.' She breathed out on a little laugh. 'I am so relieved,' she said. She put her hand to her throat and felt her hammering pulse quieten beneath her touch. 'You won't burn her,' Alys said again. 'You won't burn her.' She laughed uneasily. 'Here I was, trembling with fear that I had brought an old lady to the stake!' she said. 'I was fearful for her. But you won't burn her, even if she should be charged. Even if she were found guilty. You won't have her burned.'

'No,' Stephen replied. 'We hang witches.'

When Alys came to her senses she was lying in her bed, the dark green tester she so loved above her, the curtains half drawn around her to shade her face from the bright sunlight pouring in the arrow-slit window. For a moment she could not remember the time, nor the day. She smiled like a child at the richness of the fabric all around her, and stretched. Then she heard the soft crackle of a fire in her grate, and was aware of the warmth of the setting sun on her whitewashed walls. Then she remembered the quiet terror of Stephen's promise, and Mother Hildebrande facing a charge of witchcraft that afternoon, and she cried out and sat upright in bed.

Mary was at her side. 'My lady,' she said anxiously. 'My lady.'

'What time is it?' Alys asked urgently.

'I don't know,' Mary said, surprised. 'About five o'clock, I suppose. The people are just leaving from the trials. It is not suppertime.'

'The trials are over?' Alys asked.

Mary nodded. 'Yes, my lady.' She looked anxiously at Alys. 'Will you tell me what I can fetch you?' she asked. 'Should you not have something from your chest of herbs? You are very pale, my lady. You fainted at dinner and they carried you up here like a dead woman. You have lain still all this long time. The old lord himself came up to see you. Have you nothing I may fetch you?'

'What happened at the trials?' Alys asked.

Mary frowned. 'I have been up here with you,' she said, with a trace of resentment. 'So I couldn't see nor hear them. But Mistress Herring told me that they branded one man for thieving and Farmer Silter was warned for moving his boundary posts. Peter Marwick's son was summoned –'

'Not them,' Alys interrupted. 'The old woman charged with witchcraft.'

'They didn't try her,' Mary said. 'They questioned her under torture and she is not a witch. They released her from the charge of witchcraft.'

Alys felt a sense of ease flow through her whole body, from her aching jaw, through her clenched fists, to the soles of her feet. Her skin glowed as if she had just stepped, tinglingly clean, from a bath. She felt the blood rise up in her veins and warm her clammy skin.

'They released her,' she said, tasting hope, as sweet as new desire.

'They changed the charge,' Mary said. 'She is to face a charge of heresy. She will be tried tomorrow in a second day of the court's sessions.'

Alys felt the room heave and yaw like a sailing ship out of control. She clung to the fine linen sheets as if they were safety lines in a storm-rolling sea.

'I can't hear,' she said pitifully. 'I did not hear you, Mary. Say it again.'

'I said she is to be tried tomorrow for heresy,' Mary said loudly in her rounded country accent, like one talking to an old deaf woman. 'They say she is no witch, but a heretic. A papist. They will try her tomorrow after dinner.'

Alys lay back against the pillows, her eyes shut. The child in her belly stirred and kicked against the pounding of Alys' rapid pulse. Alys felt her sins massing against her. Her stomach churned in terror, her heart fluttered.

'Get a bowl,' she said thickly to Mary. 'I am going to be sick.'

Mary held the bowl while Alys vomited a stream of undigested pottage from dinner and then her breakfast of bread and meat and ale, and then yellow bile, until she was retching and retching on an empty belly and bringing up nothing but clear saliva.

Mary whipped the bowl out of the room and came back with a ewer and a napkin moistened with cold water. She sponged Alys' face and her neck – hot and sweaty under the heavy weight of her hair. She held a glass of water to her lips.

'Is it the sweating sickness?' she asked Alys anxiously. 'Or is the child pressing against your belly too hard? The old lord should not make you work so! Can I fetch you something to eat?'

Alys leaned forward. 'Help me up,' she said.

Mary protested but Alys threw back the covers and held out her hands. 'Help me,' she ordered.

They had laid her on her bed in her blue gown and put covers over her. The gown was hot and creased. 'Take this off,' Alys said.

Mary unfastened the gown and shook it out, laying it in the chest.

'I will wear my green gown,' Alys said.

Mary slipped it on over Alys' head. Alys stood still and let her dress her, like an old pagan stone on the moors, dressed with scarves.

Her legs were trembling and Mary helped her across the gallery and down the stairs to the great hall. The servants were pulling the tables and benches back into their usual places after the disruption of the trial. She let Mary help her to the door to the garden and then she waved her away. She stepped out of the shade of the hall on to the cobblestones of the yard and out into the garden to find the old lord. He was sitting in the arbour, enjoying the evening sunshine. Eliza Herring and Margery were sitting beside him. Eliza was playing her lute.

Alys paused for a moment, watching them. The old lord's white hair shone in the sunshine, Eliza and Margery's dresses were bright – yellow and blue, summertime colours. Behind Lord Hugh's head an espaliered peach tree was showing fat fruits. Before them were half a dozen formal flower-beds with twisting gravel paths around them edged with box. And on the left, in the far corner of the castle wall, was the tower with the staircase to the second storey and a doorway only on the second storey. The lower storey had neither windows nor door. It was a blind tower of solid stone. It was the prison tower and the only way into it was through a trapdoor in the guardroom floor down rough steps. And the only way out (they said as a joke) was in a coffin.

Alys walked across the grass, her green gown hushing around her legs, through the maze of paths, a couple of hens and a cock scattering before her, until she came before Lord Hugh.

'Alys,' he said with pleasure. 'Are you better already? You gave us a fright. I've never seen so deep a swoon. Sit down! Sit down!'

He brushed Eliza and Margery off the seat and waved them away. They curtsied and wandered off, their heads together. Alys sat on the sun-warmed bench beside Lord Hugh.

'How sweet the air smells,' she said idly. 'And how well the garden is doing.'

'It's not big enough,' Lord Hugh said. 'My wife always wanted me to lay a formal pleasure garden. But I never had the time, nor the desire to throw money away for a posy of flowers.' He flapped his hand irritably at the hens which were picking at the flower-beds. 'They'd eat them all,' he said. 'Where's the kitchen-lad? They should not be out here!'

Alys smiled. 'What was she like, your wife?' she asked.

Lord Hugh thought. 'Oh, good,' he said vaguely. 'Well-born, religious. Dull.' He racked his brains. 'She read a good deal,' he said. 'Lives of the saints, church books, that sort of thing. She had very black hair – that was her best feature. Long, thick, black hair. Hugo has her hair.'

'Did she die young?' Alys asked.

The old lord shook his head. 'Middling,' he said. 'She was forty or thereabouts – a good life for a woman. She was ill with all her childbirths. And miscarriages. Lord! She must have had a dozen. And at the end all we had to show for it was two worthless daughters and Hugo.'

A companionable silence fell between them, Lord Hugh smiling at some old memory, Alys sitting beside him, composed.

'That old woman,' she said casually. 'What became of her?'

'The suspected witch?' Hugh roused himself. 'Oh, she was no witch. They put her to question under torture and she said nothing that could be called witchcraft. Even Stephen accepted that, and he sees a warlock in every doorway.'

Alys chuckled, a strained, unconvincing sound. 'He's very enthusiastic,' she said.

Lord Hugh cocked an eyebrow at her. 'Everything to gain,' he said. 'It's the King's Church now. Progress upward and there is the King's court at the top and God's heaven beyond that. A tempting enough prospect, I should think.'

Alys smiled and nodded.

'I don't know where it will all end,' he said. 'I shan't see the end of it, that's for sure. I used to think they would go back to the old ways but I can't see how any more. The abbeys are half destroyed, the priests have all taken the oath to honour the King. Still, it is Hugo's inheritance. And he's all for the new ways. He will have to find his path through them. I don't doubt he has the skill. As Stephen ascends, Hugo rises too. They have hitched their stars together.'

Alys nodded again. 'The old woman . . .' she started.

'A papist,' the old lord said. 'Accused of heresy and treason. When they got her off the rack and drenched her with cold water until she could speak again, she denounced them all, and said she was ready to die for her faith. We'll try her tomorrow. I doubt she'll recant. She's a powerful woman.'

'Can't she be released?' Alys asked. 'Shipped off somewhere? She's such an old lady and she will die soon anyway. She's no danger to anyone.'

Lord Hugh shook his head. 'Not now she's arrested,' he said pedantically. 'She's in the court records, Stephen knows of her. His report goes to his bishop, mine goes to the council. She can't just disappear. She has to be tried and found innocent or guilty.'

'But on what you say, she's bound to be guilty!' Alys exclaimed. 'Unless she recants, she's bound to be found guilty.'

The old lord shrugged. 'Yes,' he said simply. He leaned his head back against the sun-warmed stones. 'You could bake bread on this wall,' he said. 'It holds the heat like an oven.'

'It serves no good purpose to execute her,' Alys insisted. 'She's so old and frail that people will hate you and Hugo for hurting an old woman. They could turn against you. It's hardly worth the risk.'

The old lord turned his head to Alys. 'It's out of my hands,' he said gently. 'She is accused before the court and I will try her tomorrow. Stephen will be reasoning with her and questioning her. She wanted no one to represent her. If she does not repent, take the Oath of Supremacy and acknowledge the King as head of the Church, then she has to die. It's not whim, Alys. It's the law.'

'Couldn't you . . .' Alys started.

Lord Hugh turned his head towards Alys and his look was acute. 'Do you know her?' he asked sharply. 'Was she from your old Order? Are you pleading for her?'

Alys met his eyes squarely. 'No,' she said. 'I have never seen her before in my life. She means nothing to me, nothing. I am just sorry for her. Such a foolish old woman to die for her delusions. I feel distressed that my complaint has brought her here, nothing more.'

Hugh leaned forward and clapped his hands at the hens. They scuttered out of reach. The cock flapped his wings and jumped awkwardly to the flat top of the little box-hedge. He stretched his neck and crowed.

Alys watched the deep emerald shimmer on his throat.

Lord Hugh shook his head. 'It's not your fault,' he said. 'She would have preached or taught people. She would have gathered people around her. She would have come to our attention one way or another. And then we would have had to take her up. She is an old fool looking for sainthood, that one. She would never have taken the easy route, never altered her faith and her vows to suit the times. She's a foolish old martyr. Not a wise woman like you, Alys.'

Alys walked slowly into the castle through the doorway of the great hall. After the golden sunshine of the garden the smoky darkness of the great hall was a relief. She walked without purpose, without direction. Hugo was riding out to his new house, practising archery, riding at the dummy in the tilt-yard, or trifling with one plaything or another. Hugo would make no difference. Alys paused at the top of the hall and leaned against the table where the senior soldiers sat for their dinner.

Hugo was like a child. His father's long life and power had kept Hugo as a merry child – happy enough when things were going well, sullen and resentful when his will was crossed. He would not save Mother Hildebrande at Alys' request. He would not care enough. Not for her – a poor old woman who should have died last year. Not for Alys.

There were men sleeping off their dinnertime ale in the shadows of the hall, on the benches under the tables. Alys walked quietly past them, mounted the dais and drew back the hanging over the lord's doorway. One of them turning over in his sleep caught sight of her and crossed himself. Alys saw his gesture. Superstition hung around her still. She must remember that she was not safe herself. She put a hand to her belly. Her only safety was in the baby she carried: Hugo's son. She started wearily to climb the stairs to the ladies' gallery.

She might carry Hugo's son but the old lord had planned all along to take the child from her and adopt him as his own. Alys had not thought of that. She had not known that such things could be done. She had thought that the baby boy would be her passport into the family. She paused on the stairs, waiting for her breath to come back and the dancing black spots to go from her vision.

'I am ill,' she said aloud.

If she was ill then Catherine would not insist that they share a bed, Lord Hugh would not threaten her. If she was ill and in her own bed then no one could blame her when Mother Hildebrande rushed upon martyrdom without Alys saying one word to save her. No one could blame Alys for Mother Hildebrande's hunger for sainthood, especially if Alys were ill.

'I am ill,' she said again with more conviction. 'Very ill.'

She walked slowly up the steps to the ladies' gallery and opened the door.

It was empty and quiet. Mary was sitting at the fireside, stitching some plain work. She laid it aside when Alys walked in and bobbed her a curtsey.

'Lady Catherine has been asking for you, my Lady Alys,' she said pleasantly. 'Shall I tell her you are here? Or should you lie down?'

Alys looked at her with dislike. 'I will see Lady Catherine,' she said. 'She was disturbed when she looked from her window and saw you flirting with her husband in the courtyard.'

Mary gave a little gasp of surprise.

'The young Lord Hugo will take his pleasures where he wishes,' Alys said distantly. 'But do not flaunt yourself, Mary. If you distress Lady Catherine she will turn you out of the castle.'

Mary's cheeks were blazing. 'I am sorry, my lady,' she said. 'It was just words and laughter.'

Alys' look was as sour as if she had never heard words or laughter, or seen Hugo's hot, merry smile. 'If your humour is lascivious you had better avoid the young lord,' she said coldly. 'It would go very ill for you indeed if you offend his wife. You told me yourself your father is poor and out of work. I suppose it would be difficult for all of them at home if you returned without your wages and without hope of work in service again.'

Mary dipped her head. 'I beg your pardon, my lady,' she said humbly. 'It won't happen again.'

Alys nodded and went into Catherine's room, the taste of spite very sweet and full in her mouth.

Catherine was dressed, sitting in a chair by the window, looking out over the courtyard and the garden, the sun-drenched wall of the inner manse and the tops of the apple trees in the outer manse. The smooth round prison tower stood like a dark shadow behind the little bakehouse. Alys, looking past Catherine out of the window, saw nothing else.

'How well you are looking, Catherine!' Alys said. Her voice was high and sharp, the words a babble. 'Are you feeling better?'

Catherine's face when she turned to Alys was bleak with sorrow. The old hard lines had reappeared from the rosy plumpness of pregnancy.

'I just saw you in the garden,' she said. 'Talking to the old lord.'

Alys nodded, her face alert.

'I have been a fool,' Catherine said suddenly. 'I called your girl in here and asked her if you were with child and she curtsied to me and said, "Yes, my lady," as if it were a known fact, as if everyone knew!'

Alys drew up a chair and sat down.

'Is it Hugo's?' Catherine asked fiercely. 'Is it Hugo's child? I must have been blind not to see it before. When you walked across the garden I could see how you thrust your belly forward. Are you with child, Alys? Hugo's child?'

Alys nodded. 'Yes,' she said quietly.

Catherine opened her mouth wide and began to cry soundlessly. Great drops of tears rolled down her sallow face. She cried shamelessly like a hurt child, her mouth gaping wide. Alys could see the white unhealthy furring on her tongue and the blackness of one bad tooth.

Catherine snatched a breath and swallowed her grief.

'From when?' she asked.

'June,' Alys said precisely. 'I will give birth in April. I am three months pregnant now.'

Catherine nodded, and kept nodding, like a little rocking doll. 'So it was all lies,' she said. She took a scrap of linen from her sleeve and mopped at her wet face, still nodding. 'You will not come with me to the farm, that was all lies. You will stay here and have Hugo's child and hope to rise higher and higher into his favour and into the favour of the old lord.'

Alys said nothing.

Catherine gulped back sobs like a carp bubbling in the fish ponds. 'And while I thought that you would come to love me and that you were pledged to live with me you were scheming to have me sent away so that you and Hugo could romp together in public,' Catherine said, nodding wildly. 'You have shamed me, Alys. You have shamed me before the whole castle, before the whole town, before the country. I thought that you were my friend, that you would choose me instead of Hugo. But all this morning when I was talking with you and planning our life together you were playing with me. Scheming to have me sent away.'

Alys sat still as a rock. She felt the high flood-tide of Catherine's anger and grief wash around her but leave her dry.

'You have betrayed me,' Catherine said. 'You are a false friend. You are untrue.' She choked on another rich sob. 'You act the whore with Hugo and you are sweet as a daughter to the old lord,' she said. 'You play the false friend with me and you queen it among my women. There is no truth in you, Alys. Nowhere is there a scrap of honour or truth. You are meaningless, Alys, meaningless!'

Alys, her eyes on the round tower without windows, inclined her head. What Catherine said was probably true. 'Meaningless'. What would they be doing with

Mother Hildebrande in there now? Alys rose to her feet. 'I am not well,' she said. 'I am going to my chamber to rest before supper.'

Catherine looked up at her pitifully, her sallow face wet with her tears. 'You say nothing to me?' she asked. 'You will leave me here as I am, grieved and angry? You do not defend yourself, you do not even try to explain your false faith? Your disloyalty? Your dishonour?'

Alys glanced towards the round tower once more as she turned to the door. 'Disloyalty?' Alys repeated. 'Dishonour?' She gave a shrill little laugh. 'This is nothing, Catherine! Nothing!'

'But you have lied to my face,' Catherine accused her. 'You promised to be my friend, promised to be my lover. I know you are false.'

Alys shrugged. 'I am unwell,' she said flatly. 'I am too ill. You will have to bear your pain, Catherine. I cannot be responsible. It is too much for me.'

Catherine's face grew pale. 'Are you sick as I was?' she demanded. 'Is his child turning rotten inside you, as mine did? Is that all that Hugo can father? Candlewax?'

Alys' dream of the maggot-filled roadside and then the little dolls hastening to Castleton, seeking their mother, rose very vividly in her mind. She blinked hard and shook her head to rid herself of the walking dolls. 'No,' she said. She put her hands on her belly as if to hold the baby safe. 'My baby is whole and well,' she said. 'Not like yours.'

That gesture – the simple gesture of pregnancy – broke Catherine's anger into grief. 'Alys! I forgive you! I forgive you everything! The deceit and the lies, the shame you have laid on me. Your infidelity with my husband! I forgive you if you will come with me. They will have me thrown out of the castle, I shall have to go. Come with me, Alys! We will look after your son together. He will be my child as well as yours. I will make him my heir! My heir, Alys. Heir to the manor that they will give me and my dowry which they will return. You will be rich with me. You will be safe with me and so will your son!'

For a moment Alys hesitated, weighing the odds, scanning her chances. Then she shook her head. 'No, Catherine,' she said coldly. 'You are finished. Here in the castle they are finished with you and will be rid of you. Hugo will never touch you again. The old lord will never see you. I was playing with your desires to get you to leave without making an uproar, and to do my lord a service in furthering his ends. I never meant to go with you. I never wanted your love.'

Catherine's hands were over her mouth. Her wide eyes stared at Alys over her spread fingers. 'You're cruel!' she said disbelievingly. 'Cruel! You came to my bed with Hugo, you held me in your arms this very morning! You nursed me in my sickness and kept my secret safe.'

Alys shrugged and opened the door. 'It meant nothing,' she said coldly. '*You* mean nothing. You should have drowned in the river that day, Catherine. All the destinies are coming homeward like evil pigeons. She will burn, and you will drown. There is no escaping your fate, Catherine. There is no escape for her.'

Catherine looked around wildly. 'What d'you mean, Alys? What fate? And who will burn?'

Alys' face was sour and weary. 'Just go, Catherine,' she said. 'Your time is finished here. Just go.'

She closed the door on Catherine's wail of protest and went across the ladies' gallery. The other women had come in from the garden and were taking off their head-dresses and combing through their hair, complaining of the heat. Alys went through them all like a cold shadow.

'What ails my lady?' Ruth asked, as they heard Catherine's cries and saw Alys resentful face. 'Shall I go to her?'

Alys shrugged. 'She's to leave the castle,' she said succinctly. 'My lord has ordered it. She's to be set aside, the marriage annulled.'

There was a moment's silence and then an explosion of chatter. Alys threw her hands up to fend off the hysterical questions. 'Ask her yourself! Ask her yourself!' she said. 'But remember when you give her your service that she's soon to be a farmer on a little manor at the back end of nowhere. She's Lady Catherine no more.'

Alys smiled at the sudden stillness in the room. Each one of them was silent, fearful for their own future. Slowly, one after another, they looked to her.

'I will wash before supper,' Alys said composedly. 'Eliza, order a bath for me. Margery, order them to light a fire in my bedroom. Ruth, please mend my blue gown, I kicked out the hem the other day when I was walking upstairs. Mary –' she looked around. The girl was standing by the chamber door, her eyes cast down, the picture of the perfect maidservant. 'Lay out my linen, I will wear a fresh shift.'

Alys watched them move to do her bidding. Her women.

Behind her door Catherine wept as her room grew darker. When suppertime came no one called her, and no one brought her food. She lay on her bed, sobbing into her pillow, and heard the noises of eating and drinking and laughter from the hall below. It grew darker, no one came to light her fire nor bring her candles. They left her in the cool evening air in darkness.

She heard the women come upstairs from the hall and heard their low-voiced chatter. She heard Alys' laughter, edgy and shrill. But no one came to her door. No one came to see if they could be of service to her.

The silence from Catherine's chamber put a blight on the gallery. No decision had been made but somehow the new positions had coalesced. Hugo did not ask after Catherine, the old lord had not spoken of her since the miscarriage. And now Catherine's own women, who had served her since she was a girl, looked away from her shut door and did not offer her service. It was as if she were gone to live far away over the moors already, thought Alys, or drowned and buried; and she laughed again.

'I heard an odd tale today,' Eliza said, pouring the night-time cup of ale.

Ruth glanced towards Lady Catherine's door as if she feared her still.

'Tell it!' Margery said. 'But not too frightening, I need to sleep tonight.'

'I stepped into Castleton market this morning and met a woman I know selling eggs,' Eliza said. 'She had walked the moorland road this morning from Bowes.'

Alys looked up from her cup and watched Eliza's face.

'Ahead of her in the dust in the road she saw the strangest thing,' Eliza said.

Ruth shuddered and crossed herself. 'I'll not hear talk of the devil,' she warned. 'I'll not hear it.'

'Hush,' the others said. 'Go to your chamber, Ruth,

if you have not the stomach for the tale. What did she see in the dust, Eliza? Go on!'

'She saw little tracks,' Eliza said mysteriously.

Alys felt herself grow cold.

'Tracks?' she asked.

Eliza nodded. 'Footprints. The marks of the heels of riding boots, and a pair of shoes. As if a woman and two men had been walking on the road.'

Margery shrugged. 'So?' she asked.

'They were tiny,' Eliza said. 'Tiny little footprints, the size of mice feet, she said "Tiny."'

Mistress Allingham exclaimed, 'Fairy folk!' She clapped her hands. 'Did she wish? Did she wish on the little people's tracks?'

'She followed them!' Eliza said. 'Two tracks from boots and one track from shoes, like two men and a woman.'

The women shook their heads in amazement. Alys said nothing, she sipped her ale. It went down her throat as if it were ice.

'And the little woman's footprints were dirty,' Eliza said. 'Dirty with slime like a snail. Slug juice.'

Ruth crossed herself abruptly and rose up. 'I'll hear no more,' she said. 'Nonsense to frighten children!'

The rest of the women were fascinated. 'And so?' they asked. 'What then?'

'She bent down and poked the trail with a stick,' Eliza said. 'She would not touch it.'

They shook their heads. Touching slime from one of the fairy folk could bring all sorts of dangers.

'She said it was . . .' Eliza whispered. They all leaned closer. 'She said it was like candlewax!' Eliza said in triumph. She sat back on her stool and looked around at their faces. 'An odd story, isn't it?'

Alys drained her cup. She noticed her hands were steady. 'Where were these tiny tracks?' she asked carelessly. 'On the road, which road? Whereabouts were they?'

Eliza gave up her cup to Margery who put them away in the cupboard with the empty pitcher of ale. 'Just a mile above the bridge,' she said. 'From Bowes Moor heading into Castleton. And coming closer. A horrible story, is it not? But she swore by it.'

Alys shook her head. 'Tiny tracks!' she said derisively. 'Candlewax! I thought you were going to frighten us with a ghost six feet tall!'

Eliza bridled. 'But it is true . . .'

'I'm weary,' Alys interrupted. 'Fetch Mary for me, Eliza, I'll go to bed.'

Eliza glanced at the closed door to Catherine's room. 'Should I see if she is all right?' she asked Alys. The rest of the women waited for Alys' decision. Alys, thinking of the little dolls just a mile from her door this night smiled bleakly.

'It does not matter,' she said. She laughed, a high, sharp laugh while the women looked at each other in surprise. 'Nothing is going to matter after all!' she said. 'After all this trouble. Nothing matters at all!'

Thirty-one

Hugo blundered into Alys' room as she dozed in her first sleep, making her jump awake with fear.

'Is it fire?' she demanded, coming out of sleep.

Hugo laughed aloud. He had been drinking till late in the hall and was boisterous. He pulled the covers off Alys and slapped her rump playfully.

'Heard the news?' he demanded. 'My marriage is to be annulled. I am to be wed to a girl straight from the nursery! And Stephen can get no sense out of the old woman from Bowes Moor!'

Alys snatched the covers back and pulled them up over her shoulders. 'I know all the news,' she said sourly. 'Except about the old woman. What is he doing to her? Is he hurting her?'

'Oh no,' Hugo said. 'He's no barbarian. She's an old lady. He's questioning her and arguing theology with her. It sounds as if she is holding her own. He was in a vile mood after dinner. He told me all about it over a pitcher of hippocras. They have been arguing over transubstant-transubstant-trans . . .' Hugo chuckled and gave up. 'Whether it's bread or meat,' he said vulgarly.

'Will he let her go?' Alys asked. She sat up in bed. Hugo was flushed and merry. He unbuttoned his fine doublet and tossed it towards the chair. It fell on the floor and he unbuckled his belt and codpiece, untied his hose and pulled them down and slung them all towards the pile of clothing. He came to her bedside, his shirt billowing.

'Move over, wench,' he said contentedly. 'I shall sleep here tonight.'

'Will he let her go?' Alys asked again. Hugo held her tight around the waist and nuzzled his head into her belly.

'Who, the old woman?' he asked, rearing up, his hair tousled. 'Oh, don't ask me, Alys, you know what Stephen is. He wants to do right by his God, and he wants to do right by his bishop, and he wants to do right by every simple soul, and he wants to do right by himself. If he finds she is an innocent old woman in error then he will persuade her to take the oath, let her go, and I will pop her over the border into Appleby for you and there will be an end to it.'

Alys lay back and closed her eyes. 'An end to it,' she said softly.

'Why not?' Hugo demanded. 'What matters one more old lady or no? Stephen and I will be going to London to see the little bride within a month. My father must be in his dotage. His preference for me is a child of nine, to be betrothed in name alone.' Hugo laughed. 'I care not!' he said. He patted her belly with a gentle hand. 'Catherine set aside and you big with my child. A new wife can come or wait. It matters little. As long as you give me a son which I can make my heir, and then another, until the castle is full of them. I have plenty of time to get children, Alys. There is plenty of time. Plenty of time. Plenty of wealth and land and ease for all of us.'

Alys let him rock her in time to his words and slid her arms around his back. She found she was smiling.

'You would not believe what troubles I have had today,' she said. 'Catherine has been hysterical, your father threatened to throw me out of the castle for a word spoken out of turn, I have been worried sick about the old lady, and then Eliza frightened me into fits with some horrid ghost story.'

Hugo chuckled and reached below the covers to slide Alys' shift up her body. 'My poor love,' he said. 'You should have come out with me. I was supposed to ride over to Cotherstone Manor but I saw such a buck on the way that I stopped and chased him. He led us for hours and would you believe I missed him with a crossbow? I was close, but I had sweat in my eyes and I could not see. I missed him! A clear shot to the heart and all I could see was a blur. William killed him for me in the end. I was raging! You shall have him for your dinner next week.'

He penetrated her with a gentle thrust and a gasp of pleasure. 'Be joyful!' he said, moving gently inside her. 'We shall be rid of Catherine and she can do as she pleases. My father's mind is on a new match and he can think of nothing else. Your old lady is holding her own against Stephen and needs neither your help nor mine, and these ghosts are terrors for little girls only, not a woman, Alys, not a wise woman like you.'

He sighed, and Alys felt his hand stroke her breast persuasively. She opened her legs wider.

'Are you joyful, little Alys?' he breathed. He started moving more urgently, consulting his own pleasure.

'I am well enough,' Alys said. Her mind roamed over the fears and triumphs of the day while her body moved accommodatingly under Hugo. She smiled and let him do what he would.

'Oh yes,' said Hugo.

And then they both were still.

'Alys,' Hugo said urgently. 'Alys!'

She woke at once. The moonlight was streaming through the arrow-slit in a silver bar across the green and yellow counterpane on the high bed.

'What?' she demanded, her own fear leaping up at the terror in his voice.

Hugo was white-faced. 'Mother of God,' he said. 'A dream! I had such a dream! Tell me I am awake and it was nonsense!'

The sheets were wet with his sweat. In the moonlight Alys could see his hair sticking damply to his shiny face. His eyes were wide like a man with a fever.

'Did you dream of dolls?' Alys cried incautiously. 'Little dolls coming to the castle?'

'No!' Hugo said. He stretched out his hands. They were shaking. 'Mother of God! I dreamed my fingers had gone numb. I dreamed my fingernails had gone. I dreamed my fingertips were gone. My fingers had gone, as if I had the leprosy. All I had were horrid stumps!'

Alys blenched. 'What a dream!' she said unsteadily. 'But you are awake now, Hugo. Don't fear.'

He threw his arms around her and buried his face in the warm skin of her neck. 'God alive, I was afraid!' he said. 'The tips of my fingers, Alys, they were melted away. Melted like wax!'

Alys lay very still, her arms around him, and felt him tremble. 'Hush,' she said, as if she were speaking to a little child. 'Hush, Hugo my love, my dear. Hush, you are safe now.'

After a little he stopped shaking and lay quiet in her arms.

'God! What terrors!' he said. He gave a little laugh for bravado. 'You will think me a babe in arms!' he said, embarrassed.

Alys, lying like a fallen statue in the moonlight, her belly like ice, shook her head. 'No,' she said. 'I have my nightmares too. Sleep now, Hugo.'

He settled himself like a child, his head on her

shoulder, one arm sprawled across her body. 'A dreadful dream!' he said softly.

Alys put her hand up and stroked his head, the damp, matted curls of his hair. 'I was screaming like a babe,' he said with a chuckle.

Alys gathered him closer still. Soon he was breathing steadily, his fears fallen away from him. Alys lay beside him and thought again of all the terrors, flying like pigeons with their beady, bright eyes to their homes.

Hugo's arm across her belly was too heavy. She lifted his hand to free herself from the weight, and then she paused. In the darkness she could not see well, but she stroked his fingertips with her own. The fingernails were short, surely they were shorter than they had been before. She pulled his hand into the moonlight to see better. Surely the tips of the fingers were blunt and the nails were shorter and squarer at the top, as if they had been rubbed away.

Alys gave a little moan of terror, slipped from the bed and pattered over to the fire, thrust a taper into the red embers and lit a candle. She walked back to the bed, the flickering flame throwing huge shadows all around her. She walked slowly, reluctant to know. She thought of the little doll of Hugo which she had shaped with such determination and anger all those months ago when she had wanted nothing but to be left alone by him. She had smoothed his mouth and bid him not call her. She had rubbed away the fingertips and ordered him not to feel her. She had scraped away the ears and ordered him not to hear her. She had scratched his eyeballs and ordered him to be blind to her. And now Hugo dreamed that his fingers were melting, and he had already missed his shot.

She sat on the bed and put the candlestick on the

table nearby. She did not trouble to shield the light. She had a certainty as deep and as cold as death that it would not waken him; he would not be able to see the glow of it through his closed eyelids. She took his hand and held it close to the candle so that she could see clearly what she feared to see.

The tips of his fingers were blunt as if they had been nipped off. Hugo's long strong hands were shorter, the last joint of each finger disproportionately stunted. His fingernails stopped short, square as if they had been roughly filed; shorter than the ends of his fingers, cut back. Alys shuddered. His hand looked as if someone had pruned the tips of every finger, leaving the nails clipped, the plump balls of the fingertips cropped.

She turned his hand over and looked at it as if she were reading his palm. The tips of his fingers were as smooth as the skin of his smiling, sleeping face. He had no fingerprints. They were rubbed away. On each fingertip there was nothing, no mark, just smooth, pink skin, squared off at the top like an ill-modelled statue. Alys gave a little sigh like a groan and sat with his malformed hand in her lap for a moment.

She leaned forward and held the candle high to look at his ears. Already they were tiny, the ears of a child. Only Hugo's long curly hair and the caps he always wore had prevented her from seeing it before. She looked at his lips. The sharp profile of his upper lip was blurred. The attractive, kissable bow of the upper lip and the sharp pout of the lower lip had melted. Only the perimeter of the dark shadow of stubble marked where his lips should start. The light flickered as the candle shook in Alys' hands. On an impulse she bent over him and gently shook him.

'Open your eyes, Hugo!' she said softly. 'Open your eyes a moment!'

He rolled away from her touch, mumbling something in his sleep, but when she shook him again his eyelids flickered open though he was still dreaming. In the moment before he closed them again and sank back into sleep, Alys peered closely at them. Across each dark pupil there was a tiny trail of cloudy grey as if someone had drawn a fingernail across his eyeballs.

Alys let him sleep and put the candlestick carefully on the bedside table. She slipped into bed beside him and piled the pillows up against the heavy carved headboard and sat upright, waiting for the dawn. She was cold and white but she made no move to pull the covers around her shoulders or to huddle down beside Hugo's contented sleeping warmth. Alys sat upright in her rich bed with the young lord beside her, his arm thrown lovingly across her, and waited for the dawn of another day with her face as grim and fearful as her betrayed mother Morach had looked all the years of Alys' childhood, when magic was not enough to make them safe.

In the morning Hugo was in a hurry to be off hunting. Stephen had brought him a new horse and he wanted to try its paces. The day was sunny and it would be too hot for hard riding later on. Besides, he had to be home early for the court in the afternoon. He barely noticed Alys' pale wakefulness.

'Are you well?' he asked, pausing in the doorway wearing only his shirt. 'You well, Alys?'

She blinked at him, her blue eyes strained and red-rimmed from the long night of watching. 'I dreamed,' she said. 'Bad dreams.'

'Good God, so did I!' Hugo said, remembering. 'I dreamed my fingers had gone. Gone like a leper. God! What a terror!'

Alys tried to mirror his relieved grin, but she could not. 'Show me your fingers,' she said 'Show me them.'

Hugo laughed. 'It was only a dream, sweetheart. See!'

He stepped back into the room and held out his right hand for Alys to inspect. In the bright dawn light from the arrow-slit she looked at the back of his hand. The fingernails were perfect, smooth and strong. His fingers were long and well-proportioned.

Alys gave a little hidden gasp of relief and turned his hand over. On each finger there was a perfect whorl – his fingertips were sound.

'We're both as fey as each other!' Hugo exclaimed. He bent down and gave her a quick buss on her cheek. 'Let me go, Alys! I'm going hunting!'

'Are your ears all right?' she demanded, as he went to the door.

He turned and grinned at her, as feckless as a child. 'Yes! Yes! Every part of me is well, and some parts of me are superb! Now may I go?'

Alys laughed unwillingly, her heart lightening despite her fear. 'Go then!' she said.

The door banged and he was gone. Alys pulled up the covers and slid down into the warmth where his body had lain. She shrugged her shoulders against her night fears.

'I won't think about it,' she said to herself as her eyes closed. 'I won't think about it.'

Catherine's door was open when the women came into the gallery in the morning. She was sprawled across the bed, door flung wide, waiting for them.

'I'll have my breakfast here!' she yelled. 'You, Ruth, bring me bread and ale. I'll have some roast beef or venison, and some goat's cheese. I fasted last night and I am hungry today. Fetch it for me at once.'

Eliza shot a quick irreverent grin at Alys. 'She's drunk!' she whispered. 'Good God, what now!'

Alys stepped up to the door. By Catherine's bed was the jug they kept in the cupboard of the gallery; it was rolling on its side, leaving a trail of red lees over the floorboards.

'Where did you get wine, Catherine?' Alys asked.

Catherine's face was flushed, her hair tousled, her eyes bright. 'Went down to the hall at dawn!' she said triumphantly. 'I can serve myself when I need, you know. I'm not some whey-faced child that they can torment. I've been Lady Catherine here for years. I kicked a page awake and he brought me dinner and wine. I've been drinking ever since.'

The women fluttered behind Alys in consternation.

'Downstairs in her shift,' Ruth said softly. 'Oh dear!'

Alys bit back a smile. 'You're drunk,' she said concisely to Catherine. 'You had better eat some bread and then sleep. You'll be sick enough later.'

Catherine shook her head and pointed imperiously to her window. 'I give the orders here, Alys. I am not yet commanding a pig and a cow on the edge of the moor. I am not yet set aside and shamed for the benefit of you and whatever you carry in your belly! Go and fetch me some more wine. I'll have clary wine – that's a good wine to drink in daylight. And I'll have ale with my breakfast! And then tell them to bring me a bath. I shall bathe and wear my rose and cream gown. And I shall dine in the hall today.'

Alys heard Eliza's giggle smothered from behind her hand. She turned around. 'She's impossible,' she said to the women. 'One of you sit with her. We'll have to do as she wishes. She'll pass out with the drink soon enough.'

'She can't go down to dinner like this,' Ruth said, scandalized.

Alys shook her head. 'She'll be sick long before dinnertime if she's been drinking all night.'

'My breakfast!' Catherine shouted imperiously, with the authority of the enormously drunk. 'At once, girl!'

No one had called Alys 'girl' for many months. Alys smiled wryly and nodded towards Catherine. 'At once,' she said with mock obedience. She closed the heavy carved door and pointed to Ruth and then Mary.

'You fetch her breakfast, what she wanted. It makes no difference, she'll be vomiting it up in moments. And you, Mary, go to the kitchen and tell them to set water to heat, and order her a bath.'

The two nodded. Alys led the rest of them downstairs for their breakfast, and waited in the lobby for the old lord and David to come down the stairs from the round tower.

'Good morrow, Alys,' the old lord said.

Alys stepped forward and kissed his hand.

David opened the door for the two of them and they entered the hall together.

Breakfast was a meal taken without ceremony at the castle. There was too much to do in the early hours of the day for much delay. The kitchen sent out a continuous stream of messes – four-person platters of bread and cheese and cold bacon. Serving-women and men went around the hall serving ale and hot water. People came and went, with a quick bow to the high table when one of the lords was seated and dining.

Hugo was long gone – out hunting with Stephen. Most of the soldiers were fed and at their posts by the early light. Alys sat at the lord's side and ate the best bread with him and drank a small cup of hot water with a sprinkling of chamomile on the top.

'What's the brew?' the old lord asked.

'Chamomile,' Alys said. 'For calmness.'

The lord gave a snort of amusement. 'Calmness is for the grave,' he said. 'I'd rather have panic any day. Tells me I am still alive.'

'Then you should have been born a woman,' Alys said.

He gave a quick guffaw of laughter. 'God forbid!' he said. 'What panics are you suffering, little Alys?'

'Catherine,' Alys said. 'She got hold of some wine in the night and she's still carousing this morning. She thinks of coming to dinner, primped up in her best, and winning back your affection.'

The old lord slapped the table with his hand and roared with laughter. Men taking breakfast on the nearby tables looked up, smiling, and one shouted, 'Share the jest, my lord!'

Lord Hugh shook his head, his eyes streaming. 'Women's troubles! Women's troubles!' he called back. All the men smiled and nodded.

'So!' he said, when he could catch his breath. 'When may I expect this seduction?'

Alys nipped the inside of her lips to contain her irritation and sipped her tea. 'She will come down to dinner unless someone prevents it, and she will make a scene and shame herself and shame you,' she said. 'If she spews all over you and over the young lord it will not be so merry, I suppose. We cannot stop her in the gallery. We cannot order the servants not to give her wine. She will have her own way unless you order it.'

Lord Hugh was still chuckling. 'Oh lord, Alys, don't bring me these hen-coop troubles,' he said genially. 'Give her wine and a drop of one of your sleeping herbs in the cup. Send her to sleep for a few hours and when she wakes sober and sick she'll have learned her lesson. I'll have the papers through in a few days and she can sign them and leave the castle forever.'

'In a few days?' Alys confirmed.

Lord Hugh nodded. 'Aye. So you can drink ale for breakfast and not handfuls of grass, my dear.' He chuckled again. 'Calmness. Oh Lord!'

Alys smiled thinly and broke some bread on her silver plate. 'Hugo tells me you have settled on the young girl for his bride,' she said. 'The little girl of only nine?'

Lord Hugh nodded. 'The best choice,' he said. 'I was torn. I'd have liked to see a quick wedding, bedding and birthing, but the girl's family are the very people we need as kin. And she herself is from fertile stock. Her mother had fourteen children, ten of them sons, before she died. All before she was twenty-five!'

'A fortunate woman indeed,' Alys said sarcastically.

Lord Hugh did not hear. 'The wench will come and live here and we can school her as we wish,' he said. 'If you'll be kindly to her, Alys, you can stay by her and serve her. She's no fool. She's been serving as a maid in the Howard household and at court since she was seven. She'll be fit to bed at twelve I should think. I may yet see her son.'

'And my son?' Alys pressed.

'He'll be mine as soon as he is born,' the old lord said. 'Don't fret, Alys. If he is a strong and bonny child he'll be my heir and you can stay as long as she permits and as long as we desire. This is a good outcome for you, as it happens. Your luck follows you like your shadow, does it not?'

'Like my shadow,' Alys assented. Her voice was low and quiet. Lord Hugh could hardly hear her. 'My luck follows like a shadow,' she said.

He pushed his plate away from him and a page came up with a silver bowl and ewer and poured water for him to wash his hands. Another came up with embroidered linen and he dried his hands.

'We dine early,' he reminded Alys. 'There are the rest of the trials this afternoon. I shall rest this morning. They weary me, all these stolen pigs and missing beehives. And besides, the law changes with every messenger that comes. It was better in the old days when I did just as I wished.'

'What of the old woman?' Alys asked.

Lord Hugh turned as he was going out of the door. 'I don't know,' he said. 'Father Stephen was talking with her again, after his supper last night. And this morning he went out riding with Hugo. She may not come to trial, Alys. It is Father Stephen's decision if she has no case to answer.' He grinned. 'She was leading him a merry dance as he told it at dinner last night. She is as learned as he and when he reproached her in Latin she defended herself in Greek and he was hard-pressed to follow. I suppose I shall conduct her trial in Hebrew for the purity of the language!'

'Might he release her?' Alys asked.

The old lord shrugged. 'Maybe,' he said. A mischievous gleam came into his eyes. 'Do you wish to appear for her?' he asked. 'Her learning and your quickness would be a formidable defence, Alys. Shall I tell Stephen that you will speak for her? Is it your wish to stand before us all and defend a papist and traitor, no matter what it costs?' His dark eyes scanned her face, his smile was cruel.

Alys ducked her head. 'No, no,' she said hastily. 'No, she is nothing to me. Father Stephen shall be the judge. I cannot be involved in this. I have too much to do, and my health needs all my care. I cannot be troubled with this as well.'

Lord Hugh gleamed his malicious smile. 'Of course, Alys,' he said. 'Leave it to us men. I'll let you know if we need chamomile.'

He swept out through the door, his wide flared surcoat swaying from his shoulders. Alys heard him laughing as he went up the stairs to the round tower. She finished her cup of chamomile tea in silence and then led the women back to the ladies' gallery.

Catherine was singing loudly. They could hear her from halfway down the stairs. Eliza snorted with laughter as they opened the door and saw Catherine seated in her old chair before the gallery fire, a jug of ale in one hand and a cup in the other.

She beamed as she saw them. 'My handmaids!' she said. 'My companions!'

'You must go to bed,' Alys said, stepping forward. 'You will be sick with all this drink, Catherine.'

Catherine waved the jug.

'Now Robin did a courting go –
To the leafy woods so green,
And Marion his lady-fair . . .'

'This is impossible,' Alys said through her teeth.

'I want my bath now,' Catherine ordered abruptly.

Alys looked towards Mary. 'They're bringing it,' she said, dropping a curtsey. 'But she wanted your herbs and oils in it, my lady.'

'Like last time,' Catherine said with drunken enthusiasm. 'When you bathed me in perfume flowers and rubbed me with oils and Hugo came and had us both.' There was a gasp from all the women. 'When it was so nice, Alys. When you lay on me and licked my breasts and poked me with your fingers. Like that.'

Alys shot a warning glance around the women. Eliza's face was scarlet with suppressed laughter. Ruth was white with shock and she was crossing herself against the sin of venery.

'Get the bath,' Alys said to Mary. 'She can have herbs in it.'

The women stood in silence seething with unspoken gossip while the servants carried in the heavy wooden bath-tub, draped it with linen and then poured in churn after churn of hot water. Alys fetched mint oil from her chest of goods, hoping that it would sweat the drink from Catherine's sodden blood. Catherine gaped blankly at the gallery fire and did not see the curious glances of the servants as they came and went with the hot water.

'He will return to me,' Catherine said suddenly. 'He can have me and he can have Alys. What man could resist? I have my dower lands and Alys is with child. I will accept the child. What man could want more?'

Alys grabbed Catherine under the elbow and nodded Margery to support her from the other side. 'Hush, Catherine,' she said warningly as they tottered towards the chamber where the bath was steaming and scented before the blazing fire. 'Hush. You shame yourself with this talk.'

'I will accept you,' Catherine said, looking at Alys. 'I will love you like a sister and we can all live here together. Why not? We are the lords. We can live as we please. And Hugo would be happy with us both.'

'Hush,' Alys said again. Her brain was working fast. Hugo might indeed accept a life financed by Catherine's dowry and inherited by Alys' children. The dynastic ambitions for the new young bride were his father's – it had always been his father's plots and schemes – Hugo

599

wanted his place at court, he wanted the money for his voyages and his ventures, he wanted to sink mine shafts and quarry lime, but if Catherine and Alys could make a truce and Alys bear him a son, he might abandon the venture of another wife.

'It's too late,' Alys said thoughtfully. 'The old lord is determined.'

Catherine was still rolling drunk. She staggered as Mary untied her shift and pulled it off over her head. It took three of them to steer her safely into the bath. She sat on the low stool in the tub and leaned her head back against the linen-covered side.

'You could deter him,' she said. She was slurring her words and her eyelids were drooping. 'You could persuade him. There is my dowry and your child. He wants these things.'

Alys rolled up her sleeves and roughly rubbed Catherine's shoulders and grimy neck. The folds of fat hung loosely around her body now that the baby had gone.

'Or if the old lord died,' Catherine suggested. Her voice was far too loud for safety. Margery, at the window, heard her. Eliza, waiting by the door, heard her. Mary, airing the shift before the fire, turned quickly and stared at Catherine lolling in the tub, lazy, corrupted.

'Don't say it!' Alys said sharply. 'My lord is well and will live for many years yet, please God.'

Catherine opened her drunk, unfocused eyes and smiled at Alys. 'It's true though,' she said. 'Hugo would never have the will to set me aside. Hugo likes his pleasures at once. He would never wait for a nine-year-old bride. These are not his plots and schemes. If the old lord was gone we could live well, us three.'

'Hush,' Alys said again. It was true. If the old lord

died and Hugo inherited tomorrow then Catherine would stay as nominal lady of the castle and Alys' position would be assured. Hugo had neither the energy nor the skill to rid himself of Catherine and negotiate a new marriage. And besides, he liked his comforts and his easy way of life. Catherine as lady and Alys as mistress was an ideal combination for Hugo, giving him wealth and sensual pleasure without effort.

'More hot water,' Catherine said. 'I will lie in the bath and drink more wine.'

Eliza sniggered at that, but a sharp look from Alys sent her from the room.

'Give her more hot water and a cup of watered wine,' Alys ordered. 'I am going to my room. It is too hot for me here.' She turned to Catherine. 'After your bath you must lie down and sleep,' she said firmly. 'You can dress in your rose gown after your rest. I will have you awakened in time for dinner, but you must sleep now.'

Catherine was already drowsy. Her large features, blurred in the scented steam, were soft with sleep. 'All right, Alys,' she said agreeably. 'But will you come and touch me? Will Hugo come and mount you while I watch? Like we did before?'

There was an utter silence in the room. 'You are dreaming,' Alys said roughly. 'Bawdy dreams, Catherine. Your humours are too hot. Your bath has over-heated you. You must rest.'

She turned and went quickly from the room before the others could read the guilt in her face. As she shut her chamber door she heard a soft scandalized shriek and the babble of whispers at the oriel window in the gallery, as the women fled from Catherine's room to repeat what she said.

Alys went to the arrow-slit window and looked out.

Over the bridge the white road uncurled itself around the hill and then headed straight as a Roman spear over the moor. The fields at the riverside were a dusty yellow-green. The hay was cut, the corn was in. They were tossing straw into windrows and would gather it this month. In the higher fields beyond the river there were cows picking over the hayfield stubble. Beyond them was the rough green and grey hide of moorland with a few sheep scattered across it. The heather was in flower and a traveller crossing the moor would have to wade through thigh-deep clumps of purple and walk all day in a cloud of sweet pollen. The fords would be dry, a man could walk northwards across the high hills and drop down into dale after dale – the Greta, the Lune, Cotherstone – without ever wetting his feet or finding a drop of clean water to drink.

Alys looked at the thin track of the white road and wondered where her little dolls were now, and if they were still walking wearily towards the castle, still trailing a little thread of candlewax slime behind them wherever their tiny feet pattered. They would make slow progress along the dusty road, leaping aside into the grass at the roadside for fear of cartwheels and feet and the dangerous clatter of hooves. The doll of the old lord would be hobbling, the doll of the miscarried woman trailing slime, and the doll of Hugo staggering sightlessly with his blunt insensate hands stretched before him.

In the warm air blowing through the arrow-slit Alys shivered, as cold as if she were trapped in a dank cave with flood water rising.

A flock of pigeons wheeled and turned in the sunlight, their feathers bright and golden, moving as one. They flew like a fletch of arrows straight towards Alys at the window and then wheeled at the last moment and settled out of her sight on the round tower, where the pigeon lad would settle them in their boxes and cut the messages from their cherry-red legs. Alys shuddered and drew back from the window, lay down on her bed and stared upwards at the rich green and gold embroidery of the tester above her head.

She must have dozed. She was wakened by a banging on her door and a high, sudden scream of fear, the noise of running feet, and someone calling her name in a voice sharpened with terror. Alys had jumped from her bed and torn open her door before she was awake.

'Is it fire?' she demanded urgently. Then she swayed and leaned back against the door. 'What is the matter?'

'Lady Catherine!' Eliza said. She took Alys by the shoulders and shook her awake. 'It's Lady Catherine. She's drowned! She's drowned! Come at once!'

Alys stumbled but Eliza dragged her forwards, across the gallery and to Catherine's chamber. Alys, still dazed, looked around all the faces expecting to see Morach soaking wet, her shock of white hair slicked down by river water, beaming with pride and saying 'I saved her!'

'Wake up!' Eliza said. She pushed Alys roughly towards Catherine's doorway. There were many people crowded into the gallery, soldiers and servants, all of them milling helplessly around and shouting instructions.

'Warm her up!'

'Fetch Father Stephen!'

'Put her in her bed!'

'Give her usquebaugh!'

'Burn horsehair!'

Alys, pushed by Eliza, fought her way into Catherine's chamber and fell back when she saw the bath-tub.

Catherine was blue. Her staring, blank face and all over her flaccid body was stained veinous-blue. Blue fingernails, blue feet, blue lips, white-blue face.

Someone had heaved her up out of her bath-water and then let her slide in again so her head was tipped back against the edge of the bath, limp as a doll. She looked like a dreadful parody of the sensual Catherine who had shouted for wine and more water. A woman who had given herself up to selfish pleasures and was now given up to death.

'How did this happen?' Alys asked. Her voice was still croaky from sleep. She coughed to clear it.

'We left her alone,' Eliza said. Alys could hear the grief and guilt in her harsh tone. 'She wanted to be alone and we shut the door and left her. God knows what I was thinking of. I knew she was drunk. But she was maudlin and dull. She ordered us out of the room and we went. We left her.'

'Did she fall?' Alys asked.

'I'd have heard if she had fallen,' Ruth said sharply. Her face was nearly as pale as Catherine's horrid whiteness. 'I was listening for her call. I was not gossiping about sin and lechery. If she had fallen I would have heard. I heard nothing. Nothing.' She broke off, and turned her face away, a handkerchief to her eyes and sobbed. 'Nothing,' she said.

'She was drunk,' Mistress Allingham said. 'I think she just slid under the water and could not get herself out again.'

'Can you do nothing?' Eliza demanded. 'Open a vein, bleed her! Something!'

Alys shook her head. 'Nothing,' she said slowly. 'There's no blood pumping around Catherine any more. She's dead.'

She drew back. 'Close the door. Get these people out of here,' she said. 'Send for someone to cover her nakedness and lift her out of the bath. The old lord will have to be told, and Hugo. They should not see her like this.'

There was a movement among the crowd in the gallery as they went to obey Alys.

'I'll tell the old lord,' Alys said numbly.

Ruth gave a loud, thin cry and ran to her room. Eliza turned to go after her. 'Odd,' she said. She paused and looked at Alys. 'That she should escape drowning in the winter river, bobbing with ice floes, treacherous with rocks, and then go under in her bath.'

Alys shook her head, half closed her eyes. 'It is a nightmare,' she said honestly. 'A nightmare.'

Thirty-two

They dressed Catherine's cold, water-logged body and they laid her in the little chapel which stood by the gatehouse in the outer manse, a branch of candles at her head and at her feet. Father Stephen, rushed off his horse from hunting and into his black archdeacon's gown, ordered prayers to be said for her soul, but there were no nuns and no monks to keep a vigil for Lady Catherine. All that had gone and no one knew how to mourn for the lady of the castle any more.

Father Stephen told four soldiers the prayers which should be said and they kept a vigil like a guard duty. But it was not done well. Everyone knew that it was not done well now there were neither monks nor nuns to pray for the soul of a woman drowned while deep in sin. Ruth stayed by the makeshift coffin, one hand on the side, her head bowed, fingering her rosary and saying the prayers she had learned as a child. She would not be moved away.

The other women tried to pull her away to the gallery and Eliza stood before her, trying to hide her, when Father Stephen came into the chapel. He raised his eyebrows at the murmur of Latin prayers and the click of the rosary beads but one glance at Ruth's agonized white face prevented him from interrupting her.

'What is this?' he demanded of Alys in his sharp, accusing voice. 'Is this woman a papist? I knew she was devout but I never knew she used the rosary and prayed with the old prayers. She has taken the Oath, has she not? She knows the King is head of the English Church?'

Alys nodded. 'It's the shock. She loved Lady Catherine. When she is recovered from the shock she will behave as she should.'

'And the other women?' he demanded. Alys could hear his excitement rising. 'Are the other women also steeped in Roman heresy? Do they not understand the nature of the true Church?'

'No, no,' Alys said quickly. 'We are all good Christians now. Ruth is sick with shock.'

'Take the rosary from her,' Father Stephen said.

'Is it a sin?' Alys asked in confusion. 'I thought it was allowed.'

'Some say it does no harm but I believe, and my bishop believes, that it is a graven image as bad as any other false god,' Stephen said passionately. 'It is a doorway to sin, if it is not a sin itself. Take it from her.'

Alys hesitated. 'It is her own,' she said. 'She is using it only to keep count of her prayers.'

'Take it,' Stephen said firmly. 'I cannot permit it – not even to mourn Lady Catherine. It is a doorway for sin and confusion.'

Alys waited until he had left the chapel and then tapped Ruth on the shoulder. 'Give me them,' she said abruptly, pointing to the rosary beads. 'You will have us all questioned for our beliefs by Father Stephen. You are a fool to be so open. Give me them or hide them where they cannot be found.'

Ruth's white face was twisted with grief. 'It is all I can do for her now!' she said wildly. 'All there is for me to do. She disgusted me with her talk and I left her to drown. She died in sin, I must pray for her soul. I must light candles for her and have masses sung for her. She died in deep sin, I must save her soul if I can.'

'No one believes that stuff any more,' Alys said

tightly. There was something about Ruth's outstretched hand on the coffin with the rosary clasped so tightly which was inescapably moving. 'Father Stephen says none of it is true.' Alys remembered the darkness of the chapel and the long nights of vigil which followed a nun's death. The long, sweet cadences of a Requiem Mass and the spellbinding holiness of the incense. The candlelight and Mother Hildebrande's face smiling and serene in the certainty of eternal life.

Alys snatched at the rosary and pulled it from Ruth's hand. 'No one believes that now,' she said brutally. 'Pray in silence or you will endanger us all!'

Ruth tugged back. 'I will pray for my lady as it should be done! I will keep my loyalty to her. I will give her her dues,' she cried.

Alys pulled, the string biting into the palm of her hand. Then with a sudden snap, the string of the rosary broke and the beads spilled on to the stone-flagged floor of the chapel, bouncing and dancing in every direction, scattering and rolling out of sight, under the pews, into the gratings, in a great explosion of destruction. There was a gasp from the other women and a loud cry from Ruth, who dropped to her hands and knees and scrabbled frantically, trying to gather them up as they rolled away from her.

'Oh God!' Alys said desperately.

She marched from the chapel, clutching the string and the remaining beads and the dangling cross, before Ruth could protest. Her footsteps echoed on the little stones of the aisle and her gown swished from side to side as she strode away. Alys walked with her head up, her fingers gripping the broken rosary so tight that the mark of the string was as red as a weal around her fingers when she stopped in the porch of the chapel and looked at the little wooden cross. It seemed a lifetime since she had counted beads through her fingers and said her prayers and kissed the cross. Now she snatched them from a praying woman to hand to a man who was an enemy of the faith of her childhood and the inquisitor of her mother. Alys' face was bleak as she held out the rosary to one of the soldiers at the gate.

'Take this to Father Stephen,' she said. 'Tell him there is no heresy here! I have taken the rosary away from the praying woman.'

He nodded and turned away.

'He will be with the old lord,' Alys said.

The man shook his head. 'He has gone to the prison tower,' he said. 'He told me I could find him there. There is an old woman coming for trial this afternoon and he has gone to question her and persuade her to repent of her error.'

Alys went whiter still and swayed a little where she stood. 'Yes,' she said. 'In this shock of my lady's death I had forgotten. Is the old woman still to be tried? Will they not delay the trials to mourn Lady Catherine?'

The man shook his head. 'There are too many people come into town for the trials to be delayed,' he said. 'The old lord said they would go ahead. Father Stephen thinks he can bring the old woman to repentance, please God.'

Alys nodded and turned away. 'Please God,' she said under her breath. The words were meaningless. She had robbed them of meaning every day since the night when the flickering light of the burning abbey had woken her. 'Please God,' Alys said, knowing that she no longer had a god to trust. Knowing that the gods she now served were fearfully swift and reliable in their responses – but that nothing could please them.

In the ladies' gallery they had to share their clothes to find dark gowns with dark sleeves, dark petticoats and dark hoods. Alys' navy blue gown had gone to Mother Hildebrande in the kitchen lad's bundle; it seemed like years ago. She went to Catherine's chest of clothes and found a gown of deep pine green, so dark that it was almost a black. She wore it with a black underskirt, and a high old-fashioned gable hood. As she closed the chest she saw Catherine's rose and cream gown which Catherine thought would regain Hugo's weathercock desire; the gown Alys had dreamed she would wear in a garden, walking on the arm of the young lord. Alys dropped the lid of the chest with a bang.

Father Stephen led a prayer for Catherine's soul before he said grace at dinner. He spoke in English. Alys listened to the strange, informal chatter between Father Stephen and his God. It did not sound holy. It did not sound as if it would save Catherine's soul from hell. Alys kept her head down and said 'Amen' with the rest.

She had chosen to sit at the women's table, behind the lords, for dinner. She did not want to sit at the high table, between the old lord and Father Stephen, she did not want to take Catherine's place at table while Catherine lay, blue and icy, in the little chapel, inadequately watched by four soldiers and Ruth in awkward silence. She did not want to look at the old lord and see his shielded, smiling face while he calculated how to make this new turn of events serve him. She did not want to see Hugo's careless joy at his freedom.

The women were silent at dinner. They were served with broth and half a dozen meat dishes and salads. None of them ate well. Alys, watching the back of Hugo's head and shoulders from her old place, saw that he ate heartily after his morning's ride. He had not seen Catherine, half in, half out of her bath, with her blue lips open underwater. He had not yet gone to the chapel to pray for her soul. He had not even changed his clothes, so that he was still wearing a red doublet, slashed, with white shirt showing at the slashes, a heavy red cape at his shoulders, and red breeches with black leather riding boots. When one of the serving-lads dropped a plate in the centre of the hall Hugo laughed, unaffected by gloom.

The old lord, sitting in his seat, smiled quietly. Hugo was a widower, the dowry lands were his without contest. The manor farm he would have given Catherine was his still. The marriage with the nine-year-old girl was well in hand but with Catherine's wealth and Hugo's improved status as a widower the terms could undoubtedly be improved.

The pages set hippocras and fruit and wafers on the tables. Alys took a small glass of hippocras and felt the sweet wine warm her through.

'It doesn't seem right, eating and drinking with my lady dead this hour,' Eliza said.

Alys shrugged. 'You can join Ruth in her vigil if you wish,' she said. 'But the castle will run as my lord commands. It seems right to him – I shall not argue.'

Eliza nodded. 'As you say,' she said, dropping her eyes away from Alys' cold face.

Lord Hugh looked behind him. 'Alys!' he said peremptorily.

Alys rose up from the table and stood behind his chair, leaning forward.

'Father Stephen is engaged in the arrangements for Catherine's funeral and questioning the old woman, so you shall be my clerk for the trials. Come to my room within an hour and we can prepare the papers. The trials start here at two.'

'I shall not know what to write,' Alys said unhelpfully. 'Could not David serve you better? Or even my Lord Hugo?'

'I'll tell you what to write,' Lord Hugh said firmly. 'It is all done by rote. We have a book to enter the charge and the sentence. Any fool could do it. Come to my room before two and you shall see.'

'Yes, my lord,' Alys said unenthusiastically.

'You can leave now,' he said. He shot a quick glance at her pale face. 'Not sick are you?' he asked. 'The baby is well? Catherine's death did not shock you, damage the child?'

'No,' Alys said coldly. She thought of claiming illness and avoiding the trials but she knew she could not again wait in her room knowing nothing. Mary's account of Mother Hildebrande's trial for witchcraft had been so sparse as to be worse than hearing nothing. Alys thought she would sit at the women's table at the rear of the dais with her head down, writing what Lord Hugh commanded, and then at least she would hear all that was said.

'I am well enough to be there,' Alys said. 'It is my wish to serve you.'

Lord Hugh nodded, noting the whiteness of Alys' face, the strain which showed in dark shadows around her eyes and the hard set of her mouth. 'Rest afterwards,' he said gruffly. 'You look dreadful.'

'Thank you, my lord,' Alys said steadily. 'I will.'

The great hall was packed with people. They had been waiting outside the castle gates from noon while the lords finished their dinner and sat over their wine. The trestle-tables had been dragged back against the wall as soon as dinner was finished, the fire which had burned since Alys had first come to the castle was doused and the ashes swept away so that people could sit side by side in the whole body of the room. The benches and stools were arranged in concentric rings around the high table and crowded with people sitting too close. Behind them, and pressing continually forward, was a mob of people – some of them servants in the castle, many of them from Castleton. At the rear of the hall were more benches and people standing on them in unsteady lines, leaning forward to overlook the others.

Alys sat with the women, behind the high table at the rear of the dais, shrinking back against the wall. The fine weather of yesterday and the morning had gone, the sun turned grey, shrouded in mists. The hall was dark though it was only two in the afternoon. Alys leaned back into the shadows. She had the book which recorded Lord Hugh's quarterly sessions of justice, and two pens and a pot of ink spread on the table before her. The other women sat facing the high table leaving Alys room to write.

The door behind the tapestry opened and Lord Hugh's trumpeter, stationed high in the minstrel gallery over the hall at the far end, played a flat blast on the horn. Everyone in the hall rose to their feet and a bench overturned and crashed backwards on to someone's toes, making them cry out and swear. Lord Hugh walked into the hall, wearing his best gown with the fur-lined collar, and took his seat at the high table. Hugo followed him, and sat on his right, in his usual dinnertime seat.

'Bring in the accused,' Lord Hugh said quietly.

The man was already waiting. He stepped forward: 'John Timms, my lord,' he said respectfully.

Lord Hugh looked around. 'Alys!' he said irritably. 'I can't see what you are doing back there in the shadows. Bring your book up here so I can see the entries.'

Alys hesitated. 'I prefer . . .' she started.

'Come on,' Lord Hugh said abruptly. 'We don't have all day. The sooner this is done the sooner we can have this rabble out of the castle and back to their work.'

Alys picked up her book and went to Catherine's seat on the left hand of the old lord. Eliza followed her with the ink-pot and pens. Alys seated herself and bent her head low over the page. In her dark gown and the large black gable hood she thought that she might pass unnoticed, melting into the background as a lowly, unimportant clerk.

'Write John Timms,' Lord Hugh said, pointing one finger to a column.

Alys obediently wrote. There was a long column of names, then the occupation and age, then the charge, then the verdict and then the sentence. Most of the verdicts read guilty. Lord Hugh was not a man to offer anyone the benefit of the doubt.

'Failure to practise archery,' Lord Hugh read from a crumpled piece of paper in a pile before him.

John Timms nodded. 'Guilty,' he said. 'I am sorry. The business was doing badly and I had no time and my son and the apprentices had no time either.'

Lord Hugh glared at him. 'And if I have no time to keep a pack of soldiers and the Scots come down on us, or the French make war on us, or the damned Spanish choose to call on us – what then?' he demanded. 'Fine three shillings. And don't neglect it again.'

Alys scribbled quickly.

The next case was a stolen pig, as the old lord had predicted. The accused, Elizabeth Shore, alleged that the pig had strayed into her yard and eaten the hens' feed and had thus been fed by her for free all the summer. Her accuser claimed she had tempted it away. Lord Hugh gave them some moments to squabble before slapping his hand on the table and ordering them to jointly feed the pig up, kill it and share it: three-quarters of the pig to the owner and one leg and some lights to the accused.

Next was a man accused of failing to maintain roads, then a man accused of theft, a woman accused of slander, a merchant accused of shoddy goods, a man charged with assault. Alys wrote the names and the charges and the people came and went, dispatched with speed and sometimes justice by Lord Hugh.

'Is that it?' he asked, when there was a lull in the proceedings.

An officer stepped up to the table. 'That is all the common cases, my lord,' he said. 'I have not heard if Father Stephen wished to charge the old woman from Bowes Moor.'

Alys looked up from her page.

'Send to him and ask him,' Lord Hugh said irritably. 'If he is unsure, the old woman can be released. I don't want her persecuted over some bookish detail.'

Alys bent her head down to the page again. The paper seemed very white, the letters on the page very black and spiky. She swallowed on her hope and pressed her lips together so that they would not move in a silent prayer to whatever gods might listen.

Hildebrande might be set free. If she were turned out of the castle into Castleton it would be easy to send her money and clothes and set her on her way. Southwards perhaps, or even east to the coast and to France. She would have learned now what danger she was running with her plans to work and pray in the rules of the Order. She would have been frightened, Alys told herself, and perhaps treated a little roughly. That would have warned her that the world had changed, that there was now no room for piety and devotion to the old religion. Alys pulled at the feather of the quill. Hildebrande would have learned that the old ways were truly gone. She might now be prepared to live out her days quietly, in a little farm somewhere. Alys might find her some people who would house her and treat her kindly. She might be content to be an old lady sitting at the back door in the sunshine. Now she might have learned the wisdom to take the easy way.

Alys raised her head, she could hear the guards shouting outside the double doors of the great hall. Father Stephen came in, walking slowly, his face grave, a ledger tucked under his arm.

Alys felt her heart speed. She scanned Stephen's face. Surely he was slow and thoughtful because he had to report that there was no case to answer. He had failed to incriminate Mother Hildebrande. Her learning and her old skilful wit had been too much for him. Perhaps she had even shaken his reforming zeal. Alys hid a little smile.

'Please call the old woman to account for herself,' Stephen said. He slid the ledger across the table towards Alys and motioned her to open it. 'There is the charge.'

Dumbly Alys opened the book where a dark ribbon marked the place. The old lord leaned forward to see. Father Stephen went around to the back of the dais, mounted the steps, and took a stool beside Alys at the foot of the table.

Alys looked at the Bishop's Court records in the heavy black ledger. There was a column for the date, and for the name, and for the occupation. There was a space for the charge. There was a space for the verdict. There was a space for the punishment. Alys looked along the page. There were rows after rows of names arraigned for all sorts of crimes, from adultery to heresy. Wherever it said 'Heresy', along the line it said 'Guilty', and then further on it said 'Burned'.

'Burned,' Alys whispered incredulously.

'Do you see how to write it?' Stephen whispered encouragingly. 'And this other paper, the roll, is a record of what is said here this afternoon. I will nod to you when you need to make a note of something. You can write in English, we can copy it fair into Latin later.'

'Make way for the old woman of Bowes Moor,' Lord Hugh said impatiently. He waved at the people in the centre of the hall. 'Let her through, for God's sake,' he said irritably. 'We don't have all day to spend on this.'

Alys leaned towards Lord Hugh. 'I don't want to do this,' she said urgently. 'I must ask to be excused.'

He glanced down at her white face. 'Not now, not now,' he said. 'Let's get this over and done with. It's a messy business. I like it not.'

'*Please*,' Alys hissed.

Lord Hugh shook his head, he was not listening. 'Do your work, Alys,' he said roughly. 'This is the last case. I am weary myself.'

Alys bowed her head over the ledger, writing the date with exquisite care. She was aware of the commotion in the hall, of the sound of the soldiers coming in slowly, out of step, not marching as they usually did, but delayed by a limping pace.

'Give her a stool,' Lord Hugh said impatiently. 'Give her a seat, the old woman can't stand. And give her some wine.'

Alys kept her head down. She had an insane thought that if she never looked up, if she never raised her eyes, then she would never see Mother Hildebrande sitting on a stool in the centre of the great hall surrounded by staring people. If she kept her head down and never looked, then it would not be Mother Hildebrande. It would be someone else entirely. On a different charge. A different charge entirely. Another person.

'Your name?' Stephen rose to his feet. Alys did not look up.

'Hildebrande of the Priory of Egglestone.' The voice was different, it rasped as if the speaker's throat was scraped. It was deeper, hoarser. And the speech was different too. This old woman could not speak clearly, could not form her words, lisped on her 's' and gargled the other words in her throat. Alys copied 'Hildebrande' in the space in the book for the name of the accused; and told herself that since it was not Mother Hildebrande's clear voice, not Mother Hildebrande's pure speech – it could not be her.

'Not your popish pretence of a name, but your real name,' Stephen said. He sounded angry, Alys thought, keeping her head bowed over the book. He should not be angry with this old lady with the sore throat, whatever she had done.

'My real name is Hildebrande,' the rasping voice said and stopped for breath. 'Of the Abbey of Egglestone.'

'Write: "Refuses to give true name,"' Stephen said in an aside to Alys. Laboriously she opened a bracket beneath the name she had already written, then she copied – 'Refuses to give true name'. She nodded with satisfaction. It was not her mother's voice, Hildebrande was not her name. It was someone else altogether. Above her head the questions went on.

'You were a nun at the abbey?' Stephen asked.

'I was.'

'You were there on the night that the abbey was inspected for heresy, popish practices, gross impropriety and blasphemy, and closed?'

There was a murmur from the audience. Alys could not tell whether it was moral outrage at the nuns, or resentment towards Stephen. She did not look up to see.

There was no answer for long minutes.

'I was there when the abbey was burned,' the voice said wearily. 'There was no inspection, there was no impropriety. It was an attack of arson. It was a criminal attack.'

There was a surge of speech from the crowd. The old lord banged the handle of his ebony stick on his board and shouted, 'Quiet!'

'That is a lie,' Stephen said. 'It was a legal inspection of a corrupt and dangerous nest of abuse. You were smoked out like the vipers you were.'

There was a silence.

'And where did you go, when you fled from justice and mercy?' Stephen demanded. 'Where have you been these eleven months?'

'I will not answer that question,' the hoarse voice said steadily.

'You have been asked it before with torture,' Stephen said warningly. 'You can be put to question again.'

Alys did not look up. The hall was very quiet.

'I know,' the voice said in a ghost of a sigh. 'I am prepared to die down there.'

There was a low angry mutter from the crowd. Alys, hidden behind her arm as she bent over the book, peeped up. She could see the first couple of rows of men. They were Hugo's own soldiers, but they were shifting uneasily on their seats.

'Write down: "Is shielding fellow-conspirators,"' Stephen said to Alys. Alys copied the words into the roll of paper.

Stephen changed tack. 'Were there any others who also fled from justice on that night?' Stephen asked. 'Others who have been hiding, as you have been hiding? Who have perhaps plotted to meet with you? Who planned to be with you?'

There was a silence.

'Who is "Ann"?' Stephen asked softly.

Shocked, Alys' head jerked up before she could stop herself – and then she saw her.

Hildebrande sat slumped on her stool. Her fingers were spread out over her knees, as if she were holding sinew and bone together. The old blue gown Alys had given her was bloodstained and spattered. There was a large dark stain at the hem – she had soiled herself in her agony. Her shoulders were hunched awkwardly, one side irregular where the shoulder had been dislocated and not thrust back into the socket. Her feet were bare. On the pale old skin of her feet were deep purple and red blood-bruises, perfect copies of the knots which had tied her to the rack. Her wrists were black with bruising, where the rope had tied her arms above her head. Her thin toes were stained with blood. They had ripped out the toenails. The fingernails, too, were gone. The hands spread like old bloody talons, clinging to her own body, as if to hold it together, clinging to her faith.

At Alys' sudden movement Hildebrande looked in her direction.

Their eyes met.

She recognized Alys at once. Her bloodstained mouth

opened in a dreadful smile. Alys saw the deep, dark bruises on her cheeks from the metal gag and then, as her ghastly smile widened, saw that her teeth had been pulled out from the gums, some broken and left as stumps, others leaving dark, blood-filled holes. Alys saw the smile and knew Hildebrande's revenge had come easily to her hand. Hildebrande would not suffer alone. She would not burn alone.

Mutely, Alys watched her. She said nothing. She did not plead with her eyes, she did not put her soft hands together in a secret sign for forgiveness. She waited for the horror of Hildebrande naming her as her accomplice and a runaway nun. The evidence was there. She was wearing Alys' gown, there was food from the castle at the cottage. Alys waited to be named and Hildebrande to be revenged on her for her pain of disappointment, and for the pain of the rack and the tortures.

Hildebrande's pale blue eyes in the blackened strained sockets never wavered. 'There was no one conspiring with me,' she said, her voice clearer. 'I was alone. Always. All alone.'

'Who is Ann?' Stephen said again.

Mother Hildebrande smiled directly at Alys, her old face a ghastly, toothless mask.

'Saint Ann,' she lied without hesitation. 'I was calling on Saint Ann.'

Alys dropped her head and wrote blindly, one word after another.

The old lord leaned forward and tweaked Stephen's gown. 'Finish it,' he said. 'I mislike this crowd.'

Stephen nodded, straightened up, raised his voice to a shout. 'I demand that before this court you deny your mistaken loyalty to the Pope and affirm your loyalty to the King, His Majesty Henry the Eighth, and your faith in his Holy Church of England.'

'I cannot do that,' the weary voice replied.

'I caution you that if you fail to repent now you will be found guilty of heresy to the Holy Church of England and you will be burned at the stake for your sins and burn hereafter in the everlasting torments of hell,' Stephen said in a shower of words like hailstones.

'I keep my faith,' Hildebrande said quietly. 'I await my cross.'

Father Stephen looked uncertainly towards Lord Hugh. 'Shall I wrestle with her for her soul?' he asked.

'She looks as if she has done enough wrestling,' the old lord said acidly. 'I'll sentence her, shall I?'

Father Stephen nodded and sat down.

Lord Hugh banged on the table with his stick. 'It is the judgement of this court that you are guilty of treason to His Supreme Majesty Henry the Eighth, and guilty of heresy to the Holy Church of England,' he said rapidly. 'Tomorrow morning at dawn you shall be taken from here to a place of execution where you will be burned at the stake for your crimes.'

Alys was writing blindly, seeing nothing, hearing nothing, watching the quill move up and down the paper. She felt Hildebrande's eyes on her, she felt the old woman willing her to look up, to exchange one look. She felt the weight of Hildebrande's need for the two of them to look into each other's faces once more, without deceit, without pretence, knowing what the other one truly was – as clear and as open as when Alys had been the little child in the garden and Hildebrande had seen the daughter she would never have.

Alys knew that Hildebrande was waiting for one

glance from her. One honest exchange of penitence, of forgiveness, of release.

Of farewell.

Alys kept her head down until she heard them carry the old woman out. She would not look at her. She never said goodbye.

In my dream I smelled the dark sulphurous stink of a passing witch and I pulled the smooth embroidered sheets up over my head and whispered 'Holy Mary, Mother of God, pray for us', to shield me from my dream, from a nightmare of terror. Then I heard shouting and the terrifying crackle of hungry flames and I came awake in a rush with a thudding heart and sat up in my bed and looked fearfully around the white-washed walls of my room.

The walls were orange, scarlet, with the bobbing light of reflected flames, and I could hear the deep excited murmur of a waiting crowd. I had slept too long, in my grief and confusion – I had slept too long and they had the faggots piled around her feet and they had already set them alight. I snatched for my cape and I ran barefoot through the open door of my chamber and out into the ladies' gallery, where the light was shining brightly through the coloured glass of the oriel window and the smoke was pouring in through the open casement where the women were gathered. Eliza Herring turned to me, one side of her face glowing with the brightness of the fire outside, and she said: 'We called you, but you were fast asleep. Come quick, Lady Alys, the flames have caught.'

I said nothing to her, but ran for the door, down the winding stairs and out into the courtyard.

They had set up a stake for her in the square stone-filled pit before the prison tower, and heaped small pieces of dry kindling at the base of the pile and faggots of wood, to burn brightly and strongly, at the top.

Before the fire were the soldiers and servants and Lord Hugh, Stephen the priest and my Hugo. But they had kept the townspeople away, afraid of their anger. Hugo turned and saw me in the doorway, my hair flying loose, my eyes glazed with fear. He put a hand out to beckon me, turned to come towards me, but I was too quick for him.

I raced across the courtyard towards the fire, towards the flames, and I saw through the heat haze the white tortured face of Hildebrande. The wind was blowing from the west, a clean wind with the smell of rain behind it, and it kept the flames away from me. I scrambled, like a child rock-climbing, over the wide spread of kindling and then up the faggots to the central pole, and grabbed her thin, racked body around the knees, and then found my feet and pulled myself up, and held her around the waist.

Her hands were bound behind her, she could not hold me. But she turned her face towards me and her bruised eyes were full of love. She said nothing, she was silent, as if she were at peace, like the quiet centre of a storm, as the flames came licking closer, all around us like the tongues of hungry serpents and I was choking in the swirl of smoke and dizzy with the heat and the terror.

Deep in my belly my baby churned and struggled as if he too could feel the heat, as if he too wanted, more than anything in the world, to live. I looked through the shifting heat haze of the smoke and saw Hugo's white, panic-stricken face turned towards me, and I tried to make my lips say 'Goodbye' but I knew he could not see me properly. His sight was too blurred, it is fading fast. He could not see me when I said to him 'Goodbye'.

I held firmly around her waist and tried to force myself to stand still like a woman with holy courage. It was no use. The bundles of dry wood beneath my feet were

*shifting, the flames were licking up from underneath. I
stepped from one foot to the other in a foolish dance, vainly
trying to spare my bare feet from the pain of burning.*

*'Alys! Jump!' Hugo yelled. He was beating at the
flames with his cloak. Stephen was behind him, screaming
for water to douse the fire. 'Jump off!' Hugo shrieked.*

*The old lord was close behind him, his arms held out to
me. 'Come down, Alys!' he shouted at me. 'Come away!'*

*Then Hugo flung himself past his father towards the
flames and Stephen and some other men dragged him
back. I saw them struggle with him, as I fretted from one
frightened foot to the other and the heat fanned around
me like the breath of a dragon. Through the heat haze I
could see Hugo's face looking towards me, his mouth
calling my name, and I saw in his eyes his terror of losing
me and I knew then – for the first time perhaps – that he
had loved me. And that for a little while – God knows
only a little, little while – that I had loved him.*

*I turned my face away from him, away from the castle,
away from them all. I leaned my head on her thin shoulder
and tightened my arms around her waist. The flames had
flickered up the back of the stake and the singed rope
binding her hands behind her suddenly parted. Her
broken, racked hand stroked my hair, clasped the top of
my head in her blessing. And even with the pain from my
scalding feet and the heat of the smoke in my throat and
the ceaseless, senseless thudding of fear all through me, I
felt at peace – at last – at peace. Because I knew at last
where I belonged, and because I had found, at the very
last, a love I would not betray.*

*The last thing I knew, even more powerful than my old
constant terror of fire, was her arms coming around me
and her voice. She said:*

'My daughter.'

Discover more about our forthcoming books through Penguin's FREE newspaper...

Penguin
Quarterly

It's packed with:

- exciting features
- author interviews
- previews & reviews
- books from your favourite films & TV series
- exclusive competitions & much, much more...

Write off for your free copy today to:
Dept JC
Penguin Books Ltd
FREEPOST
West Drayton
Middlesex
UB7 0BR
NO STAMP REQUIRED

READ MORE IN PENGUIN

In every corner of the world, on every subject under the sun, Penguin represents quality and variety – the very best in publishing today.

For complete information about books available from Penguin – including Puffins, Penguin Classics and Arkana – and how to order them, write to us at the appropriate address below. Please note that for copyright reasons the selection of books varies from country to country.

In the United Kingdom: Please write to *Dept. JC, Penguin Books Ltd, FREEPOST, West Drayton, Middlesex UB7 0BR*

If you have any difficulty in obtaining a title, please send your order with the correct money, plus ten per cent for postage and packaging, to *PO Box No. 11, West Drayton, Middlesex UB7 0BR*

In the United States: Please write to *Penguin USA Inc., 375 Hudson Street, New York, NY 10014*

In Canada: Please write to *Penguin Books Canada Ltd, 10 Alcorn Avenue, Suite 300, Toronto, Ontario M4V 3B2*

In Australia: Please write to *Penguin Books Australia Ltd, 487 Maroondah Highway, Ringwood, Victoria 3134*

In New Zealand: Please write to *Penguin Books (NZ) Ltd,182–190 Wairau Road, Private Bag, Takapuna, Auckland 9*

In India: Please write to *Penguin Books India Pvt Ltd, 706 Eros Apartments, 56 Nehru Place, New Delhi 110 019*

In the Netherlands: Please write to *Penguin Books Netherlands B.V., Keizersgracht 231 NL–1016 DV Amsterdam*

In Germany: Please write to *Penguin Books Deutschland GmbH, Friedrichstrasse 10–12, W–6000 Frankfurt/Main 1*

In Spain: Please write to *Penguin Books S. A., C. San Bernardo 117–6° E–28015 Madrid*

In Italy: Please write to *Penguin Italia s.r.l., Via Felice Casati 20, I–20124 Milano*

In France: Please write to *Penguin France S. A., 17 rue Lejeune, F–31000 Toulouse*

In Japan: Please write to *Penguin Books Japan, Ishikiribashi Building, 2–5–4, Suido, Tokyo 112*

In Greece: Please write to *Penguin Hellas Ltd, Dimocritou 3, GR–106 71 Athens*

In South Africa: Please write to *Longman Penguin Southern Africa (Pty) Ltd, Private Bag X08, Bertsham 2013*

BY THE SAME AUTHOR

Mrs Hartley and the Growth Centre

Statuesque Alice Hartley of the khol-eyes and the gypsy shawls can no longer arouse the interest of her pompous husband, the adulterous professor. Despite her spirited rendition of the Dance of the Seven Veils, her heightened consciousness, her organic carrot cake and her many-coloured pop-socks she still leaves him cold.

Just as she is compelled to face this chilling truth, she meets Michael, a young gullible student with an excessive libido. In Michael, Alice discovers an endless supply of all she has sought: revenge, sex and a large house suitable for conversion.

Soon the house is thigh-deep with women joyfully casting off the shackles of their middle-class oppression through aerobo-gardening, psyche-soothing massage and appropriate amounts of alcohol and magic mushrooms. Sadly, some narrow-minded neighbours and the numerous forces of the law seem completely impervious to all those healing and liberating vibrations.

But the dolphins had a great time . . .

BY THE SAME AUTHOR

Wideacre

Wideacre Hall, set in the heart of the English countryside, is the ancestral home that Beatrice Lacey loves. But as a woman of the eighteenth century she has no right of inheritance. Corrupted by a world that mistreats women, she sets out to corrupt others. Sexual and wilful, she believes that the only way to achieve control over Wideacre is through a series of horrible crimes, and no one escapes the consequences of her need to possess the land.

'The eighteenth-century woman is a neglected creature ... but, in the figure of her heroine, Philippa Gregory has defined a certain kind of wildness, of female assertiveness ... This is a novel written from instinct, not out of calculation, and it shows' – Peter Ackroyd

BY THE SAME AUTHOR

The Favoured Child

Wideacre estate is bankrupt, the villagers are living in poverty and Wideacre Hall is a smoke-blackened ruin.

But in the Dower House two children are being raised in protected innocence. Equal claimants to the inheritance of Wideacre, rivals for the love of the village, they are tied by a secret childhood betrothal but forbidden to marry.

Only one can be the favoured child. Only one can inherit the magical understanding between the land and the Lacey family that can make the Sussex village grow green again. Only one can be Beatrice Lacey's true heir.

'For sheer pace and percussive drama it will take a lot of beating' – *Sunday Times*

BY THE SAME AUTHOR

Meridon

In her night-time dreams she was the favoured child, heir to land, beloved of her family, sleeping soft between linen sheets. But during the day she was bruised, barefoot and hungry . . .

Meridon, the desolate Romany girl, is determined to escape the hard poverty of her childhood. Riding bareback in a travelling show, while her sister Dandy risks her life on the trapeze, Meridon dedicates herself to freeing them both from danger and want.

But Dandy – beautiful, impatient, thieving Dandy – grabs too much, too quickly. And Meridon finds herself alone, riding in bitter grief through the rich Sussex farmlands towards a house called Wideacre – where they await the return of the last of the Laceys.

Sweeping, passionate, unique: Meridon completes Philippa Gregory's bestselling trilogy which began with *Wideacre* and continued in *The Favoured Child*.

'Compelling . . . Philippa Gregory reigns supreme as the mistress of historical drama' – *Today*